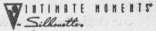

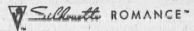

SHARON SALA

is a child of the country. As a farmer's daughter, her vivid imagination made solitude a thing to cherish. An inveterate dreamer, she yearned to share the stories her imagination created. And for Sharon, her dreams have come true. She has captured the hearts of countless readers with her award-winning novels, published under her own name as well as the pseudonym Dinah McCall.

ELIZABETH BEVARLY

is an honors graduate of the University of Louisville and achieved her dream of writing full-time before she even turned thirty! At heart, she is also an avid voyager who once helped navigate a friend's thirty-five-foot sailboat across the Bermuda Triangle. Mother of a young son, Elizabeth likes to think she has a lot in common with the characters she creates—people who know love and life go hand in hand.

SANDRA STEFFEN

Growing up the fourth child of ten, Sandra developed a keen appreciation for laughter and argument. A national bestselling author, she lives in Michigan with her husband, three of their sons and a blue-eyed mutt who thinks her name is No-Molly-No. Sandra's book *Child of Her Dreams* won the 1994 National Readers' Choice Award. She is also the creator of the extremely popular BACHELOR GULCH series for Silhouette Romance.

CHERYL REAVIS

A former public health nurse, Cheryl describes herself as a "late bloomer" who played in her first piano recital at the tender age of thirty. "After that, there was no stopping me. I immediately gave myself permission to attempt my *other* heart's desire—to write." Her Silhouette Special Edition novels *Patrick Gallagher's Widow* and *A Crime of the Heart* won the Romance Writers of America's coveted RITA Award.

SHARON SALA
ELIZABETH BEVARLY
SANDRA STEFFEN
CHERYL REAVIS

Silhouette®

Sensational

Published by Silhouette Books
America's Publisher of Contemporary Romance

SILHOUETTE BOOKS

ISBN 0-373-48406-2

Copyright © 2000 by Harlequin Books S.A.

The publisher acknowledges the copyright holders of the individual works as follows:

ANNIE AND THE OUTLAW
Copyright © 1994 by Sharon Sala

A LAWLESS MAN
Copyright © 1994 by Elizabeth Bevarly

CHILD OF HER DREAMS
Copyright © 1994 by Sandra E. Steffen

PATRICK GALLAGHER'S WIDOW
Copyright © 1990 by Cheryl Reavis

CONTENTS

Dear Reader,

When I learned that *Annie and the Outlaw*, my first
Intimate Moments title, was going to be reissued, I was
ecstatic. Despite the honors the book received, it was three
special readers that touched me most. Two of them wrote
letters, telling me their stories, and I cried when I read
them, humbled to know that something I'd written had
helped them in such a personal way.

But it was the third reader, a bookseller named
Steffie Walker, who touched me most. She appeared at my
table during an autographing session with the book in hand.
Her eyes were filled with tears but she had a smile as wide
as Dallas on her face. And she put her arms around me and
just started to hug. I'd never met her before, but there was
something about her that made me hug her back. Then she
told me of her illness, and how depressed she'd been feeling
until she'd read my book. She laughed and said that I had
given her hope, and all I could do was stand there. She kept
telling me thank-you for the story and for the uplift to her
spirit, but I was speechless, because, you see, I was the one
who received a blessing that day.

Now, six years later, *Annie and the Outlaw* is going to have
another go at the world, and for that I rejoice. A couple of
years ago I learned Steffie had died, but her spirit lives on in
such a marvelous fashion. In 1999, the Romance Writers of
America presented the first Steffie Walker Bookseller of the
Year Award to a Texas bookseller named Kathy Baker.

So, my dear readers, when you begin my story, cheer for
Annie, and for Gabriel, and if you have it in your heart,
remember a woman named Steffie Walker, who cheered for
them first.

With love,

Sharon Sala

ANNIE AND THE OUTLAW
by Sharon Sala

ANNIE AND THE OUTLAW
epitomizes a *Silhouette Intimate Moments* novel.
Silhouette Intimate Moments are known for fast-paced,
dynamic stories and the ability to sweep readers into
a larger-than-life world. Filled with intriguing heroes,
dramatic situations and mainstream excitement, these
stories will set your pulse pounding and mind racing!
Six new *Silhouette Intimate Moments* novels
appear at your bookstore every month.

During our lifetimes, someone special will cross the paths
we are on and forever after change the directions that
we take. From that day forward, we will be different.
Either in the way we think or the way we live.
And from that meeting will spring renewed faith in
ourselves and hope for the future. Without faith—with the
absence of hope—we are nothing. We have nothing.
This book is dedicated to those special people
who care enough to make the difference.

Prologue

Kansas Territory—Mid-1800s

The noonday sun was at its zenith, beaming down with relentless persistence upon the crowd gathered around the hanging tree at the edge of town. A gusty wind did its bit in making what was left of Gabe Donner's last minutes on earth miserable by blowing sand into his eyes and against his cheeks, stinging his already bruised and battered face with a rude reminder that sensations would soon be a thing of the past.

"You cain't just hang him," a woman sobbed, and cradled her belly, swollen to near-bursting with an overdue baby. She threw herself between the angry crowd and the man on the horse who was about to be lynched. "He saved my life. If it had'na been fer him, you people...you God-fearin', law-abidin' citizens woulda run me down."

"Get back, Milly," a man shouted from the back of the crowd. "He was part of the gang who robbed our bank. Just because he couldn't bring himself to hurt you, don't change the fact that his buddies have done gone and made off with our life savings."

Gabe cursed and squinted his eyes. It was a hell of a day to die. But he'd been heading toward this for most of his life, and he knew it. Somewhere around the age of twelve he'd taken a step in the wrong direction, and there'd been no one in his life who'd cared to call him back.

The woman called Milly screamed as two men pulled her out of the way. Gabe's gut kicked as the horse beneath him danced sideways from the noise and shouts. The rough fiber of the rope around his neck and hands ate into his skin like a saw-toothed rasp. He winced, aware that losing a little skin was nothing to what was about to transpire.

He stared down at the woman who'd uselessly pleaded his cause and still could not believe he'd done what he had. One minute he'd been riding out of town with the rest of the gang, just ahead of a hail of gunfire, and the next thing he knew, he found himself leaping from the horse and throwing himself onto the ground, using his body as a shield between the pregnant woman and the pounding hooves of the horses ridden by the posse giving chase. He sighed and swallowed another curse. Why the hell couldn't she have been home having that baby?

"Gabe Donner...do you have anything to say for yourself?" a man asked.

He grinned and shrugged as he looked down at the sobbing woman. "Whatever you do, lady...don't name him after me."

In spite of his dusty, blood-stained clothing, a week's worth of whiskers and a badly needed haircut, the smile transformed his face. His handsome features and devastating grin made her sob even harder. It seemed such a tragic waste of manhood.

Wrenching free of the man beside her, she dashed forward. Pressing a shaking hand on Gabe's leg, she felt the jerky tremble of long thigh muscles under stress. "May God have mercy on your soul," she whispered.

And in that moment Gabe felt one small ounce of his guilt lifted and delivered. He winked.

Then, before the stunned assembly, he took away their decision and some of their joy by doing the deed himself. He kicked the horse, sharply jabbing his spurs into the animal's sweaty flanks. The horse neighed wildly, rearing up on hind legs in sudden objection to the pain, and then burst forward, as if coming out of a starting gate.

A couple of curses and then a hush came over the crowd as the man's long, lean body jerked in the dusty wind. One by one they turned and walked away, suddenly shamed by their kangaroo court and the ruthlessness of it all.

The sobbing woman was escorted back to her house, where she fell into bed and promptly gave birth, as suddenly and painfully as Gabe Donner had died.

And then there was nothing but the creak of the rope against the tree limb as the solid weight of his body swung back and forth...back and forth.

A loud roar filled Gabe's ears. Fire swept across his face, and the smell of sulfur scalded the insides of his nostrils and burned his eyelids. Confusion was uppermost within his heat-fogged brain as he tried to decipher the words being screamed at him in a virulent tone.

"You were mine!"

The air around Gabe reverberated from the sound of the voice. He inhaled, then wished that he hadn't, as the sulfuric steam once again scalded his throat and lungs. He stood his ground, unable to move from the spot on which he'd landed.

"Right up until the last moment, your soul was mine! And then what did you do? You ruined it! It might have been excusable if it had only been the woman...but no! You had to go and save a baby! An unborn one, at that! *They still belong to* Him!"

The hiss that accompanied the accusations sucked the air from Gabe's body. He began to get the message. The voice screamed and spat, shouting obscenities Gabe had never imagined as he absorbed the implications of his situation.

I've done it now! I've gone and made the Devil mad! This is too damned scary, even for me. From the way he's spitting and cussing, it seems I don't even belong in Hell.

The voice seemed to filter through the skin over his bones, insidious by its very nature, imbuing him with a sensation of scorched flesh and degradation. Yet he saw nothing but the constant swirling clouds of fire and steam. If he hadn't been so stunned, he might have laughed. It seemed he was doomed to mess up, even in death.

"Get out! Get out!" the Devil screamed, and Gabe's body quivered from the onslaught of sound. "You don't belong here. There's nothing I hate worse than a sanctimonious sinner!"

And before Gabe could blink, the fire, the smoke, even the voice, had disappeared, and he felt himself being tossed aside as if he were so much garbage. It was as if he were left hanging in a vacuum where no one and nothing existed—except himself.

God! he thought, and with the thought came the being.

"Gabriel."

The voice was solace after sin. Grace after a lifetime of gratuitous living, and Gabe shivered.

"I never thought we'd be having this conversation," God said softly.

Gabe shivered. Neither had he.

"You surprised me, my son," God said. "You were one that I thought I'd lost. But right at the last moment, when it actually counted, you did something right."

If an immovable force hadn't been holding him up, Gabe

would already have fallen. He'd endured more than a human could bear this day, and yet he was being forced to stand and listen again to his sins and the lack of compassion with which he'd lived his life.

"However, that in itself is not enough for all your transgressions to be forgiven," He continued. "Remember, it wasn't you who begged for mercy on your soul…it was the woman."

Gabe's head dropped, his chin nearly touching his chest. *This is it,* he thought. *I'm about to get the shaft here, too.*

"No, Gabriel. Heaven does not give shafts…only second chances."

Gabe's head jerked up, his nostrils flaring as he inhaled and his mind absorbed the clear, pure sound of God's laughter. He almost smiled. If he'd known God had a sense of humor, he might have tried religion a long time ago.

As badly as Gabe wanted to, he could not speak. All he could do was stand and listen to his fate being handed out.

"This is my command!" God said, his voice deepening with a powerful force as the sentence He had decided to impose was made clear to Gabe. "You will go back. Soul intact, flesh and bones. To the human eye you will seem as all men. But heed me, Gabriel!"

Gabe's body shook, and he blinked rapidly as a blinding light sent him to his knees.

"If you can learn what it truly takes to get to Heaven, then you will be granted entrance and eternal life."

Dear God…it will take two lifetimes to undo the damage I've done, Gabe thought.

"So be it!" God commanded. "Then you shall have two lifetimes. One hundred and fifty more years on earth to right your wrongs. But…heed my warning!"

Gabe could not see, only hear and feel, as the air around his body vibrated once again. Yet this time it was as if the motion came from a multitude of wings…as if all the angels in Heaven had suddenly surrounded him and struck him blind as God continued.

"Stray from my path...ignore the way of the righteous...and you will be lost in Limbo, stranded between Heaven and Hell for all eternity with nothing but your conscience for company."

Suddenly all was silent. Gabe tried to stand, and then he felt himself being hurtled backward.

The limb cracked, and Gabe's eyes opened just in time to see the dry, dusty earth of Kansas rushing up to meet his face.

A horse's soft nicker of welcome was his only clue that he hadn't imagined what had just transpired. This was real. Gabe Donnor had come back from the dead.

With an aching groan, he rolled up and over, momentarily surprised that the ropes around his neck and wrists were in the dust at his feet. And then he shuddered, remembering where he'd been, and knew that those ropes were the least of the surprises yet to be had.

He picked up his hat from the ground, dusting the worst of the grime from inside the brim, and called softly to his horse. In minutes there was nothing left to tell of what had transpired that day but a coil of rope lying in the dirt like a snake waiting to strike.

Gabriel Donnor was gone.

Chapter 1

Oklahoma City, Oklahoma—Present Day

It was hard to tell where the man began and the machine ended. Black leather and black metal, both well-worn and dusty, covered muscle and motion as the motorcycle and its rider wove their way through the heavy weekend traffic on I-240 on the south side of Oklahoma City.

Just ahead, an eighteen-wheeler swerved to keep from running up the ass-end of a car that was barely doing forty in the fast lane of the freeway. The motorcycle moved smoothly past the near-miss as its rider guided it in and out of the swiftly moving vehicles like a bullet on its way to a target.

The rider in black suddenly shot into the far right-hand lane and geared down to take the next exit, which would lead him toward Dallas, via southbound I-35. The biker leaned into the turn, and as he did, caught his first glimpse of the altercation taking place at the corner quick stop across the street.

His frown was hidden behind the smoke-tinted visor of his helmet. But he didn't like what he was seeing. Without taking his focus from the road before him, he accelerated through a small gap in traffic and shot across all three lanes, coming to a sliding halt a few feet behind the gathering crowd.

The woman's hair was the first thing he noticed. It was a deep, rich brown. And the afternoon sun that shot through it highlighted the chestnut and amber strands until it looked like a coil of coffee-flavored taffy wound around her head.

Because of the business at hand, he manfully ignored the faint but enticing outline of long legs and a slender but shapely body beneath the white, gauzy-looking skirt and blouse she was wearing.

He yanked off his helmet and hung it on the handlebar of his bike as he dismounted. His legs were long and heavily muscled. The lower half of his body was covered in supple black leather, ending with dusty black boots adorned with old-style silver spurs.

He was rock-hard and a deep-to-the-muscle brown from countless years and endless miles on the road. As his fingers threaded through too-long hair, he lightly massaged his scalp along the places where the helmet had ridden, then let the shaggy black length of his hair fall where it would.

Bare to the waist except for a black leather vest laced loosely across his taut belly, he pulled sunglasses from his bike pack and slid them on. It was intentional that their mirrored surface hid much of what he was, while allowing him to see more of what was before him. He'd heard it said that the eyes were the mirror of the soul, and Gabriel Donner was real careful of who he let look inside the man that he'd become.

* * *

Annie O'Brien was nervous. And because of that, she was also mad as hell. She, a grown woman of twenty-nine, had let these sixteen- and seventeen-year-old boys get her goat. Granted, there were more than a few. And also granted, in this day and time, few boys of that age were the innocents that their parents would like to believe. But the gang of boys preventing her from leaving the parking lot was daunting. And as the number in the gang had grown, so had their daring. They were out of control, and she knew it. And because of that, she was afraid.

"Hey, hey, Annie-Annie," the tallest boy chanted. "You know what I'd like to do to you?"

He tossed his head, and as he did, a dirty brown lock of hair fell from behind his ear and caught in one of his earrings. Annie inhaled sharply and tried not to let him know she was afraid. He was a woman's worst nightmare come to life.

Several of the others laughed and hitched at their jeans, swaggering in thought, if not in deed, at the idea of taking this pretty lady down a notch or two, of showing her what real men were all about.

"Just let me pass, Damon," Annie said, trying again, as she had for the past fifteen minutes, to get to her car on the other side of the lot.

"Oh, now...I don't know if I can do that little thing," he said, then smoothed his hand across the fly of his baggy jeans, watching with increasing delight the way her eyes widened and the slight nervous lick she gave her bottom lip. "You're on our turf now, Annie-Annie. Here, you do what we say."

"Like hell," she said softly, and started to push past, aware that she had little time left in which to deal with this situation before it got completely out of hand.

Damon stepped forward; his pale hazel eyes seemed a reflection of his inner self, wild and out of control. And as he moved, the other seven teenage boys moved with him as if they were joined at the hip, their dilated pupils and jerky, foot-shuffling movements a sure bet that they were riding high on more than adrenaline.

Annie's heart pounded, but she ignored her own panic as she tried to push past them. She took a deep breath, certain that she was about to become another crime statistic, then watched in amazement as the boys came to an abrupt halt. All their cocky assurance slipped away as they looked up and over her head.

Someone was behind her!

Terrified that it was simply more of the same, she froze in horror. She saw the man's shadow as it moved across the pavement, covering and then passing her own shadow, to come to a stop somewhere about the middle of Damon Tuttle's knees. It was big and wide, and she had a moment's impression of being swallowed whole. And then he spoke, and she would have sworn that the air vibrated, so close was his mouth to her ear.

"Trouble?" he asked.

His hand rested lightly at the edge of her shoulder. And though the small squeeze he gave her was as much a question as what he had asked, she knew the second he touched her that he was on her side.

In answer to his one-word question, she nodded. She had trouble indeed.

It was instinctive, an urge born of relief, she knew. But she felt a sudden need to turn and bury her face against what she sensed was a big, strong chest and forget everything but the safety she knew she would find there.

Damon Tuttle was one tough dude. All you had to do was ask anybody on the south side of the city. They would tell you. And if they didn't, Damon would. He had his hand in a little bit of everything rotten that went on in the area and still managed to stay one step ahead of the law. It was tes-

timony to his probation officer's persistence that he was
even still in school.

"Okay, boys…back off!" Gabriel said, and even Annie
jumped at the tone of the voice behind her.

He didn't say where, he didn't say when, but the look on
his face made three of the boys at the edge of the gang take
several steps backward in nervous reflex.

"Move, damn it…and I mean now," Gabe said in a
softer, more menacing tone of voice. When they held their
ground, he swiftly put himself between the woman they
called Annie-Annie and the gang.

His fingers curled into fists and his stomach muscles tightened against the possibility of oncoming blows.

Annie's heart tilted. As he slid past her, she caught a flash
of a wild, handsome face half-hidden behind mirrored
glasses, a dangerous smile, and then all she had left was a
very solid view of his back.

He was tall, so tall. And he was more tan flesh and black
leather than she'd ever seen, even in a gym. She should
have been scared out of her wits, yet she'd never felt so
protected in her entire life.

Damon's skin crawled as he looked into the big man's
face. His thoughts went into free-fall, as if he'd just walked
into a whirlwind and been caught up in the dead-calm of
the eye, waiting for the rest of the storm force to catch up
and eat him alive. Yet he felt honor-bound to hold his
ground. He couldn't lose face in front of his boys, not for
just one man.

"Who do you think you are, man?" one of them sneered,
secure from his vantage point in the middle of the gang.

Damon shivered as the big man's focus shifted, turning
that hidden gaze from himself to the boy who'd spoken.
And when a slow smile slid across the biker's face, Damon's belly rolled.

"I *know* who I am, boy. I'm someone you don't want to

make mad." He took several steps forward and was suddenly nose-to-nose with Damon Tuttle.

"I'm no boy," Damon muttered, trying to maintain eye contact with the man, when he felt an urgent need to cut and run instead. Damon was the type of tough who was at his best with a backup of muscle, and he had a sudden instinctive flash that his buddies were about to bolt.

"Oh, but you're wrong," Gabe said softly.

The biker's motion was so swift, that Damon never saw it coming. He shuddered as hands locked around his arms, the grip iron-hard and unyielding. Looking up and suddenly seeing the terror on his own acne-scarred face mocking him from the mirrored reflection of the biker's glasses was a humbling experience. Damon Tuttle did not like to be humbled. Yet there was no other way to describe the fact that his feet were now dangling inches off the pavement while the biker held him suspended as if he were a child.

"That's exactly what you are…a boy," Gabe said. "And not a very good one, at that." He shook Damon roughly to make his point, ignoring the fact that the other gang members were digging in their pockets for weapons. "Boys do stupid things. Threatening a woman like this is stupid…real stupid, *boy!*"

He emphasized the taunt by glaring over Damon's shoulder at the others, who quickly slid their weapons back out of sight.

"You've gained nothing by frightening her." He dropped Damon as suddenly as he'd picked him up. "And there's something else you should remember." His last statement encompassed the entire gang as he took off his sunglasses and stared them full in the face, no longer hiding behind the mirrored lenses for effect. "Men don't run in packs…but dogs do."

The big man's quiet sneer as he slid his sunglasses back on made all eight boys turn red in anger and embarrassment as they remembered the fear on Annie's face. It suddenly didn't seem as cool as it had minutes earlier.

"Oh, hell, let's go, Damon," another boy said nervously. "No big deal, right, bro?"

"Is it going to be a big deal, Damon? It *can* be one if you need it to be," Gabe said softly.

Damon got the message. This biker could take them apart and reassemble them in new order, and they all knew it. He shook his head and dropped his gaze. He couldn't describe the relief he felt when he saw the biker relax and take a step back.

Damon Tuttle was the first to move as, one by one, the teenagers shuffled away, tossing half-hearted threats and rude innuendos over their shoulders, unwilling to completely acknowledge the fact that they'd let themselves be bested by one man who hadn't even thrown a punch.

And then Gabriel remembered the woman and turned.

"Are you all right?" he asked gently.

Annie nodded, then fainted in his arms.

He sat in the shade of the building, using his bike for a chair as he cradled the woman called Annie who was lying loose and limp across his lap. Her head was lolling against his bare biceps, and he marveled at how thick and soft her hair felt against his skin. He couldn't remember the last time he'd held a woman so intimately or been able to look his fill.

Her nose was small and straight and perfectly fit her heart-shaped face. Her cheeks looked soft, and as he held her, he absently traced the ball of his thumb across them to test out his theory. He'd been right; they were as tender and soft as a baby's lips.

He sighed and inhaled slowly, wishing away the thousand thoughts that instantly intruded, as well as the accompanying ache in his loins. After what she'd been through, what he was thinking had no place in her life, and because of who he was, neither did he.

Her mouth was wide, her lips full. They were the kind that drove a man wild and begged to be kissed without saying a word. Gabriel Donner had come too far and lived too long to turn down the unoffered invitation.

Ignoring the busy traffic on the street just beyond the parking lot, as well as the ebb and flow of customers coming and going in the store behind him, he bent down, opened his mouth just enough to encompass hers, and then groaned when she sighed and unconsciously responded.

She tasted of heat and cinnamon, and as his mouth tightened across her lips, he dug his hands into the coil of her hair, unwittingly sending the pins that had held it in place flying.

She moaned, and he lifted his head and frowned, instantly aware that he'd trespassed. It was a silent acknowledgment that the good he'd done by helping her had been wiped out in a heartbeat by the marauding manner in which he'd taken her favors without permission.

Her eyes were green. That much he remembered from before she passed out. He looked down at his fingers, buried deep in her thick, luxuriant fountain of hair, and tried not to think of where else on Annie he would like to put his hands.

Her hair fell free as he withdrew his fingers and began trying to smooth the mess that he'd made of it. Guilt at his transgression made him feel too much like the toughs he'd just run off.

She came to with a start.

"Oh, Lord," she muttered, as she realized where she was and began trying to unwind herself from the man and his bike.

But the action, as well as her panic, was wasted when he

calmly stood and then set her back on her feet without a word.

"You fainted," he said.

Annie's hands shot to her head. She felt the long, thick weight of her hair falling through her fingers. Doubtfully, she looked back up at him.

"And the pins came out of your hair," he added.

She frowned. She already knew that. It was the how of the incident that was worrying her.

"I can't see your face," she said, unaware of the nervous tremor in her voice.

His movements were as slow as honey on a cold winter morning. Annie held her breath as he leaned forward until their faces were only inches apart, then slid his glasses down the bridge of his nose and let them drop into his hand.

Oh... I had a feeling this would only get better—and worse, Annie thought.

To go with the starkly handsome features she'd seen only in profile, she now had a pair of eyes so blue that she caught her breath at the color's purity.

"That better, Annie?"

She took a step backward, then swayed. His hand shot out so quickly that she didn't even see it coming. She felt only the firm yet gentle grip as he steadied her on her feet.

"How do you know my name?" she asked.

"Damon the Terrible called you by it several times. I assumed he knew you. Was I right?"

She sighed and buried her face in her hands. Gabe frowned. There was obviously more to this incident than casual harassment.

"Well, Annie-Annie, was I right?"

"Don't call me that," she said sharply, shuddering at the fear that came back with the rude twinning of her name.

"Then what *do* I call you?"

Annie stared at him. There was no reason on earth why

she should be telling this bike-riding, leather-clad knight on shining metal a darned thing about her personal life. In fact, everything she'd been told and taught over the past twenty-nine years reinforced that fact.

"My name is Annie Laurie O'Brien."

He held out his hand, then waited to see how much woman she turned out to be. By all rights she should be scared out of her wits by his appearance.

Annie looked down at the long, strong fingers, the wide, callused palm and the tracing of scars across the backs of his knuckles. Surprising herself, as well as him, she reached out and took what he offered.

Gabriel was shocked. His eyes narrowed, and his mouth firmed. He looked down at the way her fingers had curled around his and then back up into her face. He swallowed hard. Oh damn! Not trust!

She was more woman than he'd even imagined. The thought made him angry. Not now! he thought. Don't you do this to me! Not when you know my time is nearly up. He glared up into the sky.

Gabriel, Gabriel. When will you learn? Everything that happens, you bring upon yourself, said His voice.

The quiet answer slid through his mind, and with it came the truth slapping him full in the face. He dropped her hand and sighed wearily. How many years had he been on earth, riding the roads and highways, trying to get it right?

"And your name is...?" Annie asked.

At the same time that she was waiting for him to answer, she was thinking that if he'd been accompanied by three other "horsemen" on similar metal, she would have guessed by their motorized mounts that they were the Four Horsemen of the Apocalypse. She squinted her eyes, fancying that he was about to answer by saying "Death," when his deep voice rumbled past her ear.

"My name is Gabriel...Gabriel Donner."

Her eyes widened, and her lips curved into a smile. In spite of the fact that she knew laughing in someone's face was extremely rude, it happened anyway, loud and clear.

Gabe knew there must be a joke somewhere. He waited for her to explain.

"I'm sorry," Annie said, squinting and trying desperately to wipe the accompanying smile off her face. "That was rude of me." She shrugged, still grinning. "I have this vivid imagination." She waved her hand up and down his frame as lights danced in her eyes. "An angel in devil's clothing...that's what you are. My avenging angel."

His heart skipped a beat. Angel? She thinks I'm an angel? This time it was Gabriel who grinned. Oh lady, if you only knew.

Annie thought back to the past half hour and knew that her troubles were only momentarily solved. When tomorrow came, it would be more of the same from Damon and his gang. And then she had a sudden and shocking thought. She focused on his heart-stopping smile and ignored the warning her brain was sending.

Pooh! she told herself, as she realized that what she was thinking could get her killed. So what! Everyone had to die sometime.

"So, Gabriel, where were you going when you so kindly came to my rescue?"

He shrugged. "Nowhere...anywhere."

Her pulse accelerated. Everything kept falling into place. It had to be a sign.

"How would you like a job?" she asked.

Her question caught him off guard.

"Doing what?" he asked, eyeing her carefully, suddenly realizing that he might have rescued a kook. It wouldn't have been the first time, although, to be honest, this time it would be a major disappointment.

"I've ignored the signs for weeks, but after today...I

think I need a bodyguard." She ignored the shock on his face and continued before she lost both her breath and her nerve. "I'm a teacher. And the gang you rescued me from happens to be part of my homeroom class. I'll be damned if I'll let them beat me. I will not be frightened into quitting at this late date."

Gabe was speechless.

"It would only be for a few weeks," Annie said quickly. "Then school is out for the summer. After that, you could be on your way to nowhere…or even anywhere."

The nervous look she gave him sent his heart right to his feet. He couldn't have told her no if his life depended on it.

"Let me get this straight," he said. "You want to hire me to accompany you to school and sit in on all your classes until summer vacation begins?"

She nodded. "Why are you so shocked? Surely it won't be all that bad. Just look at it as a refresher course in basic high school."

"That's just it," Gabe muttered to himself. "I never went to school."

It was hard to say who was the more shocked. Annie for what she'd heard, or Gabe for admitting it.

"You can't read?" Annie asked, trying hard not to sound as shocked as she felt.

"I can read fine," Gabriel said shortly, pushing his sunglasses back on for protection. "I've had a long, long time to read just about any and everything ever written. And believe me, I mean everything."

"Then you're self-educated," she said, somehow greatly relieved that her angel's wings had not been clipped.

"I'm self-everything," he said in disgust.

"Why am I not surprised?" Annie muttered under her breath, then glanced up. "So…is it a deal? Will you be my guardian angel for the next few weeks?" A shadow crossed her face as she lifted her chin, trying desperately not to plead. "When I start something, I like to finish it."

Her voice softened, and Gabriel would have sworn he saw her chin tremble.

"It's real important to me that I finish this school year," she added.

"I'll need a place to sleep," he warned.

The light came back on in her clear green eyes. In for a penny, in for a pound, she thought. Besides, I've never taken a single risk in my entire life. I think it's about time I started...before it's too late. Her hesitation was only slight.

"Follow me," she said as she headed for her car, her slender body swaying gently beneath the loose, gauzy-white skirt and blouse she was wearing.

At that moment he would have followed her to the ends of the earth.

Chapter 2

Her apartment was everything he'd expected it to be. Ultrafeminine. It was a tasteful display of floral upholstery, small figurines placed in random fashion around the rooms and plants everywhere. There were flowering things, leafy things, spiky stems and flowing vines. He had an urge to duck as he walked through the door, half expecting something to come flying past from her semitropical jungle.

"Make yourself at home," Annie said, and tossed her purse on top of the kitchen table.

All the way home she'd debated with herself about the utter stupidity and careless abandon with which she'd hired him. Off and on, as traffic permitted, she'd caught glimpses of him riding at a safe distance behind her on that devil-black machine, dressed in biker leather, having traded his mirrored sunglasses for a black helmet with a smoke-tinted visor. One seemed no different than the other. She sensed he was using both to hide behind.

But what Annie O'Brien had endured over the past few

months had taken some of the caution out of her life. She would finish this school year and her teaching contract, no matter what.

The front door slammed behind him as he shut and locked it. Annie turned at the sound and couldn't hide a shudder. He looked so out of place. A nervous thought occurred to her as she watched him fold his arms across his chest and stare thoughtfully around the room. Had she let the Devil into her Garden of Eden? She bit her lower lip and turned away, hurrying into the kitchen and opening the refrigerator door, then bending down to peer inside.

Gabe heard the tremor in her voice as she invited him in. A wry grimace crossed his face as he dropped his duffel bag beside the couch, then stretched. But he was unaware of her observation and wouldn't have cared if he *had* known. He was used to his appearance making people nervous.

Annie turned, a package of hamburger meat in one hand and a bowl of shredded lettuce in the other. She watched him close his eyes and reach first one arm and then the other toward the ceiling in a halfhearted attempt to work out what she suspected were muscle kinks from long hours on his bike.

"Are you hungry?"

Her question took him by surprise. His eyes opened, and he stared intently at the blank, almost innocent expression on her face. *Yes...but not for food...for you.*

The thought made him angry both with himself and at the situation. He didn't have time for entanglements, especially those of the personal kind.

"Why the hell aren't you afraid of me?" he asked quietly.

"I suppose, if I'm honest, I can't say I'm not." She hastened to add, before he got angry and left, "But let's face it. The worst you could do to me is rob me, or rape me. Or...maybe torture or kill me.''

"Good Lord," Gabe whispered, uncertain how to take her blithe assessment of his presence in her life.

"Those are givens," Annie continued. "And after what I've been through the past few months, I'm not much afraid of givens anymore. Besides..." She shrugged. "Everyone has to die...sometime."

A bitter smile twisted Gabe's face. "You'd think so, wouldn't you?" He'd watched more than one generation disappear from this earth, and he was still here to tell the tale.

She looked up, startled by his strange answer, and then shrugged off the curiosity that might have let her pursue his comment.

"I need you, Gabriel Donner. I need you to get me through the next few weeks of school. After what I've endured at the hands of those boys, I will not let them think intimidation wins wars. And believe me...this is war!''

He grinned slightly at the ferocity in her voice.

"Just stay until my job is over, and then you'll be free to go your own way," she added.

He nodded. Of course he would stay. But she didn't understand why. She couldn't. Leaving someone in trouble wasn't part of the deal he'd made with God. He was honor bound to help her whether she liked it or not.

"Where do I sleep?" he asked.

A faint flush painted her cheeks a rosy hue as she led the way down the small hall.

"This is my spare room." She opened the door and stepped aside as he moved through the doorway. Annie watched as he dropped his duffel bag by the bed and silently assessed the pink comforter draped across it.

"Sorry about all the stuffed animals. I've had them for years. Just toss them on the floor, out of your way. The room isn't much, but it has a separate bath. There are clean sheets on the bed, and—''

"It's fine," he said.

She nodded. "If you want to clean up or...or rest before you eat, feel free. I don't stand on ceremony."

"It's a good thing," Gabe said. "I don't care much for ceremonies." Frowning, he rubbed a thoughtful hand across his throat, feeling the slight pucker of his scar, a memento of a rope that had done what it could to end his life. "The last one I was at didn't serve food."

Her eyes narrowed as, for the first time, she noticed the thin ring of slightly discolored skin circling his neck. Just what and who had she invited into her home? Visions of ax murderers and serial killers sifted through her mind, but she discarded them. Her decision was made, and Annie O'Brien didn't go back on her word. She spun away and headed back toward the kitchen.

"We're having meat loaf," she called over her shoulder.

Gabe shut the door, then leaned against it, a thoughtful expression on his face. Meat loaf!

Two hours ago I was on my way to Texas, minding my own business, and now I'm in a pink bedroom full of stuffed teddy bears and about to be served meat loaf!

He began stripping off his clothes as he headed for the shower.

The evening meal had come and gone with surprising ease. Annie's matter-of-fact attitude helped. Also, Gabe had a suspicion that this was just another heaven-sent test. During the past century, he'd endured quite a few. Thrusting a teacher into his face was obviously a none-too-subtle way of telling him that he had more to learn.

He got up from the table and began gathering their dirty dishes. Unintentionally, he and Annie reached for the same bowl at the same time. His fingers slid over the back of her hand, and for a second he felt the panic pulsing through her system. But as quickly as it had come, it passed, leaving him with nothing more than the beginnings of a sleepless night. His body hardened at the thought of spending that night with her, but sanity reminded him that that was out of the question. Getting involved in any way was out of the question.

"Sorry," he said, and calmly reached for another bowl instead.

Annie shivered. His touch had done something to her nervous system that she hadn't expected. For one heart-stopping moment she thought she remembered that same hand cupping her face as soft breath feathered across her cheeks. She inhaled and closed her eyes. Certain she had to be mistaken, she exhaled and opened them, calmly meeting his cool blue gaze.

"Did you get enough to eat?" she asked, ignoring the sexual tension she felt building between them. But the moment she'd said it, she realized she'd only added fuel to the fire.

He smiled. The ache in his body increased.

Oh, damn, I shouldn't be thinking this, Gabriel thought.

Annie forgot what she'd been about to say as she stared at that smile.

His mouth, the one that had been twisted in a wry, almost cruel smirk ever since they'd met, had turned into a thing of beauty. Gabe Donner's smile had turned his mouth into the most beautiful set of lips she'd ever seen.

"What a waste," she muttered under her breath.

"Not for long," he whispered, and moved—too quickly for her to react.

Gabriel captured her between the sink and his body, then leaned down and pressed his lips against the shock of protest he saw coming.

He'd only meant to tease, but the intensity of their joining left him breathless. She tasted of the strawberries they'd had for dessert, and of passion too long denied.

He pulled back and stared long and hard into her face, missing nothing of the fact that her eyes had slipped shut and she was no longer pulling away from him. In fact, at that moment, if she hadn't opened her eyes and realized what had just happened, he knew damn well that she'd meant to slide her arms around his waist.

"Why did you do that?" she asked, trying to work up the good sense to tell herself that she'd asked for it by inviting a total stranger into her home.

"You said you wanted a taste," Gabe said, drawing a finger along the curve of her cheek. "I was just obliging."

"I did not!" she gasped. "I said—" she looked back at his mouth, remembering that only moments earlier it had been pressed against her own "—'what a waste.'"

"Oh," he said, and masked a grin. "My mistake."

"Good Lord," Annie muttered, thinking to herself how close it had come to being a mistake for both of them.

She turned away from the table with a handful of dishes and headed for the sink.

"Forget it," she said, giving him a warning look he couldn't miss.

Not on your life, Annie Laurie, he thought. But he shrugged and continued to clear the table.

"Why do those boys have it in for you?" Gabe asked as he carried the last of the bowls from the table to the sink.

Annie rinsed and loaded the dishwasher with absent skill as she thought about his question. Finally she could only shake her head.

"Honestly…I have no idea. It's been rough all year, but the last two months have been hell. Pure hell! I've been cornered in the halls, in the classroom, even in the parking lot at school. But today was the first time it happened off campus."

Gabe watched her lips tighten as a muscle jerked at her temple.

"Have you reported this to your...uh...whatever?"

"The administrator at my school? Yes."

"And...?"

She looked away. "He told me security would look into it...and to put up my hair and wear more sedate clothing in the classroom."

Gabe frowned. He might have been born in another time, but he was well aware of the implications of what she'd just said. His hand slid across her shoulder, then gently turned her face up to his.

"Are you telling me he was saying that you asked for what was happening? That it was your fault?"

"Not in so many words," she said. And then she turned in sudden anger and thumped her finger sharply against his chest. "But that's what he meant, damn it! Why do men do that?" she yelled. "What is it about the male sex that makes them blame a woman for everything they can't fix?"

Gabe caught her finger on the third jab. "Have a heart, Annie. It wasn't me." He grinned and gingerly rubbed the spot on his chest that she'd been attacking.

"Sorry," she said, and yanked her hand away, trying to forget the way his fingers had heated her skin as they'd curled around her hand.

"Why don't you go watch television or something?" she said, pointing toward the living room. "There's bound to be some sort of ball game on. All men like ball games. You're a man. Go watch one."

Oh, yes, Annie, I am a man. And, thanks to you, a very uncomfortable one.

She shrugged and turned away, mentally excusing herself for being rude. As far as she was concerned, after that kiss he'd stolen, manners were a thing of the past. And she needed him out of her space.

When her back was turned, Gabe leaned forward just enough to inhale a faint whiff of her perfume and considered the thought that he would rather watch her. But after the kiss he'd taken without asking, he didn't think she would appreciate knowing that. When she wasn't looking, he grinned and ambled out of the small kitchen.

Annie breathed a quick sigh of relief. He was so darned big that he swamped everything he came in contact with, including her. She'd never had claustrophobia in her life until he'd started helping her with the dishes. And after he'd kissed her and then turned away as if it was no big deal, it had been all she could do not to burst into tears.

And the strangest thing was, she didn't know why. Although she probably should, she didn't feel threatened by him. And if he did as he'd promised, he was going to make life a whole lot easier for her. She had absolutely nothing to cry about.

She grimaced and tossed the hand towel on the counter. If she looked at it another way, she had absolutely *everything* to cry about. She stomped into the living room, her posture ramrod-stiff and her expression furious.

"I'm going to bed," she said sharply. "Is there anything you need first?"

He stared long and hard at the anger on her face, wondering where the wall had come from that was suddenly standing between them.

"Go to sleep, Annie Laurie," he said quietly. "I'm a big boy. I can take care of myself."

As if I hadn't noticed, she thought as she walked down the hallway toward her bedroom. She couldn't forget the way that wall of man and muscle had pinned her against her own kitchen sink with so little effort.

Therein lay part of her problem. Annie O'Brien had done two stupid things today. She'd hired a total stranger to be her bodyguard. And it wasn't enough that she didn't know him. He had to be a biker…riding the biggest, blackest Harley she'd ever seen. To top that off, she'd taken him home with her like some stray animal and let him kiss her.

And therein lay the root of Annie's problem. She was way too interested for her own good in the male animal she'd brought home. The last thought she had before she finally drifted off to sleep was that he didn't look the least bit domesticated. In fact, if she wasn't careful, he might turn into some wild thing and eat her alive.

"Oh no!"

Annie's quiet dismay as she walked out of the apartment ahead of him sent Gabe bolting out the front door, expecting to have to rescue her again. Unfortunately for Annie, they'd already come and gone.

Her nearly new red Caprice had been vandalized to the point of being totaled. Three separate colors of paint had been sprayed in graffiti-like fashion all over it. All the windows were shattered, the hubcaps were missing, and the tires looked as if someone had taken a chain saw to them. The seat covers had been slashed, and a offensive odor emanated from inside the vehicle.

Gabe stared. The anger that surged through him made him shake. How had this world gotten so rotten? He had a sudden notion that he would have no regrets when it finally came time for him to leave it.

"Call the police," Gabe told her. When he saw indecision sweeping across her face, his voice grew harsh. "Do it, Annie! *Now!*"

She swung around and headed back to her apartment, her posture a vivid statement of her anger at the vandalism, as well as his bossy demand.

After a second brief phone call, this one to the school to let them know she would be delayed, they waited. Several minutes later, a squad car pulled up. The officer's gaze went from the biker who was leaning against the vandalized car to the big black Harley parked beside it.

Gabe had traded his leather pants for jeans, and, in honor of the presence of a lady, he had put on a long-sleeved shirt beneath his leather vest, but it didn't help disguise his go-to-hell attitude, the mirrored sunglasses or the old silver spurs on his well-worn boots. The officer came out of the car with his hand on his gun.

Gabe sighed. One of these days he was going to have to make a change in his appearance, if only to alleviate some of this crap.

"Put your hands in the air," the officer shouted as he slid into a half crouch behind the open door of his car, aiming his revolver at Gabe.

Annie had had enough. "It wasn't him, for God's sake!" she shouted, slamming her briefcase down on the sidewalk as she swept over to the two men. "If it was, do you think he'd be standing there waiting to be arrested? He's with me," she said, and then buried her face in her hands.

Gabe's fingers slid up the back of her neck in a gentle, reassuring squeeze.

"It's okay, Annie," he said quietly. "It's happened before."

The officer made no apology for his misunderstanding as he holstered his gun.

Less than thirty minutes later the report had been made. They watched as the officer drove away with their meager information in his possession. What they had was a vandalized car and a lot of suspicions. But as he'd told them, in his business, you couldn't take suspicion to court.

"I'll have to call a cab," she said, eyeing the ruined car and then her watch.

Gabe shook his head and pointed at her skirt. "Not if you're willing to change your clothes." Her eyebrows arched as his suggestion sank in. "Put on some pants, Annie O'Brien, and I'll get you to work on time."

Just thinking about what her superintendent would say when she arrived at work on the back of a Harley made her nervous, and then a determined glint came in her eyes, changing them to a darker shade of jade.

"Why not?" she muttered, and ran to change.

Gabe smiled. He was beginning to like Annie O'Brien more and more. She was his kind of woman. And then the smile slid off his face. He didn't have women...of any kind. It didn't pay to care when you knew you couldn't stay.

"Wow! Would you look at that?" one of the students shouted, pointing toward the motorcycle and its riders as they turned into the staff parking lot.

Allen Baker, the administrator in charge of the high school, frowned. "They can't park there," he muttered, and stomped toward the bike.

The first bell was ringing as Annie swung her leg over and dismounted. She could hear the bell's shrill peal through the helmet Gabe had made her wear.

I can just imagine what my hair's going to look like, she thought, then looked up in time to see her boss heading toward her. She grimaced. Perfect timing!

She ran her hands through her hair and sighed. It was hopeless. Settling for a redo of her outfit, she began to tuck the tail of her blue silk blouse back into the waistband of her navy linen slacks.

Late-arriving students were making a mad dash across the parking lot. Teachers were strolling through the doors on their way to their classrooms. But Gabe Donner's instincts homed in on the tall, overweight man in a plaid sports coat and navy slacks who was lumbering across the pavement toward them.

"A friend of yours?" Gabe asked, readjusting his sunglasses, then nonchalantly using his fingers for a comb as he thrust them through his wind-blown hair with casual abandon.

"My boss," Annie said, and sighed as she handed him his helmet.

"I say," Allen Baker began. "You can't park here. This is reserved for—" A stunned expression crossed his face as he recognized the face that had emerged from under the shiny black helmet. "Miss O'Brien! What on earth do you mean by arriving in such a...?"

"Mr. Baker. I'd like you to meet Gabriel Donner. He'll be accompanying me to class for the remainder of the school year. Now, if you'll excuse me, I need to hurry or I'll be late."

Allen Baker turned pasty white. He wanted to argue. But nothing more than a gasp slid past his lips as he grabbed her arm, stopping her progress, then stared fearfully at the tall, ominous-looking man who stepped between them.

"What do you mean, he'll be accompanying you to class? We don't allow people to monitor classes without special permission from—"

"I'm not monitoring anything but Annie's welfare," Gabe said quietly, gently removing Allen Baker's hand from her arm.

Baker shuddered as the big man's gaze warned him to look but not touch. As much as he would have liked to, he didn't have the guts to refuse someone who looked as if he'd climbed up from Hell to spend the day on earth.

"I don't understand," Baker said.

"I hired him," Annie said.

"Hired him for what?" Baker asked, wondering what on earth this biker could possibly do that was worthy of a paycheck.

"Bodyguard," Gabe said, daring the man to argue.

Allen Baker had a mental flash of an earlier meeting with

Annie O'Brien. He remembered her complaints about student harassment and vaguely remembered telling her to change her style of dress. He looked from her to the bike and back again in panic. This wasn't what he'd had in mind.

"You can't have a personal bodyguard," Allen Baker argued. "Whatever protection a teacher needs is furnished by the district."

"Then why didn't she get it?" Gabe asked. "Why was this woman left to deal with her problem on her own?"

Gabe didn't get an answer to his question, nor had he expected one. They left Allen Baker standing in the breezeway with his mouth agape as Annie hurried away with Gabriel Donner only a half step behind.

"The superintendent's not going to like this," Baker said, as he finally came to his senses and headed for his office. "He's not going to like this at all." And then he frowned and shuddered. "And God help us if the media gets wind of the fact that a teacher in this system felt compelled to actually hire her own security."

He began to run.

The closer Gabe and Annie got to her classroom, the louder the noise level became. Annie gave him a nervous glance over her shoulder as she started inside.

"I'm right behind you," Gabe said quietly.

The deep, level tone of his voice, as well as the reassuring touch of his hand on her shoulder, did what he'd intended. Her stomach settled, her heart rate decreased, and a calm expression spread across her face. She opened the door and walked into the room.

Damon Tuttle's hand slid up her arm, and in spite of the fact that she'd been braced to fight, she found herself being thrust against the blackboard behind her. His pale face, rank odor, red-rimmed eyes and cold stare told her more than she wanted to know. Even if he wasn't high now, he'd obviously spent most of the night that way.

"Take your seat, Damon," Annie said firmly, pushing him away from her.

He grinned and let his gaze rake her body from head to toe in a rude, sexual manner.

"I'm a little surprised to see you, Annie-Annie. Thought you might chicken..."

The sneer slid off of Damon Tuttle's face as his gaze went from Annie's nervous expression to the man who'd walked up behind her.

"Now, why would you think something like that?" Annie asked. "I haven't missed a day of school this year."

Damon flushed and looked nervously away as the big biker from yesterday pulled off his sunglasses and started toward him. In spite of his determination to remain belligerent, he felt himself backing away.

"Hey, *boy*," Gabe said softly, for Damon's ears alone. "I thought we settled all of this yesterday."

Damon tried to bluster his way out of the fact that, step-by-step, the biker was backing him all the way down the aisle to his seat, but it was no use. The obvious fact was that he was scared out of his mind.

"What's he doing here?" Damon asked loudly, and pointed toward Gabe, who refused to budge from his personal space.

"Who? Oh! You must mean Mr. Donner," Annie said in an offhand manner. "Just pretend he's not here," she said, quickly taking charge of her class. "Students, please take your seats."

Gabe grinned at Damon, and the boy shuddered at the feral gleam in the big man's eyes.

"She's right," Gabe said, sweeping his hand out to encompass the class of gaping students who'd suddenly realized he was there to stay. "You won't even know I'm around."

And then he stunned the entire class as his whispered

warning swept across the room. "But so help me, if one of you has one cross word to say to her…or looks at Miss O'Brien with anything other than a question about school on your mind, I'll take care of you myself." There was a long pause before he finished. "Have I made myself clear?"

They nodded as one, while silently absorbing the fact that their teacher had obviously hired herself a big gun. And then a tall, skinny youth at the back of the room stood up, making a subtle but daring move as he shoved his hands in his pockets while waiting for permission to speak.

Gabe's gaze swept over the young black man, and then he nodded. "You have something you need to say to me?" he asked softly.

"All I'm saying is…Miss O'Brien is one fine lookin' lady…if you know what I mean. So if you see me lookin' at her and you don't like the way I'm doin' it…then you just better bust my chops now, man, cause I can't help admiring the obvious."

Gabe chuckled, ignoring the flush that swept up Annie's face. "Yeah, man. I know what you mean, she is pretty. But the deal is to respect her, not take her apart…if *you* know what *I* mean."

The young man nodded and shrugged, then grinned and sat back down. A sprinkling of soft laughter flowed from one end of the room to the other, setting the mood for the rest of the class.

Finally the bell rang for classes to change and the students left. It was obvious from the quick, sideways glances Gabe got, and the near-silent manner in which the newcomers took their seats, that word had spread swiftly in the halls of the high school.

And when noontime came and the teachers drifted through the halls on their way to lunch, Annie O'Brien returned the favor by staring down any whispered comments about Gabe's presence and quietly introducing him to what he assumed were some of her friends and co-workers.

If it hadn't been so pathetic he would have laughed. Here he was, for the first time in his life able to experience what ordinary life was all about, and it was too late. For Gabe, it would always be too late.

The day was nearly over. Gabe sat at the back of the class, silent as a monolith, barely moving, never speaking, yet the entire day, his eyes had rarely drifted from Annie O'Brien.

He knew to the inch exactly how far up the blackboard her arm had to stretch before the fabric of her blouse cupped her breast and faintly outlined the nipple behind the cloth. He also knew that if she was facing the class when she smiled, the slight dimple at the left corner of her mouth wasn't evident. However, if her head was turned just so…and if she was really lost in what she was saying…it darted in and out like a pixie playing hide-and-seek.

He'd watched the sunlight play havoc with the hidden textures and colors of her hair until he'd had to mentally restrain himself from ignoring the fact that there was a classroom full of students watching every move he made. He'd never wanted anything in his life as much as he wanted to bury his face in her hair. To inhale the scent of her, to feel her heat and taste the texture of her skin.

He shuddered at the thought and shifted uncomfortably in his seat, stretching his long, jeans-clad legs out in front of him to ease the pressure behind his zipper.

What he'd expected to be unmitigated boredom had turned out to be a treat. He'd read history. Hell, he'd even lived part of what she'd taught earlier in the day. But he'd never expected to fall under the spell of being taught that there was more to it than dates and events. Too much of his life had been wasted just trying to survive, and when that had failed, the rest of it had been—and was *being*—spent on doing what he'd been sent back to do.

Ancient history seemed to be her favorite class. Sixth period and the Trojan War brought her to life. He, along with the students, began to visualize the great wooden horse slowly being rolled to the gates of Troy.

He smiled along with them as Annie related how the Greeks remaining outside must have waited impatiently for the soldiers encased within the bowels of the gift horse to climb out, drawing a picture with her words of how they'd emerged during the black of night and opened the great gate so that the Greek soldiers could come inside and conquer.

The great devastation of the siege that followed was presented as if she'd actually been there. Gabe wasn't the only one to be jerked rudely back to the present when the bell rang for classes to change.

"So the next time someone tells you, 'Don't look a gift horse in the mouth,' you'll know exactly what they mean." And then she added, "Don't forget that you have to finish reading *The Iliad* by Friday. It will be part of your final exam."

She laughed at their dismayed objections and took their good-natured grumbling as it was meant. One of the girls even paused on her way out the door to whisper something to Annie, and then ducked her head when Annie impulsively laughed and hugged her before shooing her out.

But Gabe was oblivious to the students' groans on the subject of finals. He was too busy trying to get past the realization of his own devastation as he watched Annie hug the teenage girl.

He was jealous. He wanted her to smile at *him* and share whispered nothings in *his* ear. And as he looked past the thought to the emotion behind it, he decided that he'd finally lost his mind.

He'd heard of the phenomenon, but mistakenly imagined

that it only befell *little* boys. But Gabriel Donner had been mistaken. Regardless of his age and the reason for his presence, he'd only spent one day in a classroom and already he'd fallen for the teacher.

In sudden panic, he grabbed his sunglasses from his pocket, slid them quickly onto his nose and glared through their darkened lenses, daring anyone to see through the mirrored reflection to the truth behind.

He couldn't be in love. For Gabriel Donner there was no future in loving. His future had ended the day the rope tightened around his neck. And regardless of the fact that he'd been returned intact to the earth on which he'd been born, for him, a future no longer existed. Only time…a waiting period that was soon coming to an end.

Annie gathered up the papers from her desk, sighing as she lifted the stack that would have to be graded tonight.

"Let me," Gabe said, and took them from her arms before she could object. "You did all the work today," he said by way of explanation, and stood aside for her to precede him from the room.

"Another day, another dollar," Annie said, and gave him a weary smile that made him stumble in his tracks.

Luckily for him she didn't notice him falter. She was too busy focusing on the two men standing at the end of the hallway.

"Oh, great," she muttered.

Gabe looked up, expecting to see Damon Tuttle and some of his friends. Instead, he recognized Allen Baker, the school administrator, but he didn't know the other man.

"Annie?"

The question in his voice stopped her progress, and she turned to face him. If he hadn't known Annie's fighting nature, he might have imagined he saw tears in her eyes. But that couldn't be. After facing down a gang of toughs and calmly dealing with the fact that her car had been demolished, surely two well-dressed men wouldn't be what it took to bring her down.

"It's the school superintendent," she said. "He's everyone's boss."

"Not mine," Gabe said quietly, and offered his elbow as they started down the hall.

Annie took a deep breath. It was odd what strength she'd gained from Gabe's two small words.

"Miss O'Brien." Censure was thick in Millard Penny's voice.

"Mr. Penny."

Annie stood steadfast, unwilling to give an inch. And with Gabe by her side, it was incredibly simple, after all.

"I don't like what I've been hearing," Millard Penny said, glaring at Gabe.

"I can imagine," Gabe answered, surprising everyone, including Annie, with his interruption. "What startled you most?" he asked. "The fact that one of your teachers was being assaulted and sexually harassed on a day-to-day basis...or the fact that Baker here chose to ignore it?"

Allen Baker stiffened, as if someone had just shoved a hot poker up his rear. Annie stifled a grin and slid one step closer to Gabriel as he continued.

"As I'm sure you've already realized, or you wouldn't be here, the media would have a field day with that information, wouldn't they?" Gabe asked.

He paused while Millard Penny digested his announcement, then grinned engagingly, tossing the problem right back in the superintendent's lap with his next remark. "What exactly did you have in mind? I can assure you, as Miss O'Brien's bodyguard, I'm willing to work in conjunction with any other security you authorize."

Penny was speechless.

And then Gabe's smile disappeared, and his eyes grew stormy. "However, you *do* realize that I am not budging from her side until she, and she alone, decides to dismiss me. I take my work seriously…very seriously."

Millard Penny stared. First at Annie, then at Allen Baker, then back at Gabriel. He wiped his hand across his face, dislodging the jowls hanging over his too-tight collar far enough that his chin quivered as he answered.

"I can see that this incident is going to take further study." He glared at Baker as if suddenly willing to lay the blame for the entire mess at his feet. "And as far as my teachers' security goes, you can rest assured that that is always uppermost in my mind."

"Thank you, Mr. Penny," Annie said. "I'm glad you've recognized my side of the problem." She stared pointedly at Allen Baker, then looked up at Gabriel.

He saw her determination being replaced with exhaustion. It was that moment when he knew that as long as Annie O'Brien had a fight that needed to be fought, he was her man. Like it or not, love be damned, she needed him. And it felt good…real good.

Gabe handed her his helmet. "Put this on, Annie. We're going home."

They left the two men arguing in the hall.

Chapter 3

After the hectic day and the constant state of defense in which they'd spent it, the apartment was a welcome haven. Gabe was beginning to understand Annie's love of plants. They were something alive with which she could share her space, and they didn't talk back.

Annie's face was pale, the tension lines around her mouth deep and drawn.

"You look beat. Why don't you take a nap?" Gabe suggested as he set the papers to be graded down on the kitchen table.

She gestured toward the stack and tried to smile, but a muscle jerked at the back of her neck, reminding her that the headache she'd been trying to ignore all day was about to take over.

"Maybe I will lie down for a minute," she said. "But I don't have time to sleep." Her lip trembled, and she looked everywhere but at Gabe. "Not yet. Not this soon."

He looked down at his watch. "At least rest until I get back. I've got an errand to run."

She shrugged and handed him her keys. "You'll need to get back in," she said, stumbling toward her bedroom as the pain at the back of her neck overwhelmed her.

Gabe looked at the keys and frowned. He couldn't understand her apparent lack of concern regarding his presence. She treated him as if she'd known him all her life. It just didn't make sense.

And as for her headache, he'd seen others like it before. He stuffed her keys in his pocket and followed her, afraid she was going to need help getting where she was going. He was right. He caught her as she staggered.

"Annie, are you all right?"

Uncertainty filled him as her head lolled against his shoulder. Only hours earlier she'd been ready to fight tigers...and Damon Tuttle. Now she couldn't even get herself to bed.

"I stubbed my toe," she mumbled, unwilling to admit how weak she felt, and covered her ears with her hands, dreading the sound of her own voice. "My head hurts."

"I know, Annie," he said softly. "I know."

Without a word, Gabe lifted her into his arms and carried her to her bed. Her face was a contorted mixture of misery and embarrassment as she struggled to help herself.

"Let me," Gabe said, and pulled off her shoes. "Got anything for the pain?" he asked, as he entered her bathroom and began shuffling through the shelves of her medicine cabinet.

"Brown bottle...bottom shelf," she mumbled, then groaned as the words vibrated against her eardrums.

Gabe picked up the bottle and frowned. Prescription medicine. No over-the-counter stuff for Annie. He read the label and frowned again. *Strong* prescription medicine. He hoped she wasn't hooked on the stuff. She wouldn't have been the first to get unintentionally addicted.

He filled a glass with water, then carried it and the bottle back to Annie's bed. The mattress gave beneath his weight, rolling her gently against his thigh as he scooted close beside her.

"Open," he ordered, and slipped the prescribed dosage between her lips. By that time her teeth were chattering from the tension, and a few drops of water slid out the corner of her mouth as he tilted the glass.

She swallowed, then dropped back onto the pillow with a groan, unaware of Gabe's fingers gently blotting the trickle of water before it stained her blue silk shirt.

He swallowed harshly as his hand touched her skin. Just as before, her body was satin to his touch. As her eyelids fluttered between the daylight and dusk hovering at the back of her mind, he cradled the side of her cheek, absently testing the pulse at the base of her neck. It was racing.

Gabe leaned back, smoothing her tousled hair away from her forehead, and felt tiny beads of sweat across her brow. Something was wrong. He hoped to God she wasn't getting sick. He knew even less about healing than he did about school, but today it seemed as if he was about to get a dose of both.

She sighed as blessed sleep claimed her, missing the tender touch of his hand and the fire that kindled in his eyes as he leaned down and kissed the curve of her cheek.

"Just rest, Annie. Rest," he whispered. "I'll be back."

Annie opened her eyes. The glow from the streetlights coming through the slats in her blinds told her that it was dark. Where had the evening gone? Then she remembered the headache and vague impressions of being put to bed like a child. She bolted up as if she'd been shot and raced out of her room and across the hall, half expecting to see that a big man and his duffel bag had gone missing. She was right.

"Oh, no," she groaned, and ran toward the living room, afraid of what she would find next. What she didn't expect was to hear the hum of her washer and dryer in the alcove off the kitchen, or the smell of warm pizza drifting in the air.

"I saved you some pizza," Gabe muttered, pointing toward a half-open cardboard box. "It's a good thing you woke up. I've graded as far as I can go. I was never much good at stuff like this, but I can at least follow your key." He waved her answer sheet in the air, then leaned back and grinned.

Annie stared. This was the last thing she'd expected to see. He was grading her papers...and he wasn't wearing enough clothes for her peace of mind. And then she remembered the pizza.

"You bought food?"

He nodded.

"I'm sorry," she muttered, running a shaky hand through her tousled hair. "You're spending your money on me, and we haven't even discussed salary."

Gabe noticed the nervous way she kept glancing at him, then remembered his disheveled state and grinned.

"Sorry about my, uh..." He waved toward his near-bare body and shrugged, as if to say he had no choice. "I'm doing laundry."

His grin told her that he was obviously lying. He wasn't sorry about a thing, and Annie knew it.

"What exactly is that you're wearing?" she asked, trying not to stare at all that expanse of tanned body and hard muscle.

"Your tablecloth. It was the only thing big enough to wrap around me. I don't think flowers do much for my manliness, but..." He shrugged and waved toward his makeshift sarong to make his point.

He could have saved himself the trouble. It was impossible to ignore his manliness...any of it. Annie tried not to stare in the direction the sweet-pea-and-ivy print was climbing, but she couldn't help noticing that it had climbed right up his leg and wrapped itself around his...

"Supreme," he said.

You certainly are, Annie thought, and then jumped as her own thoughts reminded her that she was losing control. "What?"

"The pizza," he said, pointing toward the box again. "I got supreme. And you'll have to grade this stack," he said, as he shoved the papers toward her.

"I can't believe you did that, but thanks," she said, pointing toward the papers, and then took a bite of pizza. She muttered a near-silent curse as a string of cheese fell onto the edge of her collar.

Gabe stood up. And as he came toward her, bells and buzzers began to sound. Annie's eyes widened. So much man in so little fabric.

Fear interceded as she watched him coming closer and closer. She began backing up, until the kitchen wall halted her flight and left her helpless and pinned, the slice of pizza clutched tightly in her hand.

Without saying a word, Gabe reached out, lifted the string of cheese from her collar and dangled it in front of her lips. Stunned by the unexpected action, Annie opened her mouth like a baby bird as Gabe dropped the cheese inside.

Her heartbeat rode her racing pulse like a winded jockey as she watched him, certain that he was about to eat her...or her pizza, whichever came first. He did neither.

Instead, he gently moved her aside and opened the door behind her. It was then that she realized why she'd been hearing bells and buzzers. The washer and dryer had finished their cycles simultaneously. He was merely getting his clean clothes out of the laundry.

"Why don't you sit down to eat, Annie?" he asked. "You need all the rest you can get. I never realized that teaching could be such a headache."

He grinned at his own wit as he disappeared down the hall in a swath of sweet peas and ivy. He returned a moment later, dragging long-legged blue jeans along the carpet, with a handful of white cotton briefs clutched against his chest.

"I *am* going to sit down to eat," Annie said unnecessarily, and plopped down in the chair he'd just vacated.

The chair was still warm from his body, and the suggestion it sent drifting into her mind had her out of it in seconds and into the one on the opposite side. She'd had all the excitement she could take for one day. Thinking about big bikers and their warm behinds did nothing for her peace of mind.

The evening passed without further upheaval, as did the next few days. One week turned into two, and then, before she knew it, they'd actually developed a routine of living together that was almost comfortable.

It was his proper, almost blasé attitude and her own casual acceptance of his presence in her life that—most of the time—made her forget how truly male he was. But she was reminded all too vividly one weekend when she looked up from the chair in which she was sitting to see him burst through the door, half naked and mad as hell.

"Where is your shirt?" It was the first thing that came to mind, but Annie knew the moment she'd asked that it was the worst question she could have asked.

Gabe grinned, but not with humor. He stalked past her and continued down the hallway toward his room without answering.

Annie got up from her chair, pulling absently at her white T-shirt and shorts to straighten them as she followed. It was then that she saw the small path of blood splattered on the floor in his wake and felt a moment of panic as she realized that it had to be Gabe who was bleeding.

Ignoring propriety, she burst into his room without knocking and caught him leaning over the sink in his bathroom, trying to wash a long, angry slash on the back of his arm.

"You're bleeding!"

He turned. His eyes pierced her, blue shards of icy fury pinning her in place.

"Not as much as I was before," he drawled, remembering the puddle of blood he'd left beside his bike, along with what was left of his shirt in the garbage can outside. He winced when the cold washcloth slid along the tear in his flesh.

"Oh, my God," Annie said, and moved. Before she could think, she'd taken the cloth from his hand and pushed him backward onto the commode. "Sit down," she said, and leaned forward, peering over his shoulder to see if there was further damage to his back that she hadn't noticed.

Gabe hit the seat with a sigh, wearily giving in to the exhaustion and pain he was experiencing, and wondered how much longer his body could endure what he put it through. In the same thought, he realized the silent question was moot. If his calculations were correct, his time on earth was nearly up. It was that thought, and the knowledge that he couldn't have the forever that he wanted with this woman beside him, that made him react as he did when Annie cupped his chin with her fingers and started to wipe the cool, damp cloth across his face as she would a child's.

He took the cloth from her hands and flung it into the bathtub, and before she knew what was happening, she was in his lap, and his hands were on her face. She had one moment of fear, and then it swiftly disappeared as he groaned, leaned forward and covered her lips with his own.

Annie shuddered. It was like feeling steel melt against her lips. At first his lips were hard and hot, and then they shifted, softening, testing the corners of her mouth, her chin, even the hollow at her neck.

"Gabriel," she whispered, and then, when she could

breathe again, she realized that he'd only begun. His body trembled beneath her fingers, and as her hand slid down the front of his chest, his heartbeat thundered beneath the skin, rumbling like the Harley's engine on a wild ride to heaven…or hell.

He scooped her into his arms and stood. Without words, he carried her into his room and then stopped by the side of his bed. His gaze went from her face to his bed, then back again. In spite of the question in his eyes, Annie could not speak. It was all the answer he needed.

The bedspread was cool and slick against the bare skin on the backs of her legs as Gabe deposited her with little aplomb. Annie shuddered and moaned as his hands swept down the front of her breasts, molding the thin fabric of her T-shirt to her generous curves. He straddled her body, positioning himself so that her womanhood was in perfect juxtaposition to his own aching need, and then leaned forward and pressed his mouth across the protesting bud he'd made of her nipple, which protruded upward beneath the cloth.

With mouth and hands, he moved across her body like a marauding outlaw, and just when Annie thought he would take without asking, he stopped, buried his face against her belly and started to shake.

"Gabriel?"

She traced her fingers across the taut, corded muscles of his neck and shoulders, feeling the tension and the emotion he was trying to control.

"I want you, Annie." His voice was low and guttural, muffled against her belly as he struggled with the red-hot need to rip the clothes from her body and bury himself deep inside her heat. "But it isn't fair to you. You deserve promises I can't make. A love I can't give. You don't deserve this…to be taken in want and need. And right now—" a shudder ripped through him as his fingers tightened in the flesh at her waist "—all I'm feeling is need."

It killed him to admit the truth of his feelings, but it would have been the end of him later if he'd taken her in a lie.

Tears squeezed from the corners of Annie's eyes as her hands gently stroked his shoulders and down his back until she actually felt the anger dissipating beneath her touch.

"It's all right, Gabriel," she whispered. "It's all right." *I would have been willing to settle for need,* she told herself as she watched him roll off her body and walk back into the bathroom. *There's no time in my life for promises, either. Not anymore.*

She got off the bed and walked out of the room.

It was only days later, standing in line at a local supermarket, that she learned what had happened to him. That he'd walked into a robbery at a gas station not three blocks from her home and wound up in a fight that might have cost him his life.

When she heard the story, Annie stared at the box of cornflakes in her hand and then down at her basket and tried to remember what she'd been about to do. But she couldn't. All she could hear was the woman praising an unknown biker for saving her husband's life, and all she could see were the events that had ensued.

It was then that Annie thought she understood where Gabriel's intense need to have sex had come from. It must be a natural emotion to want to feel alive, when only a short time earlier you had come so close to being dead.

The cornflakes fell from her limp fingers onto a loaf of bread as Annie closed her eyes and swallowed past a lump in her throat. She could think of no better way to feel alive than to experience the blessed rush that came from the joining of two bodies with one purpose…making love.

Time continued to pass with little mention ever made of the near miss they'd had and the wanting that hung between them. Gabe's presence in Annie's world had become so solid that she could not imagine life without him. Yet always, at that thought, came an overwhelming sadness, because for Annie, there would be no future with Gabe. When school was over, he would leave her. She had to face that fact. It was the only way she could·get through the days they had left.

Sirens screamed, matching a woman's terrified shriek. Annie sat straight up in bed, heart pounding, eyes heavy with sleep as she tried to imagine why she was still hearing a nightmare when she was wide awake.

A door banged across the hall, and Annie realized that she wasn't having the dream alone. Gabriel's footsteps moved quickly toward the living room. It was only when she heard the front door open and then slam shut behind him that she knew she was truly awake. She bolted out of bed and ran to the window.

Her first thought was that she was hearing police sirens. But when she parted the curtains and looked outside, her heart sank. Fire trucks were everywhere.

"Oh, God! The complex must be on fire," she moaned, and ran to the closet. If she was going to lose everything she owned within the next few minutes, she didn't want to be nearly naked when it happened.

In less than a minute she had on jeans and a sweatshirt. With socks and shoes in hand and shaking from the rush of fear and adrenaline, she stuffed her personal identification in the hip pocket of her jeans and ran for the door.

In the back of her mind, she was both surprised and disappointed that Gabriel had left the apartment without even warning her of the danger. But then, as she raced toward the parking lot where the other residents were gathering, she realized that she'd misjudged him completely. The danger was not to her own building, but to the one two buildings over and closest to the street.

Using the bumper of the nearest car for a makeshift seat,

she quickly put on her socks and shoes, shivering nervously as she struggled to tie the strings without making knots, still wondering where Gabriel was and why he'd disappeared so fast.

Firemen were wielding their hoses and making way for the paramedic unit that had just arrived. The paramedics rushed out of the ambulance and, with skill born of long years of practice, quickly cleared a space in the crowd as they began setting up a first-aid station. Another ambulance arrived, available, if needed, to transport the injured. And then a woman's horrified shriek silenced the crowd's rumble of dismay.

"There's a child in that apartment!"

All eyes turned toward the third-story apartment facing the parking lot. A small girl, probably no more than nine or ten, was outlined by the flashing lights from below as she stood at the window, pounding on the glass with both hands. It was like watching terror in pantomime as she struggled helplessly against the glass barrier, unable to lift the window.

The onlookers, Annie included, felt sickened and helpless as they watched the child through the glass. Gabriel's whereabouts was momentarily forgotten in her shock, until she saw a tall, dark man slip through the crowd, run past the fire fighters and into the smoke-filled doorway.

"Gabriel!" Annie screamed, but her shout was lost in the noise around her.

Few people even acknowledged her cry as they stared transfixed toward the child, who was now moving helplessly from window to window in the room.

A handful of firemen held a net directly below her, but she was still unable to break the window. The people could only watch and hope that the man would be able to rescue her in time. Annie increased her own silent but terrified pleas for help as they waited and prayed.

"Oh, my God," Annie whispered, pressing shaking fingers against her lips, unable...unwilling...to believe that she'd really seen Gabe run into the building.

Frantically, she began moving through the crowd in the parking lot, certain that any minute Gabe would grab her arm and spin her around with that heart-stopping smile on his face, chiding her for her fears. But it didn't happen, and she had to face the fact that it *was* him that she'd seen.

A local news crew, which had materialized out of nowhere, had also seen the man, and cameras were instantly trained on the last place he had been seen, as well as the girl in the window.

Fear such as Annie had never known enveloped her. This was worse than anything she'd ever experienced. Fear for herself she could cope with. But this fear for another human being, one who'd come to mean more to her than he should, nearly overwhelmed her.

Ignoring the intermittent tails of smoke that blew toward the crowd in which she was standing, Annie stared at the child in the window and prayed as she'd never prayed before.

Long moments that seemed like hours passed, and then suddenly another gasp went up through the crowd. Flames could now be seen behind the child, and they all knew it was only a matter of moments before it would be too late.

"There's someone in there!" a man shouted and raised his arm, pointing toward the child as a second figure appeared at the window.

Moments later glass shattered onto the firemen below. But they stood their ground and waited, bracing themselves and holding on even tighter to the net. Seconds later, two figures stood in the opening. A man leaned out, holding the limp body of the child. Just as the camera crew focused, he let go of the child, and she fell through the air, as silent as her earlier plea for help had been.

With hardly a thud, the firemen deftly made the catch and then transferred her semiconscious body to the arms of a paramedic, who turned and made a dash toward the waiting ambulance. The man came next. With the flames licking at his feet and no time to maneuver, he leapt headfirst out the window.

Gabe landed on his back, unable to believe that he was still in one piece as he stared up at the smoke-filled night sky.

"You crazy son of a bitch," one of the firemen said, as they rolled him out of the net and slapped him roughly on the back. "You could have been killed."

Gabe staggered to his feet as he gratefully drew long draughts of clean air into his lungs. A man in uniform began heading toward him. Unwilling to explain himself, Gabe turned and quickly lost himself in the gathering crowd.

Annie had watched until she saw him stand up. Then she buried her face in her hands and fell to her knees, unable to move for the relief that coursed through her body. Hands appeared from the crowd around her, quickly pulling her to her feet, then moving her to the edge of the pack.

"Are you all right, miss?" a voice asked.

Annie looked up into the face of a man she recognized as living in her own building. She nodded.

"You sure?" he continued. "It looks as if they've got it under control. I'd be glad to walk you back to your place."

"No, no, I'm fine," Annie muttered, and began looking for Gabe. He was nowhere to be seen.

She pulled away from her neighbor's grasp and started running. Something told her that Gabe wouldn't stick around for an interview. She headed for her apartment.

Her legs were shaking along with her hands as she struggled with the doorknob, trying to make it turn. And then finally it gave and she burst into the living room, only to hear the sound of water running in the shower down the hall. Without sparing a thought for what she was about to do, she slammed the door behind her and began to run. Seconds later she was in his bedroom.

A heavy mist floated out of the shower stall. A pile of smoke-tainted clothing lay in the doorway. The faint but unmistakable outline of a tall, male figure behind the frosted Plexiglas door was all the impetus she needed.

Gabe was leaning with arms outstretched against the wall, bracing himself beneath the flow of water, letting it wash away the acrid stench of smoke and fire. He leaned forward, closed his eyes and sighed as the steady stream rushed over his head and down the back of his neck, easing the muscles he'd strained only moments before and soothing the tiny scorched places on his skin. And then the door flew open and he moved away from the water's force, staring in shock at the look on Annie's face.

"You could have been killed," she said in a broken whisper.

Ignoring the fact that she was fully dressed and he was not, she stepped into the shower and into his arms.

"Annie! My God!" Gabe groaned, as his body betrayed him.

Water pelted down on top of them. Several seconds passed as Gabe stood in shock before he thought to reach over her shoulder and close the door to keep the floor from being flooded.

"Back off, Annie!" His voice thickened as her hands moved up and down his back in a desperate, searching motion, as if she couldn't believe he was actually there and in her arms.

But his warning was useless. She was as glued to him as her clothing was to her own body. With a muttered oath, he reached over her once again, this time to turn off the shower.

Suddenly there was only the sound of Gabriel's harshly indrawn breath as she stepped back and looked at him. Everywhere. Once again his body betrayed him, and this time there was no way he could hide what her nearness had done.

Annie closed her eyes and let the sensations of what she'd seen fill her. And when she opened them again, it was to feel him pulling her wet sweatshirt over her head.

"You have about thirty seconds to get the hell out of here," Gabe said. "Or it'll be too late...for both of us."

She shook her head and slid the palms of her hands up his chest as the sweatshirt fell to the floor of the shower with a soggy plop. Her bare breasts tingled as a draft of air moved across them, tightening the nubs in their centers to a jutting pout.

Gabriel groaned and bent forward, testing them with the end of his tongue. She sighed as his lips moved over her and leaned against his body when her knees went weak, bracing her hands on his chest, where his heart pounded wildly beneath the skin.

"It's already too late, Gabriel. It has been since the day we met."

He wasn't certain it was tears that he saw on her face. It could have been the lingering remnants of their shower. But the trembling of her lower lip told him all he needed to know.

"Annie...I can't promise you anything," he said harshly, still unable to make the last and final move toward the inevitable.

"I don't need promises, Gabriel. Promises mean a future. You and I don't have that. All we have is now...and it's all I need."

The shower door flew back, slamming with a sharp thud against the wall as Gabriel picked her up and carried her to his bed. There, in a tangle of teddy bears and bed sheets, he stripped her of the rest of her clothing and covered her body with the fierce determination of a warrior claiming his prize.

He was everything she'd imagined and more than she could have dreamed. His hands moved with gentle finesse across her body, lighting fires in places that had never been ignited before. Every curve of her skin became a flash point of nerves. She struggled beneath him, trying to return the favors of his loving, and then found herself unable to do anything but simply hang on to his shoulders as he took them both to a place where time ceased and sensation was the beginning and end of everything.

"Annie, Annie, Annie."

Her name was a chant on his lips as his hands slid between her legs. And then a roar began in her ears that blocked out everything but the feelings building beneath her skin. Fire bursts came in sudden, intense jolts, starting from the center of her being and emanating outward, melting her bones and her senses until she could no longer move or think. All there was in her world was Gabriel's hands, his lips, and the feel of his body moving up and then over... down and inside.

Gabriel slid between her legs, shuddering with every breath as his mind raced his body for control. But Annie's own loss of control was unbelievable, unexpected, and too much to resist.

Her hands said what her lips could not as she grasped his shoulders and urged him on. And when her hips lifted from the bed and begged him to come closer, he did. By then he was too far in and too far gone to remember to prolong anything but the need to breathe.

Annie's heart raced, her body burned, and Gabriel kept touching matches to the fire with intensifying thrusts.

When the first tremors began inside her, moving along his manhood in tiny, convulsive jerks, Gabriel groaned from the pleasure. Through a sensual fog, he watched as Annie closed her eyes, bit her lower lip and arched upward, trying to engulf him. And then everything exploded around them as the world tilted on its axis, and Gabriel held on to the woman beneath him to keep from flying away.

The last thing Annie remembered before falling asleep was Gabe's arms enfolding her and his faint whisper drifting across her ears.

"This wasn't supposed to happen, Annie Laurie," he kept saying. "This wasn't supposed to happen."

Hours later Annie felt herself being taken from the warm bed and carried across the hall. A sharp, unwelcome pain surfaced behind her eyelids when she realized that Gabe had put her back in her own bed. She all but held her breath, unwilling for him to know that she was awake. The hurt was too fresh and too swift as she realized that he hadn't even been willing to awaken with her in his arms.

Finally she heard his footsteps receding, and then the door to her room closed. It was then that the tears came, and with them, the knowledge that she had no reason to cry. He'd warned her that he had no room for promises in his life. And yet Annie knew that she wasn't actually crying because he couldn't promise her anything. She was crying because it wouldn't have mattered if he had.

The next morning the newspapers and television stations were full of the phantom hero who'd dared the fires of hell and saved a child from the burning building. The grainy footage of the rescue was played and replayed the entire day, but luckily for Gabriel, the thick, billowing smoke had hidden his face.

Annie didn't understand his reticence and wondered again if she was harboring a man who was on the run from something…or someone. She didn't want to think that Gabriel had a lurid past. But all she had to do was catch him unaware and look, really look, at the hard expression he wore when he thought no one was watching, and her fears came back twofold.

* * *

The intercom buzzed, an indication that an announcement from the principal's office would be forthcoming. Annie paused in the middle of her lecture and waited without looking at the back of the room, where she knew Gabriel was watching her every move. Since the night they'd made love, little more than quiet politeness had passed between them. Each evening, immediately after they got home, Gabriel would disappear into his room and come out only to eat or run the occasional errand for her. Yet his looks had gentled, and she would have sworn she saw constant regret coloring the expression on his face.

Twice she'd tried to pay him for his duties as a bodyguard, and each time she'd yanked the check back, his anger so fierce that she'd half expected to see that he'd lopped her hand off at the wrist.

While part of her understood that something had changed between them, the other part of her needed to fulfill her own promise and alleviate the guilt she felt over what had happened the night of the fire. She'd all but begged him for intimacy, and after he'd warned her there was no future in it for either of them.

She fumbled with the papers on her desk as she waited for Allen Baker to make his announcement, desperately trying to ignore the feelings that had returned with her thoughts of making love with Gabe.

Gabriel's eyes narrowed as he watched her look at everyone and everything but him. In a way he understood her need to maintain the distance between them, and in another way he resented the hell out of the fact that she'd been able to do it. Since the moment she'd opened the shower and walked into his arms, she'd been more deeply imbedded in his senses than the heat and smoke from that fire.

"This concerns all graduating seniors," Allen Baker said, his voice slightly distorted from the microphone. "Please remember that graduation practice will be right after school today. Try to attend. It will help the actual ceremony go much more smoothly this weekend.''

He signed off with a short witticism that no one laughed at, leaving the class oddly silent.

Damon Tuttle fidgeted in his seat and stared at Annie with his old hatred as she turned her back to the class and began writing an assignment on the blackboard.

Gabriel sensed an imminent eruption, and still he was surprised by the anger with which it came.

"You bitch!" Damon Tuttle shouted as he stood up from his desk and threw his book toward Annie.

Gabriel bolted for the front of the room, but not in time to stop the book. He winced, then breathed a quick sigh of relief as he saw Annie duck. Two students near the door jumped up and ran into the hall.

Gabriel heard their footsteps echoing toward what he hoped was the principal's office. He had no time to be dealing with anything except the fact that Damon Tuttle had just pulled a knife and jumped over two desks in an effort to get to Annie.

"Annie, run!" Gabriel shouted, then said a prayer as he made a flying leap, catching Damon at the back of the legs and sending them both falling across desks and then rolling onto the floor.

The piny scent of cleaning solvent came up and hit Gabriel in the face as he and Damon rolled over and over on the floor, fighting desperately with each other for control of the knife.

Damon Tuttle's pupils were dilated, his nostrils flared, as venomous curses poured from his mouth.

A security guard burst into the room, with Allen Baker right behind him. Among the three of them, they managed to subdue Damon Tuttle without anyone being injured.

And when the knife in Damon's hand fell to the floor at Allen Baker's feet, he could only stare in stunned disbelief.

The security guard slapped handcuffs on Damon as sirens were heard in the distance.

"I'll get you, you bitch," Damon kept shouting. "You won't get away with this. You'll be sorry you gave me grief!"

Gabriel shook as he grabbed the youth's arm and yanked him around to face him.

"She didn't give you anything but a chance at a better life," Gabe said.

Damon spat on Gabriel's boots, then looked up with hate-filled eyes. "She didn't give me nothin'. Anything I have...I gave myself," he yelled back, screaming and kicking out at the guard and the principal alike.

"Take him out of here," Allen Baker ordered, and then he stepped aside in undisguised fear as Damon's glare of hatred was turned on him.

Damon was still screaming and cursing when they dragged him out the door and into a patrol car.

"Is anyone hurt?" Annie asked quickly, searching the room as students began rearranging their belongings and moving desks back into place. The tremor in her voice was evident, but no fear showed in her movements. As usual, in her classroom, Annie was in total control.

"No, ma'am," several students echoed.

"Then please take your seats. Turn to the last chapter of the book and begin reviewing the quiz. Test tomorrow."

With that she walked out of the room and into the hall. It was there that Gabriel caught her.

His arm was on her wrist as she spun around. The look in his eyes was wild. A thin trickle of blood ran from the corner of his lip. Annie dug in her pocket for a tissue. She had started to blot the blood with shaking hands when Gabriel stopped her.

"Why the hell didn't you run?" Gabriel asked, his voice rough with dying panic.

"Because it was my classroom. Those are my students. If I'd run, one of *them* might have suffered, instead."

"Oh, God, Annie," Gabriel said, and pulled her into his arms. For the first time since they'd made love he was holding her, and he knew then that it wouldn't be the last.

"He hurt you," she said, and buried her face against his chest.

"He didn't hurt me, Annie. I hurt myself."

She looked up. His blue eyes were blazing with a fire she could not miss. At that moment she knew that what he'd just said had nothing to do with Damon and everything to do with them.

She sighed and then let him pull her back into his arms. For whatever time they had left, she would not deny him, or herself, anything.

Chapter 4

Their feelings were out in the open. The knowing and the wanting no longer had to be hidden. But it didn't make that first step toward each other any easier.

Glances were swift, smiles easier, but still uncomfortable, and the air between them was thick with unspoken emotions as they drove home from school.

Annie went straight to her room to change, while Gabe lingered in the front of the apartment, prowling from kitchen to living room and back again, uncertain which way to go with the shift in their relationship.

He'd promised her nothing, and she'd accepted that...and whatever else he was willing to give. But the professional Annie O'Brien was at odds with the one he saw at home. The one at school let no one intrude on her territory. She was proud and protective of all her students. Except for Damon Tuttle, she even made excuses for the troublemakers.

But that Annie didn't fit with the Annie who'd taken a

total stranger into her home, offered him a bed, and then slept only feet away with nothing more than a few yards of carpeting and a couple of doors between them. Why had she taken such chances with her own safety? He could have been far more of a danger than three Damon Tuttles.

Gabe stalked to the window and stared out into the street, fingering his lip, which had been cut during the fight, and remembering the night of the fire and the abandon with which Annie had come to him. His gut kicked as his body reacted to the memory of them together in the shower, wet and naked, and the way she'd calmly accepted his warning of "no promises."

He frowned. Either she was lying to herself or to him about her feelings, because in all his long years, he'd never known another woman who would accept his making love without also making promises. And knowing he couldn't make them made him sick. Never before, in the millions of miles that he'd traveled, had he ever regretted the fact that he couldn't say what he was sure Annie needed to hear.

He leaned his forehead against the windowpane, letting the lingering warmth from the heat of the day soothe the ache between his eyes as he wished that his life had been different. And then, at that notion, he laughed aloud.

Hell! If it had been different, I would have been dust long ago and never have known my Annie.

At the same moment that he realized he'd thought of her as his, she walked up behind him. It was the shock of that realization and the feel of her hands on his back that made him react as he did.

"Are you all right?" Annie asked, remembering the viciousness with which Damon had fought and the strength that Gabe had used to subdue him.

"No," Gabe growled, and pulled her off her feet and into his arms.

Her own reaction was instinctive. Annie held on. She had

no other choice as he carried her down the hall toward his room.

"You shouldn't be carrying me," Annie said. "You may be hurt."

"I *am* hurting," he said, as he reached the side of the bed. He turned her in his arms and slid her body slowly down against his own as he set her back on her feet.

"I hurt here," he said, emotion thick in his voice, as he took her hand and splayed it across his chest, watching with intensity as her fingers traced the feel of his heartbeat. "And I hurt here," he continued, and took her hand, moving it from his chest to the growing ache between his legs.

Annie gasped at the seductive familiarity and then found herself cupping him instead of withdrawing, instantly drawn into the promise of passion hovering behind a curtain of blue jeans.

At her touch, Gabe lost control. If only she'd pulled back or made a sound of complaint, given any indication that he'd overstepped a boundary, he might have stopped. But she hadn't moved except to trace the power of his need and caress it even more as it pushed against her hand.

"Annie!"

Her name echoed loudly in the silence, and then she began to shake as his hands tore at her clothing, yanking at buttons, struggling with zippers, furious with whatever stood between him and the need she'd created.

With every garment he pulled off, her own passion grew. By the time she was naked, her hands were trembling. She unzipped his jeans and felt him, shivering from the onslaught of feelings that swept through her. She felt omnipotent, as if she were holding on to lightning, just waiting for the thunderbolt that would take her to heaven. Her legs went weak as she tried to pull the shirt from his back, suddenly anxious for the feelings that she knew he was capable of creating within her.

"No," he groaned, as red pinpoints of light began to appear before his eyes. He was too far gone to take the time to undress. "No time," he said, and braced his legs as he lifted her up and then impaled her on his engorged manhood.

Annie's gasp slid across his senses as she braced herself against his chest.

She felt his mouth at her temple and sighed with anxious expectation for what was coming. Just as the room began to spin, she inadvertently looked down and saw how their bodies were melding. The image was staggering, and her head snapped back in an instant need to see his face, to know if what he was experiencing was as powerful and out of control as she imagined. She wasn't prepared for his desperation.

His eyes were burning, blue fire in a face gone taut with passion. His nostrils flared, and the perfect cut of his lips had thinned as his need for this woman sent him out of control.

"Don't move," Gabriel said harshly. Blood pounded against his eardrums, rocketing through his body in a wild, near-vicious flow as he struggled with his own lust in a need to give her pleasure.

But Annie didn't—or couldn't—heed the warning. Her legs wrapped around his waist, and as they did, she drew him even farther into her heat.

Honey flowed around him, moving him too far inside to pull back. With a groan, they fell onto the bed in a tumble of arms and legs, and without missing a beat, Gabriel began to thrust.

Unable to prolong the passion, unwilling to wait for the thunderous climax he knew was coming, he closed his eyes, wrapped his arms around Annie and let the storm overtake them.

The suddenness with which it struck left her breathless,

with tears washing her cheeks in wild abandon. Her neck arched, her hands clung, as Gabriel rode her toward madness.

The end came without warning. No buildup of sensations, no increasing fire. Just a blinding flash of heat that seared their bodies, then seeped through their systems, leaving them weak and shaken.

Gabriel felt her tears on his face and knew a moment of terror. Had he hurt her? How could he have used her so viciously without a thought for her own needs? With a groan, he lifted himself from her body and stared down into her face and the wild tangle he'd made of her hair.

"Annie, Annie...sweet Lord, but I'm sorry. Don't cry. Please don't cry."

She shuddered and pulled him back into her arms.

"How can I not?" she asked, as emotion shook her voice. "Beauty always makes me cry."

Her words stunned him. Shamed by the giving nature of the woman beneath him, he covered her face with gentle kisses of thanksgiving and knew a terrible moment of regret that they would never have a lifetime together.

Moments later he rid himself of the rest of his clothing and then fell back into bed, wrapping her tight within his embrace as he pulled her head beneath his chin. Slowly her body relaxed against him, and he knew almost to the moment when she fell asleep. It was only then that he could speak, and when he did, he kept repeating the same words softly...over and over.

"Annie...my Annie."

Saturday came and went with little notice. It was the next morning before Gabriel realized what Annie was doing. She'd retreated from his bed to her own room shortly upon waking. Now his brow furrowed thoughtfully as he listened to the water running in her shower.

*Just what does she have to do this morning that's impor-
tant enough to take her out of my arms?*

Gabe rolled out of bed and headed for his own shower.
If she was going somewhere, she would still need him at
her side. Although Damon Tuttle had been booked and
jailed, the judicial system was notorious for releasing the
wrong people at the wrong time.

Minutes later Gabe headed for the kitchen, wearing nothing but a pair of Levi's and a frown. He poured a cup of
coffee and then turned with it halfway to his lips as he
watched Annie come up the hallway and into the kitchen.
She looked different. Suspicion continued to grow.

"You put up your hair," he said.

It was more accusation than observation. Gabe took a
slow sip of coffee while trying to decipher her nervousness.

"Is there any more coffee?" Annie asked, knowing full
well that the pot had just been made.

Gabe rolled his eyes and handed her his cup. "Take
mine," he said. "You look like you need it worse than I
do."

Her features froze. The moment he said it, he saw her
pain. At that instant Gabe wished himself into the next century.

Annie set the cup down and turned away. Her dress billowed out around her legs as she walked toward the window. Gabe stared at the slender, seductive outline of her
body beneath the fragile yellow fabric and wished he knew
what he'd said that was so bad. He'd already learned that
when Annie hurt, so did he. That he'd caused it made the
pain nearly unbearable.

"What? What on earth did I say?" he asked as he followed her to the window, cupping her shoulders with his
hands and pulling her toward him until her back rested
against his chest. He felt her momentary slump, and then
all the muscles in her body tensed as she answered him.

"Wrong? Nothing's wrong," she mumbled. "It's Sunday. I'm just going to church…that's all."

He grew still. *Church! Oh damn.*

Even now, churches still made him nervous. All he had to do was walk into one, and every feeling he'd suffered from the time he'd been hanged, until he came to facedown in the Kansas dirt, returned in full. Everything he'd seen and heard ricocheted inside his head like a nightmare until he could exit the building.

He had a feeling that it was God's way of reminding him why he'd been given a second chance. What he was having trouble reconciling was the fact that for the first time in nearly a hundred and fifty years, Annie had given him a reason for living, and it was too late to care.

"Great…church," he muttered, unaware that she heard him.

"I don't remember asking you to go," Annie said shortly.

Gabe stared. Something was terribly wrong. If he hadn't known better, he would have sworn that she didn't want him along.

"You can't ride on the back of my bike in that dress," he said, choosing to ignore her rudeness.

"I called a cab," she said, and shrugged out of his grasp.

"I don't have anything to wear," he said.

Annie smiled in spite of herself. "That's supposed to be my line," she said, and turned.

Gabe stared down into green eyes welling with tears. Whatever was going on, he had no intention of missing it. He took her chin between his thumb and forefinger and tilted her face so that she couldn't miss what he was about to say.

"You do not go without me," he ordered, and disappeared.

Annie sighed. She should have known he would be like this. She kicked her toe furiously into the plush gray carpet and then winced when a small pain shot up her leg. How could she have known that hiring a solitary man like Gabriel Donner would become so complicated? Why did he have to come into her life when it was too late to matter?

A yellow cab pulled up into the parking lot of the apartment and honked. Annie looked out the window and then went to get her purse. She would only warn him once. If he missed the ride, it wouldn't be her fault.

"Cab's here," she said, barely loud enough for him to hear, and started out the door with her purse strap slung over her shoulder.

"Got your keys?" Gabe asked as he grasped the door at a point just above her head.

She swiveled around and glared, and then dug into her purse to check. She pulled them out and slapped them into his outstretched hand, then walked away, leaving him to shut and lock the door.

She was already in the cab when Gabe came sauntering down the walkway as if he had all the time in the world. For a big man, he moved with unusual grace. Annie tried not to stare, but it was impossible. She knew only too well how much man there was inside that denim. And in honor of the day, he'd somehow unearthed a near-white shirt and a soft brown leather bomber jacket she'd never seen him wear.

She knew his entrance was going to make a quiet commotion in church, but there was absolutely nothing she could do about it. And then later, after they'd arrived and Gabe slid into the seat beside her and quietly clasped her hand, she knew that she wouldn't have changed a thing about him if she could.

Night slid across the horizon with little fuss. A car horn sounded from the parking lot as an impatient driver tried to hurry a dawdling friend. Gabriel set the last clean glass in the cabinet and then turned. The kitchen was clean. The leftovers had been covered and stored. The evening meal had come and gone with little more than polite conversation.

He sighed and slapped the dish towel down on the counter and went in search of Annie. She'd left nearly half an hour earlier to take a phone call, and she'd never come back.

The door to her room was slightly ajar. He pushed it aside and then stood in the doorway, frowning at the small lump she'd made of herself in the middle of her bed.

Curled knees to chin, her arms hugging herself to keep from coming undone, Annie lay wide-eyed and quiet, staring without blinking at the opposite wall.

Gabe inhaled sharply. A sick feeling came and went in the middle of his stomach, although there was no obvious reason for his uneasiness. A person had a right to quiet times. He could accept that. But the memory of her fixed attention during the church service that morning, and the near-panic he'd seen more than once in her eyes as she'd listened intently to the sermon, made him wonder. He was certainly no expert on religion. But the last time he'd checked, people weren't supposed to be afraid of it.

"Annie, are you all right?"

She jerked as if she'd been shot, unwound herself and sprang from the bed.

"I'm fine," she said, and turned away to smooth the wrinkles she'd made in the spread.

"Who was on the phone?" he asked, determined to get to the bottom of her withdrawal.

She shrugged. "A policeman. He called to tell me that Damon Tuttle made bail."

A rich chorus of unusually descriptive curses fell from Gabriel's lips. Annie turned and smiled at him in spite of herself.

"It's no big deal," she said. "Besides...I don't think it's humanly possible to do what you just suggested."

Gabriel glared. "If that punk comes anywhere near you again, I'll show you—and him—what a little imagination can accomplish."

"It doesn't matter," Annie said. "In two days school will be over. After that, it's immaterial what happens."

Gabriel covered the distance between them in two strides and took her by the shoulders.

"I don't get it," he growled. "Why the apathy, Annie? For weeks you've acted like all that matters is finishing the damned school year, and now you don't care about anything...not even saving your own hide."

She yanked herself out of his grasp and turned away, unwilling to look at him when she answered.

"School matters...at least to me. Besides," she said, and bit her lower lip to keep from crying, "this time next week you'll be long gone and I'll be forgotten. Right?"

Tears blurred her vision as she pulled aside the curtain in her bedroom and looked out into the street. Cars sailed by on a river of asphalt, honking horns in warning, like buoys bobbing in a sea of darkness, to let other drivers know they were passing.

Gabe slid his arms around her and pulled her hard against him until her shoulder blades dug into his chest in mute objection. He rested his chin at the crown of her head and closed his eyes against the pain.

Now it comes, he thought. Here's where she begins to blame me for making love to her without promises.

"Is that what's wrong, Annie? Are you mad at me because I didn't say I...because I can't promise that we'll..."

She laughed and spun in his arms. He saw the sheen of tears in her eyes and felt like a heel.

"Lord, no!" she said, and threw her arms around his neck. "You are what you are, Gabriel Donner. I wouldn't want to change you...even if I could."

He let himself absorb the feel of her body against him,

tried to ignore the dampness on her cheeks as she lifted her face for his kiss, and knew that she was lying. And as he took advantage of what she offered, he hated himself for not being able to call her hand.

The bell rang. At that same instant, the entire classroom full of students erupted into a shout of gladness. School was out!

Gabe stood at the back of the room and grinned, watching as the bulk of the class headed for the door in a single motion. They were a mass of humanity on the move. The noise level was just below painful as desks scooted and students shouted playfully back and forth to one another while continuing toward the exit.

Annie fielded comments and accepted the customary token gifts from several students, while waving goodbye to others.

Gabe moved toward her with a single intent. The worry lines around her mouth had deepened during the past two days, and try as he might to assure her that Damon Tuttle would threaten her no more, he felt he'd been unsuccessful. Surely, now that the students were gone and her responsibilities would soon end, she could relax.

Although her students had become accustomed to his presence, a few that had lingered behind slipped aside as he moved down the aisle, giving him the wide berth that his icy demeanor demanded.

Gabe sauntered past her desk on his way to the window, gazing absently toward the parking lot and wondering where he went from here. Leaving seemed inevitable...and impossible.

Bits and pieces of Annie's conversations with her students floated through the air above the noise, and then suddenly he homed in on a conversation that sent him spinning toward her in shock.

"Oh, Miss O'Brien, my little sister is so excited," one of the students was saying. "She's going to be in your class next year. I told her you were the best. She can hardly wait."

Annie's expression froze. The smile on her face never wavered. But the light in her eyes went out as certainly as if someone had taken a gun and blasted it away.

"That's quite a compliment," Annie said. "But I'm afraid your sister will have to take history from someone else. I won't be here next year."

"But why? You can't leave! It just won't be the same without you," the student cried.

Annie's chin quivered. It was all Gabe needed to see.

"What's left to do here?" he asked, his deep voice breaking into the round of complaints.

Annie shook her head without answering and started needlessly sorting papers on her desk as the last of the students drifted away, murmuring to themselves about the loss of a favorite teacher. And then they were alone.

"You didn't tell me you were going to quit."

The accusation hung in the air between them. Annie looked up, her face full of anger, her words sharp, cutting the distance between them in short, staccato bursts.

"My contract was with the school district, not you. I didn't have to tell you anything. You're leaving… remember?"

Gabe slapped the desk with the flat of his hand, and Annie had to force herself not to jump backward in response to the fury in his voice.

"Why, Miss O'Brien! Is that you I hear sounding so bitter…and resentful…and just possibly mad as hell? I guess you needed promises, after all." Gabe's words stung as his drawl ate into her conscience. "Why am I not surprised?"

Annie couldn't look him in the face. After all he'd done for her, she'd been reduced to lying to keep from begging him to stay. The echo of his harsh laughter was all he left behind as he walked out of the room, slamming the door after him.

She sank into her chair, crossed her arms on the desk and buried her face in them, unable to deal with what she had done. But it was her only option. She'd already faced that and the other facts bearing down on her with ominous persistence.

A dry sob burned her throat, but she refused to let it out. An old rhyme from her childhood floated to the surface of her memory, and she found herself muttering, "If wishes were horses then beggars would ride."

But no one was there to question the insanity of the comment or wonder why Miss O'Brien, who taught history on the south side of Oklahoma City, was taking out the contents of her desk drawers and methodically throwing them into the trash.

Nearly an hour later Annie left her classroom, refusing to admit that it was for the last time, and walked into the hallway, expecting to make the long walk to the front door alone.

Her heart skipped a beat as Gabe shoved himself away from the edge of a locker and fell into step beside her without speaking. A small catch in her breathing was all the notice she gave as he reached out and took her by the hand.

"Come on, Annie Laurie. Do what you have to do and then brace yourself. Tonight I'm taking you out."

She couldn't have been more shocked if he'd told her that he was getting a haircut and buying a three-piece suit.

"But..."

He frowned and pointed toward the principal's office, where a gaggle of teachers was gathering.

"Go on...do your thing, teacher. When you're through, I'll be waiting."

Annie couldn't watch him leave. She was too focused on

not crying in front of the others as the words "I'll be waiting" echoed inside her head and then settled into a hard lump in the center of her heart.

Oh dear God, Annie thought. *Why now? Why did you do this to me now, when you know how futile it is?*

But there was no answer, and, for Annie, no hope. She moved into line, smiling and nodding, thankful that most of the other teachers were unaware of her decision not to return. It saved her the anguish of making excuses she didn't have.

With dinner on the horizon and a rumbling in her stomach that reminded her about the lunch she'd skipped in order to check in textbooks, Annie fought with Gabe for a fair share of the full-length mirror in her apartment.

It was then, between his chin and the bottom of the mirror, that she looked up.

"Where are you taking me?" she asked.

"Are you through with your two-thirds of the mirror?" he asked, smiling a little to himself as he noticed that his snide remark got her goat.

"Be my guest," she said.

"I already am," Gabe said, and winked.

Annie stepped aside, then bowed dramatically. She would bite her tongue before she let him get the best of her.

She buckled the belt on her blue jeans and then ran a fingertip down the front of her plaid shirt, checking to see if she'd gotten all the buttons when she realized that he hadn't answered her.

"So...where are you taking me?" she asked again.

Gabe stood behind her, peering over her shoulder and combing his thick, dark hair. He stopped and looked, staring intently into the mirror until she was forced to meet the reflection of his gaze.

Her eyes widened, turning them an even deeper shade of jade.

"Well?" Annie wouldn't give an inch.

His gaze slid across her face, as if imprinting it forever into his memory. The heat from his gaze made her shiver.

"With me," he said.

For Annie, it was answer enough.

Minutes later she followed him outside to his bike, and then put on the helmet he handed her without comment, wondering as she did why she'd bothered to fix her hair.

He squatted down beside the monstrous metallic ride to check it, unaware that Annie was taking in every aspect of his body and clothing.

Heavily muscled haunches stretched the denim tight across his legs as he stood and leaned across the seat to tighten a strap. Annie was thankful for the helmet's tinted visor, aware that she could look her fill without detection.

It was then that she began to realize how much Gabriel could see without being seen when he wore it himself. She shuddered. He saw entirely too much for her peace of mind as it was.

The long sleeves of his blue-and-white striped shirt were unbuttoned and rolled halfway up his forearms. He wore the same black boots he'd had when she met him, only now they bore a month-old shine. They were sporting the same single-roweled spurs.

The black leather vest he wore over the shirt was open and loose across his chest. In essence, he was still the same menacing man she'd first met in the parking lot of the quick stop. And yet, in Annie's eyes, he would be forever changed. She now saw beyond the obvious. Beyond the outer layers of his disguise to the man beneath. He had the appearance of a devil but the heart of a lion. Strong and faithful and constant.

Annie caught her breath as he moved toward her. The

setting sun caught on the crown of his head and turned it to a halo of glittering jet. He winked and smiled at her, as if he could see beyond that smoky Plexiglas to the woman beneath. She shivered at his depth of perception.

The smile was almost the same one he'd given her the day they'd met. But not quite. While the change in their relationship had added to its texture, the last two days had given it a certain caution, as if he wasn't quite sure whether to share it with her or not.

"Are you ready?" he asked, and slung his leg over the seat, straddling the bike in an unconsciously enticing movement that reminded Annie of the way he covered her in bed.

Annie nodded. There were no words to say what she was feeling inside. She simply slid on behind him, wrapped her arms around his waist and waited.

Moments later the engine roared to life beneath them, and Annie inhaled, reveling in the joy of the moment, in just being alive. As the bike threaded into the traffic, Gabe's body moved beneath her hands, a powerful ripple of man and muscle.

She swallowed, closed her eyes and let herself pretend she was in control. It was as close as she'd come to lying to herself in months, and she knew it. Gabriel Donner wasn't a man to be controlled...or loved. He wouldn't stand for the former and couldn't return the latter. Either way, Annie was on a one-way ride, with defeat as her destination.

What else is new?

A wry grin tilted the corner of her mouth, but it was lost behind the helmet.

Chapter 5

"I should be the one paying the check. You've yet to accept a dollar from me, and it's just not right, Gabriel. After all, I *did* hire you to do a job."

Annie's words held a hiss of resentment and a lot of guilt as they stood beside the desk, waiting while the cashier totaled their bill.

Gabriel didn't even bother glaring as he paid for their meal. In his mind, they'd gone way past an employer-employee relationship, and there was no going back. Besides, to him, money was nothing more than a necessary evil. He took jobs when he needed them, and when he had enough money to last him awhile, he simply crawled on his Harley and never looked back. Accumulating worldly goods had no place in his life, although Annie would have been shocked at how much he'd managed to save over the years.

He took the change the cashier handed him, stuffed it into his pocket and cocked an eyebrow at Annie, grinning when she pursed her lips and gave him what he privately thought of as her "schoolteacher look."

"It's not going to work, Annie. I'm not behind on my schoolwork, so you can't suspend me. And I'm pretty sure you're not going to fail me. After all—" his drawl held her attention long after it should have, and made her miss the look in his eyes as he continued "—some of my abilities are beyond reproach, aren't they, sugar?"

He leaned forward and, in front of everyone standing at the door waiting to be seated, pressed a firm, sweet kiss directly on her pouted lips.

"Gabriel!"

Annie blushed two shades of red and glanced nervously around, checking to see who was watching. She should have saved herself the embarrassment by not looking, because everyone else *was.* Several giggles and a chuckle or two mingled in her mind with the fact that he'd just referred to their lovemaking and they both knew it.

She stared at a spot somewhere over his shoulder, then down at the floor, and finally breathed a sigh of relief when he took her by the hand and led her out the door of the steak house.

"You are impossible," Annie said, relishing the cool night air on her heated face.

Gabe grinned. "Nothing's impossible, Annie. I thought we'd already covered that subject—in bed."

She grinned in spite of her embarrassment and made a face.

He smiled and cupped her cheek with his hand. "It's good to see you smiling, Annie. I've missed it…and you."

Breath caught in the back of her throat. This man had a way of cutting past all the excess, polite conversation. He went for the jugular every time.

"I've just had a lot on my mind," she said. "I'm sorry."

Gabe nodded and then leaned forward and whispered against her lips just before he kissed her, "Enough said.

Climb on, woman. The night's not over yet. I know where there's a soft bed, empty and waiting to be used."

Annie's heart thumped once in anticipation and then settled back into its regular rhythm. She put the helmet on, slipped on behind him and wrapped her arms around his waist in anticipation of the ride and what awaited her at home.

Gabe closed his eyes and tried to ignore the ache that had settled just behind his heart. The more time he spent with her, the harder it was going to be to leave. Yet leave he must. There was nothing in the way of permanence that he could offer a woman like Annie O'Brien. And she was the sort who deserved a forever kind of man, a home and a lapful of babies.

Damn it all, anyway, he thought. He couldn't give her any of those things. All he could do was treasure the time they had and try not to hurt her when it was time for him to go.

Gabe was the first to see the lights. The parking lot of Annie's complex was full of police cars and emergency vehicles. For a moment it was like the night of the fire all over again.

"Oh, no," Annie gasped as she jumped from the bike and yanked the helmet from her head. "Something terrible has happened! Gabe...what do you suppose...?" And then she gasped and dropped the helmet into Gabe's hands. "Those officers...they're coming out of my apartment."

Gabe followed the direction of her gaze and knew that the burning sensation in the pit of his stomach was a warning sign that their night wasn't going exactly as he'd planned.

He took her hand and moved toward her apartment, ignoring the roped-off area, as well as an officer's warning shout.

88

"Hey, mister! You can't go in there."

"My name is Annie O'Brien. I live here," Annie said, pointing toward the partially opened doorway.

"Hey, Harvey!" the officer shouted. "Get a detective out here. The property owner just showed up."

As the officer spoke, Gabe's sharp gaze quickly caught sight of a body on the ground just beyond the bumper of a parked car. A sheet of yellow plastic had been pulled over it, but the outline of a pair of tennis shoes was unmistakable.

Gabe frowned and slowly changed position so that he was shielding Annie from the sight. That was the last thing she needed to see.

"Miss O'Brien?"

Annie nodded, her eyes huge, her chin trembling as she let the detective lead her toward the breezeway sheltering the door to her home. Gabe followed.

"What happened?" Annie asked, and then swallowed a scream as she took an instinctive step back when she looked through the door.

Gabe caught her retreat and steadied her, his hands firm and reassuring on her shoulders as the detective began to talk.

"Officers responded to a break-in when your security system went off," the detective said. "They were too late to prevent what happened, but they got the perpetrator. Damnedest thing, too. When they searched the body, they didn't find anything of value on him. All he did was mess up the place and then run when he heard sirens."

"Body?" Annie began to shake. The events of the last few weeks were about to send her sanity caving in.

The detective nodded. "Some teenager. He started shooting at the squad car the minute it turned into the parking lot. Didn't even give the officers a chance to make an arrest. They didn't have a choice. No matter what their age, the perps are better armed than we are every time."

"Oh, Gabriel," Annie whispered, and stepped inside her apartment. "Who? And in heaven's name, why?"

Gabe held her firmly, afraid that she was going to come apart in his arms. Her beloved plants were lying everywhere, uprooted and broken, the dirt from their containers strewn about the carpet. Huge slashes had been made in all her furniture, and the stuffing had been pulled out through the ripped fabric until it was hanging like topping melting on a cake. Broken crockery and an open refrigerator door told him that the man had left nothing untouched. Items of her clothing were visible from where they stood, and Gabe knew that their bedrooms were probably a mirror image of this destruction.

"Miss O'Brien..." The detective pulled out a notepad and pen. "I know you're upset. And rightly so," he added. "But I need to ask you some questions. We found some jewelry on the bed in one room, and some money in another. The perp obviously saw it, but he didn't take it. From my point of view, this looks like a gigantic case of revenge."

Gabe's pulse skidded to a halt as his heart skipped a beat. Revenge! A horrible thought occurred to him as the detective continued.

"So, Miss O'Brien, I have to ask. Do you know anyone who would want to...?"

"Detective...I want to see the body," Gabe said coldly.

The interruption was unexpected. The detective glared at the big man.

"Now, see here," he began, and then he realized he didn't know the big man's name. "I don't believe I got your name, mister." His pen was poised above the pad, awaiting Gabe's answer. It didn't come.

Gabe stared down into Annie's face and watched as the same thought suddenly occurred to her. Tears welled, and she began to shake harder.

"No," she groaned. "He wouldn't. He couldn't."

"Honey, he tried to cut you apart in your own classroom, in front of a room full of witnesses," Gabe reminded her.

"Who tried to cut who?" the policeman growled.

"She'll tell you," Gabe said as he moved away, and when Annie started after him, he turned and pointed his finger at her. "You wait! I'll be right back."

The look on his face made her sick. She'd never seen so much suppressed fury in her life. Moaning softly to herself at the unbelievable string of disasters that had been dumped on her life, she staggered backward until the wall behind her stopped her progress. Only then did she allow herself to give way as she slid to the floor and buried her face against her knees, unable to face any more horror.

Gabe walked outside toward the body. His hand shook in anger as he bent over and lifted the plastic. The pale eyes staring sightlessly upward were familiar, as was the face and everything that went with it. He dropped the sheet and turned to find that the detective had followed him.

"Damon Tuttle." Gabe's voice was rough, his breathing shallow. He had an insane urge to hit something...or some-one.

The detective's eyebrows rocketed to his hairline. He obviously hadn't really expected Gabriel to come through with anything useful.

"How do you know him?" he asked Gabe.

"A few weeks ago Miss O'Brien hired me as a bodyguard because several of her students had been harassing her to the point that she'd become afraid."

"She's a teacher?"

Gabe nodded. "And that—" he pointed to the body on the ground "—was one of her students. He was arrested after he pulled a knife on her in the classroom."

"Damn." The detective scratched his head, then looked back at Gabe with new respect. "I take it you were what stopped him?"

"He made bail. The system just let him walk," Gabe accused, ignoring the detective's question.

"I guess it's a good thing she had an alarm, otherwise he might have sat inside and waited for you to come back so he could finish the job," the detective said.

"I'm taking her to a motel for the night. I've got to get her away from this," Gabe said, and headed back to the apartment, unaware and uncaring whether the officer had other ideas.

"Annie!"

His shout shook her. She looked up and saw him coming toward her. She didn't have to ask if they'd been right.

"Oh, my God," she moaned, and started to cry.

"Stop it," Gabe growled, and pulled her from the floor and into his arms. "The son of a bitch wasn't worth it."

Annie saw the room starting to spin. In reflex, her hands reached out for balance. But it was no use. For the second time in their short acquaintance, she was going to faint at his feet. The last thing she felt was his arms beneath her body and his breath upon her face.

It was the steady, rhythmic vibration of a heartbeat beneath her ear that woke her. For a moment she lay quietly, absorbing the gentleness of the man in whose arms she lay.

His hands moved across her like a shadow stealing across the floor, gently smoothing a stray hair away from her face, carefully straightening her clothing, quietly readjusting the hold he had on her to assure himself that it was secure.

But it was the gentle whispers she heard coming from his lips that made a fresh set of tears come into her eyes. He was making promises she knew he couldn't keep. And when she looked around the strange, sterile room and then up at Gabe and caught him looking back, she remembered.

"It wasn't just a bad dream, was it, Gabriel?"

"No, it wasn't a dream. But it's finally over. There's nothing and no one left to fear."

Annie tried to smile and then caught back a sob. *Oh Gabriel...if only that were true. You don't know the half of my hell.*

"Don't cry, Annie." His voice was harsh as he wrapped his fingers in the hair cascading down her back and pulled her closer against him. "It makes me crazy. I'll do anything to put a smile back on your face."

Annie looked around at the room, felt the bed beneath their bodies, and wondered where they were and how they'd gotten there. The ride she'd taken in a squad car to the nearby motel had come and gone without her notice, while she'd been blessedly out for the count. A terrible sense of doom overwhelmed her. Another tear tracked toward her chin. She was incapable of a smile.

Gabe groaned. "Baby...please...just tell me. What can I do to make this better?"

Annie felt the palms of his hands swiping across her cheeks as he tried unsuccessfully to remove the traces of her misery from his sight. And then something he'd said triggered a notion she hadn't considered. She took a deep breath, and before she knew it, heard herself telling him, "I want to go home."

Gabe sighed and nodded as he pressed a helpless kiss at the corner of her lips.

"Tomorrow...when it's light. I swear we'll go back and clean everything up. Before you know it, it'll be good as new. You can buy new plants...and you said you had insurance. We'll shop for new furniture, and..."

"No!"

Her abrupt refusal left him speechless. She'd just asked to go home and in the next breath refused. What was going on?

The headboard of the motel bed dug into the small of his

back, and he cursed softly as he tried to find a comfortable position in which to sit.

At the same moment Annie pulled away and rolled off the bed. Seconds later he caught her in his arms as she paused at the curtained window of the motel room.

"What is it, Annie? I thought you said you—"

"I want to go home...to where I was born."

Gabe was dumbfounded. "You don't have any family there. I remember you telling me once that your parents were dead."

Annie winced at the word and pulled the curtain aside, staring blindly out into the night.

"They are. But the house is still there...and it's mine... waiting beneath that stand of trees Daddy refused to cut down." She shuddered and closed her eyes, picturing the last time she'd seen her childhood home. "I miss the trees. There are lots of trees in the Missouri hills."

The curtain fell from her fingers, once again shutting the night out and them in as she gave Gabe a last ultimatum. "If you still want to help, then take me home.... Take me to Missouri."

"I don't get it, Annie. It isn't like you to run away."

Annie's short bark of laughter was anything but funny. "That's a hoot," she said derisively. "I couldn't run far enough and fast enough to escape my fate. Besides—" she wrapped her arms around herself and stared down at the shadows on the floor, made by the faint light coming through the curtains behind her "—I'm not running away. I just want to go home."

Gabriel sensed that there was more to her request than what she'd admitted, but it was beyond him to press her for answers. Not tonight.

"Then you will," he said, and unwound her arms from around her waist and rewrapped them around his. "But tonight...just let me hold you. You may not need it, but I sure as hell do.''

Annie's legs went weak. She would always need this man. For as long as she lived, she knew she would never get over that need. She buried her face against his chest and nodded her acceptance of his plea. *For as long as I live,* she reminded herself.

It took ten hours on the back of Gabe's bike. Hard, hot, grueling hours with few stops. Stops in which she crawled off the back of that bike certain she would never be able to walk again, and then, when it came time to move on, equally certain that resuming her seat behind Gabe would be impossible.

But she'd done it. And as they turned off the two-lane highway onto a narrow dirt road, Annie's stamina was disappearing as fast as the sun setting behind them.

"Is this it?" Gabe asked as the bike rolled to a stop. He stood upright, with the bike balanced but still grumbling quietly between his legs, and stared at the small frame house nestled in the midst of a thick grove of oak and pine.

"Yes."

One word. A single statement that to Gabe's ears sounded awfully flat, considering the fact that she'd been so hell-bent on coming.

He sighed, killed the engine and moved the kickstand in place with the toe of his boot. Annie got off first and handed him her helmet as she began brushing dust from the legs of her jeans and the sleeves of her denim shirt.

Gabe slid his sunglasses up, letting them rest on the top of his head as he watched her start up the walk alone. Something about the way she moved told him that she would not welcome company. Not now.

He swung his leg over the bike, untied their duffel bags and slid the straps over his shoulder. They'd traveled light, taking only what would fit on the bike. Everything that Damon Tuttle had not destroyed was being shipped. Annie had left with assurances from her insurance company that a check for her vandalized car as well as the damaged personal property would be forthcoming.

He remembered thinking it was strange that she hadn't seemed to care. In his experience, and God knew he had plenty of it, women took great stock in "things." But Annie O'Brien had simply walked away from all her belongings and ridden off on the back of a Harley with a man she hardly knew.

He cursed softly beneath his breath and followed her up the walk. Maybe here she would find peace; then he could leave knowing she was safe and well.

It was the thought of leaving that made him move angrily past her and up onto the porch, leaving the sound of his footsteps to echo loudly into the odd silence of the woods.

"I don't suppose you have a key," he growled, as he twisted uselessly at a doorknob that wouldn't give.

Wordlessly Annie moved him aside, then stood on tiptoe and reached above the door frame, running her finger lightly across it. Moments later she stepped back, a dusty key in hand. She thrust it into the lock.

"Don't ever put that damned thing back up there," Gabe said harshly, imagining an intruder hiding inside at some future date, awaiting Annie's entrance. "It isn't safe."

"No place is safe. Safety is merely a state of mind." Annie walked inside.

Dust motes highlighted by the fading light coming through the curtained window shifted as a draft of fresh air moved through the house. Everything inside was covered in draped white cloths, lying unused and lifeless, waiting, like Annie, to be needed again.

Annie hit a light switch beside the door, and, surprisingly, a dull, dusty glow illuminated the dingy room. Although the utility bills came regularly and she paid them faithfully, she still hadn't expected anything to work. She looked up and saw that only a single bulb remained in what had once been her mother's pride and joy. A small, four-section *faux* crystal chandelier hung from the ceiling, emitting all the light it could from its forty-watt source.

Gabe grunted, surprised by the fact that the power was on, and dropped their bags beside the door. Without asking permission, he went from room to room, pulling back curtains and opening stubborn windows. Soon a cool draft of air was slowly circulating through the small frame house.

Ignoring him, Annie walked with single-minded intent down the narrow hallway to the room at the end of the hall. Her hand shook as it touched the door. She took a deep breath, letting her fingers slide down the surface as they tested the texture, until they came to the knob. She gripped it and turned.

The last ten years disappeared in a heartbeat as she walked over the threshold. Were it not for the drop cloths over all the furniture, she could have imagined that it was only this morning when she'd left for school. She walked to the bed and pulled back the cloth. The faded pink coverlet was still in place, while a single old teddy bear—her first—reclined against the headboard, one ear missing, along with most of its stuffing. She tried to smile, but she hurt too much inside for the feeling to come.

She walked to the corner opposite the bed and pulled another drop cloth away. It fell to the floor in a cloud of dust, revealing antique maple and a row of snapshots lining the dusty mirror of her dresser.

She inhaled, blinking back tears as she traced the curling edges of the old photos. Her parents smiled back at her. Instinctively she returned their smiles and then realized they couldn't see. They'd been dead for years.

She bit her lower lip and moved on to the next picture,

whispering her best friend's name to herself as she remembered well the day it had been taken. Molly on graduation day! There was a picture of Rufus, her daddy's hunting dog, and one of her mother out back working in the garden. Everything seemed so ordinary...and so long ago.

"Annie...I'm going to backtrack to that little store a few miles back and get some food."

She spun around. He was silhouetted in the doorway. A dark, menacing figure of a man with a beautiful smile and a gentle voice. To Annie he represented stability and safety in a world in which she was fast losing ground. She flew into his arms before she thought.

Gabe held her. He didn't understand her fear, but he recognized it just the same. For a long moment neither spoke, and then he felt her withdraw as suddenly as she'd come.

"Are you all right?" he asked softly, willing himself not to react to her fears.

"Are you coming back?"

He drew a slow, deep breath, letting the shock and anger he felt at her question slide back to a safer place inside him.

"I'll pretend you didn't ask that," he said shortly. "And I'll be right back."

She listened to the door slam and then the sound of the bike as its motor was revved more strongly than necessary before he slipped it into gear.

"Oh, my God," Annie whispered, and turned back toward the mirror. The teenager who had been there moments ago was gone, along with the memories. There was nothing left but a woman wearing guilt on her face.

"How could you have done that?" she muttered, as she leaned forward to stare accusingly at her own reflection. "After all he's done...you still doubt him?" A bitter smile twisted her mouth. "You don't doubt *him*, you fool. It's yourself you doubt."

With that she pushed herself away from the dresser and walked out of the room without looking back.

By the time Gabe returned, Annie had cleaned the refrigerator and wiped off the stove. It was time to put the past behind her. She had no more choices to make.

After all these years, the night sounds in the hills were strange to Annie and made it impossible for her to sleep. She tossed restlessly on her bed, grimacing when the old springs squeaked protestingly under her weight.

Gabe shifted beside her in his sleep, and then unconsciously reached out, trying to settle her back safely against him. But Annie resisted the comfort of his touch, as well as the safety of his strength. He'd done what she asked and brought her home to Missouri. And although this was only their first night here, there was no way of telling how much longer he would stay.

Annie knew that she was going to have to find a way to exist without him, and there was no time like the present. The sooner she got used to being alone...and lonely...the better off she would be. With that bitter thought in mind, she rolled out from under Gabe's arm and left the bed.

The old wood floorboards creaked beneath her feet. Thorough cleaning would come in the days ahead, but the sweeping they'd gotten earlier had served its purpose. The floor was smooth and cool to the touch and, to Annie, vaguely familiar. Without thinking, she stepped over the board just left of center in the doorway, knowing that it would protest loudly under her weight.

A heavy, throbbing pressure was building at the back of her neck as she walked through the house toward the front door, a warning she'd come to recognize and hate.

Anxious for the welcome coolness waiting just outside on the porch steps, she rolled her head, rubbing her neck as she did and wincing as her muscles protested the action.

If I only had access to a hot tub, she thought. This misery had to be caused by exertion and exhaustion. All she needed was a good night's sleep and it would be better. Surely it wasn't a portent of things to come. Not yet. She wasn't ready.

Her fingers curled around the doorknob at the same instant that the first wave of pain struck. The moan that slid from her lips was soft and frightened, but it was enough to awaken Gabe, who sat up in startled silence, wondering how long he'd been alone in her bed...and why.

Wearing nothing but a pair of white cotton briefs, he bolted through the house without trying to mask the noise he made.

"Annie! Where are you?" he shouted, and then wondered why he felt such panic when they'd left the person who'd threatened her far behind and six feet under.

The pain was so sudden...and so intense. If she could have caught her breath, she would have screamed. As it was, she leaned against the door and braced her legs to keep from falling. At that moment, standing was all she was capable of doing.

"Oh, God," Gabe breathed as he saw her in the shadows, unable to walk, swaying by the door like a broken butterfly trying to fly.

And then he saw her clutch her head and tilt forward. He caught her just before she crashed to the floor.

"My head...my head," Annie groaned, and dug her fingers into her scalp. All she wanted was to rip out the pain and throw it away.

Gabe had a flashback of the first time he'd seen her in the throes of such pain and remembered the prescription medicine that had given her ease.

"Your pills! Annie! Where did you pack your pills?"

She didn't answer. Couldn't answer. Instead, she groaned and went limp against him as he slid his arms around her shoulders and tangled his hands in her hair, massaging the taut, corded muscles at the back of her neck in a helpless effort to ease her pain.

"Annie...where did you put your pills?" he repeated.

"Kitchen...kitchen...kitchen," she moaned, saying the word over and over like a litany. "Oh God, oh God, make it stop."

Her fingers dug into her hair and pulled as Gabe lifted her from her feet and quickly carried her back to her room. Tears streamed down her cheeks as he bolted from the room, leaving her alone in the dark with the pain.

Gabe hit the light switch in the kitchen with the flat of his hand as he ran past. Seconds later he had every cabinet door swinging open as he searched the dusty shelves for the brown prescription bottle he'd seen before. And when he saw it, his sigh of relief coincided with her shriek of pain.

"My God," he muttered, realizing that in his entire life he'd never been this afraid before. Not even when he was about to be hanged.

He grabbed a glass and filled it with water, unmindful of the puddle he left on the floor by the sink as he bolted back down the hall, the pills in his hand.

By the time he got back, Annie had rolled in upon herself. She was curled into a ball so tight that he had to fight her to get her upright enough to swallow.

"Open your mouth, damn it," he yelled when she fought him for making her move, because movement only increased the pain.

And somehow she heard...and obeyed. Gabe slid the pills between her teeth and chased them by pouring water down her throat, unmindful of the liquid that once again spilled, this time going down her neck and onto her gown.

Then he crawled in beside her, rolled her up into his arms and held her until the tremors subsided, her breathing slowed and the pulse he felt beneath his fingertips was no longer racing toward cataclysm. And when she finally slept, he could only hold her, staring up at the ceiling, wide-eyed and shocked, until daybreak came calling.

Chapter 6

Annie brushed the toast crumbs from the table into her
hand and then tossed them into the sink. Breakfast had come
and gone with little conversation. Gabe kept looking at her
as if he expected her to self-destruct at any moment, and
Annie kept looking away, afraid that he would learn more
about her than she was willing to reveal.

"Do you want more coffee?" she asked as she topped
off her own cup and then turned to Gabe with the pot in
her hand.

He shook his head.

"Did you get enough to eat?" she asked as she began
dumping grounds and rinsing out the inner components of
the old percolator she'd unearthed from her mother's cupboard.

He nodded.

She twisted the tie onto the bread wrapper and shoved
the loaf into the wooden bread box beneath the cabinet.
Without looking around to see if he was watching, she took

a dishcloth from a drawer, doused it into some sudsy water and began scrubbing needlessly at the countertops.

"Annie..."

She grimaced. It was the tone of his voice that warned her. That and the look he'd been wearing that she'd tried all morning to ignore. Last night had been unexpected...and it had been hell. He was bound to wonder. There was only one way to stop the interrogation before it started, and that was to take the offensive.

"Migraines are hell," she said.

Migraines? Was that what those were?

Gabe frowned. He'd heard of their ferocity. After the second episode that he'd witnessed, he could vouch for the truth of that statement—in spades.

"Are you sure that's all they—"

"Would you add dish soap to the grocery list, please? I need some. I just used up what was left."

She rinsed the dishcloth before going on to the next set of cabinets.

Gabe frowned and did as she'd asked.

"You *need* a car," he muttered, and added it to the top of the list just for spite, as if she could just walk into a supermarket and pick one off the shelves.

The thought of Annie alone up in these woods with who knew what for neighbors made him nervous. Thinking of Annie alone, period, made him angry with himself. Thinking of himself without her made him sick.

Annie shrugged. "I'll see to it in good time," she said. "There's no hurry."

He gawked at her. Her answer made no sense at all. Of course there was a hurry. "How will you get food?" he asked. "How will you get to town? How will—"

A car horn honked, interrupting Gabe's questions. Annie dropped the dishcloth into the sink and parted the curtains over the window to peer outside.

A new model electric-blue pickup truck with silver running boards had just pulled up and parked beneath the big oak at the edge of the yard. Annie watched as a hulking figure of a man squeezed himself out from behind the steering wheel and stood, looking anxiously toward the house and the big Harley parked in front.

"Davie! It's Davie Henry!" she said, and headed for the door.

So who the hell is Davie Henry? Gabe shoved himself out of the chair, abandoning the list he'd been helping her make, and followed.

The screen door banged against the wall as Annie raced outside. In three steps she was off the porch and headed toward the big man who stood waiting beside the truck with a huge grin on his face.

"Annie...Annie, it *is* you!" Davie said, and caught her on the fly, swinging her up into his arms and then turning her around and around beneath the shade tree.

Gabe sauntered out, leaned against the porch post and tried not to glare. It was obvious they were friends. From the way the man was holding her, damned good ones, at that.

A slow rage filled his belly, building layer by layer at the injustice of it all, and just when it might have erupted and ruined whatever existed between himself and Annie, she was released and set back on her feet.

At that moment Gabe felt hatred. He hated Annie for laughing with that man in a way she'd never laughed with him. And he hated the man for being able to make her do it.

"Gabe!" Annie motioned for him to come closer. "There's someone I want you to meet."

"I can't wait," he muttered, and took his time about complying.

Davie Henry's shock was evident as he looked past Annie

to the man on the porch. The smile on his face disappeared as he watched the big biker come toward him. He looked from Annie to the man and back again, unable to believe that these two were actually traveling companions.

The man she called Gabe didn't look like anyone he'd ever seen her with before. The expression on his face could only be called menacing. And even though he was wearing blue jeans and a near-white shirt that might pass for Western-style, those high-top leather boots and leather vest of shiny obsidian that matched the too-long shock of unruly hair framing his face, made Davie nervous—along with the silver spurs on his boots that jingled when he walked. Davie thought he'd never seen a more likely outlaw. He frowned and watched. The man reminded him of a big black panther stalking his prey.

Oddly enough, if Annie saw the animosity between the two men, she chose to ignore it.

"Gabe, this is Davie Henry. One of my oldest friends." She punched him playfully on the shoulder and looked up into his face. "Would you believe I used to baby-sit this big lug?"

Gabe stared. *Baby-sit? Then that meant...*

"Only until I was eleven," Davie added, and ruffled Annie's hair as if she were a puppy at his feet. "That was the year I outgrew you by six inches."

Annie rolled her eyes and slapped his hand away. "It's true," she said, turning to fix Gabe with a smile that dropped his heart to his feet. "My parents made me baby-sit a moose."

Davie laughed so openly at the joke on himself that Gabe had to grin. The man *was* big. And Annie wasn't all that tall. He looked back at her, trying to imagine her as a young child and then a teenager, and suddenly he realized how little he really knew of this woman who'd stolen his heart.

The time was nearing when he would have to leave her.

But it was suddenly a little bit easier, knowing that Annie would be among friends when he did. He held out his hand.

"Gabe Donner," he said, introducing himself. "Annie and I don't go quite that far back. But it's nice to know that she's got friends nearby."

Davie nodded and shook Gabe's hand. "Our place is just a hoot and a holler from here as the crow flies. By car, about a mile and a half."

Gabe grinned. He couldn't remember the last time he'd heard anyone talk like that. It reminded him of his life before.

"Someone's been taking care of the place," Annie said, and looked at Davie.

The blush that ran up his neck toward his ears was answer enough for her, although he verified it with a grin.

"It wasn't much," he said. "Just cut a little grass and made sure the roof didn't leak."

Annie thanked him with a hug.

"You here for a visit?" Davie asked. "I haven't seen you since your daddy's funeral."

She shook her head. "No visit, Davie. I'm moving home."

He grinned. "It'll be just like old times."

A strange shadow passed over Annie's face. Davie was too busy rejoicing in the news to see, but Gabe saw it. With Annie, he missed nothing. He saw regret and something else…something that looked suspiciously like…

Fear!

Annie was afraid. Of that he was certain. Gabe didn't know how he knew, but he did. And for the life of him, he couldn't understand why she should be afraid. What did she have to fear? Damon Tuttle was out of the picture permanently. Here in Missouri, she had a chance at a fresh start, which was more than he would ever have. So why in hell was she afraid? Everything around her was familiar. She should be waltzing on air. But she wasn't. Annie O'Brien was afraid.

"I have a girlfriend," Davie said, and then ducked his head, suddenly embarrassed that he'd announced something so personal so abruptly.

Annie hid what she'd been thinking behind a grin. "Who on earth would have you?" she teased, and then watched an odd expression come and go on Davie's face. She'd un-intentionally hit a sore spot somewhere.

"You don't know her," Davie said. "Her folks moved into town about six years ago…right after you got that teaching job in Oklahoma City. They own and operate a feed-and-seed store."

"What's her name?" Annie asked, trying to smooth whatever it was that she'd stirred up.

"Charlotte. But I call her Charlie."

Gabe walked away, leaving the pair to hash over old times. The knowledge that he had no place in the conver-sation and no place in their lives was eating at him like a festering sore.

Minutes later Gabe heard the sounds of an engine starting up, and then Annie's footsteps in the dirt behind him. He squatted down beside his bike, picked up a wrench and a pair of pliers, and began tightening stuff on his Harley that didn't need tightening. But it didn't matter. It would give him something else to do when he had to loosen it up again.

"Seeing Davie was great!" Annie said as she knelt beside Gabe and handed him a screwdriver.

He took it from her and then dropped it onto the ground with a thud.

"I don't need that," he said sharply, and refused to look at the shocked expression he knew she would be wearing.

In all the months they'd known each other, he'd never been rude to her. And yet he'd done it today with a ven-geance.

"And I don't need to see you act like a jealous baby," she said, and jerked to her feet.

She would have walked away, but Gabe caught her before she'd taken the second step.

"I'm sorry," he said. "And I wasn't jealous."

She fixed him with a stare he tried to ignore. It was no use.

"Is that your 'teacher' look?" he asked with a grin.

She shrugged.

"Okay...I *was* a little bit jealous. But not enough to count."

Her lips pursed as she continued to stare. This time she crossed her arms across her chest and waited for him to fold. He did. Like a table with three broken legs.

"Look, honey," he said, and swept her into his arms, "I admit it." He kissed the end of her nose. "Now are you happy? I saw red." He grinned against her neck as he felt her arms sliding around his shoulders. "I even saw stars. I also saw myself wiping that grin off his face and replacing it with a big fat lip. Now...does that make you happy? I have confessed my worst thoughts to you regarding Davie Henry, and I expect to be rewarded for telling the truth."

"You can quit worrying about my lack of transportation. Davie is loaning me his father's car. And I think I want you to take me to bed."

Gabe was at a loss for words. He now had to consider the knowledge that Davie Henry was about to step into his shoes by providing for Annie's well-being and welfare.

Okay...he knew the reality of leaving her. Someone had to be there for her when he was gone, and it might as well be Davie. He kicked the dirt with the toe of his boot, and then he thought about the second half of her statement. In spite of his need to stay angry, he caught himself grinning.

"So, pretty Annie, you want me to take you to bed? Once we get there...just exactly what do you expect me to do?"

She leaned forward and whispered in his ear. It was reflex that made Gabe sweep her off her feet and into his arms. But then he stopped, staring down into her face at the moisture glistening on her lower lip and the promise of passion in her eyes.

She waited. Quietly. Impatiently.

Desire for this woman turned him pale as he stumbled toward the door with her in his arms. It was one of the few times in his life that he thought to say a prayer. And his prayer was that he would make it to the bedroom in time to do what she asked before he came unglued at the thought.

"Do you know what you're asking?" he said as he set her gently in the middle of her bed.

I asked you to make love to me until I begged you to stop. But what I want is never to forget this day...or you.

"Yes, I think so. I just don't want you to forget me when you're gone," Annie said, and started to pull her T-shirt over her head.

Oh, my God. When I'm gone.

"Damn you," Gabe said harshly, and yanked the shirt from her hands. "As if I could, Annie Laurie. As if I could."

In seconds he had her naked. Within the next heartbeat he'd joined her, body to body, heart to heart, upon the bed. Now all he had to do was exert enough control over his own emotions to make certain that *she* never forgot *him*, either.

In that moment, before they joined, Gabe knew that knowing Annie and the love they'd shared would be the closest thing to heaven he would ever find on earth. And when the time came for him to leave, existing without her was going to be a living hell.

"Gabriel."

His name was a sigh on her lips. A plea to begin and, at the same time, a prayer that, for sanity's sake, it would not end too soon.

"I'm here, Annie. I'm here."

His whisper slid across her face. She closed her eyes and let herself go, giving herself up to the emotions he was so skillfully able to create, and refused to contemplate the fact that she would spend the rest of her life alone.

The rest of her life!

She sobbed once, and then reached for him.

His hands moved across her breasts, and his lips followed. She arched beneath his touch as his tongue rasped the end of her nipple. She moaned as sensation upon sensation flooded her limbs, making her weak and achy, but yearning for more.

When she would have wrapped her arms around his neck, he grabbed both her wrists, pinning her arms above her head with one hand, while he raided tender territory with the other.

Gabriel shivered at the satiny feel of her skin beneath his fingertips. He closed his eyes and inhaled the essence of Annie as his mouth closed around her breast. And when the tip of it hardened and throbbed incessantly against his tongue, he felt the wild coursing of her lifeblood and knew with joy that it was because of him.

Every touch, every caress he gave her had a rhythm that matched the one pounding wildly within himself. When he longed to plunge his aching body inside her, he sent a searching finger instead. And when honey flowed and heat increased, and muscles began winding too tight to bear the strain, he stroked her body, up one side and down the other, in long, even motions, gentling it for the release that was to come.

Gabriel was lost to all but the woman moving beneath him. The same woman who was urging him to move inside while she made a place for him in the cradle of herself. But he remembered what she'd asked of him and knew that, even if it killed him, he could give her that. He *would* make love to her until she begged him to stop. He *couldn't* promise her anything else, but he would give her that.

A harsh groan ripped up his throat and tore out of his mouth. As badly as he wanted to sheathe himself inside, in the heat, in sweet Annie's fire, it wasn't time. Before he could change his mind, he turned loose of her arms and slid down the length of her body.

Annie felt weightless. Seconds ago Gabriel had been pressing her deeper and deeper into the mattress as he drove her mad with his touch. Now cool air moved across her breasts, bringing the love-swollen nubs to tight, hard peaks. And just when she would have moved in search of him, his mouth found its target and threw Annie's body into instant spasms of satisfaction she had never expected.

"Oh, Gabriel," she moaned, and reached down.

Her fingers slid through his hair, then curled into fists. All she could do was hold on for dear life as his mouth opened, then closed, centering on the throbbing pinpoint of her arousal and yanking her backward through a tunnel of sensuality. It went on...and on...and on...until it became a pleasure she could no longer bear.

"No more. No more," she moaned, digging tighter and tighter into his hair with her fingers as her head thrashed from side to side on the pillow. But it didn't end, and still the tremors rocketed through her body, leaving her burning alive from the inside out.

"Gabriel!" Her body arched as if from a violent jolt of electricity as she screamed his name.

Perfect pleasure. Pounding pain. Where one started the other ended. Gabe had done what she'd asked. She was begging him to stop. To put out the fire of perpetual pleasure while there was enough left of her to survive it.

Her passion. He felt it. Moving beneath his lips, pounding with the rhythm of his own blood that coursed through his veins to near boiling point. And when he heard her begging

him to stop, it was all that kept him from dying on the spot.
It was what he'd been waiting for.

With a gasp, he lifted himself from where he'd been.
Before Annie could react to the abandonment, he moved up
and covered her body. The muscles in his back and arms
shook from the violent emotion of his own needs as he
braced himself above her. Before the last syllable of his
name had died on her lips, he was inside her. Just when
Annie thought there was no ability left in her to savor what
came next, the feel of him moving in and out in a desperate
rocking motion started everything all over again.

She groaned, wrapped her arms around his neck and her
legs around his waist, and knew that if this was the moment...she would and could die happy.

He climaxed, spilling into her over and over in shuddering thrusts. Bright sunbursts of light went off behind his
eyelids as he called her name. And then, like the quiet after
a storm, he collapsed on top of her, wrapped her in his arms
and rolled until she was the one on top. Only then could he
relax. Only then could he close his eyes and let exhaustion
and sleep overtake him.

Annie lay with her ear against his heartbeat, her hands
splayed across the hard, muscled expanse of his chest, and
knew that she would never feel this safe and this loved
again.

But it had been worth it, she kept telling herself. *At least
when he's gone I'll have the memories*. And then she raised
herself up and stared long and hard into the face of the man
who had stolen her heart.

"It isn't fair," she whispered. Her mouth trembled as she
lay back down and searched again for the place nearest his
heart. "It just isn't fair."

It was mid-afternoon, and Annie was almost finished un-
packing. The moving van had arrived with what was left of

her things, and the next half hour had been devoted to dealing with the meager assortment of boxes that the movers carried into the house. When the men finally pulled away, Annie was left with her clothes, a few personal mementos that Damon Tuttle had missed when he'd trashed her apartment, and a small box labeled Books that she seemed unwilling to put down.

Now Gabe sat on the edge of the bed and watched as she walked from a box of clothes to the closet and back again, methodically slipping each garment on a hanger and hanging it up in the closet before retrieving the next item.

Her shapely legs looked long and lean beneath the short cutoff jeans she was wearing. And her body, the one that he'd loved to distraction such a short time ago, moved without constraints beneath the loose pink T-shirt she'd pulled on in her haste. The bra she'd put on this morning was still on the floor where Gabe had tossed it in their haste to make love. And her bare feet padded against the floorboards with a faint, slap, slap sound as she walked.

His eyes narrowed, darkening with remembered passion as he watched. He knew her body so well, yet he knew next to nothing of what went on inside that pretty head. She shared the physical, but never the personal. And there was one thing about Annie O'Brien that just didn't add up.

No matter how organized and thorough and by the book she was in her professional life, from the moment they'd met, she seemed to have simply thrown caution to the winds and done everything a "good girl" wasn't supposed to do.

Somewhere in Annie O'Brien's background was a secret he hadn't unearthed. But unless the revelation came within the next forty-eight hours or so, he didn't think he was ever going to know the truth. He sighed and pushed himself off the bed as he noticed that the small box of books had yet to be unpacked.

"Where do you want me to put these, honey?" Gabe asked as he parted the flaps and pulled out a handful.

"Give those to me!" Annie said, and all but snatched them out of his hands.

Two of the books fell to the floor between them as Gabe stared at her expression. Panic filled her eyes. Certain that he was mistaken about her emotion, he bent down and picked up the books, casually reading the titles as he handed them back.

"*Neurosurgery in the Nineties* and *Life After Death,* two of my all-time favorites." His sarcasm sliced through the silence of the room as he dropped the books into Annie's outstretched hands. "So...now your secret's out. You like to read weird books. But don't worry, I won't tell," he drawled.

She blanched. *Could he have guessed?*

"I didn't mean to..."

"Save it, lady," he said. "No apologies necessary. Obviously I've somehow overstepped my bounds...again. You don't owe me anything...not even an explanation. I'm leaving. Remember?"

The sweet smile she loved so dearly was back to a bittersweet smirk as he turned and walked out of the room, leaving Annie alone with her guilt...and her fears. After the passion they'd shared earlier in the day, she couldn't bear to see pain on his face and know that she was the cause.

She dropped the books onto the bed and hurried after him. But before she could catch up and apologize, she met him in the hallway. He was coming back to her.

She looked up into eyes blazing with a blue-white heat, saw a muscle jerk at the side of his jaw, and wanted to run her fingers through his unruly hair in the hopes that she could smooth the frown away from his forehead in the process. Instead she did nothing. Only waited.

"You make me so damn mad," he said.

"I know." Annie sighed and shrugged, as if it were inevitable that sparks flew between them.

"I didn't mean to pry. I just wanted to help. Since the day we met, that's all I've been trying to—"

"I know," Annie said. "Please...don't apologize for something that's my fault."

"You let me do what I want with your body...but you keep your heart and soul to yourself...don't you, Annie Laurie?" Gabe's hand hit the wall with a solid slap as he spun away from her in anger, and she jumped as his accusation sliced through what was left of her conscience.

She flushed. It was too close to the truth to comment.

"Why is that, Annie? Why would a lady like you let a man like me into her life...and into her bed?" Before she could make up an excuse, he continued. "And don't give me that crap about trying to find yourself. You're the most together woman I've ever known." He turned back to her, and his anger escaped in a slow sigh as his hand cupped her cheek. "You're also the most beautiful woman I've ever known. You could have any man you wanted. Why don't you?"

"Before I met you, I wasn't looking," she said. "After I met you...you pretty much laid it on the table for me. I had a choice. I could take you as you are...or leave you." She walked into his arms. "I just chose to take what I could get, Gabriel. You can't blame a woman for that."

He groaned. Again it all boiled down to the fact that happy ever after and growing old together had no place in his life. It had never been part of the deal.

"I'm sorry...so sorry," Gabe said, and crushed her to his chest. "I wish I could explain...."

Annie shook her head and buried her nose against his shirtfront, searching for that particular spot she'd come to love. The place where the curve of her cheek fit directly over the beat of his heart.

"I don't need explanations, Gabe. I don't even need promises. I had more with you in the short time we've known each other than in all the years I've lived." Her voice shook as she wrapped her arms around his waist. "For me… it's enough."

But it's not enough for me, Gabe thought. *This is the first time since my journey began that I'll leave part of myself behind.*

He dug his fingers into the thick, heavy length of her hair, tilted her face up to meet his descending mouth and captured what tasted suspiciously like a sob.

They stood together in the hallway, absorbing each other's pain, and wondered how the hell they would survive when it was time to say goodbye.

Pain engulfed her as she watched him pack. He'd dragged it out until there were no more excuses left to use. No more reasons to stay. She was safe and snug in a house in the hills, with a borrowed car to drive. Her phone was hooked up. Her house was clean. And Davie Henry had stopped by again to give her his number as well as an assurance that he'd be Johnny-on-the-spot if she needed anything… anything at all.

The only problem was, what Annie needed, Davie Henry couldn't provide. Annie needed a miracle. And she'd long since given up believing in those.

"I still wish you'd let me pay you," Annie muttered, then refused to look away from the fierce glare he gave her.

"Well…I do," she continued. "After all, if it wasn't for me, you never would have stopped in Oklahoma. At least, not to stay," she added, on seeing him clench his teeth and viciously shove a pair of jeans into his duffel bag.

"You'll call Davie if you get frightened, won't you?" Gabe asked, and paused in the act of zipping the bag he'd been packing. He couldn't bear the thought of her alone and afraid.

"I won't be afraid," Annie assured him. "There's nothing on this earth that can frighten me."

Gabe stared long and hard at her, mulling over the odd answer she'd just given him as he watched her expression for a reason to stay. *Nothing on this earth?* It was an odd way of putting things. *As opposed to something not of this earth?* He shrugged. He was reading too much into a few simple words.

"Yeah, right. Tough little teacher, aren't you, Annie?" He tried to grin. It didn't quite make it.

"I'll write," he said.

"Don't make promises you won't keep," Annie said quietly, and bit her lower lip to keep from begging him not to go.

"Ah, God," Gabe said, and swept her into his arms.

Kisses rained upon Annie's face and neck until she thought she might faint from the power and passion with which they were delivered. Frantically they clutched each other, willing something…anything…to happen that would stop this insanity. This parting. It didn't come.

"Don't forget me," Annie said, tears sliding down her face in numb profusion. "I would hate to think I'd come and gone without one single person to regret my passing."

She tried to laugh, but it turned into a choking sob, instead. Gabe shook his head and turned away, dry-eyed and aching inside in a place too deep to heal. He walked outside with his bag slung across his shoulder, then tossed it onto the back of the bike and fastened it down with short, angry motions.

His hands trembled as he yanked his helmet off the handlebars and shoved it over his head. Without a sound, he flipped the smoke-tinted visor over his eyes and snapped the chin strap in place.

Annie watched as he swung a long, leather-clad leg over the bike, started the motor and then stood with the Harley rumbling between his legs and stared at her, imprinting her image into his brain for all time.

He looked just as he had when she'd first met him, back in disguise. The hardcase who rode the highways on a Harley. But she knew better. Beneath that leather was a man, not a monster. A man who deserved more out of life than she had to give. It was because of that knowledge that she didn't cry out when the Harley began to roll. She didn't cry, "Stop!" She didn't cry, "Come back!" She just cried.

And he rode away.

Chapter 7

Hours passed. Hours in which Annie roamed from room to room, trying to find a focus. Trying to find a reason to do something other than cry. But it didn't come. And the emptiness inside her echoed like the painful quiet of the small frame house. She was so lost in her own misery that she didn't even hear Davie drive up.

"Hey, Annie!"

The familiar voice boomed a greeting through the open screen door. Without waiting for an invitation, Davie Henry walked inside with a petite blonde in tow.

"I thought I'd stop and see if you wanted something from town," Davie said. "Mom gave me a list the length of my arm, so if you need anything, don't hesitate to say so. I'll be in that grocery store for an hour trying to find everything. Besides, I wanted you to meet my Charlie."

He grinned and winked as he looked down at the pretty young woman at his side.

"Charlie...this is Annie O'Brien. Annie...Charlotte Thomas."

120 Annie and the Outlaw

Annie smiled at the woman. She reminded her of a pixie. Turned-up nose. Big round eyes. Pouty lips and bashful dimples. Such an odd contrast to Davie's hulking appearance...and yet, somehow, perfect.

"Hi, Charlotte. It's so good to finally meet you. Davie has told me all about you." And then she grinned impishly as she added, "You do know that he's never full?"

The unexpected remark about Davie's constant state of hunger set both women into a fit of the giggles.

Charlotte rolled her eyes and nodded. "Do I ever." And then she added, "Davie's talked about you for years. I'm pleased to finally be able to meet the infamous Annie." And then she turned to Davie with an innocent expression. "Davie...she does *not* have horns and a forked tail. Shame on you!"

Davie turned red. He was dumbfounded by the fact that both women had instantly turned on him. "I never... Well, Annie, I swear it was only a joke. I wouldn't..."

They burst into laughter as Davie breathed a sigh of relief. As long as they weren't mad at him, they could laugh all they liked.

"So, Annie, do you need anything from town, or would you two rather stand here and make fun of me some more?" Davie grumbled.

"The only thing I really need is to have a prescription refilled," she said, thinking about the small number of pain pills that were left in the bottom of that little brown bottle.

"Is Parker's Drug still in business?" Annie asked.

He nodded as she handed him her written prescription.

"Wait while I get you some money."

"Naw...just pay Parker the next time you go into Walnut Shade. He knows you're good for it."

She sighed to herself as she thought, Oh, the luxury of small-town living. It felt good to be home.

"Need anything else?" he asked.

"Thanks, Davie, but I don't think so," she said, and shrugged to make her point. "I bought plenty when Gabe was still here. It'll take me a week to eat it up by myself."

The biker is gone! Davie frowned. He'd noticed that the bike wasn't out front. But he hadn't known it was a permanent absence. He'd imagined the man was off on an errand. He stared at her face and nearly missed seeing the emptiness with which she smiled back at him.

Oh damn! She was in love with the guy, he thought.

Davie recognized the signs. He should. He felt the same way about Charlotte. He looked at her, and then stared at the floor in front of his boots.

Charlotte realized something was amiss and thought to give the two old friends some privacy.

"I'll wait in the truck," she said. "Annie...it was great to be able to meet you. Come see me sometime."

Annie nodded and waved, masking regret as the tiny blonde left. *I would have liked her for a friend.*

Davie kept staring at Annie's sad expression. Something felt wrong, but he couldn't put his finger on what, or figure out a way to offer his help.

"You sure you don't need anything else?" He walked across the room, closing the space between them in three easy steps and wrapped her into a warm, engulfing hug. "You better promise me that if you ever—and I mean *ever*—need anything, you'll let me know."

Annie smiled past her tears. For a single moment she let herself imagine that it was Gabe who was holding her. That it was Gabe who was asking for promises. And then Davie turned her loose and stepped back as a cocky grin slid across his mouth. The feeling disappeared.

"Oh, right! If I ever need baby-sitting, I'll call on you. I wasted half my sunny days keeping you out of mischief. I guess it's only fair that you have to reciprocate."

A frown furrowed his forehead. "I'm not real sure what

you just said I should do...." And then he grinned and poked her playfully on the shoulder. "But if it doesn't hurt my manhood—or my feelings—I'll do it."

"'Reciprocate' means pay me back, you goof."

He flushed. "Okay, just don't be using all those big fancy words on me. I never left Walnut Shade, you know."

"But I would have sworn that before she died, Mother wrote and told me about you getting an athletic scholarship to Missouri State."

"Well, I did, but it didn't work out," he muttered, then turned away.

He stuffed his hand in his pocket as he searched for his truck keys, looking more uncomfortable by the minute. Annie couldn't imagine what she'd said that had made him so defensive.

"I better be going," Davie said, yanking out the ring of keys he'd been looking for as he headed toward the door.

A small white piece of folded paper fluttered to the floor behind him as he turned away. Annie bent down and picked it up. Tiny, unintelligible scribblings and a few, minute line drawings were written in neat, perpendicular order in three equally neat rows. She frowned. It looked like childish scribbles. It was probably nothing, but since he'd thought enough of it to keep it, the least she could do was return it.

"Davie...you dropped this," she said, and held out the folded paper.

He turned. "Oh, man, my list," he muttered. "If I'd lost that, Mom would have had a fit. I've got a good memory, but it's not that good." He grinned, took the paper from her outstretched hand and shoved it back inside the front pocket of his jeans.

"Thanks, Annie. Be seeing you," he said, and missed the look of utter shock sweeping across her face.

He climbed into his truck beside Charlotte and drove

away, leaving Annie to stare in muddled confusion at his brake lights as he slowed to turn the corner.

"List? There wasn't one single, legible word on that paper." But there was no one around to hear her, or argue with the truth of the statement.

She shrugged and walked back inside, certain that they'd just misunderstood each other. Davie hadn't looked, he'd just assumed that it was his list he'd dropped. The real list was probably safe, tucked away in another pocket. She smiled to herself, imagining him pulling out that paper and then trying to find a list of groceries amid that mess of hen scratching. He was going to be so mad at himself, she thought.

She walked back toward the kitchen in search of something to still the grumbling reminder in her stomach that she hadn't eaten all day. Hunger was the least of her problems. But starving herself and adding another problem to the already insurmountable ones she was facing was out of the question.

She opened the refrigerator and leaned down, saw a half-eaten meat loaf wrapped in plastic wrap, and caught her breath at the pain that knifed through her. It reminded her of the first meal she'd prepared for Gabriel.

"Damn you, Gabe. Are memories of you going to haunt me for the rest of my life?"

As soon as she said it, she laughed. But it was a harsh, bitter laugh. The rest of her life. That was rich.

She slammed the refrigerator door shut, her hunger forgotten in the loneliness that overwhelmed her. With a sigh, she retreated to the living room.

She stood in the doorway, watching…listening. But there were no answers to her problems in there. Her gaze fell on the narrow bookcase, where she'd stacked her books from home. Without conscious thought, she walked over to it and then paused, looking at the second shelf from the top. Her fingers traced the spines, mentally cataloging the titles as she braced herself for what she was about to do. With a forefinger, she hooked the top of the book and pulled it toward her. It slid out of the tightly fitted stack like toast popping out of a toaster.

"Okay," she muttered, as she headed for the sofa with it clutched against her chest. "If there are answers to be found, maybe you have one for me in here."

In seconds she was stretched out on the couch, the book open before her at the place where she'd stopped last.

Life After Death. She sighed, ignoring the burning sensation in the back of her throat where unshed tears hung at the ready, and began to read.

Compulsion to understand the words made her grip the edge of the book so tightly that when it came time to turn the page, she couldn't. Her fingers were stuck to the paper.

And as she read, she became lost in the images called up by the words swimming before her. Finally she slept, certain only that at some point and time in their lives, all mankind came to the same, inevitable end.

"Annie! I'm back!"

She woke with a start. The book that she'd been reading slid off her stomach and onto the floor with a thump.

"I'm in here," she called as Davie walked into the room alone.

He walked to the couch and leaned over, dangling her prescription in front of her.

Annie took the bag out of his hands. "Thank you."

She tried unsuccessfully to sit up, and Davie held out a hand, pulling her to her feet in one smooth motion. As he did, his foot kicked the book that had fallen on the floor. He bent down and picked it up.

Annie's stomach jerked, and a guarded expression crossed her face. She wasn't in the mood for explanations...or conversational detours. But she needn't have worried. Davie's actions were stiff and awkward as he slapped the book shut and held it out in front of him.

"It won't bite," Annie muttered, and started toward the kitchen with her medicine. "Would you mind putting that book back on the shelf? Just poke it in anywhere you can find space." She waved her hand in the general direction of the book shelf, and didn't look back to see if he was following orders.

Davie sighed as she walked out of the room, then looked long and hard at the book in his hand before heading toward the bookcase at the other end of the room.

In less than a minute Annie was back. Her bare feet made little noise as she walked, and she entered the living room undetected. She opened her mouth and started to speak, but the words dangled unspoken on the tip of her tongue as she watched Davie's odd behavior.

He was standing by the bookshelf. She couldn't see his face, but she saw what he was doing. And when she did, warning signals went off. She couldn't quite pinpoint the urgency of what she was feeling, but she watched, silently and intently, as Davie moved from book to book.

Reverently he touched each book's spine with his forefinger, tracing the letters in the titles with the tip of his finger as a blind man read braille, as if trying to absorb what he read by touch alone.

Annie shivered. Davie wasn't blind.

She watched him studiously struggle with the shape of each letter, tracing it over and over before going on to the next. It reminded her of something she'd seen before. Something in the classroom. Something one of her brighter students had done during her first year of teaching.

What was it? Annie pondered. *What am I trying to remember?*

And then Davie turned unexpectedly. The guilt...the

shock…the overwhelming embarrassment on his face was the last clue to the memory she'd been trying to unearth. It was the same look of panic. The same guilt that her student, Varlie Hudson, had worn when Annie had realized what was wrong.

Davie can't read!

The knowledge came swiftly. She didn't even have to ask as she watched Davie turn away in sudden horror and quickly shove the book back on the shelf.

"I'd better be getting home," he said. "Mom's ice cream will be starting to melt."

"Davie…"

Annie started toward him. He began backing to the front door, dodging chairs and grabbing at table lamps to keep them from tumbling to the floor as he tried to escape the certainty on her face.

"You know how Mom is," he continued. "She likes crisp things crisp, and cold things cold. If I dawdle, she'll nag for a week."

"Davie, don't," Annie said, and grabbed him just as he reached the screen door.

He looked away, unable to face the question he knew she was going to ask.

"You know that I'm your friend," she reminded him.

He nodded, still unable to meet the look in her eyes.

"You know that you can trust me."

He sighed. "You don't let go, do you, Annie?"

She didn't answer.

He started to talk. It came out in bits and pieces, but she understood just the same.

"I can remember anything," Davie said.

Annie nodded and slipped her fingers across the massive muscle in his forearm. It jerked uncontrollably beneath her fingertips. She squeezed once for comfort as he continued.

"I don't remember a time when I ever really understood

them…the words, you know.'' He looked away in embarrassment as he explained. ''And every time I asked a question, or stumbled over the sounds, the kids laughed and the teacher would get frustrated with me. I thought I was just stupid. I think so did my teacher.''

''Why did they keep promoting you to the next grade?'' Annie asked.

Davie smiled. But it wasn't a happy smile. It was full of pain and regret.

''I don't know,'' he muttered. ''Every year I was the biggest one in my class. It was hard being so damned big… and different. I guess they just didn't want to fix someone else's mess and kept moving me up. But I got by.''

Tears puddled in Annie's eyes. ''Why didn't you tell me? When we were kids together, why didn't you tell me, Davie? I would have helped.''

He shrugged. ''By then it was too late.''

''How on earth have you managed? How did you get a job? How did you get a driver's license? Does anyone else know about…?''

''Whoa,'' he said, and ran a hand through his curly blond hair in confusion. ''First things first, teacher.''

Annie waited.

''I can't get the good jobs,'' Davie admitted. ''Luckily there's plenty of heavy-labor, part-time jobs around. Even some farming. You don't have to be able to read to plow or cut wood. And I can write my name real good.''

''Oh, Davie, I'm so sorry.''

He shrugged. ''As for the driver's license…'' He grinned, as if it were one of his more innovative stunts. ''I walked into the office with a patch on my eye. Told them I'd hurt myself and needed an oral test. That I couldn't come back later because I was leaving town on a job. They read it to me. I only missed one question. After that, driving was easy.

I know what the shapes of the traffic signs mean. And I can drive as good as anyone. The rest was easy.''

Annie hugged him. Davie Henry had been running on guts for years. And then something occurred to her. Something so overwhelming she knew that the message had come from somewhere other than inside herself.

"Davie...I could teach you to read."

He stepped back, astounded by the thought.

"I could," she persisted. And then she added, before he could object, "No one has to know a thing. We could do it here, in my house. Everyone would think you were just helping out with odd jobs."

He swallowed harshly, his Adam's apple bobbing up and down several times before he got out the words.

"You would do that for me?"

She nodded, her eyes filling with unexpected tears. "But I can't promise anything. All the work will have to come from you."

"I'm a real hard worker," Davie said. "And I'm stubborn as hell."

"I remember," she said.

"I'll do it!" he cried, and hugged her, holding her in a near-frantic grip, as if he couldn't believe his luck or was afraid that she might disappear. "When can we start?"

"Come back tomorrow," she said. "When I have time, I'll pick up some proper books, but for now, we'll start with what I learned on," she said, remembering the stacks of children's books that her mother had saved from her childhood.

"What time?" Davie asked.

"You decide," Annie answered. "I'm here. I'm not going anywhere." *At least...I don't think so...not yet.*

"See you!" he shouted, and bounded out the door and off of the porch.

Annie smiled and waved, then went back into the house.

The weight in her heart was still there. After losing Gabe, that would never change. But a small part of the ache was gone, and she knew it was because now she had a purpose. She had a reason to get up each day. For the first time in longer than she cared to remember, she had a goal. Before it was too late...for herself and for Davie...she was going to teach him how to read.

She headed toward the kitchen, yanked the half-eaten meat loaf out of the refrigerator and began slicing it to make a sandwich. Now she had a reason to keep up her strength.

The night sounds around her home were becoming familiar. Annie had gone to bed just after sunset, weary beyond words at the emotional upheaval she'd been forced to face today.

Losing Gabe had nearly killed her. Then she thought of Davie and his revelation and knew that it had come at just the right time to save her sanity. All she had to do was focus on Davie's problem, instead of the huge, aching hole Gabe's exodus had caused. Surely she could do that.

But the tension of the day had been too much. Three hours into her sleep, she bolted awake. Heart pounding, sweat seeping from her body, hands shaking with dread at the onslaught of what was coming. And it *was* coming. She'd learned to recognize the signs.

"My pills," she muttered, and stumbled as she rolled out of bed.

The small table lamp clattered to the floor as she reached to turn on the light. A loud thud and then the tinkle of glass were enough to tell her that she would have to navigate the darkened room by instinct until she got to the light switch at the edge of the doorway.

But on the second step, she fell, going down to the floor in unexpected pain as a shard of glass from the broken lamp pierced her foot.

"Oh, no," she muttered, as the throbbing at the back of her head increased to blinding proportions.

Carelessly brushing her hand over the bottom of her foot, she swiped at the area that was causing her pain. And as she did, she broke the glass off in her foot. Ignoring the pain and the trail of blood she was leaving behind her, she staggered toward the kitchen with single-minded intent. She had to get to her pills. She had to stop the pain before it stopped *her*—permanently.

She didn't remember turning on the light in the kitchen, pouring a glass of water or holding the open cabinet door to steady herself before reaching inside to grasp the new bottle of pills that she'd placed there earlier in the day.

The cap wouldn't budge. In that moment she hated the invention of the childproof cap with a vengeance. But she continued to struggle, convinced that unless she got the bottle open, this would be the end of her.

Without warning, the cap came away in her hand, scattering tiny pills all over the countertop and at the floor near her feet. Without looking to see where the others had rolled, she grabbed the nearest pill, stuffing it shakily into her mouth. Excess water cascaded onto the front of her gown as she tilted the glass to wash the pill down.

"Now...now..." she groaned as she clutched her head and staggered, swaying drunkenly as she tried to see through the pain-induced haze. Somewhere in front of her, she knew there was a doorway that would take her back to her bed.

But she'd left it too late to move any farther. She went down in a heap near the table in the center of the room, her resting place the floor on which she'd left an assortment of pain pills, water and blood. For Annie, it was far enough. She rolled into a ball, closed her eyes and waited for the medicine to take effect, longing for the blessed relief she knew would come.

* * *

Gabe hurt. He ached from the inside out. Anger at fate and himself kept his foot heavy on the pedal while the Harley ate up the miles, widening the gap between himself and Annie.

The sun beamed down on him in relentless persecution. The blowing dirt and wind stung his bare neck and chest as he rode. Once he thought about stopping and putting on a shirt beneath that black leather vest, and then he instantly nixed the idea. He deserved misery. He'd certainly left plenty behind.

There was a crossroad ahead. He stopped to look both ways and flipped up the visor of his helmet, inhaling the hot, dry wind, relishing it over the stuffy air that he breathed behind the helmet. He frowned as a memory tried to surface. Something about this day was so familiar, and yet he couldn't quite put his finger on it.

And then he grinned wryly to himself. It reminded him a little of that hot, dry day so long ago in the Kansas Territory when this had all begun—or ended, depending on the way one chose to view it.

A girl drove by and waved, her smile and her wink nothing more than a reminder to Gabe of what he'd left behind. With an angry curse, he flipped the visor back down and accelerated across the intersection.

Miles and hours passed. And with them came the growing certainty that leaving Annie had been the wrong thing to do.

He knew the unspoken rules governing his time here on earth. He knew that to undo the wrongs of his past, he had to keep on the move. Personal happiness had to be of lesser importance in his life. Personal involvement had no part in what he had to do. And still his gut instinct told him to turn around.

"But why?"

He pulled off the interstate, hit the kickstand with the toe of his boot, then killed the engine. He hung his helmet on the handlebar and walked a distance away to get his bearings.

Stiff muscles reminded him that it had been months since he'd ridden the bike so continually. He stared blindly off into the small brushy canyon below and tried to bring some order to his jumbled thoughts.

When he'd first met Annie, the reason why he'd stayed was obvious. She'd asked. He could even, he told himself, justify why he'd stayed after Damon Tuttle had gotten himself killed. After all, he could hardly have left her in the lurch after nearly all her belongings had been destroyed. And…she'd asked him to bring her home. He couldn't turn down a personal request from someone in need. He just… couldn't.

"Oh, hell," he muttered, and bent down, grabbing a handful of gravel from the shoulder of the road, then absently tossing the pebbles one by one down the hillside. "Face it, Donner. You lost your focus the first time you kissed her."

The ache in his belly grew as he remembered. That was the day he'd first rescued her. When she'd fainted at the gas station, and he'd held her in his arms while he waited for her to regain consciousness.

He closed his eyes. Even now he could remember the feel of her mouth beneath his and how soft her skin was to the touch. He frowned as that thought brought another, more sinister, memory bobbing to the surface.

Fainting.

She did a lot of that.

Migraines.

He knew people had them. Hers had even brought on some of the fainting spells he'd witnessed. But he couldn't bear to see someone he cared for so deeply, so deeply in pain. He wondered if she'd ever had these bouts at school.

Teaching would have been impossible during one of the episodes.

With the thought of teaching, another sinister memory rose to the surface, sitting alongside the first, like little sores festering in his mind.

Books.

She loved books. She shared her love of them, and what was inside, with everyone. So why had she been so defensive about the ones he'd been helping her unpack? They were on such offbeat subjects that he would have expected her to joke about them instead of trying to hide them.

Neurosurgery…Life After Death.

He started to laugh. But the sound turned into a harsh, ugly gasp as everything he'd just assembled in his mind stirred itself into a thick, ugly heap and began steaming with possibilities he didn't want to contemplate.

Fainting…migraines…pain…pain pills. Neurosurgery… even dying.

A flashback of the day they'd attended church together in Oklahoma City set his teeth on edge. He thought of how oddly she'd behaved, and suddenly one fact became irrefutably clear.

Something's wrong with Annie! Something bad!

"Why did I decide that?" Gabe muttered, and stuffed his hands into his pockets to keep them from shaking. "What in God's name made me think of that?"

And with the speaking of His name, came the knowledge. He knew Who had made him think of that.

"No," he groaned, and looked up into the nearly cloudless sky, as if trying to see past infinity to One beyond. "Tell me it isn't so."

But no answer came. All he felt was a growing fear and the need to hear Annie deny it to his face.

He ran to the bike, calculating how long it would take

him to get back to her. If he had it figured right, he would be there around midnight.

He shoved his helmet on his head, snapping the chin strap as he swung one long leg over the bike. In seconds he was on the move. He raced across the highway, crossing the grassy median and leaving grass flying in the air behind him as the tires hit pavement on the other side.

One way or another, he and Annie weren't through with each other. Not by a long shot.

Chapter 8

Dawn was a thought on the horizon as Gabe finally wheeled the Harley into Annie's yard. After missing turns and once even taking the wrong highway in the dark, he'd misjudged the time it would take him to get back.

He slipped off his helmet and hung it on the handlebar as the motor coughed and died. After hours and hours with the sound of the wind and the roar of the engine in his ears, the sudden silence seemed like a warning.

In one motion he put the kickstand in place and swung his leg up and over, dismounting from the bike as he'd always dismounted from his horse. The rowels on his spurs jingled once as he took a step away from the bike and stared silently up the path that led to the house.

It looked the same. Nothing seemed ominous...or out of place. But if that was so, then why did he have this over-powering feeling of dread? What made him think he might already be too late?

Gabe glanced down at himself, realizing as he did that he

probably looked like hell. A day's worth of black, spiky whiskers and twenty-four hours on the back of a bike would do little toward making him presentable. But a bath and a shave would have to wait until he'd seen her...until she'd laughed in his face at his fears and cursed him for coming back just to say goodbye again.

He walked around the bush at the edge of the yard, heading for the path that led to the front door. His heart skipped a beat as he saw the light on at the back of the house.

"She can't be up already." He glanced down at his watch and squinted as he tried to read the luminous dial. It wasn't quite 5:00 a.m.

But he remembered the pain on her face as he'd ridden away, and the knot in his own gut at saying goodbye, and decided that she, like him, had probably just suffered a sleepless night.

Even though he'd already answered all his own questions, he still felt a need to hurry. Just to make sure that she was all right.

If she's so all right, then why in hell hasn't she come out to meet me?

He stopped at the door and knocked. Nearly a minute went by without a response, so he knocked again, and this time he called her name aloud. Twice. Nothing happened. No one came.

"Annie, damn it, where are you?" he muttered. "Okay...maybe you left the light on by mistake."

If she *was* asleep in her bed, checking that theory before barreling into the house seemed the sensible thing to do.

With that thought in mind, he ignored the steps and turned the corner at the side of the house on the run. Destination: kitchen window.

A faint beam of light poured out of the window and into the night, cutting the ground in a butter-colored, geometric pattern.

He leaned forward, bracing himself against the outer wall as he peered through the narrow gap between the curtain panels. From where he was standing, all he could see was her foot...and the blood...and the fact that she was motionless on the floor.

"No!"

The denial was ripped from his lips as terror spread through his system. This was what he'd been sensing! This was what had sent him riding back through the darkest of nights! She was hurt...or worse.

"Annie! Annie!"

She didn't move. She didn't answer.

He banged the flat of his hand on the window in sick frustration, and then ran back to the front door.

The door was locked. He'd expected that.

But just as he started to kick it in, he remembered the old, dusty key that she'd retrieved from above the door frame the day of their arrival. He reached up and ran his fingers along the dry, splintery wood. The key was still there! He was inside in seconds, running to Annie's aid.

As he entered the kitchen, he started to shake. Small patches of blood were spattered everywhere. She was lying halfway beneath the table, her thin, white nightgown twisted around her legs. All he could see was the back of her head and the back of her body. Silent. Unmoving.

Within the space of a second, his heart stopped and then changed rhythm to a frantic, pounding pace that left him gasping for air.

Small yellow pills lay scattered across the counter and the floor, haphazardly interspersed with the drying blood stains to form an odd, garish pattern.

Bile rose and burned the back of his throat. But his legs refused to move. In the countless years that he'd been traveling the earth, he'd witnessed almost everything. Births, accidents, even deaths. But this was something he wasn't ready to face. He didn't want to lose the woman he loved. Not now...not like this.

He'd known for weeks that Annie O'Brien meant more to him than she should. But not until now—not until it might be too late—had he been able to admit, even to himself, the magnitude of his feelings for her. For the first time in his life, he felt love for a woman.

"Annie!"

Her name became a prayer as he knelt at her side. With a sick heart and a frantic touch, his hands swept the sides of her face. And when he touched her shoulder, she rolled limply onto her back. Too quiet, too still. He shook as he searched for signs of life.

The flat of his hand splayed across the center of her chest as he felt for her heartbeat. If it was there, it was so faint that it was undetectable.

"Annie...please, baby, don't do this to me," he begged, but she didn't respond.

He leaned forward, so close that the faint, tiny pores of her skin were visible. He held his breath and listened until he heard the slight but steady sounds of her even breathing. His knees went weak, and his heavy sigh of relief echoed in the utter silence of the kitchen.

"Thank you, God," he murmured. "She's still alive."

The mess she was lying in gave birth to all sorts of implications that Gabe didn't even want to consider. There were pills everywhere. To someone who didn't know her, it might look as if she'd tried to take her life. And yet Gabe knew that the pills did not explain the blood.

"Annie...baby...if only you could talk to me."

She didn't respond, and in panic, he began to check her for further sign of injury. It was then that he noticed the seeping wound on the bottom of her foot.

"Thank God," Gabe whispered. Suddenly the blood made sense. Whatever had happened to her must have been an accident. "I've got to get you to a doctor," he said, and started to pick her up from the floor.

But his intentions were momentarily forgotten as Annie's eyelids fluttered, and with a soft moan, she opened her eyes.

"Gabe?" Her chin quivered, and she blinked over and over, unable to believe what she was seeing. "You're gone...not here...just a dream. Bad dream."

"Ah, damn." Regret tinged his voice as he lifted her into his arms and pressed hot, thankful kisses across her face and neck, tasting the place where her lifeblood pulsed. "It's not a dream, honey. I'm here. What happened?"

"Head...headache."

He cursed beneath his breath. With a frown, he carried her toward the bedroom. This didn't look good. In fact, it was just as he'd feared. The headaches were becoming too frequent, and each time they occurred, the pain seemed to be more intense.

He moved through the house, her head bobbing limply against his arm as he held her carefully within his embrace. But when he walked into her bedroom and saw the lamp shattered on the floor, his reaction was anything but proper.

His curses were few but colorful. And he made no apologies for them. There was nothing else that would describe his emotions so well.

Imagining Annie alone and in pain made him sick to his stomach. He turned on the light, and as he did, she moaned.

"I'm sorry, Annie," he said softly, and quickly laid her on her bed. "Let me get you settled. I want to get a better look at your foot."

Confused by his reappearance, in addition to fighting the aftereffects of the painkillers, Annie struggled against the weight of his hand on her shoulder.

Gabe gently pushed her back into a reclining position while angling her foot for a better look.

"Don't move, baby. Let me look."

She lay back on the bed with a moan and swallowed a mouthful of tears. His gentleness was her undoing.

"Oh, God. Why did you come back? I can't take any more goodbyes."

Gabe's vision blurred. The pain in her voice was an echo of the pain in his chest. But he didn't have time for recriminations, from her or from himself. He was too busy trying to ascertain the extent of her injuries. His fingers shook as he examined her foot for the place where the blood had originated. But there was so much of it that it was difficult to tell.

"How bad did you hurt this time?"

Annie opened her eyes and peered down the length of her body. Her foot was propped on Gabe's lap.

"Hurt what? My foot?"

"No, damn it! Your head. How bad was it? Was it worse than before?"

She didn't answer. With a muttered oath, Gabe got up from the bed.

Annie looked away as he walked into the bathroom. Moments later, the sound of running water told her that he wasn't through with her foot…or her. She didn't like this. She didn't like it at all. His questions were too pointed for comfort.

He walked back into the bedroom with a wet washcloth in his hand. From the corner of her eye, Annie saw a look on his face that she didn't want to decipher.

She refused to meet his gaze. Gabe wanted to shake some sense into her.

The mattress gave beneath his weight as he maneuvered her foot back onto his lap and carefully began washing away the blood.

"I said…how bad was the headache this time?"

Once again, he waited for an answer that didn't come. And then he let her silence slide as his fingers traced the initial wound and finally found the reason for the continuous blood seepage.

"Annie, there's still glass in your foot. It's got to come out. Do you want me to help you change, or do you want to go to the emergency room dressed like that?"

She sat straight up in bed, shock chasing away the last remnants of the painkiller. Her answer was short and succinct.

"I don't want to go to the hospital," she said.

He frowned. "You don't have a choice, lady. We go like this or you can change. But either way, we go."

A very unladylike curse split the air. Gabe smiled and raised his eyebrows at her opinion of his ultimatum.

"I've heard that one before," he said. "Don't get me started. You'll lose."

She flushed and then waved her hand toward her closet. "If you're so insistent on doing this, at least hand me some clean shorts and a shirt."

Moments later he tossed the garments, as well as fresh underwear, into her lap.

"Want some help?" He started to bend down.

"You can either leave or turn your back."

Hurt beyond words that in less than twenty-four hours she'd completely shut him out, he could only mutter, "I've seen it all before."

"That was then...this is now," she said.

He turned his back, closed his eyes and tried to ignore the spreading pain in his gut. Leaving her had obviously been the wrong thing to do. For her to behave like this, whatever trust she'd had in him must be gone.

He seethed in angry frustration. It was back to square one with Annie O'Brion. At the moment, giving her space seemed to be wise.

"I'm going to clean up the kitchen while you finish dressing." He walked out before she could argue.

By the time he'd rebottled the pills and wiped away the blood, the sun was just coming over the horizon. A vivid slash of fiery orange coupled with an undulating swath of hot pink clouds painted a welcome on a new Missouri sky.

Gabe parted the curtains and looked outside, wondering as he did how many more sunrises and sunsets he had left in him, and how difficult they would be to endure without Annie's love.

"I'm ready," she called.

The curtains dropped back in place as he stepped away from the window. He started out of the kitchen, then made a sudden U-turn. Retrieving the brown bottle of pills from the cabinet, he stuffed them in his pocket and went to Annie.

Davie's loaner was an older model car, and for that Gabe was grateful. The back seat was larger and roomier than a newer one would have been. It gave Annie plenty of space to recline, and the pillows Gabe stuffed under her ankle kept her foot elevated. The constantly oozing blood made him nervous. From what Annie had told him, the accident had happened around midnight. The fact that it was still bleeding told him that it was very deep.

"We're here," he announced unnecessarily as he turned the car into the hospital parking lot.

Annie grumbled beneath her breath from the back seat and started to open her own door. Gabe bounded out and caught her in mid-scoot.

"You're not hurting me by acting like this, Annie. You're hurting yourself. Now stop it, damn it, and let me help you."

She flushed. His rebuke was justified. The simple truth was that she wasn't mad at Gabe for coming back. On the contrary. She'd been overjoyed when she'd opened her eyes and realized he was truly there.

It was fear that made her act as she did. Fear that he

would find out what she'd been trying to hide, and that pity
would replace what they'd shared. No matter how fleeting
their relationship had been, Annie treasured it.

"Gabe?"

The sound of her voice was soft, almost nonexistent. He
sighed and pressed his chin against the crown of her head
as he lifted her into his arms and started carrying her toward
the emergency room entrance.

"What?" he asked, and kissed a curl that slipped across
his lips, wishing it was Annie's lips he was kissing instead
of her hair.

"I'm sorry."

He stopped in mid-step, looked down, then nodded his
acceptance of her apology.

Her lower lip trembled, and he sighed and smiled gently
as his gaze swept down her face. Her eyes were dark, nearly
jade, and her hair seemed to catch fire as the morning sun's
rays played hide-and-seek within the tangles of her curls.
She looked vulnerable and miserable and so damned beautiful it made his heart hurt.

"It's okay to be scared, darlin'," he whispered. "I should
know. I've been scared so many times in my life I can't
even count them, and yet all of them stacked together were
nothing to the scare you gave me when I saw you on that
kitchen floor."

"I'm sorry for behaving so badly. Really, really sorry."

"Don't apologize to me. Save it for the man who's going
to dig that glass out of your foot. If you give him half of
what I got this morning, he'll be the one needing an apology."

She groaned and made a face at the thought.

"Let's get this over with," she muttered.

And then, as he started toward the door, she spread her
hand across his chest, found the spot where his heart beat
loudest and closed her eyes in silent thanksgiving that he

was back. For whatever reason...and for however long...she would take it as the gift that it was and appreciate it.

At the sound of the emergency door opening, a nurse looked up. She raised an eyebrow at the sight of the big, leather-clad biker who'd just entered, carrying a woman whose injury was leaving persistent drops of fresh blood in their wake.

The nurse read the look on his face and made an instant decision. This man was not the kind who would willingly wait to fill out the necessary papers.

"This way," she said, and motioned them into a curtained-off area near the door. "You can put her down here. The doctor will be in shortly. There's a waiting area right down the hall, if you'd care to—"

"No. I'll stay here," Gabe said, and gave the nurse a cool look, daring her to argue.

She didn't. If someone wanted him moved, someone else could move him. She was a nurse, not a policewoman. She took down the patient's name, made note of the time and the type of injury, then left the chart at the foot of the bed.

Minutes later, a doctor arrived.

"What have we here?" he asked, and gave them a confident smile.

"I stepped on some glass," Annie said.

"She passed out," Gabe interrupted.

The doctor looked from the big man to the smaller woman and masked a weary sigh. With one on the defensive and the other ready to argue, this looked like it was going to be a nuisance.

"Let's start over," the doctor said. "I'm Dr. Pope." He picked up the chart that the nurse had started. "And you're Annie O'Brien?"

She nodded. "This is my...um, my friend...Gabe Donner."

Gabe hated it. They didn't even have a way of categorizing their relationship. He wasn't just her friend, damn it. But there was no getting past the fact that although they'd made love with sweet abandon, he'd never given Annie reason to think there was anything emotional in their relationship.

"So, Mr. Donner. You're telling me she passed out," he said, as he bent down and began examining the cut on the bottom of Annie's foot. "How do you know? Did you witness it?"

"No. But I saw her lying unconscious on the floor with blood everywhere and *assumed* she didn't choose that location in which to spend the night."

Dr. Pope's eyebrows drew together at the sarcastic tone of Gabe's voice.

"So you're telling me that you weren't there when this happened."

Gabe swiped an angry hand across his face and cursed beneath his breath.

"No...I wasn't there. I left yesterday morning." Gabe stuffed his hand in his pocket and pulled out the bottle containing Annie's pills. Her harsh gasp as she saw what he'd done told him more than he wanted to know. "She takes these for pain...headache pain. She says she has migraines. I didn't know people could pass out from headaches."

Elevated eyebrows were the only sign of surprise that Dr. Pope allowed himself as he took the bottle from Gabe's hands and read the prescription, as well as the dosage.

Gabe turned and fixed Annie with a hard, pointed stare.

Her eyes were wide, the pupils transfixed. All color had drained from her face as she waited for the doctor's reaction.

Dr. Pope looked up. Annie shook her head once in a negative motion. He assumed she didn't want anything further said about the matter, and because she was his patient, he recognized her right to privacy.

Dr. Pope set the pills down on the table beside her bed and resumed his inspection of her foot.

"Let's get some local anesthetic around this cut and then clean out the glass. I think it'll need a few stitches, too, but I can't be sure until I see how deep the glass is. Wait right here, Miss O'Brien. I'll get the nurse."

Annie rolled her eyes and flopped back onto the bed. *Where on earth would she go—and how?*

She looked up at the ceiling, then over at the door. Everywhere and anywhere except at Gabriel's face.

"You're mad at me, aren't you?" he asked quietly.

"No. Of course not," she said shortly. "Whatever for?"

He almost bought it. Almost...but not quite. Because no matter how sweet her smile or how innocent her look, he still saw a deep and abiding fear in the depths of Annie's eyes. Before he could press her for more of an explanation, the nurse arrived with an ominous-looking tray bearing an assortment of bottles and needles.

"You'll have to wait outside," she announced.

Gabe glared. Annie intervened.

"Please, Gabe," she said. "I'll be fine. You did your job by getting me here. Now let them do theirs."

He nodded—reluctantly. Then, before he changed his mind, he leaned over and kissed her gently on the lips.

It was unexpected, and because of that, Annie reacted before she had time to hide her own feelings.

When their mouths merged, sighs traded places. Gabe reluctantly tore away from the seductive pull of her lips and walked away without looking back.

The nurse raised her eyebrows and winked at Annie. "He's a tough one, isn't he?" she asked, eyeing the stiff, unyielding back of the man in black.

Annie didn't answer at first, and then when she might have, she was too busy trying to get past the sharp little needle jabs around the cut on her foot, as the nurse went about her business of deadening the area for the stitches that were to come.

The waiting room chair was small and uncomfortable as hell. But Gabe was unaware of anything or anyone except the muted sounds of conversation going on between Annie and the doctor. He could hear their voices, but not clearly enough to discern what was being said. It was making him crazy. If he could only get a little bit closer, he knew that he would have the answers to his own questions regarding one Annie O'Brien.

He sighed and shifted restlessly in his seat. It wasn't going to happen. Not here. He'd been relegated to being on the outside looking in, and for now, that was the way it would have to be.

A small, determined smile slid across his mouth. But, he told himself, there was always later, after he got Annie home. After she'd rested. When she wasn't in so much pain. Then she had some explaining to do, and he wasn't going to be happy until she did.

"All done," Dr. Pope said a little while later, coming to stand in front of Gabe.

Gabe stood.

"You can take her home," the doctor continued. "I want to see her again in seven days. Earlier if she has unusual soreness or swelling around the area. I gave her an antibiotic. She should be fine."

"What about the headaches? What about the pills? Is that normal?"

A weary, time-worn expression of sympathy moved across the doctor's face. He could see that the man was sincerely worried. His concern for Annie O'Brien was obvious.

But a long time ago the doctor had taken an oath to be faithful to a patient's right to privacy. And this patient had certainly been adamant about hers. He simply shoved his stethoscope into the pocket of his lab coat and answered Gabe's question without actually revealing any confidential information.

"The pills are Miss O'Brien's regular medication."

He'd told the truth...as far as it went. It was up to Miss O'Brien to reveal the rest...if she chose.

"Exactly what *is* her condition?" Gabe persisted.

The doctor shrugged. "You should know better than to ask me that. If you want to know more than what I've told you, it will have to come from Miss O'Brien, not me."

He walked away, leaving Gabe to read between the lines of his vague remarks. And what he read there didn't make him feel any better. In fact, it made everything worse. It seemed to confirm his own worst fears.

"Annie...are you ready?" he asked as he stepped inside the curtained cubicle.

She nodded.

"I'll get a wheelchair," the nurse said.

"It won't be necessary," Gabe answered, and scooped Annie gently from the bed.

Moments later, they were gone.

He watched her sleep.

With her still groggy from the painkillers and the shock of the accident, it had been all he could do to get her inside and in bed before she succumbed to exhaustion. The moment her head hit the pillow, she rolled over on her side, curling up like a child in prayer, with her hands clasped beneath her chin. She never knew when he left the room.

He hadn't gone far, and he wasn't gone long. As soon as he was satisfied that all was as it should be within Annie's domain, he went back to her room. And there he remained, slumped down in another chair too small for his large frame, staring at each separate feature on her face, trying to understand what made her so special to him.

Dissecting her face with his eyes, feature by feature, was a revealing experience for Gabe. He saw past the externals to the woman beyond, and he finally realized that what he loved most about Annie was what was invisible to the human eye. It was a combination of her spirit and her unswerving trust in the face of what should have been insurmountable odds.

He groaned quietly and buried his face in his hands. She was so loving, and too giving, and he couldn't help but wish their lives had been different. He wanted to stay here forever. To go to sleep each night holding her in his arms and wake up each morning by putting a smile on Annie's face. But it wasn't going to happen, and the sooner he faced it, the better—for himself as well as Annie. Giving her false hope was the cruelest thing he could have done, and despite whatever reasons he'd given himself for coming back, it had already happened.

Without thinking of the consequences, he crawled into the bed beside her, then slid one arm beneath her head and the other around her waist. It didn't take much. Just a scoot and a shift before he had her right where he wanted her. Right where he needed her. He closed his eyes, unaware of the painful smile that cut across his features as she relaxed against him.

My Annie.

It was his last conscious thought before weariness claimed him, too, and they slept. But only Annie dreamed.

Fateful dreams and flights of fancy had no place in Gabriel Donner's life. He was here on sufferance only, his days marked by a ticking clock and the number of times that he tried to right a wrong. It was what he did, who he was, but this time it wasn't going to be enough.

Chapter 9

"Juh...Juh-ack and Juh-aisle..."

"That's a short *I* Davie. Try again."

"Juh-ill..."

"Right! Good job! Now continue."

"Juh-ack and Juh-ill wuh...wuh." Davie grimaced in frustration, as he continued. "...Wuh-int up the huh-ill to...Jack and Jill went up the hill!"

The expression on Davie's face was priceless. The sudden understanding of what he'd been trying to read colored his expression with joy. She smiled. That look was the single reason she'd chosen teaching as a profession.

"Oh God, Annie. I read that whole sentence, didn't I?"

Annie nodded. She patted his arm, then pointed to the next line. "You sure did, Davie. But now's no time to stop. What comes next?"

Eagerly he leaned forward, his forefinger still positioned below the last word he'd read so as not to lose his place, and began sounding out the syllables.

Annie's thoughts wandered as she absently listened. It had been a week since their lessons had begun. And in that week, so much had occurred in her life.

Gabe was back and, except for the time she spent with Davie, never far from her side. The stitches had come out of her foot. And Davie Henry was making progress, actual visible progress in learning to read. She should have been the happiest woman on the face of the earth. But she wasn't. Day by day, she became more anxious, more certain that, for her, time was running out.

Each night she was loved to sleep so deeply and so thoroughly that she often found herself pretending that this way of life was going to go on forever. But when morning came and she had to face herself in the mirror, she couldn't lie... not even to herself. It wasn't forever. And it was all because of the secret she was keeping from Gabe. The secret that was eating her alive.

The ragged grumble of the Harley's engine broke her wayward concentration. Annie blinked, looked at the clock on the wall and then over at Davie, who was quickly closing the book he'd been reading from.

"I'd better be going," he muttered, still embarrassed for anyone other than Annie to know about his problem.

"Take this with you," she said, shoving the book toward him. "Practice reading aloud. Sound out the letters the way I showed you, and we'll do the next page tomorrow."

Davie nodded, glancing nervously toward the back door as Gabe's footsteps sounded on the porch.

"He won't interfere," Annie said, and she squeezed Davie's arm reassuringly, remembering the understanding with which Gabe had received the news of Davie's handicap. "So what," he'd remarked. "I was older than him before I learned. It's the learning that counts...not when it happens."

Annie sighed, wishing she could share that bit of Gabe's

conversation with Davie. She suspected it would go a long way toward making him feel better about himself.

The two men passed each other with nods and furtive smiles. Gabe imagined Davie didn't approve of him and his relationship with Annie, and Davie imagined that Gabe could see into his soul and read his shortcomings in a single glance.

Gabe stopped just inside the doorway, his gaze sweeping across Annie's face as the screen door banged behind Davie Henry's exit.

Her familiar smile was in place. Everything about her seemed so open and aboveboard. But instinct told him that she was hiding something. Something she was afraid to tell him about.

"I'll be right back," Annie said, and gently touched Gabe's shoulder before following Davie to his truck.

Just as she left the kitchen, the phone rang in the front part of the house. She paused in the doorway, indecision catching her in mid-stride.

"I'll get it," Gabe offered. "Go tell Davie whatever it is he needs to know."

She nodded, waved her thanks and hurried out the door, anxious to give Davie some more last-minute instructions regarding his lessons.

Gabe picked up the receiver on the third ring.

"Hello…O'Brien residence." Then he frowned. The man's voice on the other end was unfamiliar, the tone of his question far too serious for Gabe's peace of mind as he answered, "Yes, she's here, but she's outside. Could she call you right back?"

A slow sigh slid through the line and into his ear. For some unknown reason Gabe shivered. And then the man spoke again.

"So…she's actually there…as, in residence?"

Gabe frowned. "Yes, of course," he answered. "If you'll wait—"

"I can't right now," the man answered. "I'm due in surgery." And then, as if he felt compelled to continue, he said, "My name is Dr. Peter Barnes. Miss O'Brien is… was…my patient. She's missed her last two scheduled appointments, and I was extremely concerned about her welfare. In fact, I was actually relieved to know that she missed them because she moved, not because…well…"

Gabe inhaled slowly. His belly muscles clenched as he closed his eyes and said a small, silent prayer. Something told him that if he handled this right, he would get the answers he'd been wanting, and no one would be the wiser.

"That's too bad," Gabe said. "I wish I'd known about her appointments. I would have made sure she'd called and let you know about the move. We made it together, in fact." He let the doctor digest the information he'd planted before he continued. "So…how did you find out where she was?"

He thought he could hear Dr. Barnes shuffling papers. "I had a request for the transfer of her medical records come across my desk today. I took a chance and called Walnut Shade for a number. After I realized that a doctor there…a Dr. Pope…had already treated her, it only made sense that she had to live nearby."

"Right, that was late last week," Gabe said. "When she had one of her fainting spells and cut her foot. I took her to the emergency room myself."

Gabe imagined that he could actually hear Dr. Barnes absorbing this news. "So…you know something of her condition, then?" he asked.

Gabe bit his lip. What he was about to say wasn't a lie. He did know something. He just didn't know why or how it mattered.

"Yes, I do," Gabe said. "And it's a constant worry to me. I care very deeply for Annie. I could be wrong…but it seems to me that her episodes are more frequent and more intense than when we first met.''

Dr. Barnes sighed heavily into the phone. And as he did, Gabe absorbed the sound with a sick shudder.

"That's to be expected. Does she still have plenty of medication?" Dr. Barnes asked.

My God...to be expected? What the hell did the man mean?

"Yes," Gabe assured him. "We make sure she's never out of those. I don't think she could survive without them."

"Unfortunately, as you know, the time will come when that point is moot. I'm really sorry about that. I liked Miss O'Brien immensely."

Liked? Why the hell did he say it in the past tense?

Gabe blinked in shock and turned his attention back to the doctor's comments as soon as he realized that the other man was still talking.

"It's a damned shame that something like this had to happen to someone like her...someone in the prime of her life, with so much to offer," Dr. Barnes continued.

Gabe grunted. But it wasn't in agreement, it was from pain. Had Dr. Barnes been able to see the look on Gabe's face, he would have realized that what he'd unwittingly revealed had provided the worst kind of shock.

"Please tell her that I wish her well, and if she has any questions regarding her condition, she should feel free to call me and talk anytime. Even though she's asked for Dr. Pope to be her doctor of record in the last phases of her illness, I can't help wishing she hadn't moved. There's going to come a time when even the strongest medications won't help. After that, as I'm sure you know...it's only a matter of time."

Gabe went weak. *Last phases of her illness.* He felt himself sliding down the wall with the receiver still held against his ear. *Only a matter a time.*

He knew he must have been saying all the right things, because he vaguely remembered hearing Dr. Barnes telling him to call if he needed advice, then hanging up. But the memory of what he'd said was gone. All he could hear was the echo of Dr. Barnes's statement.... *"It's only a matter of time...only a matter of time."*

"Oh, damn...oh, Annie. Not *my* Annie."

But there was no one around to refute the horror of what he'd learned. Only an overwhelming sickness that kept threatening to engulf him.

The edge of the chair rubbed the back of his legs, just at the bend of his knees. Luckily for Gabe, it stopped his fall. He found himself sitting in it rather than sliding all the way to the floor, and was oddly thankful for its unexpected presence. It was a less-compromising position in which to be as Annie walked back into the house, calling his name.

"Gabe, where did you...?"

Whatever she'd been about to ask was lost as she walked into the room and saw him sitting in the chair with the telephone receiver lying on his lap.

His long, jeans-clad legs were stretched out in front of him, as if bracing him against sliding out of the chair. As usual, he'd rolled up the sleeves of his long-sleeved gray shirt and had only buttoned it halfway, revealing more of the taut muscles across his chest and belly than would have been considered polite out in public.

Annie smiled. She knew Gabe. It was obvious to anyone who cared to look that Gabriel Donner cared little for society's demands. And because she knew him so well, she saw past the obvious to the shock on his face and felt an unnamed fear.

"What is it? Is something wrong?"

Gabe couldn't answer. All he could do was look at her and remember the doctor's words. *It's only a matter of time. It's only a matter of...*

He loved that dress she was wearing. The skirt was softly flared and moved with her body as she walked. The sleeveless bodice showed off her narrow waist and slender, tanned arms to perfection. The narrow red-and-white stripes that ran throughout the fabric reminded him of peppermint sticks, one of the few Christmas presents that he'd ever received as a child back in the Territory. Her hair was loose and full around her face, and bounced when she walked like the coils of a spring. Her eyes were sparkling with joy, full of...*life?*

"When the hell were you going to tell me?"

The question was harsh, the words guttural, torn from deep inside in short, jerky clumps.

Annie took a step backward in defense against the unexpected anger of his attack.

"What are you talking about?" she asked. "I already told you why Davie comes to the house...and why you have to leave. I thought you understood."

Gabe tried to smile. But the smile was lost as he was forced to grit his teeth to keep from shouting at her. Rage and an ungovernable sense of injustice swept over him.

He picked up the phone and held it out to her in a taunting gesture. "You missed your call," he said harshly.

Annie felt sick. She didn't know what had happened, but whatever it was, she knew it had made Gabriel as angry as she'd ever seen a man.

"Did they leave a number?" she asked.

Gabe laughed harshly, but the joke was on himself.

"No. You already have the number." He stood up jerkily. "In fact, you have everybody's number, as well as all the answers...don't you? The only problem is, you just weren't of a mind to share."

She was afraid. What terrible thing had happened that had changed Gabe from the tender lover of last night to the cold, angry man standing before her now?

"What are you talking about?" Annie asked. "And stop shouting at me, damn it! You're scaring me."

Her chin trembled, but she held her ground. And as her words hit home, she watched Gabe's defenses crumble.

"Well, excuse the hell out of me, darlin'," he whispered sarcastically, and wiped a shaky hand across his eyes, as if trying to remove the traces of what he'd learned from his mind. It was no use. He knew that the horror of the last few minutes would stay with him forever.

"Who called?" Annie asked.

His hands trembled, and he shook his head, as if in denial of her question. His arms dropped limply to his sides as he stared at her.

Annie watched his eyes turn cold, boring into her until she couldn't look away. Finally he answered.

"It was your doctor."

She turned pale. "Dr. Pope?"

"No, Annie. Dr. Barnes. Dr. Peter Barnes from Oklahoma City. You missed your last two appointments."

Her lips moved, but no sound came out. Understanding began to invade her mind. In sudden terror she started to shake.

"When were you going to tell him that you'd moved, Annie? Or were you planning to give him a dose of the same medicine you've been giving me and just wait? Were you going to let us find out the hard way? Were you going to wait until you died in my arms and he read it in a paper somewhere?"

"Oh...my...God."

Her worst fears had been realized. He knew! The room began to spin around her.

Gabe grabbed her by the shoulders, pulling her toward him, pressing her intimately against him in fierce denial of what he'd learned.

"Annie." Her name was torn from his lips. "Please! Tell me it isn't so!"

Gabe winced as she buried her face in her hands. He knew then that every harsh word, every cruel accusation he'd uttered, was true. He heard her struggling to breathe past the overwhelming shock and realized that he'd gone too far.

"Dear God, sweetheart, I'm sorry. I didn't mean to say it...not like this. But have mercy, Annie...." His lips moved across her cheeks as he shoved her hands away from her face and made her look at him. "Were you ever going to tell me?"

"No."

He groaned. The pain of her admission nearly doubled him over.

"Why?" he begged as his thumbs traced the tracks of her tears.

Her voice shook as her hands wrapped around the edges of his vest, holding on to the only stable thing in her world. Holding on to Gabe.

"I only wanted your love, Gabriel. Not your pity. If I'd told you...I couldn't have had the one without the other. It was my choice to make. I made it. You don't have to approve...but you have to understand." And then her voice broke as she clutched at him. "Tell me you understand."

Blind to everything but the pain in her voice and the touch of her hands, Gabe wrapped his arms around her shoulders and held her.

"I can't believe Dr. Barnes told you," Annie whispered, as Gabe's hands stroked across the width of her back in a gentling motion. "He shouldn't have. He wasn't supposed to tell."

He drew back. The guilt on his face was impossible to miss.

"He didn't actually come right out and say it. Mostly I

tricked him into believing I already knew what was wrong.
What he said was too simple to miss. What he didn't say
was impossible to ignore.''

"Damn you," she said, and struggled to pull away from
his touch. "I needed to do this by myself."

Gabe shook. "Why, Annie? Why cheat the people who
care for you most?"

She shrugged and looked away.

"Because…ultimately, Gabe, no one can help me do this.
It's a trip I'll have to make alone."

His eyes closed in sudden shame. The truth of her statement was too close for comfort. And then the need to know
more—to know everything about this woman—drove him
on.

"Exactly what is wrong with you?" Gabe asked.

"What did the doctor say?" she countered.

"That it was only a matter of time."

The words hung heavily between them. Annie struggled
through the anger and injustice of the moment to find the
right way to say what was in her heart. Finally she decided
there was no easy way to say what had to be said and just
started talking.

"There is something growing inside my head that doesn't
belong there. A tumor. Ultimately, it will kill me."

Gabe groaned softly and threaded his hands through the
thick tangles of her hair, feeling the silky strands bounce
against his fingers and wondering, as he did, how something
this beautiful could hide something so unwanted and ugly.

Annie closed her eyes, relishing the touch of Gabe's
hands as she continued, letting everything spill out in a rush
before she lost her nerve.

"It will only get worse, and, in time, one of the episodes
will be my last."

At the moment the words were uttered, Gabe saw her wilt.
It was then that he knew what strength of character, what

strength of will, it had taken her to hide the fears she'd been living with.

He had a sudden flashback to the Sunday morning weeks ago when they'd gone to church. He remembered how quiet and uptight she'd been on the way. And then how she'd focused on the pastor's every word, and the intense way she'd had of listening to every nuance of his voice. He remembered the books that he'd seen and the way she'd reacted to his discovery of them. The way she hid her pain and denied the reasons for its existence. Suddenly it all became clear.

Annie was afraid to die! He knew it as surely as he knew his own name. And in that moment, he also knew why God had sent him back to her. If there was anyone on earth who could show Annie O'Brien how to die, it would be him. After all, he'd been where no living man had gone before and returned to tell the tale. He alone knew the beauty and the peace of what awaited Annie.

He slid his arms around her waist and held her close as she tried to regain her composure.

"It'll be all right, darlin'," he whispered. "I promise. It'll be all right."

"I didn't want to tell you, because I didn't want you to feel sorry for me. If you couldn't stay with me when I was well, then you shouldn't stay with me just because I am…just because I will…"

"I came back, didn't I?"

She grew quiet, then finally nodded.

"I came back before I knew the truth, too, didn't I, lady?"

She nodded again.

"Then you can't tell me…you can't accuse me…of staying out of pity. I came back because I had to, Annie. I came back because leaving you behind became impossible to bear."

Annie began to sob.

"Life isn't fair," she said, and felt his arms as they enfolded her.

Gabe closed his eyes and buried his lips in the crown of her hair. Together they stood, rocking back and forth within each other's embrace, and knew the full measure of truth in Annie's words.

Life was anything but fair. But it *was* for the living. And if it was the last thing he did, he would make damn sure that Annie O'Brien's last days on earth were full and perfect.

"Gabe, this is crazy."

Annie's hissed complaint was coupled with a soft giggle as she bumped into his backside when he stopped unexpectedly on the path in front of her.

"Slow down, woman," he teased, and then peered carefully through the inky darkness of the trees before them, searching for the path that had been highlighted only moments earlier by moonlight. "That damn cloud came out of nowhere," he muttered, wishing again that he'd thought to bring a flashlight.

But when they'd left the security of Annie's house for their nighttime excursion to the hilltop behind her home, there hadn't been a cloud in the sky. Only the bright, beaming face of a three-quarter moon shining down to light the way.

Annie smiled to herself and hooked her fingers over the waistband of his jeans. "Whither thou goest and all that stuff," she said.

At that moment the cloud slid away, and the moonlight illuminated Annie's face. She seemed rejuvenated by the short respite.

"Finally," Gabe muttered, and started back up the path through the trees, hurrying now that the light had returned, anxious to get where they were going before it disappeared altogether.

The safe thing to do would have been to return to the house, retrieve the flashlight he'd left behind and venture back through the trees with light in hand. But safe wasn't necessarily the wisest move. Not anymore. A man—or a woman, as the case might be—could waste precious hours practicing safety. When there were no hours left to waste, safety could go begging.

Annie's pulse quickened with excitement as well as apprehension. She could see only as far as Gabriel's ramrod-straight back. She had to squint to see the slim, muscled curve of his buttocks, as well as the long, lean legs she knew were there. He was too big, and it was too dark to see more. But it was her opinion that there were a lot of worse things than having to look at his backside.

She hooked her fingers a little tighter in the belt loop on the back of his jeans and let him lead her up the slow, sloping Missouri hillside toward the bald knob, framed by a ring of trees that shone silver in the moonlight.

"We're here."

This time, when he stopped, she was ready. She unhooked her fingers and then turned, looking for the first time down the hillside toward the shallow valley where night shadows hid everything but the highest treetops from view.

She turned in place until she'd made a complete three-hundred-and-sixty-degree turn. And when she had, she found herself looking up into his face. From the shadowed expression he was wearing, Annie realized that he was anxiously awaiting her verdict. It wasn't long in coming.

"Oh! Oh, Gabe! It's so beautiful!"

His smile was a slice of silver in the moonlight as he grinned at her delight.

"Then it was worth the climb?"

She threw her arms around his neck. "It was worth everything,'' she said. ''I've lived here all my life, and I never—absolutely never—knew that this place was so beautiful in the dark.''

Gabe slid his arms around her shoulders and pulled her close to him, letting himself revel in the way she melted against him with no reservations.

''I just wanted you to know you don't have to be afraid, Annie. The dark isn't something to fear. It's just another way of looking at the world in which we live.''

She sighed and smiled through her tears, unwilling for him to know how moved she was by his constant need to lessen her fears of her final destination.

''You don't fool me,'' she said as she watched him move away from her and begin spreading a quilt that he'd brought with them on the ground. ''You just can't wait to get me naked.''

Surprise came swiftly, followed by a desire so fierce that he nearly choked on the sound of his own laughter. He took a deep breath and hoped that she hadn't noticed. If he hadn't known himself better, he might have thought it sounded like a sob.

But Gabe didn't cry. He hadn't cried in so long that he'd completely forgotten what it even felt like. He vaguely remembered that, as a child, he'd cried once for a beating he hadn't deserved. But that was long ago in the Kansas Territory. Long before he'd taken that wrong road and gotten himself into the mess that had started this whole cycle of regret. Long, long ago, before Annie.

The quilt was a pattern of smoky shadows—pale, fuzzy blues, foggy whites and misty yellows—densely bordered with darker shadows of reds and browns that looked black in the moonlight. It made a perfect bed upon which to lie.

Annie stepped out of her slippers and then walked into the center of the patchwork pattern, doing a quick little two-step of delight from the joy of it all. She turned and clapped her hands, smiling and laughing at Gabe as she did, and caught a look of regret and sadness on his face before he had time to hide it.

"Don't," she begged, and held out her hand. "Not tonight. You've shown me something so special...so very, very wonderful. Don't let things get in the way."

He grinned, ignoring the blinding pain in his chest as she smiled up at him, and pulled off his boots, joining her on the quilt before he had time to think.

Her nightgown was soft and sheer, and the fabric felt slick against his fingers as he pulled it up and then over her head. She lifted her arms to help him. At the moment the gown fell away, it left her arms upraised toward the beckoning moon in a gesture of supplication.

Gabe caught his breath and stared down at her slender beauty. She sighed and dropped to her knees. Seconds later Gabe shed what was left of his clothes and went to meet her.

"Annie, I..."

Her fingertips moved across his face and caught the words before he'd finished.

"No vows or promises. Just love me."

Gabe groaned as he moved across her body, pinning her to the quilt with gentle finesse.

Love her?

That was the easy part.

Telling her that he loved her?

Knowing what he did about his own fate...that was improbable.

Letting go when it was time?

Impossible to face.

A swift and sudden wind gusted across the hillside, fanning the edges of the quilt and Annie's hair. It tugged haphazardly at the curls around her face, blowing them gently across Gabe's lips and hands, flirting like a wayward lover as it made impossible tangles in the silky length of them.

Gabe buried his face in their heavy depths, savoring the lingering aroma of lilac-scented shampoo, and knew that for the rest of his life, no matter how far he rode, whenever he saw lilacs he would remember Annie...and the hillside... and their love.

Annie laughed aloud into the night from the simple joy of being one with this man. Of knowing that with nothing more than a nudge from her body or the touch of her hands, he would come undone. That she could bring him to an aching hardness with only a look, or make him lose complete control with nothing more than a whispered word.

She arched her body up to meet the forceful demand of his mouth, clasping his head against her breast as she stared up and over his shoulder to the inky depths of the starlit sky above them.

Gabe had given her something truly wonderful by showing her this night. It was up to her to give something special back.

She was fire and rain, sweeping across his senses in a maelstrom of emotions too fierce to contain. Consuming him by degrees, she burned for him far into the night. Then, raining kisses upon his weary body, she washed away the might-have-beens that hovered in the nighttime, beyond the quilted square upon which they lay.

Sometime during the early morning hours, when the dew was gathering on the grass and soaking persistently into the patchwork of their quilted dreams, they gathered themselves and their belongings, and made their way along the path that led down the hillside.

And when they quietly entered the small frame house that had patiently waited for the lovers' return, they knew that the night had been magic. It had been with them like a friend, filling their memories with only the best of what had been, sifting out the fear of what was to come.

Chapter 10

"Gabriel, come look."

Poised in the act of tightening a nut on the bike, Gabe wiped a bead of sweat from his forehead and turned to see what Annie was up to now. The last time he'd noticed, she'd been cleaning fallen leaves from the chrysanthemum bed that lined the front porch. Now she was nowhere to be seen.

"Annie? Where are you?" He dropped the crescent wrench he'd been using and straightened up to look around.

"Up here. In the tree."

Gabe walked to the porch, then tilted his head back until he was staring up into the wide, overhanging branches of the old oak that shaded the front of the house, peering intently through the thick growth in search of Annie.

She was perched about halfway up the tree, sitting in the fork of a branch while her feet dangled downward in thin air. All he could see was a bright splash of yellow that he knew to be her shirt and shorts, and an expanse of bare arms and legs.

"You'll fall," he said, and instinctively reached up as if to catch her.

"No, I won't." Laughter was rich in her voice. "As a child, I used to spend hours upon hours up here. I never once fell."

"That was then, this is now," Gabe reminded her. "Come down...please?"

She smiled. Bracing her arms against the limb that was her seat, she leaned down and blew him a kiss.

His heartbeat jerked, a painful reminder that the world was never going to be the same without Annie's smiles, and that he was never going to be the same without her kisses.

"Okay, I'm willing to concede you're part monkey." He shrugged and put his hands on his hips in pretend defiance. "If you didn't intend to mind me, lady, then what the hell did you want?"

Annie grinned. His anger was all bluff. And he knew that she knew it.

"I hadn't realized until I got up here that the leaves are turning. I wanted you to see."

Annie reached out and picked a leaf from just over her head, then let it drop slowly downward, drifting through the gaps in the limbs until it came to rest at Gabe's feet.

He bent down and picked it up. It was still soft and supple to the touch, but she was right. The colors were changing. A faint hint of wine red and burnt orange highlighted the places between the leaf's fragile veins.

Gabe's anger came unexpectedly. Time was running out. The season was changing and taking Annie with it. He looked away, suddenly in need of something else on which to focus, and tried to ignore the fact that he was looking at the world through a blur of tears.

"Fall is great...but winter is my favorite time of year," Annie said, and then leaned back and stared up through the

branches to the bits and pieces of clear blue sky overhead.
"I like the snow…and I love Christmas."

Gabe stared down at the leaf in his hand and then slowly
crushed it in his fist.

A low string of curses filtered up through the branches,
to the spot where Annie was sitting. Shocked by his unexpected reaction, it took several moments for understanding
to come. And when it did, she, too, felt an overwhelming
sadness.

Unwittingly she'd just reminded them both that these
were the last leaves of fall she would see. That she might
never see this year's first snow or enjoy another Christmas.

"Gabe!"

It was no use. He was already gone. She looked down
through the branches in time to see him walking away toward the creek below the house.

Annie leaned back and looked up, taking a last look
around at the world from above, and then scrambled down
through the branches. The lowest limb was her last firm
handhold. To get down from there, she had to let herself
dangle, then drop to the ground, trusting that it wasn't too
far.

The bark of the branch was rough against her palms as
she scissored her legs to find the perfect landing. From
where she was hanging she was enveloped by leaves, a thick
umbrella above her, another multicolored barrier between
her and the ground below. Yet Annie knew firm ground
awaited. All she had to do was trust her judgment and then
turn loose. She held her breath, closed her eyes and let go
of the limb.

Small clumps of leaves brushed against her underarms
and the sides of her face as she slipped through the opening
and dropped to the ground, landing safely upright just as
she'd known she would.

Dusting her hands on the seat of her shorts, she started

to run after Gabe when something stopped her. She turned in mid-stride and stared back at the heavily laden branches of the old oak tree that she'd just vacated.

"Oh!" Her gasp was soft as understanding came quickly.

She'd known before she climbed the tree that there was a way down. And when it had come time to vacate her perch, she'd known that all she had to do was trust in the obvious.

"All I had to do was believe that the ground was there," Annie whispered.

Her eyes grew round and her mouth went slack with surprise as she stared intently at the tree. There was nothing else to consider, because she had just been given the answer to something she'd been trying to come to terms with for months.

She'd faced everything about her illness except how she would behave when it ended. All along she had been—and still was—dealing with the pain. Another bridge that she'd already crossed was the knowledge that she would be leaving things and people behind that she'd come to love.

But the one thing—the single most important thing—that she hadn't understood was what she had to do. What was her part in leaving going to be?

She'd made herself sick worrying about the way it would happen. Where would she be? Would it hurt? Would she even know it was coming? The unknowns had been driving her mad.

"That's it!" Annie said as a slow sigh of relief flooded her system. "I don't have to know when or where. All I have to do is trust. A firm foundation has already been laid. All I have to do is let go, just like I did when I climbed out of the tree. I won't fall. Someone will be there to catch me."

And with that thought came the knowledge that it wouldn't be Gabe. He was part of what had to be left behind.

Tears shifted across her vision, but she blinked them back with rough determination. She had no time for tears. There was too much left to do to waste time crying over things that couldn't be changed. She remembered where she'd been going, turned toward the creek and began to run. He needed to know that she was going to be all right.

Somewhere between the tree and the creek, Gabe had started undressing. A grease rag lay on the ground where he'd dropped it. His vest was hanging from a low branch, dangling from the armhole where he'd looped it. She saw his shirt hanging across a bush in a haphazard fashion where he'd obviously tossed it.

And then she saw him, bare to the waist, with water droplets running from his seal-black hair down the middle of his back and onto his jeans. His head was thrown back in a gesture of defiance, his legs braced for an invisible blow only he saw coming. He stood without moving, staring blindly down into the gentle flow of water while the world went on without him.

Annie felt his pain as if it were her own. The love she held for him went deep and was without reservation. Everything about him was at once familiar to her and, at the same time, unique, right down to the stillness that was so much a part of him. The strength of his body, as well as his character, that she'd come to rely on more each day. She knew him so well…and yet he was very much a stranger.

She accepted the secrets that were a part of him, because she understood his need. The unabashed way in which they made love was what kept her going from day to day. For Annie there was nothing else left in this world that mattered to her except this man.

And yet, in spite of his constant denials, she knew that staying with her was killing him. She saw his pain. She felt his regrets. She, after all, was the one doing all the taking.

She took what he offered, knowing that she had nothing left to give back. And he never complained.

Unobserved, she continued to watch, but when he drew back his arm, she saw for the first time the thick, clublike stick he held in his hand. Uncertain what to expect, she was not prepared for the rage that exploded within him.

Anger came up and out of him in a roar, a painful denial of Annie's fate that went out with the stick he threw into the air. It crossed the creek with deathlike force and exploded against the side of a tree trunk. Helpless to deal with his fury, he let it tear through him. With the release of his rage came an ebbing of adrenaline that sent him to his knees.

"Gabe...don't!"

In seconds Annie was at his side, wrapping her arms around his neck, absorbing the shudders that ripped through him while he held her in desperation.

"I don't know how to let you go."

His heartbroken words wounded her and, at the same time, consoled her. At that moment, the depth of his love for her was unmistakable.

"You don't have to, Gabe. I finally understand what you've been trying to show me. I know that I don't have to worry about anything. When it happens, I'll know what to do."

"No, no," he begged, and pulled her roughly across his lap. "Surely there's another way. Another doctor. Someone else with a..."

Annie closed her eyes against the pain of his words, realizing, as she did, that she was also closing herself off from everything that could have been. It didn't bear thinking about. The decision had already been made.

"Stop it, Gabe. Please don't make this any harder than it already is."

Her quiet plea was all he needed to get his maverick

emotions in check. And the only way he knew to change the subject was to pick another one she couldn't ignore. It was all he could do to laugh through the pain, but for Annie's sake he made the effort.

He jiggled her lightly on his lap and nuzzled her neck. "So...you don't want this any harder?" he asked.

Annie flushed, knowing full well what he was referring to.

"What I *want*, at this minute, is beside the point." She gave him her best teacher look for good measure.

A wry smile changed the expression on his face from one of despair to one of beauty.

Annie caught her breath, and then, before she thought, she clasped his face in her hands. "You are so beautiful," she whispered as their lips met, then danced back and forth in little nips and tastes, savoring each other as passion built.

Gabe nearly blushed. "Oh, hell, Annie, men aren't beautiful."

"Tell that to your mother, then," Annie said, and sighed with regret as the smile slid off his face. "What? What did I say?"

He looked away in shame, remembering his life before. Old fears and bad memories came calling. And then he thought of Annie and knew that whatever she saw in him, she saw through the eyes of love.

"I never knew my mother," Gabe said. "Or my father...or any single person who I might be related to."

Shocked by the unexpected revelation, all she could ask was, "Who raised you?"

Gabe shrugged. "Mostly I raised myself. There was an old trapper...and a few others. It was a long time ago... lifetimes ago, darlin'. You wouldn't understand."

Annie leaned forward and pressed her mouth against the faint pucker of scar tissue ringing his neck. She felt his shock beneath her lips. Blood raced and muscles jerked as

his throat worked and he tried to speak past the surge of
emotion her touch had aroused.

"I would understand anything about you, Gabriel. Even
how you came by this." Her fingers traced the edge of the
scar. "When you love someone, anything is possible."

Everything faded except the sound of Annie's voice and
the wide, green stare of her eyes. He was stunned by her
admission.

She watched anxiously for his reaction. It was the first
time that either had said aloud the thing that was in their
hearts. Emotion filled him.

"So...you think you love me?"

Shyness accompanied the joy in his voice as he looked
into Annie's face.

She laughed softly. "I don't think. I know. And why
shouldn't I?"

He took her fingers and laid them against the scar at his
throat. "Because you just shouldn't. Because I don't deserve
it," he said quietly.

Annie shook her head in denial. "What you were doesn't
count, Gabe. You could have been an outlaw for all I care.
What matters is that right now...for as long as it takes...
you're my outlaw."

He laughed wryly and rolled her beneath him before she
had time to think.

Outlaw. Oh, Annie, if you only knew.

"I'm going to make love to you, Annie Laurie."

She looked up, startled by his announcement.

"Right here? In broad daylight?"

He grinned. "Sure, lady. That's what outlaws do."

Nearly a week had passed since the incident at the creek.
And in that time Gabe had almost been able to convince
himself that Annie was getting better. It had been weeks
since she'd had any pain. Her days were spent in doing

whatever she wanted. All she had to do was think it and he would put the thought in motion.

He went to bed each night with her in his arms, and then lay awake watching her sleep, trying not to think of a world without her in it. Everything revolved around Annie's wants and wishes. Everything else had been put on hold. To him, she was all that mattered.

Her days were full of immediate plans. And each day a certain portion was set aside for Davie and his lessons. Watching his progress and knowing that she was partly responsible was a large part of what kept her going. Because of Davie's need, she had something to look forward to…a purpose in life. It seemed as if, while Davie still needed her, Annie refused to give up and give in to the thing growing inside her head.

"Gabe! You're still here!"

Annie's shock was evident as she stared at the part he'd removed from the Harley and the oil dripping from his fingers. A nervous glance toward the clock on the wall told her that Davie would arrive almost any minute for his reading lesson.

He waved the length of tubing as he walked past her toward the kitchen sink. "Fuel line's clogged. I'm not going anywhere today."

"But…Davie will be here any minute. What's he going to think when…?"

"I think Davie's a big boy," Gabe said shortly. "He'll survive."

Annie resisted the urge to stomp her foot. It wouldn't do any good, and she knew it. When Gabe got that look on his face, there was no changing him. Obviously the fact that his bike was on the fritz had put him in a disgruntled mood.

"Oh, Lord," Annie muttered, as Davie pulled up and parked beneath her climbing tree.

She peeked out the window. Even from here she could see the frown on his face as he neared the front door clutching his small stack of books. There was only one thing to do, and that was to pretend nothing was different.

"Hi!" she said as she went to meet him. "Come in. I'm on my way to the kitchen. I was just taking brownies out of the oven."

"Why is he still here?" Davie muttered, glaring over his shoulder at the black Harley still parked at the edge of the yard.

"He's working on his bike," Annie said. "He won't bother us."

Davie stopped short and stood in the doorway. "Maybe I should come back tomorrow," he said, and started to make a U-turn.

"Hey, Davie, how's things?"

Gabe's simple question stopped him from leaving and left the trio standing at the door, staring mutely at one another while Gabe waited for his answer.

Davie shrugged and tried to grin. "'Bout the same, I guess," he said. "Can't complain."

"Well, I sure can," Gabe said, holding up the piece of tubing. "I thought this thing was clogged. Now I find it's got a pinhole in it somewhere. The darned bike sucks air instead of fuel."

Davie frowned. "You know...I just might have something in the toolbox behind the cab. Come on outside and we'll look. Might save you a trip into Walnut Shade."

Gabe nodded and walked past Annie, giving her a slow wink that Davie missed.

Annie watched them go through the doorway, their heads together like two little boys with one frog, and smiled to herself at the mental image.

One was blond, broad and brawny, the other tall, dark

and deceptively deadly. And yet, somehow, she knew that in another time, another place, they could have been friends.

"Sorry," Gabe said as he watched Davie digging through the odd assortment of bits and pieces in his toolbox.

"What for?" Davie mumbled as he shoved a greasy glove and a half-used box of shotgun shells aside. "I know I've got some tubing somewhere. I'm just not sure if it's the right size."

"I'm sorry you're going to miss your lesson because of me."

Davie grew still. A deep red flush stained his face and neck as he backed away from the toolbox. "Damn it, she promised," he said, glaring at the ground as shame overwhelmed him.

"She didn't actually tell me anything," Gabe said. "I just recognized the signs. I've been there myself."

Davie looked up. Shock spread across his face as his gaze swept up and then down the big biker.

"You? You didn't know how to...I mean you couldn't...?"

"Oh, hell. Come out and say it. I couldn't read. I never even went to school until I was full-grown. You're not so damned special after all, are you?" Gabe grinned wryly to lessen the sting of his words.

Davie sighed. "Thanks to Annie, I'm getting real good at it," he offered.

Gabe clapped his hand roughly on Davie's shoulder and grinned. "I know. Congratulations."

Davie grinned back. "When I can read the want ads in a newspaper, I'm going to ask my girlfriend to marry me."

The smile died on Gabe's face. A sudden and intense surge of jealousy filled him as he considered the simplicity of Davie Henry's life.

Davie had a problem. His problem was that he couldn't

read. All he had to do was learn how and his problem was over.

Annie had a problem, too. And it wasn't going to be cured by learning anything. In fact, the more they learned, the worse her situation became.

Gabe cursed softly and spun away, unwilling for Davie to see his pain and anger.

"That's good. Really good. I'm happy for you. A man needs to have a place to call home and a woman to come home to," Gabe said quietly.

"So, what's between you and Annie, then?" Davie asked, then resisted the urge to take a quick step backward. The look Gabe gave him as he turned was anything but friendly.
"And I'm not going to apologize for asking," Davie said. Instinctively he curled his fingers into fists and waited for the blow that never came.

Gabe's anger dissipated when he saw how fiercely Davie would have defended Annie. And he knew Davie's reasons for asking were fair ones. After all, he'd known Annie all her life.

"There's a lot between Annie and me," Gabe said. "But that's where it's going to stay...between us." He fixed Davie with a cool blue stare. "I can't help it if you don't like that answer, but it's the only one I've got to give."

Davie shrugged. "None of my business, really," he said. "If Annie's happy, I'm happy."

"That just about sums it up for me, too," Gabe said. "Now...about that tubing."

Minutes later Davie dashed back inside the house, using the scent of brownies to lead him to Annie.

"Where's Gabe?" She looked past Davie toward the open doorway.

"I loaned him my truck to go to town. The tubing I had didn't fit."

"Oh."

Davie grinned and pointed toward the brownies cooling on a rack. "Do I get any of those?" he asked.

"What happened between you two?" Annie asked, ignoring his question in favor of another.

"Not much," Davie said, and helped himself to two brownies without waiting for her approval. "When you get to know him, I guess he's a pretty decent guy. Right?"

Annie nodded and sat in the nearest chair with a plop, unable to mask her surprise. Would wonders never cease?

Thunder rippled through the hills and down the valleys, running with the storm front that was moving across the state. Lightning cracked as it tore across the skies, rocking the lamp on the bedside table and rattling the glass in the windowpanes.

Gabe rolled over and, at the same time, reached out for Annie. The flat of his hand slid across her pillow and then down the length of the bed.

Seconds later he was crawling out of bed in panic. She was gone! He stepped into his jeans as he walked out of the bedroom, calling Annie's name.

The wind whipped her nightgown, molding it to her slenderness like a second skin. Annie tilted her face, catching the first raindrops as they began to fall upon the thirsty earth. She closed her eyes and inhaled slowly, letting her skin savor the moisture in separate, single increments. It was as if every cell in her body had come alive, dancing with the same electrical force as the lightning that threaded the skies.

The thunder, an angry grumble of nature, rumbled overhead. Annie's toes curled against the rough-hewn boards of the porch as she felt the house quaking from its power.

Like a daring child, she stood at the edge, just beyond the safety of the rooftop, and let the storm have its way with her. In those few moments, before the full onslaught of the rain, she felt joyously alive...and knew no fear.

And then she heard his voice and turned toward the sound, waiting on the edge of the steps for him to come to her. To become part of the immensity of what she was experiencing.

"Annie! Annie! Answer me, damn it! Where are you?"

"I'm here," she said softly, knowing that he would hear her voice and follow it with unerring instinct.

He walked outside, intent on nothing more than rescue, when a bolt of lightning slashed through the darkness just beyond the trees and momentarily illuminated her in a glow of eerie light.

It was then that he saw her face and knew that she was locked under the spell of the elements in which she stood.

"What the hell are you doing to yourself?" Gabe growled as he grabbed her by the forearms and hauled her back beneath the safety of the porch.

His hands ran rapidly up and down her body, touching, testing, to assure himself that she was still in one, albeit fragile, piece. That she was not as storm-tossed as she looked.

"Feeling the storm," she whispered. "Oh, Gabriel… come feel the storm with me!"

He couldn't tell her no.

She took him by the hand and led him to the edge of the porch, where the wind whipped wildly beneath the overhang, digging through the thick, damp tangles of her hair. She turned to him, needing to know that he understood. That he felt what she was experiencing in the same special way. The look on his face made her knees go weak.

The wind caught and lifted the dark, heavy length of his hair, whipping it back and forth across his face and into his eyes in stinging fury, and yet he stood unmoving, watching Annie's joy. Rain began to come down in earnest, pelting against the broad, muscled strength of his chest and belly, only to slide downward in rivulets toward the spiral of hair that began just below his navel, visible in the V of his un-zipped jeans.

Annie's eyes narrowed, and she took a step forward, fascinated by the path of the rain and its destination. She splayed her hand across his chest and watched, eyes widening with desire, as the wind-driven water hammered against her own skin, too. She closed her eyes and breathed deeply, imagining that she was melting into him, becoming part of him, always with him.

"Annie."

Her name was a prayer as she came to him, unto him. And when her rain-slicked body moved against him, he knew he was lost.

"Come inside," he urged, and started to move her toward the doorway.

"No," she whispered, and pressed her mouth against the curve of his lips, letting him feel, as well as hear, her words. "You come inside. Inside me."

Denial was impossible.

With little loss of motion, he let the wind tear away what was left of her gown as he pulled it up above her waist. Shaky with desire, he groaned as she laughed aloud, lost in the driving need and the rain pelting down upon them. And when she wrapped her arms around his neck and her legs around his waist, the pleasure and the passion nearly sent him to his knees.

Staggering backward in desperation, now buried so deeply inside the woman in his arms that he feared he might lose the way back, he felt the porch post behind him and knew a moment of thanksgiving that they wouldn't fall.

With legs braced, he centered her once again on the hard, jutting thrust of his body, and relished the cry of delight that flew out of her mouth and into the night. With a shaky groan he took them both over the edge and into the storm, and never knew which ended first, the rain or their pleasure.

All he remembered was struggling for breath and feeling a cool wind drying the last raindrops from his bare back. The rest was a blur. Just a collage of lightning, power, the touch of Annie's hands, her laughter and the rain upon her face. It was only later that he thought to wonder if it had been tears, and not the rain, that he'd seen running down her cheeks.

But it didn't matter, and it wouldn't have changed a thing. Sometime during the night, he'd taken Annie on a ride to heaven and back. Much later, as he set her in bed, he watched her curl up in weary satisfaction against his passion-spent body. Annie seemed to be at peace with herself and the world. It was Gabe who now struggled to find the sense in it all.

Annie's life mattered so much to so many, and yet it was about to end. His had been of no consequence in the beginning, and now, no matter how long he rode and how hard he tried, he feared he would never know the peace of heart that Annie possessed.

Chapter 11

"Annie! Annie! You'll never guess."

Annie looked up from the book she'd been reading and smiled at the man who burst through the front door.

"Don't you ever knock?" she asked, and grinned at the shock that came and went on Davie's face as Gabe's arm slid off her shoulder and back into his own lap.

"Oh...yeah...right," Davie mumbled, suddenly embarrassed by his behavior. "How ya doin', Gabe?" It was such an obvious afterthought that Gabe laughed, catching Davie off guard.

It was the sight of those black boots propped up on the coffee table alongside Annie's sock-covered feet that told him he might have walked in on a serious hugging-and-kissing session.

"Am I interrupting anything?" he asked, knowing full well he probably was.

Gabe stood up and stretched. "Just the possibility of a nap. It's too cold outside for anything else."

Davie nodded, and then remembered why he'd come.

"Annie! I've got great news!"

"You won the lottery."

"Nope!" Davie grinned and shoved his hand through his hair, ruffling the thick wheat-colored curls even more than they already were. "Guess again."

"You're getting married."

Davie blushed as Gabe laughed softly from across the room.

"Well, yeah, actually I am, but that's not it, either," he said.

"Okay, I give up," Annie said, and spread her hands in defeat. "What's the big secret?"

"The head of the history department at Walnut Shade High School just quit. There's going to be an opening next semester. What do you think about that?"

The smile froze on her face.

Gabe's stomach turned as he looked at Annie.

Twice she started to speak, and both times the words wouldn't come.

"Son of a bitch," Gabe said succinctly, and walked out of the room, unable to watch Annie's pain.

Davie was in shock. "What? What did I say?" he asked, and touched her anxiously on the shoulder.

Annie shrugged and tried to smile, blinking over and over in rapid succession to clear her vision of a sudden spurt of tears. "Nothing," she said, and hugged him to prove her point. "Absolutely nothing at all."

"Then why's everyone so uptight?" he persisted. "Something made Gabe madder than hell, and I'm the only new face in the room."

"It's complicated," she said. "But it's nothing you did, I promise."

Davie shoved his hands in his pockets and shrugged.

"Okay, okay. I get the message. I'll drop whatever it was I said...if I can figure out what it is I'm supposed to drop."

A small niggle of pain dug into the muscles at the back of Annie's neck. She rolled her head and winced, trying to loosen the tension before it became full-blown.

"Davie...about the job." Annie struggled to find the right words. "Thanks, but I don't think I'd be interested." The smile on her face broke. Unable to contain her misery, she turned and walked out of the room.

"Well, I'll be damned," Davie said.

But there was no one around to hear him, and rather than risk another outburst, he left the same way he'd come in. Unannounced.

He was halfway up the path when he saw Gabe walking toward the creek behind the house. In seconds he'd made the decision to follow him and find out what was going on. He would get answers out of that damned biker or know the reason why.

Gabe hurt from the inside out. Every step he took was a step away from Annie's pain, but it didn't lessen the impact of what he'd seen in her eyes. He would have bet his life—if he'd had one left to bet—that she wanted that job, and badly.

He knew how important teaching was to her. He'd witnessed her determination in the classroom back in Oklahoma. He'd seen her willingness to risk personal safety just to fulfill a contract, as well as her duty to the students. He'd also seen the life go out of her when they'd had to leave Oklahoma City. At the time, he hadn't understood.

The real inner joy, the thing that kept Annie motivated, had returned only after she'd discovered Davie's handicap. It was after that that she seemed to have taken a new lease on life. Looking back, the reasons for it were so simple, so obvious. Annie was at heart a teacher. She needed to be needed.

Even with the knowledge that Davie would be her last student, she'd still dealt with the disappointment of giving up a much-loved career. Day by day, she'd struggled with the fact that she had to let go, a little bit at a time. And she'd done it.

But that was before Davie Henry had come barreling through the door offering something she desperately wanted, something she couldn't have. A future.

Heavy footsteps pounded the trail behind Gabe. He turned, his fists doubling instinctively, then relaxed almost as quickly.

It was only Davie. But when he saw the concern on the big man's face, he cursed softly to himself, sickened by the entire mess. He should have known Davie would want answers. In his place, he would have done the same.

"Donner! I want to talk to you!" Davie shouted.

Gabe waited for him to catch up.

"What's the damned deal with Annie? She hardly ever leaves the house, and when she does, you're always with her. You have no job, and she expects me to understand, without any explanation, that she isn't interested in teaching. *Why?*"

"What did she tell you?" Gabe asked, ignoring all of Davie's accusations except those concerning Annie.

Davie spat angrily, then ground the moisture into the dirt with the toe of his work boot.

"She didn't tell me a thing. She just started crying."

"Damn. I was afraid of that." Gabe looked away, unwilling for Davie to see his pain.

Davie grabbed him by the arm and spun him around. A long, slow minute passed while the men took each other's measure.

Finally it was Davie who made the first move by loosening his hold on Gabe's arm. "All I want to know is, what the hell's going on," he muttered.

"I can't tell you more than Annie wants people to know," Gabe said. "And that's all I'll tell you. If you find out more, it'll have to come from her."

"What are you saying? What's the big secret?" Davie shouted.

"It's not my secret to tell," Gabe said softly. "You above all others should understand that. After all, you asked Annie to keep your secret, and she did. Why do you expect me to do less for her?"

But Davie still persisted. "What could be so bad that she doesn't want it told?" he asked.

Gabe didn't answer. He couldn't. All he could do was turn away and try to focus on something—anything—besides the pain eating away inside him.

"Okay," Davie said shortly. "But if I find out later that you've had anything to do with Annie's problems...anything at all...I swear I'll fight you to hell and back."

Gabe turned. All sound unexpectedly ceased. The mockingbird that had been scolding from a tree limb took sudden flight. The squirrels that had been playing above the creek bank, jumping from limb to limb like furry acrobats, disappeared from sight.

Sunlight haloed behind Gabe, making his shadow larger than life. Davie shuddered. He had a moment's impression that Gabe was not of this world, and then he scoffed at his own flight of fancy as Gabe's deep voice echoed within the silence on the creek bank.

"There's no coming back from hell. Pick another location."

Davie's eyebrows arched, and then he laughed abruptly. His anger was gone as quickly as it had come.

"Damn, but you're a cool one," he said.

Gabe shrugged. "I am what I am. Just know this. What I do, I do for Annie's best interests...always." He took a step forward until he was nearly toe-to-toe with Davie. "For as long as I'm with her, she's safe. I'll kill the next man who harms her. Know *that* for a fact."

Thou Shalt Not Kill!

The celestial warning sifted through his mind, but Gabriel shrugged it off as he continued to stare long and hard into Davie Henry's eyes.

"The next? What happened to the first?" Shock splintered the concern on Davie's face.

"The cops got him," Gabe said shortly, aware that what he'd revealed was something about her life in Oklahoma City that Annie had obviously kept to herself.

"Cops?"

"Just remember what I said," Gabe warned, ignoring Davie's wild-eyed, slack-jawed expression. "No one messes with Annie. She's been hurt more than any woman should have to endure. If you want to know anything more about her business, you'll have to ask her yourself."

Gabe turned and walked away, disappearing into the thicket of trees above the small spring-fed creek, leaving Davie Henry alone with the warning still echoing in his ears.

For two days Annie moped around the house, no longer able to find joy in the little things as she previously had. All she could think about was Davie's news and the fact that she couldn't even consider the job. Anger and self-pity for what fate had dealt her crept back into her daily routine and held on with insidious persistence.

Gabe found himself being rebuffed for even offering to do the smallest things for her, and he was at a loss as to how to fix what ailed Annie. But then an advertisement in a local paper gave him an idea. He began to set his plan in motion, remembering that spontaneity had worked before. Why not now?

When she was busy at other tasks, he began packing a bag for what would amount to an overnight stay. Little by little, he secreted her belongings, along with his own, in the duffel bag.

Just after dark, while she was taking a bath, he buckled it onto the back of the bike and then hurried inside. He yanked off his boots and jeans and crawled quickly into bed, excited about the prospect of what he planned. He took slow, deep breaths to calm his racing pulse, anxious that when Annie came back, she would not suspect he'd ever been gone.

A few minutes later she came out of the bathroom, her nightgown billowing around her legs as she walked. With only a dim light in the hallway to serve as illumination, she sat down on the edge of the bed to brush her hair.

At first glance she looked unbearably young and innocent, all white lace and long, rambunctious curls. And then she turned slightly as she struggled with the length of her hair, trying unsuccessfully to brush out the knots. The incoming light silhouetted her sensuous shape against the sheer fabric of her gown and left Gabe in no doubt as to how much of a woman Annie really was. It made him want. It made him hard.

She lifted the hairbrush again and began to brush another swath through her hair when she came to a tangle and winced. The motion of her arms unintentionally pushed her breasts tightly against the thin, cotton fabric. Gabe's swiftly indrawn breath was the only clue to his instant desire.

Unashamed of his nudity or the obvious ache in his manhood, he rolled over onto his knees and took the brush from her hands, scooting her gently until she was braced against his body.

Annie sighed and let her head loll back against his bare

chest with relief. Everything she did nowadays seemed to take too much effort to bother.

"Let me," he begged, and began to pull the brush through her tangles in slow, firm strokes.

"Be my guest," she said shortly, and then blinked quickly to stifle the film of moisture that distorted her vision.

She was being rude and she knew it, but it was beyond her to accept his gentleness without bursting into weak tears. She hated herself for feeling it, let alone thinking it. She didn't want to be weak.

Damn it! I want to be well!

"Your hair is so beautiful," Gabe whispered softly, feathering kisses along the curve of her ear as he pulled the brush through her hair, letting it rake lightly against her scalp in a sensuous motion. "It's one of the first things I noticed about you."

Annie shivered. She remembered the first thing she'd noticed about him. His size...and his mouth. How a smile had changed his appearance from menacing to marvelous simply by turning it up at the corners.

"There's something I want to tell you," Gabe said.

He dropped the brush onto the table and slid his hands around her shoulders toward the front, cupping his palms to fit the thrust of her breasts beneath the gown.

For days he'd been living with the knowledge that, for whatever it was worth, he was in love with Annie O'Brien. And yet telling her without making her think it was said out of pity was impossible. He'd struggled with the how of it for so long that he ached.

"Don't talk to me, touch me," she begged and leaned a little farther back, allowing him easier access. Within an instant of his touch, she became lost in the sensuality of Gabriel's hands.

Gabe shuddered as his body answered the call by thrusting uncontrollably against the softness of her backside. He closed his eyes and swallowed harshly, imagining her cupped tightly behind him on the back of his Harley without this ache being eased. It was impossible. He had to make love to Annie before they rode or he would land them both in a ditch.

They would ride. Of that he was certain. But that would be later. After he'd healed both their respective aches and pains.

And then he forgot what he'd wanted to say. He forgot about everything except his need to lay claim. Gently his hands feathered across her body in seeking strokes, in much the same way as he'd brushed her hair only moments before.

"Annie, Annie...so much woman..."

"...And so little time."

He paused in mid-stroke, stunned by the finality of how she'd ended his sentence for him.

"Damn you," he groaned, and rolled her beneath him. "Damn you for making us both remember."

A sheen of tears puddled across her eyes. Even in the faint half light, he saw her lips trembling around a smile.

"Then make me forget," she whispered, and slid her arms around his neck.

"I don't want to forget," he said harshly, as he yanked her gown up and off her body. "I don't want to forget a thing about you...ever."

Annie's sob was lost as he lowered his lips to hers. Tears blended with passion as he swept across her body, moving like a marauder through the night, taking what he needed from her to survive, leaving behind a trail of pleasure for which Annie burned.

She took what he gave and tried not to wish for more. And while she could hide it from Gabe, she could not hide it from herself. Just once...even if he didn't actually mean it...she would have given a precious minute of what was left of her life just to hear him say he loved her.

Gabe left his trail across her body. A path of mind-drugging kisses that left her shaking and breathless and yearning for more. His hands coaxed and caressed her to the point of explosion and then gentled her back into a waiting game.

And as he rebuilt the fire within Annie, his own body ached, pulsating to the point of explosion as her tiny cries of pleasure echoed in his ears. When it was nearly too late to make the move, he lifted himself up and then thrust. Falling too deep to pull back, he came apart in her arms.

Ripple after ripple of pleasure exploded within him. Gabe shook from the exertion of his release. Unaware of Annie's arms around his neck, unaware of her legs around his waist, he buried his face against the curve of her neck and knew that the tears upon his cheeks were not his own.

"You're mine...mine. You're my love," he muttered over and over as shudders racked his body, forgetting, in his weakened state, that he'd meant to keep that secret to himself.

Her heart stopped as his soft, urgent whisper nearly missed its target.

Oh, Gabriel, Annie thought, as she clutched him to her in desperation. *If only you meant it. If only I'd met you sooner...before it was too late. I might have had the nerve to take the chance.*

But Gabe was unaware of her thoughts. He was too lost in the feeling of having died and been reborn in Annie's arms.

They slept. An hour before dawn, Gabe woke with a start, knowing that it was now time to implement his plan. He rolled out of bed and quietly began to dress. Soon he was ready.

A small, indistinct sound filtered through Annie's mind. Sleepily, she rolled over and then sat upright, staring directly at the shadow of the man who was standing in the doorway across the room.

Just when she thought about screaming, she realized that it was Gabe. And as she did, she knew that the sound that had awakened her was the slight jingle his spurs made when he walked.

Spurs! That meant he was dressed!

"Gabe? What on earth are you doing?"

"Kidnapping the school marm."

She imagined she saw his smile, although it was really too dark for her to have done so. But it was there in the sound of his voice just the same, and it reassured her as nothing else could have done.

"It's still dark outside," she said, and then began backing up against the headboard of the bed as she saw him coming toward her.

"The better to steal you away, teacher dear."

This time she was certain he was smiling. She heard a distinct chuckle as her back connected with the headboard.

"Nowhere left to run, girl. You're mine. All mine."

With a practiced growl, he swooped, lifting her from the bed in a tangle of bed sheets and laughter.

She struggled weakly, laughing too hard to put up much of a fight. But truth be known, she was too intrigued by what was happening to argue.

"Go do your thing, woman," he grumbled in a gentle but teasing voice. "You've only got minutes to spare before I come in after you."

Annie headed toward the bathroom to "do her thing," as he'd suggested. She had a sudden suspicion that it would be hours before he let her off that darned black Harley.

She stared at herself in the mirror over the sink, realizing as she did that the woman who looked back was laughing and full of anxious anticipation. Her eyes sparkled; her hair was a wild, sleep-tossed tangle. Her lips were still slightly swollen from last night's passion. She should have looked like hell. But Annie knew she'd never looked better.

"You've got two minutes, and then I'm coming in after you," he warned.

Annie squealed in mock fright and began running water and yanking on clothes with wild abandon.

On the other side of the door Gabe grinned sadly to himself. God willing, this trip would be perfect. It had to be. It might very well be their last. At the thought, he went to double-check, just to make certain that he'd packed that damned brown bottle of pills.

It was a heady thing to ride in the dark, with the throttle on the Harley wide open and the sound of the engine roaring in your ears. Annie imagined that it was like flying blind, trusting that instinct would keep you on the right path and luck would get you to your destination.

She inhaled deeply, reveling in the freedom of the moment and pretending that if they went fast enough, she could outrun the inevitable. For Annie, sitting behind Gabe on the back of the Harley was her past, present and future. Wherever he went, she was ready for the experience.

Sunrise was waiting for an audience. Through his mirrored sunglasses, he saw the faint rosy hue and the change in the texture of the air just above the horizon. Without announcing the fact, he wheeled off the highway onto a small lookout point above the autumn hues undulating throughout the thickly wooded valley below. He nudged Annie with his shoulder to get her attention.

Thankful for the opportunity to divest herself of the ungainly helmet, she pulled it up and off, unaware of what she was about to witness. At Gabe's insistence, she turned in the direction he was pointing and stared.

It came over the treetops in a burst of color, moving up and out in a spasm of rebirth. A soft, pure white and thick, creamy gold, with a faint crimson lining to remind the onlooker that pain as well as joy came with new life. The day had begun.

"Oh!"

Her gasp of delight was all he needed to hear.

"So beautiful," Annie sighed, and rested her forehead against the bulge of muscle on Gabe's arm, unaware of the tension beneath her cheek or the tight grip he still had on the bike.

Just like you, my love, Gabe thought.

She smiled up at him, then saw that he was still wearing the glasses, still hiding his feelings behind those mirrored walls.

Oh, Gabe. You never let me in. And then her thoughts became lost as she watched his face.

His lips tilted into a gentle smile. Something told her that he was feeling more than he was saying. It had to do with the muscle jerking along the cut of his jaw and the way the skin seemed to tighten across his cheekbones.

But you care. You can't make me believe you don't care, Annie thought.

"Seen enough?" Gabe asked roughly.

It was for damn sure he had. Feeling Annie's soft body pressed firmly against the back of his for mile after mile had done nothing to ease his aching libido. Seeing the beauty that sunrise had put on her face made everything worse...and at the same time made everything better. This trip was meant to take her out of herself and her worries. From the way she was smiling, he'd done it in spades.

"The prelude was spectacular. What's next?" she asked, still willing to play along with the game.

"Breakfast in Branson," he said, and handed her the helmet.

"Branson? I haven't been to Branson in years. Especially not since it's become the 'New Nashville.'"

Nearly every country and western singer of any merit, plus half the entertainers who had once played solely in Las Vegas, played Branson, Missouri, now.

Elaborate music halls had sprouted up nearly overnight and dotted the small, cramped hillsides surrounding the tiny town to the point that tourists drove bumper to bumper on a quest to see their favorite stars.

"Me either," Gabe said. "Besides breakfast, there's something I want you to see."

"What?" she asked, her stomach suddenly growling at the mention of food.

Gabe grinned. "Food first. Surprises later. Now, quit asking so many questions. You're supposed to be my prisoner, remember?"

She smiled beneath the smoke-tinted visor of the helmet and wrapped her arms around his waist as the Harley's powerful engine made the bike leap forward beneath them.

Chapter 12

Gabe sat in the small café with his back to the wall, nursing a cup of coffee. He watched with satisfaction as Annie cleaned the last of her biscuits and gravy from the plate and then looked around the table to see if there was anything left that she might want to eat.

It was the most food he'd seen her eat in a week. Their outing had put color in her cheeks and a growl in her belly, but there was no way he could stop the destruction that was happening inside her head.

She looked up from her plate with a smile on her face. But it was impossible to look at her and not see the shadows beneath her eyes or the deepening hollows in her cheeks. Annie's health was failing, and there wasn't a damn thing he could do to stop it.

"You're frowning at me," Annie accused, and nodded when the waitress sailed by with a fresh pot of coffee and stopped to top off her cup.

"No, baby, only at how much you ate," Gabe teased. "You ate the last biscuit."

She laughed. "Some kidnapper," she chided. "You let me have it."

He leaned close until his lips were only a whisper away from her face before he answered. "I'll let you have it all right, darlin', but not now...and not here."

A woman in the next booth choked on her food. At the same time, Gabe and Annie turned to look. They saw the guilty expression on her face and knew that she'd been eavesdropping. Gabe's sexy innuendo had left her gasping for air.

Annie leaned over and whispered conspiratorially to the curious woman, "He's real good at it, too."

Gabe grinned as he hauled Annie out of the chair. "That does it. You're coming with me, lady. Remember...you're my hostage for a day. Now let's go before you get me into something I can't fight my way out of."

Annie's eyes sparkled. Gabe was a wonderful kidnapper.

"I can hardly wait until later," she whispered as he dug in his pocket to pay for their meal.

His eyes widened and a grin slid across his face. He could tell by the look in her eyes that she wasn't through playing with him.

"What happens later?" he asked, and knew the moment he'd asked that he'd fallen right into her trap.

"That's when I pay my ransom. What did you have in mind? A little bondage, or just some—"

Her feet barely touched the floor as Gabe yanked her out the door.

"Lord, lady. You're gonna get me arrested yet," Gabe swore, then looked around nervously to see who else might be listening to their byplay.

Annie shrugged. "Can't help it. That's what usually happens to the bad guys."

A strange expression crossed Gabe's face. "Not always. Sometimes they just string 'em up and ask questions later.

Here, put this on," he ordered, and stuffed the helmet in her hands without waiting for her to respond.

Annie tucked in the strands of her hair and did as she was told. But she couldn't help wondering what she'd said that had put that guarded look on Gabe's face.

"Gabe...?"

"What?"

"If my teasing embarrassed you, I'm sorry. I was just..."

He lifted the visor of her helmet and leaned inside.

Lips met. His hard and demanding. Hers soft and ready to please.

Gabe groaned as he reluctantly released her from the kiss.

"Gee, Miss Annie, for a schoolmarm, you're a real good kisser."

She blushed.

Gabe laughed and then added, "And you ought to know that you can't embarrass an outlaw, darlin'. Now mount up. We're ready to ride."

The grin was back on his face. She sighed with relief. Whatever she'd unwittingly said had been forgiven.

As he guided the Harley out into traffic, Annie slid her arms around his waist, searching until she found her familiar handhold. Locking her thumbs into the two front belt loops of Gabe's jeans, she leaned forward, bracing herself against his back, ready for whatever was to come.

An hour or so later she heard him gearing down and looked around in surprise. As they pulled off the highway and into a huge parking lot, she craned her neck, trying to see where they were going. All she could see was row after row of cars.

"What on earth?" And then she saw the sign up ahead and started to smile. "Oh, Gabe!" She squeezed him in delight. "It's Silver Dollar City."

Gabe heard the excitement in her voice and knew he'd chosen wisely. But Annie would be surprised to know the real reason he'd chosen to visit the old-time, frontier-style theme park.

Annie waited impatiently while he buckled down and locked up everything they weren't taking inside.

"I haven't been here in years," she said.

He stuffed his sunglasses in his front pocket, then used his fingers for a comb, roughly shoving the black, shaggy length of his hair away from his face in haphazard fashion.

"Me either. I came once, a long time ago, when it first opened. It made me homesick," Gabe said quietly.

And then he slid his hand along her neck, tugging gently at the silky thicket of hair hanging down her back. "It's only fair that a man show all he can about his past to the woman he loves."

Annie's eyes grew round. Her lips parted, but no words would come. Her heart pounded, and she clasped her hands together to keep from throwing herself into his arms.

"Don't look at me like that," Gabe growled, and pulled her into his arms, anyway, ignoring the constant influx of tourists pulling into the theme park.

"Oh, Gabe," she whispered, moved beyond belief that he'd admitted his feelings to her.

"I know, darlin'," he said softly, and bent down. "It takes my breath away, too."

When their lips met, she was smiling. When he came up for air, Gabe was smiling back.

"Don't get me wrong," Annie said, as they walked toward the entrance gate. "I love being here. But how can bringing me to Silver Dollar City have anything to do with your childhood? This kind of life-style disappeared over a hundred years ago."

"By all rights, I should have, too." He gave her an odd sort of grin, one that held more regret than humor. "Don't ask me to explain, honey. Just know that I'm more comfortable with the way of life in there than what's out here."

Annie nodded, accepting him on his word alone, as she'd done since the moment they'd met. It was a fact that, by all rights, their meeting each other, much less becoming lovers, should never have happened.

She sighed and leaned her head against his shoulder as they walked through the entrance gates to the theme park nestled deep in the verdant hills of southern Missouri. She didn't care that they came from two different worlds. She didn't even care that he was an enigma she couldn't explain. Gabriel Donner loved her. It was all that mattered.

And so they walked the narrow streets of the town, marveling at the reclamation and resurrection of an older and slower way of life, and pretended, as did everyone else who ventured inside, that they were in another world.

Their footsteps echoed on the wooden sidewalks as they crunched candy apples and savored the hand-pulled saltwater taffy only hours old. And all through the day, as Annie saw the old mountain town through Gabe's eyes, she realized that she was also seeing another man emerge.

Gone was the cynical tough who'd climbed off a Harley and into the middle of a gang of hoodlums without giving it a second thought. Gone, also, was the daredevil who'd run into a burning building and rescued a child without thought for his own life. She tried to picture this Gabe walking into the middle of a robbery with fists doubled and couldn't quite make it fit. The Gabe who dared life to take him down seemed to have disappeared. In his place was this young-hearted, easy-spoken man from another era.

More than once, Annie found herself turning around to tell him something, only to realize he was no longer walking beside her. And when she checked to see where he had gone, invariably she would find him standing somewhere behind her, lost in thought as he stared wistfully at the old-time displays in the store windows, not even aware that Annie had gone on without him.

The wood-carver's shop fascinated him. Deep in a discussion with a clerk over the price of a figurine, Annie heard laughter and turned to see Gabe kneeling on the floor in the wood curls and sawdust. With two small towheaded boys for an audience, he was showing them how a hand-carved wooden man could dance on the flat of his hand. Annie grinned in delight. At that moment it was difficult to tell the adult from the children.

Soon afterward, as they walked outside in the cool autumn air, she saw Gabe stop and listen. An eager, almost boyish expression crossed his face, and before she knew it, he was dragging her down the street, through the crowds, all the while coming nearer and nearer to the sound that had caught his attention.

It was the village blacksmith, bare to the waist, covered with an old-fashioned leather apron, hammering a piece of iron he held fast upon an anvil.

"Would you look at that forge!" Gabe said, and whistled softly through his teeth.

Before she knew it, Gabe had ducked under the roped-off area, taking the blacksmith by surprise as he was about to demonstrate an old-style method of foundry work, pouring hot pig iron into a mold that had been buried in the earth.

Within minutes Gabe had talked the blacksmith into letting him try his hand. A crowd gathered, and they, along with Annie, watched in fascination as Gabe shed his shirt, donned the leather apron to protect him, and picked up a hammer and tongs. The onlookers watched as Gabe eagerly pulled a piece of hot iron from the fire.

Annie held her breath, unable to believe what she was seeing. Gabe hammered with skill, placing firm, steady blows on the iron, constantly bending and shaping, reheating and then hammering some more. He never seemed to tire or lose his concentration. And before her eyes, a perfect horseshoe began to take shape.

Heat from the fire seared the tan of Gabe's skin, and sweat began to run across his forehead and down onto his belly as the blacksmith obligingly pumped the bellows to keep the fire in the forge at optimum heat. But Gabe was oblivious to everything but his task.

The blacksmith's bushy beard parted in a pleased smile of surprise as he watched Gabe work. "That's quite a feat," the man told Annie. "It took me years to learn to do that. What's he do for a living, anyway? And don't tell me he's a stockbroker or it'll break my heart."

Annie laughed at the blacksmith's joke and made light of the fact that, when Gabe wasn't rescuing people, she didn't know what he did with his life. Along with the onlookers, she was stunned by Gabe's obvious and unexpected abilities.

What *does* Gabe do for a living? she wondered.

To Annie, he was something between the love of her life and a guardian angel. He often seemed to be a man with a past he kept trying to outrun. She frowned as she watched him finishing his work. What she knew about Gabriel Donner could have been written on one page with space left over.

Suddenly Gabe plunged the horseshoe into a bucket of water. The hot iron hissed as it was engulfed, sending a small cloud of steam into the air. Then he yanked the shoe out and held it up for approval while the water dripped from the tongs and ran down his elbow.

"Good job!" the blacksmith cheered. "Mister, if you ever want to change occupations, just let me know. You could work here any day. That's the best piece of iron work I've seen in a month of Sundays."

Gabe grinned as he relinquished the hammer and apron the blacksmith had loaned him. "It's been a while." And then he laughed aloud. "Ah, hell, who am I kidding? It was a whole other lifetime. But it was fun."

Suddenly he remembered Annie, and a spurt of guilt surfaced. "Sorry, honey. I sort of got carried away. What do you want to do next?" he asked as he dried himself off and then dressed.

For a moment Annie didn't answer. She was too busy fixing his expression firmly in her memory. She didn't ever want to forget how he'd looked filled with excitement and laughter.

"I want to have our picture taken," she said, remembering a studio they'd passed earlier that had period costumes for the customers to wear while being photographed. "I want to remember this day for always."

He grinned and hoped that his smile was steady. Because when she'd said "for always," he'd had a sudden urge to grab her and run and never stop. Maybe if they ran far enough and fast enough, they could outrun Annie's fate.

"Okay," he said, and let her lead him back the way they'd come. "But I get to pick what you wear. I distinctly remember seeing a red satin dress in the window. The one with black feathers around the neck and hem. I think I once knew a Sue from Santa Fe who had a dress just like it."

"Oh, you," Annie said, and punched him lightly on the arm, unaware that, for once, Gabe was telling her the truth, the whole truth and nothing but the truth.

Annie pulled at the neckline, trying to tug it up to a more respectable position. It wasn't going to happen. She blew at the feathers tickling her neck and chin, and rolled her eyes. Gabe hadn't been kidding about picking out her dress. It *was* red satin and as flagrantly gaudy as it could possibly have been.

She made a face at herself in the full-length mirror and then grinned, imagining what her old principal back home would have said upon seeing her dressed like this. School-teacher material she was not. If she knew Gabe, he was probably going to love it.

"I'm ready," she called.

"So am I, little lady," Gabe said quietly as he walked up behind her.

Annie looked up. The smile on her face froze in place. "Oh, my."

It was all she could manage to say. The outfit she'd picked for him to wear had been chosen in jest. She'd had no idea that he would come out of the dressing room looking as if he'd walked out of one of the daguerreotypes hanging on the studio walls.

Devils danced in his eyes, making them seem brighter and bluer than before. Suddenly his much-needed haircut was no longer an issue. The slightly longer style now fit him to perfection.

His black frock coat bounced against the backs of his thighs, and his matching black pants made his legs seem even longer as he pranced around the studio, testing his appearance in first one mirror and then the next. The white ruffled shirt was a crisp and vivid contrast to the all-black suit, and the red string tie beneath his chin was just right for the riverboat gambler that he'd become.

Annie's eyes widened, and her lips parted on a slow sigh as she watched him jam a black flat-brimmed hat on his head and then buckle on a double holster. She grinned at her sudden urge to fan herself before she went into a fit of the vapors.

"Here you go," the photographer said as he led Gabe toward an array of fake firepower. "Pick your weapon. How about these fancy pearl-handled revolvers? Everyone seems to favor those."

Gabe shook his head and reached for two plain, long-barreled pistols instead. The only thing remarkable about their appearance was the shiny, blue-black sheen to the metal.

"I'll take these," Gabe said, flipping back his coat-tails and sliding the guns into place with little wasted motion.

Annie shuddered as she watched him handling the pistols. They fit too easily in his hands and slid too slickly from the holsters as he fanned them in and out to test his draw. Somewhere between the dressing room and now, she'd lost the Gabe she knew.

She glanced back at herself in the mirror, trying to get in the mood of the moment as deeply as Gabe had done. But it was no use. She was out of place in this silver dollar town, while Gabe looked as if he'd been born here.

"Now...about the pose," the photographer muttered to himself as he began moving Gabe and Annie around like mannequins. "Sir, how about you sitting down in this wing-back chair pretending to hold the cards you've been dealt, with the little lady leaning over your shoulder, as if she's peeking at your hand?"

Annie looked at Gabe and shrugged, suddenly out of her element. A few minutes ago it had seemed like so much fun. Now she felt a certain uneasiness.

Gabe sensed Annie's dilemma and thought he knew the reason why. He was too at home in this place. Instead of playing the curious and interested tourist, he'd become a part of the place. The last thing he'd meant to do was make her afraid.

He turned to Annie and held out his hand. She came to him without a word.

"Just take the picture. We'll do the rest," Gabe said.

The photographer shrugged. It was all the same money to him. He fiddled with his cameras and lighting, but finally he was set.

"Are you ready?" he finally asked.

"Do it," Gabe said.

Annie held her breath as his arm slid around her shoulder, then squeezed her gently. Without thinking, she looked up and found herself reading his lips.

"I love you, lady," he whispered.

Lights flashed. The moment was caught forever on film. It seemed as if a dark, devil-may-care rake was about to kiss the woman he loved. Only by tilting the photo a certain way could you see the tears that had been running down her face.

Annie sat in the middle of the motel bed, looking over the array of mementos from their outing. Unable to resist it, she'd bought the small wooden dancing man from the wood-carver's shop. She fiddled with its floppy, jointed legs, trying to make it dance as Gabe had done, and then let it fall onto the bed with a plop. It obviously took a skill she was lacking.

Next to it was the rag doll that Gabe had insisted they buy. She'd resisted playfully until he'd pointed out that the doll had green eyes just like hers. The doll had gone into the bag with the little wooden man.

But it was the picture of them together in costume that she kept coming back to time and again. She picked it up and stared long and hard, unaware, as she looked, of the despair etched upon her face.

Gabe came out of the bathroom, still slightly damp from his shower, to find her sitting among the day's treasures. She should have been tired and happy, but all he could see was defeat.

"Annie, are you all right?"

Gabe's deep voice was husky, suddenly anxious that today had been more than she should have endured.

She looked up, unaware that she was smiling through tears. "Better than all right. Today was perfect, absolutely perfect."

Gabe sighed with relief and made a place for himself on

the bed beside her, moving their prizes to a safer place on the bedside table.

"You're probably exhausted," he said, eyeing the clock on the table. It was nearly midnight. "Did you really have a good time today?"

She nodded. "It was practically perfect."

He grinned. "Only practically?"

"Well—" the drawl in her voice should have alerted him "—for a kidnapper, you sure lose sight of what you're doing."

His eyebrows arched, and a sexy grin slid across his lips. "Just what am I doing wrong, teacher?"

"Forgetting to demand a ransom, that's what."

"Oh, no, lady, I haven't forgotten a thing. I'm just still trying to decide what it'll take to get me to let you go."

"Oh, Gabe," Annie whispered, and threw her arms around his neck. "Don't do it! Don't ever let me go."

His hands cupped Annie's shoulders as he held her tight within his grasp. "I won't ever leave you, Annie," he whispered as he pulled her into his arms. "Wherever you go, I'm right behind you. Don't you ever forget it. Not for a moment."

The picture slid onto the floor as Gabe pinned her beneath him on the bed. Then there was nothing between them but the truth as Gabe stripped them of their clothes and made slow, perfect love to her until the sun came up.

And when morning came, they packed their bags in silence, climbed back on the Harley and headed back to reality. For a short while Gabe had done the impossible. He'd stopped time and given Annie one perfect day to remember.

Annie dug through the package that had arrived by post only minutes ago. Inside were the special books that she'd ordered to supplement Davie's reading material. She sorted them by subject matter, leaving the ones she knew he would view as work, putting the ones that she knew he would enjoy on top.

A nagging pressure at the base of her skull kept reminding her that time waited for no man...or woman.

If only Davie continues with his studies after I'm gone.

She slammed the stack of books on the table and then winced at the noise. Day by day, the knowledge that she was growing weaker was impossible to ignore. Each morning it seemed to Annie that it took more effort to get up than it had the day before. Often she caught Gabe watching her, as if he were gauging her strength and measuring her weakness, and, in a strange way, she hated him for doing it. She lacked even the privacy to die in peace.

A book slid out of her fingers and onto the floor. With a muttered oath, she bent over to pick it up, and as she did, she felt the room spin beneath her feet.

"No," she muttered, and grabbed hold of her knees until the spinning stopped. "No, damn it, no! I'm not ready for this to happen."

The sound of a truck pulling into the yard warned her that Davie had arrived for his lesson. It was the first time since they'd begun that Annie dreaded his appearance.

"Hey, Annie," he yelled as he burst into the house in his usual fashion. "Ready or not, here I come."

Annie straightened and pasted a smile on her face, determined not to let her weakness show.

"Look what came," she said as Davie began digging through the books. "They'll help you immensely in your studies. Promise me you're going to use them."

Davie grinned and shrugged. "Sure I will, teach," he teased. "And if I don't, you can always give me a failing grade."

Annie frowned. "I won't always be around to give you a kick in the pants, Davie. You'll have to push yourself to gain the skills you're going to need."

His smile died on his face. "Where are you going?" he asked. "Somewhere with Gabe?"

A sharp pain twisted inside her chest. *If only I could run away with Gabe.*

"I'm not going anywhere. I just want you to realize that I'm no longer your baby-sitter...and I won't be your teacher forever. Soon you'll be at the point where all you'll need to do is just practice. You won't need me for that."

"Whatever," Davie said agreeably. "Let's get busy. I've got a hot date with Charlie as soon as we're through."

Annie grinned at his enthusiasm.

"Where's Gabe?" Davie asked as he sat down at the kitchen table and opened his book to the spot where they'd stopped yesterday.

"He's outside somewhere," Annie said. "He won't bother us, remember?"

Davie nodded and began to read. His brow furrowed in concentration as he read the sentences aloud. Soon he was lost in the story, unaware that Annie was less than focused on what they were doing.

Oh God, Annie thought. *Not now. Not in front of Davie.*

But the dull ache ignored her warning and spread across the back of her head, pushing persistently behind her eyeballs. She closed her eyes and took a long, deep breath, hoping that she was wrong about the impending attack.

Motioning for him to continue, she pushed back her chair and started toward the cabinet. By the time she touched the countertop, it was all she could do to reach up and open the door. Her fingers curled around the bottle of pills at the same time that the pain burst behind her eyes. The last thing she remembered hearing was the sound of breaking glass and Davie's shout of alarm as she fell to the floor.

Annie curled into herself, digging her fingernails into her scalp as she mindlessly tried to tear out the pain that was killing her by degrees.

She needed her pills. The blessed pills. The reliever and the seducer…the thing that took away what she treasured most, her ability to function.

Davie dropped to his knees in a panic. Unsuccessfully, he tried to pick Annie up. He couldn't believe her strength as she fought his touch. Twice he almost had her in his arms, and both times she arched her back and screamed, in so much pain that he was forced to lay her back on the floor.

Finally, Davie thought of Gabe. "Don't move, Annie. I'll get Gabe."

But she didn't hear. And she wouldn't have reacted if she had. She was too lost in the pain that was ripping her apart.

Gabe grunted as he tightened the last bolt on the new carburetor he'd just put in Annie's car. With the weather turning cooler by the day, riding on the back of his bike was becoming less and less of a pleasure.

He'd heard Davie arrive, and imagined that he and Annie were now deeply engrossed in sorting through the new books that she'd ordered.

It was a day like all others until he heard Annie's scream. He was on his feet and running toward the house when he saw Davie bolt onto the porch, his face a dull, pasty white.

Gabe pushed past him and in seconds was on the floor at Annie's side.

"I don't know what happened," Davie kept saying over and over as Gabe knelt beside her. "One minute she was fine, the next thing I know, things are falling on the floor, dishes are breaking…"

"Her pills. Where the hell are her pills?" Gabe muttered, as he tried to sort through the broken crockery on the floor and keep Annie from hurting herself in the progress.

"Pills? I didn't see any…"

As he spoke, he accidentally kicked an unbroken and overturned plate. Beneath it lay a small brown prescription bottle that rattled as it rolled toward the cabinet.

Gabe grabbed it with a thankful oath and seconds later was trying unsuccessfully to push one of the small tablets between Annie's tightly clenched teeth, unaware that Davie was calling for an ambulance.

"Oh, damn," he muttered when he realized that her pain was so great that her muscles had gone into spasm. "Annie...baby, please! Open your mouth!"

Sweat beaded Gabe's forehead as panic began to set in. This was by far the worst episode that he'd witnessed. He couldn't even face the implications of that knowledge.

Harsh, aching gasps of air tore through her windpipe and down into her lungs as she tried to remember to breathe. It would be so easy to just stop. It would be so much simpler to just give up now. *No,* she thought, and opened her mouth wide enough to pull in the next breath.

"Thank God," Gabe whispered, and dropped the tiny pill deep into her mouth, knowing that when she next swallowed, it would go down where it belonged.

And then he braced himself against the cabinets, with his back to the doors and his boots digging deeply into the floor, and held her with a grip that death couldn't have loosened while he waited for the pill to take effect.

Davie sank to his knees on the other side of the room and stared blankly at the mess in front of him, trying to assimilate what he had witnessed. "What's wrong? What in hell's wrong with Annie?"

Gabe shuddered and began to rock her gently, back and forth in a slow, gentle motion. He breathed a sigh of relief as he felt her body beginning to relax. Twice he looked up at the shock on Davie's face and knew that the man deserved an answer. But each time that he tried to speak, nothing came out. It was impossible to say aloud what he knew was happening.

"I called the doctor," Davie finally said. "The ambulance should be here any minute."

"It won't help," Gabe said. He buried his face in her shoulder. "Nothing will help."

Annie moaned and rolled limply against him as the painkillers began to kick in.

"What the hell do you mean, 'It won't help'? Have you lost your mind? She needs attention. She needs it now."

Gabe maneuvered himself to his feet and then shifted Annie's limp body carefully as the distant sounds of a siren became obvious. He glared at the younger man, directing his anger at Davie to keep from crying aloud in despair.

"No doctor can fix what's wrong with Annie," he said harshly, unaware of the sheen of tears in his eyes. "Damn it, Davie, she's dying." His voice broke. "She's dying, and I can't stop it. No one can."

With that, he walked outside to the ambulance that had just pulled up in front of the house. Moments later, the ambulance pulled away, with Gabe on his Harley, only seconds behind.

Chapter 13

The waiting room was too warm. Gabe sat in a hard-backed chair against the wall and watched the sweat beading across Davie Henry's forehead. He knew that the small blond woman who sat beside him was Charlotte. He'd been introduced. That was as far as the relationship had progressed.

He watched them whispering to each other, trying to get past the bitterness of knowing they had each other and the rest of their lives, when he and Annie had nothing.

Charlotte clutched Davie's hands in her own, touching the worry lines on his face, patting his knee when he fidgeted restlessly in the chair, and every now and then leaned over and murmured in his ear.

Gabe wished to hell that they were somewhere else. He didn't want to see them. Not here. Not now. And yet he knew that Davie cared deeply for Annie, that begrudging him the right to be here was petty. But he couldn't help what he was feeling.

Oh, Annie...they don't love you like I do, Gabe thought, and buried his face in his hands.

In doing so, he missed seeing Dr. Pope enter the waiting room. He jerked in surprise when the doctor touched him on the arm.

"How is she?" Gabe asked. "When can I take her home?"

"She's stable. But her condition has progressed a little faster than we'd expected. I'm not sure home is the best place for her at this time," Dr. Pope said.

"Exactly what does that mean?" Davie asked.

"It means that for her to be able to go home and... function normally...she's going to have to be on a stronger medication. That in turn means that she'll sleep for longer periods of time, which in turn means that she's close to needing round-the-clock care."

"Son of a bitch."

Gabe's curse startled them all, and left them staring in shock as he bolted from the chair and stalked out into the hall.

The quick tears that shot to his eyes shamed Gabe. He didn't cry. He never cried. He couldn't let go of his emotions, not even for Annie. If he did, he would never be able to stop.

Dr. Pope followed him into the hall.

"I'm sorry, Mr. Donner. I wish I had better news to give you."

"Hell, Doc, so do I," Gabe said shortly, then shoved his hands in his pockets, and started toward Annie's room. Suddenly he stopped and turned.

A tiny jingle from the rowels on his spurs was the only sound that warned Dr. Pope he was coming back.

"Doc..."

"What is it?" Dr. Pope asked.

"How long?"

"It's hard to say...maybe a month, maybe three."

A month? A mere thirty days?

The doctor's prediction was a death knell that knocked the wind from Gabe's lungs. He knew that he staggered, because he remembered seeing the floor tilt. But he never saw the doctor reach out and steady him. All he felt was the firm, reassuring grip, and then the world coming back into focus.

"If you were planning a big Christmas, I'd advise an early celebration," the doctor said, and patted Gabe roughly on the shoulder.

Shock bled the color from Gabe's face. "Christmas," he repeated blankly, as if unable to contemplate a celebration of any kind. His life was never going to be the same. Not without Annie.

Davie and Charlotte came out of the waiting room hand in hand. Gabe saw the way their heads nearly touched as they leaned together, sharing whispered words of comfort as they drew near. In that moment he hated them for having the rest of their lives together.

"It doesn't make sense," Gabe muttered. Annie's life should still be beginning, and instead it was coming to an end.

Doctor Pope overheard Gabe's remark and misunderstood the reason for the comment. And in doing so, he inadvertently revealed the last of Annie's secret. The part she'd never meant to share.

"I agree," Dr. Pope said. "It doesn't make sense. And I told Miss O'Brien so, the first time I examined her. You remember…the day she cut her foot and you brought her in to see me."

Gabe nodded absently and stared at a small water spot on the ceiling, trying to focus on anything but the news at hand.

"There *is* a risk involved. Actually, a big risk. But to blindly turn it down without giving herself a chance…" Dr. Pope shook his head. "I don't know her very well, but it surprised me. I imagined her to be more of a fighter."

Gabe's attention slowly refocused. He turned and stared, suddenly very attentive to the rest of Dr. Pope's opinion.

"Annie *is* a fighter," Gabe argued. "I've never known anyone quite like her."

Dr. Pope shrugged. "That may be. But I was still surprised when she refused to consider the possibilities of surgery."

Gabe's belly turned. What he was hearing didn't bear contemplation.

"Are you trying to tell me that Annie had a choice? That she didn't have to die?" Gabe asked.

Dr. Pope looked startled as he realized that he'd revealed confidential information.

"I thought you knew," the doctor muttered. "This wasn't my news to tell."

Gabe grabbed the doctor by the shoulders. Without thinking, he shoved him against the wall. "I want the truth," he whispered. "I'm sick and tired of hearing everything in bits and pieces. Talk to me...now!"

Davie saw the commotion and ran toward them without waiting to see what would happen next. From the expression on Gabe's face, it could have been almost anything.

"What the hell do you think you're doing?" Davie said, and started prying the doctor from Gabe's grasp.

"Answer me," Gabe said softly, refusing to let go of the man until his question had been answered. "Are you telling me that Annie could have been cured?"

Davie froze. He, too, stood silently, awaiting the doctor's diagnosis.

Dr. Pope shrugged. "There was a chance. It was a slim one, but it was better than no chance at all."

"And she refused to consider it?" Shock was thick in Gabe's voice.

The doctor nodded. "So it would seem," he said.

"Why? Why would she choose to die?" Gabe asked.

"She said the risk was too great. She didn't want to be just alive. If she couldn't be active, she didn't want to live."

"She chose death? She could have changed her own fate, and she chose death?"

Gabe couldn't believe his ears. He'd heard the doctor saying it, but he wasn't processing it as thoroughly as he should. All he could see was Annie, withering away before his eyes, and it had been by choice.

"I don't believe it," he said, and turned away.

"Is it too late now?" Davie asked.

Gabe listened intently for the answer, although he couldn't look at the doctor's face when it came.

Dr. Pope shook his head sadly. "I would guess that the chances now are reduced by more than half. It's hard to tell whether she would even survive the surgery, let alone in what condition."

"Oh, damn," Gabe groaned, and felt his legs go weak. He hadn't been this scared in his whole life. Not even the day he'd been hanged.

"At their best, what were her chances of coming out alive and well?" Davie asked.

"There was about a twenty percent chance of a total cure, maybe less," the doctor said.

"Then that means that Annie now has less than a ten percent chance of living through the surgery," Davie repeated.

"And that doesn't take into consideration what shape she'd be in if she did," the doctor reminded them.

"So what?" Gabe shouted. "Without it, her chances of living are zero."

He slammed his hand against the wall, ignoring the fact that it echoed down the hall and brought several nurses scrambling to see what was happening.

"Damn her! She cheated." Gabe's voice went from angry

to empty in one breath. "She lied to me. But what was worse, she lied to herself."

He walked away, leaving Davie and Charlotte to console each other as best they could. For Gabe, there was no consolation, only the overwhelming fact that Annie had given up on life without a fight.

The walls of her room were yellow. A pale, placid color that reminded her of a plate of butter that had sat out too long and lost its shape and consistency. The view wasn't the most appealing she could have had, either. It made her lonesome for her little frame house and the thick ring of trees surrounding it, for the clear running water in the creek and the big moss-covered rock below the spring.

And she missed Gabe. She vaguely remembered hearing his voice when she'd been brought in, but she couldn't remember if he'd visited since.

She shrugged. It was to be expected. She'd lost most of the last twenty-four hours to pills and shots. But no more. Annie wasn't ready to sleep what was left of her life away.

She threw back the sheets and swung her legs out from under them, letting them dangle for a minute off the edge of the bed, just to make sure that the vertigo she'd experienced earlier was gone.

Nothing happened. The room didn't spin. Her head didn't feel as if it was about to explode. *Okay...now I'm going to get dressed.*

And then the door swung open and Gabe filled the doorway with his presence.

"Gabe! I'm glad you're here," Annie said, her attention entirely focused on the fact that her means of escape had arrived. She didn't notice his expression. If she had, she might have been ready for what ensued.

"Hand me my clothes, will you? They're in the closet."

He didn't move. He didn't speak.

"I can't wait to get home," she said, unaware of his lack of cooperation. "I'm going to soak in a tub for—"

"I didn't take you for a coward."

Shock spilled across her thoughts like beads of water dancing on a hot griddle. She slid back into bed and pulled the sheets up beneath her chin. It was an unconscious and useless gesture. She had no way of hiding from Gabe or the truth. And from the look on his face, the truth had finally come out.

"I don't know what you're talking ab—"

"Bull."

"You don't understand."

Gabe came toward her, the rowels on his spurs jingling with each long, slow step he took. And when he got to the edge of the bed, he placed an arm on either side of her body and leaned forward until Annie saw her own reflection in the cold blue glare in his eyes.

"Make me understand," Gabe whispered. The bed shook gently from the movement of his body as he slid onto the edge beside her. "Damn you, lady. Make me understand."

Her chin quivered, but it was the only sign she gave of how deeply his behavior moved her.

"I've been alone for seven years," she said.

"And I've been alone for more than two lifetimes," he countered, uncaring of how odd his rebuttal might seem.

Annie tried to glare. It shouldn't have been necessary to defend her decisions about her life to anyone.

"When I first got the news, I was devastated," Annie said. And then her chin tilted in a defiant gesture, as if daring him to begrudge her her fear. "Actually, I was scared out of my wits."

Gabe heard the tremble in her voice, but he gave her no evidence that he cared. He couldn't. He needed her to see her life from another perspective.

"And...?" he said.

"They gave me my options, such as they were. Actually, it was pretty cut and dried." Annie's eyes teared up as she remembered sitting in the doctor's office while her world came shattering down around her. "I could have an operation. But there was a less-than-twenty-percent chance that I'd survive, and even less than that, that I would survive intact. *If* I survived, I might be blind, immobile, unable to speak, unable to think, or—" bitterness colored her last remark "—a combination of the above."

Gabe looked away. He didn't want her to see the sympathy he was feeling.

"So...I chose to go out the way I came in. All in one piece."

The bravado in her voice made him furious. He turned and glared. "It all sounds so damn easy. Is that the way you've gone through life? Taking no chances, always choosing the easy way out?"

Annie leaned toward him, her voice shaking with fury. "No! Once in my life I took a hell of a chance, Gabe Donner. I took you home, and I fell in love."

He flushed, unwilling to admit that she'd scored.

"That wasn't much of a chance, lady," he whispered. "You had nothing to lose when we met. How can you look on our relationship as any kind of a risk? You'd already signed your own damned death warrant. There wasn't anything I could do to you that you hadn't already done to yourself."

Annie gasped. Cruelty from Gabe was something new. Something she didn't know how to fight. It made her angry. In fact, it made her fighting mad.

She kicked out and actually pushed Gabe from her bed with her feet. "Get out!" she said, swinging her legs over and then off the bed. "I don't need your help. I'll get myself dressed."

"So it's like that, is it, teacher? Do as I say, not as I do?"

"What do you mean?" she asked.

"Everyone needs help at one time or another in their life, Annie. I can vouch for that. I've had more help than you'd ever believe. But not you! Oh, no! You're willing to help everyone else, but you won't help yourself."

Annie stomped to the closet and started grabbing her clothes from the hangers in fits and jerks.

"All the years that you taught, you made such a difference in your students' lives," Gabe said. "Look at the ones you left behind in Oklahoma City who'd looked forward to having you for a teacher next year. You walked off and left them without a single thought. And why? Because you were too busy feeling sorry for yourself to fight."

Annie threw a shoe at him and screamed in frustration when it missed.

"Look at Davie. He'd still be hiding behind a wall of ignorance, afraid to tell the woman he loved that he wanted to marry her. And why? Because he couldn't read. You changed all that for Davie, but you aren't willing to change anything for yourself."

Annie pushed her feet angrily through the legs of her jeans, wishing she had enough hands to dress herself and still cover her ears. She didn't want to hear this. She didn't want to face the truth of what Gabe was telling her.

"You have so much to offer, Annie," Gabe said softly as all the anger and fight suddenly went out of him. "Life has so much to offer *you*. How can you give up without a fight?"

Annie slumped forward and buried her face in her hands. But no tears would come. There was no way of hiding from the truth of what he'd said.

"Oh, Gabe," she whispered. "I wish I'd met you sooner. Before all this happened. If I'd had you to come home to, I might have been strong enough to give myself a chance."

"No! No, you don't," he said, his voice harsh and unforgiving. "You don't use me for your scapegoat. You don't choose to live for me, Annie. You either choose life for yourself or not at all."

Annie stared, dry-eyed and sick at heart, as Gabe turned and walked out the door. Long, silent seconds slid by as the echo of his accusations rang in her ears.

Annie shuddered, then stared slowly around the room, as if coming out of a trance. She moved toward the bed, walking as if every muscle in her body ached, and when her knees hit the mattress, she collapsed. Crawling beneath the covers like a recalcitrant child, she turned over on her stomach and buried her face in the pillow, unable to look at the truth of what she'd done.

Gabe sat on the bank of the creek below Annie's house and stared off into the trees beyond. The ground on which he sat was cold, and the seat of his jeans felt damp, but he didn't care. Moving took too much effort. He was weary clear down to his soul and heartsick beyond belief.

"I've been here too long," Gabe muttered, and buried his face in his hands.

"Does that mean you're leaving me?" Annie asked, and then clasped her hands in front of her like a child waiting to be chastised. What she'd overheard had made her panic. She couldn't lose Gabe. Not now, when so much depended on his strength.

Gabe bolted to his feet, then grabbed her by the arms, raking his gaze across her face and then down her body to assure himself that she was really there.

"I didn't mean I'd been too long with you, Annie. That's not what I meant." He stopped there, unable to explain any further. And then he realized she'd come home from the hospital...without his aid.

"How did you get home? Why didn't you call? I would have come for you."

Annie sighed and spread her hands in defeat. "I wasn't sure if you would even talk to me, Gabe, never mind play chauffeur. I called Davie. He and Charlotte brought me home."

He took her in his arms. Unable to hide his pain when she relaxed against him, he groaned softly and pressed a kiss against a curl that strayed across his lips.

"I'm sorry. I'm so, so sorry," he said. "I had no right to say the things I said to you. Please…just chalk it up to shock and an inability to mind my own business."

"No," Annie said and pushed him away. "You had every right. And you were right to say what you did."

Gabe closed his eyes against the truth of her words. Being right didn't make what would happen later any easier to bear.

"Come to the house," Annie said. "I have something to show you."

She held out her hand, and Gabe took it. Together they walked back through the trees, then up the path that led to Annie's house.

He shivered slightly as they walked inside. It was the first time they'd been here together since he'd found her on the floor at Davie's feet.

And then he forgot everything he'd been thinking at the shock of what he saw in the middle of the living room floor. There were boxes everywhere.

"What's all this?" he asked, and watched as Annie began opening and sorting boxes with calm deliberation.

"Mother's Christmas decorations. I had Davie get them out of the attic before he left. I want to put up a tree."

"A tree?"

"A Christmas tree," she said, then continued to sort through tissue and tape.

"Davie's father has lots of cedar growing on their place.

He's bringing one over this evening after he gets off work. He and Charlotte are going to help us decorate. It'll be fun."

"A real Christmas tree?"

Annie paused in the act of unwinding an old string of lights and stared at Gabe. "I know it's early," she said. "But I thought it would be obvious to you why I'm doing this." She handed him the string of lights. "Here, see if you can get these untangled. I want to test them before we put them on the tree."

Gabe sank into a chair as Annie dropped the string of lights in his lap. He stared down at them, then up at her, as a slow smile spread across his face.

Even though she'd seen it plenty of times, Annie still caught her breath at the amazing beauty of his smile. It made him seem almost angelic. She laughed to herself at the thought and turned back to her task.

"I've never had a Christmas tree."

Annie almost didn't hear him. She stopped what she was doing and turned. Gabe was holding the lights and staring at them as if they'd suddenly turned to gold.

"What do you mean, you've never had a Christmas tree? Surely you've had a—"

"No. Never. It just didn't seem like a thing to do alone."

Annie stopped what she was doing and dropped to her knees beside Gabe's chair. "Gabriel Donner...I love you. Very, very much. And for the rest of our days, whatever we do won't be done alone. Somehow it only seems fitting that we share your first Christmas together."

The words were never spoken, but they both heard them just the same.

Gabe pulled Annie into his lap, settling her amid the tangle of wire and bulbs, and then held her face between his hands.

"I don't deserve you, lady," he whispered, then feathered a kiss across her lips.

"I know," Annie said with a sigh, and leaned against him, nuzzling her cheek over his chest until she came to the place where his heart beat loudest.

He chuckled, and Annie heard its origin from deep down inside his chest and smiled.

"We'll put up the tree tonight and open presents tomorrow. And then whatever comes after that, comes. At least we'll have celebrated together. Deal?"

The anxious look on her face made him angry. He'd put it there, and for that he would never forgive himself. Gabe hugged her lightly, willing the swelling pain in his chest to hell, where it belonged.

"Deal, darlin'," he whispered. "Whatever comes."

Annie smiled. With Gabe at her side, she *could* handle whatever came.

"Open mine first!"

"Okay, okay," Annie said. "Hand it to me."

Davie was like a puppy with a new bone. He'd gotten into the excitement of the early celebration as if he'd thought of it himself. His request was duly noted as Annie picked up the small flat box and shook it for effect.

Gabe watched the two old friends and tried to smile, hoping that no one noticed he wasn't nearly as excited about this event as he should have been.

It was impossible not to notice Annie's drawn expression or the dark hollows in her cheeks. When she thought no one was looking her eyelids drooped; she was constantly sleepy from the heavier doses of painkillers she was now forced to take.

Gabe stared at the scene unfolding before him and tried not to let his feelings show.

"Look, Gabe. It's a picture frame. I'm going to put our picture from Silver Dollar City inside. It'll be perfect."

"Now mine," Annie said, handing Davie a wrapped box.

He tore into it with enthusiasm, and his face lit up as he pulled out an old nursery rhyme book.

"It's one of my favorite books," Annie said. "And it's the first one you learned to read. I thought you should have it so that you can read to your own children some day."

"Man..." he whispered, suddenly choking on emotion as he gently turned the pages of his gift. "You've changed my life, Annie. Because of you, I'll never be ashamed again."

"Here," Gabe said, offering Davie some punch. "Annie spent all afternoon mixing this stuff. You'd better check to see if she's spiked it."

Annie smiled as her heart swelled with pride. Gabe was trying so hard...and all for her.

"Okay, you next," Gabe said, and handed Annie a small oblong box. There weren't many gift choices in Walnut Shade, but when he'd seen this, he had instantly thought of her.

For a moment Annie just held the box, letting the love with which it had been given seep into her soul. She needed all the strength she could get to finish this day. And then the rest of her life was going to be in someone else's hands.

She lifted the lid and pushed back the tissue. When she saw the tiny apple-shaped charm and the long gold chain, she began to smile.

Gabe lifted it from the box and then draped it around her neck while he fastened the intricate clasp.

"An apple a day keeps the doctor away?" Annie asked, and caught the small, golden charm as it dangled in the valley between her breasts.

"No, honey. It's an apple...for my favorite teacher."

Gabe leaned over and kissed her lightly on the lips before turning to pour himself some of that punch. Suddenly he, too, was suffering from a lack of words and too much emotion.

"Oh, hell," Davie said, and took another big gulp of punch.

Annie laughed. "You're both pathetic," she said. "I'm not done for yet."

Gabe grinned past the knot in his throat. Damned if this woman wasn't something. She was thumbing her nose at them and at her fate. He couldn't let her down. Not when she was trying so hard.

"Where's mine?" Gabe asked, and began poking playfully beneath the branches of the tree.

Annie clasped her hands together in her lap and took several slow, calming breaths before she began. It was, after all, why she'd planned this elaborate get-together.

"It's here," she said, and slipped an envelope from behind her back. "I was hiding it. I knew you'd peek."

Gabe grinned and took the long white envelope as she handed it over, wondering as he did about the near-panic he thought he saw on her face.

He made a big issue of turning it over and over several times before slipping his finger beneath the flap and pulling it up. And then, just to prolong the issue, he peered inside twice before pulling out the contents.

Davie muttered softly in disgust, and Annie laughed aloud.

Gabe grinned. He'd done his bit toward putting a smile back on her face. It was time to end the ordeal. With an elaborate flourish, he pulled the piece of paper from inside the envelope and began unfolding it with relish.

"Probably a letter from the IRS," he teased as he unfolded the first flap.

"Naw...it's from one of those sweepstakes places," Davie offered, slapping his leg in jest. "You just won the jackpot."

The smile on Gabe's face stopped in mid-formation. Quickly he scanned the printed page, and Annie held her breath, waiting for his reaction. She didn't have long to wait. The paper shook in his hands as the blood drained from his face.

"Why? Why now?" Gabe asked.

Annie shrugged. "Why not?" she retorted. "After all, what you said was the truth."

"What is it?" Davie asked.

"It's a copy of my preadmission form," Annie said, her voice a little too bright and a little too light to fool anyone. "I'm admitting myself tomorrow. Surgery the day after that."

"But I thought…"

"Shut up, Davie. Just shut up." Gabe's voice shook as he leaned over and picked Annie up in his arms.

She slid her arms around his neck and rested her head against the curve of his cheek as he shifted her to a safer place within his embrace.

"Davie…" Gabe stared at the sheen of tears in Annie's eyes.

"What?" Davie asked.

"Let yourself out," he said, and walked out of the room with Annie in his arms.

"So, do you like your gift?" Annie asked a few minutes later as Gabe laid her down upon her bed.

He shuddered as he crawled in beside her and then wrapped her so tightly within his arms that it was hard to draw a breath.

Long minutes passed, and Annie thought he was never going to speak. Where once he'd been the one who gave comfort, now it was her turn to do the same.

Gabe shook. Great, shivering contractions that jerked his muscles and rattled his teeth. The tighter he held her, the colder he felt. He didn't think he would ever be warm again.

And in the moment that he thought it, he knew why he'd reacted as he had.

If Annie died, all the light and warmth would go out of his world. That piece of paper was simply a reminder of the awful fact.

"It's not my present to keep," Gabe finally whispered, and buried his face in the warm, thick tangles of her hair. "No one's life can belong to another. The only thing you can give away is love, Annie. Only love."

"Then it's yours," she said lightly. "Now, remind me of what I've got to live for, Gabriel. Make love to me now, while there's still time."

"My God, Annie. I don't know if I can. I've never made love with a broken heart."

He choked on his words and felt her tremble as he wrapped her in his arms.

"Then try. That's all anyone can do—just try," she whispered.

So he did.

Chapter 14

The house was cold and quiet. Inside, it looked and felt a little bit like it had the day that they'd arrived: drab and lonely. And now it sat empty, just waiting for someone to come back and add the spark to it that made a house a home.

Gabe walked from room to room, making certain that everything was turned off and unplugged.

All morning Annie had gone through the rooms, folding up linens and making up beds, anything she could think to do that would postpone her trip to Walnut Shade. She'd fussed with the little things until she'd made herself sick and ended up leaving Davie with a list of instructions he faithfully promised to complete.

But now she was gone.

Gabe inhaled deeply as he walked into her bedroom. The scent of her bath powder still lingered, as well as a few small, unnecessary items that she'd left behind when she'd packed her bag.

He leaned against the door frame and closed his eyes,

recalling his last image of Annie and how small she'd looked as they'd strapped her down in the gurney and lifted her into the helicopter.

MediFlight was airlifting her back to Oklahoma City, to the specialist who'd first begun her treatment. Walnut Shade and the good doctors there simply didn't have the specialists and facilities available for the delicate neurosurgery she needed.

Gabe pushed himself away from the door and cursed softly, trying to forget how pale she'd looked and how frightened she'd seemed when the helicopter lifted off.

He'd watched until it was nothing more than a tiny black speck in the sky. And then a sudden sense of urgency had sent him driving back to the house in a cloud of dust. He couldn't shake an overwhelming urge to race the helicopter to Oklahoma City. Annie might need him.

Because he owned little and traveled light, Gabe had nothing much to pack. What he'd left until last, he now stuffed haphazardly into his bag, anxious to get back on the road.

He started out of the room, then stopped and turned, taking one last look around at the place where he and Annie had loved.

The old stuffed teddy bear, her first and her favorite, was propped against the pillow shams on her bed. Their picture, the one they'd had taken at Silver Dollar City, was safely mounted in the frame Davie had given her as a gift and now sat in a place of prominence in the center of her dresser.

Gabe looked at it from across the room and felt a sense of timelessness, as if all things come full circle. It was as if someday another couple might come upon the picture and know that once upon a time, in another life, a man and a woman had loved as they did now.

"God willing, my Annie, you will be back."

He walked away, his bag over his shoulder, and missed

seeing that she'd hung the long gold chain with the little apple charm over the corner of the frame. If he had, he would have known then that Annie had already made peace with herself and her fate. The necklace hadn't been off her neck for a moment since he'd put it on. And yet it was the first thing she'd left behind.

The front door slammed behind him as he walked out on the porch. Gabe dropped his bag and reached up over the door, letting his fingers trace the dusty path until he came to the old, rusty key.

He poked it into the lock and then turned it. The tumblers clicked into place. Carelessly Gabe put the key back onto the narrow ledge, paying little attention to its location, and picked up his bag. With Annie gone, there was nothing here that needed to be kept safe.

In two steps he was off the porch and running toward his bike. He tossed his bag onto the back, strapped it in place and jammed the helmet on his head. Seconds later the engine fired, and the big, black Harley roared out of the quiet little yard, leaving dust and dry leaves flying in its wake.

Hours later Gabe crossed the state line and absently read the sign at the side of the road. Welcome To Oklahoma. He didn't feel welcome. He didn't feel anything at all.

Sometime later he crossed another, smaller state highway to get to the southbound on-ramp leading to Interstate 40. The wind beneath the helmet roared in his ears as he focused on the next leg of his journey. Destination: Oklahoma City—and Annie.

It was nearly midnight when Gabe got off the elevator. A night nurse doing rounds looked askance at his shaggy black hair, dusty boots and faded jeans, then shrugged and entered the next room on her list. In her job, she saw all kinds.

Gabe's spurs made tiny jingling sounds as his long legs quickly covered the distance to the nurses' station.

"Annie O'Brien's room," he said as he stopped in front of the desk and waited for further directions.

"I'm sorry, sir," a nurse said. "But visiting hours were over long ago."

"She's expecting me," Gabe persisted. "I've been on the road since early this morning. I don't think she'll rest until she knows I'm here."

The nurse frowned. She'd already familiarized herself with the case history and couldn't quite fit this big biker with the young school teacher who'd been brought in by helicopter earlier in the day.

Gabe saw her frown and knew it for what it was, disapproval of his appearance, rather than anything that he'd done.

"Please," he insisted. "My name is Gabe Donner. I have to see Annie. I'm all the family she has."

"You're *that* Gabriel? Miss O'Brien's angel of mercy?" She grinned. "Sorry. You just didn't quite fit the image I had in mind." And then, to soften the rudeness of her remark, she added, "I was expecting maybe…wings?"

Gabe grinned wearily. "That's one I haven't heard before." And then the smile disappeared and the shadows came back into his eyes. "Please…I need to see Annie."

"Room 353, down the hall and to the right."

Gabe disappeared so quickly that the nurse was left wondering if she'd imagined him. And then she heard the faint but distinct jingle of spurs and knew that he'd been real. She resumed her work and hoped that Gabriel Donner could withstand some shocks. Miss O'Brien's appearance had undergone a drastic transformation.

Nervous anticipation made him shake as he pushed open the door to the private room, then walked inside. Thick, dark shadows surrounded the bed, making everything, including Annie, seem small by comparison.

A mere lump beneath the covers, she slept in her old familiar position, with her knees drawn up and her hands beneath her chin in a gesture of prayer. Gabe caught his breath and swallowed his shock.

He leaned over and kissed her cheek, trying not to look at the small white cap she wore over her head, trying not to notice that she looked more like a newborn baby than the woman he'd made love to with total abandon only a day ago.

Annie stirred, as if sensing Gabe's presence. She reached out into the darkness and found him reaching back.

"They cut off my hair," she whispered, unaware of a small tear that trickled down her nose.

Gabe hurt from the inside out. "It will grow back," he whispered, and kissed the tips of her fingers before covering her hand with his own.

She sighed and seemed to settle. Gabe sat on the edge of the chair and held Annie's hand in the safety of his own. When he could no longer look at the damage that had been done to her in his absence, he leaned forward, resting his head against the edge of her bed, and closed his eyes.

Twice he swallowed, trying to get past the pain before he was able to talk. "Sleep, Annie. Rest while you can. I'll do the worrying for both of us now."

She seemed to smile and then sighed.

The sigh sounded too deep, too final, and Gabe found himself holding his breath in fear, unable to rest again until he'd heard her inhale. And when she did, he went weak with relief. It was the assurance he needed that she was still breathing.

Guilt overwhelmed him. If he'd minded his own business and accepted Annie's decision about her life, she would be back in Missouri in her own house, in her own bed, waiting for fate to catch up with her. Not here, shorn of her pride, poked and prodded and hooked up to too many machines with too many beeping lights and multicolored wires.

"Annie...Annie." His heartbroken plea slipped into the silence of the room. "What have I done to you?"

But she didn't answer. And the night passed away.

They came with morning, unannounced...unexpected. Bolting in through the doors of her room like the sun springing up from below the horizon. Wearing surgical greens, laughing and talking about the movie they'd seen last night and the pizza they'd had. Making light of the fact that someone had gone off a diet while another had gone off the wagon.

Gabe wanted to shout. He wanted to cry. He wanted to lash out at their lack of compassion for the pain that he was in. He wanted to rail at them...to ask them why it mattered that someone had gained a pound or drank too much, when Annie's desperation should have been foremost in their thoughts.

Were they blind to the way she clung to him as they moved around the room? And when they lifted her with little finesse from her bed to the gurney, Gabe felt empty...without purpose, knowing she would soon be gone.

He didn't know that they suffered with him, that they truly sympathized with Annie's pain. He didn't know that their loud, raucous jokes were the only way they could deal with daily doses of lives gone wrong. He didn't know, and at that moment he wouldn't have cared. The only thing in his world was Annie, and they were taking her away.

"Gabe!"

She called out in panic, reaching for a last touch of his hand as they wheeled her from the room.

His fingers curled around her wrist and then instantly loosened as he felt her fragility.

"I love you, sweetheart," he said huskily.

"Will you wait?" Annie asked.

Gabe shuddered. She hadn't asked him if he'd wait *for her.* She'd only asked him if he would *wait.* Wait until the verdict was in, whatever it might be.

"Sure I will, honey," he said, forcing himself to smile when all he wanted to do was crawl into a hole and pull it in after him. "Forever, if that's what it takes. But you already knew that, didn't you? Outlaws don't run from love, just the law."

"Remember," Annie whispered as they wheeled her from the room. "Remember me."

Gabe had stared at her face until they'd taken her away, too lost in the depths of those unblinking green eyes to tell her that her last request had been unnecessary. Remember Annie? How could he ever forget?

A nurse came in and started to strip the bed. Gabe turned and stared, unable to make even the simplest of remarks.

"I'm just going to make up her bed," she said gently. "There's a waiting room across the hall, and a cafeteria on the basement level. Why don't you go get yourself some breakfast...at least some coffee? Her surgery will take hours, and they haven't even started."

Gabe wiped a shaky hand across his face. The thought of food made his stomach roil.

"I might get some coffee," he said. "But I'll be just across the hall. When you have news, you'll come and get me...won't you? I won't be far."

She smiled sympathetically. "I promise," she said. "Someone will find you. Until then, you need to take care of yourself...for her."

For her.

He looked up to see Davie and Charlotte almost running down the hall.

"You just missed her," Gabe said, and pointed toward the end of the hallway.

"No, we didn't. We saw her just as they were putting her on the elevator. We got to say goodbye."

Anger overwhelmed him at Davie's careless words. He shook as fury enveloped him, and then he cursed helplessly, knowing that he was searching for an excuse to take his fear and anger out on someone else. He shook his head and shrugged, telling himself that what had been said, had been said without malice.

Davie flushed. "I'm sorry," he muttered. "I didn't really mean...goodbye as in forever. I just meant..."

"Save it," Gabe said. "I knew what you meant. It's hard to find the right thing to say."

"Come on," Davie said. "Charlie and I brought you some coffee and doughnuts. We can eat in the waiting room."

Gabe followed them. It was the simplest thing to do. Having to explain why he would rather be alone would have been impossible...and selfish.

The waiting room quickly became a prison. The longer he sat, the sicker he got. Imagination was making him crazy. Any minute Gabe expected to look up, see that damned doctor wearing pity and mouthing excuses, and know that it had all been for nothing.

Davie and Charlotte were at it again. Heads together, touching, whispering, even now and then having the unmitigated gall to laugh quietly about things, when he was bleeding to death from uncertainty.

"I'm going to get some coffee. I'll be right back," Gabe said shortly, then jumped to his feet and stomped out of the waiting room before anyone could offer to go with him.

Within seconds he'd made it to the elevator without losing his mind. He pushed the button, then leaned against the wall, taking slow, deep breaths while he waited.

The car came quickly, and when he got on, he was thankful he was alone. Conversation was the last thing he could face. The doors closed behind him as he reached out to punch the button for the ground floor.

His finger never touched the panel. Instead, all around him, the air inside the car felt strangely charged and too rich to breathe. Gabe staggered then fell against the back wall as the pressure inside the car changed from heavy to light.

Suddenly he found himself being drawn upward, quickly now that motion had started, faster and faster toward a bright white light.

Gabe's thoughts spun outward, flinging themselves into the atmosphere until there was nothing left inside him but one single, desperate cry.

"No-o-o!"

But it was too late, and he'd gone too far to be heard. Gabriel Donner was gone.

The Voice came through the air, and when he dropped into the light, he knew who was waiting for him to appear.

"Gabriel."

Oh, God. Why now?

"Because it is time. Welcome, my son," God said. "I've been waiting for this day."

Gabriel felt weightless and knew that somewhere along the way he'd left his earthly body behind. And with that thought came the knowledge that he'd also left something else...something infinitely more important. Annie!

I wasn't ready.

"Oh, but you are," God said, and joy filled the air around them as his laughter echoed within the clouds. "You've done all that I asked and more during your time on earth. You've earned your rest, Gabriel, my son. Come...follow me...and the sound of my voice."

Wait!

God gasped, and the air was suddenly filled with the sound of his displeasure, rumbling across the skies like so much thunder.

"Gabriel! What manner of foolishness is this? You don't *wait* to get into the Kingdom of Heaven. You come when you are called."

Annie! What about my Annie?

God's sigh blew the thunder from the heavens, clearing the skies and the air with a single breath.

"She's no longer *your* Annie, Gabriel."

No-o-o! I have to know. I can't leave without being sure. Will Annie live? Please...will she live?

God's answer was kind, his voice benevolent, and yet Gabriel heard the certainty with which he spoke.

"Her fate is no longer your concern."

An overwhelming pain sent Gabriel to his knees. There at the Gates of Heaven, he felt the first onslaught of tears as they began running down his face.

He never cried. Not even on earth when it had mattered, and here he was, crying at the feet of God.

Please. Don't let her die!

God hissed, and the heavens stirred, as with a tumult of thousands upon thousands of angels' wings moving in constant motion, fluttering in unison. And with the wind came a sound, a wailing unlike anything Gabriel had ever heard.

"Now see what you've done," God said.

The accusation in his voice became a violent reverberation of judgment that made Gabriel unable to look up.

"You've made my angels cry. For shame!" He cried as the air was rent with sound. "For shame! There can be no tears in Heaven."

But she has no one. No one but me, and now I'm gone. I have to know...will she live?

"I tell you now! Come forward into the light."

The voice was once again a command and a demand, yet

solace to Gabe's aching soul, peace where none had been. But taking that first step away from Annie was still impossible for him to do.

He lay at the feet of God. Prostrate with grief. Unable to do what his Master had commanded.

Send me to hell. Cast me from heaven forever…leave me in Limbo, lost between Heaven and Hell for all eternity…just let Annie live.

The cry came from Gabe's heart.

God heard and at once understood that the man He'd sent back to earth to right all his wrongs had indeed grown in stature and grace. He'd done more than penance, he'd learned the meaning of true sacrifice.

God's manner changed. His voice became the sound of purity overflowing with patience, and yet it held a warning Gabriel could not miss.

"You would willingly exist alone—for all eternity and more, without the sight or sound of another living soul—just to know this woman's fate?"

Yes…oh, yes.

"You would never know the meaning of rest, never feel an inner peace, never—"

Yes! Yes! Yes! I would go now. I would go willingly. If you will only let Annie live.

"Without you?"

Without me.

God smiled. And in that moment Gabriel felt the tears drying upon his face. Felt the wind around him moving, turning, faster and faster, a whirlwind of motion that pulled him up and then flung him out.

Gabe forgot to be afraid. He forgot to say that last goodbye to Annie in his heart. Everything exploded within him, and he felt, rather than saw, a blackness enveloping him.

So, this is now my existence.... This is my Limbo.

"No, my son! This is life!"

The elevator came to an abrupt stop that sent Gabe to his knees. He reached out as he fell, expecting to touch the empty space of Limbo and instead felt the floor of the elevator coming up to meet his face.

"Where am I?" he muttered as he rolled over and then pulled himself to his feet, thinking that Limbo couldn't be an empty elevator car on its way to nowhere.

And then he heard the squeak of the elevator cables and heard a receptionist's voice coming over the hospital intercom and into the car, patiently paging a doctor by name.

He reached up, felt the tears on his face and knew in that moment that everything he'd imagined had been true. He *had* stood at the feet of God. He *had* been called Home. Then *why* was he back? Why was he *here*?

Because you cared.

Gabe started to shake. He knew as well as he knew his own name that God had just spoken to him.

"So...how long do I have this time?" Gabriel whispered, almost afraid to ask.

You are now as other men, my son. Live your life. Love your love. When it's time... you will come to me. I will never again come for you.

The elevator door opened. Davie all but jerked him out of the car and began running with him back toward the waiting room.

"Where the hell have you been?" Davie muttered as he turned a corner with Gabe in tow.

"Talking to God...I think," Gabe said.

"Oh! Right. I didn't think to look in the chapel," Davie said. "Sorry." And then they entered the waiting room, where a weary young doctor, still wearing his surgical greens, stood up at their arrival.

"I found him!" Davie shouted, almost shoving Gabe toward the man. "Now...tell him what you just told us." Davie was almost dancing with relief as he pulled Charlotte into his arms.

The doctor smiled and motioned for Gabe to sit.

"I'll stand, if you don't mind," Gabe said softly. "I'm still trying to get my land legs back."

They all smiled at his joke. They had no idea how close to the truth it was.

"It's like this," the doctor said. "We had all the tests results. MRIs, CAT scans, EEGs, every test known to man. We had every reason to believe that the mass inside Miss O'Brien's head was becoming aggressively invasive."

Gabe ignored his own advice and sank into a chair. What were they all smiling about? This sounded like hell.

"But..." the doctor continued. "When we got in-side—" his face lit up, and he began gesturing with his hands to describe what had happened "—the damned thing was just...just sitting there. It all but fell out in our hands, so to speak. I don't know what it was we saw on the X rays—shadows...bad films...I can't explain it. All I can say is, in surgery today...I saw a miracle. I can't explain how or why, but Miss O'Brien should recover with few, if any, lingering effects."

Gabe buried his face in his hands. He could have explained it.

A miracle. Divine intervention. Or just a plain, old-fashioned gift from God.

He didn't care what they called it. Annie had been given back to him. And in a way none of them could ever have known, he'd been given back to Annie.

"Thank God," Gabe whispered, and reached up to shake the doctor's hand.

You're welcome.

Gabe smiled. The Big Man always had the last word.

Epilogue

Sunlight was warm on Gabe's face as he carried the last of the groceries into the house. He passed through the hall on the way to the kitchen and caught a glimpse of himself in the hall mirror. He almost laughed. The outlaw he'd been was nowhere in sight.

His leather and his spurs had been packed away, his haircut was almost ordinary, and he was going to be late for work if he didn't hurry.

Work! It still amazed him that the old skills he'd once thought were useless had been the single most important reason for landing him a job as one of Silver Dollar City's employees.

If old-style, wooden shingles needed to be hacked by hand, he was their man. He also blacksmithed, trading days with another blacksmith who also knew how to make soap, a job Gabe politely refused to do.

Now and then he was even a stand-in for the gunslingers when an exhibition shoot-out was performed. But there was one thing he refused to do. He wouldn't pin on a star to save his life. Being a lawman, even playacting as one, was a little too close to the bone for Gabe.

"Gabe...you're going to be late for—"

"I'm never late for the things that count, am I, Annie Laurie?"

He dropped the sacks onto the counter and swung her up into his arms, ruffling her short, thick curls and mussing her makeup just to hear her fuss.

She did. But not because she cared. She did it because he expected her to.

"So your timing is almost perfect," she said, and grinned when his eyebrows shot up into his hairline.

He laughed. The little devil. She wasn't talking about his damned job, and they both knew it.

"What do you mean...almost?" he asked. "I give good love. Remember...you said so yourself."

Annie blushed, then opened her mouth for the kiss she saw coming.

Gabe sighed and wrapped her in his arms as she snuggled within his embrace. "What?" he asked. "Why, my dear wife, do you always wiggle when I first hold you?"

"I'm just finding my spot," Annie said, surprised that he'd even had to ask.

"What spot?"

Annie smiled and moved the flat of her hand across his chest until she found the spot she'd been searching for.

"This one," she said, and laid her cheek against it. "It's the place where your heartbeat's the loudest. It makes me feel closer to your heart."

"My God," Gabe whispered, and dug his hands deep within the baby curls framing her face. "Closer to my heart? Annie. You couldn't be any closer, darlin'. You *are* my heart. Without you, it isn't capable of beating."

She sighed and relaxed in his arms.

"When I get a little better, I'm going to teach again, you know. Then we won't have all this special time together."

"Then we'd better enjoy it while we can, honey."

Reluctantly he set her aside with a sweet farewell kiss. And when she whispered a naughty promise in his ear as he started to let her go, he laughed uproariously and began swinging her around and around the room like a doll.

It was during their dance that Annie looked up, laughter rich upon her face, and saw them shining in his hair.

"Gabe! Gabe! You have to stop. You won't believe what I just saw."

He stopped and stared, thinking that she'd truly lost her mind.

"What is it now?" he asked. "And don't make up stories. I really can't be late for work. One of the men is out sick."

Annie grabbed him by the hand and dragged him back out into the hall, pushing and shoving until she had him square in front of the oval-shaped mirror.

"Look!"

He bent over and peered carefully. All he could see was the same old face.

"See what?" he asked. "I don't see anything different."

Annie turned his head and then plucked a lock from above each ear and held it out from his head like little horns.

"Look! There! You have gray hair!"

An emotion swept over him that was at once so fierce and so joyful, he didn't know whether to laugh or cry.

"Where? I don't see it!" he said, and tilted his head even closer to the mirror, desperate to see the proof.

She tilted his head in the other direction and then tugged once again at the thick tufts of hair between her fingers.

"There…just above your ears…on each side. Like little wings. See?" And then she smiled as she had a thought. "You know how I always call you my guardian angel…well…you finally got your wings. I guess this makes it official.'' She laughed, pleased with the comparison she'd drawn. Gabriel would forever be perfect in her eyes.

"Oh, my God! I see them! They're beautiful," Gabe whispered, and feathered them beneath his fingers, testing the feel against the smoother texture of the rest of his hair. "They're honest to God fantastic!" he shouted.

Annie stared. She'd expected any kind of reaction other than excitement. Some men might have ignored their appearance. Some might have dyed their hair back to a more youthful state. Some might even have panicked and yanked the gray hairs out, unwilling to face the evidence of their mortality. But not Gabriel. She should have known that he would be different.

But Annie would never know exactly what a precious sign this was for Gabriel. It was the final and physical proof that, after more years than he cared to remember, he was at last a man like every other, and he was growing old...along with Annie.

* * * * *

Dear Reader,

I was so delighted to hear that Silhouette would be reissuing *A Lawless Man*. It's definitely one of my personal favorites, and its hero, Griffin Lawless, is, without question, one of the top five heroes to ever pop into my brain. What can I say? I just love a guy in jodhpurs. And black leather gloves. And shiny black boots. Straddling a motorcycle. A *big* motorcycle. A *really* big motorcycle.

Um...where was I?

Oh, yeah. The reissue of *A Lawless Man*. Another reason I was so pleased Silhouette chose to reprint it is because it's one I hear readers frequently requesting. I guess they love a man in jodhpurs, too.

But mostly, I'm glad the book is seeing another go-around because its initial release date was the same month my son was born. As a result, I was just a *tad* preoccupied with other things at the time, and I kind of missed seeing it in stores. So it will be fun to see it on the stands this time, especially since I'm in such amazingly good company, included in a collection with some of my very favorite authors.

I did have an awful lot of fun writing about Griffin and Sarah the first time around. And I hope you have as much fun reading about them this time.

My very best wishes,

Elizabeth Bevarly

A LAWLESS MAN
by Elizabeth Bevarly

Originally appearing in *Silhouette Desire*,
A LAWLESS MAN is a delightful example of the
powerful, passionate and provocative novels in this
contemporary line. These sensual, emotional,
believable stories are meant to appeal to today's
woman, who is not afraid to go after what she wants.
Look for all six new *Silhouette Desire* titles
each month and catch the sizzle!

For Brownie Troop No. 920.

See? I told you all I was thinking up a story
while the police lady was talking.
(Now, let your moms hang on to this book
until you all turn eighteen.)

Chapter 1

The sound began as a faint whine, scarcely noticeable above the music blaring from the car stereo. Sarah Greenleaf simply tuned it out and turned the knob on the tape deck to the right, until Graham Parker was singing to her even more loudly about stupefaction. A warm wind burst through the open window on the driver's side, tossing her short, blond curls fiercely about her head. The sunny afternoon was hot and pleasant, just the way she liked her spring days, and unless she thought about what lay ahead when she reached her destination, she hadn't a care in the world.

Until the faint whine grew louder, and she glanced into her rearview mirror. Immediately she realized the whine was actually the screech of a siren—a siren attached to a police motorcycle. She also noticed that the policeman sitting atop the motorcycle was closing in on her fast.

Thinking he must be hot on the trail of some evildoer, Sarah downshifted and urged the brake pedal carefully toward the floor, edging her car to the side of the road as she slowed enough for him to pass. The policeman kept moving forward, but instead of shooting past her and off to right some wrong, he pulled alongside her car and offered her a very stern expression. Jabbing a leather-clad finger toward the right, he also mouthed the words "Pull over." Only then did she realize the evildoer he was pursuing was apparently none other than she herself.

She reacted as he requested, more out of shocked surprise than any sense of duty or submission to authority. She'd been doing nothing wrong—of that she was certain. No doubt this was some mix-up that would soon be rectified, and then she could be on her merry way. As she rolled her little Volkswagen Beetle to a halt, she glanced at her watch and frowned. She was already fifteen minutes late for lunch with Wally. Her brother was difficult enough to deal with when he'd been kept waiting. Now Officer Motorcycle Man was about to make Sarah even later, and the afternoon with Wally would be even more strained than usual as a result.

She glanced anxiously in her rearview mirror again, pushing back her overly long bangs, watching every move the policeman made. He seemed to take his time in steadying the big machine beneath him, his foot clad in a shiny black leather boot pushing down the kickstand with much familiarity. Nearly everything about the man was black, right down to the skintight jodhpurs and short-sleeved shirt that had earned the Clemente, Ohio, Police Department some strange fashion award two years in a row. As he drew nearer, she saw that his helmet, gloves, mustache and aviator-style sunglasses were black, too, the final item reflecting the sun as if two fiery orbs burned behind the lenses. Sarah swallowed with some difficulty as the policeman paused by her window, then she pushed her sunglasses to the top of her head.

"Hi," she greeted him cheerfully. "Is there a problem, Officer?"

"Turn the music down, please" was all he said in reply.

Obediently she punched the cassette from the tape player and switched it off.

"License and registration," he stated efficiently.

Even his voice was dark, she thought as she leaned across to the passenger side for her purse. When she'd extracted her driver's license from her wallet, she reached for the glove compartment to search for her registration.

"Move slowly, please," the policeman added in a no-nonsense tone of voice. "No sudden moves."

Sarah turned to gape at him. What did he think she was going to do, pull a gun on him? He must be joking. Sarah Rose Greenleaf-Markham-back-to-Greenleaf-again, den mother, room mother, PTA representative, coordinator of the annual Fulton Street bake sale and all-around normal citizen, packing a piece? Honestly, it was too funny even to consider. Without commenting, she reached for the glove compartment again and punched the metal button with her thumb. But instead of flipping open, the door remained steadfastly shut. She stabbed the button once more, to no avail.

Sarah sighed in frustration. She dearly loved her thirty-year-old Volkswagen Beetle. Unfortunately, time had not been good to the little car. She still carried fond memories of her teenage revels in the yellow Bug, and of driving it to college out of state for the first time.

But these days, the Bug was no more a bright, excited kid than she was. Both of them had left their shining youths long behind. Sarah was three years older than her car, a divorced mother of two, and her little VW had become more of a liability than a fun possession. She dreaded to think how she would stand up to a similar comparison.

Still, anything that went wrong with the Bug she could pretty much fix herself. She even knew how to rebuild the engine if times called for such an overhaul. The fact that she knew how her car worked better than she understood the workings of her own mind was what had kept her from trading it in for something new and unfamiliar. That and the fact that she just couldn't afford something new right now.

Optimistically she tried to curl her fingertips under the glove-compartment door and yank hard as she pushed the button one last time. But the effort was futile. The door remained fixed tight.

She turned back to offer the policeman a nervous smile. "It's jammed," she said unnecessarily. "This, ah, this happens a lot. Well, not a lot, actually. But sometimes." She kept her gaze level with his as she repeatedly bashed the oblong piece of metal with her doubled fist. "When it's... most...inconvenient."

The policeman did not seem to be amused. With a sigh that fell somewhere between impatience and resignation, he surveyed Sarah intently, one hand settled on an intriguingly trim hip, the other placed menacingly on the butt of his gun. It was a position she duly noted, and she couldn't help herself when she held up her hands in a gesture of surrender that was only half-joking.

"The registration is in there, I swear it," she told him. "I just can't get the stupid door open." After a moment's pause, she added hopefully, "Maybe...maybe you could give it a shot?"

"Lady, I—"

He stopped speaking as quickly as he'd started, sighed deeply again, then shook his head as if he couldn't believe what was happening to him. For the first time, Sarah noticed the name tag pinned to his shirt above his badge. Lawless, it said. She wondered if that was indeed his name, or some kind of dubious honor the department had bestowed upon him.

"Your name is Lawless?" she asked before she could

stop herself, unable to halt the smile she felt forming. "A cop named Lawless?"

"Yeah," he replied wearily.

His tone assured her he had been through this before and did not intend to go through it again with her. Sarah chose not to pursue the subject and instead worried her lower lip with her teeth. Out of nowhere, she wondered what color his eyes were behind the dark glasses. Probably black, just like everything else about him, she thought. Gingerly she extended her license toward him in silence, but Officer Lawless didn't take it right away. He only continued to stare at her in that maddeningly accusatory manner.

"I'd give you the registration, too, but I can't get the glove compartment open," she reminded him.

The policeman drew in a deep breath. "Unlock the passenger-side door," he told her. She got the feeling his statement was pulled from him reluctantly.

As he made his way around the front of the car to the other side, Sarah could have sworn he was mumbling to himself. He jerked open the door opposite her, bent forward and struggled with the glove compartment in much the same way she had done only moments earlier.

"See?" she said, not quite able to keep herself from gloating. "I told you so."

Officer Lawless glared at her. At least, Sarah thought he was glaring. It was hard to tell with those dark glasses hiding his eyes. No matter what, though, she could sense without a doubt that he was getting pretty steamed.

He folded himself into the car seat beside her, and suddenly the little vehicle seemed microscopic. She hadn't really noticed how big the policeman was when he was standing outside her window. Everyone seemed tall when one was sitting—especially when one was sitting in a Volkswagen Beetle. But now Officer Lawless was sitting, too, and he still seemed to tower over her. In the close confines of the car, with the sun beating through the windshield, she could feel the heat radiating off his body in enticing waves. His black leather boot creaked when he pulled one foot inside the car for leverage, and she noted almost absently the silver handcuffs shoved beneath his belt.

An odd thrill of excitement wound through her as she envisioned herself sharing an activity with Officer Lawless for which those handcuffs were never intended.

Sarah marveled at the waywardness of her thoughts, feeling her skin heat all over as she tried unsuccessfully to push the graphic image away. Clearly she had been too long without the attentions of a man, she thought. Or maybe she just wasn't getting enough calcium. She'd been reading about that lately.

As she pondered the curiousness of her uncharacteristic fantasy, Officer Lawless gave the glove compartment one final thump with the heel of his hand, and the door sprang open. Her delight with his success was quickly compounded by her embarrassment when the entire contents spilled out into his lap. Amid the occasional necessities like maps, flashlight and tissues, there fell a seemingly endless cascade of ketchup and soy sauce packets, abstract Lego creations, socks, GI Joe action figures, lipsticks and mismatched earrings.

Sarah grabbed up one of those last items. "Well, would you look at that?" she asked no one in particular. "I've been searching all over for this." She clipped the earring into place and shook her hair back so that she could inspect the effect in the rearview mirror. "What else is in there?" she added as she spared a glance at Officer Lawless's lap.

Why did no one carry gloves in their glove compartment? she wondered idly as her gaze picked absently through the assortment of stuff that had spilled. Her eyes finally settled on a perfectly square, foil-wrapped packet that had fallen into a *very* significant place on the policeman. A condom?

she gasped inwardly. Heavens, where had that come from? It must be one of Michael's. But she and Michael had been divorced for more than three years. Just how long had it been since she had cleaned out the glove compartment?

Sarah started to reach for the item in question, until Officer Lawless seemed to realize where she was headed and intercepted her hand before it made contact with its target. He gripped her wrist fiercely with one hand sheathed in black leather and scooped up the condom with the other. Lifting it to eye level, he turned his attention to her more fully, then cocked his left eyebrow with much interest.

"I—it must belong to my husband," she stammered. "I mean…he's not my husband, but…"

Officer Lawless's right eyebrow joined his left.

"I mean…uh…" Oh, dear. Just what did she mean?

"Never mind," Officer Lawless said. He dropped the condom into the glove compartment and began to gather up the remaining contents and return them to their original resting place.

Griffin Lawless couldn't believe this was happening to him. He picked gingerly through the assortment of odds and ends on his lap as if they were radioactive, all the while wondering what kind of person would drive around with so many unnecessary accoutrements. He stared at the woman beside him as he tried to figure her out. He had noticed the moment he'd sat down in her car that she smelled wonderful, a strangely floral fragrance he found incongruent with her ragged jeans and T-shirt. Her hair was a riot of blond curls falling over her forehead and spilling down around her ears, and her brown eyes were as dark and guileless as a beagle puppy's.

Absently he realized his fingers still encircled her wrist, and he glanced down at her hand. Strong-looking, raw-boned, with nails bitten down to the quick and Band-Aids on her index and ring fingers. Probably because she had hangnails, he thought. He released her then, and watched as she anxiously brushed her hair behind one ear. Still wearing the one long, dangling earring, she looked, for some reason, like an abandoned street waif.

Griffin frowned. He did not care for women like her—women who had no concern for their appearance, no control over their nerves. This was just what he needed after the kind of day he'd already had. One more bizarre encounter in a string of bizarre encounters. The condom had been an interesting touch, though. She didn't seem the type to carry something like that around. And who was this guy who was, then wasn't, her husband?

He was still wondering about that when he realized the woman beside him had started helping to collect her things and put them back in the glove compartment. Nimble fingers skimmed over his thighs in a way that made Griffin hold his breath and swallow hard. She seemed to have no idea of the possible implication behind her activity. When her fingers began to travel a little higher than they should, he jumped up and struggled to get out of the car, spilling the few items left in his lap onto the floor and bumping his head severely. Fortunately he was still wearing his helmet. That didn't help him, however, when he slammed the car door shut and caught the end of his finger in the process.

''Ow, dammit,'' he cursed as he cradled his injured hand in his good one.

He made his way back around the front of the car, eyeing the woman in the driver's seat suspiciously. Some college kid, he guessed. She gazed back at him steadily, but looked plenty worried. Which of course was fine with him. Why should she be comfortable when he was feeling so agitated himself?

When Griffin stood beside the driver's-side window once again, he squared his shoulders resolutely, flexed the fingers of his injured hand and stated, as if the past several minutes had never occurred, "License and registration."

The woman beside him smiled nervously again, then reached across the seat and began to pick through the glove compartment. He watched her intently, assuring himself his interest was only idle curiosity. The way her yellow T-shirt strained against her back let him know she wasn't wearing a brassiere, and his eyes lingered at the waistband of her faded blue jeans before dipping lower to inspect the slight flare of her hips. She was a little slim by his standards, but not too bad. He was still considering that fact when she turned back around and caught him ogling her, and her triumphant expression at having found her registration quickly turned sour.

"See anything you like?" she snapped.

Griffin reached for the registration without comment, then extended his hand for her license, as well. The woman slapped it into his palm silently, her eyes flashing with a combative fire.

After he'd scanned both documents, he asked, "Ms. Greenleaf, do you realize how fast you were going back there?"

"About thirty-five?" she asked hopefully.

"Try forty-five."

She shook her head vehemently. "There's no way I could have been going that fast. I—"

"Forty-five in a school zone," he clarified further.

"A school zone? That's not a school zone. Not now, anyway. Not at noon."

"Yes, ma'am, at noon. A lot of those kids go home for lunch."

Well, this was the first Sarah had ever heard of that. Of course, she didn't normally drive this way when she was meeting her brother for lunch, but since she'd been running so late, she had opted to try for a shortcut. She was about to explain that to him, but Officer Lawless had disappeared with her identification, and she realized belatedly he had returned to his motorcycle, presumably to run a check on her. The thought that he could be so suspicious of her character insulted Sarah as much as anything else he'd said, and she fumed silently as she awaited his return.

"Officer, I can explain," she said when the policeman stood beside her window once again.

He said nothing in reply, but cocked his left brow in that curious way again. The gesture, along with his silence, indicated to Sarah that he was at least willing to listen.

"I was running late for an appointment," she began.

She could tell immediately that she'd lost him with that. No doubt he'd been hoping for something really creative and juicy—that she was being followed by body-snatching pea pods from outer space, or was on her way to meet Elvis, who had been spotted working as a pastry chef at the local thrift bakery. Officer Lawless dropped his gaze back to her license and registration, then pulled a ticket book from nowhere and began to write.

"No, really," she said, trying again. "I was supposed to meet my brother, Wally, twenty minutes ago, and he hates to be kept waiting. Actually, he's kind of a jerk, but it's only because he's so insecure. If I told him that, though, he'd go through the roof. Besides, I'm always late when I'm supposed to meet my brother. I suppose that's psychologically significant, but, then, how many brothers and sisters get along, you know? Of course, Wally would probably blame my always being late on the fact that my parents divorced sixteen years ago, and then he'd ask me if I ever called that analyst he recommended, and I just don't want to get into that with him again...."

Sarah's voice trailed off when she realized how hysterical she was beginning to sound. Honestly, the moment she got nervous, she always started running off at the mouth like nobody's business. When she saw that Officer Lawless was no longer listening, she tried a new tack.

"Would you believe I was being followed by aliens?"

His pen paused about halfway down the page on which he was writing, but he didn't look up.

"Or that I was on my way to meet...? Oh, never mind."

The pen began to scratch back and forth again.

Sarah sighed. This was just what she needed. She couldn't afford to be late meeting Wally. She couldn't afford another one of his long-winded monologues about how badly she'd screwed up her life since her divorce. Most of all, she decided further when Officer Lawless stuck the ticket book and pen under her nose with a silent demand for her signature, she couldn't afford a seventy-five-dollar speeding ticket.

"Seventy-five dollars?" she cried when she saw the total.

Officer Lawless remained his usual stoic self as he nodded. Sarah felt moisture forming under her arms and between her breasts, noted that he still seemed as cool and collected as ever, and wondered what it would take to make him break into a really good sweat.

"Yes, ma'am. Seventy-five dollars is the fine for going twenty miles an hour over the speed limit in a school zone."

"But I told you I wasn't going forty-five."

"And I told you that you were."

Sarah narrowed her eyes at him fitfully. This was not going well—not well at all. She'd always had a problem with authority figures, ever since she'd been sent to the principal's office in first grade for throwing spitballs at Bobby Burgess, even though Bobby had started it. That was probably what had gone wrong with her marriage. Not that she threw spitballs, of course, but that her ex-husband had always pulled an authoritative routine that had nearly driven her mad.

"Well, I can't afford seventy-five dollars," she told Officer Lawless, handing back the ticket and pen without signing, as if in refusing her signature, she would no longer be responsible for her transgression. "Sorry."

But instead of taking the ticket back, Officer Lawless only continued to stare at her. "You could always opt for traffic school," he suggested.

"Traffic school," Sarah repeated. "I've heard about that. Isn't that where they put you in a dark room and show you that gory, horrible film about reckless driving, with children getting decapitated and animals being run down mercilessly until there's nothing left of them but an oily spot on the road?" She thought for a moment. "Or do the animals get decapitated and the children get run down...? Well, anyway, thanks, but I can see that stuff at my local cinema at my own convenience. I don't think I want to go to traffic school."

She noticed a slight twitch in Officer Lawless's jaw before he set his teeth more completely on edge. He bent forward until his face filled the driver's-side window, and suddenly Sarah wondered what madness had overcome her to make her spar with him in the first place.

"Well, then, Ms. Greenleaf," he said in a low, level, utterly dangerous voice, "in that case, I could take you downtown in handcuffs right now and tell everyone you resisted arrest."

Sarah opened her mouth to argue, decided quickly that such a reaction would get her nowhere—except maybe booked into a suite at the Hoosegow Hilton—then scrawled her name illegibly on the ticket beside the place where Officer Lawless had so thoughtfully provided her with an *X* to mark the spot.

"I'm going to argue with the judge over this, you know," she assured her tormentor as she handed the ticket book back to him.

Officer Lawless smiled for the first time as he tore off her copy of the ticket, and Sarah became furious with herself that she found his smile so appealing.

"Well, then, Ms. Greenleaf," he said as he dropped the ticket through the window and into her lap, "I look forward to seeing you in court. Have a nice day."

Only after he'd turned and walked casually back to his motorcycle did Sarah bravely whisper the word *Pig*. She watched in her rearview mirror as he straddled his big motorcycle and shoved back the kickstand with his boot, throttled the machine to a rousing roar, then sped off past her, spewing gravel in his wake.

Sarah wadded up the ticket and stuffed it into her purse, grumbling about fascism and police states, ill-tempered brothers and men in general, then urged her own little car to sputtering life. She was not having a nice day. Worse than that, she knew it wasn't going to get better anytime soon.

Late that Friday afternoon found Griffin Lawless sitting on a bench in the locker room at the police station, staring thoughtfully into his locker. Man, it had been a bitch of a week. Vaguely he noted the calendar taped to the inside of the scarred metal door, a collection of dates that seemed meaningless now somehow. He had a dentist's appointment next Thursday...a date with that new redhead in homicide tomorrow evening...that Cub Scout career-night thing on Monday.

His eyes wandered over all these appointments until his gaze fell on one date marked in bright-red ink, circled five times for effect. His great-grandfather's ninety-fifth birthday would have been next Friday. It was the day Griffin was to have met the old man for the first time. Now he never would. Because his great-grandfather had never made it back to the States from wintering in New Zealand, and now the old man's body was resting quietly at sea.

An attorney had telephoned last week with the news of Harold Mercer's death, and to confirm that Griffin Lawless was the sole living relative and heir to the Mercer holdings. It was strange to think now, that the family name so famous for wealth and refinement around the suburban community of Clemente, Ohio, would turn out to be Griffin's own. He'd grown up knowing of the Mercers as everyone else in Clemente had, as the town's richest, most illustrious citizens. Who would have ever guessed that he was one of them?

He wadded up the black uniform shirt in his hands and stuffed it unceremoniously into a wrinkled duffel bag. The boots came off next, falling to the floor with a slow *thump...thump,* then Griffin pushed himself up from the bench with a ragged groan to remove his black jodhpurs. He rotated his left shoulder to alleviate the stiffness still present from his wound, then headed for the showers.

He leaned into the swirls of steam that rose around him, letting the moist heat rush into his pores and sore muscles, easing the tension that resulted from a combination of many things—the remnants of pain from a gunshot wound that was scarcely two months healed; the frustration of finding a family he never knew he had only to lose it again so quickly; the odd, sudden realization that life was passing so quickly, too quickly for him to stop and enjoy it for a while...

The lingering fragrance of flowers he couldn't quite dispel from his memory, a fragrance that brought with it the reminder of coffee brown eyes full of spirit, and blond curls that had seemed to beg him to touch.

Griffin pushed the memory away. He'd *ticketed* the woman, for God's sake, he reminded himself. Even if there was some obscure chance he might run into Ms. Sarah Greenleaf again, she wasn't likely to be receptive to any romantic overtures on his part. Still, he couldn't help but smile as he recalled the expression on her face when that condom had come tumbling out of the glove compartment along with a number of other personal belongings. He couldn't remember the last time he'd seen a human being blush with embarrassment. There weren't many people left who felt such a thing anymore.

"Griffin? You in here?"

He recognized the voice of his friend and co-worker Mitchell Stonestreet and called out, "In here, Stony."

Stony materialized through the rolling white fog, dressed in his nondescript plainclothes detective wear, his white-blond hair scarcely visible amid all the steam. His impenetrable black eyes were as piercing as ever, though, and Griffin marveled at the way they made an otherwise innocent-looking man seem utterly menacing.

"Got good news for you, pal," Stony said, holding up a white, legal-size envelope. "Captain Pierce sent me down with this for you. Your orders came through. They're bumping you upstairs. Fraud squad. Although why you'd want to hang out with us bunco guys is beyond me. You could have taken homicide or vice. What's wrong with those? Not enough man for them?"

Still naked and dripping wet—very comfortable with his masculinity, thank you very much—Griffin strode toward his friend and took the proffered envelope, running damp fingers under the flap. The paper he withdrew was engraved with the Clemente, Ohio, P.D. letterhead and quickly grew limp in the humid air. Nonetheless, the words it contained were precisely the ones he wanted to read, and he smiled.

"Homicide's a bit too grim for my tastes," he said. "And those vice guys are lunatics. But fraud... Now that's what I call a good time. Besides, Stony, I miss seeing your ugly mug every day now that you're gone from the cycle unit. Anyway, I put in for a transfer out of uniform almost two months ago. It's about damned time this came through."

He thrust the letter and envelope back toward his friend,

then returned to the shower head to rinse the remnants of soap from his body. When he was through, Stony tossed him a towel, and Griffin knotted it carelessly about his waist.

"There weren't any openings until now," Stony told him. "You're replacing Tommy Gundersen. His wife got some big promotion, and they're moving west." He smiled as he added, "You and me, Griff, we'll be partners again."

"Just like old times. I hope the department knows what they're doing."

Stony chuckled. "They want you to report for duty two weeks from Monday," he said as he followed Griffin back into the locker room. "Think you can stay out of trouble on your bike until then?"

Griffin nodded impatiently. "Yeah, yeah. I'll do my best."

"No more trying to shoot it out with the bad guys one-on-one?"

Griffin scowled as he rubbed unconsciously at his shoulder again. The skin was still pink, puckered and raw-looking on both his chest and back where the entry and exit wounds had healed. "No worries there. I hope I never have to look down the barrel of a gun again. Why do you think I put in for a transfer? Uniform duty is getting too dangerous."

Stony looked at his friend doubtfully. "Too dangerous? Did I hear you correctly? This from a man who vacations in the desert just so he can go night biking without a headlight?"

Griffin smiled grimly. "Nobody shoots at me in the desert. Too many things can happen out on the streets. I want to live long enough to enjoy my retirement."

He held up a hand when Stony appeared ready to object. He knew what his friend was going to say. What was the point of retiring when he had nothing to retire to? Unfortunately Griffin couldn't quite contradict that line of thinking. Both his parents were dead, and he had no other family.

Not anymore, anyway, he amended reluctantly, recalling his great-grandfather's death. He was a thirty-seven-year-old man who had very little to show for his time on Earth and no big plans in the making. Why start thinking about the future now?

Griffin tucked his black T-shirt into well-worn jeans, shoved his feet into low-heeled boots and threw his duffel bag over one shoulder before allowing himself to form an answer to his question. And the answer that finally came wasn't one that sat well with him. He was starting to think about the future now because, for some reason, lately he'd been able to think of little else.

"You got plans tonight?" he asked his friend as he collected his nondepartment-issue motorcycle helmet from the top shelf of his locker.

Stony shook his head. "Elaine's not speaking to me this weekend."

Griffin made a face. "Again? What did you do this time?"

Stony sighed with much confusion. "I have no idea."

Griffin smiled as he slammed his locker door shut. "The usual, then, huh? Want to grab a bite?"

"Sure. Why not?"

The two men chatted as Stony gathered his things, then they filed out of the locker room and into the balmy spring evening.

"You know," Stony began as they paused beside Griffin's sleek, dark Harley Davidson, "maybe you can help me figure out the feminine mystique. You've had more than your share of experience coping with it."

"Yeah, 'coping' is the appropriate word, too." Griffin donned his helmet and straddled the big machine. "And believe me, I don't understand women any better than you do. So, meet you at Delgado's?"

Stony nodded. "Whoever gets there first buys the first round."

Griffin nodded back, then slammed his foot down on the pedal, bringing the bike to roaring life. For some reason, the motion reminded him of the woman he'd encountered earlier in the afternoon, the one who had glared at him from her rearview mirror and silently mouthed the word *Pig*. He smiled when he recalled that. She probably didn't realize he'd been able to see the comment she'd made. He wondered what she would have done if he'd returned to her car, yanked her out for arrest and given her a thorough body search.

Griffin's smile broadened. She probably would have pressed charges of police brutality and sexual harassment and landed his butt in the can. Still, he thought further, remembering the smooth expanse of back beneath her yellow T-shirt, a few years in the pokey might be worth it.

Chuckling to himself, Griffin Lawless slipped his sunglasses on, urged the throttle forward and sped away. Ms. Sarah Greenleaf would just be a memory from now on, and there was no reason for him to dwell on her anymore.

Still, he thought, she had smelled wonderful. And he didn't think he'd seen anyone with eyes that brown before. He wondered if her hair was as soft as it had looked....

Chapter 2

"So how was lunch with your brother on Friday?"

Sarah looked up from icing a lopsided chocolate cake to throw her friend Elaine Bingham a grim look. "Same as always. Wally just can't understand why I'm not as wildly ambitious and successful as he is. He's convinced I ruined my life when I divorced Michael."

"Well, tell him to lay off," Elaine said. "Just because he's a contractor doesn't mean he can run everything, especially your life."

Sarah nodded her agreement, wishing it were that simple. "All in all, though, I guess lunch was no worse than usual. Certainly no worse than what I experienced on the way."

Three days had passed since she had signed her name to a speeding ticket she was still certain she didn't deserve, but the passage of time had done nothing to improve a dark mood that had followed Sarah all weekend. Every time she remembered Officer Lawless in all his black glory, her back went up like a startled cat's. She didn't know why he continued to raise her hackles so long after the fact, or why she couldn't stop thinking about him, and her confusion at her behavior only enhanced the tension she felt. Now as she prepared for her house to be invaded by fifteen little Cub Scouts, she could only shake her head in wonder at her odd reaction.

"What happened before lunch?" Elaine asked from the dining room, where she was setting out paper cups and plates.

Sarah bit her lip as she tried to even out a big lump at the center of the cake. She never had been much of a cook. She was an even worse baker. "I got a speeding ticket," she said.

Elaine's expression was incredulous when she returned to the tiny kitchen from the dining room. At one time, Sarah had thought her kitchen huge. Of course, that was back when she and Michael had moved into the four-bedroom Cape Cod from a two-room apartment with a kitchen the size of a closet. Nowadays, amid all the clutter, even painting every visible surface in her kitchen white had done little to create an impression of size. And with Elaine looming in the doorway, Sarah felt the space grow even smaller.

"*You* got a speeding ticket?" her friend asked. "In that dinky car of yours? That thing doesn't go faster than ten or fifteen miles an hour, does it?"

"Very funny," Sarah said, swiping a finger across her cheek. "I don't want to talk about it."

Elaine shrugged and went back to her task. "Okay, fine. By the way, although it's really too late to be asking, you did get your four guys lined up for tonight, didn't you?"

"Yes, I got my four guys lined up for tonight," Sarah replied obediently. "And I think I did pretty well. I have an accountant, a claims adjuster, a computer programmer and a mortician."

Elaine came back into the kitchen and wrinkled her nose.

"Sarah, we're having career day for a den of Cub Scouts, for God's sake. What are those guys going to talk about with a bunch of little kids?"

Sarah lifted her chin defiantly. "They all have perfectly lucrative jobs. Jobs that will definitely be in demand in the future, I might add."

She couldn't help but feel a little defensive. She thought she'd done pretty well, considering the fact that she didn't know that many men to begin with. And it hadn't been easy to get these guys lined up for the meeting tonight. She was going to have to go out with two of them. "What kind of guys did you get?" she asked Elaine.

The other woman beamed, shook back her long, dark hair and smoothed a graceful hand over the widow's peak that Sarah so envied. "I got an air-force fighter pilot, a baseball player—from Cincinnati, no less—a fireman and a cop."

"A cop?" Sarah sneered.

Elaine laughed. "Well, if I'd known you were going to have a run-in with the law..."

"Ha, ha."

"Anyway, Jonah is really looking forward to tonight, and I'm sure the other boys are, too."

Sarah smiled, her defensiveness fading as she thought of her own sons. "Yeah, Jack and Sam can't wait to see what we have planned. How on earth did you manage to draw guys from such glamorous fields? I mean, come on, Elaine, a baseball player? A Cincinnati Red?"

Elaine threw her a self-satisfied smile. "Oh, I just called a few numbers in my little black book."

Sarah shook her head. "You and that little black book. I'm going to have to sneak a peek inside one of these days."

"Hey, I've offered to set you up," her friend reminded her. "Remember? There was that guy from the circus who was dying to meet you."

"The human cannonball? No, thanks. Life with Michael

was explosive enough. I want some nice, sedate, normal guy. No adventurous types.''

''Mm-hmm,'' Elaine remarked. ''Like an accountant, maybe? Or a claims adjuster? Or a mortician?''

Sarah nodded. ''Yeah, maybe. What's so terrible about being involved with a quiet man?''

''Nothing—if you don't mind being bored to death,'' Elaine rejoined.

''I refuse to get into this with you,'' Sarah said as she surrendered to the cake. It would just have to remain lopsided. ''You're a woman who thinks bungee jumping is a passive sport.''

''Well, it is.''

Sarah couldn't help but laugh. In many ways, the two women were very different people. Elaine was tall and well rounded in all the places women were supposed to be, her black hair spilling in a straight cascade to the middle of her back, streaked with silver as if touched by a fairy's paintbrush. Her gray eyes reflected an adventurousness and passion for life that Sarah wasn't quite sure she could claim herself, as much as she might like to.

Sarah Greenleaf and Elaine Bingham had become fast friends nearly two years ago when they'd met as room mothers for their children's class. Back then, Elaine had been enrolling her son, Jonah, in the same first-grade class as Sarah's twins. Six months ago, about the same time the two women had bought an antique business together, the three boys had joined the same Cub Scout den. When asked if they'd be interested in sharing den mother duties, Sarah and Elaine had resoundingly replied yes. Nowadays, the three boys together were more like brothers than close friends, having forged a bond as immediate and as strong as the two women's had become.

Like Sarah, Elaine was also divorced, and in addition to sharing the business and the Scouting duties, the two mothers also found themselves frequently trading off baby-sitting and dinner patrol, thus allowing themselves the occasional free time where they might not have it at all otherwise. All in all, their friendship had become as efficient a working system as their antique business was gradually becoming.

"Oh, gosh," Elaine said suddenly as she opened the freezer door to retrieve the ice trays. "I almost forgot to tell you."

Sarah put a cover over the offending chocolate cake so she wouldn't have to look at it until later, then brushed her hands off on her shirttail. "What?"

The other woman's smile was huge. "We have an appraisal job. One of the guys who's coming tonight—the cop—recently inherited his great-grandfather's house here in Clemente, along with everything in it, and he wants us to catalogue and appraise the collection."

"*Us?*" Sarah asked, unable to mask her surprise.

Elaine made a face. "Of course us. Why not us?"

It was a fair question, Sarah thought. "Well, because our shop just opened last year, that's why. We still don't have all the bugs worked out of the system. Let's face it, Harper's Antiques has been a Clemente fixture for decades. They usually get all the good jobs. Why would this guy hire us?"

Elaine's eyes sparkled. "Maybe because I quoted him a price that's half what Harper's charges for an appraisal."

"Ah. Good reason."

"Plus," she added a little reluctantly, "he's a good friend of Stony's, so it's kind of a personal favor."

Sarah narrowed her eyes at her friend. "I thought you and Stony were on the outs right now." She'd only met the man in question once, but he seemed nice enough. Still, he and Elaine seemed to have their share of tiffs.

Elaine shrugged. "Outs, ins, ups, downs... Everyday brings something different. But getting the appraisal isn't the best part," she said, rushing on before Sarah could comment further.

She smiled, her friend's good humor infectious. "What's the best part?"

"Wait until you hear what house the guy inherited."

"What house?"

"The old Mercer place."

Sarah's eyes widened as she whistled low. "Wow. I'd give my eyeteeth to get a load of that old mansion up close."

The Mercer place had lain vacant for years, but Sarah remembered that when she was a child growing up in Clemente, it had been occupied by a woman named Meredith Mercer, the unmarried daughter of Judge Harold Mercer, retired. The judge had spent most of his time in the Canary Islands or someplace, and when his daughter had died, single and childless, he'd simply closed up the house and it had sat dormant and unoccupied for years.

Sarah had never really given much thought to the place, except on those rare occasions when she drove by and gazed at it longingly, wondering what treasures were hidden beyond the front door. She supposed she had assumed it was tied up in probate somehow, and that someday the old house would either change hands or be torn down. Now it appeared as if the former would be the case. Apparently Judge Mercer had been the father of more than one child. And now it looked as if Sarah's dream of inspecting the Mercer treasures might just become a reality.

"Well, it seems you're going to have the opportunity to look inside without risking dental trauma," Elaine said, voicing Sarah's thoughts out loud, "because the guy who inherited the place signed a contract with us this afternoon."

"Just like that?"

Elaine nodded, her smile reflecting her utter delight. "Just like that."

Before Sarah could ponder her friend's assertion further, the back door slammed open, and in ran three streaks of blue, laughing and shrieking as they sped by in a hurried blur. As quickly as the tumult had erupted it disappeared, and the two women could only shake their heads in wonder as they stared in the direction into which the chaos had fled.

Sarah was the one who broke the silence. "If we could harness that energy, we could heat the entire northeastern United States for a hundred winters to come."

The three boys reappeared then, Jonah a mirror image of his mother with his black hair and silver gray eyes. Jack and Sam, on the other hand looked little like brothers, let alone twins. Jack was a repeat of his father, with unruly brown curls and eyes the color of amber, while Sam resembled Sarah with his pale blond hair and dark brown eyes.

"Mrs. Stevens just pulled up with Mark and Devon," Jack announced.

"When does the pilot get here?" Jonah demanded.

"Is the cop going to bring his gun?" Sam wanted to know.

Good heavens, Sarah thought. If Nellie Stevens was already here, the other boys would be right behind. Belatedly she realized she wasn't even close to finished with all she had to do before the meeting's commencement. She glanced over at her friend for help, but only sighed with frustration. Elaine looked professional and organized in her Scouting blues, but Sarah hadn't even changed her clothes yet, and her blues were of the more casual variety—well worn and ragged jeans coupled with an equally bedraggled and much oversize chambray shirt, now generously spotted with chocolate.

"Elaine? Can you handle these guys while I go change?"

"Sure," her friend told her.

As Sarah fled down the hall, she heard the other woman tell Sam, "Yes, the cop will bring his gun. All the men coming tonight are going to wear what they would normally wear to work, so that you boys can get a well-rounded view of their professions.''

The doorbell buzzed at the same time the back door rattled with another entry, and since Sarah was passing the living room, she automatically went to answer the door. Her first thought when she saw Officer Lawless standing on her front porch was that he had come to take her downtown and book her for some heinous crime like illegal use of a spatula or trying to pass off bad cakes as culinary creations. Then her gaze fixed with those same dark glasses that had so frustrated her attempts to gauge his reactions Friday, and she wondered once again what color his eyes were.

He was dressed exactly as he had been three days earlier, all black and leather. But now as Sarah stood face-to-face with the man, she noticed a few more things about him that she hadn't noticed before. With his helmet off, she realized his hair was short and razor straight, a realization that surprised her for some reason. Somehow he seemed the type to prefer long hair. Maybe short hair was a department rule. She also hadn't noticed Friday the way the muscles of his upper arms strained against the short sleeves of his shirt, or the dark hair that peeked up out of his open collar below the hollow of his throat. A few strands of silver mingled with the black of his mustache, and there was a scar on his chin that was too big to have resulted from a shaving accident. Somehow she was sure he had won the decoration in a fight, and such a certainty only made him seem that much more dangerous.

"Officer Lawless," she said before she could stop herself. "Was there something else I didn't do Friday that you forgot to cite me for?"

Instead of answering right away, Griffin took a single step backward and glanced up at the numbers above the front door. He frowned. Yeah, this was the right house all right. Dammit.

This was just what he needed. Another run-in with the intriguing, infuriating blonde who had haunted his thoughts all weekend. How the hell had he managed to end up here? He was doing this favor for a friend of Stony's because Stony had been assigned to duty tonight. And Stony's friend's name hadn't been Ms. Sarah Greenleaf. Griffin would have recognized that in an instant—and fled screaming in the other direction. So what was Sarah Greenleaf doing here?

She was every bit as enticing as he remembered, perhaps even more so when he considered what appeared to be a big glob of chocolate smeared across one cheek and more chocolate staining a good portion of her man-size shirt. She didn't look like the kind of den mother he'd had when he'd been a Cub Scout himself too many years ago to remember. Scouting had sure come a long way in three decades.

"Officer Lawless?" she asked him again. Only then did he realize he had yet to offer her some kind of greeting.

Before he could stop himself, Griffin reached out a hand and wiped the glob of chocolate off her cheek with his thumb, then pressed his thumb against his lips to suck the icing into his mouth. Her eyes widened in surprise at the intimate gesture, and he smiled.

"Could use a little more sugar and a little less salt," he said as he moved past her and into the house.

"Are you talking about the icing or about me?" he heard her ask from behind him.

Griffin spun around to meet her gaze levelly with his. "Oh, the icing is fine," he said without hesitation.

He could tell she was about to retaliate with something he was sure to find interesting, so he whipped off his sunglasses in order to get a clearer view of her pique. When he did so, her expression changed dramatically, and the mouth that had opened to voice a protest quickly snapped shut in concentration.

"Is there something wrong, Ms. Greenleaf?" he asked.

She shook her head slowly, but remained silent, staring at him in fascination, as if he'd just grown another head.

"What is it?" he insisted.

She took a tentative step forward, lifting a hand almost absently toward him. "Your eyes," she said softly as she came to a halt a few inches in front of him. "They're so..."

Her comment was, to say the least, the last thing he had expected to hear. Still, he encouraged her. "So...?"

She sighed, a sound that was restless and full of longing. "Blue," she replied quietly. "Your eyes are blue. For some reason, I thought they'd be dark, but they're not. They're..."

Her voice trailed off then, and Griffin was left wondering what else she had intended to say.

He felt an involuntary shudder wind through his body at the way Sarah Greenleaf was looking at him. For just the briefest of moments, her expression was completely open, utterly free of any ill will or pretense. And for that one stark moment, he saw in her eyes an absolute hunger like nothing he'd ever seen before. Her reaction made him feel more than a little uneasy, because he realized he was responding to her in exactly the same way. Sarah Greenleaf made him feel hungry, too. Hungry for something he couldn't quite identify, hungry for some unnameable something that he didn't until that moment realize he needed desperately in order to survive.

And then the moment was gone. Sarah returned to her earlier wariness, taking a step away from him again to close the front door.

"Excuse me," she said hastily, "I have to go change."

And as quickly as she had come into his life again, she was gone. Griffin felt strangely out of place in her home, noting his surroundings absently. The house looked like any number of other middle-class suburban homes he'd been inside in his line of work. The furnishings were big, boxy and functional, with a few personal touches in the form of plants, photographs and scattered toys. He should have realized right off that Ms. Greenleaf was married with children. Hadn't she mentioned a husband on Friday? He couldn't quite remember now. At any rate, a man would have to be crazy to come across her and let her get away.

Yet if that was the case, why had she thrown him such a longing look only a moment ago? Griffin wondered. Could it be that Mr. Greenleaf wasn't exactly adept at meeting all his wife's needs? Better yet, he wondered further, maybe her old man had taken a powder somewhere along the line.

"Whoa, who're you?"

The small voice came from behind Griffin, and he spun around to find five young boys staring at him in awe. He smiled. He knew what kind of imposing figure he appeared in uniform. Hell, being imposing had become one of his most effective weapons over the years. And knowing that adults reacted with some degree of fear, he could only imagine what a little kid might think of him. He didn't want to frighten a child, naturally, but he didn't mind if one was impressed. Too bad he'd been utterly ineffective in impressing the elusive Sarah Greenleaf to the same degree. Although, he thought further with a smile, maybe he wouldn't mind frightening her just a little. At least as much as she frightened him.

"I'm Officer Griffin Lawless," he introduced himself. "Clemente P.D. Motorcycle unit."

The tallest of the boys strode confidently forward, hand outstretched. "I'm Jack Markham. This is my little brother, Sam."

"I am not your little brother—I'm as old as you," Sam

said quickly, stepping forward with considerably less
aplomb than his brother.

"Nuh-uh, you are not," Jack contradicted him. "I came
fifteen minutes before you. Mom said so. I'm oldest."

"Are not."

"Are, too."

"Are not."

"Are, too."

"I'm Jonah," a third boy piped up while the other two
continued to disagree. "Jonah Bingham. You know my
mom."

"Elaine," Griffin said, recalling the name of Stony's on-
again, off-again lady friend, the one he seemed to be seeing
more of than women he normally dated.

"Right."

"So who do your two argumentative friends belong to?"
he asked, unable to prevent his smile at what he had de-
duced was an old argument between the twin boys.

"Those two are mine."

Griffin looked up to find that Sarah had rejoined the
group, and his smile broadened at the picture of efficiency
she presented in her Scouting outfit. He knew the last thing
that should seem erotic to him was a den mother's uniform,
but for some reason, her cool blue togs made his blood race.
The chocolate was gone from her face, and her riotous curls
had been brushed back and tamed by a simple leather head-
band. Yet the image of control and aloofness only made
Griffin want to turn her as inside out as he was feeling
himself.

Before he had a chance to comment further, the room
began to fill with people, and amid a flurry of introductions
and instructions to quiet down, the group was called to order. The rest of the evening passed in an atmosphere of
barely controlled chaos, until every man present had been
offered an opportunity to speak and answer questions about

his occupation. Then the group dispersed to enjoy refreshments and mingle a little more.

All in all, Griffin enjoyed himself immensely. Normally he had little reason to be around kids beyond the occasional police-department function, and he recalled now how much he generally liked children. He wondered, as he inevitably did when confronted by kids, what it would be like to have one or two of his own.

Not for the first time, he reflected on the fact that Sarah's two sons shared last names different from hers, and he couldn't help but feel optimistic. She must be divorced, he decided. Unless, of course, she had never taken her husband's last name to begin with. He had noted almost immediately the absence of a wedding ring on her left hand, and no telltale indentation that one had ever been worn. Still, some people didn't wear wedding rings, so her lack of one was no surefire indication that she was single.

Of course, he could just come right out and ask her about her marital status, he reminded himself. But she would no doubt interpret the question as a social interest on his part—which of course it was—and considering the fact that she was seventy-five dollars in the hole because of him, her reaction to his interest might not be as favorable as he'd like.

So instead Griffin contented himself by watching and wondering, and waiting for some cue from her. As the night began to draw to a close and he hadn't yet received one, he concluded he must have made a mistake earlier in the evening when she had studied him with such interest, and decided it might be best if he simply withdrew from the chase.

Until he looked up with the intention of telling her that it was time for him to go and saw her staring back at him with that strange, yearning expression a man would have to be a fool to misinterpret. She was as interested in him as he was in her. And Griffin decided then that there was no reason he had to leave just yet.

Sarah was nearly at her wit's end by the time the last mother left with the last child. Elaine offered to stay and help her clean up, but Sarah insisted she could manage on her own and sent her friend packing with Jonah. She wanted to be alone for a while, to contemplate her sanity and to wonder why on earth she had experienced such a major sexual awakening in the middle of a Cub Scout meeting.

All night long she had been unable to focus on anything except the way Officer Lawless's jodhpurs so lovingly fitted every hard plane of his lower body. It was criminal, really, how incredibly sexy that man looked in the uniform of a public servant. The only thing she had been able to think about all evening was what it would be like to indulge in raw, unbridled passion with him and his handcuffs. Lawless, indeed. No man had ever been named more appropriately.

As she tossed the last of the paper plates and cups in the trash, she listened vaguely to the sounds of her sons playing in Jack's room upstairs. That sound was followed by another, much closer—the whisper of creaking leather. Somehow it was a sound that didn't quite come as a surprise to Sarah. Somehow she had known Officer Lawless would still be in her house.

She turned to find him leaning oh-so-casually in the doorway between the kitchen and the dining room. He stood stock-still in all his cop regalia, eyeing her intently, his expression belying nothing of what he might be thinking. Sarah was still wondering how it would feel to lie naked and panting beneath him, and her breathing was a little shallow and ragged as a result.

"You're still here," she said quietly, her statement sounding silly in light of the obvious answer.

Yet it didn't prevent him from replying. "I hung back

from the others. I thought maybe I could help you straighten up."

Sarah shook her head. "That's okay. There's not that much. Thanks for offering, though."

Instead of interpreting her assurance and thanks as an indication that it was time for him to leave now, Officer Lawless took two measured strides into the kitchen, pausing by the table.

"How come your sons have a different last name than you?" he asked.

His question didn't seem as odd as she might have thought under different circumstances, so she replied without hesitation. "They have their father's last name."

He nodded thoughtfully, then took a few more steps forward, his boots scraping quietly across the tile as he approached her. "And why don't you have their father's last name?" he asked further.

Sarah swallowed with some difficulty. With every step he took toward her, her pulse quickened with dangerous speed. "I took back my maiden name when I got divorced," she told him, unable to break her gaze free from his as he drew nearer.

"So you're single?"

He had come to a stop a scarce inch in front of her. Sarah nodded mutely in reply, unable to get words past the lump that was fast forming in her throat.

When he reached toward her face, she instinctively began to draw back. He seemed to notice her skittishness, because he frowned. Yet still his hand came forward, until his fingers curled lightly over her throat and beneath her jaw.

"Officer Lawless," she began to object in a breathless whisper.

"Griffin," he corrected her.

"Griffin. I don't think—"

"I've never seen a woman so prone to getting food on

herself," he interrupted her, drawing his thumb over the corner of her mouth.

"What is it?" She tried once again to draw away.

But Griffin's touch followed her, until his thumb raked across her lower lip. "There, that's got it," he told her softly.

Before Sarah could reply, he was leaning forward, and then his mouth was pressed against hers, his lips rubbing gently over her own, the soft bristles of his mustache tickling her skin. At first she was too surprised to respond, and only stood before him, letting him kiss her. Then, when she realized what was happening, she did indeed react with a vengeance. Only instead of pushing him away, as her rational mind insisted she should do, her traitorous hands rose to clutch at his shirt, her fingers somehow finding their way to tangle in his hair.

And then Griffin responded, too, deepening the kiss until Sarah was pressed back against the kitchen counter, his legs insinuating themselves between her own, his pelvis pressing urgently against hers. The hand at her throat moved to cradle the back of her head, tilting it until he could slant his mouth more fully over hers. She felt another hand at her waist, then on her ribs, until finally his warm palm curved completely over her breast, rhythmically thumbing the peak to expectant life. Sarah groaned at the electrical explosions his touch set off on her skin, a sound that Griffin repeated as he tasted her more deeply.

For long moments, the two struggled to see who could consume the other fastest, neither certain where their passion had come from or where it would lead. Sarah had settled her hand on the buckle of Griffin's belt when she heard something thump loudly upstairs. Immediately she remembered her sons and, with one savage gesture, pushed Griffin away.

At first she was unable to speak, so stunned was she by

her behavior. All she could do was try to catch her breath and shake her head in silence, wishing more than anything in the world that she could turn back the clock five minutes and start all over again. But not because she wanted the outcome to be different, she realized to her dismay. Because she wanted to relive that kiss over and over again.

"Why...why did you do that?" she finally managed to whisper.

Griffin met her gaze levelly, his own breathing as ragged as hers. "Because you asked me to," he said.

Sarah shook her head in silent denial.

"You're doing it now, too," he told her. "Every time you look at me like that."

"But—"

"Mom! Jack hit me!"

"I did not!"

"You did, too!"

"Did not!"

"Did, too!"

Her sons' voices, raised in childish anger, awakened similar feelings in Sarah. She resented the way Griffin had so easily insinuated himself into her arms, was confused by her own willingness to let it happen and worried that she had so easily forgotten the presence of her children in the house. She was also angry as all get out that every nerve in her body was as aroused as hell thanks to Griffin Lawless. Consequently her words were edged with anger when she spoke.

"I think you'd better go."

"Have dinner with me tomorrow night."

Sarah wasn't sure what bothered her most—his ignoring her request that he leave; his stating, instead of asking, that she go out with him; or her own desperate desire to say yes.

"I can't," she told him.

"Why not?"

Not for the first time, she wished this night had never

happened. Drawing in a deep breath, she met Griffin's gaze levelly and said reluctantly, "Because I already have a date." Roger, her claims adjuster, had talked her into going to a movie with him in exchange for his appearance tonight.

Griffin's expression changed drastically at her statement. "Oh. I see," he said, pushing himself away from her.

Sarah knew she should be grateful for the distance he seemed suddenly willing to place between them, but instead she felt inexplicably cold, despite the warm spring breeze sifting through the open window. When she felt herself wanting to explain the situation to Griffin, to ask him if maybe he was free Wednesday night, instead, Sarah forced herself to keep the words in check.

This was a man who had cost her seventy-five bucks she couldn't afford, she reminded herself. A man who was self-confident to the point of arrogance, who probably never heard the word *no* from a woman. What kind of message would she be sending him if she just jumped into his arms three days after he'd ticketed her for a crime she hadn't even committed?

Pushing aside the realization that that was precisely what she had just done, Sarah repeated her earlier statement. "I think you'd better go."

Griffin nodded silently and turned to leave, but she could tell her announcement that she was seeing someone else didn't sit well with him. Still, it was probably better this way. Never in her life had a man caused her so much turmoil in such a short time. Getting involved with Griffin Lawless would be dumb, she assured herself. He was too sexy, too overpowering, too authoritative, too everything. What she needed was a quiet man, an unassuming man, a safe man. Like Roger, she thought blandly, waiting for even the slightest twinge of excitement the name might arouse.

Instead the only arousal that came was the one that hammered through her body as Sarah watched Griffin Lawless go out the door.

Chapter 3

"Your first assignment, Griff. Make us all proud."

Griffin glanced up at Stony, then down at the manila folder the other man had tossed onto his desk. He smiled. "No sweat. What is it?"

"A contracting company here in Clemente called Jerwal, Inc.," Stony told him. "We've had the owners under surveillance for about three months now. There's reason to believe they're running a scam on some local businesses and private citizens. Gundersen and I put a lot of time in on this. I don't want to see it wasted."

Griffin shrugged. "Like I said, no sweat."

Stony nodded. "Read over the file and let me know if you have any questions. It's all pretty self-explanatory stuff. They don't know we've been watching them, but it's only a matter of time before we go public with this. A couple of months at most."

Griffin opened the manila folder and began to scan the information contained inside. The moment he saw the names of the two men he would be investigating, his palms grew damp, and his assurance of "No sweat" suddenly betrayed him. One of the men was named Jerry Schmidt, an inconsequential name, as Griffin had never heard of the guy. But the other man's name was Wallace Greenleaf. And in a town the size of Clemente, it was a pretty safe bet that anyone who carried that last name would be somehow related to Sarah.

He recalled the long spiel she had offered in explanation when he'd pulled her over two weeks ago. Hadn't she said something about going to meet a brother? he thought. He closed his eyes, thinking hard, trying to remember if the brother's name had been Wallace. He didn't think so. Wally, maybe? Griffin's eyes snapped open. That was it. Wally. Terrific.

He threaded his fingers through his hair, leaned back in his chair and stared at the ceiling. Well, he hadn't exactly expected to be seeing Sarah again socially, anyway, had he? Considering the less-than-promising origins of their acquaintance, and the fact that she had made it clear that night in her kitchen that she wanted nothing more to do with him, and her assertion that she was seeing someone else, this added little setback shouldn't be of any concern. Hell, he hadn't seen her for two weeks. There was no point in wanting to get close to her, anyway, right?

Wrong, he immediately answered himself. Considering the fact that he had been able to think of little other than the way she had felt melting into him in her kitchen two weeks ago, he had every reason to want to get close to her again. As close as a man could get to a woman without being burned alive.

Great. This was just great, he thought. He looked down at the file again and began to read, all the while wondering how he was going to work this out. It wasn't as if he could avoid Sarah. He had hired her and Elaine, after all. The two women were already invading his great-grandfather's house to appraise its contents.

How was he supposed to keep his hands off of her, when all he wanted was to drown one more time in her warmth and softness? He was already having trouble sleeping at night. Now, faced with certainly seeing Sarah again and wanting to know her better, and armed with the knowledge that he was investigating her brother for something that, if proven, could land the guy with a serious stint in jail, Griffin felt a little...well, lousy.

It figured, he thought. Just his luck. He'd managed to land the job he wanted and meet the potential woman of his dreams in the same week, and now it looked as though one would cancel out the other. How was he supposed to salvage something out of all this?

As he began to read the file once again, Griffin shook his head hopelessly, absolutely certain he heard all the gods laughing at him.

The Mercer house smelled musty, old and empty when Sarah entered it late in the afternoon two weeks to the day after she and Elaine had signed an agreement with Griffin Lawless. He had given them a key when he'd hired them so that they could come into the house while he was at work and begin the long process of cataloging and appraising the huge assortment of antiques Judge Mercer and his daughter had collected over the years. So far, only Elaine had come to the house, to survey its contents and estimate the size of the project the two of them were about to undertake. Sarah would begin the appraisal the following day and had decided to stop by on her way home to get a feel for the place, instead of entering it cold in the morning. Still, she crossed the threshold now with more than a little trepidation.

One of the main things that had drawn Sarah and Elaine together two years ago was a common affection for antiques.

While Elaine's expertise lay in the area of furniture and jewelry, Sarah had always had an interest in and proficiency with serve ware—china, crystal, silver and linens. When the two women had pooled their meager resources to purchase the antique shop in the historic section of Clemente, they had been seizing upon an opportunity neither had ever thought she would see. The owner, looking to retire, had put the establishment up for sale lock, stock and barrel, and because of his anxiousness to sell and escape to the balmier climate of Orlando, had agreed to a price that was quite beneficial to the two women.

They had added quite a bit more to their stock by taking in auctions throughout the Midwest, and they currently boasted a nice assortment of pieces. And although Sarah and Elaine weren't getting rich off of their new acquisition by any stretch of the imagination, they were managing to make ends meet. They looked forward to the summer ahead, when tourism thrived in historic Clemente, and were banking that they could make it through the lean winter off their fat take in the summer.

Naturally, any jobs they might encounter as appraisers only added to the till, and their current contract with Griffin Lawless was a real plum. The publicity alone could potentially double their business. Better than that, though—at least for Sarah—was the fact that she was finally going to have an opportunity to become utterly involved with the pieces she was inspecting.

She had loved antiques for as long as she could remember. Unfortunately, being the daughter of good—and poor— country people on both sides of her family, there were no Greenleaf heirlooms to speak of save the occasional hat pin or doll. Buying the business with Elaine had been a dream come true, but sometimes it hurt like hell to part with the items they stocked in the shop.

Sarah was fascinated as much by the history of a piece

as by the skill used in creating it. And too often, pieces came and went too quickly for her to truly research their character and genesis. Certainly she knew quality when she saw it and could identify origins and manufacture, but she was seldom given the chance to trace an item back to its original owner or the circumstances for its coming into being.

Now she had the opportunity to really delve into an entire collection, one that no doubt spanned centuries. She could scarcely wait to get started.

"Hello?" she called out experimentally, unsure why she was bothering. Elaine had already told her there probably wouldn't be anyone home.

Griffin, she'd said, had offered no indication that he intended to move into the old house, nor had he bothered to be present when Elaine had come by the first time. The entire appraisal would take months, perhaps as long as a year, depending on the items in question. By trading off times they would work at the Mercer house, the two women were still able to run the shop, but Sarah's duties also meant she would be tied to Griffin Lawless for some time.

She had tried not to think about the kiss they had shared in her kitchen two weeks ago. Tried and failed miserably. Every time she closed her eyes at night, all she could see were Griffin Lawless's blue eyes filled with longing as he drew nearer, and all she could feel was the mind-scrambling heat that had shot through her body the moment he'd touched his lips to hers.

"Hello?" she called out again, hoping she imagined the nervous trill in her voice. "Is anybody home?"

The front-door hinges creaked ominously as she closed the door behind her, and Sarah couldn't help but be reminded of any number of Gothic novels she'd read as a teenager. Novels in which young, naive women succumbed to the seductions of dangerously sexy men in old, menacing houses where they were kept locked away.

She pushed the thought aside. She was neither young nor naive, and the Mercer house was anything but menacing. Of course, Griffin Lawless was dangerously sexy and appallingly seductive, but Sarah could handle herself there.

Hah! a little voice inside piped up unbidden.

Ignoring the little voice, she squared her shoulders resolutely, smoothed a few nonexistent wrinkles out of her sleeveless beige front-button sheath and strode forcefully into the house, hoping she exuded more confidence than she felt. The late-afternoon sun, slanting through windows that lined the wall above the front door, threw long beams of golden light across the entry hall. It reflected off scattering motes of dust as if fairies danced within. Dark wood paneling soared up twenty feet above Sarah in the entry hall, and a richly colored, very old Persian carpet cushioned her feet below. The house was every bit as beautiful as she had hoped it would be, and the thought of exploring its treasures made Sarah's blood race warm and lively.

To the left of the entry hall was a huge living room, while to the right was what appeared to be a sitting room or parlor. Between the two rooms, a wide staircase swept upward, separating into two sections that led to the second-floor gallery. Beside the stairs on the first floor, a long, mahogany-paneled hallway beckoned, so Sarah walked forward, her flat-heeled pumps echoing the leisurely pace of her footsteps.

The hallway ended in two French doors that were closed. Naturally curious, she reached for the brass handle of one and pushed it downward. The latch gave easily, and the door opened inward, almost of its own free will. The sweet scent of old books assailed Sarah then, and she smiled. A library. How wonderful.

The library was a repeat of the rest of the house—dark

paneling, high ceilings, exquisite furnishings. She was
standing in the center of the room, when she detected another aroma—that of a rich, expensive cigar. Her ex-
husband had smoked them occasionally, and Sarah had always loved the fragrance. It was one of the few nice
memories she carried of her marriage.

"So, Ms. Greenleaf, you've come at last."

She whipped around in panic at the masculine voice, even
though she recognized it very well. Griffin Lawless sat in a
leather-bound chair near the fireplace, looking very incon-
gruous in the formal room. He wore extremely faded blue
jeans, ripped across one knee, and a white, vee-neck T-shirt
stretched taut over his muscular abdomen. He affectionately
rolled a cigar between the thumb and index finger of one
hand, while the other cradled a delicate crystal snifter of
brandy. Sarah's heart hammered double-time at the picture
he presented. She'd never seen a more striking man.

"I-I'm sorry," she stammered. "I would have knocked,
but I, uh, I didn't realize anyone was here."

"No doubt," he quickly replied. "Had you realized I was
here, you probably never would have come in."

Assuring herself that he was completely wrong, she said,
"I won't be long. I was actually on my way home from the
shop, but I wanted to come in and have a look around before
I begin cataloging tomorrow."

Griffin nodded but said nothing in reply. His eyes never
left hers as he placed the cigar in his mouth and inhaled
deeply, holding the smoke in his lungs for several long moments before exhaling it in a slow spiral of white. Then,
still watching her, he lifted his brandy to his lips for an idle
sip, again swirling the liquor in his mouth to savor it before
swallowing. The knowledge that he took such pleasure in
sensual stimulation made Sarah's head spin, and she swallowed in vain to alleviate the dryness in her mouth.

"Drink?" he asked, lifting his glass in invitation, apparently noting her preoccupation.

She shook her head. "No, thanks. I haven't eaten since this morning, and it would go straight to my head."

Griffin wasn't sure that was such a bad thing, but he said nothing in reply. The thought of being present when Sarah Greenleaf lost control was oddly appealing. Why had this woman so thoroughly unsettled him? he wondered. Why did her face seem to be indelibly imprinted at the front of his brain? And why, dammit, could he think of little else other than the way her body had responded to his touch two weeks ago?

"So you'll be coming to the house, after all," he said. "I was beginning to think you were trying to avoid me."

"Me?" Sarah chirped with a high-pitched, anxious chuckle, diverting her gaze from his. "Why would I be avoiding you?"

Her nervousness was almost a palpable thing. Griffin smiled. "Because you've been thinking as much as I have about the manner in which we parted ways a couple of weeks ago."

Her eyes snapped to his again, and she inhaled deeply, the gesture making her breasts strain against the thin fabric covering them. His fingers twitched as he recalled the warm, soft flesh he had cupped briefly in his hand. Still clearly nervous, she began to fiddle with the top button of her dress, and his gaze fixed on the movement.

"I don't know what you mean," she said softly.

He placed the smoking cigar in a crystal ashtray on a side table, then set the snifter of brandy beside it and stood. Sarah took a giant step backward as he did so, so Griffin took a few giant steps forward to close the distance between them. His hand covered the one she had hooked into her buttonhole, while his other crept around her waist to press insistently at the small of her back until she was in his arms again. Then he kissed her, long and hard and deep, pulling back only when she uttered a soft sigh of surrender.

"Now do you remember?" he asked, his voice rough and ragged as he tried to tamp down his desire.

Sarah's breathing was a little raspy, but she managed to whisper, "Yes, I think it's coming back to me now."

He slanted his mouth over hers again, and she was lost in the smoky flavor of cognac and the sweet fragrance of tobacco that clung to him. Once again she felt the odd brush of his mustache above her lips and she tilted her head some to enjoy the full effect of his kiss. The hand covering hers loosened the button from her grasp and reached for the one below it, slipping the flat disk through the buttonhole before moving lower. When she realized Griffin had every intention of undressing her right there, Sarah finally managed to pull away, gripping his upper arms fiercely with her fingers as she held him at arm's length.

The fact that he allowed her to do so was simply a symbolic gesture, she knew. There was no way she was physically strong enough to hold him back. The muscles beneath her fingers were as hard and taut as bands of iron, the heat seeping from them into her flesh as searing as molten lava. For a long time she could only stare at him and fight for breath, and wonder how long this madness was going to last.

Griffin was too busy trying to gather his thoughts to wonder about anything for the moment. Sarah's dress gaped where he had managed to free three buttons, the champagne-colored lace of her camisole making him want to reach out and touch her again. Good God, what had come over him to start pawing at a woman he barely knew? He had to regain control of himself. This thing with Sarah Greenleaf was getting far too out of hand.

"Why do you do that?" she whispered after a moment.

"Why do you just step up and take whatever you want without asking first?"

He shook his head silently, having no idea how to answer.

She dropped her hands to her sides, then lifted one to shove a handful of curls off her forehead. "This…this *thing* between us has to come to a stop right now, before it goes any further than it already has."

"Why?"

She stared at him incredulously. "Why?" she repeated.

Griffin nodded. "Why?"

She emitted a sound of disbelief. "Well, because…"

That scrap of creamy lace beneath her dress still taunted him, so he slowly strode forward and extended a hand toward it. When Sarah didn't flinch or try to move away, he touched a fingertip to the third button. He could see her pulse thumping wildly in her throat, and more than anything he'd ever wanted in his life, he wanted to undo the rest of the buttons and spread her dress open wide as he urged her body to the floor. Instead, with no small effort, Griffin forced himself to loop the button back through its hole, then repeat the gesture for the other two. But he couldn't resist tracing his thumb over her pulse before he pulled his hand away.

"Again, Sarah," he murmured, "I ask you why?"

It was the first time he had spoken her first name, and the sound of it coming from his lips made Sarah's heart do funny things.

"Because I'm not the kind of person who does things like that," she finally said.

One corner of his mouth lifted beneath the black mustache, an action she supposed was something of a smile. "Oh, no?" he asked.

"No," she insisted. "I'm not. Not usually, anyway. Usually I'm an incredibly normal, middle-class, suburban, divorced mother of two, whose life consists of the most mun-

dane of tasks. Now, maybe I've been overextending myself
for the past few months, but I'm not stressed out enough to
do something totally crazy and self-destructive like get involved with a man like you.''

''A man like me,'' he repeated. His jaw twitched in a
barely perceptible way. ''And just what kind of man is
that?''

Sarah drew in a deep breath and shook her head slowly.
''Look, never mind. I should go.''

She turned to leave, but Griffin's voice halted her.

''Don't,'' he said quietly. ''Don't go yet. It's kind of
nice...'' His voice trailed off, and he didn't complete his
statement.

''What?'' Sarah asked as she pivoted slowly around
again.

''It's kind of nice having someone else here for a
change.'' He rubbed the back of his neck restlessly and
surveyed the big room. ''This house is so empty. So lonely.
As beautiful as this place is, I don't feel I belong here. I
don't know that I'll ever be able to call this place home. It
just doesn't feel like me.''

Sarah's gaze followed his. As much as she hated to admit
it, he didn't exactly look like the lord of the manor in his
ragged jeans and T-shirt. He did, however, exude a raw
power and confidence that commanded attention, something
she was sure was a direct result of the Mercer genes. In that
way, at least, Griffin seemed right at home in his surroundings.

''I've heard about what happened,'' she said, her quiet
words sounding to her like thunder in the otherwise silent
room.

His gaze locked with hers. ''You mean about my mother
being the lost Mercer,'' he said.

Sarah nodded. ''When Elaine first told me you had inherited this place, I figured you must be related to an off-

spring of Judge Mercer's that I didn't know about. But Meredith was his only child, wasn't she?''

His expression was inscrutable as he said, ''She was my grandmother and I didn't even know it.''

Sarah tried to gauge Griffin's mood by the tone of his voice, but could detect nothing in the deep, resonant sound. Before she could comment, he continued.

''I found out about it just before Christmas. Apparently sometime around Thanksgiving the judge was overcome by a feeling of nostalgia and his own mortality and wanted to do right by the grandchild he'd never known.''

He ran a hand through his hair and sighed. ''The way the story came to me, Meredith Mercer was only fifteen when she fell in love with a boy from town who worked for the judge after school doing odd jobs. Needless to say, the old man wasn't too happy about the development, because the kid had no prospects, and he wanted something better for his daughter. When she got pregnant, the judge pretty much locked her in the house and brought in a tutor so no one would know. She had my mother when she was sixteen, and the judge immediately had the baby taken away and put up for adoption.''

''The baby was your mother,'' Sarah said.

He nodded. ''She was adopted by a couple from Cincinnati, and when she married my father, they moved to Clemente for his job. That's where the story becomes so ironic. For years, Meredith's daughter lived only a few miles away, yet neither ever knew it.''

Griffin returned to his chair, picked up his cigar and inhaled deeply once again. He silently indicated the chair opposite his, and Sarah moved toward it. He seemed to want to talk about what had happened, and she had to admit she was curious. Not only about the story, but about his reaction to it. She couldn't help but wonder how all this made him feel. She couldn't imagine what it would be like to learn in her adult life that she had an entire family history she'd never known before.

After she seated herself, Griffin sat, too. "Do you blame him for everything?" she asked softly. "Judge Mercer, I mean."

He took another thoughtful sip of his brandy. "To be honest, I'm still not sure what I feel about this whole thing. I suppose he was as much a victim of circumstance as Meredith and my mother were. The times he lived in, the position he held in the community... I try to reassure myself he did what he thought was best. In the end, he did try to make amends."

After a moment, he added, "I would have liked to know my maternal grandfather, though. My mom's adoptive father had died by the time I was born. I'll never know what her birth father's name was. He might even still live here in Clemente. It's a strange feeling. Both my folks are gone now, and the family I never knew I had is gone, too. There might just be one other man out there I could call 'Gramps,' but I'll never know for sure."

"You don't have any brothers or sisters?" she asked.

He shook his head. "A handful of aunts and uncles and cousins scattered around, but I've never been particularly close to any of them."

"Family is important to you." Sarah's comment was a statement instead of a question, because she could already tell it was a fact.

"Yes, it is," Griffin told her. He studied her curiously. "Isn't it important to you?"

Sarah emitted a single, derisive chuckle. "You're talking to someone whose parents split after more than twenty years of marriage, telling me and Wally that they'd hated each other for most of those years and had only stayed married because of us kids. My brother and I get along about as well as a cobra and a mongoose. My own marriage was really over before it had a chance to begin, so maybe I'm not the person you should be asking that question."

"But you love your sons," he concluded.

"Of course I do," Sarah replied wholeheartedly. "But—"

"Then family is obviously important to you, too."

She thought for a moment, then began to smile. "Yeah, I suppose it is, now that you mention it. Funny, though, I never would have thought that before."

Griffin smiled back, and his face changed dramatically as a result. She hadn't thought him especially handsome. Attractive, yes. Striking, certainly. Sexy, by all means. But he was too rugged-looking to be handsome. Too rough around the edges. Too…too tough. But when he smiled that way… She sighed against her will. He was quite breathtaking.

"So which one are you?" he asked suddenly. "The cobra or the mongoose?"

Her brows drew downward in puzzlement. "What?"

"You said you and your brother get along as well as a cobra and a mongoose. I just wondered which one you are."

Sarah chuckled. "Oh, the mongoose, by all means," she said. "They're cuter."

"So they are," Griffin agreed, his smile broadening. Then, as suddenly as he had brightened, his expression became sullen again. "That would make your brother the cobra. A snake, so to speak."

She shrugged philosophically. "Wally's not a bad sort, really. He's just way too ambitious for his own good. It will ruin his life one day—mark my words."

He nodded again, and for a moment Sarah got the distinct impression that he knew something she didn't. Ridiculous, she assured herself. He was just preoccupied by thoughts of his own past.

"Look, I have to get going," she said as she rose from

her chair. "My sitter only stays until six, and I'm sure it's almost that now."

Griffin glanced down at his watch. "Ten till," he told her.

Hastily she gathered up her things, trying to talk herself out of asking him the question she found herself so wanting to ask. Intending to tell him she would be back at the house in the morning to begin cataloging, what she actually said was "Do you have plans for dinner?"

When their eyes met, each could see clearly how surprised the other was by the question, and then they began to laugh.

"Actually, no, I don't," Griffin said, stubbing out his cigar. He lifted the brandy snifter to his lips and swallowed what little remained. "Why, Ms. Greenleaf, is that an invitation?"

She lifted a shoulder a little shyly but nodded. "Yes, I guess it is. Would you like to come home with me and join me and the boys for whatever is most convenient to thaw?"

"Love to."

As Griffin followed her out of the library and down the hall of his house—God, it still felt strange to think of the big building as such—he watched the subtle sway of her hips and the way she tossed her curls out of her eyes. He was supposed to be meeting Stony for dinner in an hour, he thought. He wondered if Sarah would mind if he used her phone once they got to her house.

Chapter 4

Sarah wasn't sure when she did it why she'd asked Griffin Lawless to join her and her family for dinner. Nor was she any closer to an answer later at her house, as she watched her sons make a huge fuss over him, demanding to know all about his motorcycle, asking what it was like to be a cop. Griffin had just looked so forlorn, so lost, sitting there in the Mercer library, she recalled now. She hadn't been able to resist.

She'd always been a sucker for stray animals. And maybe that's exactly what he had become to her. A stray animal who wasn't quite certain how to handle the blows the world was dealing him. She, on the other hand, was no stranger to unfair experiences. And if her experience in handling them could maybe help Griffin in some way, then she was obliged to take him under her wing, right?

The only problem was that this particular stray was far more dangerous than any other Sarah had ever brought home. This one was a predator, pure and simple, and somehow she wasn't quite sure she would be able to escape him should he set his sights on her. Would she be taking him under her wing? she wondered. Or would he wind up making a meal out of her first?

"Mom, can we go for a ride on Griffin's bike?" Jack asked.

Sarah stood on the front porch and eyed the big motorcycle dubiously. "I don't think so, sweetie," she said decisively. "Maybe when you're a little older."

"Aw, Mom…"

"And you should address Officer Lawless as 'Officer Lawless,'" she added when she realized how familiar the boys were already becoming with Griffin.

"But he's not an officer anymore," Sam joined in. "He just told us so."

"Of course he is," Sarah said, realizing guiltily that she hadn't followed much of the conversation because she'd been too preoccupied with thoughts about the man in question. "He's—"

"I'm actually Detective Lawless now," Griffin told her with a sheepish grin. "I got promoted a couple of weeks ago. Sorry I didn't tell you earlier. It just didn't come up in conversation."

She felt a momentary tug of regret when she realized she wouldn't be seeing him in his cute little motorcycle outfit anymore, but tried to remain philosophical. Detectives still carried handcuffs, didn't they?

The wayward thought caused her to stumble over her next words. "Oh. I see. Uh, well, then. Then you should call Officer Lawless 'Detective Lawless,'" she told her sons, hoping none of them saw the blush she felt creeping up from her toes to her hairline. "I mean, you should call *Detective* Lawless 'Detective Law—'"

"Really, 'Griffin' is fine," he interrupted her. "There's no reason to stand on ceremony."

Jack and Sam beamed at him, clearly suffering from a severe case of hero worship all over again. Sarah hoped she hadn't done the wrong thing in bringing Griffin home. She didn't want her sons to get used to having him around, any more than she wanted to get used to that herself. It was probably too late, though, she realized as she watched Griffin help Sam sit on the big motorcycle, steadying her son with one hand, the bike with the other. Too late for the boys, anyway. Certainly she could keep herself in line. Couldn't she? Of course she could.

With one final, worried look over her shoulder, she entered the house. "I'll just start dinner, why don't I?" she said through the screen door.

"Sounds great," Griffin replied, smiling at her before turning to address a question Jack asked him about something called "c.c.s."

As she searched through the eclectic assortment of pre-packaged food in her freezer, Sarah pondered her almost daily concern about whether Jack and Sam were getting all the masculine attention they needed. Michael hadn't sought custody of his sons when the couple had divorced, but he had been granted liberal visitation. The boys spent a month every summer with him—and now with his new wife, too, Sarah remembered—not to mention an occasional weekend here and there. But Michael and Vivian lived in Pennsylvania now, so he wasn't close by if the boys ever needed him in a pinch.

And those pinches had been coming more and more frequently as Jack and Sam got older. They had questions now that Sarah was certain would be answered much more appropriately by a man, but there just weren't any men in her life she trusted with the boys in that way. She wouldn't even let Wally spend time alone with them lest she infect them with his aggressive workaholic philosophy. She wanted her sons to enjoy their childhoods and make the most of every moment of every day, and she'd done her best to see that they did. But she couldn't help thinking that little boys needed strong male role models, just as little girls needed strong women to inspire them. Sarah knew she was a good mother. But it was tough trying to be the father Jack and Sam needed, too.

Her attention was caught by the sound of Sam's laughter erupting outside the open window. She smiled. The boys had taken to Griffin immediately at their Cub Scout meeting. He had clearly captivated the entire group much more completely than any of the other men had. And when the two boys had come barreling out the front door tonight to discover their mother had brought Officer—or rather, Detective—Lawless over again, they had been clearly delighted.

Sarah pulled a family-size bag of chicken breasts out of the freezer, then located a big bag of ready-to-mix, stir-fry vegetables. If something had to be microwaved more than fifteen minutes or boiled more than twelve, there was a good chance it wouldn't be found in her kitchen. She wished she were one of those women who could work all day without mussing her hair, stop by the market on the way home and come breezing through the door with fresh everything, throw it in a pot and whip up a gourmet feast in fifteen minutes flat.

"Hah," she muttered as she wrestled with one of the plastic bags to open it. "Women who can do that always wind up in the loony bin before their thirty-fifth birthdays."

Tossing the frozen assortment onto the counter, Sarah went to work. Maybe she wasn't the most organized woman in the world, but she could sure whip up a mean stir-fry at a moment's notice.

As she prepared dinner, she wondered again about the immediate union her sons had seemed to strike with the compelling Detective Lawless. Must be something in the Greenleaf genes, she thought. Because as much as she dreaded to admit it, she'd struck something of an immediate union of her own with the man. And where the boys would probably end up with a friend for life in Griffin, she couldn't help but wonder—and worry about—what her relationship with the man might wind up being.

She had a good appetite. Griffin watched in silent admiration as Sarah piled a third helping onto her plate. Of course, he remembered she'd told him that she hadn't eaten since morning, but most women, when dining with a man for the first time, would probably have been less willing to let him know how completely they could put their food away. But Sarah Greenleaf made no apology for being hungry. Griffin liked that. It made him wonder what other appetites she had, and whether those appetites were as voracious and slow to be satisfied as this one clearly was.

"So how come you're not a motorcycle cop anymore?" Jack, who was seated to Griffin's left, asked around a mouthful of food.

He looked down into the pale amber eyes of the eight-year-old and smiled. The two boys were like color negatives of each other—Jack with his dark curls and light eyes, and Sam with golden hair and eyes the color of coffee. They were opposites in other ways, as well, he'd noted. Jack was the outgoing one, almost showmanlike in the way he presented himself. Sam, on the other hand, seemed content to hang back a bit. Certainly he had no qualms about piping up when he wanted to know something, but, like his mother, he tended to wait and see what would happen before plunging in.

They had good names, too, Griffin thought. Jack and Sam. Straightforward, solid, old-fashioned names, completely at odds with the recent yuppie habit of selecting upscale, trendy and sometimes bizarre-sounding monikers. He wondered briefly whether Sarah or her ex-husband had chosen the names, and decided almost immediately it must have been Sarah. She was simply straightforward, solid and, yes, a bit old-fashioned, too.

"I'm not a motorcycle cop anymore," he said when he remembered he'd been asked a question that required an answer, "because I thought detective work would be a lot more interesting. And a lot more fun."

"Do you still get to have a gun?" Sam asked.

"Sam…" Sarah groaned.

Griffin smiled. Clearly she was none too happy about her son's preoccupation with firearms. "Yes, I do," he said.

Sam's eyes brightened. "Do you have it with you now?" he asked.

Griffin shook his head. "Nope. It's locked up. It's not a toy, Sam. Not something to be carried around by just anyone. Guns should only be allowed into the hands of those who are responsible enough and smart enough to know how to use them. And that doesn't include very many people, I'm afraid. Mostly law-enforcement officers. Few others."

The little boy's face fell. "Does that mean you won't teach me how to shoot it?"

Griffin glanced up at Sarah for a moment, already knowing how he would answer the question, but wanting to communicate he respected her wishes, too. "No, Sam, I won't. Guns don't belong in the hands of children."

Sarah relaxed, throwing him a small, grateful smile. He smiled back.

"See?" Jack said, wadding up his napkin to throw it at his brother, seated opposite him at the table. "I told you Griffin wouldn't have his gun with him."

"You did not," Sam shot back.

"I did, too."

"Did not."

"Did, too."

"Boys," Sarah interrupted. "If you're finished with your

dinner, why don't you go outside and play? It's a lovely evening tonight, and tomorrow it's supposed to rain.''

Two chairs scraped away from the table, and the boys continued to argue through the kitchen toward the back door.

Sarah shook her head mutely as she watched them leave. Seeming to remember something suddenly, she called out, "And don't slam the door on your way—''

The back door slammed shut behind them with a vigorous shudder.

"Out," she concluded with a soft sigh.

She looked at Griffin and shrugged. "Boys," she said simply, as if that explained everything.

He nodded. "I was exactly the same way when I was a kid. The only difference was that I didn't have brothers or sisters to fight with. I had to grapple with the neighborhood kids instead.''

"You sound like you miss not having had a sibling," Sarah said as she stood to clear the plates. "How ironic. I spent most of my youth wishing I were an only child."

Griffin rose to help, but she gestured him back down. "You can help me with the dishes later," she told him. "I think I'd like some coffee first. How about you?"

"Coffee sounds great."

As Sarah went about the motions, Griffin watched, marveling at what a good time he was having doing almost nothing at all. He smiled at her matter-of-fact assurance that he would help with the dishes. By feeding him dinner, she'd made it clear he was a guest in her home—but not so formal a guest that he wouldn't be expected to pull his own weight. Her frankness was something else he liked about her. Sarah Greenleaf was different from most women he knew. And her differences intrigued him.

"I can't imagine growing up an only child, though," she said when she returned to the table. This time she ignored the seat she had previously occupied opposite his, and instead sat in the chair to his left that Jack had just vacated. "Even though Wally and I didn't get along a lot of the time, there were moments when the two of us could get beyond our sibling rivalry and have fun together. Christmases were always especially nice. Wally would help me figure out how my new toys worked, showed me how to put in the batteries or read the instructions to me when I was too young to read. And on Halloween, he always held my hand when we went trick-or-treating and ignored the bigger boys who razzed him about being stuck with his kid sister."

Griffin grunted noncommittally. He didn't want to hear anything nice about Wallace Greenleaf, didn't want to know what a protective brother he had been. In order to shift the conversation away from the man he was investigating, he said, "It really wasn't so bad being an only child. I was always the center of attention and never had to share anything. I never had to fight with my brother or sister over who had dibs on the TV or stereo, and I had a room all to myself. But sometimes..."

"Sometimes?" Sarah said, encouraging him to continue.

He shrugged. "Sometimes I wonder how it would have been to have someone else around. Especially now that both my parents are gone. It's strange, being the last of the Lawless line." After a moment, he added, "And now evidently the last of the Mercers, too."

Sarah watched Griffin closely, wondering what he was thinking about. This was the second time today their conversation had turned to the subject of family, and she couldn't recall on either occasion what had caused the topic to arise. Perhaps it was simply foremost in his mind right now, she thought. Certainly the recent turn of events in his life would warrant a rethinking of what family meant.

The coffeemaker wheezed as it gasped out the last few drops of the dark brew, and Sarah rose to fill two generous mugs. She returned to the table, offered him cream and sugar and, when he shook his head, sat down again. She drank hers black, too.

"Did you really become a detective because you thought it would be more interesting?" she asked. "More fun? I'd think riding around on a motorcycle all day would be better than sitting behind a desk in a crowded, poorly ventilated office."

He had lifted the mug to his lips, but hesitated as he thought about her question. After a deep swallow, he smiled. "You know, that's a strange comment coming from a woman who's out seventy-five dollars because of my riding around on a motorcycle all day."

When Sarah made a face at him, he chuckled, a deep, rusty sound that seemed to erupt from the very depths of his soul. A thrill of something warm and unfamiliar ran down her spine, and as much as she wished she could toss off a witty comeback, her mind was a complete blank. Only the rich, rumbling echo of his laughter resounded like a warm wind.

When she didn't reply, Griffin continued, "I was never given a court date, so I can only assume you paid your fine." His eyes sparkled like pale blue diamonds. "Unless of course I missed it somehow and you didn't show, and now they've issued a bench warrant for your arrest. In which case, Ms. Greenleaf, I'm going to have to run you in."

How could he make such a playful threat sound like such an incredibly erotic promise? Sarah wondered. "That won't be necessary," she said in a shallow voice. "I paid the fine. It just seemed easier and less time-consuming. Of course, now I won't be able to get that big book on Baccarat crystal I was saving up for, but…"

"I'll make it up to you," Griffin told her.

From the tone of his voice, she was afraid to ask what he had in mind for repayment. Instead she told him, "You already have by hiring Elaine and me to appraise the judge's collection.''

His face clouded a bit at the mention of the man who had prevented him from knowing so much about himself. He dropped his gaze to stare down into his coffee, seeing something Sarah was sure she wouldn't see herself. Before their conversation could be steered to a subject he probably wanted to avoid, she jumped back to the one she had meant to raise earlier. ''So why did you really become a detective?''

She wasn't sure, but she thought Griffin looked grateful when his eyes met hers again. ''A few months ago, I was shot in the line of duty,'' he told her bluntly.

She flinched at his statement, spilling hot coffee over the side of her cup. ''Shot?'' she asked, a soft whisper all she was able to manage.

He nodded, but seemed less concerned than she was herself. ''In the shoulder,'' he said, lifting a hand absently to the body part in question, rolling the shoulder as if testing it. ''It wasn't life-threatening, but it made me…reevaluate… a few things. I decided detective work would be less dangerous.'' He dropped his hand back to the handle of his coffee cup. ''Let's face it. Riding around on a motorcycle all day isn't exactly safe in itself. Add to that the dangers that go along with police work anyway, and you have a real good combination for bringing on a premature end to life.''

Sarah opened her mouth to ask more, but Griffin stopped her with a question of his own.

''How long have you been divorced?'' he asked.

It took a moment for her brain to adjust to the change of subject, but she eventually replied, ''A little over three years now.''

''Does your husband still live in Clemente?''

Griffin told himself his curiosity was nothing more than a desire to divert the conversation away from himself. Unfortunately, he knew such an assurance was untrue. He wanted to know all about Sarah's past and present and, worse, wanted to help her make plans for the future. It wasn't a good idea, he tried to tell himself. Not only was he investigating her brother—a fact she might find less than appealing—but she simply wasn't the kind of woman with whom he should find himself mixed up. She just wasn't his type.

So why the intense attraction? he wondered. And just why hadn't he told her about the investigation? Doing so would certainly precipitate an end to their time together, wouldn't it? If that was what he wanted, why didn't he just tell Sarah her brother was under investigation for bilking half the town and be done with it?

He tried to assure himself that he didn't tell her because it was against police procedure. She might tip her brother off, after all, and Wally would undoubtedly start trying to cover his tracks, something that would make Griffin's job more difficult than it already was. A simple response for a simple question.

But somehow things just didn't seem that easy. Griffin had a feeling he was less concerned about Sarah tipping her brother off than he was about the fact that she would be out of his own life faster than a streak of lightning if she found out about the investigation. And although being done with her was precisely what he *should* want first and foremost, it was in fact the last thing he wanted.

For some reason, he wanted to keep Sarah close at hand for as long as he possibly could. At least until he figured out what the hell was going on between them. And for that reason, not the more logical professional one, he decided to keep his mouth shut on the subject of her brother. Unless she came right out and asked him point-blank if he had on his desk a file that specifically mentioned Wallace Green-leaf. He wasn't sure if he could lie to her flat out.

He realized then that Sarah was speaking, and shook his errant thoughts from his brain to focus on their conversation once again.

"Michael remarried a few months ago and moved to Pittsburgh, where his new wife works. It's kind of funny, really," she added, staring at some point past Griffin's shoulder, "how he could never accommodate a single request *I* made while we were married, but he left his job, his home, his children, his whole life here to make her happy."

Realizing how bitter she sounded, Sarah tried to smile. "I shouldn't complain, though. Divorcing Michael was probably the smartest thing I ever did."

"What went wrong?" Griffin asked.

She sighed, toying with her coffee cup, for some reason unable to meet his gaze. "Probably we never should have married in the first place. I was still in college and wanted to graduate before we tied the knot. Michael talked me out of it, talked me into getting married, instead. For a couple of years I didn't do anything except be 'Mike's wife.' I thought about going back to school, but about the time I decided to enroll, I realized I was pregnant."

Sarah smiled then. "Jack and Sam are wonderful—they've always been good kids. I wouldn't trade them for anything. But Michael kept me so stifled after they were born. Don't get me wrong," she hastened to add. "I honestly don't think he did it consciously. Certainly he was never mean or patronizing. He just didn't want me doing anything except raising the boys."

"And that wasn't enough for you?" Griffin asked.

Sarah finally looked up, thrust out her chin defensively and stared him right in the eye. "No, I'm afraid it wasn't. God knows I love being a mother. But I have to have something else, too. Is that so terrible?"

He shook his head. "Not if it's what you want."

She gazed down at her hands again. "I guess I was happy

enough when Jack and Sam were little and needed me. But once they started school, started becoming more independent, I wanted to put my energies into something else that needed me. Michael just never could understand that. Of course, he had a career that demanded his attention almost twenty-four hours a day.''

"And now you have that, too," Griffin concluded.

She nodded. "A career, anyway, though not one that commands so much of me that I have time for little else. The antique business with Elaine has been perfect. With both of us being single mothers, we understand each other's needs, and we can swap duties and juggle our time. It's worked out very well."

"Elaine certainly seems to know what she's doing," Griffin said. He leaned forward in his chair, resting his elbows on the table and tucking his hands under his arms. The motion brought his face to within inches of hers, and she forced herself not to pull back. "And now, Sarah," he continued, a suggestive smile tugging at his lips, "I guess I'll get to find out if you know your stuff as well."

His quiet voice set her pulse to racing and her heart thumped madly behind her rib cage at the look on his face when he'd made his comment. Why did she suddenly feel as if "knowing her stuff" encompassed far more than her command of her job? Without her realizing it, Griffin Lawless had become a very important part of her life. Not only was he a client who would probably be responsible for turning her business around, but he was a man she was beginning to find more and more attractive, despite the questionable way in which she had met him.

She had thought it bad enough that her encounter with the infuriating Officer Lawless would cost her seventy-five dollars. Now she was beginning to wonder if the expense would be far, far greater than that, a price higher than she could afford and in no way connected to a monetary amount. And suddenly she began to worry that paying this fine might just do her in completely.

Chapter 5

"Sarah, you're passing up the chance of a lifetime here."

Sarah stared at her brother blandly as she withdrew a bunch of broccoli from a brown paper grocery bag and stowed it in the vegetable crisper. His coloring was similar to hers, but he had lost vast amounts of his curly hair, and his scalp shone brightly beneath what little was left. The spare tire around his middle seemed to be inflating a little more every time she saw him, and she wondered if he was still seeing Dr. Rowan for his blood pressure. She knew better than to ask, however. Wally was nothing if not confrontational where his health was concerned.

"Wally," she began, trying to hold on to her patience. Why did he always stop by on Saturday mornings, when she had a million things to do? "You know better than this. You know I'm having trouble making ends meet now. The shop is just barely turning a profit, and I don't have any money lying around to invest in some risky scheme of yours."

"This isn't a risk, Sarah—it's a sure thing. You'd be making an excellent investment."

She glared at him doubtfully. "A roller-blade rink for toddlers doesn't sound like a sure thing to me. It sounds like something only an idiot or a swindler would promote."

Wally looked absolutely flabbergasted. "Why, Sarah, how could you say such a thing about your own brother? You wound me. These roller rinks are the wave of the future." He paused for only a moment before launching into another idea. "Okay, if you don't like that project, how about this one? A topless cafeteria. All the servers would be nude."

Her quick, efficient movements came to a halt, and she turned around to gape at her brother. "You have got to be kidding."

He shook his head, beaming. "Isn't it a great idea? I came up with it myself. Think of the appeal to conventioneers. Cheap eats, naked girls, everything a man wants when he's on the road. Puts Jell-O salad into a whole new perspective, doesn't it?"

Sarah shook her head ruefully. Wally was such a jerk. She couldn't believe the two of them had resulted from the same gene pool. "Now, you *do* know better than to ask me to invest in something like that. Even if I did have the money, which I don't. Wally, you should be ashamed of yourself. What would Mom think?"

"Mom's in for ten grand."

She rolled her eyes heavenward. "Well, I'm not in at all."

"All right, all right, I won't ask you about my projects again unless you come to me first," he promised her. "But you know, you wouldn't be in such dire financial straits if you had stayed married to Michael. The guy was worth a bundle."

Sarah sighed fitfully. So they were back to that again,

were they? She knew it was pointless to argue with her brother, but she simply could not let his comment go unanswered. "First of all, Michael wasn't worth a bundle."

"He pulled in seventy-five thou a year."

"Which I hate to tell you, dear brother, isn't as much as it sounds like when you've got a mortgage, two cars and the care, feeding and future of two kids to think about. Second of all, what happened between me and Michael is none of your business. And third," she said, hurrying on before he could object, "you spend an awful lot of time speculating on my marriage, when you've never even come close to making a commitment like that yourself. If you're so keen on the institution of matrimony, how come you're still a single guy? Now, I know a woman who would love to go out with you—"

"Gosh, is that clock right?" Wally interrupted, jumping up from his lazy position at her kitchen table. "I didn't realize it was getting so late. Gotta run."

He kissed her quickly on the cheek and then dashed out the back door. Sarah heard the rumble of his sports car, then the squeal of tires as he hightailed it out of her driveway. She smiled. Yes, her brother was annoying sometimes. But she knew exactly how to handle him when he started to overstep the bounds. She should be careful, though. Someday he was going to call her on that "I know a woman" business and ask to be introduced. Frankly Sarah didn't know anyone who was interested in meeting Wally, despite her best efforts to fix him up. Still, that didn't mean she had to stop trying.

She hummed softly as she put the rest of her groceries away, scarcely noting that the song she'd chosen was something about highways and adventure and motorcycle riders who were born to be wild.

It was nearly a week later when Sarah saw Griffin again. She was standing at the center of an attic in the Mercer house, hip deep in opened crates, with dust and bits of straw swirling madly about her. A bare bulb swinging laconically above her provided the only illumination in the cramped, slant-ceilinged room, and she was hot. Her perspiration-soaked, red T-shirt clung to her like a wet animal, and her faded jeans felt loose, as if she'd sweated off ten pounds since morning. Yet her discomfort did little to distract her.

Because she had found a treasure.

Each of the crates contained a cache of fine china, every bit of it representative of a generation in the Mercer family. Some of the pieces dated back at least two hundred years, most of the collection was European in manufacture and all of it was in exquisite shape, with more than a few museum-quality pieces.

Why was all of this packed away? she wondered. Why was none of it in use? Or on display? If the Mercers had no longer felt any need for it, why hadn't they arranged for others to enjoy it? There must be tens of thousands of dollars' worth of china here alone. And, she reasoned further, there was probably crystal, and perhaps silver, to match these assortments, as well. Where were those?

She shook her head in wonder that one family had amassed such a collection. She couldn't imagine what Griffin would want to do with all this. Sell it, most likely, she decided. Truly, that was probably the most logical thing for him to do. Still, it seemed a shame no one would use any of this to entertain anymore. At one time the Mercer home must have been filled with people for holidays and family gatherings. Whoever had been madam of the house then would have made certain all the nicest of her pieces were polished and piled high with food. This old place must have been lovely in its heyday, Sarah thought. Too bad it hadn't seen much life for the past several decades.

She wondered if Griffin would sell the house. Probably.

It was a large residence by contemporary standards, especially for one person. And despite their talks about the importance of family, he didn't seem the type to settle down and have a passel of kids. No doubt the house would go on the block, just as everything inside would. The sale of his newly inherited belongings would bring Griffin a tidy sum, to be sure, but somehow, she didn't think he was the type to be much changed by his wealth.

She bent down to reach into another crate and withdrew a stunning piece of Limoges. She skimmed her fingertips over the creamy china, tracing the cobalt stain and gold trim. Bernardaud, she decided before allowing herself to inspect the marking. Probably about a hundred years old. Flipping the dinner plate over to read the bottom, she confirmed her assumption. She turned to carefully place the piece beside another that matched it, and when she pivoted around, saw a large figure looming in the doorway.

Griffin filled a room without even entering it, she thought as he stood there without speaking. Instinctively she lifted a hand to smooth over her hair, cursing herself for caring how she looked in his presence. The perspiration-soaked curls sprang right back when she removed her hand, and Sarah saw bits of straw clinging to her fingers. Oh, great. She must look really terrific with straw and dust sticking to every last inch of her.

"Aren't you hot up here?" he asked by way of a greeting.

His standard uniform of ragged jeans and T-shirt had been replaced by loose-fitting cotton khakis, rumpled white shirt, nondescript, neutrally colored jacket and a skinny, outdated necktie that must have belonged to his father. He looked like a combination of Columbo and Joe Friday. But his blue eyes burned in the stark light provided by the naked bulb, and Sarah felt her temperature rise even more. Hot? Yeah, she was hot. But it had nothing to do with the oppressive heat of a southern Ohio summer.

"Just a little," she said, hoping her voice sounded less limp than she felt.

He crossed the threshold and approached her slowly, ignoring the mess she'd made to focus on her instead. With every step he took toward her, Sarah found it more difficult to breathe. By the time he came to a halt before her, her lungs felt empty. He lifted a hand and curved it around her neck, rubbing his thumb along her jaw. When he pulled his hand away, she could see that his fingers were wringing wet. When he picked a piece of straw from her hair, he smiled.

"You don't look just a little hot," he told her. "You look like you're about to dehydrate. Come on downstairs. I'll fix you something cool to drink."

He turned then and began to walk out, and the crazy moment that had tied Sarah in a knot passed as quickly as it had begun. She had no choice but to follow him, because suddenly all she wanted was to be close to him again.

Griffin was already standing in front of the open refrigerator door by the time Sarah caught up with him. He called himself a fool for having run out on her that way, but if he'd stayed up there with her a minute longer, he would have done something he shouldn't. Like tumble her to the floor and have his way with her. She'd just looked so damned sexy up there in her tight, wet T-shirt with no brassiere underneath. He'd seen every curve and shadow of her breasts as if she'd been wearing nothing at all, and he'd wondered if her lower extremities were as intriguing.

When he turned to find her standing scarcely a foot away from him, still damp, still sexy as hell, he realized coming downstairs into the air-conditioning hadn't helped at all. He still wanted her. Only now, he wanted her even more.

"There's soda or beer," he told her, forcing himself to concentrate on the contents of his refrigerator instead of the way her blue jeans hung low on her hips. "Which do you prefer?"

"Actually, ice water sounds better than anything," she said, swiping again at her damp curls.

Griffin nodded, pulled some ice from the freezer and went to the sink. Instead of emptying the tray, he withdrew only a few cubes, tossed them into a glass and filled it with water from the tap. Sarah took it and drank thirstily, and he watched, fascinated, how her throat worked over the swallows.

"Thanks," she said when she had drained the glass.

"More?"

She nodded, handing the glass back.

When she did so, Griffin's hand closed over hers for a moment longer than was necessary. He had promised himself he wasn't going to do this. That he wouldn't be so fascinated by her, so wrapped up in thoughts of her, so affected by her presence. The more he uncovered in his investigation of Jerwal, Inc., the more he was convinced Wallace Greenleaf was into some pretty shady dealings. It wouldn't be fair—not to mention ethical—to court Sarah while he was trying to put her brother behind bars.

But as he pulled his hand away from hers, he knew it was pointless even to try to stay away from her. There was something burning up the air between them—that much was undeniable. And judging by the look in her eyes, she was as eager as he was to explore the attraction further.

Sarah slowly sipped her second glass of water as Griffin put the ice away. She wondered what he was thinking about. Ever since he'd come in, he'd been looking at her as though she was something worth looking at. An awkward silence loomed between them, and for the life of her she had no idea what to say to end it. The only thoughts that popped into her head now were of the physical variety, and all included Griffin Lawless. To speak now might make her say—or do—something she'd regret later.

"How's it coming?" he asked, and she hoped her sigh of relief wasn't audible.

"Very well," she told him. "I've discovered some wonderful things upstairs."

He nodded, but said nothing more. Just as she'd suspected, he obviously wasn't overly concerned about the enormous collection that now belonged to him.

"How long do you think it will take to get everything itemized?"

"Still hard to say, really. There's another attic on the other side of the house, and I haven't even looked inside it yet."

He nodded again, seemingly satisfied. "You busy tomorrow night?"

Sarah had been ready for more queries about the progress of her work, and this question threw her for a moment. The last time they had been alone together was when he had eaten dinner at her house. The evening had ended awkwardly, with the two of them parting ways at the front door while Jack and Sam watched TV only a few feet away. There had been a palpable tension in the air. Sarah had been thinking about the kisses they had shared earlier in the afternoon, and had known Griffin was remembering them, too. As much as she hated to admit it, she had been wanting to kiss him again. She should have been thankful the boys were there to prevent something like that. Instead she had wanted to pack them off to bed early.

Right now, of course, her sons were nowhere near her and Griffin. Right now, if she wanted, Sarah could step forward and plant a kiss on him that he wouldn't likely forget. But she only shook her head and said, "No, I'm not busy tomorrow night. Why?"

Griffin shrugged, but she could tell that the gesture was anything but casual. "There's a softball game then. The men and women in my precinct—the first precinct—are playing the second precinct. It's a grudge match. They took the city tournament from us last year.'' He seemed to be preoccupied by an old stain on the kitchen counter as he added, "I just wondered if you and the boys might want to come and watch."

She smiled. "Jack and Sam would love it."

"And their mother?" he asked as he looked up to meet her gaze. "Would she love it, too?"

Sarah caught her breath at the expression of utter longing in his eyes, fearful that what she saw was nothing more than a reflection of her own desire. Without hesitation, she replied, "Yes, Griffin, she would. She's probably looking forward to it more than the boys will."

He suddenly seemed relieved for some reason. "Good. I have to get back to work—I just came home on my lunch hour to see how you were getting along. How about if I pick you all up around five tomorrow? We can grab a quick bite to eat on the way."

Sarah's gaze lingered on the clock hanging on the wall behind Griffin. Only twenty-eight and a half hours stood between her and five o'clock tomorrow. She could probably stand being alone until then. Probably. "Five will be fine. We'll be ready."

He pushed away from the counter and began to walk past her, then stopped. Turning back around, he lifted a hand to her cheek and smiled, then bent forward and brushed his lips softly, swiftly, over hers. "See you tomorrow," he said quietly as he left.

Sarah raised two fingers to her lips, as if in doing so, she might be able to preserve the lingering effect of the kiss. But as quickly as Griffin was gone, so was the sensation. She told herself she should remember that pleasure was always a fleeting thing. Instead she couldn't stop grinning for the rest of the afternoon.

* * *

"Eh, batter, batter, batter, batter...suh-*wing*, batter."

As Griffin poised himself in right field, he shook his head and smiled. Sarah stood in the stands with her palms flattened over her eyes against the glare of the setting sun, doing everything within her power to annoy the opposing team. Every time a member of the second precinct approached home plate to bat, she was there chattering like a Little League mother, trying her best to blow the batter's concentration. Jack and Sam sat on each side of her, as intent on the game as she was herself.

He knew she'd be the type to balk at being called cute, but...she sure was cute. Her unruly curls smashed out from beneath a navy blue ball cap identical to the ones his team wore and that Sarah had donned backward. Her cropped white T-shirt offered a tantalizing glimpse of tanned torso, and faded cutoffs showcased her long, bronzed legs.

"Ball?" she yelled through the chain-link fence at the umpire. "Ball? What are you, blind? That was a strike, even in my grandma's time. How can you call that a ball? Kill da ump!"

Griffin chuckled. She was nothing if not enthusiastic about her sports.

The thump of a bat brought his attention around, and he looked up to find a softball descending in a perfect arc toward him. He caught the pop fly easily, then glanced over at third base in time to catch Denny Malloy trying to steal a run, so he hurled the ball home. When the dust settled, and the umpire called the runner safe, Griffin rolled his eyes heavenward, waiting for what he knew would come next.

"Safe?" Sarah shouted. "What are you, nuts? Here, pal. Here's a quarter! Call the home for demented umpires and book yourself a padded room, 'cause you're crazy! The guy was out by a mile!"

"Hey, Lawless," Stony called out from his position at shortstop. "Looks like you got yourself a live one there."

Griffin grinned back at his friend, lifted his cap and swept back his damp hair before putting the cap on again. "Yeah, she is that," he said with a sigh.

The two teams waited patiently while Sarah and the umpire engaged in a brief, but heated, difference of opinion. Griffin watched with his hands settled casually on his hips as the umpire threw his hat into the dirt and jammed a finger through the chain-link fence at Sarah, then watched Sarah press her face toward his and yell back. She'd make a hell of a coach, he thought. Team loyalty was job one.

When the little set-to ended, and the umpire's ruling stood, Sarah stomped back to her seat and the game progressed again. But as the pitcher wound up on the mound, one sound rose above all others in the crowd.

"Eh, batter, batter, batter, batter..."

Griffin sighed and waited for the pitch.

"You were great out there tonight, Griffin," Jack said as he chewed methodically on a wedge of pizza two hours later at Ferd Dante's Pizza Inferno. "That was some home run."

Griffin rubbed absently at the dirt stain streaking the right leg of his jeans from knee to thigh. He could already feel a bruise forming beneath.

"Yeah, the winning run, too," Sam added enthusiastically.

Griffin smiled at the two boys. "Well, I couldn't have done it without your mom's team spirit. She had me all fired up."

And not entirely because of her enthusiasm for the game, either, he thought. Every time the breeze had picked up and lifted her shirt to reveal a generous view of her smooth torso, he'd felt a rush of electricity spark through him like nobody's business. There was no doubt in his mind that's what had generated his final burst of energy. All that pent-up sexual awareness.

Sarah had the decency to blush sheepishly. "I, uh, I guess I should have warned you that I'm something of a sports fanatic," she said softly. "The boys' Little League coach has threatened to bar me from their games on more than one occasion. He doesn't think I take school sports in the spirit in which they're intended."

"Yeah, Mom's a fanatic, all right," Jack said. "Dad could never understand it. 'Course he would never even pitch to us, either, but we could always count on Mom."

Griffin couldn't help but wonder what kind of man would neglect the needs of his two children. Especially children who were as lovable and well adjusted as Sarah's clearly were.

"Hey, I've got no complaints about your mom's performance tonight," he told them. "It's been a long time since we've had a cheering section as enthusiastic as you three were." It had also been a long time since they'd won a game, he thought further. Tonight had been the first precinct's first win of the season. Griffin was fully willing to consider the two facts entirely related. He smiled at Sarah. "You must be a good-luck charm."

She smiled back, ready to reply, when the small group was interrupted by another group of people.

"Yo, there's the slugger!"

Stony clapped Griffin's right shoulder soundly, making him wince. Until that moment, Griffin hadn't realized he'd slid home on his arm, too. He was going to be a wreck tomorrow morning.

"Nice run tonight, Griffin," Elaine commented as she and Jonah joined Stony.

The three pulled up a vacant table near the others and sat down. Stony dropped a familiar arm around Elaine's shoulders and drew her close, a gesture that made Griffin's eyebrows arch in interest. Last he'd heard, Stony was washing his hands of the woman. But now his partner's behavior suggested the relationship was back on steady ground.

"Thanks, Elaine," he said, hoping his voice belied none of his curiosity.

She looked at Sarah then and added, "We saw Leonard at the bar as we came in. He was tossing back rattlesnakes. We asked him to join us, but when he heard you were going to be here, he declined and ordered another round."

"Leonard?" Sarah asked.

"The umpire," Griffin told her.

"Oh."

Stony chuckled. "I think what really got to him was when you suggested his mother had enjoyed a little fling with a blind fruit bat before he was born."

Sarah colored becomingly. "Well, that *was* a lousy call he made on Griffin. The ball was in bounds by a mile."

"Hey, you get no complaints from me," Stony told her. "But it may take Leonard a few days to recover from this game."

"Listen, Sarah," Elaine began again, "Jonah was wondering if Sam and Jack could spend the night at our place tonight. If it's all right with you, that is. I certainly don't mind."

"Yeah, Mom was the one to suggest it in the first place," Jonah told them. "I couldn't believe I didn't have to beg for a change."

Griffin wasn't sure which he noted first—Elaine's downcast eyes or Stony's puzzled expression as he watched her. But clearly there was something going on with his partner and Sarah's best friend, and he made a mental note to ask Stony about it at the next available moment.

"Uh, well," Elaine stammered, "I just thought, you know, that the boys might want to have a little more time together."

This time Stony was the one to look down, his gaze focused on a spot on the floor he nudged with his toe. "Look, I'd better get going," he said suddenly, pushing himself away from Elaine to stand. "I just remembered someplace I gotta be. See you later, Elaine. Bye, Jonah. Everybody."

And with that he left, weaving his way quickly through the crowd, until he'd disappeared from view. Griffin and Sarah exchanged bewildered looks, then turned their attention to Elaine, who still sat silently, as if Stony's behavior was nothing unusual.

"So what do you say?" she asked, her voice sounding unsteady and too bright. "Jack? Sam? You guys want to spend the night at our place?"

"Yeah!" the two boys answered in unison.

Sarah studied her friend for a moment, then reached quickly for her purse. She withdrew two dollars' worth of change and thrust the coins at her sons. "Here, guys. You and Jonah go play video games for a little while. Griffin?" she added pointedly. "You want to go with them?"

The three boys each snatched up a piece of pizza and their sodas and headed off for the game room. Griffin threw her a look that indicated he wasn't at all pleased to be dismissed along with the youngsters, but he said nothing. He only rose and picked up his beer and followed slowly in the direction the boys had disappeared. Sarah waited until they were all well away before turning to her friend again.

"Elaine? Is everything okay?"

Elaine's expression was inscrutable when her gaze met Sarah's. "Sure," she said simply. "Why wouldn't it be?"

"Well, because things seemed a little tense between you and Stony a minute ago. Then he stormed off for no reason. Kinda made me wonder if there was something wrong."

Elaine sighed deeply and shook her head. "Stony's just acting like a child because he wants something he can't have."

"And what's that?" Sarah asked.

"Me."

Sarah closed her eyes and opened them again slowly, only to see Elaine staring back at her with a level look. "What do you mean?" she asked.

"Just that Stony wants to get more…intimate…than I do right now."

"Oooh." Sarah nodded her understanding.

Elaine shoved a handful of hair restlessly over her shoulder and toyed with a pepperoni on the abandoned pizza. "Look, I thought inviting the boys to sleep over would keep Stony from trying to wrangle an invitation like that for himself. Earlier this evening, he suggested I send Jonah to your house for the night, and I told him that Jonah had already asked to have Jack and Sam over. I lied, all right? But I didn't know what else to say."

"Maybe you should just be honest with Stony," Sarah suggested. "Tell him how you feel."

"I can't."

"Why not?"

"Because I'm not sure how I feel."

Sarah opened her mouth to say something more, then snapped it shut again. For some reason, Elaine's dilemma sounded vaguely familiar, and for some reason, commenting on it right now made Sarah feel like a hypocrite.

"So you just thought it would be better to avoid the situation altogether," she concluded.

Elaine nodded, looking miserable. "And now he's mad at me."

"He'll get over it."

Elaine seemed to remember something then, because she turned to Sarah with a worried expression. "Hey, me having your kids over to my place isn't going to put *you* in a bind or anything, is it?"

"A bind?" Sarah asked, unsure what her friend meant.

"With Griffin, I mean."

"I don't follow you."

Elaine sat back in her chair and eyed her friend speculatively. "Well, I know you and Griffin aren't...you know. At least, I don't think you are. Are you?"

Sarah narrowed her eyes, puzzled. "Aren't...what?"

Elaine rolled her eyes in exasperation. "You know..." She made a gyrating motion with her hand to encourage her friend along.

Sarah shook her head.

Her friend uttered an impatient sound before fairly shouting, "Sleeping together!"

Now Sarah's eyes widened in shock. She threw two hasty glances left and right to make certain no one had heard her friend's outburst, before whispering loudly, "Of course not! Elaine! How could you even ask such a thing? He and I hardly know each other. Honestly."

Elaine smiled. "The way the two of you stare at each other all the time makes a person think you might know each other *very* well."

Sarah tilted her chin upward defensively. "What way?"

Elaine smiled. "Oh, like you can't wait to get home, tear each other's clothes off and cover each other with chocolate syrup. That way."

"Actually," Sarah began slowly, "it isn't so much chocolate syrup that preoccupies my thoughts as it is... handcuffs."

Elaine laughed. "I beg your pardon."

"Look, it's just a fantasy, okay? Lots of women fantasize about motorcycle cops and handcuffs and leather gloves. Happens all the time."

"I've never fantasized about that. My fantasies almost always involve food. Food and, on rare occasions, Nerf balls."

Sarah's brows arrowed downward at her friend's admission. "Yeah, well, I've read all about the handcuff thing.

Nancy Friday says it's perfectly normal. And so does Dr. Ruth.''

Elaine lifted the slice of pizza she'd nearly destroyed with her nervous fiddling and took a generous bite. "So you don't think there's any chance Griffin will put the make on you tonight?" she asked when she'd swallowed. "Now that the boys will be out of the way?"

"Well, I didn't say *that*...."

The two women looked at each other for a moment, then began to laugh.

"Look, I can handle Griffin Lawless," Sarah said as her chuckles subsided.

Elaine sighed. "You sure?"

She nodded. "Positive."

"Good. Because he's coming this way, and he doesn't look too happy."

Sarah pivoted quickly around to see Griffin approaching fast. She hadn't meant to dismiss him like a child when she'd asked—or rather told—him to join the boys. But thinking back on it now, she supposed that's exactly what she'd done. Naturally he'd be a little angry with her right now. Only for some reason, he seemed less angry than he did...intent. Just what that intention was, she could only wonder about right now. No doubt she'd find out soon enough, she thought.

The words she had just offered so carelessly to Elaine came back to haunt her. Could she indeed handle Griffin Lawless? she wondered. She was beginning to think such a feat was impossible. Unless "handling" him took on an entirely new, decidedly *literal* meaning. In which case, Sarah thought, she would probably be better off if she just stood up right now to face him—and ran away with all her might.

Chapter 6

Sarah's house was always so quiet when the boys were gone. Sometimes she found the break in the chaos a wonderfully relaxing change. Other times—like now—the silence rather unnerved her. Although, she conceded as she studied the man glowering at her from across the room, maybe her discomfort now was less a result of her children's absence than it was Griffin Lawless's presence.

He had scarcely spoken a half-dozen words to her since leaving Ferd Dante's Pizza Inferno a half hour ago. Elaine and Jonah had followed them home to collect Jack and Sam and their sleeping bags, but once that chattering group had left some moments ago, Sarah and Griffin had done little more than stare at each other. She supposed their sudden lack of communication should come as no surprise to her, considering the fact that the two of them had never been completely at ease when they were alone together. But for some reason, she felt as if the unsaid words hanging in the air between them tonight were much more important than what they usually didn't say to each other.

"I'm sorry," she finally said, hoping not only to get the conversation started, but also to bridge the gap that had formed between them. "I shouldn't have excluded you earlier tonight by sending you off after the boys. I was just worried about Elaine, and I didn't think she'd open up in front of you. You and Stony are such good friends, after all, and..." Her voice trailed off when she realized she wasn't sure how much she should reveal.

Griffin nodded, but said nothing.

Sarah tried not to be discouraged. "I don't blame you for being mad at me, but—"

"I'm not mad at you."

It was the longest string of words he'd offered her since she'd sent him away with the boys. She smiled, suddenly feeling encouraged. "Then why aren't you speaking to me?"

Griffin crossed the living room in a few easy strides, dropped his hands onto Sarah's shoulders and stared intently into her eyes. "Because ever since Elaine asked Jack and Sam over, ever since I realized I was going to have you to myself tonight, all I've been able to think about is..." He looked away briefly, drew in a deep breath and expelled it slowly. When he met Sarah's gaze again, he concluded unsteadily, "Is making love to you. And quite frankly, the thoughts I've been entertaining have left me a little speechless."

His bluntness startled her. She would have been lying if she said she hadn't been thinking about the same thing, but she certainly wasn't the kind of person who would come right out and announce it. She should have realized Griffin would be, though.

She opened her mouth to comment on his roughly uttered declaration, but all she was able to manage was "How about some coffee, hmm?"

He only continued to gaze at her, but she thought she detected a faint twitch at one corner of his mouth.

"Or...or a glass of wine?" she said, trying again. "I think that would be nice, don't you?"

"Sarah, I—"

She pulled quickly away from him and sped toward the kitchen, stepping up her speed when she felt Griffin following closely behind. She opened a cabinet by the sink and stretched up to rummage fitfully through its contents.

"Sarah," Griffin began again.

"I know I still have a nice bottle of something that I got for a Christmas present," she interrupted him as she pushed aside boxes of wild rice and cans of soup. "Something red. Elaine gave it to me, and she knows all about wine."

"Sarah."

"Her ex-husband owned a wine shop, you know."

"Sarah."

"I just need to remember where I—"

His arm suddenly appeared alongside the one she had thrust into the cabinet, corded with muscle and sprinkled with dark hair where her own was slender and smooth. He circled her wrist with strong fingers, but made no other move. Faced with such rigid differences in their physiques, Sarah felt something set to racing in her midsection. Griffin stood directly behind her, his body pressed intimately and without apology against hers.

Suddenly dizzy, she closed her eyes and inhaled deeply, only to find her lungs filled with the scent of him, a scent that was stark and masculine and utterly primal. Somehow she managed to continue with her search, his fingers curling around hers just as she located the wine she had been seeking. Together, they pulled the cool green bottle from its resting place and set it carefully on the counter.

Sarah began to reach up again, to retrieve two glasses from the top shelf, but Griffin's hand covered hers once more and halted her progress. Wordlessly she turned to face him, but dropped her gaze to the floor when she found it difficult to meet his eyes. Hesitantly he bent his head toward hers, and when she still did not look at him, brushed his lips against her temple. Instinctively she tilted her chin up toward the caress, and when she did, he touched his lips briefly to hers before pulling away. Then he repeated the gesture—another soft, quick brush of his lips on hers. Followed by another. Then another. And another.

Sarah flattened her hands against his chest, telling herself she should push him away. But beneath her fingers, she felt the warm, hard steel of his chest and the ever-quickening pulse of his heart, and found herself bunching the soft, faded fabric of his T-shirt in her fingers, pulling him even closer, instead. He wound an arm around her waist, then tangled his fingers in the curls at her nape. Finally, she did turn her face to his, and lost herself in the pale blue depths of his eyes.

For just a moment, she thought she saw a flicker of confusion in those eyes, thought she saw Griffin shake his head slowly in what appeared to be bewilderment or even denial. Then the look was gone, and he was kissing her again, this time with more insistence, this time with more aplomb.

She told herself she was crazy for letting him do it, called herself every kind of fool. Griffin Lawless was not the kind of man for her, not the kind who would want to settle down with a ready-made wife and family. She'd been so careful not to get involved with fly-by-night men since her divorce. In fact, she'd been careful not to get involved with any men at all. He was no different from the others, she tried to assure herself. There was no future in what they both obviously wanted to do tonight.

Then why did she want to do it so badly? she asked herself. She should want him to stop kissing her, should want to make sure things didn't go any further than they already had. But really, she had to admit when she felt the tip of his tongue touch the corner of her mouth, what she wanted to do was kiss him back.

So she did. With all the wanting, need and desire he exhibited himself. For long moments the couple remained locked in an embrace Sarah hoped would go on forever. She threaded her fingers through his hair, cupped his rough jaw in her palm and explored every solid inch of his arms, shoulders and back. Griffin, too, took time to investigate his discovery, lingering over every soft curve and smooth plane he encountered.

Suddenly, deftly, he switched their positions until he was the one leaning against the counter, then curved his hands possessively over her derriere to pull her into the cradle of his thighs. Sarah groaned, a wild little sound of surrender, and kissed him more deeply.

Griffin's head was spinning. He wasn't sure how it had happened, but he was on the verge of completely losing control. He knew what he was doing was crazy, knew he shouldn't have Sarah Greenleaf in his arms this way when he was investigating her brother for fraud. But he was a man who thrived on dangerous behavior, he reminded himself. And ever since meeting her, she had filled his head with thoughts of the most dangerous variety. He wanted her. Badly. And being with her now, like this, he could feel how badly she wanted him, too. So what was wrong with two people who wanted the same thing indulging in what each had to offer the other? They were consenting adults who clearly turned each other on. What was the harm in enjoying each other?

He felt her hands at his hips, clinging wildly to the belt loops of his jeans as if trying desperately to prevent her exploration of his body from venturing further. Knowing he'd be sorry for what he was about to do, Griffin covered her hand with his and loosed it from its grip, then placed her palm over the rigid crest that had risen under the zipper of his jeans.

Immediately her fingers took possession of him, and he groaned aloud at the exquisite shudder that wound through him at her touch. After that, all thoughts of the Wallace Greenleaf investigation fled, along with any doubts he might have had about making love to Sarah. As she raked her fingers slowly over him, he knew there was nothing that would stop him from doing what he had set out to do from the beginning—have his way with Sarah Greenleaf.

"Where's your bedroom?" he asked, wondering where he was finding the ability to speak coherently.

His question seemed to pull her out of the haze into which they had both apparently descended, but she met his gaze levelly with her own. "Through the dining room, at the end of the hall," she replied without hesitation.

Griffin nodded, then took her hand and led her in the direction she'd indicated. He found himself in a softly-lit room filled with old, feminine things—ornate Victorian furniture with flowery cushions, plants tumbling from antique pots, vintage botanical etchings and, tucked unobtrusively into the corner, a small bed draped with fine, delicate linens.

Suddenly he realized that while the rest of the house was a family dwelling furnished with the basic necessities and equipped to handle the roughhousing of two young boys, Sarah's bedroom was clearly her own exclusive haven. Somehow the knowledge that she had allowed him to penetrate the sanctity of her room humbled him a little, and he began to feel just the slightest touch of uncertainty about what they were planning to do.

But before he could question his concern further, Sarah came into his arms and kissed him, winding her arms around his neck, twining her fingers in his hair. And suddenly all his uncertainty fled. He dropped his hands to her waist, dipping below the cropped T-shirt for the first time to allow

himself a sampling of the warm, soft skin beneath. He
strummed her ribs as if playing a symphony upon them, then
hesitated when he cradled her breast in the curve created by
his thumb and index finger. With one gentle swipe upward,
he caught her breast fully in his hand, smiling at the sound
of Sarah's slight gasp.

"Oh, Griffin," she whispered unevenly.

The fingers in his hair gripped tighter, tipping his head
toward hers. Instead of kissing him, however, she only
pressed her forehead against his own and sighed deeply.

"It's been a long time for me," she said softly.

"Has it?" he said simply, aware the confession had been
offered reluctantly.

She pulled her head away from his and nodded. "Not
since… I mean, I've gone out with men since Michael, but
I haven't…you know."

"You haven't been with anyone since your husband."

She shook her head and continued to avoid his gaze. "No.
In fact, there was no one before Michael, either. I've only
been with one man in my entire life. Pretty funny, huh?"
she added with a nervous chuckle that afforded not a trace
of amusement. "I, uh, I guess I'm not exactly the kind of
woman you're used to dating."

Griffin curled a finger beneath her chin and turned her
head until she was facing him fully, but her eyes remained
downcast. Finally he said, "Hey."

Dark blond lashes lifted slowly, until he was gazing down
into the seemingly endless depths of her brown eyes. For
the first time he noted a few flecks of gold that shot out like
sunbeams from her pupils.

"I'd like to think I'm not the kind of man you're used
to dating, either. At least, I hope I'm not. I don't expect—
or want—you to be like anyone other than yourself. If I
wanted a different woman, I'd be with someone else right

now. I want *you*, Sarah. And I can only hope you want me, too.''

Sarah studied his face for a long time before replying. *Want* was actually a pretty tame word for what she was feeling for Griffin, she decided. But until she could come up with something to describe the galloping, frenzied heat that was burning her up inside, she supposed *want* would suffice.

"I don't understand what it is I feel for you, or why," she finally said, reaching for him again, "but I don't think I've ever wanted anything as much as I want you."

She watched as his lips curled into an easy, languorous smile. "Then take me, Sarah. I'm yours for the night."

She swallowed hard at his command, wondering what madness had come over her ever to think that she could handle the situation. *For the night*—that's how long he had said he was hers. The three little words bounced around in her head like a ceaseless echo. She tried not to dwell on the finite length of time those words indicated. Don't think about later, she told herself, dropping her hand to his belt buckle. For once in your life, just take something for yourself and revel in the moment.

Her eyes never left his as, with one gentle tug, she freed his belt from the buckle, then unfastened each of the buttons on his button-fly jeans. She stifled a groan when she realized he wasn't wearing any underwear, and focused instead on how to pull his T-shirt from the waistband. When her fingers stumbled over the task, Griffin reached behind himself to grab a fistful of the shirt, pulling it over his head with one quick gesture. He messed up his hair in the process, but Sarah had never seen a more glorious-looking man.

Every rigid muscle of his abdomen was clearly defined beneath a rich scattering of dark hair that covered his chest and torso and disappeared into his open jeans. Her hands were drawn like magnets to explore each tantalizing inch of him, and she marveled at the contradictions of soft skin and hard sinew, of coarse hair that sprang to life beneath her fingertips. Her fingers lingered at the pink, puckered skin on his shoulder, a quick bolt of fear shimmying down her spine as she realized how close she had come never to having this man in her life. She pressed her lips briefly against the scar, then ventured lower in her explorations.

As she took her time becoming familiar with him, Griffin seemed to grow impatient. After dropping his hands to unfasten her cutoffs, he caught the hem of her T-shirt and pulled it up over her head. Before she realized what was happening, Sarah was standing flush and half-naked against him, an infinitely more intimate touch than anything she could have anticipated.

"You know, that bed of yours seems awfully small," Griffin said suddenly. Only then did she realize his attention had been drawn to something beyond the agitated state of arousal that had risen between them.

Before she could answer, he pushed his hands down past her waist, under the waistband of her jeans and beneath her panties, cupping the bare flesh of her fanny fully in his warm palms. All she was able to manage for a moment was a softly uttered, "Oh." Then Griffin began to walk toward the bed, leaving Sarah no alternative but to walk backward with him, clutching his big biceps to keep herself from stumbling. As they moved, his hands continued to stroke the soft contours of her derriere, but what caught her attention even more was the rigid swell of him pressing against her belly.

"Yeah, it's a small bed all right," Griffin went on as he came to a halt beside the piece of furniture in question. "I guess we're just going to have to stay real close to each other."

He kissed her as he tumbled her to the bed, shucking her cut offs and panties as they fell. Always fair-minded, Sarah pushed insistently at his jeans until they, too, lay in a heap on the floor, then struggled to turn down the bed—no easy feat amid their squirming bodies. The shedding of those final garments was the abandonment of what few apprehensions either may have had left, and they came to each other with urgent need.

Her senses caught fire at each place Griffin touched. He seemed to be everywhere at once, his lips nibbling hers while his fingers toyed with her breasts and explored parts of her she barely knew herself. The soft bristles of his mustache introduced an entirely new realm of sensual experience, and more than once she found herself giggling with ticklish delight. But as his ministrations became more insistent and extravagant, her laughter eventually faded.

When he rolled her onto her back and rose above her, Sarah suddenly panicked. She remembered vaguely that there were often repercussions of the sexual act that came about later—two of those repercussions happened to be spending the night with their best friend tonight. She tried hastily to calculate the days that had passed since her last period, but discovered quickly that in the state she was in now, she was scarcely familiar with her own name, let alone the biological comings and goings of her reproductive system.

She faltered when Griffin began to kiss her neck and skim his fingers along the inside of her thigh to encourage her legs apart. Oh, who cares? she thought briefly. But on the heels of that thought came another, that of a bouncing baby girl with black hair and blue eyes identical to her father's—a father who was nowhere to be found in the picture.

"Wait!" she cried.

Griffin lifted his head from between her breasts and gazed down at her through narrowed eyes. "Wait?" he repeated. "May I ask for what?"

Sarah smiled at his expression, loving him for it. She

knew if she called it quits right now, he'd abide by her wishes. He wouldn't much like it, but he'd go along with her. She touched her finger to his lips, realizing there was more truth to her reaction than she had first thought. She did love him for it. She was beginning to understand that she loved him for a lot of reasons. When it had happened or how, she wasn't sure. But somehow she had let herself fall flat on her face in love with Griffin Lawless.

She removed her finger and raised her lips to his for a quick kiss. "I, uh, I just remembered that there's every possibility I could wind up pregnant for this."

His eyes widened in surprise, as if he, too, had forgotten just how babies came into the world. "Oh, yeah. I don't suppose you, uh, you know…have something."

"Well, I'm sure I still have a diaphragm around here somewhere. But there are necessary, ah, *accessories,* shall we say, that go with it, and I don't have any of those right now. And a diaphragm isn't guaranteed effective without them."

Griffin nodded. "Well, don't take this the wrong way, but…I do sort of carry some protection with me all the time—in my wallet, no less."

Sarah laughed. "How could I take that the wrong way? You forget you're talking to a woman who carries a condom around in her glove compartment."

"Yeah, without even realizing it."

"Griffin?"

"Yeah?"

"Shut up and get moving. Or do you want me to go through your pants for you?"

He grinned as he pushed himself away from her. "Seems to me you've already done that once, and look where it got us."

"Well, hurry up so we can get back there again."

He did, and they were. Seemingly without missing a beat,

Sarah found herself back in his arms, with her fingers buried in his hair and his lips wreaking havoc on her senses. And then suddenly, without warning, he was inside her, pushing himself deeper and deeper until completely sheathed in the delicate contours of her body. She cried out, marveling at the strength of him springing to life. He pulled away from her for only a moment, then plummeted inside again. Almost of their own free will, her legs circled his waist, and she matched his rhythm in a sensual dance as old as nature.

Together they climbed higher, sensations multiplying all along the way. Just when Sarah thought she could no longer tolerate the exquisite fire burning through her, Griffin drove her further, taking them to a place that nearly sent them both over the edge. Yet before she could let herself go, she felt the tension inside her build again, until she nearly went mad demanding satisfaction. With one final burst of energy, they went spiraling out of control, clinging to each other lest they become lost forever. For several long moments, they continued to cling to each other, their hearts pounding in unified rhythm, their breath commingling as it stirred the air around them.

"Wow," Sarah said when she was able to manage speech again. "That was amazing."

Griffin nodded, but said nothing. He buried his head in the damp, fragrant hollow where her neck and shoulder joined, placing a kiss on her salty skin. Something inside him had snapped at some point while he was making love to Sarah, and he still hadn't quite come to terms with what it was. He didn't want to think about it, didn't want to wonder what it meant. So instead he tried to do what he always did after he'd just made love to a woman. He tried not to let it get to him.

But to no avail. For some reason, this time it had gotten to him good. Sarah Greenleaf was inside him now, in some deep place that he hadn't known existed until this moment.

He lifted his head and gazed down at her, shaking his head at the expression on her face and the look in her eyes. Whatever was happening between them hadn't affected him alone, he thought. He smiled at her, but for some reason the smile felt false. So he lifted a hand to brush away the damp curls clinging to her forehead, and pressed his lips to her temple.

"Griffin?"

"Shh."

He would think about it in the morning, he thought, pulling the covers up over them and nestling in beside Sarah. Wordlessly he turned her so that her back was against his front, draping a strong arm around her waist, pulling her close.

Tomorrow, he thought again. Surely by then, everything would make sense.

Sarah awoke slowly, not quite sure where she was at first. The early-morning sun slanting through the bedroom window felt warm on her bare back, and she wondered vaguely what had happened to the pajamas she usually wore. Her antique sleigh bed—larger than a single but smaller than a double—felt different somehow, more...intimate...than usual. She stretched her arm across the mattress and clenched a fistful of sheet in her fingers, murmuring in delight at the pleasant sensations wandering through her body.

What a magnificent dream she'd had. All night long, her brain had played host to wondrous images—scenes of her body tangled up with Griffin Lawless's in a most intriguing sexual encounter. She sighed deeply, marveling at how his scent seemed to cling to the pillow and how even the sheets felt warm from his body. It was amazing, she thought blissfully, how some dreams seemed so real.

Hearing the sound of the shower switch on in the next

room, Sarah snapped her eyes open. That had been no dream, she recalled suddenly. All those erotic visions she'd been playing back in her brain were in fact her memories of the night before. She groaned as she rolled over onto her back, dropping her arm over her eyes. She was lying naked in her bed amid a virtual war zone of messed-up sheets, and Griffin Lawless was in the adjoining bathroom, taking a shower after having done things to her that had made her feel more exquisite than she could ever have imagined feeling.

What have I done? Sarah asked herself wildly. How had this happened? The answers to those questions came readily enough. She'd finally allowed herself to completely cut loose with a man who had her tied up in knots, and it had happened because she fancied herself in love with him.

"Oh, boy," she muttered to no one in particular.

She lifted her arm away from her face and stared at the ceiling. She told herself she should feel guilty, tried to berate herself for having done something so stupid. Unfortunately, try as she might to regret what had happened, Sarah could only smile, instead. She wasn't some starry-eyed teenager the morning after the prom worrying about what would happen next. She was a mature adult, a grown woman capable of raising two kids and running a business, a woman who was realistic about the future and knew how to take responsibility for her actions.

She wondered what Griffin would like for breakfast.

It was Sunday, she remembered, and the shop was closed. How convenient. Surely Griffin didn't have to work on Sunday. They could spend the whole day together. Maybe they could stop by Elaine's and pick up the boys and head to the park for a picnic. Or the four of them could go to a movie. And then Griffin could stay for dinner. Of course, it would be nice if he could stay the night again, too, but with the boys home, that would be impossible. Still, there would be other opportunities for the two of them to be alone together.

For the first time in a long time, Sarah was actually excited about what the day ahead held for her. Moving quickly, she rolled out of bed, grabbed a pair of khaki shorts and an oversize red T-shirt from her dresser and headed for the hall bathroom to wash her face and get dressed. She had just switched on the coffeemaker and was about to inspect the contents of her refrigerator, when a series of loud raps shook the back door.

Who could possibly be dropping by unannounced at eight a.m. on a Sunday? she wondered. Before she even opened the door, she knew.

"Wally," she greeted the man who stood on her back porch. He was dressed in his golf clothes—lime green slacks and a canary yellow polo shirt, with a red-and-purple plaid driver's cap poised precariously on the back of his head. She squinted at the color combination, placing a hand over her eyes to shield them. "It's a little early, don't you think?"

He ignored her comment, kissing her briefly on the cheek as he pushed past her. "Great, you're making coffee. I've only had two cups this morning and can barely see straight."

Instead of closing the door behind him, Sarah left it open, standing pointedly beside it with her hands on her hips, glaring at her brother.

"What?" he asked.

She shook her head in disbelief. "Has it ever occurred to you that it might be nice to call before you drop by? Or better yet, not to come by at all until you're invited?"

He made a face at her. "Sarah," he said. His tone of dismissal put her teeth on edge. "It's me—Wally. I'm your brother, remember? We don't have to stand on ceremony."

With a dry smile, she replied, "Oh, come on, Wally. Sure we do."

He waved his hand at her as if she'd just made a wonderful joke. "Frankly, though, I'm surprised to find you up and at 'em this time of morning. I figured you'd still be in bed."

Sarah gave in, closed the back door and went to the cupboard for two mugs. Wally would find out soon enough why she was up this early, she thought with a smile. Neither of the cups she held was for him.

"Then why did you stop by?" she asked. "Obviously you weren't too concerned about waking me up."

"I got a letter from Mom yesterday, and she figured she'd save on postage by sticking one for you in the same envelope." He reached into his back pocket and extracted the missive in question.

"A woman who would invest good money in a topless cafeteria suddenly wants to save twenty-nine cents by doubling up on her mail," Sarah muttered as she took the letter from him.

"You know Mom."

"Yeah, I do."

She was about to comment further, but the appearance of Griffin at the door connecting her kitchen to her dining room stopped her. He wore only his jeans from the day before. His hair was still damp from the shower, but he had run a comb through the thick, unruly tresses. Tiny droplets of water clung to the hair on his chest, winking in the light like miniature diamonds, taunting her until they disappeared beneath the waistband of his jeans. Muscles roped and corded his arms and chest, and she couldn't help the sigh that erupted from somewhere deep inside her soul. Good heavens, had she really made love with such a man the night before?

"Sarah, I—"

His words halted abruptly when he saw Wally. Sarah held
her breath as the two men evaluated each other. Almost as
if daring Wally to say something, Griffin raised his arms to
brace them against the doorjamb, leaning forward in a way
she could only call menacing. Wally's only concession to
Griffin's defiant stance was to straighten in his chair and
uncross his legs. For long moments, no one spoke. Griffin
eyed Wally. Wally eyed Griffin. And Sarah eyed them both.

"Uh, Griffin," she finally said, breaking up what she
feared would be a never-ending silence, "this is my brother,
Wally. Wally Greenleaf."

Griffin's posture changed immediately. She didn't know
why, but for some reason, she was certain he became uncomfortable when he discovered who the intruder was. More
than uncomfortable, she amended when she noted the way
his eyes flashed at the other man. Almost hostile. How odd.

She supposed his reaction was only normal. What man
would want his first meeting with a woman's family to occur
immediately following what had clearly been a night of
lovemaking? Still, it wasn't as though she was some blushing virgin. She'd been married, after all, and had two children. It was no secret that she must already know *something*
about the sexual act. And late twentieth century morality
did not dictate that a brother had to fight for his sister's
honor. Nowadays a brother's sister was perfectly capable of
fighting for herself. Usually.

"And, Wally," she continued quickly, "this is Griffin
Lawless. My, uh…"

Well, now, that was a tricky one, she thought. Just what
exactly was Griffin in the scheme of things? Calling him
her "boyfriend" seemed a little silly, since he was clearly,
in no way, a boy. "Lover" was too presumptuous—although she was fast falling in love with Griffin, she wasn't
certain how he felt about her yet. "Significant other" was
too trendy, while "beau" was too old-fashioned. "Hunka

hunka burnin' love'' was the phrase that came most readily to Sarah's mind, but that was probably more than Wally needed to know. Yet she had better come up with something before her brother took it upon himself to draw his own conclusions and think Griffin was just some guy she'd picked up in a bar the night before.

"My, uh…" she said, trying again.

"I'm a friend of Sarah's," Griffin answered for her, stepping into the kitchen to offer his hand to Wally.

There was a wariness about the gesture that Sarah couldn't ignore, but she didn't dwell on it, because she was too busy fretting about Griffin's classification of himself. He'd called himself her friend. Was that all he considered himself to be? Did most friends do what the two of them had done the night before? Sarah had never done it with any of her friends. She hadn't even *thought* about doing that with her friends. But maybe Griffin did. Maybe what happened last night was nothing new for him at all. Maybe all his women friends wound up in his bed. Or he wound up in theirs. Or…

She sighed fitfully, trying to push the thought away. Men were supposed to be the ones who hated the phrase "Let's be friends," she reminded herself. Women were bigger than that, weren't they? At the moment, she wasn't sure.

Wally stood as he shook hands, but seemed no more amiable about doing so than Griffin appeared to be. Sarah didn't know what was going on. Some guy thing dictated by the laws of the animal kingdom, she supposed. Brother looks out for sister while predator licks his chops, or some such thing.

"So, Wally, won't you stay for breakfast?" she asked sweetly, already knowing the answer.

"Uh, no. No, thanks. I'm meeting Jerry for breakfast at the club." He glanced down at his watch. "In fact, I'm running late as it is."

"Don't rush off on my account," Griffin said. But his smile suggested he wished Wally would rush off—right off a bridge at high speed.

"Thanks, but I really should get going. Sarah," he added as he kissed his sister goodbye and hurried out the back door, "I'll see you soon."

"No doubt," she said as the door slammed shut behind him.

She turned to smile at Griffin, but her smile quickly fell. His expression was anything but happy. In fact, he looked as if he wanted to hit something. Hard.

"Coffee?" she asked, the question ending in a near squeak.

He nodded once. "Please."

Griffin watched Sarah's movements closely, wondering if she could detect the tremors of anger spiraling through his body. He wasn't angry at her. Hell, he wasn't even angry at her brother, if truth be told. He was angry at himself. Angry that he'd conveniently chosen to forget that the woman he'd spent the night making love to was the sister of a man he was investigating, a man he was *this close* to putting behind bars for a good stretch.

She turned wordlessly and handed him his coffee, remembering that he took it black. Griffin sipped it slowly, stalling as long as he could before talking to her, wondering how he had managed to botch something up so thoroughly.

When he had awakened that morning to find Sarah nestled beside him, he had been nearly overcome by how utterly right the position had felt. She had been curled against him with her head tucked into the hollow of his chin, the fingers of one hand curled into a loose fist against his chest, while the other hand cupped his hip. His arms had been looped around her waist, the one she was lying on numb due to a lack of circulation. He hadn't minded a bit, though. She had been warm and soft and redolent with the lingering aroma of the lovemaking they had shared, and Griffin had wanted nothing more than to wake her up and start all over again.

He should be able to awaken in such a way every morning, he thought. Memories of the way in which they had turned to each other time and time again during the night nearly knocked the breath right out of him. They had responded to each other as if they were two halves of one whole, a unified body that had been separated for far too long. He had wanted to join them together again. But quite frankly, he hadn't thought he'd be able to manage it just yet.

So he had placed a quiet kiss on her forehead and disengaged himself as easily as he could to slip off to the shower. He had halfway hoped she would remain asleep for most of the morning, just so he could come out and watch her for a while. But when he'd emerged from the bathroom, she'd been gone. Now she stood before him, looking soft and rumpled and confused, and all the anger that had welled up inside him at Wallace Greenleaf's surprising appearance gradually began to fade.

But it didn't go away completely.

"What would you like for breakfast?" she asked then.

Griffin tensed. It was her tone of voice more than the question itself that disturbed him. The question implied her certainty that he would be staying for breakfast, and he wasn't quite sure how he should interpret that. But her voice, so matter-of-fact sounding when he felt so confused inside... That was what put him on edge. Part of him—a *big* part of him—wanted to spend the rest of the day with Sarah and her family, doing all the things that families normally did together on Sunday. And he could see clearly that such a pursuit was exactly what Sarah had on her mind, too.

But another part of him knew it would be a big mistake to let this thing between them go any further than it already had as long as he was tied up with the investigation of her brother. It wasn't ethical, it wasn't moral and it sure as hell wasn't nice. But then he noted the way Sarah was looking at him, noted the way her thin T-shirt draped lovingly over the swell of her breasts, remembered that one wild sound she had made just before she'd lost herself to her passion, and his conviction began to waver.

"Coffee," he forced himself to say before his thoughts could race beyond his control. "Just coffee is fine. I can't stay."

Her expression fell at his announcement. "You're leaving?"

He made himself nod in the affirmative, even though he wanted more than anything to reply in the negative. "There's a case I need to work on today."

"What kind of case?"

She would ask, Griffin thought. He sipped his coffee again to stall. "I really can't talk about it. The guy we're investigating doesn't know it." Yet, he added to himself. But any day now...

"Oh."

The one-syllable reply was almost Griffin's undoing. That single, tiny sound had the effect of a bazooka shot off right beside his ear. He heard disappointment, uncertainty, regret and not a little fear all tied up in that simple, softly uttered interjection.

"Sarah," he began, trying to think of some way to explain.

"No, that's all right," she assured him. "I understand. I should have realized. You must be very busy."

He inhaled a restless breath and expelled it slowly, wishing he could think of something that would allay her concern, but completely at a loss as to how he could explain without revealing the nature of his investigation. "I'm sorry," he said, instead.

She arched her brows in resignation. "Yeah, me, too."

"Look, Sarah, I—"

But she cut him off. "It's okay, really."

She lifted one shoulder in what he supposed was meant to be a careless shrug, but it missed the mark by a mile. Any fool could see that she was hurting inside. And seeing as how he was probably the biggest fool of all, Griffin couldn't miss the reaction. She thought he was abandoning her. Thought he was the kind of man who would sleep with a woman, then desert her the following morning. Then again, he supposed, in a way she was right. Because as things stood now, he couldn't allow what had happened last night to happen again.

Sarah was wrong, he thought. It wasn't okay at all. He'd managed to muck things up royally. But he'd make it up to her, he promised himself. Then immediately, he saw the irony in that. Just when was he likely to make it up to her? As long as he was investigating her brother without her knowing about it, he was effectively lying to her. Some foundation for a relationship. So maybe he could make it up to her after the investigation was concluded, when he'd been responsible for putting her brother behind bars. Oh, yeah. No doubt Sarah would be really happy to cozy up to him then.

"Look, I really should get going," he said suddenly. "Thanks for the coffee."

Sarah nodded mutely, but didn't meet his gaze. More than ever before, Griffin wished he knew the right thing to say to put things back the way they were before. Before he had gone and fallen halfway in love.

"I'll call you," he said.

"Sure you will." She stood stoically with her arms crossed over her abdomen, giving him the impression that she was trying to hold herself together. Still she refused to look at him.

He placed his coffee cup on the counter and took a step

toward her, then curled his fingers firmly around her nape.
When she didn't respond, he rubbed his thumb softly up the
column of her throat, then followed the line of her jaw.
Sarah stirred a little, shifting her weight from one foot to
the other. He felt her pulse quicken beneath his fingertips
and felt a little better. Bending forward, he pressed his lips
to her temple for just a moment before pulling away.

"I'll call you," he repeated.

Sarah nodded again, lifting her head to finally stare into
his eyes. "You'd better."

Griffin managed to lift one corner of his mouth in a smile
before releasing her. He allowed himself the luxury of tangling his fingers one last time in the silky curls at her nape,
then turned to collect his things from the bedroom. He still
wasn't sure how he was going to work this situation out,
still didn't know what the hell he was going to do about
Wallace or Sarah Greenleaf. But one thing was certain. He
wasn't going to let either of them get away.

Chapter 7

"Thanks for the coffee," Sarah mimicked angrily to herself as she watched the door close softly behind Griffin. "It was the least I could do!" she called out after him, knowing he couldn't hear her. "You creep!"

Sure, he was going to call her. She'd heard that one before. Maybe she hadn't dated extensively since her divorce—or before her marriage come to think of it—but every woman in her right mind knew what the phrase "I'll call you" meant. It was the big brush-off, pure and simple.

How could he do that to her after the night they'd spent together? she asked herself. Hey, she was a realist—she hadn't been expecting miracles this morning, that she'd wake to hear him murmuring his undying devotion to her and swearing he couldn't live without her. But she'd assumed he would at least stay for breakfast. She glanced over at the still-steaming, half-full cup of coffee on the counter. Breakfast, she repeated to herself with a rueful shake of her head. He hadn't even finished his coffee.

She jumped when the phone jangled behind her, and for one brief moment, a flicker of hope ignited in her heart. Then she realized that unless Griffin had a cellular phone on his motorcycle, it probably wasn't going to be him at the other end of the line.

"It's Elaine," her friend said in response to Sarah's greeting. "Are you up yet?"

She sighed. "I'm up."

"What's wrong? You don't sound so good."

Sarah wondered how much she should tell Elaine, then decided she wasn't in the mood to discuss anything about Griffin Lawless right now. "Nothing. I'm just not awake yet."

"Do you, uh, have any…oh, plans for the day?" Elaine asked further, clearly fishing for information.

I wish, Sarah thought. "No, no plans."

"Oh. Sorry."

"It's no big deal," she lied. "Griffin said he had to work on some case. Have you heard from Stony?"

"No, but it's still pretty early in the morning for him to be up and alert enough to figure out the phone. Not to mention that our parting last night might keep him quiet for a while yet."

"Maybe he's working, too."

"No," Elaine replied quickly. "He said something yesterday about he and I taking Jonah to the Natural History Museum, but we never finalized anything."

"But he's Griffin's partner, isn't he?" Sarah asked.

"Yes."

"So if Griffin had to work on a case, wouldn't Stony be working with him?"

Elaine's hesitation before replying told Sarah more than she really wanted to know. "Well, not necessarily," her friend said in that tone of voice women use when trying to let each other down as easily as possible. "Just what exactly happened between the two of you last night?"

"Something that shouldn't have," Sarah replied reluctantly.

"Oh."

Fearful her friend might launch into some tea-and-sympathy routine, Sarah continued hastily, "Maybe we could take the boys to a movie or something."

Elaine hesitated before replying, and Sarah held her breath, willing her friend not to pursue the topic of last night. Elaine seemed to get the message, however, because she said, "There's a movie called *Firestorm* they want to see. I read the review in this morning's paper. It's loaded with high-tech weaponry, lots of explosions, bloody dismemberments, the foulest language known to man and women with big hooters."

"I think the Hanlon Theater is showing a Disney double feature," Sarah remembered. "*Old Yeller* and *Davy Crockett*."

"The boys will hate it."

"So what are we waiting for?"

"I'll pick you up at noon. We can eat lunch first."

Sarah hung up the phone feeling a little better than she had after Griffin's sudden departure. She and Elaine were *not* taking their frustration with the adult male population out on their sons, she assured herself. But wasn't it nice to know that there were still *some* males in the world over whom women had control. At least until they were grown-ups, she amended as she went to take a shower. At which point their mothers generally turned them loose to bother someone else.

At six p.m. two Mondays later, Griffin sat in the living room of his apartment, sipping a beer and thinking about Sarah. Or, more specifically, about making love to Sarah.

Or, even more specifically, about the way Sarah's skin had tasted and smelled when he'd touched his tongue to her—

With a heartfelt groan, he jumped up from his seat, upsetting the coffee table and bashing his knee in the process. When he instinctively jerked down to cradle his injured joint, his beer bottle went flying, spilling a wide amber wake across the hardwood floor before splitting clean in two. He swore colorfully, hobbled to the kitchen for a towel and thought about Sarah some more.

More than two weeks had passed since he'd seen her, and he hadn't called her once. But he'd wanted to. Not a day had gone by that he hadn't reached for the phone to punch the numbers that would connect him to her. Even stronger had been his desire to stop by the judge's house while she was working there. Or rather, *his* house, Griffin amended uncomfortably, still unused to his ownership of the Mercer home. He remembered how she had looked the day he'd surprised her there, the way her wet T-shirt had clung to her body and how her damp curls had fastened to her forehead.

But inevitably, such a reminder also roused memories of how Sarah had looked after the two of them had made love, something he just shouldn't have allowed to happen. Yet.

The investigation into the illegal doings of Wallace Greenleaf was really heating up. He and Stony were only days away from being able to petition for a search warrant, and once that happened, Wally and his sidekick, Jerry, would be history. Their little cheat-the-public and money-for-political-favors machines would be effectively and permanently shut down.

Griffin couldn't help but wonder how much Sarah knew about her brother's professional life. He got the impression that although the two siblings saw each other from time to time and spoke civilly, even affectionately, to each other, they weren't particularly close. Not in the sense that they shared a good portion of their lives with each other. And

Wally Greenleaf didn't exactly seem the type of man who would let his sister in on his shady dealings. Nor did Sarah seem the type of woman who would stand by and let her brother get away with cheating people.

No, Griffin was sure she had no idea what Wally and his partner were up to. And what they were up to was bribing public officials and bilking gullible citizens out of their life savings. It left a bad taste in Griffin's mouth to realize there were people in the world capable of taking advantage of others in such a way.

What Wally Greenleaf and Jerry Schmidt did was convince unsuspecting people—usually the elderly or those who were struggling to build even the tiniest of nest eggs and desperate for fast cash—to invest every nickel they had in some scheme the two owners of Jerwal, Inc., had no intention of following through on. They pretended to invest the money in hiring and contracting, then bribed some local government figure to block the project with a lot of legal hoo-ha. And then all that was left was to tell the investors that their money was gone, their investment a bust, thanks to a lot of legal and political tangles that no one could have possibly foreseen. So sorry about that, but maybe they'd be interested in another project Jerwal had going.

Griffin wiped up the last of his spilled beer and carried the broken pieces of bottle to the kitchen. He felt edgy and anxious, trying to think of some way to work off his tension.

Immediately he remembered a terrific way to work off tension—diving deeply into Sarah while she cried out her demands with a ragged desperation that rivaled his own. As quickly as the graphic image entered his mind, he pushed it away. There was little chance she wanted to see him right now. Nor after the way they'd parted two weeks ago, with his telling her he'd call her and never following through.

Dammit, why did this have to be so complicated? he wondered, lifting a hand to rub at the knot forming on the back of his neck. He suddenly felt the need to get out of his apartment for a little while. He would go nuts sitting here thinking about Sarah all night. He grabbed his helmet from the top of the refrigerator and headed out the back door. Maybe he couldn't release his tension making love to Sarah, he thought, but a man had other alternatives.

Sarah looked through the passenger-side window at the big, marble, romanesque building that housed the first precinct. The place was quiet, not surprising for a Monday night, but a few people came and went through the heavy doors, some in uniform, some in plainclothes. None of them was Griffin, though, she realized, then immediately chastised herself for even bothering to look for him.

She sighed impatiently before asking, "Elaine, why did you bring me here?"

"I didn't bring *you* here, I brought *me* here. I have some stuff I promised I'd drop off for Stony."

"Can we go in, too?" Jonah asked from the back seat. He turned to Jack and Sam. "I've been in the police station before," he announced proudly, his voice suggesting that his presence was the result of a number of felony offenses. "Lots of times."

Elaine rolled her eyes and gazed at her son in the rearview mirror. "Twice," she corrected him. "And neither time because you were in trouble. Only because we were meeting Stony."

Jonah frowned at his mother, feeling what Sarah supposed was his disappointment that Elaine had ruined what would have been a beautiful story of an eight-year-old's lawlessness and adventure.

"And no, you may not come inside," Elaine added. "I don't want to be here all night. It'll be past your bedtimes before long."

"Aw, Mom..."

"Aw, Mrs. Bingham..."

The complaints were offered in a petulant, off-key chorus, and Elaine turned to Sarah in a silent plea for help. Sarah shook her head in defeat. "Oh, let them go in. I'll keep an eye on them while you look for Stony."

"You have no idea what you're getting yourself into," Elaine cautioned.

"Hey, I've got *two* of them," Sarah countered. "I know *exactly* what I'm getting myself into."

All five exited the car at the same time, but the boys were well into the squad room before the women caught up with them. Jonah took a seat atop Stony's desk and concentrated on balancing a pen on his index finger, while Jack and Sam inspected a bulletin board full of wanted posters, trying to discern whether they knew any of the men portrayed in the grainy black-and-white photos. Jack was certain one was Mr. Pike, the gym teacher at their school, but Stony managed to reassure him otherwise.

Sarah couldn't help but smile at the scene, curious about her friend's misgivings where Stony was concerned. He was clearly a man who loved children, and by the expression in his eye when he looked at her, was also clearly devoted to Elaine. Sarah wondered if Griffin would be as patient with the boys, then remembered how attentive he had been at her house the night he'd come over for dinner. Griffin, too, would make a good father. Jack and Sam adored him, and he appeared to be a natural with the boys. Too bad he didn't seem to show the same interest in their mother, she thought morosely, recalling for the thousandth time that he hadn't called her as he'd promised.

"Griff's in the exercise room," she heard Stony say, and she realized he and Elaine had been speaking for some moments while she'd been lost in thought.

"What?" she asked, turning to Stony, although she had understood his statement perfectly well.

He smiled, and Sarah could have sworn there was a some-what devilish quality about it. He pointed toward the other side of the room.

"Through those double doors, down the stairs at the end of the hall, first door on your left."

It rather annoyed Sarah the way her heart took off at the realization that Griffin was in the same building. What difference did it make? she asked herself. He had no desire to see her, or he would have called. Whether or not he was in the building was immaterial. She would not go looking for him when he obviously did not wish to be found by her.

She met Stony's gaze and shrugged. "So next time you see him, tell him I said hi."

"Why don't you run down and tell him yourself?" he asked. There was an underlying challenge in his voice.

Sarah lifted her chin defensively, never one to back down from a dare. "All right," she said. "I will."

And with that, she spun on her heel and headed in the direction Stony had indicated. When she first entered the exercise room, she thought it was empty. The equipment looked bleak and skeletal with no one using it, and garish fluorescent light tinged everything with an odd, vaguely blue tint that threw harsh black shadows everywhere. The silence was deafening. She was about to turn around and leave, when she heard something, a hollow, irregular *thump, thump…thump-thump*. Seeing a door on the other side of the room, she made her way to it and discovered it led into a gymnasium. And on the other side of the gym, she saw Griffin. Looking very angry.

He was barefoot, wearing only a pair of ragged gray sweatpants and well-worn boxing gloves. He pounded his fists brutally against the leather punching bag, perspiration streaming down his face and chest. When she noted his teeth were clamped down hard on a smoldering cigar, Sarah smiled. Some workout.

She pushed through the door silently and leaned against the wall, watching him. His footwork was impressive. He feinted and danced gracefully before heaving his fists into the bag of sand. The bag swayed backward, the chain holding it jangling a bit, then swayed forward to be hit again. Griffin slugged it five or six times in quick succession, then skipped backward before lunging forward once more.

Sarah found the movements fascinating. Muscles bunched and rippled in his arms and abdomen every time he came forward, then relaxed when he moved away. And each time his fist made contact with the bag, he made a sound—not quite a groan, not quite a cry—but something primal and masculine and utterly arousing.

She must have made some sound in reply, because suddenly Griffin glanced up and saw her. Immediately he began to move toward her, his motions fluid, deft and confident, making Sarah feel like some small, defenseless prey. In a matter of seconds he stood before her. His black hair was wet with perspiration, falling forward, clinging to his forehead. His blue eyes seemed deeper than usual somehow, bright with exhilaration at the flow of blood that must be zinging through his system.

She watched, fascinated, as a trickle of sweat rolled down his cheek, curved past his jaw and down his throat, winding over his chest to disappear in the dark hair that spiraled down his abdomen. She wanted to follow that route with her tongue, to taste the life she felt pulsing from him, to lose herself completely in Griffin Lawless. Helplessly she closed her eyes and inhaled deeply, growing dizzy from the scent of him and at having him so close again. When she opened her eyes, he was still there, studying her with a maddening intensity and any number of unasked questions. She stood silently, not certain how she should answer them.

He shifted to rest his weight on one foot, his gloved hands settled on his hips and his cigar jutting from the corner of his mouth, but he didn't speak right away. For long moments they only stared at each other, and Sarah wished with all her heart that she knew what he was thinking.

Finally he asked, "What are you doing here?"

"Looking for you," she replied without thinking. She hurried to clarify, "I mean, I'm here with Elaine and the boys. She had to drop something off for Stony."

Griffin shrugged, ignoring the last part of her statement when he said simply, "So you found me."

"So I did."

When she didn't elaborate, he reached for his cigar, surprisingly adept at removing it from his mouth, considering he still wore his boxing gloves. "What is it you want, Sarah?"

He emphasized the word *want* as if it promised satisfaction to every desire she would ever have. Her mouth suddenly felt dry, and she licked her lips in an effort to ease the sensation. She noted that her action caught his attention and held it, and her heart trip-hammered against her rib cage at the lascivious thoughts burning up her brain.

"You never called me," she said.

He frowned. "I know, and I'm sorry. I've been working on a—"

"A case," she finished for him. "I know. A difficult case. A case I would think Stony would be working on with you."

"He is."

"But Stony isn't working right now," she said. "And neither are you."

"I know, but—"

Before she realized what she was doing, Sarah took Griffin's gloved hand in hers, removed the cigar and threw it on the floor, stamping her foot on it to put it out. Then she unlaced his glove and jerked it clumsily from his hand, tossing it to the floor, as well. She placed his loose fist at the center of her chest, over her heart. His eyes widened at her gesture, but instead of pulling his hand away, he opened it, splaying his fingers over her breast.

"This is my heart," she said softly, holding his hand more tightly against her. With a shaky smile, she added, "You break it, mister, you've bought it."

Griffin opened his mouth to say something, but evidently decided against it. Instead he held up his other hand, silently encouraging Sarah to remove that glove, as well. She did so immediately, her fingers fumbling over the task this time because his hand curved over her breast completely, making languid circular motions that nearly drove her mad. The moment his other hand was free, Griffin swooped down on Sarah, pulling her into his arms and kissing her within an inch of her life.

She circled his neck with her arms to pull him closer, conveniently choosing to forget all the turmoil he'd caused her. His bare back was slick beneath her fingertips, and the perspiration on his chest soaked through her shirt to mingle with the dampness that had risen on her skin. She felt Griffin's hands under her shirt, skimming over the planes of her back, and she cried out with longing when they strummed over her rib cage and breasts. All at once, she remembered that they were standing in the gym at the police station and that anyone might wander in at any moment, including her friends and family. Immediately she pushed herself away from him, struggling to get herself under control.

"So," she said when she was able to manage speech again, "you, uh, you got any plans for the rest of the evening?"

His chest still rose and fell in an irregular rhythm, but he smiled. "Oh, yeah. You bet I have plans for the rest of the evening."

When he began to move toward her again, Sarah held up a hand and backed away. "Great. I'll see if Elaine can han-

dle having the boys spend the night twice in one month."
When he took another step forward, she took another step
back. "And I'll wait for you while you shower and
change," she added pointedly.

Griffin stooped to pick up the discarded boxing gloves
and smashed cigar. "You know, this was a Cohiba," he
said wistfully, indicating the crumpled heap of tobacco in
his palm. "The last one in my great-grandfather's humi-
dor."

"I'll get you another one," Sarah said apologetically. "A
whole box of them."

He shook his head. "You can't get them here. They're
Cuban."

She smiled. "Aren't Cuban cigars illegal in the U.S.?"

"Highly."

"Why, Detective," she cooed. "You are a lawless man,
aren't you?"

He smiled back. "Well, my thoughts right now are anything but licit, that's certain."

He pushed past her and headed for the double doors
through which she had come.

"Oh, Griffin," she called after him.

He turned, his expression inquisitive, but he said nothing.

Sarah chewed her lip nervously for some moments before
voicing the question burning itself at the forefront of her
brain. When he only stared at her silently, she drew in a
deep, fortifying breath and asked, "Would you, uh...I
mean, could you, er...that is..."

"Spit it out, Sarah."

"You won't by any chance have your...handcuffs...with
you tonight, will you?"

The look on his face was positively profligate, and Sarah
felt her temperature rise.

"Oh, Ms. Greenleaf," he said in the no-nonsense voice
of efficiency she remembered from their very first encoun-

ter. "Just what kind of thoughts have you been entertaining?"

She lifted a shoulder in a noncommittal shrug, but said nothing. Griffin laughed, a deep, sensuous sound that reminded her of dark chocolate, then turned once again. She thought he would leave without replying, then he quickly spun around, returned and pulled her into his arms. With a single, roughly offered kiss, he released her and started off again.

She staggered backward and watched him go, wondering if she was as crazy as she felt, pursuing him this way. She'd never run after a man in her life, and discovered that there was a strange, heady delight that came with the chase. What she'd had with Michael had been a mutual admiration from the moment they'd met, and she hadn't met a man since her divorce who seemed worth the trouble. But Griffin was, she thought. He was something special, something wonderful, something she'd be crazy to let get away.

She was still tingling when she went to find Elaine and Stony. For the first time in her life, she thought, maybe, just maybe, something was going to work out the way it was supposed to.

Griffin felt good. Better than good—great. He stuffed the shirttail of his white T-shirt into faded Levi's and buttoned them up, hastily thrust his feet into well-worn boots and dragged a comb through his still damp hair. He was in a hurry. He had a date. A date with a woman who had tied him up in knots for weeks, a woman he couldn't get out of his head, a woman who would probably keep him feeling like a lovesick fool for the rest of his life.

As he collected the last of his things and zipped up his duffel bag, a flash of silver winked at him from the top shelf of his locker. He smiled as he reached up and lifted the handcuffs from their resting place. He wasn't sure if Sarah had been joking or not, but he sure as hell wasn't going to take any chances. Unzipping his duffel, he dropped the cuffs inside, then zipped it shut again and slung it over his shoulder. For some reason, he felt like belting out a few choruses of "Tonight, Tonight," but managed to contain himself. Taking a deep breath, he made his way out of the locker room and up to the squad room, where Sarah would be waiting for him.

As he took the steps two at a time, he thought about the night ahead. For the past sixteen days, he'd thought of little other than his one night with Sarah, had replayed in his head every touch and stroke over and over until he thought he would go mad with wanting her again. He'd planned what he'd do the next time they were alone together, had gone over it in his mind until he'd choreographed their lovemaking like a pro. All that was left was Sarah's input, and he had a feeling that her offering would be more than generous.

Tonight, he thought, would be even better than the last time. Tonight would be outstanding, unbelievable, amazing. Tonight...

He pushed through the double doors that led into the squad room and searched for Sarah, finding her immediately. She was watching him, smiling nervously, as if she, too, had been thinking about the night ahead. Oh, yes. They were definitely going to have an adventure.

"Griffin!"

A chorus of three small voices went up around him, and he suddenly realized Sarah wasn't alone. Jack and Sam sped out from behind Stony's desk, followed immediately by Jonah Bingham. The three boys rushed him, circling him like wild animals, inundating him with exclamations and questions.

"Jonah's spending the night with us tonight," Sam said.

"Mom said you might take us to the drive-in," Jack

added. "They're showing *Bloodbath* and *Bloodbath, Part Two*."

Sarah quickly intervened. "I said we would *not* go see that, Jack. We'll let Griffin choose a movie." She looked up at him hopefully. "If he wants to."

Griffin stared at the four of them, confused, puzzled and utterly annoyed. "Uh, Sarah?" he asked softly.

She arched her brows inquisitively. "Yes?"

"Could I talk to you for a minute?"

"Certainly." She looked at him silently, expectantly, but did not move from her frozen position.

"Alone?" he clarified.

Her eyes widened, giving her an almost panicked look, but she nodded quickly. Still, however, she did not move. He lifted his left hand palm up, closing his fist except for his index finger, which he crooked in that ages-old, somewhat ominous gesture.

"Boys?" Sarah said to the still-squirming youngsters, her voice cracking a little on the word. "Can you sit quietly here at Mr. Stonestreet's desk while I have a little talk with Griffin?"

"Sure," Jack said with a shrug before leading the others back to the bulletin board. He pointed to one photo, urging Jonah to look more closely. "It's Mr. Pike, I tell ya. Look at the guy's nose."

Griffin took advantage of their rapt attention elsewhere to grab Sarah's wrist and pull her along behind him. When they were safely out of earshot, he turned, settled his hands on his hips and demanded, "What the hell is going on here?"

"I'm really sorry," she began. "But when I got back up here, Elaine and Stony were having a kind of, um, *intense* conversation, and Elaine asked me if I could keep Jonah for the night."

"And you said yes?" Griffin asked incredulously. "After we...I mean, after the plans we made?"

Now Sarah placed her hands on her own hips, mirroring his challenging posture. "Well, I couldn't very well say no, could I?" she replied. "She kept Jack and Sam last time so that you and I could..." Two bright spots of pink colored her cheeks when she halted. "So that you and I could be alone," she finished hastily. "Tonight she and Stony needed some time alone, and it's my turn to take sleep-over duty. But if you dislike my children so much—"

"Oh, no, you don't," he said. "I like your kids just fine and you know it. It's just..."

"What?"

Griffin drew in a deep, impatient breath, and raked his fingers through his hair. "I wanted *us* to be alone. I wanted to..." He cupped his hands over her shoulders and started to pull her close, looked past her to see her two sons and their best friend watching them intently and dropped his hands back to his sides again. "Dammit, I wanted to make love to you tonight."

Sarah bit her lip, and he could tell she was trying not to laugh. "You hopeless romantic, you. You really know how to sweet-talk a girl."

"No, Sarah, I meant—"

But she held up a hand to stop him. "I wanted that, too," she said with a smile. "But you're about to learn that when you have kids, you can't always have what you want. In fact," she added, glancing over her shoulder, "you hardly ever get what you want."

"Then why don't you send them off to boarding school?" he asked, only half-joking.

She laughed. "Well, the subject of the military academy did come up frequently between Michael and me, but..." She shrugged. "So what do you say, Griffin? You want to go to the drive-in with me?"

"With you and three other guys?"

She nodded.

"I suppose necking in the back seat would be out of the question."

"Completely."

He sighed again. "Oh, all right. But you have to buy the popcorn."

She threaded her fingers through his and pulled him along behind her as she went to rejoin the boys. As she herded the three youngsters out ahead of them, she turned back to tell Griffin, "Did I mention that they usually fall asleep during the first half?"

He felt a flicker of optimism ignite somewhere in the dark recesses of his heart. Maybe, just maybe, there was hope for the night yet.

Chapter 8

Sarah listened to the chaotic thumping and squealing of three excited—and wide-awake—boys in her sons' bedroom upstairs, stared at Griffin stretched out fast asleep on her living room sofa and sighed. She supposed she should wake him and send him home; it was past one o'clock. But he looked so peaceful lying there—as if this was the first decent night's sleep he'd had in ages. She couldn't quite bring herself to rouse him. So she sat in the big club chair opposite him and watched him sleep, trying to ignore how utterly right it felt to do something so simple and harmless.

She couldn't recall a single moment during her marriage when she had felt as peaceful as she did at that moment. Virtually from day one after marrying Michael, she had experienced some anxiety, some feeling that she'd made a mistake, however small the fear may have been. But from the second she had seen Griffin Lawless standing in her kitchen doorway the night of the Cub Scout meeting, the second she had realized he had every intention of kissing her, she had known—somehow she had just *known*—that whatever was going to happen between them would be the right thing.

He stirred a little, uttering a soft, sleepy sound as he shifted on the sofa, then brought one muscular forearm up to rest it over his eyes. Yet he did not awaken.

"Griffin?" she asked quietly. She didn't want to disturb him, but knew she really should make some effort to wake him. When he did not reply, she tried once more.

"Oh, Griffin?" she asked again, drawing his name out on a long, low whisper.

He grunted, but offered no further indication that he'd heard her.

Sarah stood and went to a closet in the hall, pulled down a lightweight blanket and returned to the living room. He had removed his boots while she was upstairs getting the boys settled down, and now the dusty, creased leather accessories sat on the floor beside the couch. So she draped the blanket carefully over him from chest to toe, switched off the lamp at his head and tiptoed quietly out of the room.

"Good night, Griffin," she said over her shoulder as she left.

"'Night, sweetheart," he mumbled after her in his sleep.

Griffin awoke to a very strange noise—that of children laughing. Or more specifically, he realized as he opened one eye, children laughing at *him*. Standing over him were Sarah's two sons and their friend, who he had last seen in Sarah's living room the night before when she had ordered them all upstairs to bed. So what were they doing in his apartment now?

Griffin opened his other eye and fixed his gaze on a huge ceiling fan swirling laconically above him. He didn't have a ceiling fan, he recalled vaguely. Staring down at the lightweight blanket clutched in his hands, he remembered that he didn't have any bed linens that were pink, either.

"Mom!" Jack shouted only inches away from Griffin's ear. "He's awake! Now can we ask him?"

He heard Sarah's reply from the kitchen, but couldn't quite understand the words. He looked to Jack for clarification.

"You want syrup or jam with your waffles?"

"Waffles?" Griffin asked, still a little fuzzy. He'd never been one for quick coherence in the morning.

The boy nodded. "Mom's fixing waffles, but she's running late for work, so you gotta pick fast. Syrup or jam?"

"Syrup," Griffin answered automatically. Immediately the three boys ran off, and he was left to wonder yet again what the hell was going on.

He jackknifed up into a sitting position, scrubbed his hands quickly over his face and shook his head to clear it. Slowly memories of the previous evening began to form an orderly picture in his mind. He had fallen asleep on Sarah's couch, he realized, something that wasn't supposed to have happened. He had intended to wait for her while she got the boys tucked in and then he had planned to neck with her on this very couch for a long, long time after the three little imps had fallen asleep. Apparently, however, the three little imps had outlasted him.

He stumbled to the kitchen and saw Sarah standing at the counter beside the toaster, eyeing it expectantly and waiting for something. She was wearing a bright red, dress-for-success suit, sheer hose and no shoes. In one hand she held a dinner plate, in the other a blunt knife covered with what looked to be strawberry jam. Griffin was about to say good-morning, when the toaster clicked, two amber squares shot up from its slots and she caught them deftly on the plate before slathering them with jam. This was clearly a routine she had choreographed with great results some time ago, and he marveled at her graceful moves as she set the plate down in front of Sam.

"Thanks, Mom," the little boy said before digging into his breakfast.

"Good morning," Griffin said as he watched her shake two more frozen waffles from a box and tuck them into the toaster.

She turned to greet him with a quick, shy smile. "Good morning. Would you like some coffee?"

"Please."

The mug she pressed against his palm was warm, the coffee inside smelling strong and rich. The fragrance alone did wonders in bringing him back to life. He placed his fingers over hers as she transferred the mug to his possession, reveling in the touch, however brief.

"Sorry I fell asleep on you last night," he said. "I guess I was more tired than I realized."

She shrugged it off. "That's okay. I was going to wake you, but you were sleeping so soundly, I didn't have the heart to disturb you."

He nodded, sipped his coffee and tried to think of something to say. He'd never awakened in a woman's home to find that woman's children looking on. He would have thought such a situation would feel awkward and uncomfortable. He would have thought he'd be annoyed to find himself surrounded by a bunch of little kids when all he really wanted to do was wrestle Sarah to the floor and have his way with her.

Instead he was overcome by a giddy sense of well-being unlike anything he'd ever felt before. Of course, he still wanted to have his way with Sarah, but knowing he'd have to wait, knowing he'd be forced to tolerate the anticipation, somehow made the wanting even more intense—more pleasurable—than usual.

When he still could think of nothing mind-boggling or

earth-shattering to say, he simply voiced the first thought that popped into his head. "You look incredible."

Sarah glanced up and ran a quick hand through her tousled curls. "Thanks," she said softly. "I have a meeting with a client this morning."

"I'll say you do."

She blushed, then chuckled a little nervously. "No, not you." He hoped he wasn't imagining that regretful tone in her voice. "I mean a different client."

"Oh." He also hoped his own disappointment wasn't too obvious.

She was about to say something more, but the toaster clicked again, and she rushed back to retrieve her breakfast. For a moment, Griffin thought she was going to miss the waffles fast descending from their graceful arc through the air, but she managed at just the last minute to get the plate into position.

"I suppose I really should take the toaster in for repairs," she said. "Surely this isn't the way it's supposed to work."

"Nah," Griffin countered. "That would take all the fun out of breakfast."

"True. Have a seat," she instructed him as she set the plate before one of the two remaining empty places at the table. "Sorry they're frozen, but the last time I tried to make waffles from scratch, uh..." Her voice trailed off as she went to refill her coffee cup.

Jack completed the sentence for her. "The firemen made her promise she'd never do it again," he said before stuffing another bite of waffle into his mouth.

"It really wasn't my fault," Sarah said. "It was the waffle iron. A frayed cord. Honest. The explosion had nothing to do with the recipe. It was my mother's recipe, for pete's—"

"Explosion?" Griffin interrupted.

She nodded, but didn't elaborate further.

He shook his head. "Well, as long as no one was injured."

"No, not really."

"Mom just got her eyebrows singed a little is all," Sam said. "They grew back okay, though."

Griffin couldn't help but laugh as he reached for the syrup. "In that case, I urge you not to go to any trouble for me. I usually skip breakfast entirely."

"Eat fast, you guys," Sarah said to the boys. "Mrs. MacAfee will be here any minute, and I want to have the dishes done before she arrives." She glanced at her watch, her expression anxious. "And if she doesn't get here soon, I'm going to be late."

"Why don't you go ahead?" Griffin told her. "I can keep an eye on the boys until your sitter gets here. And I promise to wash the dishes."

"Oh, thanks, but I couldn't ask you to—"

"It's no trouble. I don't have to be at work for another hour."

"But you have to go home first, and—"

"Sarah," he interrupted her again. "I wouldn't offer if it was going to be an imposition."

She smiled gratefully. "Thanks. I owe you one."

He smiled back. "I'll be sure to collect. Soon."

She hurried from the kitchen, but not before throwing him a lascivious look. Griffin smiled at how easily he seemed to have become a part of her morning routine. He studied the boys surrounding him at the table, then looked down at the food on his plate. This morning was unlike any other he'd ever spent, and he liked the feeling of starting the day off in such a way—with other people. Especially other people like Sarah and her kids.

"So what do you guys have planned for today?" he asked the boys.

Jack replied enthusiastically, "They're building a new

subdivision over off Heath Lane, so we're gonna ride our bikes over and watch.''

"Then what are you going to do?"

Jack shrugged. "After they leave for the day, we can play on the dirt piles.''

Griffin nodded. He vaguely recalled a time in his life when he could spend an entire day in one place, finding a million things to do. "Sounds like fun," he said, wishing for some reason that he could take the day off and join them at the construction site, watching the bulldozers shift the earth and hurling dirt clods in a fight to defend the neighborhood.

Sarah came in amid a clacking of heels on the tile floor, affixing a gold earring in her ear. She treated each of her sons to a kiss on the forehead, wiped a slathering of jam from Sam's face, then, with a hastily offered farewell, headed for the back door.

"Hey," Griffin called after her, rising to follow.

As she pivoted quickly to face him, he wondered if what he intended to do was wise. Wise or not, however, he couldn't keep himself from framing her face in his hands and leaning forward to kiss her briefly on the lips. He knew the boys were watching with great interest, knew she would probably belt him for making the intimate gesture in their presence. But kissing Sarah goodbye as she left for work seemed like the most natural thing in the world for him to do.

"Have a good day," he said softly. "And be careful."

She covered his hands lightly with her own, but did not push them away. In her eyes, he detected any number of confused, conflicting emotions, emotions he figured pretty well mirrored his own. He smiled, hoping his expression was more reassuring than he felt.

"Thanks," she replied quietly. "I will."

They both dropped their hands back to their sides, then

stood staring at each other awkwardly. Their relationship had just taken a giant step forward with that one brief kiss, and now neither of them seemed to be sure where to go next.

Sarah was the first to glance away, turning her attention to the boys. "You all be good for Griffin, okay? And don't give Mrs. MacAfee a hard time, either."

Three pairs of very wide, very curious eyes gazed back at them, and all three boys nodded enthusiastically. Griffin could tell she was trying to hide her smile when she turned back toward him.

"'Bye," she said.

"'Bye."

And then she was gone, and all that remained was a faint scent of flowers and a warm feeling that spiraled up from somewhere deep in Griffin's heart. He felt the penetrating gaze of the three boys as he went back to his seat, but he said nothing, instead opting to see what their reaction would be. Jonah quickly went back to eating, while Sam and Jack exchanged interested looks. Jack would be the first to speak up, Griffin thought. It was simply the boy's nature to be the bold one. He held his breath and waited.

He didn't have to wait long.

Jack studied him intently as he asked, "Do you like my mom?"

Griffin nodded. "Yes. Yes, I do."

"You gonna marry her?"

Griffin's fork halted halfway to his mouth, syrup dripping from the waffle. Well, that was a question he hadn't expected to hear. Obviously he had underestimated the power of a child's curiosity. "Uh," he began.

"Well?" Jack asked.

Griffin recalled those awkward moments as a teenager, when he had been forced to undergo the third degree of a worried father before being allowed to date the man's

382 A Lawless Man

daughter. He had never been comfortable stating his intentions toward a girl. And now as he levelly met the gaze of the freckle-faced eight-year-old seated opposite him, his palms began to sweat.

"'Cause Mom likes you, too," Jack went on. "I can tell. I think you should marry her."

"She's not a very good cook," Sam added parenthetically, "but she's kinda pretty."

"And she likes baseball," Jack said.

"And basketball."

"And hockey, too."

"She's real funny."

"And she buys Snickers candy bars to give out on Halloween."

"And," Sam concluded, as if this were the most important quality of all, "she might let you have a puppy if you can keep your room clean for a whole year."

Griffin stared at the two boys, wondering how in the hell he'd gotten himself into this one. "Well, boys," he began, stalling for time. "Your mom's great and all. I like her a lot. But I'm not sure if—"

The telephone rang then, delivering him like a miracle descended from the heavens. Griffin leaped up to grab it, barking out a grateful hello, then frowned when no one replied from the other end of the line.

"Hello?" he asked again.

"Hello?" the voice replied. Whoever she was, Griffin thought, she sounded like she was at death's door. "I'm trying to reach Sarah Greenleaf."

"This is the Greenleaf residence," he said. "Sarah's gone to work. I'm staying with her sons until the sitter gets here."

"Well, I'm Dana MacAfee, the sitter," the woman said. "And I'm calling to tell Sarah I won't be able to make it in today."

"Oh?"

"No, I'm sorry. I've come down with something perfectly horrible and no doubt highly contagious. I don't think it would be a good idea for me to sit with the boys."

"I see."

"I hope this won't create any problems."

"No, none at all," Griffin said, wondering what to do.

"Please give Sarah my apologies."

"I will. And I hope you feel better," he added as an afterthought, before hooking the phone receiver back into its cradle.

Now what? he wondered. He had no idea where Sarah was going to be, and he couldn't very well leave three eight-year-old boys to their own devices all day. Could he? No, of course not. Even if they'd be doing nothing more than running around the neighborhood on their own, there had to be someone here for them to contact if they got hurt or into trouble. That gave Griffin pause. What if one of them did get hurt? The very idea made him cringe.

"Who was that?" Jack asked.

"Mrs. MacAfee," Griffin told him. "She's sick. She won't be able to come over today."

"Yaaaaaaay!" The cheers went up all around him, and he had to hide his smile.

"You shouldn't cheer when someone's sick," he told the boys. "It's not very nice."

They sobered somewhat, but not much.

He sighed, recognizing only one solution to the problem. "So I guess that means you're stuck with me for the day. What would you three like to do?"

Why he had just appointed himself baby-sitter, Griffin had no idea. Certainly Stony and his sergeant wouldn't be too thrilled about his missing a day of work to keep an eye on three kids. Still, the Jerwal case was just about tied up. Stony could gather the loose ends on his own, and by tomorrow, they'd probably be ready to make the arrests. The realization that he would be arresting the uncle of two of the boys he'd be watching today—not to mention the brother of the woman in whose life he was feeling so unbelievably comfortable lately—did not sit well with Griffin, so he pushed the thought away. Instead he focused his attention on the youngsters who stared back at him.

"Well?" he asked. "What'll it be?"

He watched as all three boys exchanged glances, then was amazed as three identical smiles broke out in unison. Griffin smiled back, but for some reason felt a little wary. There was something about those smiles...

"*Firestorm!*" the boys shouted as one.

"Firestorm?" Griffin asked. "What's that?"

Jack lifted a shoulder in a nonchalant shrug. "Oh, it's just a movie is all," he said.

Griffin was relieved. He'd been afraid it was some dangerous new ride at the amusement park. "Oh. Okay," he said. "We'll go see *Firestorm*."

"Yes!" the boys chorused with high-fives all around.

This was going to be a piece of cake, Griffin thought. If all they wanted to do was go to the movies, they'd go to the movies. This kid stuff was kid stuff. Nothing to it. He thought about what would happen later, when Sarah came home to find that he had spent the day with her children and had taken them to a movie they'd wanted to see. He thought about how pleased she'd be by the new camaraderie. He smiled.

"Just let me make a couple of phone calls," he said to the boys. "Then we can be on our way."

The last thing Sarah expected to see when she arrived home from work was Griffin Lawless standing barefoot in her kitchen, wearing a frilly apron covered with a cat print over his khaki shorts and navy blue T-shirt and stirring something that smelled wonderfully like barbecue. Nevertheless, that was exactly the sight that greeted her when she came through her back door Tuesday evening.

"Hi," she said as she latched the screen door behind her.

Griffin turned quickly at the sound of her voice, looking extremely guilty about something. His movements were jerky as he tapped the spoon against the pot and laid it on the spoon rest, and he made no move to approach her. Instead he leaned back against the counter, gripping it fiercely as if it were trying to escape. And although he smiled, his expression was in no way happy or reassuring.

"What's wrong?" she asked. "What are you doing here? Where's Mrs. MacAfee? Where are the boys?"

Evidently he chose to answer her questions in the reverse order they were asked, because he began, "The boys said they were going to ride over to the new subdivision, but I told them to be home by six. Mrs. MacAfee called in sick. Since I didn't know where to reach you, I took the day off to watch the boys."

"Oh, Griffin, I am so sorry about that," Sarah apologized. "You could have called Elaine at the shop. She could have told you where I was. Or better yet, she could have come for the boys herself."

"Elaine had to work, too," he said.

"And so did you," she reminded him.

He shrugged off her concern. "It was no trouble to take the day off. Stony understood."

She doubted it had been as easy as he made it sound. "I owe you another big one."

For the first time, his smile was genuine. "This is becoming a pretty big debt you owe me. We'll have to start discussing the terms of repayment soon."

Sarah felt herself grow warm at the way he was looking at her and, in an effort to steer the conversation back into safe waters, said, "So if everything worked out all right, how come you look like you spent the day on a chain gang?''

Griffin's smile fell again, and he turned his attention back to whatever it was he was cooking. "I, uh," he began. He glanced up quickly, but apparently was uncomfortable meeting her gaze, because, just as quickly, he glanced down at the pot again. He inhaled a deep breath, released it slowly, then tried once more. "I think I may have done a bad thing today."

Sarah doubted he was capable of doing anything bad, in spite of his bad-boy appearance, which had at one time so intimidated her. "Well," she began as she kicked off her shoes and shrugged out of her jacket, unbuttoning the top two buttons of her blouse. "Considering the fact that you spent the day with my kids, that's not entirely surprising. What was it this time? Grand-theft auto? Civil rebellion? World War III?"

"Ah, actually," Griffin said, "it was a movie."

Knowing her sons as well as she did, she immediately understood. "Don't tell me, let me guess. You asked them what they wanted to do, and they told you to take them to see that new adventure flick."

"*Firestorm,*" he stated apologetically.

"That's the one."

"Sarah, I promise you I had no idea what kind of movie it was. I thought it had those turtle things in it or something. If I'd known about the other stuff—"

"The women with big hooters?" she supplied helpfully.

He halted, mouth gaping, as if this newly offered bit of information was too troubling to consider. "There were women with big hooters in that movie?"

"Don't tell me you didn't notice."

He shook his head. "I gathered up the boys less than a half hour into the movie and hurried them out because the violence was unbelievable. And the language..." He shook his head helplessly, as if still haunted by the memory. "I mean, I don't hear stuff that bad in the locker room at the station. Good God, if I'd had to explain to the boys about hooters, too..." He shuddered visibly. "What are people thinking to make movies like that?"

Sarah's heart turned over at his undeniable shock and horror at what the situation with her children might have become. She stood on tiptoe and kissed his cheek. "You're a good guy, Griffin," she said before pulling back.

But he didn't let her go far. Before she could get away, he cupped his hand around her neck and pulled her back toward him. She was assailed by the spicy, masculine fragrance that was so essentially Griffin, felt the heat of his body mingling with hers. Her pulse rate quickened as she drew nearer, and she closed her eyes lest she be overcome by the desire winding its way up from somewhere deep inside her. It was amazing, she thought vaguely, how quickly things could go from harmless to dangerous where such a lawless man was concerned.

"So you're not angry with me for jeopardizing the moral well-being of your children?" he asked her softly, his mouth scant inches away from her ear.

She smiled, opening her eyes again simply to enjoy the sight of him. "With you?" she replied, hoping she didn't sound as breathless as she felt. "No, I'm not angry with you. You couldn't have known what you were getting yourself into. Jack and Sam, on the other hand, knew exactly what they were doing. I told them quite specifically that that movie was off-limits, and they suckered you into taking them, anyway."

Now Griffin smiled. "Don't be too rough on them. I would have done the same thing when I was a kid."

Sarah knew she would have, too, but that was beside the point. Her sons were in for a good talking to. "So is this why you're in here cooking dinner? Because you feel guilty about exposing my sons to the seamier side of life?''

With his free hand, Griffin tangled his fingers with hers, then lifted her hand to his lips. ''Well, that and the fact that I wanted to impress you.'' He touched his tongue to the juncture between her thumb and index finger.

Sarah closed her eyes as a shudder of delight worked its way through her body. ''Impress me?'' she managed to whisper.

''Mm-hmm.''

He skimmed his lips over her palm, kissed her wrist, then journeyed up her arm to the inside of her elbow. As he moved higher, Sarah pulled her sleeve back to grant him more complete access, then curved her hand over his nape to pull him closer. She sighed when he straightened and kissed the side of her neck.

''Oh, I'm very impressed,'' she said softly.

''Really?''

She nodded, the scrape of his day-old beard against her sensitive skin raising goose bumps. ''Mmm'' was all she was able to manage in response.

''You know,'' he began, his voice a quiet vibration against her neck, ''Jack mentioned something today about how he and Sam spend a month with their father every summer. I, uh, I don't suppose that month is coming up anytime soon is it?''

Sarah shook her head slowly, trying to get a better focus of her muddled, feverish thoughts. ''What day is this?'' she asked.

''I'm not sure,'' he said. ''The twenty-eighth? Twenty-ninth?''

''They won't be going to stay with their father until the first of August, so that's what…?'' For some reason, with Griffin nibbling on her earlobe that way, she was having trouble figuring her math.

He groaned. "Four weeks away."

Sarah glanced down at her watch. "You, uh, you told the boys to be home at six?" It was only five-twenty. That gave them a whole forty minutes to—

"Yes," Griffin interrupted her racing thoughts.

She tugged at the apron strings knotted behind his waist. "You know, a lot can happen in forty minutes."

He nodded, lifting his hands to work at the pearly buttons on her blouse. "Yes, it can."

The apron fell to the floor just as he freed the last button from its loop. He pulled her fiercely against him, kissing her with a hunger and need that rivaled her own. Sarah tangled her fingers in the dark silk of his hair, pulling him closer, until she felt the fullness of him pressing against her belly. When she realized how ready he was for her, she moaned, dropping her hands to his taut buttocks to pull him closer still. He curved his hand over her breast, thumbing the sensitive peak to life. She was just about to suggest they turn off the stove and duck back into her bedroom, when she heard the squeak of a bicycle kickstand out in the driveway beyond the back door, followed by Jack's high-pitched yell.

"Mom! Sam fell off his bike again and skinned his knee!"

The couple sprang apart as if someone had just doused them both with a fire hose. Griffin scooped up the apron from the floor and quickly tied it around himself again, and Sarah hoped the thin scrap of fabric would be enough to camouflage his condition. She fumbled with the buttons on her blouse until they were—she hoped—suitably refastened, then pushed a handful of blond curls back from her face. Unable to meet Griffin's gaze, she worried instead about striking what she hoped would be a nonchalant pose before her sons came bursting through the back door.

She gave Sam's knee a brief inspection, pronounced the

wound not life threatening, then, with a quick kiss on his cheek, sent the boys off to the bathroom for the disinfectant spray and a Band-Aid. Sam was sniffling a little, more scared than hurt, she thought, and Jack draped a reassuring arm over his brother's shoulder as they made their way down the hall.

"They're good kids," Sarah said as she turned to Griffin. "But they have very bad timing."

He smiled at her, then looked at the pot on the stove and sighed deeply. "It's just as well. The barbecue is starting to burn."

Sarah bit her lip to keep from commenting that the barbecue wasn't the only thing in the house burning. Instead she said, "I'll just go check on Sam. Make sure Jack hasn't bandaged him within an inch of his life."

She waited for Griffin to reply, but he only nodded. She made it as far as the doorway before he called out her name. She halted, glancing back over her shoulder.

"I won't wait until August 1," he said without turning around.

She drew a shaky breath. "You won't have to," she told him. And before either of them had a chance to comment further, she bolted from the room.

Chapter 9

The following Thursday found Sarah picking through the last of the items she'd discovered in the china cabinet of Judge Mercer's formal dining room—formal, as opposed to the smaller, more intimate family dining room in another wing of the house. Since she'd never done an appraisal for anyone before, she had tried to be organized for once in her life while performing the task for Griffin. She had started in the west wing of the house, working from the attic down. Now, more than four weeks after beginning her task, she had just begun to explore the first floor of the house. One thing was certain. No matter what happened between Griffin and her in their personal lives, she would be tied to him professionally for a good while yet.

Because she was no longer digging around in crates and straw-filled boxes, she now tried to dress as professionally as possible for work, and had opted today for a white blouse and no-nonsense, tailored blue skirt. Nonetheless, she hadn't been able to keep herself from kicking off her shoes and now sat barefoot before the china cabinet. She was dismayed that she had still managed to pick up a few smudges of dust and grime, and was rubbing at a spot of black on her hem, when she looked inside the cabinet and saw something wonderful. The light from the chandelier above her glinted off a crystal vase as if it had been manufactured from stardust. Sarah held her breath as she reached inside.

She pulled the piece slowly from its resting place and gave it a thorough inspection before confirming the conclusion she had already leaped to. What she held was a Lalique vase, approximately twenty-four inches in height, crystal clear at the top, etched with a frosty rendition of Artemis and animals where the belly flared out. It was signed and numbered by the artist and looked brand-new. But the artist in question had created pieces for the company more than a century ago, and although his work had been coveted in the collecting community, very little of it remained. Should the piece be authentic—and she was certain it was—the vase was worth several hundred thousand dollars.

She whistled low under her breath, turning the piece carefully in her hands, lifting it in the direction of a window to let the clear segment of the crystal catch the light. She gasped as a single ray of sunshine exploded into a brilliant cascade of rainbow hues that danced on the wall above her. The vase should be in a museum, she thought, suddenly realizing the enormity of what she held in her hands. She wondered how long it had been in the Mercer family, wondered how much had originally been spent to acquire it.

"Wow."

The word thundered through the cavernous, empty room from somewhere behind her, and so rapt had been her attention on the vase that Sarah started at the sound of Griffin's voice. For the briefest of moments, the vase began to slip from her fingers, and she quickly wrapped her free arm around it and pulled it to her breast. She rose up on her knees and twisted around to look at him. He was leaning in the doorway on the opposite side of the room, wearing his detective uniform of rumpled gray trousers, rumpled white shirt and wrinkled necktie. She wondered if he owned an iron.

"Oh, God, Griffin," she groaned. "Don't ever sneak up on me like that again."

He smiled as he pushed himself away from the doorjamb and started toward her. "Why not? I like to watch you jump."

"Yeah, well, my jump this time could have cost you more than half a million dollars."

He stopped in midstride, his gaze wandering from her face to the crystal vase she still clutched in her arms like a newborn baby. *"What?"*

She nodded, extending the piece out as far as she dared for his inspection. "This little trinket right here could net you a very tidy sum. I mean, collectively speaking, the contents of this house have already made you a millionaire several times over, but if Judge Mercer has anything else like this stowed away, you could be looking at some *really* serious dough."

Griffin stared at Sarah for a long time, letting her words sink in. Until that moment, he honestly hadn't allowed himself to consider the magnitude of all that his until-recently-unknown relative had left to him. But as he heard her voice it in such matter-of-fact terms and saw the undeniably exquisite richness of the vase she held in her hands, the knowledge of what had befallen him hit him like a ton of bricks, and he felt his knees begin to crumple beneath him.

Before he embarrassed himself by toppling over, Griffin dropped to sit on the floor beside Sarah, extending a finger to trace it carefully over the fine crystal vase.

"Half a million?" he echoed.

She nodded. "At least."

"That's unbelievable."

"Believe it."

He shook his head in wonder, trying his best to cope with the montage of emotions swirling around in his head. He had come to the house to find Sarah because he and Stony had finally received the warrants for the arrests of Wallace Greenleaf and Jerry Schmidt. He had wanted to tell her what was going to happen before he and Stony swooped in to cart her brother off to jail. He knew a confrontation with Sarah would doubtlessly ensue. He knew she'd be angry with him and might not want to see him for a long time. And hell, he wouldn't exactly blame her.

But he had wanted to prepare her, and had wanted a chance to state his case before she drew the wrong conclusions. And, he admitted sheepishly, he'd wanted to let her know just what a crook her brother was before Wally had a chance to defend himself.

Okay, so maybe that wasn't very nice of him, being a part of the justice system as he was. But some things were more important than technical legalities, right? Love, for example, was supposed to conquer all, was it not?

But somehow, the words that Griffin needed to speak escaped him. As he looked at Sarah, sitting in this magnificent house—a house that was his but didn't feel as if it was—holding a work of art worth so much money, a work of art that was also his but didn't feel as if it was, Griffin wanted to claim Sarah as his own, too. Unequivocally, irretrievably. He didn't feel as if he belonged amid the glorious Mercer holdings. But he did feel as if he belonged with Sarah. He only hoped she'd still want him after she realized what he'd done.

Without thinking about his feelings, he reached out and cradled the vase in his hands, then placed it carefully back inside the open china cabinet. Moving quickly, so that he didn't have time to think about his actions, he rose and extended his hand to Sarah. She looked at him questioningly before touching her fingers to his, but his silence must have encouraged her to remain quiet, too.

He helped her to her feet and immediately pulled her into his arms, ducking his head to kiss her. But what he'd intended to be a simple gesture, a soft caress, was nothing less than a heart-stopping joining of his mouth with hers. He kissed her hard, fast, deep and long, because for some reason he suddenly couldn't get enough of her. His fingers entwined around her nape, then tangled in her blond curls, pushing her head even closer to his so that he could plunder the dark recesses of her mouth more fully. But still it wasn't enough.

Finally Sarah tore her mouth from his, gasping for breath. "Griffin, please. I can hardly breathe."

But instead of accommodating her request, he kissed her again, with all the ferocity of the first time. He wound an arm around her waist, working feverishly at the buttons on her blouse with his free hand. She helped him yank her shirttail free of her skirt, then guided his hand to the front clasp of her lacy brassiere. Her skin was warm and soft, and he felt her heartbeat raging out of control beneath his fingertips. He moved his hand to the right until he cupped her breast in his hand, then traced his thumb in slow, insistent circles over the taut peak.

She moaned at the intimate touch, arching against him to give him freer access. An explosion of white light burst somewhere in Griffin's brain, and afterward all coherent thought fled him. All he wanted was to be with Sarah. Nothing, nothing else in the world, mattered otherwise.

"I love you, Sarah," he whispered against her mouth.

He wasn't sure he wanted to hear her response, so he kissed her again, as deeply as before. He felt her tugging frantically at his belt, and pulled away from her enough to facilitate her efforts. With deft fingers, she found her way inside, cupping what she could of him in her palm before stroking her fingers up and down against him.

This time Griffin was the one to groan, pausing in his exploration of Sarah to enjoy the exquisite sensations her hand wreaked upon him. He didn't understand the sudden intensity of his desire for her, couldn't fathom why she above all others should be the woman he couldn't live without. He only knew he needed her, right here, right now, for as long as it took to satisfy their hunger, for as long as it took to make them both happy forever.

"Upstairs," he managed to whisper as he panted for breath. "There are bedrooms upstairs."

Sarah, too, was panting, but tilted her head back to look at him. "Did you come as prepared this afternoon as you were at my house that night?"

He smiled and nodded.

She smiled back. "Did you bring your handcuffs?"

He chuckled. "They're out in the car."

"Pity." She sighed wistfully. "Well, next time for sure."

Griffin scooped her up in his arms and headed for the stairs, taking them two at a time and stopping at the first door he encountered. The bedroom smelled dusty and old, but the bright afternoon sun beat down through the window, throwing an irregular rectangle of light across the flowered coverlet on the bed. He wondered briefly who the room had belonged to so many years ago, wondered if perhaps it was Meredith's room, the room where his mother had been born.

But his thoughts quickly turned toward a new avenue when he looked down at Sarah, at the blond curls mussed by his touch, the lips reddened by his kisses. Their disarrayed clothing reminded him of how close he was to completely losing control. He released her slowly, rubbing his body languorously against hers as he set her down, then swooped in to kiss her again.

Sarah was blindsided by that kiss. One minute she was

leaning heavily against Griffin, gripping his big biceps to prevent her knees from buckling beneath her, and the next she was lost in a wondrous embrace. He cupped his hands over her shoulders, pressed his flattened palms intimately down her back, then curved his fingers over her derriere and pushed her insistently against him. She felt the swollen length of him pressing against her abdomen, and recalled in an unusually vivid memory what it had been like to feel him inside her the first time. Her temperature soared at the reminder, heat writhing through her before pooling at the juncture of her thighs. She tangled her fingers in his hair to pull him closer, returning his kiss as deeply as he had offered it, trying to devour him before he could consume her.

She struggled with his necktie until she had yanked it free of his shirt, then fumbled to undo his buttons. After a moment she felt his fingers join hers in the task, then she splayed her hands wide over the warm, rigid expanse of his chest as Griffin shrugged out of his shirt. He was a magnificent creature, she thought vaguely, marveling again at the way the muscles bunched and moved beneath her fingertips as if they were alive. Her fingers tripped down over his rib cage, pausing at the waistband of his trousers before venturing onward. Griffin caught her hands in his before she could explore further, however, and he chuckled low.

"Not yet," he said softly. "I'm liable to go off like a bazooka, and I don't want that to happen until I'm finished with you."

Her heart thumped wildly at the promise of more intimacies to come, but she smiled. "Oh?" she asked. "And just what did you have in mind for me?"

He smiled back, a smile that was at once salacious, seductive and serene. "Just you wait and see."

Without a moment's hesitation, he pushed her blouse and brassiere from her shoulders, ignoring the garments as they floated to the floor in a white heap beside his shirt. Carefully, as if he were reaching for the crystal vase he had so recently cradled in his hands, he covered her breasts with warm fingers. At first he only held her that way, his eyes never leaving hers, then he thumbed the tumid peaks to greater life. She was helpless to prevent the single sound of delight she emitted, and Griffin smiled. He bent forward and pressed his lips against the flesh he touched, drawing one velvety breast to his mouth, circling her with his tongue before tugging her more deeply inside.

For long moments he suckled her, driving her closer and closer to the brink. Just when she thought she could no longer tolerate the sensations shuddering through her, he pulled away, pausing to place one quick kiss over her heart before turning his attentions elsewhere.

He reached around behind her and tugged down the zipper on her skirt, kneeling before her as he shoved it down around her ankles. Before she could step out of it, he gripped her waist in his hands, holding her in place. He leaned forward, pressing his mouth to the soft cotton fabric of her panties, exhaling a hot, damp breath before kissing her through the thin fabric. Then he hooked his thumbs in the waistband and pulled them down, too. But instead of rising, he lifted one of her feet from their confinement, urged her legs apart and settled his hands on her waist again.

It had been hot in the bedroom when they'd entered, Sarah thought absently as she cupped her hands over Griffin's shoulders to steady herself. But not nearly as hot as it became when she looked down to watch Griffin's dark head descend upon her again. With every piercing stroke of his tongue against that most intimate part of her, the bedroom grew warmer, until she was certain it had become engulfed in flame. She squeezed Griffin's shoulders more tightly and tilted her head back to gaze at the ceiling. The bedroom was fine, she noted as her eyes fluttered closed. It was only she who had succumbed to the fire.

Just as she reached the white-hot center of that heat, she cried out loud, and Griffin finally ended his onslaught. He kissed her flat belly, dipped his tongue into her navel, then raked his hands up over her rib cage to cover her breasts. Slowly he rose, towering over her, and she wondered how on earth she had ever gotten by without this man in her life. She started to speak, but he lifted two fingers to her lips, halting any words she might have uttered. He reached for her hand, twining their fingers, then rubbed her open palm over the rigid swell in his trousers. He gasped, tilting his head back, and Sarah took a step closer.

When he released her hand, she continued the primal rhythm he had started, until she could no longer tolerate the distance between them. Together they removed what remained of his clothing, and together they moved toward the bed. They had scarcely pushed the covers to the foot, when Griffin was upon her, kneeling behind her and touching her in all the places he'd missed so far. Sarah sighed at the sensations coursing through her body, feeling more wanted and cherished than she'd ever felt in her life. And loved, she realized with no small amount of wonder. Griffin made her feel that, too.

She turned on the bed to face him, both still kneeling, circling an arm around his neck to pull him down for a kiss. As he drew nearer, he pushed her backward, until she was flat on her back and he was lying atop her, bracing himself on his strong forearms. She hooked her legs over his, curling her fingers over his taut thighs, and silently bade him to enter her welcoming warmth. He needed no further encouragement. With a single, fierce thrust he was inside her, and both cried out at the perfect consonance of their union.

Deeper and deeper Griffin ventured inside her, reaching places in Sarah that had never been touched before. He bent near her ear to murmur erotic promises, then carried them out, one by exhausting one. For what seemed like days, he

gave her pleasure, the rectangle of light on the bed growing
longer and dimmer as the time passed. Finally he came to
her one last time, burying himself completely inside to
rocket them both over the top.

What had begun as a fast, demanding need ultimately
ended in a slow, languid satisfaction. Sarah and Griffin lay
still and silent for a long time, each too overwhelmed to
break what fragile hold they held on the afternoon's encounter, each too frightened by the tenuous fragility of their
newfound intimacy to risk spoiling it by saying the wrong
thing.

As Sarah lay nestled against Griffin, she marveled at what
stroke of luck must have thrown this man into her path. She
grinned when she recalled that she had originally considered
their first meeting anything but fortuitous. Had someone told
her then that she would wind up falling madly in love with
the infuriating Officer Lawless, she would have laughed out
loud. Now, however, all she could do was smile.

There was a question she wanted to ask him but was
completely uncertain how to approach it. She twined her
fingers in the dark hair swirling about his chest, then decided
it might be best simply to be straightforward. "Griffin?"
she asked softly, her voice sounding muted and mellow in
the warm, close air of the bedroom.

"Hmm?"

"Did you mean what you said a little while ago?"

She felt him stir beside her, felt his arm tighten to keep
her close. "Did I mean what?" he asked.

She took a deep breath, voicing her next words as she
quickly exhaled. "Did you mean it when you said you loved
me?"

Sarah felt more than heard him gasp, and wished immediately that she could take back her question. But before she
had the chance to try, Griffin responded.

"Yes," he said. "Yes, I meant it."

She squirmed beside him until she was able to see his face completely. He looked tired and uneasy, and not a little scared. She cupped her hand over his rough jaw and grinned.

"Really?" she asked.

He nodded slowly. "Really."

"Then say it again."

"I love you, Sarah," he replied immediately.

She snuggled back against him, feeling a new, different kind of heat seep into her body. "I love you, too, Griffin," she said softly. "I love you, too."

Her quietly uttered words were almost Griffin's undoing. How the hell was he supposed to tell her about her brother now? *I love you, Sarah. Oh, and by the way, I'm arresting your brother this evening. I kind of neglected to mention that I've been investigating him virtually since the day you and I met. He'll be spending the next few years in the state pen because of me, and you'll only be able to see him on visiting days. He'll lose a number of the basic rights you and I enjoy, and his life will never be the same again, as a direct result of my activities. Just thought you'd like to know.* Yeah, that was sure to keep her right here by his side.

Griffin sighed, opened his mouth to say something, quickly changed his mind and snapped it shut again. How had he managed to get himself into this? he wondered. Of all the lousy luck.

"What time is it?" Sarah asked sleepily beside him.

Automatically he glanced at his wrist, only to find it watchless, then looked around, uncertain what had happened to the timepiece during their lovemaking.

"I think I put it on the nightstand after I removed it," she said, evidently reading his mind.

But it wasn't there, either. He leaned over the side of the bed and saw his watch winking up at him from the floor.

Reaching for it, he chuckled and said, "I guess you kicked it off when your foot went flying while I was—"

"Oh, yeah," she interrupted him, blushing furiously. "Now I remember. I think I broke that bud vase, too. But don't worry," she added quickly. "It was strictly cheap carnival glass. Those pieces are a dime a dozen."

He laughed. "I don't care if it was worth half a million," he said. "It was worth it to have you—"

"Griffin..." she groaned, silently begging him not to bring up their recent sexual gymnastics. "Just tell me what time it is."

His grin turned to a frown when he saw the time. "You're not going to like it."

"Why not?"

"It's after six."

"Omigosh," Sarah gasped as she jumped up from the bed. Hastily she circled the room and began to gather her clothing, trying to put it on as she hurried about. "Mrs. MacAfee's going to kill me for being late again. I wouldn't blame her if she quit. Do you know how hard it is to find a decent sitter? It's next to impossible. It took me months to find her. All the other applicants had names like Charlie Manson or Betty Mussolini. Or they looked like they'd just caught the last boat off the Island of Dr. Moreau."

"Sarah, you can't leave yet," Griffin told her. "There's something we have to talk about."

She finished buttoning her blouse, looked down to see that she had skipped a button somewhere along the line, then rapidly began to unbutton it again. "I can't," she said as she completed the task once more, this time with greater success. "I really have to go."

"But, Sarah—"

"Why don't you come home and have dinner with me and the boys?" she asked as she haphazardly stuffed her blouse into her skirt and zipped it up. "We can talk afterward."

He shook his head. "I can't. I have to meet Stony in about half an hour."

"Well, Stony could come, too. We can invite Elaine and Jonah."

"No, that's impossible," Griffin told her. "Stony and I have to make an arrest tonight."

Sarah's head snapped up and she grinned at him. "Oh, that sounds so exciting. Bagging some crook to make society safer for innocent folks like me."

He seized upon her words. "Yes!" he exclaimed, sitting up straighter in bed. When the sheet dipped low around his hips, and Sarah's expression grew speculative, he clutched it behind him like a toga. "That's right," he went on quickly, hoping he sounded more effective as a law-enforcement officer than he felt at the moment. "That's why I'm going after this guy. Because he's a crook and has forfeited his right to be a member of the law-abiding community. And don't you forget it."

Sarah leaned forward and kissed him briefly on the lips. "And I love you for it," she said before turning to leave.

"Sarah!" he called after her.

At the bedroom door she turned, her face a silent question mark. He opened his mouth to say so many things that needed to be said, but was suddenly overcome by a sense of helplessness that almost crippled him. "I love you, too," he said softly, knowing it probably wouldn't be enough.

She smiled at him, a beautiful, happy, carefree smile, then lifted her fingers to her lips, blew him a kiss and was gone. Griffin wished he could feel as uninhibited and unencumbered as Sarah must feel right now. But all he could think about was what the night ahead of him held. All he could do was envision Sarah's face the next time he saw her, knowing it would hold none of the qualities she'd shown him only moments ago. The next time he would see hurt, betrayal and anger. And all of it would be because of him.

He heard the front door downstairs close behind her, and it seemed such a sad, conclusive sound. Throwing the bed-clothes aside, he rose to dress, but without the hasty excitement of his companion. Griffin was in no hurry to get where he needed to be. He only wished the night ahead of him was over. Over so he could get back to living his life the way he'd lived it before all this had begun—alone. Funny how it hadn't occurred to him before to be lonely in his solitary existence. But now that he'd have memories of Sarah Greenleaf to haunt him, loneliness would be a nec-essary side effect.

He couldn't let her go, he told himself. No matter what happened after tonight, he had to hang on to her. She might be Wallace Greenleaf's sister, but she was Griffin Lawless's love. And through whatever means necessary, legal or not, he would see to it she remained in his life forever.

Chapter 10

Later that night, just as Sarah was finishing up the dinner dishes, the telephone rang. Certain it was Griffin, she yelled to her sons to turn down the television in the living room and reached for the receiver, murmuring a quick hello.

"Sarah, I've been arrested."

She gripped the phone more steadily in one hand, trying with the other to shift the plate she was washing under the stream of rinse water. "Wally?" she asked. "Is that you? What did you say?"

"I've been arrested," her brother repeated from the other end of the line, his voice sounding distant and tinny, carrying none of the swaggering confidence it normally displayed.

"*What?*" she exclaimed, dropping the plate back into the soapy water. He had her full attention now. "Arrested? What for?"

"My attorney is in Grand Cayman until the end of the week," he went on without clarifying. "You're going to have to come down here and bail me out."

"Bail you out?" she echoed, still unable to believe what her brother was telling her. "Why? What are the charges?"

"Trumped up," he was quick to reply. "Look, it's all some mix-up, I assure you. And it will all be straightened out soon enough. Then I'm going to sue the hell out of the Clemente P.D. for false arrest and take a nice long vacation in Tahiti on the proceeds. When can you get here?"

Sarah shook her head, trying to clear out the cobwebs. "I don't know. I mean, how much money do I need to bring?"

"Well, they've set my bail at fifty thousand dollars—"

"Fifty thousand dollars!"

"But you only need to have ten percent of that."

"Five thousand dollars?" she gasped, amazed that she'd been able to perform even that simple mathematical task.

"Yeah, so how long before you can get down here with it?"

She *might* be able to scrape up fifty bucks, Sarah thought, trying to remember what the balance in her checking account was. But five thousand? Who did her brother think she was? Nelson Rockefeller? "Wally, I don't have five thousand dollars."

"What do you mean, you don't have it?"

His proprietary, self-important tone of voice came back with a vengeance then, raising Sarah's hackles with its arrival. "I don't have five thousand dollars," she repeated, speaking slowly, as if to a toddler. "I'm not made of money, you know."

"Come on, it's just five gees. You mean to tell me you don't even have access to that amount of money?"

"Of course not."

Wally was quiet for a moment, then said, "They'll take deeds to property. You own your house, right? You got it in the divorce. Just sign that over to them."

"Wallace Greenleaf, you are out of your mind if you

think I'm going to put my house on the line for bail money. You haven't even told me what you're under arrest for.''

''I'm good for the money, Sarah. You know I am.''

Sarah was torn. She wanted to help her brother, but how on earth was she supposed to do that without the means? ''Why don't you call Mom?'' she suggested. ''She's all fired up to invest in your projects. She must have that kind of money she could wire down to you.''

''Not since she invested in the cafeteria,'' Wally told her.

''You took Mom's last dollar to invest in that crazy scheme of yours?''

''It wasn't exactly her *last* dollar,'' he said. ''And besides, the turnover on that cafeteria will be enormous. You should throw some of your own cash into the pot.''

''Yeah, well, like I said, Wally, I don't have any to spare.''

Something was wrong here, Sarah thought. Her brother might be many things, but she couldn't imagine a single one of them being something for which he would be placed under arrest. As much as she sometimes wished it were, being a persistent jerk wasn't illegal. So why was Wally so resistant to telling her exactly what the charges were?

''Tell me what you've been arrested for,'' she said. ''And then I'll decide whether or not I'll put my house at risk.''

''Sarah...''

''Wally...'' she mimicked in his petulant tone.

He sighed, a loud, exasperated sound that was even more annoying thanks to the phone's distortion of it. ''Bait advertising,'' he finally told her.

Sarah frowned. ''Bait advertising? I've never heard of that. What is it? It doesn't sound so bad. It sounds like a misdemeanor.''

''It is.''

''They set your bail at fifty thousand dollars for a single misdemeanor?''

He sighed again, an even more exasperated sound this time, and continued, "They've also charged me with deceptive business practices and commercial bribery."

Sarah's stomach clenched into a knot. "Those charges sound more serious."

"They're still misdemeanors," Wally told her. "Just as most of the other charges are."

"*Most* of the *other* charges?" she parroted. She was getting tired of her brother's games. "Wally, just spit it out, will you?"

"All right, all right. I've been charged with thirty-seven misdemeanor counts."

"Oh, Wally."

"But nothing that's going to stick," he was quick to add.

"What's the big one they got you for?" she asked him, more than a little afraid to discover what it would be.

He paused for a long moment before replying. "Bribery of a public servant," he finally said. "A felony. Class *D*. Fourteen counts."

"Oh, Wally," she repeated miserably.

"But I've been framed, Sarah," he assured her. "I swear I have. You know me. I am *not* a crook."

Sarah shook her head slowly. Frankly, she didn't know what to believe. Her brother had done some dumb things in his life, and she honestly wouldn't be surprised to discover he was still at it. But bribery? Of a public servant, no less? Something that was clearly a major legal no-no? Was he truly capable of committing such a crime? Was he really that stupid?

This time it was Sarah who sighed, a long, weary, expulsion of breath. She ran a hand through her hair and thought for a moment. Immediately Griffin came to mind, and she smiled. He was a cop. He'd know what to do. He could help her out.

"Look," she told Wally, "let me call Griffin and see—"

"Who?"

"Griffin," she repeated. "Griffin Lawless. He's that, uh...friend of mine you met at the house a few weeks ago. He's a cop, and maybe he can—"

"Oh, man, I *knew* that guy looked familiar."

"What?"

"I got news for you, little sister. One of the cops who arrested me was your pal."

"*What?*"

"Yeah, the whole time he was reading me my rights and handcuffing me—"

"He, uh, he handcuffed you?" Sarah interrupted, assuring herself that her interest was only idle curiosity. Then she quickly chastised herself for forgetting the seriousness of the situation at hand. She adopted a more outraged tone as she clarified, "I mean, he *handcuffed* you? How despicable."

"Yeah," Wally went on, evidently not noticing her slip. "And the whole time he was doing it, I kept telling him, 'You look awfully familiar. Have we met?' And he just ignored me."

"Are you sure it was Griffin?" she asked. "Griffin Lawless?"

"Positive. In fact, I remember saying something about how ironic it was, him being a cop named Lawless and all."

Oh, and he'd probably loved that, Sarah thought. He'd probably thrown Wally that same perturbed expression he'd given her on their initial meeting when she'd made the same observation. Then she immediately remembered that the man she was recalling so affectionately, the man with whom she'd made love only hours ago, the man she'd said she loved and who claimed to love her back, had just arrested her brother. He had told her outright that afternoon that he was making an arrest tonight, but had conveniently neglected to mention that the arrestee was none other than her brother, Wally. A brother he'd met in her kitchen less than two weeks ago, she reminded herself further. A man there was no mistaking was a member of her family.

Griffin Lawless had lied to her.

The realization hit Sarah in the head as if someone had smacked her. Before arresting someone, a cop had to investigate that person, right? She'd learned that much from television shows. So Griffin must have been investigating Wally for some time. How long, she had no idea. But she couldn't help wondering if the beginning of his interest in Wally's activities coincided directly with his interest in her life. Was that why he'd gotten close to her in the first place? Because she was Wally's sister and he wanted to use her to uncover more about her brother's life?

No, that couldn't be, she decided. She couldn't remember a single time when he'd even mentioned Wally's name around her, let alone asked her any questions about him, other than the normal, curious, personal ones that arose whenever the two of them were discussing their families. If he'd wanted to know more about Wally's professional life, he would have asked.

Another, more troubling thought struck her. Was she, too, under suspicion of some kind? Was that why Griffin had insinuated himself into her life? Was he hoping to uncover something illegal about her, as well? He had ticketed her for speeding, after all. In his eyes, that probably indicated she had a congenital propensity for breaking the law. Naturally he would be suspicious of her, she thought. But did the police actually carry their investigations so far that they wound up in the suspect's bed?

"Sarah? Are you still there?"

She shook her head to clear it and replied with some distraction. "Yes, Wally, I'm still here."

"So now that *your* cop pal has hauled my butt down to jail, what are *you* going to do about it?"

Wally's demanding, reproachful voice, so clearly condemning her for something he'd gotten himself into, set Sarah's teeth on edge. That did it. She'd had it. Had it with brothers, had it with cops, had it with men. She'd go down to the police station and see what—if anything—she could do to expedite Wally's release. And while she was there, maybe she'd look around for Griffin, because she had more than a few questions for him. And if Wally insisted on behaving like a child, and if Griffin's responses didn't meet with her satisfaction, she fully intended to wash her hands of both of them.

Griffin had a headache. A mind-numbing, earsplitting, shoulder-tensing migraine that had come upon him the moment he'd rapped his knuckles against Wallace Greenleaf's front door. One that simply would not go away. He swallowed a fourth aspirin—knowing the tablet would probably do little more than eat a hole in his stomach lining—propped his elbows on his desk and cradled his head in his hands. If bad days were wild horses, he thought, he had just been stampeded into mush.

"I'd like to have a word with you."

It was a voice he'd been expecting to hear all night, but one he had dreaded nonetheless. He dropped his hands to his desk, glanced up to find Sarah glaring back at him and tried to smile.

"Hi," he said. "Is there a problem, Ms. Greenleaf?"

She was wearing those tight, short cutoffs that had nearly driven him mad at the softball game and a loose-fitting, purple T-shirt that read My Mom Went To Atlantic City and All I Got Was This Lousy T-shirt. Her hair was a mess, her face devoid of all makeup, and she was angry. Very, very angry by the looks of it. Griffin didn't think he'd ever wanted anything more than to pull her into his arms and kiss her senseless that instant. But he looked beyond her to see that Jack and Sam were seated with uncharacteristic quiet on a bench behind her—safely out of earshot—watching intently every move he and Sarah made. So instead he cupped his hands behind his head, leaned back in his chair and waited for her to tear him apart.

"You lied to me," she said without preamble.

"No, I didn't."

She tugged the strap of her purse more forcefully over her shoulder, leaving her fingers curled around the length of leather. He wasn't sure if she was fearful of having her purse snatched by some questionable lowlife in the police station, or if she simply felt the need to have something— even something as slender and nonthreatening as her arm— creating a barrier in front of her.

"Yes, you did, too," she insisted.

"I'm sorry, Sarah," he began again. "But I beg to differ. I never lied to you."

"How long had you been investigating Wally before you arrested him?" she demanded.

"About six weeks, but—"

"Right around the time you started sniffing around my front door," she interrupted. "I'd say that gave you ample opportunity to tell me you were investigating my brother."

"I'm not at liberty to divulge the specifics of an ongoing investigation to laypeople," Griffin said, wishing at the last moment that he'd chosen another word besides *laypeople* to indicate Sarah. It was an impossibly inappropriate gaffe, one she'd evidently noted, because a red flush that had nothing to do with embarrassment crept up her throat and darkened her cheeks.

"Yeah, and I guess that's all I was to you, wasn't I?"

Griffin rose from his chair with enough force to send it toppling backward. Sarah flinched, but did not move away from him. If anything, her posture became more challeng-

ing. She settled her hands on her hips in the ages-old gesture
of defiance.

"That's not true and you know it," he snapped, somehow
managing to keep his voice low. He had already noted that
the two of them were generating much interest among both
her sons and the other detectives in the squad room. "I
entered the investigation into your brother's activities long
after it had begun."

"But you knew Wally was my brother. You knew you
were..." She paused, dropping her gaze to the floor, suddenly unable to meet his gaze. Her voice, too, was quieter
when she spoke again. "You knew you were getting involved with the sister of one of your suspects, but you did
nothing to stop that involvement. To me, that smacks of
unethical behavior if nothing else. Although I myself have
a few other words I could call it."

Griffin knew he shouldn't ask, but couldn't help himself.
"Such as?"

She jerked her head up again and studied him levelly.
"Such as lowdown, sneaky, calculating, self-serving, cold-
hearted—"

"All right, all right. I get the gist of it." He rubbed at a
knot in his neck and sighed. "Look. I'm no more thrilled
about how this all turned out than you are. But the fact is,
your brother is a criminal who's landed himself in a lot of
trouble. I had nothing to do with that, Sarah. I'm just the
guy they assigned to bring him in."

She stared at him for a long time without speaking, and
he could tell she was thinking hard about something. "This
isn't about Wally," she finally said.

He arched his left brow skeptically. "No?"

She shook her head. "No, not entirely. This is about the
fact that you lied to me. That you were investigating him
while you were sleeping with me." She held up a hand to
stop his protest before he could utter it. "Because you'll

never convince me there was anything more to your feelings for me than wanting sex. If there had been, you would have been honest with me. Maybe not from the start, I'll grant you that. But the least you could have done, Griffin, was warn me about what was going to happen."

"And risk you tipping off your brother before we could arrest him?"

"I wouldn't have done that!"

"Wouldn't you?"

Sarah started to immediately deny Griffin's allegation, then paused to give the question more thorough consideration before replying. She had come down to the police station full of fire and indignation, ready to nail him to the wall for what he'd done. She'd been mad about her brother's arrest, and madder still about the fact that Griffin had known all along what was going to happen and hadn't even clued her in. She'd been mad that he had gotten involved with her while he was investigating Wally. But right now, she wasn't sure what made her maddest of all.

"Why couldn't you have just waited?" she asked him softly. "Why couldn't you have just gone about your business, done whatever it was you were obligated by your job to do, then called me to ask me out when it was all over?"

"Oh, right," Griffin replied sarcastically. "Like you really would have gone out with the man who'd tossed your brother's keester into the can."

She lifted a hand to her forehead, rubbing vigorously to dispel an ache that throbbed between her eyes. She was hurt, confused and angry, and she had no idea what to think. "Was it really that important to you?" she asked. "That I go out with you?"

"Yes," he responded immediately. "It was that important. You've become more important to me than anything else in my life ever has."

She sighed, suddenly feeling more exhausted than she

could ever recall feeling. "Oh, Griffin. You've ruined everything."

He came around the front of his desk, curved his palms possessively over her shoulders and held her until she looked up to meet his gaze. What she saw in his eyes made her stomach clench into a knot. His reaction to the situation mirrored her own, she realized. But he was less willing to give up hope than she was.

"How on earth have *I* ruined everything?" he asked.

"Well, obviously there's going to be a trial now," she said.

"Yes."

"A trial that will put you and Wally on opposite sides of the fence."

"Yes."

"You'll be doing your damnedest to put him behind bars, and he'll be fighting for his life. Because no matter what happens with this thing, Griffin, his life will never be the same after it's all over."

"So what's your point, Sarah?"

"Don't you see?" she pleaded with him. "Maybe I haven't always seen eye to eye with my brother. Hell, I don't know if I've ever seen eye to eye with him. And even if he's guilty of what you say he is..." She lifted a hand into the air as if groping for help, doubled her hand into a fist, then dropped it helplessly back to her side. "He's still my brother," she finished softly. "And he's always been a part of my life. He always will be."

"And I won't." Griffin spoke aloud what she had left unsaid.

"I don't know if you will be or not," Sarah told him honestly.

"So it is about Wally, after all."

"No, Griffin, it's about us."

He shook his head silently, and she could tell he didn't understand.

"I won't be able to see you for a while," she said, shrugging his hands off her shoulders and taking a step backward. "Not during the trial. This will be difficult enough to go through without the added burden of...of sorting out my love life."

"Sarah, don't do this," he pleaded. "Don't just throw away what you and I have together."

"As it stands right now, we have nothing except a couple of great sexual encounters that were based on deception."

He shook his head. "No, what we have is a love for each other like very few people ever know."

"You can't have love without trust, Griffin," she was quick to point out. "And you can't have trust where there's been deception."

"I swear to you, Sarah, I never meant to—"

"But you did anyway," she interrupted him. "Didn't you?"

Griffin looked at Sarah, looked at the two boys seated so still and so clearly worried behind her. With the three of them, he had begun to think he might find something he'd thought he would never have. He had hoped he'd finally found a family. He didn't know what he could say or do that would change Sarah's mind. He tried to put himself in her place, tried to sympathize with how she must feel. But all he could see was his future slipping away from him, a future he hadn't until that moment realized meant more to him than anything in the world.

"What can I do?" he asked her desperately. "What can I say that will make everything the way it was?"

But Sarah only shook her head silently. "It will never be the way it was. Never again." She took another step backward. "Now I have to go see about getting my brother out of jail. Don't try to contact me, Griffin. I need some time. A lot of time.''

"But when will I see you again?" He took a step after her, hesitating only when she turned around to face him again.

She lifted her fingers to her brow. It was furrowed in worry, and if he didn't know her better, he would swear Sarah Greenleaf was about to burst into tears.

"I don't know," she told him softly. "I just don't know."

"What you and I had, Sarah," he began, lowering his voice to a near whisper, "it wasn't just sleeping together." He tried to ignore the fact that he had just used the past tense in referring to the two of them. But apparently his slip didn't pass by Sarah.

"What we *had* is right, Griffin. Now we have nothing. And as far as what the future might offer us…"

She shrugged, a gesture he found unbearable to watch. It suggested that she was willing to just let it all go, that she would give it all up without a fight.

And with that she spun around again, gathered her sons with one arm around each of them and hurried out of the squad room. Griffin watched the double doors swing back and forth a dozen times, until they finally stilled completely. All around him phones were ringing, typewriters were clacking, computers were beeping and people were shouting. The squad room was busy for a weekday night. But Griffin had never felt more alone.

Chapter 11

The trial two months later was actually much less eventful and dramatic than Sarah had anticipated it would be, and nothing at all like those Matlock movies on television. The lawyers involved were rather bland-looking, long-winded men who seemed to go on and on about nothing at all. They spoke a lot of legalese she couldn't begin to understand, and even more confusing business and corporate mumbo jumbo.

Wally never had spelled out for her precisely what the charges against him involved or how they had come to be pressed in the first place. Instead he had used most of his breath complaining about how honest, hardworking men went to prison while the streets were rife with the lowest form of riffraff that no one bothered to bring to justice. In reply, Sarah had agreed that the justice system was indeed in a sorry state—as was her bank account—and had told Wally that unfortunately he was just going to have to stay in jail until his lawyer returned from his vacation and could get him out.

And now as she sat in the courtroom studying the back of her brother's head, she still had no idea what was going on. She knew only that Griffin Lawless had shown up about fifteen minutes ago, and it had taken all the energy she possessed to keep her eyes from straying to the other side of the room where he sat. She had automatically glanced over her shoulder at the sound of the courtroom door opening behind her, only to find her gaze fixed with his. He was wearing a dove gray lightweight suit unlike anything she'd ever seen him wear, his blue eyes seeming even paler matched with the light color.

For a moment that seemed to stretch to eternity, they had studied each other, until Sarah had finally forced herself to look away. She fiddled with the buttons dotting the front of her gold suit jacket and tried to forget she'd seen him. But every scrape of his shoes against the floor as he'd walked toward his seat had resounded in her ears like a thunderclap. And she was positive she somehow managed to pick up his scent, even from such a distance. Of course, she knew she was crazy. She hadn't seen him for more than two months. She wasn't sure she even remembered how he smelled.

Oh, who was she kidding? Sarah demanded of herself. She could remember every inch of Griffin Lawless's body, every sound he'd ever made, every word he'd ever spoken. The man had haunted her everywhere she went. Her house was full of memories of him. Even driving in her car afforded her no escape. She constantly found herself glancing into the rearview mirror, hoping he would appear behind her on his motorcycle, as if she could rewind the past few months and start all over with him again.

She wished he had at least *tried* to contact her since their last parting.

The air in the courtroom suddenly felt very hot and confining, and Sarah rose to exit as silently and unobtrusively as possible. Outside in the wide corridor, the hustle and

bustle of people stirred the cooler air around her, and she
welcomed the change of scenery. She relaxed for a moment—until she felt the presence of someone standing behind her. Without turning around, she knew it was Griffin.
And when she made no move to acknowledge him, he
walked around to stand in front of her.

"I won't go away just because you ignore me," he told
her.

She met his gaze, scrambling for something light, breezy
and indifferent to say. Unfortunately, light, breezy and indifferent was in no way how she felt at the moment.

"And I won't go away just because you tell me to, either," he added quickly, as if fearful that such a statement
would be the first words out of her mouth.

"Hello, Griffin," she finally said, resigned to the fact that
she was going to have to speak to him sooner or later. "How
have you been?"

Her question seemed to rankle him, because he frowned
at her. "How the hell do you think I've been? Do you even
really care?"

She wanted to shout, Yes! Of course she cared! That not
a night passed when she didn't lay in her bed, staring at the
pillow beside her, wondering what he was doing elsewhere
and with whom. She wanted to tell him how frequently the
boys asked about him, how their enthusiasm for nearly everything had diminished significantly since Griffin had disappeared from their lives.

She wanted to tell him how much she missed him. How
much she loved him.

But instead she only said, "I hope you've been well."

One side of his mouth lifted in a sarcastic twist. "Yeah,
I'll just bet you do."

Sarah had no desire to stand around sniping. If these were
to be the last words they spoke to each other—and she
feared terribly that such might just be the case—then she

didn't want to waste time arguing. "Was there something you wanted, Griffin?"

He laughed, a completely humorless sound. "Want?" he repeated lasciviously. "Oh, yeah. There are one or two things I *want*. But nothing that can be described in polite society."

She flattened her mouth into a thin line. How could he reduce what they'd had to nothing more than the sexual? she wondered morosely. Maybe, she then answered herself reluctantly, because that's exactly what she had done the last time she'd seen him.

Unhappy with her realization and anxious to remove herself from an uncomfortable situation, she said, "Then if there's nothing else...?" She started to turn, searching for a suitable escape route, wondering where the nearest women's room was. If she didn't get out of there soon, she was going to do something really stupid. Like cry. Or throw herself into his arms and make him promise never to leave her again.

"You haven't been to the house in weeks," he said, his words no longer cool and swaggering but edged with a longing and wistfulness that tore at Sarah's heart. "Every time I stop by, Elaine is there, instead."

She hesitated in her retreat, meeting his gaze once again. Her voice was quiet when she spoke, free of the sharpness and accusation she wished she could feel. "Under the circumstances, we thought it might be better if she took over the appraisal for a while. After she's done with the furnishings and jewelry, I'll come back and finish up the rest. Don't worry," she found herself adding. "I should be out of your hair before the end of the year."

"I don't want you out of my hair," Griffin said. "I want you to talk to me. To let me explain. Dammit, to listen to reason."

"There's nothing for us to talk about," she insisted.

"Oh, I think there's *plenty* for us to talk about," he countered.

"Griffin, I told you two months ago that I can't do this until after the trial."

"And two months ago I thought I could handle that. But I've changed my mind. I need to talk to you. Now."

She drew in a deep breath, gestured at an empty bench, then made her way toward it, assuming he would follow her.

Griffin took a moment to watch Sarah as she walked away from him, noting the subtle sway of her hips that her boxy gold jacket and straight skirt did nothing to hide. He smiled as he followed her to the bench. Sarah Greenleaf sure had some way of walking—confident, self-assured, unwilling to be messed with. Just this once, he wished she'd feel some niggling sense of uncertainty. Just enough to put them on equal footing, since he was beginning to feel anything but sure of himself.

He took his seat beside her, deliberately leaving a solid six or eight inches between them so that she wouldn't feel threatened. But he couldn't keep himself from stretching an arm along the back of the bench behind her. He would just have to find the strength somehow to keep his fingers from tangling in her hair and pulling her head close to his so that he could kiss her. That shouldn't be so tough, should it? he thought. Surely a man with as much self-control as he possessed could be trusted to behave himself, right?

"I can't stop thinking about you," he blurted out before he could stop himself, grimacing at the tone of desperation he knew he hadn't been able to disguise. He was sure he had planned to start this conversation in an entirely different manner, but somehow he had wound up uttering the first thing that had come into his head. Nonetheless, he continued frankly, "I miss you, Sarah. And I want you back in my life."

She sighed deeply, closing her eyes as she tipped her head back and leaned it against the wall. "Well, we can't always have what we want, can we? If we could, I'd have hair like Cindy Crawford's, and I'd be sitting on a beach in Saint-Tropez, sipping a pīna colada while some young stud who spoke not a word of English fanned me with a palm frond."

Griffin couldn't help but smile. "Well, I could take you to the pool at the Y, buy you a Dreamsicle and try to remember my high school Spanish, if that would help. As long as you don't mind me whispering sweet nothings like 'Juan is at the library' into your ear. And I could fan you with the latest issue of *Sports Illustrated*. Frankly, I think your hair is perfect."

He saw Sarah fighting a smile, but she didn't look at him. Still, it was a good sign.

"Why do you have to be so nice and wonderful, when I'm doing my best to hate you?" she asked.

Griffin shook his head, reaching over to wind a blond curl around his finger. "Just my nature, I guess."

She opened her eyes and studied him then, but didn't pull away. "There's something that's been bothering me all along about all this," she said.

"Just one thing?" he asked. There had been a lot of things bothering him about it. "What's that?"

"If it was so important to you to ask me out, that I be a part of your life, then why didn't you request that you be removed from the case they were building against Wally? You could have still kept the information from me, but at least I would have known you tried not to compromise our relationship."

"I did put in a request to be transferred to another case," Griffin told her.

She lifted her brows in surprise, sitting up straighter in her seat. "You did?"

He nodded. "But there was no one else who could take

it. The department is shorthanded to begin with, and everyone was overloaded with cases. Plus this was my first case—I was low man on the totem pole. I couldn't very well refuse.''

"And Stony knew all along, too, that Wally was my brother?''

Griffin shook his head. "No, he didn't. No offense, Sarah, but he couldn't even remember your last name after he met you the first time. He knew you only as Elaine's friend, Sarah, and as my, uh, my girlfriend, I guess. I never made the connection for him.''

"Why not?''

He shrugged. "I guess I didn't want him to think I was a creep, either. Investigating the brother of the woman I was involved with.''

"Then why did you get involved with me?'' she asked him again.

He fixed his gaze on hers as he said softly, "I couldn't resist you, Sarah. From the moment I laid eyes on you, I couldn't stop thinking about you. You got under my skin the minute I saw your face. And when you asked, 'Is there a problem, Officer?' I wanted to drag you out of the car, kiss you until we both couldn't see straight and say, 'Yeah, a big problem. Now, what are we going to do about it?''

She watched him in silence for a long time. He wished he could tell what she was thinking, wished there were some way to know exactly how she felt. "I love you, Sarah,'' he said, uncertain when he'd decided to speak. "And I don't know what I'll do without you.''

Her eyes betrayed her then. One minute they were studying him with frank assessment and the next they were filled with tears. She still loved him, too, he thought as he lifted a finger to trace the delicate line of her cheekbone. He could feel it as surely as he could feel the soft warmth of her skin beneath his fingertip. So why didn't she say it out loud?

"You're still thinking about your brother," he said, dropping his hand back to his lap. "You're still thinking you should be loyal to him."

Sarah dropped her gaze to the fingers twisting nervously together in her lap. "I don't know what to do, Griffin. Even if he's guilty of the crimes you say, he's still my brother. My family. I never really thought much about that before I met you, but I guess the ties that bind us by blood are stronger than I thought."

"Even stronger than the ties that bind us by love?"

She didn't answer one way or the other, something Griffin tried to tell himself was an encouraging sign. Nonetheless, they were no closer to a resolution to their problem now than they had been two months ago. He closed his eyes and pinched the bridge of his nose in an effort to ease the throbbing between his temples. Man, he'd been getting a lot of headaches lately.

"Griffin?"

When he opened his eyes again, it was to find Sarah staring at him intently. "Yes?" he replied.

"Tell me exactly what it is Wally did that was so wrong."

He looked at her curiously. "Hasn't he already told you about the charges?"

She shook her head. "Not really. I mean, he's told me what they are, but he never really said what he did that got him into trouble in the first place."

Griffin sighed deeply. Where should he begin? How did one politely tell a woman that her own brother was a liar and a cheat and a thief? "Well," he began, "what Wally and Jerry did was encourage people to invest in schemes of theirs that they knew from the beginning would never materialize. They took thousands of dollars from people—usually elderly people who were easy targets, or people living off their savings who were in desperate need of a financial jolt—assuring them that the project Jerwal was developing would give them a fast return for their investment that would exceed their wildest dreams.

"They told the investors their money was being used to acquire land and rent equipment, when in fact the cash was just being socked into a bank in the Bahamas. Then your brother and his partner bribed local government officials to sign phony documents that would legally prohibit the construction of whatever they claimed to be building. Which gave them the means to tell the investors that the project had been forced down for legal reasons completely beyond their control, and that the investments had gone bust through no fault of Jerwal's. It was an obvious case of fraud, Sarah. They had a clear intent to swindle people from the outset."

Sarah listened to Griffin's account of Wally's activities, wishing with all her heart that she could rush to her brother's defense with righteous indignation. Unfortunately she couldn't quite convince herself that Wally hadn't done what Griffin said he had. Her brother *was* ambitious. And he *did* have a very intense desire to get rich quick. What Griffin described was, sadly, not beyond the realm of possibility.

"What kind of schemes?" she asked softly.

"What?"

Sarah tried to speak a little more loudly. "What kind of schemes did Wally and Jerry get people to invest in?"

"Well, when we nailed them, they had two major ones in the works. One was some roller-blade rink and another was—if you can believe this—a topless cafeteria."

Sarah's head snapped up at that. She looked over at Griffin, but he was looking away.

"I mean, can you imagine people actually putting up good money for such a thing?" he went on before she could speak. "Sometimes I think people who are conned over something that stupid deserve to be fleeced."

"This topless cafeteria," Sarah said, "are you sure it was a scam?"

Griffin looked at her curiously. "Absolutely. They'd collected hundreds of thousands of dollars from investors, and had books phonied up to make it look like they had already begun construction. But there was nothing concrete—no land, no equipment, no building. It was definitely a scam. We have proof. Why?"

Sarah shook her head and emitted a single, humorless chuckle. "Because my brother Wally convinced my mother to invest ten thousand dollars in that cafeteria," she said. "And he tried to get money from me, too."

"He asked his own sister and mother to invest in a phony project?"

She nodded. "I'll kill him."

"That won't be necessary," Griffin told her. "What he did isn't a capital offense. But he *is* going to jail—there's no question of that. And although it will be one of those minimum-security facilities, where he can learn to crochet and work on his backhand, he won't get out for a while."

"I can't believe he'd take his own mother like that," Sarah said, still unable to fathom what Griffin had told her. She'd known Wally could be a jerk, but this...this made him a world-class creep, too.

Family, Sarah repeated to herself with a rueful shake of her head. Oh, yeah. That was a tie that bound, all right. And to think she'd almost allowed it to ruin what was truly a vital bond to Griffin. She suddenly realized that there was more than blood involved in making a family. A lot more. There was loyalty and faith. There was trust and dependability. There was affection and absolution.

But most of all, there was love.

"Ah, Griffin?" she said quietly, scooting toward him until she had closed the small distance between them.

She could tell he was surprised by her sudden shift in

posture, and she smiled encouragingly. "I just remembered that I left something at the Mercer house that I really need to get back. Could you, uh, could you by any chance give me a lift over there?"

He arched his brows in surprise. "Right now?"

She nodded. "Unless you have to stay and be a witness for the prosecution. Something, incidentally, that I'm thinking of becoming myself."

He smiled. "We wouldn't ask you to testify against your own brother."

She gritted her teeth at the door leading to the courtroom where Wally's trial was still in session. "I wouldn't mind. Honest."

Griffin chuckled. "We won't need you, I promise. And I'm not going to be called as a witness until tomorrow."

"Then you could take me home?" she asked. Quickly she clarified, "To your place, I mean."

He studied her for a moment before responding. "What exactly was it you left there that you need to get back right away?"

She smiled at him, curling her fingers around his neck, pulling his head toward hers. "My heart," she whispered before she kissed him softly on the mouth. "I left my heart there somewhere, and you have to help me find it."

"Here it is," Griffin said several hours later as he pressed his lips to the heated flesh between Sarah's breasts. He looked up at her and smiled. "I've found your heart, Sarah. Now, what do you want me to do with it?"

She smoothed back his damp hair and returned his smile. "Hold on to it," she said softly. "Keep it safe."

He straightened in bed until he lay beside her. The late-afternoon sun spilled through the window in what they had come to think of as Meredith's room, bathing them in a soft pale yellow that warmed Sarah's naked skin. She nuzzled closer to him, tucking her head into the hollow below his chin, opening her palm over his heart. The steady *thump-thump-thump* was a reassuring sensation, and she sighed. All her worry and fear of the past two months had evaporated the moment she and Griffin had come together, and now she was satisfied that nothing would ever come between them again. At least, she hoped not.

"Griffin?" she asked.

"Mmm?"

"What's going to happen now?"

He tilted his head until he was staring down at her, and she could see that he was puzzled. "What do you mean?"

"I mean with me, and you, and us, and this house and everything."

He lay back with his head resting on the pillow and stared at the ceiling. "You're still going to work on the house, right?"

She nodded.

"So I'm still your client?"

She nodded again, grinning. "Among other things."

His chest shook beneath her hand, rumbling with laughter. "So I am," he said.

"And us?" she said to encourage him further, feeling just a twinge of uncertainty. She had begun to assume that the two of them would be tangled up together like this for the rest of their lives. But she'd learned, thanks to her brother, that it was best not to assume anything. What if she'd been wrong about Griffin, too?

"Well," he began slowly, "I was kind of wondering what your sons would think if you and I moved in together."

Sarah frowned. Moved in together? she repeated to herself. That wasn't exactly what she'd had in mind. Not entirely, anyway. "They'd probably love it," she replied ex-

perimentally. "It would give them the run of their own
house with no adult supervision."

"Well, naturally I was assuming that they would move
in with us, too."

"Oh."

"So what do you think?"

"I, uh…" She what? Sarah thought. Oh, for pete's sake.
she'd never been accused of hiding her feelings. Why didn't
she just come right out and say what was on her mind? With
a deep, fortifying breath, she quickly said, "Frankly, Griffin,
I was rather hoping you'd ask me to marry you."

He turned on his side to look at her. "I thought I just did
that."

She narrowed her eyes at him curiously. "No, you didn't.
You just asked me to move in with you."

He made an exasperated sound. "Well, it's the same
thing, isn't it?"

She chuckled. "Boy, you're a lot more old-fashioned than
I thought."

"Look, will you marry me or not?" he demanded, clearly
losing patience.

Sarah laughed harder. "Okay, okay. I'll marry you.
Sheesh. I just hope you realize what you're getting yourself
into. You'll not only get a wife, you'll get two kids, too."

He smiled and leaned down to kiss her. "Three for the
price of one," he said. "Sounds like a real deal to me."

She kissed him back. "You'll soon discover that what
you're calling a bargain will cost you a lot more than you
think."

"Then we'll just have to make the expense worthwhile,
won't we?"

His eyes fairly glowed with some unknown fire, as if he
knew something she didn't. Sarah found herself growing
warmer, but for the life of her didn't know why.

"What do you mean?" she asked.

He shook his head. "Nothing. Just that maybe we ought to add a couple more to the fold is all."

Her eyes widened at the thought. "You want to have more kids?"

He lifted his shoulder in a gesture she supposed was meant to be a shrug, yet seemed to her anything but careless. "Sure," he told her. "If you want to."

She smiled. "I do."

He smiled back. "I can't wait to hear you say those words to a minister."

She circled her arms around his neck, pulling him close again. "I can't wait to say them."

As he tucked her body in next to his, Griffin remembered that Sarah had asked him about the house, too. He knew she loved the old building, knew she'd hate to part with it. But he didn't think he could live here for the rest of his life. It was too big, too formal, too full of reminders of the family he'd never had. It simply wasn't a family dwelling.

"About the house, Sarah," he said, before they could lose themselves in passion again. "I don't want to live here."

He was surprised by her expression—one of profound relief.

"Oh, thank goodness," she whispered.

"You don't want to live here, either?"

"Oh, gosh, no," she assured him. "Can you imagine what Jack and Sam would do to this place?" A shudder wound through her body. "The antique community would never forgive me."

Griffin laughed, feeling relief wash over him, as well. "I was thinking about turning it into a museum," he said. "Donate the house and most of the furnishings and everything to the local historical society and let them worry about it. There are one or two things I wouldn't mind hanging on to—mostly Meredith's things—but for the most part, I'm just not comfortable in this place."

Sarah nodded her understanding. "Could there be just one stipulation in your agreement with the historical society?" she asked.

"Sure. What?"

"I'd like to play a part in overseeing the collection. If it's all right with you," she hastened to add. "I've become somewhat attached to the old place. It is, after all, what brought us together."

Griffin smiled. "You can play as big a part as you want," he told her. "But, Sarah, I have to disagree with you. This house isn't what brought us together."

"No?"

He shook his head, then leaned in close. "You breaking the law—that's what brought us together."

"What?" she said, outraged.

He laughed. "In fact, you're the most lawless woman I've ever known." He grinned lasciviously as he added, "And you know what we have to do with lawless women, don't you?"

She grinned back, evidently following his train of thought. "Lock them up?" she asked hopefully.

He nodded. "In handcuffs."

She sighed. "Oh, boy…"

Epilogue

Ah, spring. When a young man's fancy turned to thoughts of…softball. Griffin Lawless stretched languorously as he stepped out of the dugout. Although, he corrected himself, a man didn't have to be so young to be preoccupied by fancies. Nonetheless, for the past few months, he had been feeling like a kid again.

He lifted his arms over his head and pushed them backward, arching his back into the stretch. Then he selected a bat from the half-dozen or so leaning against the fence and took a few practice swings. Stony was about to strike out, and somebody was going to have to clean up his mess. Newlyweds, Griffin thought with a rueful shake of his head. They didn't know squat about how to play the game.

He looked toward the stands where Elaine, Jonah, Jack and Sam had raised their fists with index fingers extended all of them shouting that the first precinct was number one. Then Griffin turned back to the dugout and smiled at the new coach. She was a cute little thing with her stubby blond ponytail and cap turned around backward. And the slight swell of her tummy rising over the life that had been growing inside her for the past five months only added to her charm. But she had a mouth on her...

"Strike!" she shouted at the umpire. "What do you mean 'strike?' I could see that was a ball all the way over here."

Sarah came stomping out of the dugout, brushed past Griffin and marched over to home plate. She wedged herself between Stony and the umpire, standing on tiptoe until she was nose to nose with the latter.

"I've gone up against better umps than you," she began, jabbing a finger against his ample stomach. "And I made mincemeat out of 'em. Now, you'd better get your act together, pal, or you'll be outta here faster than chili through a Chihuahua."

Griffin sighed and leaned on the bat. Might as well take a little break for a minute, he thought. This would go on for a while. He inhaled deeply, reveling in the aroma of freshly mown grass, corn dogs and dust. The hot sun beat down on his face, and arms, soothing sore muscles and easing his soul. He smiled. Life had never been this good before. And it only got better every day. He had a wife, two great kids and another on the way, and a life-style that pretty well guaranteed he'd be around for a long time to enjoy it.

No stress, he thought. No problems, no worries, no regrets. Never again. After the game, he and his family would go for pizza. Then they'd go home, to the two-story colonial they'd all chosen together last fall, and they'd spend the rest of their Saturday doing all the things families did together. It was a new way of life for Griffin, one he never wanted to see change.

Sarah came stomping back past him then, grumbling about why the umpire association would allow the admittance of lunatics. Griffin caught her in his arms before she could pass him and pulled her close. She made a halfhearted effort to brush his hands away, then snuggled close against him.

"Griffin," she murmured against his shoulder, "what will everyone say? They'll think I'm showing you favoritism."

He kissed her temple. "Well, aren't you?"

"Of course. But we don't want everyone else to know that."

"Why not?"

Sarah couldn't think of a very good answer, so she just shrugged and nestled even more closely into her husband's embrace, draping her arms around his waist. "I love you," she said softly.

He squeezed her briefly, then loosened his hold. "I love you, too."

"If you really loved me," she said with a smile, "you'd go out there and hit a homer."

She felt him chuckle, and her smile broadened.

"I'll see what I can do," he told her.

"Strike three!" the umpire called as Stony swung at air.

Sarah inhaled a deep breath to argue with the call, but Griffin halted her objection by pressing his mouth to hers. It was a brief kiss, but a thorough one. Enough to make her dizzy and lose her place in the scheme of things. The spectators erupted in applause, and Griffin went to take his turn at bat.

Sarah shook her head once to clear it, then turned her concentration to the pitch. It was low, inside, with just a bit of a curve, and her husband smacked the heck out of it. With a dull, but definite *thump,* the softball arced high into the air, gaining momentum as it rose until it soared out of sight over the fence. Griffin winked at her as he took off for first base.

Her heart hammered hard in her chest as he rounded third, and by the time he slapped his foot against home plate, she was running to meet him. She hurled herself against him, and he caught her to his chest, kissing her again.

"Gee, I guess you really do love me," she said breathlessly.

He nodded. "More than you could possibly know."

"Oh, I think I know," she assured him.

The rest of the team joined them in congratulations then, along with a few fans from the stands. There were still two innings to go, but Griffin had brought in two other runs with his, and now the first precinct claimed a substantial lead.

Sarah laughed as he spun her around one last time before setting her on her feet. "Way to go, Lawless," she said.

"Thanks, Coach."

They walked back to the dugout hand in hand, and fell onto the bench together. Hoping to find a candy bar, Sarah reached for Griffin's duffel bag, and heard a strange clinking sound inside. She smiled at him knowingly.

"You brought your handcuffs home from work again," she said.

He smiled back. "Well, the boys are staying with Jonah and the Stonestreets tonight, aren't they?"

She nodded.

"Well, then."

"Well, then," she repeated. She opened her palm over her softly protruding belly. "You remember what happened last time," she said. "I couldn't get to my diaphragm."

Griffin's hand splayed over hers. "Yeah. My plan worked perfectly."

She dropped her mouth open in surprise. "You planned that?"

"Naturally."

She was about to say more, but felt a flutter of something inside her. She laughed, and quickly reversed the positions of their hands. "There," she whispered. "Feel that? That's our daughter."

She watched Griffin's expression change from concentration to surprise to delight to awe. When his eyes met hers, they were shinier than she'd ever seen them. "That's Meredith?" he asked.

Sarah nodded. "That's her."

She hooked her arm around his neck, pulling his head down beside hers, thinking this moment the most perfect she'd ever spent.

"This Meredith will be happy," Griffin said quietly.

Sarah nodded again. "I know. Just like her mother."

"And her father."

Neither paid much attention to the game after that. After all, Sarah conceded with a grin, there were one or two things more important than softball.

* * * * *

Dear Reader,

Once upon a time, *Child of Her Dreams* was my dream. I wrote this novel years ago, before I had a publisher, an editor or an agent. A lot has changed since then—in my life, and in my career. My husband and I have moved, and our four sons are nearly grown. I look at them, and I'm filled with so much pride and wonder. I've written well over twenty books since *Child of Her Dreams* graced the shelves. Still, every time I see my words in print, every time I gaze at a new cover, I'm filled with another kind of pride and wonder.

Child of Her Dreams marked the beginning of the relationship I have with my publisher, who's been wonderful, my editor, who's a peach and a pretty smart cookie, and my agent, who's become a good friend. Best of all, *Child of Her Dreams* marked the beginning of my relationship with you, dear reader.

I was thrilled the first time this book was printed. I was thrilled when it won the prestigious 1994 National Readers' Choice Award. And I'm so pleased that it's being reissued. As of this moment, you have my dream in your hands. Enjoy.

Always,

Sandra Steffen

CHILD OF HER DREAMS
by Sandra Steffen

Whether it's the magic of first love or the wonder of
a second chance, *Silhouette Romance* knows the power
of heartfelt emotion. CHILD OF HER DREAMS
features the tenderness of family bonds,
an emotionally satisfying story and the spirit of pure
romance that exemplify *Silhouette Romance* novels.
Each month, six titles invite you to experience
the enchantment all over again!

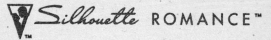

To my parents,
Denis and Mary Lou Rademacher—
thanks for everything,
especially for not stopping with three

Chapter 1

"Callie's missing!"

Pressure built in Lexa's chest as she watched the man who'd uttered those two words come closer. She couldn't be sure of the color of the stranger's eyes, but the rest of him was dark. Dark hair, dark brows, tan-darkened skin and an expression darkened by an unreadable emotion.

Within seconds she knew his eyes were dark blue, nearly the same shade as the Atlantic on a cloudy day. Even if the restaurant had been empty and her sixth sense hadn't told her not to fear him, she couldn't have turned from the raw emotion in those eyes.

"Is Callie your daughter?" she asked.

He was still standing, and Lexa tilted her head to keep from breaking eye contact as the pressure in her chest increased. She'd come to accept the pressure, and the dull ache of foreboding that seeped past it down to her stomach where it spread outward in her veins like ice.

He cleared his throat as if he was going to speak, but

nodded, instead. Pain and worry etched his face, and for the first time, he glanced at the two local men watching him from behind their beers on the other side of O'Toole's Fish Restaurant. He lowered his eyes to the table where he placed a crumpled paper sack, and took a seat opposite her.

"Did someone take your daughter?"

She watched closely, and he nodded a second time. "Is Callie your daughter's given name?" she asked in a voice she hoped was soothing.

He seemed to inhale half the air in the room in one breath, and his eyes bore directly into hers for a full five seconds before he answered. "Her full name's Carolina Joy Sullivan."

"That's a beautiful name, Mr. Sullivan."

He stirred uncomfortably in his chair and swallowed hard. "It's Cade. Cade Sullivan. Will you help me find my baby?"

His voice shook with the effort to keep his desperation in check, and Lexa closed her eyes against the cold sense of anguish awaiting her if she answered yes. But in her heart she knew she had no real choice. She couldn't turn away from a parent searching for a missing child. For the past four years, it had been her life, the only life she could remember.

She took a deep breath of her own, and leveled her gaze on Cade. "Yes, Mr. Sullivan, I'll help you find her. But first I have to ask you a few questions."

He didn't protest, but his gaze probed hers so intensely she wondered what he saw behind her eyes. "Who sent you to me?"

His gaze narrowed slightly, but his voice was controlled. "I contacted Dr. Jacobiac at the University of North Carolina at Chapel Hill. He directed me here."

Lexa trusted Daniel Jacobiac. He'd been her surgeon nearly four years ago. His skilled hand had saved her from the tumor in her brain; his compassion had saved her from the psychiatrists and parapsychologists who'd probed her mind and tried to declare her a fraud.

"Then you're familiar with my successes—and my failures."

"You're my only hope. The woman who took Callie intends to keep her. She won't be bringing her back on her own."

"And the police?"

"They don't have a clue. Neither does the private detective I hired."

Lexa studied the man seated across the small table. He looked as if he hadn't slept for a decade. Worry for his child was evident. He didn't appear happy to be placing his faith in something as unproven and unscientific as clairvoyance. Yet that was exactly what he was doing. In that instant Lexa felt a slender delicate thread form between them. In the days that followed, that thread would be their one and only link to his daughter.

"This woman who took your daughter," she began. "Is she Callie's mother?"

"No!"

The table shook beneath the slam of his fist and Lexa jumped to her feet, her hand flying to her throat in surprise. Cade glanced from Lexa to the two patrons on the other side of the room, who were now watching him openly.

"Everything okay, Miz Lexa?" one of them called.

"Everything's fine, Ramsey," she answered before turning back to Cade Sullivan.

Cade took a deep breath, ran his hand across his chin and scowled. He'd shaved off his beard three days ago, and he felt naked without it, even with the day-old stubble he hadn't bothered with this morning. Slowly rising from his chair, he said, "Is there someplace we can go to talk? Someplace a little more private?"

"Follow me." She spoke in a weak and tremulous whisper, then turned and with head held high walked toward the exit. She favored her right leg, but so slightly and with so much grace it was almost indiscernible.

These past five days had been a living hell for Cade. But watching her, he couldn't help but think she was preparing herself for her own kind of hell. The doctor said her "visions" were hard on her, and Cade was beginning to understand what he'd meant. Guilt sank to his chest like cold ashes. He didn't want to make her life any more difficult, but dammit, he had to get Callie back. And this looked like the only way.

Lexa waited for him at the door without looking back to see if he was following, and he wondered if, as a clairvoyant, she already knew he would. According to Dr. Jacobiac, she didn't read minds. She had visions, or dreams, in which she "saw" people and places in another dimension, in another place.

He grabbed the paper sack and crushed it to his side, then hurried around the tables as he made his way toward her. She led him through the door and along a winding path leading to a small stone house fifty yards behind the restaurant. It was the end of March, and already warm on the other side of North Carolina near Hendersonville, where Cade lived. But the ocean wind blew cold here on Roanoke Island, and when they passed beneath a yaupon tree, he saw Lexa shiver.

She opened the door, and he followed her inside. Her house was tiny, and nothing like he thought a clairvoyant's house would be. But then, neither was she. He'd somehow expected her to look like a Gypsy, with dancing dark eyes and bright-colored clothing and jewelry adorning her neck, wrists and ears.

She looked nothing like a Gypsy. She was thinner than he'd imagined, almost fragile. Her hair was smooth, and light brown in color. She wore it brushed away from her forehead and loosely secured at her nape with a wide cloth band. Nothing about her was brightly colored. Not the pastel skirt she wore, nor the matching sweater. She wore no jewelry, not even a watch. Her skin was pale, her lips untinted. Her eyes were large and gray and very mysterious.

She let him look his fill, seeming to understand his need to study her feature by feature, before placing his child's welfare in her hands.

"Let's go into the kitchen," she suggested. "It's brighter there, and warm."

She turned away then, and Cade took a deep breath before following. *She's beautiful,* he thought, and cursed himself for noticing.

"I'll brew a pot of tea," she called. When he didn't immediately answer, she poked her head around the doorway. "Is tea all right, Mr. Sullivan?"

His first choice would have been Scotch, straight up. He wasn't a tea drinker, but what did it matter? "Yeah, sure," he mumbled, walking into the kitchen and pulling out a chair at the wooden table.

She turned on the gas beneath the kettle and took two cups from a shelf. "Initially I'd like to try to get a feel for your daughter, Mr. Sullivan. I don't want you to tell me anything about her. But I'll need something of hers. An article of clothing or a favorite toy."

Cade opened the paper bag and pulled out a tattered blanket. He clutched the fabric in his fist before sliding it across the table. When the tea was brewed, Lexa placed a round pot between them and took the blanket in her hands. She closed her eyes, holding Callie's blanket to her heart.

From above the stove, the clock's second hand caught on every groove, ticking, ticking. Otherwise, the room was completely silent. Cade's chest ached with the air he held there. But he'd sooner explode than break her concentration, thereby destroying the possibility that she might be able to tell him where he could find his little girl.

He watched her, willing her to "see" Callie, to tell him where she was, to assure him she was safe. She finally spoke, in a voice that sounded as if it came from far away.

"I can't see her face, but I see a child with dark hair. Not a baby, though. A little girl, maybe three or four years old. Someone's holding her hand, pulling her, running—"

"Lexa!" The door burst open, shattering the quiet. "Lexa, are you all right?"

Lexa's eyes jerked open, and Callie's blanket fell to the table. "Berdie, I'm here. In the kitchen."

"Where are they, Lexa?" Cade demanded. "Where are they running to?"

She looked down at the faded blanket and her expression became somber. "I don't know," she whispered. "The vision's gone."

What started as dread quickly ignited into anger. Cade glared at the woman who'd ruined Lexa's vision and slammed his fist against the table. "Who in the hell are you?" he rumbled.

The woman placed one hand on her ample hip and poked one dark brown finger into the air between them. "You listen here. The last time a Yankee swore at me I took a switch to his backside."

"Berdie…" Lexa interrupted.

The black woman swiped her hand in Lexa's direction but didn't remove her steely gaze from Cade. "What's your name, fella?"

"This is Cade Sullivan, Berdie," Lexa admonished, "and he's here because his daughter is missing."

"Oh," the woman named Berdie said, letting her eyes dart away from Cade's for the first time.

"And this is Berdette O'Toole, Mr. Sullivan," Lexa declared, finishing the introductions.

Berdie's entire demeanor had changed in the blink of an eye. She no longer waggled a finger at him, had in fact buried both hands in her apron pockets. "People round here call me Berdie. You might as well, too. Your first name's Cade?"

"Yeah."

"Well, Cade, that's a strange name, but with my name being Berdie and all, I'm hardly one to talk. Didn't mean to barge in here just now. But Arnie and Ramsey told me somebody was giving Lexa some trouble. Y'see, tourists and Yankees are welcome in these parts nowadays. But not necessarily wholly trusted."

"Who are you calling a Yankee?" Cade sputtered.

"Were you born and raised in the South?"

"I've lived here for ten years."

"That don't make you no Southerner. People from the North just visiting are Yankees. Them that move down here are damn Yankees," Berdie stated emphatically.

"You've lived in North Carolina for ten years?" Lexa asked.

Cade nodded. "I grew up in Ohio, but moved here ten years ago. People tell me my accent's all but disappeared."

Lexa fingered the blanket on the table as she said, "Berdie can tell from the drawl and rhythm of a person's speech where they're from, whether it's Ohio or California, the Hatteras or Roanoke Island."

"I kin even tell which side of Roanoke Island a person's from," Berdie boasted.

"And can you tell me where my little girl is?"

Both women suddenly went still. Cade could feel Lexa's eyes on him, but kept his trained on the other woman as she said, "That's Lexa's department."

"I know. You interrupted her first vision."

"You've seen his li'l one?" Berdie asked Lexa.

"I've seen her, but not clearly." Lexa touched the blanket again. "Tell me. Was this one of her favorites?"

Cade nodded.

"That's odd. My visions are usually clearer, especially when I hold a possession dear to the missing child. Let's try again with something else."

"This is all I've got."

"This blanket is the only article you brought with you?" Lexa asked.

"It's all I have left."

Something nagged at the back of Lexa's mind. There was something Cade Sullivan wasn't telling her, something important. But she accepted his statement and placed the blanket over her heart and closed her eyes.

The clock ticked. And no one breathed. But Lexa saw nothing. She opened her eyes, placed the blanket on the table, and stood. "It's no use. I'll have to try again later."

"What do you mean later? You saw her before. You can see her again. We have to find her!"

The desperation in Cade's voice tormented Lexa. She understood his desperation and felt the pressure in her chest increase. Leaning against the counter, she turned to face him. "Cade," she murmured, "I'll try again. I promise. But right now it won't do any good. I can't see her."

"What do I do in the meantime?"

Berdie answered. "You wait."

Lexa watched him run his hand across the stubble on his chin, watched him take several deep breaths and watched him stuff his daughter's blanket into the paper sack. He'd walked as far as the kitchen doorway before turning to her again.

He stared at the sack in his hands, the paper crinkling beneath the pressure of his grip. "You'll need this later if you're going to try again."

Lexa took the sack, cradling it in her arms like a newborn

baby, and her breath caught in her throat at the look in Cade's eyes. She could see him hurting, aching, and she knew handing over his daughter's blanket had cost him dearly, especially if it really was all he had left of the child.

She wanted to reach out to him, to offer him comfort in his pain. But she couldn't guarantee they'd find his little girl. There was one thing she could offer him, one thing that had kept her going these past four years. Her visions had given her hope. She'd give Cade the same thing. "The fact that I've already seen her is a good sign, Cade. In the past, when I've seen a child once, I see her again."

He looked into her eyes for several seconds, and Lexa recognized the faint glimmer there. He was afraid he'd never see his child again and was afraid to place his trust in false hope. After a long pause he asked, "You honestly believe you'll see her again?"

"Yes, I honestly do."

He continued to look at her, wordlessly at first, until his eyelids lowered, and his lips lifted into a tired smile. "Then there's hope." He stared at her for a moment longer, then his gaze dropped, as did his voice. "I'll need a place to stay, at least a place to sleep."

An unexpected warmth settled over her, and Lexa wondered if he had any idea how strongly the sensuality of his voice drew her. She had no memory of her life before her surgery, but she knew no man had drawn her, not in this way, in the four years since.

"You aimin' to stay here on Roanoke Island?" Berdie asked.

Lexa had been so entirely caught up in her new-felt emotions she'd forgotten Berdie was even in the room.

"Yes. I'll wait if I have to, only because I have no choice. But I'll do it nearby."

"There are inns and resorts up and down the Outer Banks," Lexa said.

"There's a room over the restaurant," Berdie declared. "It has a tiny bathroom, and even though it ain't much, you're welcome to it."

Both Lexa and Cade turned to stare at the older woman. "Why d'you both look so surprised?" she asked indignantly. "It's true that a North Carolinian is more proud than humble, but I ain't turned a man out in the cold yet, and I don't aim to start now. Go out and get your things, Cade Sullivan. You must be tired and hungry after your long drive all the way from Hendersonville."

"How did you know I'm from Hendersonville?"

Berdie didn't bother to explain. She simply placed a hand on one hip and crowed, "You gonna do as I say or ain't ya?"

He opened his mouth to speak and closed it again. Lexa wasn't sure whether the curve of his lips was from the curse he was biting or the beginning of another smile.

"Who woulda thought something as simple as offering you a roof over your head would leave a hardheaded, hardworking man like yerself speechless?" Berdie crowed.

A chuckle found its way through his uncertainty, and Lexa smiled as that little touch of humor changed his entire appearance. He relaxed, and Lexa could have hugged Berdie for the gift she'd just given him.

"How would you know I'm hardworking?"

"Noticed you didn't dispute the hardheaded part," Berdie huffed.

Cade laughed again, then looked into Lexa's eyes. He immediately averted his gaze, but not before she saw his smile fade into nothing. She watched him walk away, watched him close the door behind him and, through the window, watched him follow the path to Berdie's restaurant and disappear inside.

"I ain't seen eyes like his since my Tucker, God rest his soul, buried his mama, papa and older brother all the same year. Something's haunting that one, Lexa. And it ain't just his li'l girl.''

Lexa hummed an answer while she removed the lid from the china teapot and poured the lukewarm tea down the drain. The pressure was back in her chest, pressure to find Cade's missing daughter and pressure to alleviate a parent's torment. If his eyes were this haunted because Callie was missing, she hated to think what would happen to him if she couldn't find his child, if he never got his baby back..

Lexa paused in the doorway, unsure what to do or say. She hadn't been particularly quiet coming up the narrow stairway, yet Cade seemed unaware of her presence. When her knock on the open door didn't draw a response, she tried again, calling his name.

It was her voice that finally seemed to reach him. He turned from the window, as if in slow motion. Once again she was struck by the darkness of his looks. He stood in the shadows of the late afternoon, and although she knew he stared at her, she couldn't see his eyes.

Lexa stepped into the room, her low-heeled shoes tapping on the old wood floor. "Berdie sent me up here with strict instructions to make this room habitable for Yankee or king." She walked to the center of the narrow room and placed fresh sheets and blankets on the stand near the double bed.

Reaching past him, she pushed aside the curtain and tugged at the tall window. He leaned to help her, and the window raised easily, the cool ocean breeze immediately freshening the stale air.

Lexa straightened and found herself shoulder to shoulder with Cade. She had an instinctive response to him and saw a flicker of warmth in his blue eyes. The moment stretched into two, and Lexa barely breathed. Her heart hammered in her breast, his nearness a pleasurable pull to her senses. He raised his hand, and for a moment she thought he might touch her. Instead, he pressed his hand to the windowpane and pulled away.

Mixed feelings surged through her. She was slightly relieved and largely disappointed, even though she knew better than to become involved with the parent of a missing child. Tensions were high and emotions too close to the surface to be acted upon. Evidently Cade Sullivan knew it, too.

Lexa turned to the bed. In one full swipe, she stripped the mattress of its dusty spread and old sheets.

"I'll do that," he said.

"You've had a long day," she replied, fitting on a fresh bottom sheet. "Besides, I don't mind."

"I mean it!" he sputtered. At her startled look, he added, "I need something to do. I've never been very good at waiting."

Lexa had a feeling that was an understatement and was about to tell him as much. But before she spoke, her gaze met his, and her smile slid away with the words. He implored her with his eyes, those blue haunted eyes, and a knot rose in her throat. A deep-rooted sorrow seemed to weigh him down, and the knot sank to her chest. He seemed as alone as she.

He resumed making the bed where she'd left off, and she wandered to the long narrow window. Holding the billowing curtain aside, Lexa stared out at the ocean waves.

"You haven't had another vision?"

Cade watched her turn away from the view. Her faint smile held a touch of sadness, and he knew, even without the slight shake of her head, that she hadn't "seen" Callie again.

Voices rose from the kitchen below, Berdie's louder than the others. Lexa shook her head again, this time in tender humor. "That's Arnie and Ramsey. Berdie's baking her famous half-moon pies. She still measures by hand and taste, and old Arnie and Ramsey never miss the opportunity to sample her wares."

Cade felt a numbing comfort in her soft voice, in the normalcy of this place. Life goes on. And when he found Callie, his would, too.

He tucked in the last blanket and found Lexa watching him. His heart nearly tripped in its beat, and it was all he could do to look away. "Do Arnie and Ramsey live around here?" he asked.

"They both have cottages up the island, but they spend most of their time here. Arnie never married, and Ramsey's wife died a long time ago. I guess Berdie and Tucker just sort of took them in. Tucker died before I came here, but the way Berdie tells it, he was as strong as Paul Bunyan and a hundred times more handsome, with a heart as soft as dandelion fluff. Of course, Arnie and Ramsey say that isn't so."

Cade doubted she knew how her eyes glowed with affection for the people whose voices drifted from below. Her voice, and that light in her eyes, warmed him in ways that surprised him. It was comforting, and it wasn't.

"They look out for you."

She smiled, a soft sad kind of smile. "I don't know how much Dr. Jacobiac told you about me, but I haven't always been clairvoyant. I'm told I led a normal life prior to four years ago."

"A normal life?" he asked.

"You see, Cade, I wasn't supposed to survive the surgery to my brain. There was an eighty-percent chance I wouldn't live through it, and another fifteen-percent chance I'd be permanently disabled. I could have been left severely brain damaged, little more than a vegetable."

"Yet you went through with it."

"Yes. I must have had an incredible desire to live," she whispered. "I'm not sure I'd take such a risk today."

Cade heard the strained tone in her voice. Her words chilled him. The surgery had taken her memory. In its place, she'd been given a "gift." But her clairvoyance wasn't really a gift. It was a tremendous responsibility. Without it, he might never see Callie again.

"Cade, you said the woman who took Callie isn't her mother."

"That's right. My housekeeper took her."

"Why?"

He took his time forming an answer, trying to weigh the whole structure of events that had taken place these past three years. "Because she wants to be Callie's mother. And when I found out what she was trying to do, I fired her."

"What about Callie's mother?"

The suitcase Cade had reached for bounced on the bed. He stilled his movements and said, "What about her?"

"Where is she?"

"She's gone."

"Gone?"

"She died. Shortly after Callie was born."

Lexa paused, not wanting to probe an open wound. It was obvious his wife's death was not a subject he wanted to discuss, and Lexa thought Berdie had been right when she said something was haunting Cade Sullivan, something besides worry about his missing child.

This case was different from the others. This child hadn't been taken by a divorced parent, nor by a complete stranger. Something had been nagging at the back of Lexa's mind, something she didn't understand. "You're sure your housekeeper took her?"

"Yes, my father saw Winnona leave the house."

"He saw her take Callie?"

Cade took a deep breath, running his hand across his chin,

over his face and into his hair. He felt like a caged animal, and anger sent him pacing to the far side of the room. "No, Pop didn't see her actually take Callie. Winnona was thorough. She already had Callie and had come back for the rest of her clothes and toys."

"She even took her toys?"

"She took everything, Lexa. Her baby things, her photographs. Everything."

"Except Callie's favorite blanket?"

"She was trying to get it when Pop unexpectedly showed up. He didn't know Callie was missing, but he knew I'd fired Winnona. The blanket was in my car and she was trying to get it, actually had it in her hands, when Pop pulled into the driveway. The wind blew the door shut on the corner of the blanket, and she fled without it."

"But why? Why would she risk getting caught in order to take everything?" Lexa asked.

"So I'd have nothing left."

The voices from below rose again, this time in laughter. Cade's heart was thumping madly, and he did what he could to keep his anger in check. He felt betrayed that Winnona would do such a thing, and guilty as hell. For three years he'd trusted her with his daughter's life. He hadn't believed she was capable of stealing his child. He'd been wrong.

Momentarily lost in introspection, Cade hadn't noticed Lexa coming closer. Once again it was her voice that drew him from his dark thoughts, that smooth soft voice. He was keenly aware of her scrutiny and hoped she didn't see the wistfulness that stole into his heart at her touch.

Her hand barely grazed his arm, and Cade's gaze traveled from the softness of her fingers to the softness of her face. Her skin looked so pale beneath the stark light of the bare overhead bulb. Fine hairs blew against her neck, billowing like the thin curtain still partially covering the window. His anger evaporated beneath her soft touch, her soft gaze, and his heart picked up its beat. His guilt dissipated, his thoughts fragmented, until he was aware of nothing but the woman before him. Her eyes were as gray as the gathering dusk and full of mysteries that beckoned to him irresistibly.

A door squeaked open from below, and dishes and cutlery clattered in the kitchen beyond. Berdie's voice called up the darkening staircase. "Lexa, when you've finished making the Yankee's bed, bring him downstairs. My half-moon pies are done, and I swear they're the best I've ever tasted!"

Lexa pulled her hand from his arm and smiled. "She'll be the first to admit she's a true old-fashioned North Carolinian, Cade. Which, among other things, means she brags loud and often."

"Lexa, girl," Berdie called. "I heard that. Now, are you coming down or ain't ya?"

"I'll be right there, Berdie."

"Well, you'd better hurry or there'll be none left for you and Cade, and old Arnie and Ramsey here will be as fat as mainland possums."

A deep voice drifted up from the stairway. "Who you callin' old?" Cade could hear Berdie's voice as she answered her friend, but couldn't make out the words she used.

Lexa took a couple of steps toward the stairs at the end of the hall, then stopped and turned back to Cade. "Even if your housekeeper had managed to get your little girl's blanket, she wouldn't have succeeded in taking everything, Cade. You still have your memories. And memories are more precious than most people ever realize."

A shudder passed through him, and his heart felt as if it were being held in the grip of a large fist. "I know how precious memories are, Lexa."

His simple reply seemed to surprise her. She continued to look at him as if unsure what else to say. Her words had reminded him of how much he took for granted, things as common as his memories. Things she no longer had.

"I'll do everything I can to help you find your daughter, Cade."

He stared into her eyes, her gray shadowed eyes, and for the first time in days he felt hopeful. His eyes clung to hers, and he watched as her gaze slid to his mouth. He smiled, and watched the effect it had on her. At first, surprise widened her eyes, and when the surprise left them, he noticed the shadows had, too.

Cade closed the door to his room behind him, and headed for the stairs where Lexa waited. "Come on. I want to see if Berdie's half-moon pies are really as good as she claims."

Lexa turned away from him and descended the stairs, graceful in a way that squeezed his heart. She disappeared into the kitchen, and Cade followed the sound of her voice, then Berdie's, and the deeper voice of the man called Ramsey.

At the bottom of the stairs, Berdie cornered Cade, poking her bony brown finger inches from his face. "Lexa here tells me you ain't convinced my pies are the best in all of North Carolina. Sit down, Yankee, and prepare to eat them words."

Cade glanced at Lexa and caught her coy wink before she took a bite of her own pie. Feeling better than he had in the five days since Callie had been missing, he returned her wink and did as Berdie said.

Chapter 2

Cade swung his jean-clad legs off the bed and paced to the door. Fatigue weighed his steps, but sleep wouldn't come. How in the hell was he supposed to sleep with the waves pounding the shore?

Goose bumps skittered along his bare chest as he strode to the open window and slammed it down. He scowled at the ocean, but knew his insomnia wasn't the fault of the sea. It was this god-awful waiting. He released the curtain and turned away. Stopping in mid-motion, he swung around and looked again.

Cade wasn't the only person awake at this late hour. Lexa's slender form was silhouetted in the faint moonlight. She stood statue-still, facing the ocean. Her hair blew free in the wind, and he saw she still wore the pale skirt and sweater she'd worn earlier.

What are you thinking? What do you see? Can you see Callie in the dark waves of your inner eye?

She hugged her arms close to her body, and Cade saw

her shiver. He cursed aloud before clamping his mouth shut. After poking his head and arms into a thick sweater and his bare feet into worn loafers, he grabbed a jacket from the back of a chair, squared his shoulders and crept down the stairs.

Footsteps crunched on the stone path. Unafraid, Lexa turned slowly, watching as Cade strode toward her. The wind blew her hair across her face, momentarily blinding her. She felt him place a jacket on her shoulders and immediately shrugged into its warmth before facing the ocean once again, aware that he did the same.

"You shouldn't be out here in the cold," he said.

"Berdie tells me that all the time. This is my favorite time of the day, when I can stand here at one with the night. Don't worry, I won't stay out long."

Lexa loved the lack of color of night. In the moonlight, there was only black and white and silver. She found it comforting, the night more a place than a time, a place where she could be alone with her thoughts. She was a little surprised that Cade's presence didn't infringe in any way on her peacefulness.

He seemed to accept her words, and for reasons she didn't understand, she felt soothed by his acceptance. They gazed at the darkness in companionable silence, each it seemed, lost in their own thoughts. At last Lexa spoke.

"I held her blanket close for a long time tonight."

"And?"

"And I saw exactly what I saw before. A dark-haired child and a large-boned woman. I couldn't see Callie's face, but she didn't appear to be afraid."

"Thank God. At least she's safe. I didn't think Winnona would harm her. Not on purpose."

"And yet she took her from you."

"Yes."

"What do you know about Winnona?"

Cade hesitated before answering, unsure where to begin. He looked all around them, then turned his head slightly so he could see Lexa's profile. "She answered an ad for a housekeeper I'd placed in the newspaper. Her full name is Winnona Smith, and she told me her husband was dead. I checked her references, and at first she seemed too good to be true."

"What do you mean 'too good'?"

"Callie was still a baby when I hired her, and Winnona was wonderful with her. Pop had his reservations at first, but he couldn't fault her behavior and in time came to accept her."

"Does your father live with you?"

He nodded and looked away. "We own a large peach and apple orchard not far from Hendersonville. Berdie was right about where I live."

"Berdie would be the first to tell you she's usually right." Lexa smiled. "What went wrong? With your housekeeper, I mean."

"After several months, she asked if she could stay in the spare room now and then. Said it would be more convenient for all of us if she didn't have to drive home every night. By the end of the second year she was living in the house with Pop and me and Callie. And she was gradually trying to phase Pop out of our lives."

"She wanted you and Callie to herself," Lexa whispered. Cade nodded.

"And did your father leave?"

"No. Pop raised me, and Callie has him wrapped around her little finger. But nobody's ever going to push him around."

"And how did Winnona react to this?" Lexa turned to face him, wanting to see his expression, if only in the faint moonlight.

"That's just it. She didn't react. I thought it was a wonderful trait, the way she never got angry. I never worried about her shouting at Callie, or hitting her."

"Never? She never showed her anger?" She placed her hand on his arm, and his gaze slowly traveled from the sand and the waves to her face. Despite his closed expression, she sensed his need and his deep vulnerability.

"The only time she even came close to anger was when I..." He looked into her eyes and his voice trailed away.

Beneath the faint moonlight, her entire body seemed to swell with feelings she'd thought long dead. For four years, Lexa had wondered about her sexuality, wondered if Dr. Jacobiac might have removed it along with the tumor in her brain and her memories of the past. Now she knew he hadn't, for it warmed her chest and stirred feelings deep in her belly.

"When I walked into the house and found her..." Once again his voice trailed away.

She inched closer and let her hand trail up his soft cable knit sweater. Cade moved closer, too, and Lexa took in his powerful presence and the powerful emotions quaking through her. "You walked into the house and found her doing what?" she asked on a sigh as his hands found her shoulders and his gaze bore into hers.

With heavy-lidded eyes Lexa watched as, like a man in a trance, he slowly lowered his face to hers. "I walked in and found her putting all...all my wife's things away."

Mention of his wife hung in the air between them, and Lexa was the first to pull away. His words were barely more than a whisper, but they couldn't have broken the spell more completely if he'd screamed them from the top of his lungs. She closed her eyes and turned her head back toward the sea. "And did Winnona put those things away?"

"She did. But I took them out again."

"And does it help? Does being near your wife's things help?"

"What do you mean?"

"I don't mean to pry, Cade, and you don't have to answer if you don't want to. But memories fascinate me. I know my losing my memory was a small price to pay for my life—and my gift. But tell me, do your memories of Callie's mother keep her alive to you?"

Lexa didn't think he was going to answer, had all but given up when his words finally came. "Sometimes my memories of her are comforting, and sometimes they're painful reminders that she isn't there." His deep voice was at one with the waves lapping the shore and the wind whispering along the Outer Banks.

"What was she like?"

"She was full of life. She was strong-willed and beautiful, and she loved to laugh. She had a crazy laugh, almost impossible to mimic. Just listening to it used to make me smile. I think I miss that more than anything."

"Does Callie look like her?"

"Only in the eyes. Callie's dark like me. But she inherited her mother's love of bright colors. Red and purple and yellow, the brighter the better."

Cade brought his wife alive just talking about her, and Lexa couldn't help but smile at the image his description evoked. "Was she tall? Was she thin?"

He laughed. "She was neither. Her skin was the color of our ripe peaches, and although she wasn't fat, she was never classically thin. Pop used to tease her, saying she was built for comfort, not fashion magazines, that hers was a beauty that never went out of style, not in any man's eyes."

Lexa thought his wife had been very lucky. She'd been deeply loved by her husband and by her father-in-law. They may have buried her, but it was obvious Cade's love for her hadn't faded.

"I promised her I'd keep Callie safe."

As quickly as it had come, the laughter in his voice disappeared. His guilt about what happened to Callie was real. It was there in his voice, as real as the wind and the waves on the ocean. He blamed himself for Callie's disappearance and for placing his trust in Winnona Smith. Above all else, he blamed himself for breaking the promise he'd made to Callie's mother.

Lexa wondered if Cade understood the impossibility of anyone's keeping such a promise. "I've seen your daughter twice," she said, "and I sensed she was safe both times. So, Cade, you haven't really broken your promise to Callie's mother."

Cade stared at Lexa's profile. Her serenity was all-encompassing. He was in awe of her power, in awe of her quiet tranquillity. He'd read several books on metaphysical mysteries both before and after he'd gone to see Dr. Jacobiac. He wanted to trust her vision, her sixth sense, but was afraid to trust his judgment. Most of all, he was afraid to get too close, afraid it might in some way impede her visions of Callie.

Cade shivered and caught himself glancing over his shoulder into the darkness up the beach. Callie's disappearance had thrown him, and Lexa's power amazed him. But awe-inspiring or not, the darkness of the night and the noise of the ocean gave him the creeps. He was coming to believe in her power, but if she levitated, he'd come unglued or run like hell. Or both.

She caught his gaze and looked deeply into it, and he did neither. His breath caught in his lungs, and he shivered a second time. Without understanding why, he again glanced over his shoulder, peering deep into the darkness.

"Cade, what is it?"

"I'm not sure, but I feel like I'm being watched."

Lexa looked all around and found nothing unusual in the

darkness. "It's probably Berdie. Not much goes on around here that she doesn't see."

With that, the light at the back of the restaurant flashed off and on, and off again. And Lexa laughed. "See what I mean? That's Berdie's way of telling me it's time to go inside."

She slipped his jacket from her shoulders and handed it to him. He took it from her fingers and cast another look into the darkness.

"Well, good night," she murmured.

"Lexa."

"Yes?" Her heart hammered in her chest, and she waited for him to continue.

"You'll tell me if you 'see' her again? No matter what time it is, I want to know. I need to know."

She lifted her eyes to his and felt an odd sense of wistfulness settle in her stomach. It wasn't the same as the thickness she felt in her chest each time she had a vision, or the emptiness she'd felt inside since waking from her surgery, and she decided this was probably empathy for his feelings of guilt.

"All right," she murmured. "I'll tell you. I promise. Now try to get some sleep."

Cade told her he'd see her in the morning and waited for her to go inside her small cottage before climbing the stairs to his own room. From his second-story window, he watched the path Lexa had taken to her cottage across the way. He couldn't actually see inside the small dwelling, but he saw the lights flick on and then off, as she made her way from one end of her house to the other. He assumed it was her bathroom light that stayed on the longest and wondered if she was taking a shower or a long soothing bath.

The image of her sliding into a warm bath brought his dead senses to life—and he suddenly pulsed with new feeling. Cade scowled. If he'd had trouble getting to sleep before, this was going to make it impossible.

Lexa's bathroom light finally went out. Moments later faint lamplight flickered on in the corner bedroom. He didn't leave his vigil at the window, not until every light in her house had been turned off.

In total darkness, he crawled between the sheets Lexa had helped put on the bed and waited for his body to relax. For years he'd managed to keep his sex drive in check. It had been fairly simple. His wife wasn't there and he'd wanted no one else. Attempting to find a comfortable position, he scowled again. He punched the center of his pillow with a fist and rolled to his side. He willed the condition away and realized it might be a long time before sleep finally came.

Lexa pulled the blankets up to her shoulders, snuggling onto her soft pillows. Moonlight cast a pale glow through the gauzy curtains at the window, and her eyes fluttered closed. She lay in the drowsy warmth of her bed and smiled, thinking about Cade Sullivan. Her bath had soothed her, relaxed her, and because of her relaxed state, the events of the day found their center, and she was able to put them into perspective.

She, Lexa Franklin, was drawn to Cade Sullivan in a completely sensual way, and she reveled in the feeling. He'd almost kissed her tonight. It didn't matter that he hadn't. It didn't matter that he was still in love with his wife. His nearness had brought her senses alive, and she gloried in the feelings of normalcy his touch had evoked. She was twenty-eight years old, yet she couldn't remember ever feeling more like a woman. She knew better than to act on these new feelings, but she was, oh, so happy to be feeling them. It was as if she'd found something she'd lost, something she could pull up like a down-filled comforter on a cold winter night.

She reached for Callie Sullivan's worn blanket and smiled into the darkness, wondering what the new day would bring. Running her fingers along the satiny edge, Lexa imagined that Callie Sullivan had done the same countless times in the past. *Sleep soundly, little Callie. Your daddy's going to come for you.* Lexa imagined father and daughter together again, her last waking thought before sleep came.

The child sat on the ground beneath a tree, her legs pulled up tight to her body, a paper sack clutched in one hand. On the front of the crumpled sack were the letters MNT. She shivered in the cold, and her lips formed the word "Daddy." Her little chest heaved as with a great sorrow. She looked behind her and shook her head no. A moment later a woman grabbed up the sack, looking all around her into the darkness. She crumpled the paper into a ball, then took the little girl's hand and drew her to her feet. The child went reluctantly, but over her shoulder, she mouthed the words "Daddy, Daddy, Daddy..."

Lexa opened her eyes slowly. She placed her hand over her rapidly beating heart and noticed Callie Sullivan's blanket was already there. She knew it wasn't an ordinary dream that had awoken her. The pressure in her chest could mean only one thing. She'd had a vision. She'd seen into another dimension, had seen Cade's daughter as clearly as if she'd been only a few feet away.

The vision was gone, and Lexa lay there for several minutes, committing what she'd seen to memory. Callie hadn't appeared to be in immediate danger, but Lexa recognized the sadness and yearning in her quivering lips as she'd silently called for her father.

Lexa drew air past the pressure in her chest. Deep in thought, she ran her fingers over the child's blanket. Then she slid her feet off the bed, donned her long robe and padded to the kitchen.

She turned on the dim light over the stove and considered brewing a pot of tea. It was only four in the morning, but she knew it was useless even to try to go back to sleep. Walking to the window facing the sound, she gazed into the darkness. Hours earlier she and Cade had stood outside gazing into the same darkness. His words came back to her, and she remembered the tone of his voice when he'd told her about his wife, when he'd talked about his little girl.

Taking deep relaxing breaths, Lexa tried not to think about the heaviness in her chest. Instead, she thought of Cade. She knew very little about him, but she knew he was a man of deep emotions. She'd heard the love in his voice, the love for his daughter and the love he still felt for Callie's mother. It was that deep-seated emotion that drew her to him. Lexa understood Cade's desperation to find his child. She felt the same desperation each time a parent came to her, each time they needed her vision to find their loved one.

She walked through the small cottage to the front window and, pushing the curtain aside, peered up at the window in Cade's room. She doubted he'd slept much since Callie had been missing and wondered if he was sleeping now.

You'll tell me if you see her again? No matter what time it is, I want to know. I need to know.

All right, she'd murmured. *I'll tell you. I promise.*

She stared at his darkened window as the pressure in her chest began to subside. Cade Sullivan believed in promises. So did she.

The curtain swished back over her window as she moved away. In her bedroom, she slid her feet into her slippers. At the last minute, she plucked the child's blanket from her bed, then slipped out the cottage door.

The wind had died down and the ocean was nearly quiet.

The moon lighted her way along the path, but once she was inside Berdie's restaurant, she had to rely on touch to find her way. Lexa knew that Berdie, who lived in the small apartment attached to the restaurant, was a light sleeper. Being careful not to make even the slightest noise, Lexa felt along the wall in the dark until her hand came into contact with the archway that opened onto the back stairs.

The stairway was dark, but rather than search for the light switch, Lexa crept up silently. At the top, she trailed her hand several feet along the wall until she found the door. She turned the knob and the door opened.

The window was an elongated shape in the moonlight, the only source of light in the room. She stood in the open doorway for several seconds, listening for some sound from Cade, anything that might indicate he was awake. The only sound in the room was his even breathing.

"Cade?" she whispered. "Are you awake?"

She listened, straining her ears for his reply. When none came, she walked farther into the room, toward the bed, which appeared white in the moonlight. As her fingers came into contact with the curved iron at the foot of the bed, she called his name again. "Cade. It's me. Lexa. Can you hear me?"

Her only answer was the pounding of her heart. On tiptoe, she followed the sound of his breathing and with gentle fingers leaned to touch his shoulder. He moved, rolling onto his back, and brought his hand to his pillow. She strained against the darkness to see into his face and found him watching her.

"You came." His voice still raspy with sleep, he murmured, "I hoped you'd come to me tonight."

Lexa breathed lightly between parted lips, her mind reeling. *He hoped she'd come to him tonight.* The sincerity of his words lingered in her mind as his hand slid to her shoulder and gently pulled her down toward the mattress. His fingers warmed her skin through the thin fabric of her robe. This close, she could see into his eyes, and her entire being seemed to fill with waiting. Her emotions whirled at his touch, and the expression in his eyes moved her very soul.

She shivered and he misinterpreted the reason. "Come here," he whispered. "You're cold."

The hand at her shoulder drew her closer, while his other hand slid around her waist. Her slippers fell silently to the floor, along with Callie's blanket, but Lexa didn't bend to retrieve them. Instead, she pliantly leaned toward him, his hands steadily easing her closer until her entire body was next to his, she on top of the covers, he partially beneath them.

For a long moment the burning look in his eyes held her still. Lexa thought of nothing, except the way he made her feel and how right it felt to be held by this man.

He didn't speak, at least not with words. His touch was warm and possessive, and his look so galvanizing words weren't necessary. His hands slid up to her face, gently tracing a line across her cheekbones and over her ears before delving into her hair. He smoothed her hair away from her face and off her shoulders, letting his fingers glide through its length, down her back and up again.

Lexa gave in to his touch, instinctively and completely. She pressed her palms to his chest for leverage and whispered a kiss along his chin. His chest heaved beneath her palms, and she reveled that her power to excite him was as great as his.

She spread her fingers wide across his chest, savoring the steady rhythm of his heart beneath her palm. Her lips climbed higher and her hands slid lower, and the last of Cade's patience disappeared. Lexa gasped as she felt the bed beneath her back and Cade's heart beating a rhythm against her own.

He kissed her with an urgency that shouldn't have surprised her. Her body became restless with that one indelible kiss. She moved her legs across the blanket and her hands down his back, the muscles there and along his waist well defined yet pliant beneath her wandering touch. He inhaled a deep breath and pressed his lips against hers again in a slow drugging kiss that would never be enough.

He pulled her underneath him, and even with her gown and robe and layers of blankets, she felt his arousal. She brought her hands to his neck and pulled his face down to hers. Her calm shattered beneath his kisses, and her heart swelled with feeling, her body with need.

Lexa knew she wasn't a virgin. Daniel Jacobiac had told her she'd been married briefly before her surgery. Even though she couldn't remember with her mind the pleasures to be found between a man and a woman, her body hadn't forgotten. She allowed her instincts to transcend what her mind couldn't recall and her body already knew.

Cade closed his eyes and reveled in her eagerness. She moved her legs and body against him, provocative as only a woman could be. He pressed his hands to her back and slid her robe from her shoulders. Whispering a kiss there, he inhaled her lovely scent and closed his eyes as she sighed in the darkness.

It had been such a long time since he'd felt this way, and he wondered if his heart might burst from the exertion and from the feelings overflowing there. Cade knew Lexa had given up her memory and her past, for her clairvoyance. Her surgery had taken her memory, but she hadn't forgotten how to be a woman, a woman who was coming apart in his arms. When her lips found his he also knew, at this moment in time, she wasn't a clairvoyant but an enchantress. And he doubted she was aware of the extent of her power.

His body throbbed for release, but he was reluctant to let this end. He kissed her lips and trailed kisses along her jaw. He whispered unintelligible words into her ear and took her breasts in his hands. She was slender, yet her breasts filled his palms as her groan of pleasure filled his senses.

"So beautiful, so soft," he murmured, his breath caressing her jaw.

Lexa moved her cheek against his chin with the same rhythm her hands stroked his chest and moved lower. He made a sound deep in his throat, and she saw his lashes lower and slowly rise again. She felt his lips against her cheekbone, and his hands slide inside the bodice of her gown.

His hands stilled as hers crept lower. His breathing all but ceased. As her fingers found what they'd been searching for, he inhaled a sharp breath, murmuring sounds of encouragement. Lexa turned her head into his shoulder and smiled against his flesh. "You like that?"

"Oh, yes…it's been so long…I've missed you so much… I've missed you, oh, how I've missed you."

His words echoed through her mind, and realization dawned. *I've missed you so much.* Lexa doubted Cade knew what he'd said. But she knew. His words were like a slap, and they brought her from her trance.

She'd reveled in the way Cade made her feel, and in her own newfound sensuality. It hadn't been important that he didn't love her. But if she made love with him, it had to be *her* he was thinking of, responding to. It had to be *her* he wanted. Not his dead wife.

She wasn't surprised he'd felt her stiffen. Even as deeply in the throes of passion as he'd been, it would have been impossible not to sense the change in her. "Look at me, Cade," she whispered. He took a deep breath and complied. "I'm not her. I'm sorry, but I'm not. And I can't be her replacement."

"Lexa," he rasped. "I'm sorry. I know, Lexa. I know."

She felt every one of his muscles tense, but it took only the tiniest push against his chest and he moved to the side, and let her go. Almost. His fingers encircled her upper arm, but she didn't turn to him in the moonlight.

"Lexa, I'm sorry. I don't want to hurt you."

He didn't want to hurt her, but he was still in love with Callie's mother. He didn't say it, but he didn't have to. She'd heard the love in his voice when he'd said, *I've missed you so much.*

"Don't go." She heard the hesitation in his voice and felt it in his fingertips.

"I can't stay."

"Why?"

Finally she tilted her head to one side and looked at him, and found herself whispering in the darkness. "Because it isn't me you want, Cade."

He didn't deny her statement, and Lexa hoped her hurt didn't show.

"What about what *you* want?" he asked. "We're both lonely. Can you deny you want this as much as I do? Isn't that why you came to me tonight?"

Her feet found the floor and she spun around. With a sharp intake of breath, she searched the floor for Callie's blanket. Going down on her hands and knees, she said, "Turn on the light. I can't find Callie's blanket."

Mention of his daughter set Cade in motion. He reached for the lamp on the bedside table and pulled the chain. "What does this have to do with Callie?" he asked the instant the lamp illuminated the room.

"I saw her tonight. In another vision. That's why I came here, because I promised you I would."

His feet hit the floor, and Lexa straightened, coming to a standing position with Callie's blanket clutched in one hand. Her gaze swung to him, then slid away again. She turned, as if his nakedness embarrassed her, and Cade scowled. She'd had her hands all over his body only moments ago and now wouldn't even meet his eyes.

He strode to the chest of drawers and deftly pulled on a pair of sweatpants. By the time he'd turned back around, she'd donned her robe and was holding Callie's blanket in both hands. Cade took a calming breath before asking, "What did you see, Lexa? Is she all right?"

"It was dark outside and she was sitting near a tree, clutching a paper sack. She was rocking back and forth, and her little chin was quivering. Winnona took her hand and pulled her away, but Callie looked over her shoulder. Her lips moved."

Anguish washed over Cade. Goose bumps snaked across his body and he was filled with dread. His baby. His poor frightened baby. "What was she saying?" he asked Lexa. "When she looked over her shoulder, what was she saying?"

He watched Lexa close her eyes and saw the tears glistening there when she opened them again. "She was calling for you. 'Daddy, Daddy, Daddy.'"

He closed his eyes and let his head drop forward. An incredible feeling of inadequacy and dread washed over him. Blood pounded in his temples and drowned out the sound of his own breathing. Lexa's voice seemed to come from someplace far away. But he listened to it, let it pull him from his misery.

"She's alive. Focus on that. She's alive, and she's being cared for. And it's only a matter of time before we find her."

He opened his eyes and let her words soothe the fear in him. He'd get Callie back. He had to. "Do you have any idea where she is?"

"I saw no street signs or words on buildings that might give us a clue to her location. But I did see three slightly crumpled letters, MNT, on the paper sack in Callie's hand. Winnona crushed it, but not before I'd seen the letters."

"MNT? What could those letters mean?"

Lexa shortened the distance between them. "I don't know. They could indicate a word or place, a store or a town. Callie was sitting under a tree, holding the sack, but Winnona led her away."

"What kind of tree? Was it unique? Did it stand alone or were there many?"

"I don't know. It was dark. But the tree and those letters are our first clues."

Cade watched her slide her feet into her slippers, first her left foot and then, a little more stiffly, her right, and he was reminded of what she'd given up because of her surgery. Her memory of her past wasn't all she'd lost. In that instant he realized she'd lost her future, too. She lived for the present, to help parents like him find their children. How could he ask her to make such a sacrifice? How could he not?

She folded the blanket over her arm and handed it to him. "Would it make you feel better if I left this with you for a while?"

Her skin was pale, her eyes the darkest gray he'd ever seen, and his heart swelled with feeling at her thoughtfulness. "Thanks. But I want you to keep it."

She turned to go and he grasped the iron bed frame with both hands as she walked past. Her slippers barely made a sound, but he called her name before she'd reached the door. She turned and so did he. For a heartbeat he gazed at her. The lamp cast a glow over her skin and hair, and shadows beneath her eyes. Her lips were still pink from his kisses, and he wanted to ask her to stay. Instead, he said, "Thank you for coming here tonight and for telling me about your vision. I'm sorry about the rest. I'm sorry I spoiled it for you. I don't want to hurt you, Lexa."

She looked at him across the room and he saw her shoulders sag with fatigue. Casting him a tremulous smile, she said, "You didn't ruin anything, Cade. You can't help the way you feel. It's over. I think we should both just forget it.'' A moment later she was gone.

Cade stood there grasping the bed frame without moving, straining to hear every step Lexa took. Did she really believe he'd be able to forget what had transpired between them only minutes ago?

He heard the downstairs door click shut and, after turning off the lamp, strode to the window. The moon had moved, and Lexa now walked in darkness. He switched off the light so he could see into the night and watched her hurry along the path, watched her look over her shoulder before increasing her pace. At her door she hesitated and looked up at him.

Cade doubted she could see him in the darkened window, but didn't doubt she knew he was there. It wasn't her clairvoyant power that enabled her to know, but her feminine power, her seductive power, the power that had made him hard and her as soft as the cotton that grew near his orchards back home.

She disappeared inside her cottage, but Cade didn't leave the window. Lights came on throughout the cottage, and he knew she didn't plan to sleep any more that night. Neither did he. He'd said that he was sorry, that he didn't want to hurt her. Such inadequate words. His body still strummed with unspent desire. She'd told him to forget it. But a man didn't come as close to making love as he had tonight, then simply forget it.

He wanted her. And she wanted him. Forget it? Not unless she convinced him she had. Not unless she convinced him she didn't want him, didn't want what had nearly happened between them.

He ran his hand over the light stubble on his chin, then up and across his eyes, trying not to focus on the pounding in his head. Lexa had said the tree and those three letters were their first clues to locating Callie. The thought of Callie crying tormented him, but Lexa was right. His daughter wasn't in immediate danger. For the first time in five, make that six, days, Cade began to feel hopeful, even slightly confident that it was only a matter of time before he and Callie were together again.

He turned away from the window and found himself staring at the old-fashioned double bed. The blanket hung to the floor on one side, and both pillows were indented where two heads had rested. He strode to the bed and lifted a pillow to his nose. Lexa's scent clung to the case. Cade recognized that scent. It was jasmine, the scent of the pomander still hanging in his closet at home.

Forget what had happened between them tonight? That was the problem. Cade couldn't forget. Even if he'd wanted to.

Chapter 3

Lexa didn't glance up when Cade walked into the restaurant kitchen the following morning. She knew without looking that he'd showered and shaved, and it had nothing to do with clairvoyance. She'd caught a whiff of his shampoo and after-shave as he'd stalked by on his way to the coffeemaker. He didn't utter so much as a good-morning. Cade Sullivan was obviously not a morning person. Evidently his shower hadn't helped put him in a more amiable frame of mind.

She continued rolling out the dough on the floured counter, not quite certain what to say to him this morning. She'd sat at the table in her own kitchen for a long time after leaving Cade's room early that morning, thinking about his touch. More specifically, her reaction to his touch. For almost four years her sexuality had lain dormant, and one touch from this man and, *wham*, she felt alive with new vitality. She almost wished her sexuality had remained in a coma. But not quite. Lexa smiled to herself, feeling more sensuous than she had in nearly four years. A lot of good it did her. The only man she'd reacted to in her entire scope of memory was still in love with his dead wife.

She pressed the cutter into the dough and deftly dropped the circles into the hot oil bubbling on the stove. She loved the smell of doughnuts deep-frying, loved the warmth of the big old cook room, as Berdie called it.

"*You're* making doughnuts?"

She glanced sideways at Cade, trying to understand what had put the sarcasm in his voice. His hair was still damp from his shower, and his face clean shaven. Neither detracted from the mysteries in his blue-shadowed eyes. Nor did the mug of coffee he was sipping appear to be helping to ease the scowl from his face.

"I don't just sit around and wait for a vision, if that's what you're thinking. Berdie took me in, and I help out in any way I can. I make a huge batch of doughnuts every Thursday morning. Berdie sells them to shops and inns in the area. It helps supplement her income until the tourist season begins."

Warily eyeing him, she suggested, "Why don't you go on through to the dining room and have breakfast?"

"Maybe I'm not hungry." He slammed his mug on the counter to emphasize his mood.

Berdie had been right on several counts where Cade Sullivan was concerned. He missed his daughter. He missed his late wife. And he was as hardheaded as they came. The man needed to learn how to lighten up.

Lexa pressed the doughnut cutter into the soft dough, and Cade practically stomped to the other side of the kitchen. He evidently hadn't missed the expression on her face, because if flippancy were liquid, his next words would have been dripping with it. "Eating breakfast would be better than standing around doing nothing, while Miss Suzy Homemaker here makes doughnuts."

Cade turned toward the door, silently cursing himself for his misguided temper. He'd spent the first part of the night tossing and turning and the last part of the night alternately worrying about Callie and trying not to think about what he and Lexa had almost done. He knew he was in a foul mood. Worry had never been conducive to a sunny disposition. Neither had unspent desire.

A slight breeze stirred the hair above his ear as a small object whizzed by his cheek, missing him by a fraction of an inch. Cade looked down to see what it had been and, *thud,* something warm and soft hit him square in the back of the head.

He turned and for a full five seconds was too stunned to move. He merely stared, tongue-tied, at the madwoman flinging dough balls at him from across the room. He eyed her cautiously, trying to gauge her next move, inching his way toward the dining-room door. The warm glob that bounced off his nose sent him into action.

Three dough balls had landed on the floor near his feet, and Cade scooped them up. He crouched behind the old-fashioned workstation near the side of the room and popped his head over the top for a quick look. He dodged the ball Lexa threw at him and jumped to his feet.

Lexa screeched when the first dough ball missed her chin by mere inches, then laughed out loud when the second hit its mark. She made a grab for the dough and flung several more balls in Cade's direction. He caught two of them in midair and flung them back at her, then dived for the others closest to him on the floor. Lexa quickly picked up those he'd shot at her, flinging every ball of dough she had in one throw.

"What's goin' on in here?" Unsuspecting, Berdie walked directly into the center of the room and was immediately pummeled, front and back, with soft balls of dough.

Her appearance on the scene had similar effects on Cade

and Lexa. Both stopped in their tracks, hands poised to throw, as surprise widened their eyes. The similarities stopped there. Lexa was appalled at her behavior, while Cade appeared to be enjoying himself immensely.

His voice was low and surprisingly deep with laughter. "Bull's-eye. Right in the a—" As Berdie fixed him with a sharp glare, he mumbled, "Er, make that ample posterior. Of course, I meant ample, as in all the right places."

Lexa, momentarily speechless beneath Berdie's glare, turned to the stove where the first batch of doughnuts was ready to be removed from the oil. Finishing that task, she turned back to Berdie, ready to take the tongue-lashing she undoubtedly would receive.

For what was probably the first time in her sixty-two years, Berdette O'Toole was struck speechless. Like children handed a reprieve, Lexa and Cade took full advantage of her silence. They both scurried to pick up every last dollop of dough and had deposited them in a metal dishpan in the sink before the older woman could find her voice. "This is the thanks I get for opening my home to a Yankee?"

Cade didn't seem to see any point in explaining the circumstances leading to the little skirmish. He eyed the back door and made noises about having seen a pile of wood that looked as though it needed splitting.

"That's a good idea, Cade Sullivan. A little hard work might just get you back on my good side."

He cast another look at the big kitchen, more specifically at Lexa, who still hadn't said a word. His dark face was unreadable for a moment, then split into a wide grin.

Lexa was glad the daggers in Berdie's black eyes weren't being directed at her, and even more relieved that Cade didn't appear to be suffering beneath that glare. He winked at Lexa, shrugged at Berdie and turned toward the door. "She started it," he declared over his shoulder on his way outside.

"Yeah? That's probably what Grant said about General Lee when the war was over and the South was little more than a pile of burnin' rubble." The door slammed, and Berdie seemed content to have had the last word.

She turned her shrewd gaze on Lexa, and Lexa had a feeling she wasn't going to fare as well as Cade had. "You mind tellin' me what that was all about, missy?"

Sprinkling more flour on the counter, Lexa resumed her task of rolling out fresh dough. "He's a grouch in the morning. I did what I had to do to loosen him up."

Berdie's irritation wouldn't have surprised her. Her laughter did. Her rolling pin poised in midair, Lexa raised her eyes as the older woman threw back her head and let out a loud peal of laughter that brought old Ramsey and Arnie scurrying into the kitchen.

"What's she all fired up 'bout so early in the day?" Ramsey asked Lexa.

"Yeah," Arnie added. "Ain't heard her laugh this hard in the morning since the time she chased poor ole Tucker out the back door waving a frying pan."

Berdie swiped at the tears on her round cheeks, wagging a finger in Lexa's direction. "You best be watchin' that batch of doughnuts, Lexa. Smells done to me."

"Where's the Yankee?" Arnie asked.

Berdie huffed. "*Cade* is outside, doin' the job *you* promised me you'd do last week. Now go on, both of ya. Lexa and I have another batch of doughnuts to make."

"Come on, Arnie," Ramsey mumbled. "I haven't beat you at checkers since yesterday."

"I wouldn't be counting them chickens, if I was you," Arnie scoffed. The two old men each swiped a warm doughnut from the rack on their way by, muttering, "Best doughnuts in all of North Carolina, Miz Lexa," before disappearing from view on the other side of the swinging kitchen door.

Berdie set about frying hotcakes and sausage and thick slices of ham for the few locals who had come by for breakfast. She paused a moment, and Lexa was aware of being openly scrutinized. Berdie was going to have her say, and there wasn't a lot she could do about it.

"So he really had it comin'?"

Lexa placed another batch of doughnuts into the hot oil and answered without looking up. "Yeah, he really did."

The browbeating didn't come. Berdie's silence drew Lexa's gaze. Watching the shrewd look settle on Berdie's face, she thought a good scolding would have been better than whatever it was Berdie had up her sleeve.

"He said you started it. That so?"

"I threw the first pitch, if that's what you mean. But Cade had it coming, believe me. Even a shower and a cup of coffee didn't help his sour mood this morning."

"Many a man with a good heart is a mite grumpy in the mornin'. My Tucker was one of them."

Lexa continued to cut out doughnuts, and Berdie continued to cook breakfast at the big stove. "Haven't seen this much color in your cheeks in all the time you've been here, girl. And I was just wondering if it was all due to that little dough fight or if it had something to do with the noises I heard coming from Cade's room in the wee hours of the mornin'."

Not much got past Berdie O'Toole. Lexa wished this had.

"You gonna tell me what happened between you and the Sullivan fella?"

Lexa stood shoulder to shoulder with Berdie, Lexa placing more dough into the big pot, Berdie turning the sausages and ham and hotcakes in the skillet. Lexa was glad she didn't have to look into her friend's shrewd eyes.

"Nothing happened, Berdie."

"You telling me you didn't go up to his room?"

"No, I'm telling you why I went to his room. At least I'm trying to tell you why."

Berdie wasn't an easy woman to stop, especially when she was on a roll. "You don't have to tell me all the details. Some things between a man and a woman should be sacred. But I saw the way you looked at him this mornin', and—"

"I went to his room because I promised him I'd tell him if I had another vision."

Berdie stopped what she was doing and turned her full attention to Lexa. "You saw his li'l girl again?"

"I saw her. Now that I'm thinking about it, her face wasn't completely clear. But I saw her dark hair and her mouth, and her hands and body."

"What was she doin'?"

"She was calling for her daddy."

Berdie's hands flew to her cheeks. "Oh, that poor child. And her poor daddy." Her black eyes probed Lexa's. "Listen to me. Oh, Lexa, honey, I'm so sorry. You must be exhausted. And here I am going on an' on."

"I'm fine, Berdie."

"You should be resting."

"I couldn't, even if I wanted to. What I really need to do is keep busy."

There was a sound Berdie made without opening her mouth or moving her lips. It came from the top of her mouth and said more than words ever could. She made that sound, then flipped the hotcakes onto a platter and removed the ham and sausage from the pan. She didn't say another word until she'd reached the swinging door. "You sure all you did was tell Cade 'bout your vision last night? 'Cuz, Lexa, your cheeks are a pretty shade of pink, and I know from experience it usually takes a man to put that particular brand of color there."

The door swung shut before Lexa could think of a reply. She placed her hands to her cheeks, feeling the heat there, and knew it hadn't been caused just by the heat of the stove. This warmth came from within. And Berdie had been right. Cade Sullivan was the reason. He'd ignited something within her last night, with his touch, with his kiss. His mention of Callie's mother had sent her scurrying from his bed, but it hadn't put the fire out. Lexa wondered what would.

An hour later she balanced the metal dishpan on one hip as she pushed through the back door. She tried to be quiet as she removed the lid from the trash can behind the small shed. For reasons she didn't want to examine, she hoped Cade, who was splitting wood nearby, wouldn't notice her presence. The metal lid grudgingly gave way, but not without jangling and echoing loud enough to wake the dead. The noise by the woodpile ceased, and Lexa had a feeling her efforts to go undetected had been thwarted. She glanced over her shoulder to confirm it and saw Cade moving toward her.

From the back, she would have called his walk a swagger. From the front, he looked like a man who knew his own masculinity and knew the effect it had on women, one woman in particular. Lexa dumped the leftover dough—the dough she and Cade had hurled at each other earlier—into the can and replaced the lid. Turning, she found Cade leaning on the ax, watching her.

"Did she let you off as easily as she did me?"

She felt an eager affection coming from him, and her awareness of him grew. It was an awareness she enjoyed because it was so new, but one she hoped he didn't see. "Surely, you're kidding! I doubt I'll ever live this down, while *you've* risen to near-sainthood because, Tucker, 'God rest his soul,' was a grouch in the morning, too."

"What do you mean *too?*"

"Never mind."

"Lexa, wait."

She turned to go, but he caught her hand in his own and

gently pulled her around to face him. The dishpan clanked against the stones at her feet, and she stammered for something to say. "I've told you all I know about my vision," she confessed. "I know the waiting is difficult..."

The expression in his eyes stilled her words. Chopping wood had alleviated his pent-up energy, and she saw heart-rending tenderness in his gaze. For a long moment he looked into her eyes without speaking, and his words, when they came, were so deep she wondered if they came straight from his heart.

"I just want you to know I believe in you, in your power. I know you didn't ask for your gift any more than you asked me to come here with my problems."

He hadn't released her hand, and she wondered if he was aware that his thumb stroked her palm, that his slightest touch sent her senses on emotional overload. Why did he have to go and turn nice? Cade Sullivan, the hardheaded, hardworking grouch, had been difficult enough to resist. Could she resist him when he was like this? Sensitive and caring?

As if he suddenly realized he was still holding her hand, Cade let it go and took a step back. Anxious to escape his watchful gaze, she leaned down for the pan on the ground, murmuring, "Berdie will be looking for me." Hoping he didn't recognize the feeble excuse for what it was, she hurried along the path toward the door.

With each step she told herself there was no need to feel so uneasy simply because she reacted to this man's touch. Although she couldn't remember, she knew she'd been married. She wasn't a virgin. When Cade had touched her just now, she hadn't felt like a virgin. She felt like a vibrant desirable woman,

Just inside the kitchen door, Lexa looked back at Cade. A cool wind blew through his dark hair and rippled the black T-shirt and faded jeans against his body. He raised

the ax high in the air like a man familiar with hard work.
The ax made a sharp crack as it sliced through a chunk of
wood. He leaned down for another log, then raised his ax
high again.

"He's got a killer smile, that one. And nice buns, too."

Lexa started, realizing she wasn't alone.

"Why thank you, Berdie!" Ramsey beamed from the
other side of the kitchen.

"I wasn't talking about you, you old coot. I was talking
'bout the Yankee Lexa's staring at."

"I'm not staring." She wasn't anymore, anyway.

"I wasn't born yesterday, you know," Berdie sputtered,
stirring a big pot of stew simmering on the stove. "I recognize a glowing flush when I see one."

No, Berdie hadn't been born yesterday. But Lexa felt as
if *she* had. Or at least as if her sexuality had been.

"Is this so, Miz Lexa? You got yerself a thing for the
newcomer?" Ramsey asked.

"Of course not," Lexa protested.

"They took a li'l stroll in the moonlight last night," Berdie insisted.

"We didn't walk, Berdie. We just stood there. Talking.
He told me about his daughter."

Berdie made that sound again, the one she made without
moving her lips, and Ramsey grinned. "Spring is in the air,
Miz Lexa," he teased. "It was spring when me and my
Rebecca first met."

Lexa glanced at Arnie, who was quiet, like her. His age
was indiscernible to her, his skin a shade darker than Berdie's, and his face a kind of handsome that was timeless.
He winked at her, and she remembered Cade doing the
same. Cade's wink had confused her, while Arnie's quiet
presence soothed her. In a much calmer voice, she said,
"That's nice, Ramsey. But, even if I did have 'a thing' for

Cade, he's only here because he needs me to help him find his little girl. When he gets her back, he'll leave."

"You sure about that?" he asked.

Lexa nodded. "He'll go home to his orchard. It's where he lives and works, and it's where his memories of his wife are."

"He's a mite young to be burying hisself with his wife, don't y'think?"

Lexa smiled. "Look who's talking. You and Berdie have both been alone for a long time, and I don't see you looking to replace the ones you loved." She glanced at all three of her friends. Ramsey and Berdie were suddenly interested in the toes of their shoes, but Arnie was looking directly at Berdie, as if waiting for her to deny the fact that she was content to live with only her memories. *Could Arnie have feelings for Berdie?*

Ramsey pushed a thinning shock of what was once red hair off his still-freckled forehead and stood up, hiking his pants higher on his waist. Berdie replaced the lid on the big kettle without looking, and Lexa followed the path of their stares. They were watching Cade swing the ax again. He bent to pick up the split pieces of wood and Berdie mumbled, "Seems a shame, such nice buns goin' to waste."

"Why, thank you, Berdette!" With a wink and a toothy grin, Ramsey did his version of a man's man swaggering from the room.

Berdie's voice called after him. "I wasn't talking about your bony buns, you old coot!"

Lexa noticed that Arnie didn't say anything. She'd always assumed he was just naturally quiet. Maybe there was more to his silence than she'd thought. Maybe Berdie didn't know everything that went on on the island, after all.

Cade watched Lexa shake the wrinkles from a full skirt and deftly clip it to the clothesline, watched her bend toward the basket for another garment. She wasn't the only islander hanging laundry outside this morning. Shirts and trousers, sheets and towels flapped from lines up and down the Outer Banks like flags in the wind. But she was the only one he was watching.

Everything she owned seemed to be muted pastels, blouses in creams and blues that matched the sky this morning, skirts and slacks in heathery fabrics of pink and lavender and gray. Her sheets weren't white, but ivory, her towels peach or pale yellow. She seemed to go for softness rather than flair, even in the underclothes she'd clipped to the line a moment ago. The bras and panties weren't black or brightly colored and shouldn't have been lust-arousing. But as they waved in the breeze, they might as well have been red flags the way his body tightened.

She stood back to view her handiwork, then turned and found him watching. "Good drying weather," she called.

He stayed where he was on Berdie's back stoop, watching from a distance the way the wind blew wisps of hair across her cheek, the way it fluttered the fabric of her loose-fitting dress. The breeze outlined the curve of her breasts and the length of her legs, and he remembered his hand following the same course during the middle of the night.

Instead of disappearing into her house, she walked toward him, and he pulled his drifting thoughts together. He'd thought her dress was plain yellow, but as she drew closer, he saw it was flecked with tiny threads of gray, the same gray as her eyes. Her hair was woven into some sort of braid and secured with a plain yellow ribbon. She stepped up to the first step and gestured outward with her hand. "I think spring is really here now."

Since this was the first time Cade had been to the Outer Banks in early spring, he couldn't comment on that. Besides, he was more interested in her than the island. "Do you always dry your clothes outside?"

"Whenever I can."

She took another step, this time with her right leg, and she teetered the tiniest bit. Cade reached out his hand and felt her fingers tighten around his arm. She let go a second later and lowered herself to the top step near him.

"Dr. Jacobiac told me you went through physical therapy following your surgery."

"Then you've noticed I have a slight limp."

"Too slight to be called a limp." He waited for her to say something, to talk to him, maybe confide in him about her physical therapy. When it became obvious she wasn't going to do so, he asked, "Where is everyone? This place is as quiet as a crypt."

"Berdie went to deliver her baskets of doughnuts and half-moon pies to her regular customers. And Ramsey and Arnie both went home. I promised Berdie I'd stay nearby in case a customer wanders in or the phone rings."

"You're good to her."

"I've found a sense of peace here. Here, a person can be different, yet fit in. They don't treat me like a leper because I'm clairvoyant, just as Arnie doesn't treat Ramsey different because their skin's a different color. They've been best friends most of their lives, for so long I don't think they even see the differences anymore."

"How did you end up here on Roanoke Island?"

"Berdie opened her home to me, gave me a place to stay when I had nowhere else to go."

They sat out of the wind, and the late-morning sun warmed him everywhere it touched. Lexa's smile pulled at his heart, but she spoke with an air of calm that soothed him as much as the physical exertion of splitting wood had.

She moved her shoulders and arched her back like a cat stretching in a patch of sunshine. She folded her hands between her knees and drowsily tried to decide how to explain what had happened to her before Berdie took her under her motherly wing.

"I came here searching for a missing child. As it turned out, it was all a hoax. The child wasn't really missing. It was just another *test* one of the parapsychologists decided to put me through to *prove* I really was clairvoyant."

"He didn't believe in you?"

She laughed, and even after all this time, Lexa felt the hysteria lurking in her voice. "According to scientific theory and knowledge, ESP is possible but not likely. This particular scientist was trying to prove the latter."

Cade mumbled two words, and Lexa laughed again. This time it was genuine. "That describes him pretty well."

"How did he explain your visions and the missing child you'd already found?"

"I think he called it luck."

Cade swore again. "He believes in luck but not in clairvoyance?"

"At first I didn't even believe in it myself, Cade. There were times I thought they were right. I believed I might have been going crazy."

"Is that what they said?"

"Some of the parapsychologists were wonderful, and others...weren't. ESP is difficult to define, let alone prove. There's telepathy, precognition, psychokinesis and clairvoyance. Then there's precognitive telepathy and mind-reading and psychic research. It's all so confusing. It doesn't help that no two people have exactly the same powers. Parapsychology deals with ESP, and there is a relatively small number of scientists willing to work with it."

"Why is that?"

"They just can't see it."

Cade didn't plan to laugh, but her humor was so unexpected, the sarcasm so rich, his own sense of humor took over and he let out a chuckle that amazed even him. Just when he thought there was nothing left of his heart, or at least the part that swelled with feeling for a woman, she threw him off guard. She surprised him with a little one-liner or responded to his touch.

He watched a smile pull at her lips, watched her eyelids close and open again. For a moment he thought she might go to sleep, her shoulder leaning against the railing, her entire body relaxed in the warm sunshine.

She was beautiful, and he doubted she knew. It didn't matter that her hair wasn't short or her body was slender, instead of curvaceous. She was lovely exactly as she was. But it wasn't just on the outside. Her beauty transcended the physical, lurking behind her smiles, in her voice and beyond her serenity. She drew him, and he was sure she wasn't aware that clairvoyance wasn't her only power. He needed her clairvoyant power to find Callie, but it was her feminine power that could break his heart. It had already been broken once, and Cade couldn't risk it happening a second time.

"Mine is especially unusual."

Cade panicked like a kid caught reading comics in history class. Her *what* was especially unusual? He could think of several things about her that were unique, but doubted she was referring to the way she'd felt in his arms last night, or the way her kisses still lingered in his thoughts. He looked into her eyes and was glad she couldn't read minds. If she could, he'd have a difficult time explaining what was going on in his.

"I mean, how many clairvoyants do you know who temporarily lost their power when they tried to learn about their pasts?"

He shoved his hands into his pockets and hunched his shoulders. "Not many, but then, my exposure to clairvoyants has been rather limited." After a time he asked, "Is that what happened to you?"

She nodded. "I was still in rehab when I had my first vision. A nurse was telling me about her son and how her ex-husband hadn't brought him back from his weekend visit. I didn't understand what was happening to me, but I saw a little boy at a train station. The letters on the ticket were so clear. I told the nurse what I'd seen, and the police picked up her son later that same day."

"That nurse must have been very happy she confided in you." Cade wished finding Callie could be that easy but knew it wasn't. His situation was much more complicated.

Lexa nodded. "News spread throughout the hospital, and suddenly psychologists and psychic researchers were probing my mind, and people were sneaking into my room to ask me about their missing loved ones, both dead and alive. They were thrusting photographs and clothing into my hands and shouting out nicknames and descriptions even as orderlies were removing them from my room."

Her words were like a weight on his shoulders, and he wished he could have been there to help her through those days. He tried to console himself with the reminder that he'd been going through his own kind of hell right about then. He'd known nothing about newborn babies and was suddenly caring for his alone. But he'd had his father, and his daughter. And Lexa had had no one.

"Is that when you came here?" he asked.

"No. I came here months later. I remember holding a child's toy, a child who'd been taken from her father by her mother. I'd already had one vision, but physically I was very weak. I remember staring at my reflection in the mirror, feeling as though I didn't know the person looking back at me. And it wasn't only because my hair hadn't grown back or because I walked with a limp and was as thin as a rail. I couldn't remember *who* I was.

"Dr. Jacobiac was worried about my physical and mental state. He was wonderful throughout the entire ordeal, full of encouragement and hope, and listened as I told him how empty I felt inside, as if I'd lost something more precious than my life. You see, Cade, I was mourning my past, a past I couldn't even remember.''

Cade heard no desperation in her voice. Only calm acceptance for what had happened to her. "And did Dr. Jacobiac tell you about your past?"

"A little. I'd just had another vision of the missing child. I was crying because I had this incredible pressure in my chest and was afraid I was going crazy. He calmed my fears and began to tell me what little he knew, which was what I'd told him before my surgery. He said my mother had died, and my father had left a long time ago, that I'd come from the western part of North Carolina and had broken all ties to the people I'd known prior to my surgery. As he talked, the pressure in my chest lessened. When he told me I'd been married but was now divorced, the pressure left completely. My vision was gone, Cade. And to this day, that child hasn't been found.''

That child had never been found. What if they never found Callie? A suffocating sensation tightened his throat and burned in his chest, but he tried to hold the raw emotion in check. "Did you learn more about your past?"

Lexa shook her head. "I was still weak and was fighting to strengthen the muscles in my right side. I felt as if my hold on my sanity was tremulous, and the image of the child I'd seen in my vision, the vision I'd lost when I'd learned about my past, haunted me. The psychologist who visited me suggested I take it one day at a time, and that's what I did. Every day I went through rigorous physical therapy, and every day I waited for someone from my past to come to me.''

She smoothed her skirt over her legs and tucked it behind her knees, which were drawn up close to her body on the next step down. After a time she continued, ''I read as many books as I could find on ESP, clairvoyance in particular. Did you know Lincoln *dreamed* his own death? And Ernest Hemingway had an out-of-body experience during World War II? I learned that clairvoyance often occurs after a person has suffered a serious trauma to the head, like a fall or accident. In some people it comes and goes, in others it occurs once or twice and never again. The vision I'd lost when Dr. Jacobiac told me about my past continued to haunt me. To this day I can still see her father's tears.''

"You didn't find that child," Cade murmured. "But you've found others since then. It wasn't your fault, Lexa. Losing that child wasn't your fault.''

"I know that in my mind, but in my heart…''

"What did you do?''

"I had to find out if I'd lost all my powers or only my vision of that particular child. Another parent came to me, gave me a photo of her little boy. After a few minutes I saw him, and I knew I still had my power. Within a few days, the child was reunited with his mother. A new feeling of peace settled over me then, as if fate had brought me to that point in my life. Dr. Jacobiac told me I'd never get my memory back. That part of my brain had been injured during surgery. But he said he'd find out everything he could about my past, said it wouldn't be that difficult. He told me it was my decision. My choice. My past, or my power.''

Her voice was soft and controlled, and he marveled at her inner strength. She'd felt alone and abandoned after surgery, and when no one from her past came forward, she'd chosen to continue to help parents find their missing children. Even though she didn't speak of self-sacrifice, Cade knew what the choice had cost her.

The phone jangled from the kitchen wall behind them, and Lexa stood up. Her skirt brushed his arm, and Cade turned his face toward it. She slipped through the screen door, but the clean scent of her lingered. It was the scent of sunshine and ocean breezes, and it drew him, just as surely as the soft clear tone of her voice drew him inside. "Cade," she called. "The phone's for you. The voice sounds familiar."

Realization dawned, and Cade reacted with speed and purpose. He found his feet and was through the door almost in one motion. He grabbed the phone from her hand and spoke into the mouthpiece. Only three people knew he was here. The police, the detective he'd hired and his father, and Cade prayed the voice Lexa had heard wasn't his father's.

It was. "Yeah, Pop. I'm here." The suffocating sensation was back in his throat. He tried to listen to what his father was saying and study Lexa at the same time. He had to see if hearing his father's voice had affected her. She watched him closely, but he couldn't tell what she was thinking.

Lexa could see the tension in his shoulders and in his fingers as he gripped the phone. She listened to his side of the conversation and knew they were speaking about Callie and Winnona. From the look on his face, whatever he was hearing wasn't good news. She braced herself for what was to come, and waited for Cade to hang up the phone.

He replaced the receiver in its cradle and turned to her. Lexa's misgivings increased by the second.

"The detective thinks he's spotted a woman and child fitting their description in Charlotte."

She waited for him to continue, waited for some indication, some reason for his sudden tension. None came. "But that's good news. Cade, what's wrong?"

He breathed deeply, and Lexa was reminded of the way he'd breathed when he'd first told her his daughter was missing, as if he'd sucked half the air in the room into his lungs in one breath.

"Charlotte's a big place."

So that was it. He wasn't a patient man, and what little patience he possessed had run out. "Charlotte might seem huge to you right now, Cade, but the size of a place doesn't matter. As long as I have Callie's blanket, I'll be able to see her. And at some point, I'll see a landmark or a street sign. We'll find her. I can feel it."

He continued to look at her for a long moment. Lexa knew the instant he accepted her words, for the tension in him lifted like a helium balloon. "I didn't expect her to take Callie to Charlotte. Winnona hates big cities. I thought she'd take her to the mountains. I thought that's what those letters you saw meant."

"Sometimes the last place we expect them to go is the exact place a child is taken."

Cade walked to the other side of the kitchen and gazed out the window. Nothing had changed in the past few minutes. Waves still lapped the shore, Lexa's clothes still billowed on the line, and she hadn't lost her power. So far, he was safe. His chances of finding Callie were still good.

Berdie came bustling into the kitchen with a huff of air and a flurry of activity. She replaced the baskets she'd used to carry her baked goods and washed her hands at the sink. "I just talked to Annabel over at Shady's Resort, and she was telling me she already has two boarders. They arrived yesterday…"

Lexa listened with only one ear. The rest of her attention was trained on Cade, who kept his back to the room while he stared out the window. Without looking at them, Berdie hustled about the cook room, telling them the latest gossip sweeping across the island. When she'd finished her tale, she asked, "Did anybody stop by or call while I was gone?"

"Just one," Lexa answered. "A phone call for Cade."

Cade turned, and Berdie stood still, looking from one to the other. "Well, what is it? What's wrong? You two are too quiet for it to be good news."

"Oh, no, Berdie," Lexa answered. "It was Cade's father.

The police think they might have seen his housekeeper and his little girl in Charlotte.''

"And?"

"And nothing," Cade cut in.

"What would they be doin' in Charlotte?" Berdie asked.

"I don't know. As far as I know, Winnona used to live someplace east of Grandfather Mountain, near Boone. She has a sister living in Raleigh, and a detective is watching her place. But Winnona is afraid of big cities, and I thought she'd head for the mountains. If she didn't go to her sister's, why in the hell would she go to Charlotte?"

"Don't make sense to me," Berdie sputtered. "But then why anybody would take a li'l girl that didn't even belong to them in the first place don't make no sense to me."

Cade ran his hand over the stubble on his chin and scowled. It didn't make any sense to him, either.

"What ya gonna do?" Berdie asked him.

"Nothing I can do but wait."

Berdie bustled to the broom closet, took out a mop and pail and pressed both into Cade's hands. "Nothing makes time go slower than sitting around waiting. Here, you might just as well keep yerself busy."

She handed a stack of clean tablecloths to Lexa and told them both to hop to it. Mopping floors had never been one of Cade's favorite pastimes, but it beat doing nothing. So did washing windows and fixing the leaky faucet in Berdie's kitchen. Berdie kept them both busy and kept them both fed, ladling hot stew into bowls and urging them to eat every last drop.

By seven that evening, Cade thought he was going to explode, odd jobs or no odd jobs. Lexa had made herself scarce in the past hour or so, but when the phone finally rang at eight, he turned and found her standing just inside the kitchen door.

Berdie answered the phone in the middle of the second ring and immediately handed it to him. "Your daddy."

Minutes later Cade hung up the phone. "It wasn't them." He spoke to both women but looked only at Lexa. "The police found the woman and child, but they had identification. It wasn't Callie, after all."

With that, he turned and headed upstairs to his room. Lexa heard his door shut just short of a slam. Berdie wiped her hands on her apron before saying, "I've seen a lot of people in my day, but I ain't never seen one quite like him. Something's eating at him, all right, and it ain't just his li'l girl. That man's keeping secrets. And I can't help but wonder why."

Lexa sat down heavily at the kitchen table, thinking about what Berdie had said. She remembered the way Cade had looked the first time his father had called, remembered the tension in him and, for a moment, the fear.

What are you afraid of, Cade Sullivan? And why can't you tell me what's wrong?

Berdie's soothing voice drew her from her thoughts. "You look wrung out, child. Go on home now and get some sleep."

Lexa placed her own hand over the darker one squeezing her shoulder. "I'm twenty-eight years old, Berdie. When are you going to stop calling me 'child'?"

"Probably never. You're just like one of my own. Now go on and do as I say."

Lexa pushed to her feet and smiled at her friend. "I think I'll do that, Berdie. See you in the morning."

She cast a final look up the quiet stairway, then opened the back door and followed the path to the little cottage she called home. She prepared for bed, but couldn't shake the feeling that something wasn't right, and that whatever it was, it was staring her in the face.

Chapter 4

Cade tried to tell himself he wasn't sticking close to the restaurant the following morning just to get a glimpse of Lexa. He'd come downstairs before daylight, started a pot of coffee and dialed his number back home. By the time he'd hung up the phone, he felt better. Talking to Pop always had that effect on him. It wasn't just because Pop had kept him abreast of the police department's and the detective's findings, either. They'd talked about Callie, yes, but they'd talked about other things, too. Like the new peach trees they'd planted last year, and the record crop their orchards would produce if the weather held. Talking to Pop reminded Cade that he and Callie had a life to go back to.

He filled a mug with coffee and went to stand at the window. Talking to his father this morning also reminded him of their conversation yesterday. He remembered the feeling of panic that had nearly overtaken him when Lexa had said the voice over the phone sounded familiar. It might not have had such a drastic effect if she hadn't, only minutes before, told him she'd lost her vision of a missing child because she'd learned something about her past.

He'd overreacted. Of course hearing Pop's voice wouldn't affect her. Hearing *his* voice hadn't.

Berdie walked into the kitchen before he'd finished his second mug of coffee, took one look at him and sputtered, "I figured you'd still be in bed. What ya doing up so early?"

Cade cast a look toward Lexa's cottage and answered, "Couldn't sleep." He heard pots and pans clank as Berdie bustled about, but he didn't turn to see what she was doing.

"My favorite time, too—the calm of the day," Berdie declared. "It's a good time to gather your thoughts." She rattled on, and Cade nodded when it was expected of him, but he couldn't have recited a single word she said. Until she said, "You can stop watching the door. Lexa ain't up yet."

He turned then and looked at the plate Berdie was pushing his way. "It takes deep thoughts to keep a man from noticing the smell of bacon frying."

He took the plate heaped with bacon and eggs, grits and pancakes, as Berdie continued. "Her light was on till late last night, and I'm glad she's sleepin' in this mornin'."

Cade knew Lexa's lights had been on late into the night. In fact, he knew the exact time she'd turned them off. He'd told himself he was waiting for her to have another vision of Callie, but he knew that wasn't the only reason he'd watched her windows. She'd come to his room the night before, and there was a glimmer deep inside him that couldn't let go of the hope that she'd come to him again.

He dug into his breakfast and Berdie clucked like a mother hen. "Does my heart good to see ya eating. Glad your worries ain't affected your appetite."

His worries hadn't affected either of his appetites.

"And to tell ya the truth, I kinda like having a little company first thing in the mornin'. Tucker, God rest his soul, used to love to watch me work in the cook room first thing in the mornin'. 'Course, he didn't say so, not in words, 'cuz he wasn't a mornin' person, either..."

Cade finished his breakfast and sipped another mug of coffee, thinking you could learn a lot about a person by simply listening. Berdie rattled on about the potato pudding she planned to make for supper, or "suppah," as she pronounced it, about her daughter who'd married and gone to live on the *mainland*, and her son who was "the spittin' image of his daddy" and had a career in the navy and hadn't been home in three years.

Cade couldn't help noticing her unusual use of the English language, but kept the observation to himself. She talked about younger days when she and Tucker-God-rest-his-soul were first married. When her topic of conversation turned to Lexa, he couldn't have moved if he'd wanted to.

Berdie told him how weak Lexa had been when she first came to O'Toole's. "Scientific research to prove there's really such a thing as a third eye!" she grumbled. "'Clairvoyance' is what Lexa calls it. I swear them there researchers are dumber than a box of rocks. 'Course there's more 'n five senses. It don't take no college degree to know that. My mama had an eighth grade education, but she had a wealth of knowledge them scientists couldn't hold a candle to.

"Birds migrate, don't they? And fish swim in schools. Even horses have horse sense. Which is a site more sense than that so-called scientist had who sent Lexa here on a wild-goose chase."

Cade wouldn't have minded five minutes alone with that particular scientist. He had a feeling Berdie wouldn't have, either.

The older woman talked on, telling Cade about those first months when Lexa had come here, telling him how she'd grown stronger, how Berdie had grown to love her like a daughter. "She's healthy now, mind and body. I can't help but worry about her, though, when she's looking for another missing child. It takes a lot out of her. She don't eat right, or sleep. Why, just last night I sent her home early to get some rest, but her light was on long into the night."

"If you saw her light on until late, you must have been awake, too. Don't you sleep, Berdie?"

She took his plate and made a sound he'd never heard before. It was the darnedest thing. Cade could have sworn her lips didn't even move. "When you git to be my age, you don't need a lot of sleep."

"What do you mean *your age?*" Cade admonished. "You have more energy than any woman I've ever met. I haven't seen you sitting still since I've been here. Maybe you should find a man who can appreciate that."

"You're a fine one to be talking," she muttered, but he noticed she smoothed her curly hair away from her face, preening like a schoolgirl. "You Yankees always know just what to say, y'know that? Besides, maybe you should take your own advice. Maybe you should be looking for a woman, one who could put up with and appreciate a hardworking, hardheaded, good-looking man like yerself."

Cade picked up his mug. The outer door opened and Lexa walked into the kitchen. Her gaze slid over his and the coffee never made it to his lips.

She wore a flowered dress in muted colors of blue, lavender, periwinkle and gray. The fabric looked as soft as the colors and as feminine as the woman wearing it.

Berdie jumped up and headed toward the stove. "Good mornin', child. Have a seat and I'll fix you something to eat."

"Thanks, Berdie. But I'm not very hungry."

"Nonsense. You sit down and I'll fix you a plate." The older woman made that sound again, but Cade noticed it didn't deter Lexa from taking the pitcher from the refrigerator and helping herself to a glass of orange juice. She'd breezed past him without a sound, but her scent, the scent of jasmine, lingered. He gradually became aware that he was holding his mug of coffee in midair and lowered it to the table without looking.

If Cade was a man parched by the hot sun, the sight of Lexa was like cool shade and a mountain stream. He couldn't deny the real reason he'd hung around Berdie's kitchen so long. He'd been waiting for a glimpse of a woman he knew he couldn't have.

She'd done something different with her hair. The sides were pulled up and secured on top with a wide barrette, and the rest was pulled to the back where it hung like satin from a loosely tied bow. She looked very Southern, very beautiful. She still wore no makeup, at least none that he could see, and no jewelry, and Cade decided that hers was the type of beauty that needed no adornment. She poured a mug of steaming coffee, then leaned against the counter to drink it.

Berdie was talking, and Lexa was answering, which allowed Cade to look to his heart's content. His gaze traveled over her face and settled on her mouth, and something intense flared in him. She moved to one side, settling herself more comfortably against the counter, and his gaze followed the gentle flow of her dress as it swished into place around her legs. She raised her mug to her lips, and his gaze followed. It was at that moment she looked at him, that moment she cast him a small smile and that moment his heart turned over in his chest. He rose from the wicker-backed chair as if propelled by an incredible force and tamped down the feeling, because he knew where that particular feeling would lead.

Straight to heartache.

"Where you going?" Berdie asked.

"Out back to finish stacking that wood."

"Nonsense," Berdie admonished. "Today's Sunday, a day of rest."

"There's no rest for the wicked," he returned.

"That's 'no rest for the weary,'" Berdie declared.

"Whatever," he called over his shoulder, and was out the door before anyone could say another word. Taking the ax in hand, he raised it high above his head. It whizzed through the air and the blade grated into the wood, much like the thoughts grating through his mind.

He hadn't realized today was Sunday. That meant Callie had been gone for seven days. An entire week of her life he'd missed. How many more days would he miss before she was back safe and sound? How many more days would he have to hold his emotions in check?

Half an hour later, the restaurant's screen door banged shut, and Cade looked up as Lexa stepped out onto the back stoop. He brought the ax down hard, wedging it into a log.

"Berdie doesn't like it when people work on Sunday, Cade," she called.

"So I gathered," he replied. Instead of taking up the ax again, he watched as a soft breeze swirled her dress, lifting the hem past her knees, then letting it fall back into place. "You going anyplace special?"

She moved down another step and lithely turned toward her cottage. "I'm going to church in Manteo. When I get back, I'll show you the island if you'd like."

She disappeared into her house, and Cade stood alone on the gravel path, casting a look around. Lexa was the one with the clairvoyant powers, yet apprehension snaked up *his* spine. He appeared to be the only person outside. No one was clipping laundry to clotheslines, and no one was working in their small yards. Not another soul was in sight on this quiet Sunday morning, yet he could have sworn he was being watched. He'd felt the same way two nights ago but had blamed it on the darkness and the noise of the ocean. It was broad daylight now, but for some reason this place still spooked him.

A doorknob rattled behind him, and he turned to see Lexa placing her key in her bag. She waved as she walked away, and Cade watched her go.

She was going to church. That explained her dress and shoes. It didn't, however, explain the reason for his uneasiness. Something nagged at him. He felt as if he was overlooking something of grave importance. He didn't need to ask if she'd had another vision. He knew she'd tell him the moment she had. What was it, then? What didn't he see?

Cade finished splitting the wood and began to stack it behind the shed. He hadn't gotten far when a pair of strong dark hands began to help. "I told Berdie I'd split this here wood," Arnie stated. "Since you did it, instead, I figured the least I could do is help ya stack it."

Cade nodded, but neither man said another word. They worked on in silence, as if both knew words weren't necessary. When the stacking was done, they brushed the dirt from their hands and clothes. Eyeing the older man's fingers, Cade said, "Those are calluses a man earns. How did you earn yours?"

For a long time Cade thought Arnie wasn't going to answer. He wouldn't have blamed him, for Cade respected a man's right to his silence. But Arnie did answer after a time in a clear proud voice. "Ninety percent of Dare County's population works in the fishing industry. I was one of 'em."

"A fisherman."

"Yep. Worked side by side with Tucker and Ramsey for over forty years." Arnie cast a look at the restaurant, and Cade followed his gaze just in time to see Berdie disappear around the front of the building.

"Does Berdie know how you feel?"

Arnie looked at him hard, and his smile was a long time in coming. "No. She knows ever'thin' else that goes on around here. But not that."

"Why don't you tell her?"

"Why don't you tell Miz Lexa?" Arnie must have read the look on Cade's face, because a smile slowly crept across his weathered features. "It ain't always easy for a man to love a woman."

"Your situation is different from mine. But you might be surprised at Berdie's reaction if you told her."

"Thought about it a time or two, but nah, I don't wanna rock the boat."

Cade watched Arnie walk away, down the shell-paved road toward his cottage farther along the bank, thinking what a sorry pair they were. He'd told Arnie their situations were different, but he hadn't told him why. Arnie was alone because he didn't want to rock the boat. Cade was alone because he had to be if he ever wanted to see Callie again.

Lexa was surprised to see Cade waiting for her after church. He was leaning against the wrought-iron fence surrounding the old cemetery. He'd changed his clothes and looked even taller and broader-shouldered in the navy pants and white cotton shirt he now wore. He appeared relieved to see her, and she asked him if everything was all right.

He cast a look around, then murmured, "I don't know. I can't shake the feeling that someone's walking across my grave."

She lowered her voice, being purposefully mysterious. "Don't ever say that when you're practically standing on someone else's." She inclined her head at the cemetery and began to walk, letting her hand trail along the iron railing.

"This is a beautiful old cemetery," she said softly. "I've walked through it many times."

"You like cemeteries?"

"I like this one. It's peaceful. I read the names and dates on the stones and try to imagine what their lives were like, how these people dressed, what they did and who they loved."

He didn't say anything, and she looked up at him to see if he'd heard. There was tension in his shoulders and in the way he rubbed his hand across his clean-shaven jaw.

"How long ago did you shave off your beard?" she asked.

He sucked in a quick breath. "How did you know I had a beard?"

For several moments she looked at him. "You rub your chin as if it's still there."

"I shaved it several days ago, two days after Callie was abducted."

She didn't understand the tension in his shoulders, in his face, didn't understand what she'd said to put it there. He gazed at the old cemetery with its leaning markers and shady paths, and one possibility came to mind. "Do you find a sense of peace when you visit your wife's grave?"

"No."

He stepped away from her, and she was uncertain whether he'd meant, no, he didn't visit his wife's grave or, no, he found no solace there.

"This cemetery is well tended," she said when she'd caught up with him. "I wonder if my mother's grave is tended as well."

Cade glanced at her, and asked, "Your mother's grave?"

"Dr. Jacobiac told me my mother died when I was eighteen. He said I'd told him she'd gone peacefully, after suffering a very long illness. I have a photograph of her, obviously taken before her illness had progressed. It's signed, 'For my darling Lexa.' That photograph was sitting on my bedside table in the hospital and was the first thing I saw when I opened my eyes after my surgery.

"Dr. Jacobiac said I'd placed the photo there as a reminder. Isn't that crazy? It's like tying a string around my finger, then forgetting what it was supposed to remind me of."

"You saved nothing else from your past?" Cade asked.

"Very little. Just my mother's photo, some clothes that no longer fit and a small box filled with dried flowers. Forget-me-nots. I don't know why I took those with me to the hospital, but I still have them on the shelf in my closet."

It dawned on Lexa that she'd saved the photo and dried flowers for much the same reason Cade hadn't wanted his housekeeper to put his wife's things away. As a reminder of a love that was no longer around. The realization lingered at the edges of her mind, and she felt as if she and Cade shared a very special bond.

They walked on without speaking and were nearly back to Berdie's when she found Cade looking at her. She knew the neckline of her dress wasn't low, but wide, swooping in a gentle arc from shoulder to shoulder. The sleeves were long, the waistline tapered. She watched as Cade's gaze followed the sweep of material, and her emotions whirled like a leaf in the wind. It suddenly didn't matter that she couldn't remember her mother's voice. She felt her love in her heart. It didn't matter that she didn't know where she'd gotten those dried flowers. What mattered was the look in Cade's eyes and the way she felt when she was with him.

When they reached O'Toole's, Lexa started up the back step. Noticing that Cade didn't follow, she turned and said, "You aren't coming in?"

He shook his head. "Thought you promised to show me the island this afternoon."

"So I did." She took another step, calling back over her shoulder, "I'm going to tell Berdie we're back and are leaving again, and then I think I'll change out of this dress."

Cade watched her go, wishing he had the right to ask her

to wear the dress for him. He loved the way she looked in that damn dress, graceful and feminine. She was beautiful. He'd love to see her gray eyes glow when he told her so— if only he could.

He'd thought his heart might burst when she'd wondered out loud if her mother's grave was well tended, and he'd almost grasped her shoulders and told her about the wild-flowers growing there. But he couldn't tell her. He cursed her power, then cursed himself. She'd made her choice nearly four years ago, and seeing her now, he knew what that choice had cost her. She'd suffered because of it and grown strong in spite of it. If he uttered the words that would ease Lexa's mind, it would jeopardize her power, and that was something he simply couldn't do.

In minutes Lexa was back, Berdie not far behind. "I gave Lexa here strict instructions to show you the Outer Banks. Sunday's a day of rest and relaxation, and I want you both to enjoy it."

"Does Lexa always do as you say?"

"When it suits her." Berdie shivered in spite of the April sunshine and looked over his shoulder. Cade did the same.

"What is it?" he asked.

"Don't mind me. I'm always jumpy when Lexa's waiting for another vision. Felt the same way when my daughter was expecting her first baby, and rightly so. Turned out to be twins."

Lexa didn't bother to change her clothes, and she laughed all the way to Cade's car. Inside, she searched for her seat belt and found it knotted at one end. She tried to work the knot loose, but Cade's hand stilled her movements. His powerful fingers slid across the top of her hand, and she felt his fingertips tremble.

"I knotted this around Callie's car seat. I know she's old enough not to need a car seat, but she's small for her age, and I didn't want to take any chances."

She searched his face, and what she saw there was like a stab to her heart. He'd done everything in his power to keep his child safe. Everything except keep his housekeeper from taking her from him. "Winnona took her car seat?"

His answer was like a growl of derision until she encircled his large hand with both of hers. "She didn't get everything, Cade. We still have her blanket. It's locked up safely inside my cottage. And I don't believe Winnona's moved on. I think she's staying in the same place, the place I saw in my last vision. And do you know what else I think?"

She watched his eyes probe hers, watched the hope she'd ignited there grow with her words. "I think she's going to make her move soon. And when she does, we'll find her."

She let her gaze trail down, over his strong chin and throat, down the row of buttons in the center of his crisp white shirt, to his left hand, which was still enveloped in both of hers. "You still wear your wedding ring," she whispered. Rather than seeing it as a painful reminder that he still loved his wife, Lexa felt his ring was a testimony to the depth of his feelings and the strength of his commitment. That strength was what made him the man he was, and drew her to him.

He turned his palm, slowly splaying his fingers through hers. With his touch, tension arced between them, the kind of tension between a man and a woman, the kind of tension that was soothing and curiously bracing. He took a steadying breath, and the pressure of his fingers increased. Her gaze collided with his, and he smiled, slowly and thoughtfully. He leaned toward her as she leaned toward him, and breathed a kiss along her mouth.

There was a dreamy intimacy inside his car and her eyelids fluttered down. Lexa was aware of his strength and his warmth, and she tipped her face so she could touch her lips to his cheek. His breath fanned her face for but a heartbeat before his lips found hers again.

Cade's appearance in Lexa's life had unleashed a strong passion from within her. His name slipped through her thoughts, and a tiny glow started deep inside her, past her heart and beyond her soul, in a place that had no name.

He ended the kiss as slowly as it had begun and touched his forehead to hers. "That was for knowing just what to say to give me hope. And for wearing that dress."

The smile that followed was all male. That smile, along with his words, ignited the spark he'd started deep inside her, and she felt her heart swell. He made her feel things she couldn't remember feeling before. It was all so new, like the very first spring, and Lexa knew she was going to miss him when he left.

He settled himself behind the wheel, and Lexa clicked her knotted seat belt into place. She directed Cade north to U.S. 64, saying, "I'll show you Roanoke Island last. It's not very large, only twelve miles long and about three miles wide, but rich with folklore and history."

Cade took the bridges and causeways east across Roanoke Sound as Lexa explained, "Next weekend marks the beginning of the tourist season. From April to December you'll find everything from sailboarding regattas to surf-fishing tournaments, from street fairs and blues festivals to hang gliding." The Southern lilt of her voice worked over him, much the way her kiss had stolen into his heart.

Driving past a sign that read Nags Head, he lifted a brow in her direction. "That's really the name of a town?"

"People in these parts claim that in the early days of the settlement land pirates deliberately tried to wreck ships. One stormy night they allegedly tied a lantern to the neck of an old nag. A ship mistook the light for a beacon and was lured to the treacherous reefs where it was looted by the wily shoremen."

"Dangerous times," Cade murmured.

"You've heard the legend of the headless horseman? It's

folklore that supposedly originated here. Legend has it that the headless horseman still gallops silently over these dunes."

Cade watched the dunes slide by his windows. Periodically catching glimpses of the Atlantic, he drove on, listening to Lexa's clear Southern voice.

"Some people still believe that the spirit of the white doe, said to be the reincarnated Virginia Dare, who was the first English child born on American soil, still roams these hills and is visible only at the stroke of midnight. This tale deals with magic and claims that Virginia was loved by two men, a young brave and a magician. To thwart his rival, the magician changed the young woman into a white doe. A magician of another tribe gave the brave a silver arrow that would magically restore the maiden to human form if it pierced her heart. The brave shot the doe through the heart, and a mist arose, revealing the form of Virginia Dare. Dead."

Cade's heart thudded at the unhappy ending to her tale. She spoke of magical folklore, but the real magic was in her voice, in her touch and in the way her gentleness penetrated his soul. Of course he didn't really believe the tales were true, didn't believe in incantations and sorcerers and magic silver arrows. But he believed she'd seen Callie in another dimension, from one place to another. He believed in her power and in her strength.

He'd tried to shore up his heart before coming to Lexa. He had in truth come here for one thing and one thing only. To get Callie back. He hadn't planned on being attracted to her, not anymore. He certainly didn't want to fall in love ever again, but didn't know how much longer his heart could withstand being pummeled with her gentleness.

"Just up the road a ways is the Wright Brothers National Memorial. Are you interested in aviation, Cade?"

"Cade?" she repeated a few moments later.

He turned and found her looking at him. He made a sound that meant, *What?* and she asked again, "Are you interested in aviation? Because if you are, we're not far from the place where the Wright brothers made their first flight. What do you say? You interested?"

He was interested in her. And it worried him. A lot.

He shrugged and she said, "Here I am going on and on. I'm probably boring you to death."

"No," he said. "Believe me, you're not." He glanced from the road to her eyes. She stared back at him wordlessly, and he again thought how miraculous it was that her clairvoyance had brought him here, that with her inner eye she could see his child. He wondered if she could also see into his heart.

They passed a sign stating the distance to other towns up the banks, and Cade said, "Kill Devil Hill and Kitty Hawk? Do you know how they came by their names?"

"Kill Devil Hill supposedly received its name from a brand of rum so potent it was considered strong enough to kill the devil. Some say the name Kitty Hawk was derived from the mosquito hawks that swarm here during certain seasons."

She filled the time with folklore, and he marveled at her ability to spin a tale. They turned around at Duck, a small coastal town, and headed south past the places she'd already told him about, past Kitty Hawk and Kill Devil Hill and Nags Head.

Lexa pushed the button and lowered her window, turning her face into the breeze streaming by. Driving over the causeway crossing the Oregon Inlet, Lexa grew quiet. The sunny weather and warm breeze was making her drowsy. She imagined she could have easily closed her eyes and fallen asleep, and wished she'd brought Callie's blanket along. Maybe she'd have had another vision in her relaxed state.

"Wake up, sleepyhead."

They were no longer moving. It was Lexa's first thought when she opened her eyes. She turned her head and found Cade smiling at her. "Where are we?"

"We're someplace on Hatteras Island. I almost woke you up when I came across a sign for Chicamacomico. Wondered what the story behind *that* name is."

"Why didn't you?"

He looked at her, and she saw the tenderness in his gaze. "Berdie told me you don't sleep well when you're waiting for a vision, and I didn't want to disturb you," he replied.

He was disturbing her now. And she reveled in the sensation. It made her feel young and alive and new. It made her feel feminine. It made her feel. Period.

"How far do you want to go?"

"How far?" she repeated. Thoughts of how far she wanted to go with this man sent X-rated images through her head.

Her stomach chose that moment to rumble, and he said, "You read my mind."

She hoped he hadn't read hers. "Your mind?" she asked, wondering if she sounded as crazy as she felt.

"Figuratively speaking. Your stomach just rumbled. You're hungry, and so am I."

He opened his door and she did the same. They both found their feet, both groaned as they stretched. In the distance Lexa saw Cape Hatteras Lighthouse. "Buxton's not far from here," she told him. "There's a fish-house restaurant there where you can see boats and ducks and even working fishermen. Do you like seafood?"

His expression stilled and grew serious, and for the life of her, Lexa couldn't understand what she'd said to effect that change. Berdie always said you had to keep a man fed to keep him happy, and Lexa wondered if that applied to Cade, as well.

At the restaurant they both ordered the special, which was a huge plate of fresh king crab legs, scallops and spiced shrimp. They drank mugs of strong coffee and for dessert ordered half-moon pies, which were fried and made from peaches and apples.

"These are good," Lexa whispered. "But Berdie's are better."

Cade smiled, and her heart nearly turned over. "I hate to admit it, don't you?" he asked. "The only person who can make a better half-moon pie than Berdie is Pop. And that's probably because he uses our own peaches and apples."

Before her sat a man of rare smiles and deep thoughts. She'd only known him a few days, would probably only know him a few more. Their time together would be short, she knew, but that didn't keep her from wanting to learn more about him.

"You love your orchards, don't you?" she asked.

"My favorite place in the world," he whispered. "Row after row of trees, and no matter what the season, there's a sense of tranquillity there. In the spring the scent of blossoms is pure heaven, surpassed only by the scent in late summer when the fruit is ripe. When the breeze is just right, the scents of apples and peaches mingle, much like the flavors mingle in these half-moon pies."

He'd probably just uttered more words in a row than he had since she'd met him. And they had all been about his place back home. Love of his home came through in his words and voice, in the almost reverent way he spoke of his orchards. "You make it all sound very beautiful, Cade," she murmured.

He looked into her eyes for a long time without speaking, and she felt transported to the clouds. Although she couldn't remember with her mind the special attraction between a man and a woman, she felt it now. It was an emotional sensation that turned into a physical want. Looking into

Cade's eyes, she knew he felt it, too. Even though he still wore his wedding ring on his left hand, Cade Sullivan was attracted to her, and she reveled in the knowledge.

The waiter asked if there was anything else he could get them. Lexa shook her head and Cade told him no. After another long moment, Cade was the first to look away. He reached into his back pocket for his wallet and made noises about heading back. He told the owner of the restaurant the dinner was delicious, and Lexa said, "When you say 'dinner,' it's a dead giveaway that you're not a true Southerner. Northerners have dinner. Here in the south we have 'suppah.'"

His chuckle set the mood for the return to Roanoke Island. She told him stories of the people, or Bankers, as they're still called, who live up and down the coast of North Carolina's Outer Banks. At Rondathe, they smiled at the shoes drying on picket fences. "Some folks here still celebrate the birth of Christ on January 6. It's called Old Christmas, or Twelfth Night, and has been a custom for generations."

"How is it that you know so much about the Outer Banks?" Cade asked.

"Most of it I've picked up from Arnie and Ramsey. They've fished these waters for decades. And I've spent many a Sunday afternoon listening to their tales. Believe me, nobody has more stories to tell than a fisherman. But I've been up and down these banks many times. When I'm not helping Berdie or looking for a missing child, I poke around in Bankers' folklore."

As they took the causeway over Roanoke Sound, Lexa said, "If Berdie was here she'd say 'Evenin' is a pinkin'-in.' We've been gone for hours and I should be getting back before she starts to worry about me. I'll have to show you the island another time."

The day suddenly seemed over too soon, and Cade felt a

moment of panic that his time with Lexa was drawing to an end. "We'd probably have time for one more stop," he said.

His voice washed over her like a warm wave, and she replied. "There's a lot to see on Roanoke Island. But it has only two towns, Manteo and Wanchese, named for two Indians who lived here in 1584. Which one would you like to see?"

Cade searched her words for some clue to the uneasiness that suddenly crawled up his spine, but found nothing that should have put it there. He pulled onto a dirt road and stopped, and his unease turned into another feeling.

She looked at him, and he explained, "You can show me those towns another time. I don't want Berdie to worry, so I'll take you back in a minute. But first I want to look at that view."

They both got out of the car and walked a short distance to where the sun was visible through the trees. They stopped, Lexa a few steps ahead of Cade, and gazed at the ruby ball of fire in the sky.

She'd had a wonderful day, better than she'd had in a long, long time. She didn't want the day to end, but knew it must. If there was one thing she'd learned these past four years, it was to take each day as it came, to enjoy what she had and find the strength from within to live without the rest. Today was a day to be cherished, a memory to add to her growing collection. And one of her most precious memories, she knew, was going to be Cade, this silent, big-hearted man who'd come into her life and changed her in the most subtle of ways.

On emotional overload, she heard his deep intake of breath, heard the tiny squeak of his shoe as he stepped closer. With the sun at her front and Cade at her back, Lexa felt truly warmed. He grasped her forearms and she felt the roughness of his hands through the fabric of her dress. He kneaded her flesh and moved his palms up to her elbows, then up farther where his thumbs were but a hair's breadth away from the sides of her breasts. When he'd reached her shoulders, he kneaded gently, and Lexa felt as if her entire body was wrapped in an invisible luxurious cloak.

She moved her head to one side and found the protective curve where his neck met his shoulder. Leaning back, she fit her back to his front. They stood that way for a moment, the only sound that of cars far in the distance and their own beating hearts.

He removed the loose bow from her hair and slid his hand underneath to her nape, where he splayed his fingers wide, lightly stroking her scalp before combing through her hair. Lexa heard his sudden intake of breath and a moment later felt him press his lips to the hair that grew in an even line along the scar on the back of her head. Her lids fluttered down, and a deep sigh filtered up from her chest.

Lexa stiffened, and the moment shattered. She jerked her shoulders up as her hands instantly covered her ears. For a moment she didn't move, not even to breathe.

"Lexa! What is it? What's wrong?" Cade's hands covered her own, and his voice slowly penetrated to her consciousness.

She opened her lids, and even though she didn't remember turning around, she found herself staring directly into Cade's blue eyes. "What's wrong?" he repeated.

She lowered her hands from her ears and took a shuddering breath as her heartbeat began to return to normal. "I heard a child's voice."

Cade glanced all around. "I didn't hear anything."

"No. No, you wouldn't. The voice is in my head."

"Whose voice?" he asked.

"I'm not sure. But it's the same voice that called me back to the living when I died on the operating table."

"You died?" His voice was so deep, so emotion-filled, the words were barely more than a whisper.

"Yes. I remember it clearly."

"How often do you hear this voice?" Cade asked.

"I hear it each time I get close to finding the child I'm looking for. It used to haunt me, but each time I hear it, I know I can't give up my power."

"What does the voice sound like?"

"That's the crazy part. I can't describe it. I'm not sure whether it's the voice of a boy or a girl. I'm not even sure what the child is saying. All I know is that the voice is calling out to me. At first I thought it must have been the voice of the child I was searching for. But after I find the child, I listen, and the child's voice is never the same as the one I hear in my mind."

"You said you hear it only when you're close to finding the missing child. Does that mean you'll find Callie soon?"

Lexa went very still. She looked all around her, and finally at Cade. "I didn't mean close in a time sense. I hear the voice when the child is nearby."

"Callie is nearby!"

She stopped, peering suddenly at a sign visible through the trees. Manteo—1 mile. Wanchese—5 miles.

"MNT. The letters on the sack Callie was clutching in her hand. The sack might have been from a shop in Manteo. And the child's voice I heard a moment ago. Oh, Cade, what if she's been right here all along?"

In the same instant they both turned and scrambled the short distance to his car. Cade felt an ache of foreboding, as sharp as a blade through his heart. He started the car and gunned the engine, the tires spinning in the loose gravel.

They didn't speak during the two-mile drive to Berdie's restaurant. White-knuckled, Cade grasped the steering wheel with both hands while Lexa hung on to the door arm with one hand and spanned her ribs with the other.

520 *Child of Her Dreams*

They roared into the driveway and gasped at the sight of the police car's flashing light and the shattered glass in Lexa's front door.

Chapter 5

"She was here. Right here!"

Cade's window was down, and Berdie's words penetrated the noise of the engine and crunch of tires as he slammed on the brakes.

"I saw her with my own two eyes," Berdie cried in a tear-smothered voice.

"You saw Callie?" Cade lunged from the car. "Where? Where is she?"

"I don't mean your li'l girl, Cade. I saw the woman who took her. She was right here!" Berdie spread her arms wide to encompass the driveway and Lexa's cottage.

She'd said *was*. Fear knotted Cade's vocal cords, making it nearly impossible to speak. He noticed two uniformed men walking toward them and Arnie and Ramsey standing a short distance away, talking with several neighbors who had come over to see what the commotion was about. The place was crawling with people, when what Cade wanted was to be alone. Alone where he could nurse his despair and disappointment, and tamp down the fear that had arisen like a jagged stone from someplace deep inside him.

Lexa stepped closer to Berdie and asked, "What did you see, Berdie? Tell me exactly what Winnona did and said."

The Dare County deputies pressed the onlookers back, and when it became obvious that Berdie was having a difficult time calming herself sufficiently to speak, Arnie walked silently to her side and began, "Ramsey and I were playing a game of checkers in the cook room where Berdie here was fixin' suppah. We heard a sound like glass breakin' and we all looked up at the same time."

Berdie cut in, rushing on, "We listened real hard but didn't hear no other sound, so we walked on outside to take a look."

"Didn't notice nothin' unusual at first," Arnie said.

"But I glanced at your cottage, Lexa, and I caught sight of movement inside." Berdie's voice shook with emotion as she continued. "I started for the door when I noticed the glass was broken. That's when I saw her, me on one side of the door, her on the other."

"You saw Winnona?" Lexa asked.

"I saw a big woman with round eyes and straight hair. 'What are you doin' in Lexa's house?' I yelled. She stepped back, and that's when I saw the li'l one's blanket in her hands. I rushed toward her, and she backed up. Ramsey yelled, 'Berdie, don't go in!' But I didn't listen. Winnona took one look at me inside Lexa's house and her eyes rolled back in her head like she'd seen a ghost. 'Bird in the house!' she screamed. And took off through the back door."

"Where did she go?" Cade asked in a voice so low it sounded as if it came from the bottom of his lungs.

"Arnie and Ramsey and me all ran after her down the banks. But we ain't as young as we used to be, and we just couldn't catch her. We heard a car start and caught a glimpse of yer li'l girl. And then they were gone. You gotta find yer daughter. She can't stay with that woman. She was pos'tively frightening.''

"How long ago?" Cade asked. "How long ago did she leave?"

Berdie looked down, and it was Arnie's voice that finally answered. "An hour at least."

An hour. Winnona had taken Callie's blanket, Cade's last link with his daughter, and she'd driven away an hour ago. That meant she had an hour's head start, when Cade had no idea which direction even to begin looking.

The deputies searched the entire area, then questioned Cade and Lexa and asked Lexa to go through her house and report anything missing. She found nothing out of place, nothing except the glass from the front door and the back door, which was still swinging from its hinges. The only thing missing was Callie's blanket.

"MTN," Lexa whispered to Berdie. "The letters I saw on the sack in Callie's hand. Cade and I both think they were part of the word 'Manteo.'''

"You think she's been right here all along, child?"

Lexa nodded, and Berdie sputtered, "Merciful heavens! The boarders Annabel told me about when I delivered her doughnuts and half-moon pies! Said it was a mother and her li'l girl."

Lexa practically had to run to keep up with her friend, who repeated this to the deputies. Moments later she found herself seated between Berdie and Cade in the back seat of the police car as it sped to Shady's Resort and Berdie's friend Annabel.

Cade kept his body perfectly erect, every muscle rigid. His features were so hard they could have been chiseled into a mountain. Lips drawn into a thin line and chin set, the muscle clenching in his cheek and the look of pain in his eyes revealed his frustration and utter disappointment. Watching him, Lexa wished she could put her arms around him. She wanted to offer him something, some small token of hope, but without Callie's blanket, she doubted she'd be able to see the child again.

Berdie was out of the car before it had come to a complete stop, Lexa and Cade and the deputies not far behind. "Annabel!" she called. "Annabel!"

"Berdie O'Toole, what is it?" A voice called through the screen door.

"I need to talk to you," Berdie shouted. Annabel took one look at her friend and the others following close behind, and she opened her door wide, ushering them all inside.

"That boarder you told me about. Is she still here?"

The woman shook her head, and Lexa cast a look at Cade. Before her eyes his face closed, locking all emotion inside.

"Checked out this morning. Her and her daughter. Cutest li'l thing I ever did see. Beautiful eyes, that one."

Cade stepped forward and in a controlled voice asked, "Did she tell you what her name was?"

Annabel cast a questioning look at Berdie, and Cade scowled. She'd let a kidnapper stay in her inn but she didn't trust *him* enough to answer a simple question.

"It's okay, Annabel. Tell him what you know," Berdie coaxed. One of the deputies took out a pad and began writing.

"Well, that's sorta strange. Said her name was Wanda, but I swear I heard her daughter call her Winna or some such name. At first I thought she couldn't talk plain and 'Winna' was her way of saying Mama, 'cuz each time she said it, the woman would correct her, saying *Mama*. The child never did say it, though. She'd just cross her li'l arms and set her lips in a straight line."

Cade's heart raced like a freight train, blood rushing through his veins until he could barely hear. Lexa's hand on his arm cut through his fear. He looked into her eyes and found hers brimming with tears.

"Callie refused to call Winnona *Mama*, Cade. She hasn't given up. You can't, either."

"Winnona," Annabel said. "Yes, that's what the child called the woman. But the mother said her li'l girl's name was Allie, not Callie."

"Callie is *not* Winnona's daughter!" Cade shouted.

For a moment the room was silent, all eyes trained on Cade. Lexa's voice drew their gazes as she explained, "The woman isn't Callie's mother. She was Cade's housekeeper, and she stole his little girl."

While Berdie explained the circumstances, Lexa walked to the back door and stood gazing at a tree not far from the inn. Cade joined her at the window. "Is that the tree you saw in your vision?"

She nodded and Annabel gasped. "You already saw her here in your vision?" Lexa nodded and Annabel turned to Cade. "You poor man! But don't worry. Lexa here will see your li'l girl again. Don't you worry."

The deputies asked for a complete description, but Cade already knew the woman and child who'd stayed here in Manteo had been Winnona and Callie. Now they were gone, and for the first time since arriving on Roanoke Island, he felt real fear, the kind of fear that ate at a man's insides and brought him to his knees.

There was little moonlight tonight. It didn't matter. Looking out over the dark waters of Roanoke Sound, Cade realized nothing mattered. Callie was gone. Winnona had won.

A dual. That's what this had been. A dual Winnona had begun three years ago when she'd first walked into his home. For three years she'd worked and schemed to finally a place in his life. For a time Cade had been under the impression that it was him she'd wanted. He hadn't loved her. He couldn't. He now realized it hadn't mattered to her.

The only person she really wanted was Callie. She'd answered his ad in the newspaper three years ago because she'd found out he had a young daughter. It was Callie she'd wanted. Right from the start. And now she had her.

Oh, what a difference a few hours made! It had been only a matter of hours since he'd spent the afternoon with Lexa, an afternoon when he'd harbored an illusion that Lexa might fall in love with him, that together they'd find Callie and they'd all be a family. Again.

An illusion. That's what it had been. And Winnona had shattered it as surely as she'd shattered the glass in Lexa's front door. She'd destroyed his illusion, and she'd taken Callie's blanket, thereby shattering his hope of ever seeing his child again.

Cade wanted to slam his fist into something. Anything hard would do. At the moment, physical pain would have been a welcome diversion to the emotional agony he was in, the more painful the diversion the better. Flexing both hands, he looked around in the darkness, but found nothing to hit, nothing except the ocean, the sky and the sand.

"I thought I'd find you out here."

He closed his eyes in the darkness, trying to close himself off from the gentleness in Lexa's voice. She didn't try to touch him, and Cade was relieved. He didn't know how much more his emotions could take before he crumbled like the sand at his feet.

"Arnie and Ramsey finally left a little while ago, and Berdie's worried about you. Why don't you go inside where it's warm?"

"I don't want to be warm."

She didn't speak for a long time, just stood within touching distance of him staring straight ahead, like him, seeing nothing.

"Did you finally get through to your father?"

He ran his hands across his cheeks and up the sides of

his face. Didn't she realize he didn't feel like talking? He wanted to be alone.

"What did your father say?"

Cade finally looked at her. Although he could barely make out her profile in the darkness, he saw the angle of her chin and her jaw set in determination. He might as well answer her. She wasn't going to go away. Not until she was good and ready.

"Not much he could say. Told me we'd find another way, the usual father kind of talk." The truth was, hearing Pop's voice had only added to his frustration, his sheer desperation. Because, for the first time in Cade's life, hearing Pop's voice didn't bolster his confidence, didn't make him believe things would eventually turn out.

"I should have known."

She stepped closer, but still didn't touch him. "What should you have known, Cade?"

"I should have known Winnona was nearby. I felt her watching me, here on this very beach. Three times, I felt her eyes on me. It gave me the creeps, but I didn't recognize what was wrong."

"You couldn't have. She never made her presence known to you."

Cade swore. Vehemently. But it didn't make him feel any better. Nothing could.

"Callie was this close." He held up his thumb and finger in the darkness. "A few blocks away from this very restaurant. And I wasn't here. I should have been here, dammit!"

Finally she touched him, and it was all Cade could do to keep the wrenching sob from escaping his lips. As if realizing he wasn't ready for a human touch right now, she removed her hand from his arm. She spoke softly, and instead of touching him with her hand, she reached out to him with her voice, down inside him to a place he thought had been closed off forever.

"You said she was thorough, Cade. She'd meticulously boxed up all Callie's belongings, planned this to the tiniest detail. She followed you here, then watched your every move. Do you really think it would have mattered to her if she had to wait another day or two for you to leave?"

Cade didn't want to talk. It hurt to talk. But there, in Lexa's quiet presence, thoughts began to race through his mind. After a time, he found himself uttering them out loud. "I didn't think Winnona would hurt Callie. But taking her from me *is* hurting her."

Lexa remained quiet, as if waiting for him to continue. He closed his eyes and let his head fall forward. "She didn't take her to her sister's in Raleigh or to the mountains like we thought." His words stopped there, but his thoughts raced on.

She'd lain waiting for me to leave, and she'd moved in for the kill, the opportunity to take Callie's blanket, my last tie to my baby. The thought of such a woman raising his little girl brought bile to his throat. He had to find his daughter. But how?

He made a sound of derision. "The police and detectives haven't had a clue to their whereabouts from the very beginning. It was as if they'd disappeared from the face of the earth. But they hadn't disappeared. Winnona simply did the last thing any of us expected. The entire time the police and detectives were searching for her, she'd been following me. And now that Winnona has Callie's blanket, you won't be able to see her."

"No one disappears from the face of the earth. They're here, Cade. Somewhere."

Maybe there was something to this talking, after all. He'd been sure he wanted, needed, to be alone. But while he'd been alone, his mind had been blank, his body numb. Now, little by little, the blankness in his head was evaporating like fog in the sun, leaving thoughts to form in his mind. A cool wind blew through his shirt, and a shiver crawled over him, chasing the numbness away.

"You won't be any good to Callie if you catch pneumonia," Lexa said. "Come on, Cade, it's time to go inside."

"I can't. That room upstairs closes in on me."

"Then come into my place. I'll brew a pot of chamomile tea."

The thought of tea didn't appeal to him, but the lure of her voice drew him from the shore. They followed the path to her cottage, and he grimaced at the board Arnie had nailed into place over the broken window. Just inside the door, he watched as Lexa leaned to turn on a light. The lamp cast a yellow glow across her cheeks as, unobtrusively, she placed a hand on the sofa to steady her step. The muscles in Cade's own legs suddenly flexed. It was all he could do not to reach out a hand to help her.

She moved briskly by him toward the kitchen, saying, "Make yourself comfortable while I brew that tea."

He turned slowly, taking in her living room, the pale-colored sofa and soft throw pillows. Four doors led from the square room. One was the front door, another the kitchen where he could hear tap water streaming into a kettle. The lamplight spilled onto the floors where the two other doors led, the black and white tiles of the bathroom and the white-washed wooden boards of her bedroom.

Silverware and dishes clinked in the next room, but Cade didn't follow the sound. Instead, he wandered over to a small desk and picked up a silver-framed photograph of Lexa's mother. He remembered thinking the room was nothing like he'd expected a clairvoyant's living room to be. Now, he realized it was exactly like Lexa. Pale, serene, and dominated by an incredible sense of calm.

Scanning the books on her shelves, he found her collection was small but varied. He'd expected to find books about ESP, but was surprised to find them interspersed with old

books of North Carolina folklore, a book of poetry, a guide
to shipwrecks along the Eastern shores and a book of jokes.
But the shelf that really caught his attention was the one
lined with assorted framed photographs. All of them of children.

He studied each photograph. There were children of several ethnic groups, boys and girls, some younger than Callie,
others in their early teens. She obviously loved children very
much. She'd have made a wonderful mother. Cade swallowed the lump in his throat and felt a heavy sadness that
Callie would never know her.

Cups rattled behind him. He turned and saw Lexa place
a tray on a low table. Inclining his head toward the shelf,
he asked, "Friends of yours?"

She stepped around the coffee table, and for the first time
he noticed she'd changed her clothes. Instead of the flowered dress she'd been wearing all day, she now wore a one-
piece outfit in pale blue. She'd taken the barrette and bow
from her hair, which now hung loose about her shoulders.

She walked closer, but didn't answer his question until
she'd let her gaze rest on each of the photographs lining the
shelf. "These are my children. The children I've found with
my gift."

The faces beneath the glass and frames took on new significance as she told him each of their names and a few
circumstances and traits that made them special and unique.
He listened to the soft cadence of her voice as she said,
"There are twelve so far, twelve children who've been reunited with their loved ones because of my gift."

He followed her gaze to another shelf that held two more
frames, one of a stocky man and a curly-haired little girl,
and one of empty glass. Lexa pointed to the first. "This is
the child I never found, the one I'd seen but lost when I
began to learn about my past. Her father gave me this photo.
I still receive a card from him every Christmas. He's re-

married and now has a baby son. But he hasn't given up looking for his daughter. I doubt he ever will.''

"She's been missing for nearly four years?" Heaviness centered in his chest as he imagined living without Callie for that long, not knowing where she was, how she was.

Lexa nodded. "He believes he'll find her. I pray he does.''

Cade looked at the photograph long and hard. Lexa called her inner sight a gift, considered her clairvoyance a magical power. But looking at the photograph of the child she'd never found, he knew her power was no gift. It was a cement block tied to her ankles, keeping her from happiness, keeping her from him. It wasn't his idea of magic.

Magic was what her smiles did to him, what her voice and her touch made him feel. Since the moment he'd learned Winnona had taken Callie's blanket, thereby severing Lexa's only means of finding her, he'd felt his hope of finding Callie begin to die. But outside tonight, when Lexa's voice had reached down inside him, he knew he wouldn't give up. He'd find a way to find Callie. And he'd thought perhaps in the process he'd find a way to tell Lexa the truth.

Looking at her photographs now, he knew he couldn't tell her the child she was searching for was her own daughter. Twelve families had been reunited because of her visions. She kept photographs of each child as a reminder of the power of her visions. The photograph of the child she hadn't found was just as powerful a reminder, for it reminded her what would happen if she lost her visions.

With that, a realization, stark and vivid, crystallized in his mind. He couldn't tell Lexa the truth. Not now, not ever. Somewhere, sometime, another child would be taken, and another parent would come to Lexa for hope, and another photograph would be added to her shelf.

With blunt-tipped fingers, Cade pointed to the other one, the empty frame. "What is this one for?"

"This frame is for the next child I find."

Cade closed his eyes. That child should have been Callie.

Lexa turned and went back to the sofa where she began to pour their tea. He walked to the sofa and accepted the cup of tea she offered. He remembered the tales she'd told him earlier today, tales of how local towns had gotten their names. One town in particular came to mind. Kill Devil Hills. She'd said the town was named for its potent rum, potent enough to kill the devil. Cade wasn't a drinking man, but he wished he had a bottle of that rum now. If it was strong enough to kill the devil, maybe it could take the edge off the helplessness and fear that threatened to squeeze the air from his lungs. He sipped the brewed tea and tried not to grimace, even though he knew the expression he was hiding wasn't wholly from the bitter taste of the tea, but from the bitterness he felt inside.

Lexa sipped her own tea, the clock in the kitchen the only sound in the entire room. She left Cade alone with his thoughts for a time, then slowly began to draw him into inconsequential conversation. But as she'd expected, it didn't take long for the topic to turn to his child.

He told her amusing tales of his daughter's life, happy times, laughter-filled moments, memories he obviously treasured. He spoke of her sweetness and of her stubborn streak, which he claimed had been evident at birth.

Lexa laughed and said, "Even Annabel mentioned Callie's stubborn streak. Winnona probably thought 'Allie' was close enough to Callie's real name, so close that it wouldn't take all that much for her to become familiar with hearing it."

"But she didn't," Cade said. "She also stubbornly refused to call Winnona 'Mama.'"

"Your daughter obviously takes after her father."

He heard the smile in her voice, and Cade wished he could tell Lexa that Callie had inherited her goodness from her mother, her inner beauty and her warmth. His eyes were drawn to the row of photographs on the shelf, and he knew he could never tell her.

The realization sent a kind of sadness mixed with admiration through his body. He looked into Lexa's eyes, and knew why he'd fallen in love with her seven years ago. He also knew their time together was running out. Now that Winnona had Callie's blanket, it was useless for Cade to stay here on Roanoke Island. He'd hire more detectives, he'd send fliers. He'd search every inch, every town, every ridge.

He'd leave. And Lexa would stay. This would be their last night together, their only night together.

His gaze met hers for an emotion-filled moment. His thoughts filtered back to the day he'd first met her seven years ago, and then to the time he first saw her again, mere days ago. His instinctive response to her had been the same both times. He'd wanted her then. He wanted her now.

Cade placed his teacup on the table, reached for hers and placed it near his own. She leaned toward him and traced his lips with her finger, then moved her hand across his face. He closed his eyes against the emotions quaking through him. He hadn't come here for this, not to the island, not to Lexa's house. Finding Callie had been his reason for coming, his reason for living.

"For this night, live only for the moment," she murmured as her hand slid to the back of his neck and she whispered kisses along his chin. He pulled back slightly and searched her eyes, thinking she must be able to read minds, after all, until he realized he'd spoken his thought out loud, and she'd answered from her heart.

Lexa felt her heart begin to hammer in her chest, felt her chest expand with feelings and her body soften beneath his look.

"I don't want to hurt you," he said.

"You'd never hurt me, Cade," she replied. "I always feel safe with you."

He kissed her, and her body grew heavy and warm. His hands slid over her, molding her soft curves more tightly to the contours of his hard body. She let her hands trail down his chest, over his arms and shoulders and down his strong back. He pressed his cheek to her breast, and a passionate fluttering rose to her throat.

The heaviness she'd felt when she'd seen his child was gone. In its place were myriad emotions, desire, and a deep-seated caring that could easily turn into more. Lexa smiled a woman's smile, but kept her thoughts to herself and simply gave herself up to the feelings his touch evoked.

He stood, and she was suddenly lifted into his powerful arms. Her hands went around his neck, and her gaze never strayed from his. She didn't recognize the powerful emotion lurking in his eyes. She doubted it was love, but knew it was nearly as strong, a kind of admiration mixed with desire. This time she had no doubt that he knew it was her he was with.

With long strides, Cade strode to her bedroom and didn't stop until he'd reached her double bed. There, he let her slide from his arms slowly until she felt her feet touch the floor, felt the bed at the backs of her knees.

Drawing his face close to hers, he whispered, "For this moment, there is only you and me."

She closed her eyes, and her head tipped back to accept his kiss. His hands pressed her closer, gliding up her back, then came around to the front of her body, fumbling at the buttons at her throat. Lexa reveled at his impatience and pressed a smiling kiss to his shoulder.

"Let me," she murmured, taking a small step away from him.

The light from the living room cast an elongated shape over the foot of the bed, but left the rest in semidarkness.

His eyes had no color in the dim room, but there was no disguising the sexual intent in their depths. She unfastened the top button, then the next and the next, her gaze holding his all the while. When she reached the button below her waist, his gaze left hers, traveling down the expanse of skin now visible.

Gently, he eased the material from her shoulders, letting it fall to her hips in a soft *swish*. His hands covered the lacy cups of her bra, and her breasts surged at the intimacy of his touch. She pressed a kiss to his throat, another an inch lower. A moment later, he pulled his shirt from his pants, jerked the buttons open and tossed the shirt behind him.

She heard the squeak of his belt, the metallic clink of his buckle and the rasp of his zipper. He kicked off his shoes and stepped from his pants and briefs.

It was Lexa's turn to gaze, Lexa's turn to appreciate the beautiful male before her. She took in every solid inch of him and was filled with an incredible sense of anticipation. He drew her against him, and she felt the full extent of his desire for her. Her emotions ran as deep as her desire, both so new, so vital, and a little frightening.

His hands went to her back, where he made short work of the clasp of her bra, and moved on to her hips, where he slowly slid her remaining clothing to the floor. She moved against him and heard his deep intake of breath. Cade gently lowered her to the bed. Following, he kissed a path down her ribs to her stomach and up again. His hands worked magic, moving in opposite directions along her body, and her fear evaporated beneath his touch.

Lexa worked her own magic across his body. She abandoned herself to the moment, to the wonderful sensation of being a woman, of feeling at one with a very special man. Her palms slid down his shoulders, kneading the taut flesh of his chest, down farther over the rippled muscles of his stomach and below. His hands on her body stilled, and she heard him inhale a choppy breath. She stroked him, letting her emotions and her instincts lead her to a place she couldn't remember with her mind.

Lips met lips, then trailed kisses and murmured words of praise along flesh heated in passion. Lexa lost all perception of time and place, and felt her emotions transport her to another dimension entirely. Words weren't necessary and were spoken sparingly on sighs and whispers.

At some point, she found herself on her back. She opened her eyes and found Cade watching her. His eyes were heavy-lidded, his breathing barely controlled. She closed her eyes and pressed against him. Moving her legs, she urged him inside, welcoming him.

There was a tingling deep inside her as he began to move. Pulse points pounded, emotions whirled. Beneath her closed eyes was only darkness, inside her ears only the sound of her beating heart. His name echoed through her mind and settled into her heart. There was no earth, no heaven, no past and no future. There was only her and Cade, and this moment in time.

When she thought the tremor deep inside her would send her careering through space, completion burst all around them, and the darkness behind her eyelids turned to light. She murmured his name over and over, not aware that she spoke out loud.

"I'm here," he answered. "I'm here."

She breathed in deep drafts of air and gradually became aware that he'd shifted his weight to his side, one leg still draped over her possessively. Lexa didn't know whether to sing for joy or weep with wonder. She did neither. Never before had she experienced such emotion, never before had she been so far beyond words.

When the air began to cool their skin, they snuggled beneath the warm blankets, where they lay for a long time without talking. Lexa wanted the night to last forever, but her lids grew heavy, her body languid in Cade's arms.

These past four years, she'd come to believe in fate. The photographs on her shelves were constant reminders of its power. She believed fate had brought Cade to her, and she knew his search for his daughter would take him away again. They would have this night, and this night alone. She'd learned to enjoy the moment, for she had little past and the future was unclear. For this moment, she was warm and sated and secure in Cade's arms. He'd given her something tonight, a memory more precious than she'd believed possible.

Drowsy with sleep, she murmured, "I just want you to know, Cade, you're my first. In all my memories, there will only be you." The pillow came up to cradle her head. She turned into its comfort, and sleep came.

Cade lay there in the dark, his heart thudding in his chest and Lexa's words echoing through his mind. She accepted him so completely, with few questions and no reservations. She'd come apart in his arms tonight, more magnificent and resplendent than ever before. She thought this time was their first. He knew that wasn't true. Or was it? She was different now. And it was more than just the length of her hair or the color of her clothes. She possessed a serenity she hadn't had before.

He stayed close to her for a long time, listening to the sound of her even breathing. She'd told him to live for only this moment, and that's what they'd done. But the moment was over. He had to leave to find Callie, and she had to stay, to wait for another parent to come to her.

Cade didn't expect the anger that came crashing through him at the unfairness of their situation. Lexa didn't deserve his anger. God only knew why he felt it. But gut-wrenching anger consumed him. It was there each time she asked him some innocent question, like their daughter's name, where he was from or what kind of fish he liked. It reminded him that she couldn't remember his love. And he couldn't forget hers.

Being careful not to disturb Lexa, he eased out of bed and pulled on his clothes. Quietly he walked from her bedroom and looked around her living room one last time, his anger now dulling into acceptance. The lamp was still on, and Cade studied the room, studied the row of photographs on her shelf. He finally understood why she'd left him.

Gazing at the photo of her mother, he remembered how Lexa had cried when she'd told him about her mother's long, slow and painful illness. She'd said the woman had suffered, not only from her illness, but because she couldn't be there for her only child, couldn't nurture her, prepare her breakfast, fix her hair, mother her in a thousand different ways. As her daughter, Lexa had suffered, as much from her mother's emotional anguish as from her painful illness. Lexa had taken on the role of caregiver at an early age, helping her mother dress and eat and bathe.

Cade remembered the look on Lexa's face four years ago when the specialist had told them Lexa's chances were slim that she'd live through her surgery, slimmer still that she'd ever fully recover. At the time he hadn't fully understood why she'd forced him and Callie from her life, why she'd wanted him to promise not to subject their newborn daughter, Carolina Joy, to a mother who couldn't be there for her.

He'd promised her he'd raise Callie to be independent and strong like her mother, but he couldn't promise Lexa he'd go on with his life without her if she survived the surgery but was changed. He'd told her he couldn't let her face surgery alone, would never stop loving her, no matter how much the surgery changed her.

He hadn't realized how her mother's illness had hurt Lexa, how she'd feared and dreaded putting her own daughter through that kind of pain. He hadn't realized, and he hadn't promised to let her go.

So she had left.

Cade had been frantic. He'd gone to see her doctor, but the surgeon told Cade he didn't know where she'd gone. Cade didn't believe him, but there was nothing he could do. Lexa had left behind divorce papers and a note promising she'd come back if she could. If she didn't, she begged him to go on with his life.

At first he'd told himself it was simply a matter of time before she came home to him. But she hadn't, and his fear and dread grew heavier each day. He imagined her in a hospital room, hurting and alone. Other times he feared she'd died during surgery. The police were no help; she'd left of her own free will. Finally in desperation he went to her former doctor again, begging for answers. The man hadn't been lying, after all. He hadn't seen Lexa. He must have understood Cade's desperation, because he told him the name of a surgeon who might have some information.

Cade went to see the surgeon the same day. Daniel Jacobiac had looked deep into Cade's eyes and said, "I'm sorry, Mr. Sullivan. I've taken an oath I can't break. I can't tell you where Lexa is, but I can tell you she's safe. Her surgery was successful. But she doesn't remember you or your daughter or anything about her past. She's undergoing intense physical therapy and is emotionally, as well as physically, weak. I'm afraid you have no choice but to respect her wishes and go on with your life without her."

"Does she know she has a child?" Cade asked.

The older man shook his head. "Try to remember that Lexa doesn't know what she was like before her surgery. She's very thin now, and her body bears no outward signs of pregnancy or childbirth."

Cade had left the surgeon's office knowing Lexa was alive, knowing she was lost to him. At first he'd grieved as if she'd died. But as the months passed and Callie grew, he began to feel abandoned and angry. Staring at Lexa's photographs now, he realized how misplaced those feelings had been. Lexa had done what she'd thought was best for her child. She'd truly suffered. He wondered if she realized she was still suffering beneath the weight of her power.

Cade strode to the door, leaned down and turned off the lamp, then quietly opened the door and shut it behind him. He slid his fingers into his pockets and lowered his chin against the chill of the night. Letting himself in the restaurant's back door, he took the stairs in the dark.

Upstairs in his narrow room, Cade didn't undress or crawl into bed. He knew it was useless to try to sleep. He stood at the window overlooking the sound and Lexa's cottage, and waited for daylight to streak the black sky, waited for the longest night of his life to end.

Lexa knew something was different before she'd even opened her eyes the following morning. She felt as if she were floating, and wrapped in a silken cocoon at the same time. Moving her shoulders and rotating her hips, she was reminded why she felt different this morning. She and Cade had made love. The tenderness she felt in certain parts of her body was one reminder of the extent of their passion. The tenderness she felt in her heart was another.

Her thoughts filtered through the pleasures she'd found in his arms, and she savored the feeling of satisfaction she still felt. But mixed with her happy thoughts was the realization that their night together was over. Today Cade would have to leave.

Lexa hurried from her bed and donned her long robe, remembering the night she went to his room, the night she'd awoken with her vision of Callie. She remembered how the passion between them had already been building.

She made short work of her shower, then dried her hair

as quickly as possible. Cade was leaving, and she had to see him before he left. She had to look into his eyes one more time. She had to tell him goodbye.

The atmosphere in Berdie's kitchen was subdued. Four pairs of eyes turned in her direction the moment she stepped into the room. Ramsey and Arnie immediately went back to their game of checkers and Berdie back to the stove, but Cade's gaze didn't waver from hers. For the most part, his expression was closed. But looking at him, she watched the tense lines on his face relax, and she smiled. Eyeing the suitcase by his feet, she said, "What time are you leaving?"

"Soon."

She searched his gaze for hidden messages and searched her heart for the right words to convey what she felt. Looking around her, she decided she didn't want to broadcast her feelings, not in front of an audience. Besides, words weren't necessary. She could tell him how sorry she was that she hadn't found his little girl. But somehow she believed he already knew.

"Have a seat, child," Berdie ordered. "I'm just about done fixing all of us a nice big Southern breakfast before Cade leaves."

Lexa took a chair next to Arnie, and Cade pulled out the one next to Ramsey, who made a triple jump, practically cleaning the board of his opponent's checkers. "Give it up, Arnie. You ain't no competition this mornin'."

When Arnie offered no resistance and no words of retaliation, her gaze was drawn to her dear friend's face. He wasn't looking at Ramsey. Instead, he peered thoughtfully at Cade.

"What is it, Arnie?" she asked.

"I'm not sure. But I cain't help but think we're overlookin' something of grave importance."

Berdie placed a heaping platter in the center of the table,

and Ramsey pushed the checkerboard aside. But Cade and Arnie didn't move.

"What could we be overlooking?" Cade asked.

"Don't know for sure. Yet."

Berdie bustled to the counter and brought back plates and cutlery. When Lexa offered to help, the older woman made the sound she made without opening her mouth and gestured for Lexa to be silent.

After a time, Arnie finally spoke again. "Why would yer old housekeeper go to so much trouble to take ever'thin'? Every dang article, every toy, every single thing yer li'l girl ever touched."

Lexa had wondered about that, too. Cade had told her Winnona had done it so he'd have nothing left. She now wondered if there was more to it. But what other reason could there be?

"And why did she risk getting discovered coming all the way over here just to get her hands on the li'l one's blanket?"

Berdie was the one who answered. "Because she's superstitious, that's how come. That woman is from the mountains. I knew it the minute she opened her mouth. And mountain people are superstitious folk. Some of 'em still weave their clothes and make their own soap by the phases of the moon. Why, one man from Cullowhee once told me a possum gives birth to its young by way of its nostrils."

"Berdie," Ramsey sputtered, "not while I'm eating!"

"You men can clean a fish with one hand and eat with the other, but mere mention of childbirth and yer green around the gills," Berdie said. "B'sides, that Winnona woman looked positively crazed when I walked into Lexa's house. 'Bird in the house,' she screamed. Y'see, she musta heard Ramsey call me Berdie, and for a person in the hills, a bird in the house is the most feared omen there is."

"Too bad she got away with yer li'l girl's blanket," Ramsey mumbled. "Yer sure you don't have nothin' else?"

Lexa noticed Cade hadn't taken a bite of his breakfast. Neither had she. She followed his gaze and found him staring into Arnie's black eyes. "Yer sure she took ever'thin'? You've looked through every box, every drawer? She didn't even leave one tiny picture of your daughter?"

"I can't think of anyplace I could have missed." Cade's voice was deeper than Lexa had ever heard it. She could practically see him reliving everything he'd done, every place he'd searched.

"Do you have a video camera?" Lexa asked, remembering how one parent had brought her a home movie of her child. Cade nodded, and she continued. "She took the tapes?"

He nodded again. "Every last one. Even took the camera."

"What about photos?" Lexa asked.

He shook his head, and Arnie asked, "What about somebody else, a relative or neighbor who might have a picture of your child."

"There's only me and Pop and Callie. Winnona took all the photo albums. She even took my camera and the film inside."

Cade went perfectly still. Lexa watched his mouth move, but he made no sound. His chair fell backward in his haste to run to the phone. His fingers shook as he dialed a number, and swearing, he had to try again. This time Berdie didn't admonish him for his language. Everyone waited, hearts thumping, eyes trained on Cade, new hope flickering to life in their breasts.

Chapter 6

Cade's knuckles, as he gripped the phone, were white. Lexa felt his tension, and even though she didn't know why he'd suddenly marched to the counter and grabbed for the telephone, she shared his resurgence of hope.

"Pop?" Without another word he slammed the phone down and swore under his breath about blasted rotary phones.

Realizing what had happened, that he'd reached a wrong number, Lexa hurried to his side. Placing her fingers over his, she murmured, "I'll dial."

She quickly dialed the numbers he recited, then stepped back to give him room as he waited for his father to answer. After what seemed like an eternity, he rasped, "Pop, is that you?" There was a moment of silence while Cade listened to his father. He looked at Lexa, mumbled a noncommittal answer and said, "Remember that camera, the one you bought a few years back? Do you still have it?"

Cade listened, asked a few questions and answered a few

more in monosyllables. From his tense body language, Lexa wasn't sure whether his father's words gave him hope or not.

He finally turned to the others in the room and said, "Pop's looking. He bought a fancy camera a few years ago. Thought he wanted to take up a new hobby. But he said newfangled contraptions were too complicated and gave it up. I haven't seen that camera in a long time. I hope he saved it, and I hope the film inside is still good."

Looking directly into Lexa's eyes, he added, "You said you've been able to see a missing child from a photograph. If I can get one of Callie, do you think you'll be able to see her?"

For reasons she didn't understand warmth surged through her, and she offered Cade her most encouraging smile. "In the past I've gotten a clearer image if I have an article of clothing. But I've seen children from photos. It's worked before. It could work again."

After what seemed like hours but was actually only a matter of minutes, Cade's fingers visibly tightened around the telephone again. He mumbled something Lexa couldn't hear, glanced at the watch on his wrist and, turning his back to the others, replaced the phone in its cradle. She watched his chest expand with the deep breath of air he took and wanted to cry out for him to tell her what his father had said.

Berdie was the one who finally groused, "Well? You gonna keep us in suspense all day?"

He turned and ran his hand across his chin before answering. "He didn't get rid of the camera, even though he claimed a person needed to take classes to learn how to use it."

"And yer housekeeper didn't take it?" Berdie asked.

"I assumed she had, but Pop said he remembers now. He bought it while Winnona was in Raleigh visiting her sister a few years ago. He didn't want to keep using it, but he didn't want to lose it, either. He put it in his strongbox in his closet so it wouldn't get misplaced. He keeps that box locked. Even I don't know where he keeps the key.''

"And he took pictures of Callie?" Lexa asked.

Cade nodded, and Ramsey let out a loud whoop. Everyone laughed, and Lexa thought she knew how the more than one hundred men and women must have felt when they first set foot on Roanoke Island more than four hundred years ago. After a long and perilous journey, they finally had ground beneath their feet and hope in their hearts. That's what that undeveloped film had given Cade. Renewed hope. And hope, Lexa had learned, was precious. Until now, she hadn't realized it was more precious even than memories.

"So, what happens next?" Lexa asked.

"Pops's going to a store that develops film while you wait. He's probably already on his way."

Ramsey said it was ironic that Cade's father had put that camera away because it was too technical, and now those photos would be developed in a matter of minutes because of high technology. Lexa didn't think it was irony. She firmly believed it was fate. "Your father will call you as soon as he knows?" she asked Cade.

He nodded, and Berdie said, "In the meantime we're back to waiting."

Everyone present already knew how Cade Sullivan felt about waiting. He wasn't a man who did it well. Patience wasn't one of his strengths. This time they could hardly blame him.

Fifteen minutes later Arnie, Ramsey and Berdie had made a good-sized dent in the food on their plates, but Cade and Lexa merely pushed theirs from one side of the plate to the other. Berdie refrained from comment when she took their dishes away, and Arnie and Lexa stood to help her with the cleanup.

Ramsey brushed the crumbs from the table and pulled the checkerboard to the center. "Move on over there, young fella. May as well do somethin' 'sides sit around waiting for the phone to ring. Ain't played checkers with a Yankee since 1953. Seems to me he cheated."

Lexa laid her hand on Ramsey's shoulder and said, "If he did, I'll bet he learned it from you."

The old fisherman pushed a thinning lock of white hair off his forehead and guffawed. He winked at Cade, saying, "Nobody but Miz Lexa here could ever git away with sayin' things like that."

Cade hadn't played checkers since he was a kid. And today, at thirty, that seemed like a lifetime ago. In the first game, Ramsey cleaned the board of Cade's checkers in record time. "Come on, Yankee, even a cheatin' man is more competition than you. Y'gotta concentrate."

After losing the third game as quickly as the first and second, Cade scowled and jerked from his chair. Three pairs of eyes were on him like glue, and he stalked to the windows on the far side of the room. Lexa and Berdie went about cleaning up the kitchen, and Ramsey strummed his fingers on the tabletop, patiently waiting for Arnie to take Cade's place at the other side of the checkerboard.

Head held high, shoulders straight and eyes trained on Cade, Arnie walked to the window and said, "He'll call."

Cade looked into the older man's dark eyes and saw that Arnie's gaze was as steady and direct as his words had been. A fragment of his tension evaporated. Arnie was right. Pop would call. And it was only a matter of time before he had a snapshot of Callie, only a matter of time before he handed it to Lexa. And only a matter of time before she had another vision.

Cade stayed at the window and Arnie went to the table where an intense game of checkers had begun. A short time later a commotion at the door drew their attention and had

Berdie sputtering, "Merciful heavens! What are you doing here?"

"I used to live here!" Berdie's daughter, Louisa, sputtered in return.

Pointing to Louisa's ten-year-old sons and five-year-old daughter, Berdie asked, "Why aren't the kids in school?"

Berdie's daughter arched her eyebrows and said, "I've had warmer welcomes at K-Mart, Ma. The kids have the day off. Now, what's going on?"

Cade was introduced all around, and Berdie told Louisa about Callie and Winnona and the stolen blanket. The boys made a beeline for their grandma's warm biscuits and honey, and the little girl climbed onto Lexa's lap.

The child put her chubby arms around Lexa's neck, and Cade's throat seemed to close up. His heart felt as if a newly healed wound had been sliced open. The anger that came crashing through him was nearly blinding in its intensity. Callie should have been the child on Lexa's lap.

The phone rang, and Cade went still. It was the sound he'd been waiting for, but now that it had come, he looked at Lexa, worried it might be bad news. What if those photos hadn't turned out? What if Callie wasn't in any of them?

Lexa stared wordlessly back at him, and before her eyes he seemed to come to his senses, grabbing the phone off the wall in the middle of its third ring. He spoke in monosyllables, but this time there was no mistaking his expression. His smile was pure sunshine, and his "yea-hah!" brought a round of cheers from Berdie's old kitchen. Even the children rejoiced, although they had no clear idea what about.

Without a word, Lexa watched Cade hurry toward the door. One by one, she and Berdie and Arnie and all the others followed. At the bottom of the back stoop, she stepped aside, letting everyone else pass. She wasn't sure what she waited for until Cade turned. The tears swimming in her eyes intensified the look in his. There was a glint of steely determination, yes, but also a glow that spoke of what had happened between them the night before. He hadn't forgotten. Neither had she.

"It's about 350 miles to Hendersonville, and Pop's meeting me halfway, so I'll be gone at least six hours. But I'll be back. I promise."

He spoke to everyone, but Lexa knew the promise was for her. "I'll be waiting," she said.

Arnie cleared his throat and Ramsey kicked at a shell on the driveway. Berdie made her own special sound and bustled into the house, only to bustle back out again seconds later. Pressing something into Cade's hands, she said, "Here, I wrapped up these fresh biscuits for your trip."

Cade took the biscuits, cast another look at Lexa and opened his car door. Tires spun as he backed from the driveway and turned around in the street. Berdie's granddaughter fit her small hand into Lexa's, and Cade disappeared around a corner a few blocks away.

Looking into the distance, Berdie said, "There's something goin' on inside that one's head, something besides finding his li'l girl. That man's keeping secrets. And I still ain't figured out why."

Lexa stared at the spot she'd last seen Cade, thinking that if he was keeping a secret, he must have a very good reason. Berdie's voice filtered through her thoughts. "And I'm worried about you, child. This case is different from the others. It ain't your health I'm worried about. This time I'm afraid you're going to end up with a broken heart."

Lexa cast a look in Arnie's direction and found him gazing at Berdie with an open look of longing. For a moment she wondered if she might not be the only one to end up with a broken heart this spring. Finally meeting Berdie's eyes, Lexa murmured, "Try not to worry, Berdie. I'm going to do everything within my power to find Cade's daughter,

en I do, I know they'll leave. And I'll stay here, until
xt parent comes to me.''

Berdie placed her arm around Lexa's slender shoulders
and together they walked back inside. "Come on, child.
Maybe you can get in a little nap before he comes back.
Noticed your light was on again until late last night, and I
heard Cade take the back stairs in the wee hours of the
mornin'. I just hope you're right. When he leaves, I hope
he don't take a piece of yer heart with him.''

The children ran inside ahead of them, and Lexa placed
her arm around Berdie's waist and squeezed. "You're a
wonderful friend, Berdie O'Toole.''

Berdie snorted an answer. Once inside the kitchen, her
grandchildren captured her attention, and Lexa stepped to
the counter and said, "I know today's only Monday, but I
think I'll make up those doughnuts a little early. If I see
Callie Sullivan, I might not be here on Thursday.''

"I thought I told you to rest!''

Lexa took a large bowl from a shelf and went about mixing up a batch of dough. Berdie didn't move, didn't continue, until Lexa looked up.

"Yer a stubborn one, Lexa Franklin.''

Lexa mimicked Berdie's snort, but the older woman
didn't laugh as she'd expected. Instead, her eyes narrowed,
and Lexa could practically see thoughts flashing in those
dark brown eyes. "What is it, Berdie? What's wrong?''

Berdie looked away, mumbling, "Oh, I was just thinkin',
but never mind. It was nothing.''

By the time Cade pulled into the parking lot in Sanford
almost four hours later, his jaw hurt from clenching his
teeth. He'd lost precious time due to lowered speed limits
in highway-construction zones, and he'd pushed his accel-
erator to the limit in between.

His father slid from the old truck before Cade had brought

his own car to a complete stop beside him. Walt Sullivan had nearly the same build as his son, but his temperament was all his own. He slapped Cade on the back and proclaimed, "I might just take up photography again after you bring Carolina Joy back home. Take a look at these pictures, son."

Cade took the photos from their envelope but had to blink several times to bring his eyes into focus beneath the water that suddenly brimmed there. His jaw hurt, his head hurt, his heart hurt. But those aches had been worth it, because there before his eyes was Callie—on her second birthday with frosting all over her face, in the orchard with the new kittens, dressed up in her Easter dress and the bright purple shoes she'd loved so much, grinning, gray eyes shining in every one.

"How is she?"

Cade took a deep breath and returned the snapshots to their envelope before answering. He knew Pop was asking about Lexa, but Cade had no idea how to respond. She was beautiful inside and out. She was quiet and serene. She was different, yet in ways he couldn't put his finger on, she was much the same.

"She's well."

"She has no idea who you are?"

"None."

Pop's gaze followed a minivan across the parking lot as he said, "That explains it. You look like hell."

"Yeah, well..." Cade's voice trailed away. What could he say? He'd gone to Roanoke Island carrying an ache deep inside him, an ache that had been building for nearly four years, an ache for the woman—Lexi, he'd always called her—he'd married. But Lexi had worn her hair short and had loved bright colors. She was boisterous and quick to laughter. He'd driven away hours ago with another ache, this one for a woman with clear gray eyes that sparkled in the moonlight, for a woman who wore muted colors, who thought before she spoke, and who rarely laughed. This time he ached as much for her as for himself.

"Does Lexi think she'll be able to help you find Callie?"

Cade nodded, then hiked his foot to the running board on Pop's truck. "Twelve kids. That's how many children she's found, Pop."

His father gave a long slow whistle, and Cade continued, "When she left I thought it was just a matter of time, that somehow, some way, if she was alive, she'd eventually come home. But she didn't, and I began to wonder if I was waiting for a ghost.

"Then, after I saw that newspaper photograph last month, the one of Lexa with that senator's child she'd just found, my hope became real to me again. I thought, *Maybe now she'll come back.* Even after I spoke with Dr. Jacobiac again and he told me about Lexa's clairvoyance, I still hoped she'd come back to me. Now I know that isn't going to happen. Her memory isn't something she's lost and will someday find again. She came out of her surgery changed. Her past is gone. Forever. She has a new life now, a life that Callie and I will pass through, but will never be a part of."

"If only Winnona hadn't seen that photograph," Walter declared, "none of this would have happened."

"Seeing that photograph of Lexa and learning of her clairvoyance were probably what propelled Winnona to act, and know enough to take all Callie's possessions, Pop—though I think it was only a matter of time before she took Callie."

His father clasped him in a strong hug. "I wish you'd let me go back with you, Cade."

"I know, Pop, but we have no idea what Winnona will do next. Someone has to stay home in case she brings Callie back there. Besides, I know how much you've always cared about Lexa, and I'm not sure you could keep those feelings to yourself. She can't suspect, Pop, or we may never get Callie back.''

"Bring Callie home, son. I'll be waiting."

"I'll try, Pop. I promise." Cade climbed back inside his car, the envelope of photos clutched safely in his hand. He waved to his father before heading back for Roanoke Island.

I'll be waiting, his father had said, and so had Lexa when he'd driven away earlier today.

I'll be waiting. She'd meant she'd be waiting for him today. Not for the rest of her life. His and Lexa's paths would run parallel for a time, but Cade knew it wouldn't be long before they forked in opposite directions. This time forever.

Arnie and Ramsey had gone on home, and Berdie's daughter and grandchildren had returned to their place on the mainland. With their departure, the restaurant had suddenly seemed too quiet. Lexa had adjusted items on shelves and poked through the utensil drawer and straightened the pantry. At Berdie's insistence, she'd taken a short walk before going home to try to rest.

The walk hadn't helped her relax. She swept her hand across the new glass Arnie and Ramsey had installed in her front door, then wandered through her small house, tired but too wound up to sleep. Cade had said the trip would take at least six hours. He'd been gone nearly eight.

Bleary-eyed, she stepped beneath the gentle spray of her shower, letting the warm water wash the weariness from her muscles. She scrubbed her face and towel-dried her hair and body before sliding her arms into her pale pink robe and her foot into slippers.

Lexa knew Berdie was right—she *should* try to rest. She hadn't slept much these past nights, the first few because she was waiting for a vision, and last night because she'd been with Cade. She thought about stretching out on her bed, but knew better than to try to rest now. The anticipation of seeing Cade again wouldn't allow sleep to come.

Instead of lying down, she drifted out to the living room where two teacups, both of them nearly full, and a small round pot still sat on the coffee table. Lexa placed the items on the tray and carried them into the kitchen, where she poured the tea down the drain. This was the second time she'd poured out the tea she'd brewed for Cade. Smiling, she remembered why they hadn't drunk it this time. They'd abandoned their tea for the whirl of passion they'd found in each other's arms, and even now, Lexa savored the feeling of satisfaction their hours together had given her.

She brewed another pot of tea for herself, and carried it into the living room, where she sat on one end of the sofa and curled her legs underneath her. Sipping her tea, she thought about Cade. He'd made love to her last night in the real sense of the expression. He'd touched her body, yes, but he'd also touched her heart.

Berdie said he was keeping secrets. While that might have been true, he was also open with his wants and needs. He loved his daughter and he wanted her back. And last night he'd wanted *her*. Now she found herself wondering just what it was she wanted from him.

Bits and pieces of the conversations they'd had these past few days filtered through her mind. Images and feelings gradually became clear. Yes, he'd touched her heart last night, but he hadn't uttered any words of love. She knew better than to expect any. They both knew this wasn't permanent. When they found Callie, he'd leave. The thought sent a flicker of pain through her, but she knew her life was here. And his wasn't.

Being held in his arms last night had filled the emptiness she'd felt in her heart these past four years, but only partially, not completely. Lexa didn't know what the emptiness signified, but she'd come to accept it and live with it.

She'd meant what she'd said last night, *For this night, live only for the moment.* She couldn't offer him her future, and he hadn't asked for it. She had little past to give him. Only the present. It would be wise if she kept that in mind.

With that, she took the empty cup and teapot back to the kitchen. After rinsing them both, she turned off the tap and stopped.

There had barely been any sound. Just the ticking of the kitchen clock and the muted thud of the door, nearly indiscernible in the twilight. She knew without turning, without looking. Cade was back. It wasn't ESP. It wasn't precognitive anything. She hoped it wasn't love.

Like the first time she'd gazed at him in Berdie's restaurant, she was struck by the darkness of him. From this distance, she couldn't see the color of his eyes. Now she knew they were deep, deep blue, flecked with a warmth that made her heart pound with tenderness, and a masculine appreciation that made her feel infinitely special.

She held out her hand to him and saw him hesitate. An odd twinge of disappointment stung her heart at his reluctance, but she decided that maybe it was for the best. What they'd shared last night was over.

"Did you get the snapshots?"

He walked closer, and Lexa knew she wasn't the only one suffering from lack of sleep. It was taking its toll on Cade, as well. His eyes were red-rimmed, as if he'd rubbed them often during the long drive back. Deep grooves cut into the sides of his face. He hadn't bothered to shave, and the stubble on his chin added to the look of weariness.

Without a word, he took an envelope from his pocket and placed it in her outstretched hand. Lexa felt the pressure build in her chest, felt it try to squeeze the air from her. But it didn't keep her from taking those snapshots from their envelope. It didn't keep her from gazing at the photographs inside.

The tea and lack of sleep had made her feel drowsy. Gazing at the first picture of little Callie Sullivan, Lexa felt the drowsiness change. Her mind went blank, the pressure in her chest increased, and the image of Cade's child formed on the screen of her mind.

Lexa had no idea how long she stood there. She knew her eyes were open, but she didn't see what was in front of her. Instead, she concentrated on Callie Sullivan. She *saw* the child stroke her blanket and tiredly lay her head on the back of her seat. Her little chin quivered, and Lexa felt the pressure in her own chest increase.

Gradually she became aware of Cade standing before her, of the ticking of the kitchen clock and the sound of her own heart pumping in her chest. "I've seen her. She's safe."

He let out a pent-up breath and waited for her to continue. "She's riding in a car, secured in the seat you told me about."

"Where, Lexa? Do you have any idea where she is?"

She thought for a minute, going over everything she'd seen. "There were no signs. No numbers. Callie was holding the blanket Winnona took from my room. Her chin was quivering, and although I couldn't see her eyes clearly, I had the impression she was squinting."

"Squinting?" Cade asked.

"Yes." Lexa looked out her kitchen window. "Squinting. Against the sun. That sun, Cade." She pointed outside. "Callie was squinting into the sun. That means they're heading west."

He grasped her shoulders and swung her in a half-circle. "West. They're heading west. At least we know which direction to begin looking."

They came to a stop in the doorway, and Lexa followed Cade's gaze. He was looking across the living room to where her bedroom door stood open. His gaze came back to hers, and she knew from the warmth in his eyes, he was thinking of last night.

He dropped his hands to his sides, and his gaze strayed to the photo still in her hand. It was as if he knew that last night was over, and today they shared a singular purpose.

"If you see Callie again..."

"I'll tell you. No matter what the hour."

At the door, a thought came out of nowhere and she added, "Cade? Did your wife like your scruffy look?"

"Scruffy?" he asked.

"The couple of days' stubble on your face."

He shook his head. "No, she always liked me clean shaven."

"Then we have something in common, she and I."

He stumbled from her house, unsure how he'd managed to leave. Just when he'd reconciled himself to the fact that Lexa was different from his Lexi, she innocently voiced her opinion. With few words, she let him know she preferred him without the stubble of a beard. It was something Lexi would have done, but something he wouldn't have expected of *Lexa*. Not in a million years.

He'd known who Lexi Sullivan had been. And he thought he knew who Lexa Franklin was. He sure as hell thought he knew who she wasn't. Now he didn't know what to think.

Cade opened his eyes in the darkness. He hadn't expected to sleep, and now didn't know what had awakened him. Bringing his watch close to his face, he pressed the tiny light. Four in the morning. His muscles felt stiff, as if he hadn't moved since he'd closed his eyes a little before midnight. He must have been more exhausted than he'd realized. He punched his pillow and rolled to his side. Then he caught a movement from the corner of his eye.

"Cade?" Lexa called from the doorway.

An ache started deep inside him just from looking at her. Slowly he rose to one elbow. "You've seen her again?"

She nodded, and he sat up without bothering to bring the sheet up to cover him. "Come here."

Instead of moving closer, she stayed in the doorway. From there, she said, "I think it would be better if we both went downstairs."

Her voice had been velvet-edged. Cade listened for a hint of worry or anguish in it. He heard no fear and felt no sense of apprehension. Whatever she'd seen of Callie wasn't earth-shattering. "I'll be right down."

He found his feet and turned back to the doorway. Lexa was already gone.

He'd taken a long hot shower after leaving her place last night. The bathroom was incredibly small, and after he'd wiped the towel across the mirror, he'd stared at his reflection for a long time. With a twist of his lips that could have been a grimace or a smile, he'd dug his razor from his bag and shaved.

Bending over the sink now, he bumped into the shower door with his backside and shook his head at his close confinement. He pressed his face into a hot washcloth and brushed his teeth. And shaved again.

Within a matter of minutes he'd pulled on a pair of black jeans and a green shirt. Not bothering with a belt or socks, he slid his feet into worn loafers and took the narrow stairs to the kitchen.

Lexa was at the windows on the far side of the room. She turned in the semidarkness when he entered, and he asked, "Have you started the coffee?"

She shook her head. Holding up a glass, she said, "I'm still working on my orange juice. Berdie insists I drink it every day."

Cade took a filter from the shelf and filled the coffee-maker with tap water. He measured the coffee by guessing, eyed it and added a little more before turning on the machine. He leaned against the counter, the coffeemaker hissing behind him, and watched as Lexa took a seat at the work station in the center of the room.

"You've had another vision?"

She pressed a hand to her chest just below her throat and nodded. "I've been having visions all night."

The dark circles under her eyes reminded him what this was doing to her. She was suffering beneath the burden of her responsibility, her power. And, dammit, there was nothing he could do to help.

Cade had thought he'd felt blind desperation before. When he'd searched for Lexa almost four years ago he'd nearly come apart at the seams. But the desperation he felt now was even worse. He'd loved her before, completely but not unselfishly. He loved her even more now, more than words, more than mere feelings. He wanted her, but knew she'd never again be his, not really. Her power would always own her. He wanted to curse it but couldn't. Her inner eye was his only link to Callie.

"Did you get any sleep at all?" he asked.

"A little."

Damn little. She was wearing the same yellow dress she'd worn a few days ago, the one she'd worn while hanging her laundry out to dry. He'd thought she was beautiful then. She was even more beautiful now. This morning her eyes were an even deeper shade of gray than the flecks in her dress. As before, she'd brushed her hair off her forehead and secured it loosely partway down her back with a pale yellow bow.

Her brown lashes appeared darker this morning and cast a soft shadow on her cheeks as she lowered her gaze to the glass in her hand. The coffeemaker made one final sputter, and Cade reached for the pot and poured the black liquid into two mugs.

"What was Callie doing? In your visions, I mean."

She sipped her coffee before answering. "I saw her asleep several times. They must have slept in the car, because Callie thrashed about as if she wasn't comfortable. At one point Winnona must have spoken to her, because I saw Callie's chin jut out stubbornly. You might have trouble with that child when she's sixteen, Cade."

Her words gave him gentle assurance, reminding him of her belief in her power, in her belief that they'd find Callie, that he'd take his daughter home where she'd grow to be the kind of young woman who'd make her father proud. He reached across the counter and grasped Lexa's hands in his. Squeezing gently, he murmured, "What else did you see?"

She left her hands in his as she told him of her other visions. One in particular gave him renewed hope. "It was dark outside. In my vision I saw Callie slip from the car. I think she was trying to run away from Winnona, Cade. But Winnona was suddenly there."

Cade knew he didn't have to worry about Callie's accepting Winnona as her mother. That little girl was a spitfire, as strong-willed as her father. And her mother.

Lexa yawned, and his heart swelled with feeling. No wonder she looked exhausted. She hadn't had a full night's sleep in days. "Lexa," he murmured, "Berdie isn't up yet, and I think you should go back home and try to sleep."

She was shaking her head before he'd finished. "I can't go back there alone, Cade. If I have to pace those floors one more time, I'll come right out of my skin."

He studied her before saying, "All right. Then come upstairs with me."

Her eyes widened, and she drew away.

"Lexa, what is it?"

"It's just... I'm so...afraid."

"Afraid of me?" he asked.

He watched her gaze search his and breathed a sigh of

relief when she finally shook her head and began to speak. "This is all so new to me. It's not that I'm afraid of you, Cade. I'm afraid to love you."

He took a deep breath and let it all out, his thoughts churning. It hadn't occurred to him that she'd be afraid to love him, but then, as far as she was concerned, she'd only known him a matter of days, and she thought he was still in love with Callie's mother. Of course she was afraid to love him!

Standing there in the kitchen, Cade thought maybe it was just as well. He'd be better off if he didn't become too attached to her, either.

None of that changed the fact that Lexa was exhausted. He didn't want to make her more afraid. He only wanted to help her in any way he could. "It's not what you're thinking, Lexa. Don't think for a minute I wouldn't love to make love with you. But I won't. You'll be safe with me, safe to rest for a few minutes. Right now I think you need your rest. More than anything else."

He led her up the stairs to his room, past the tiny bathroom and over to his bed. He kicked off his shoes, and she did likewise. Then she hesitated. He hadn't turned on a light, and what little moonlight filtered through the window barely penetrated the early-morning darkness.

"Do you trust me, Lexa?"

For a moment he felt her tension. Then her shoulders dropped, and she relaxed. "I trust you," she whispered. "I don't understand it, but I do trust you."

Neither of them removed their clothes. Cade fluffed the pillows and propped them behind his back, pulling Lexa close to his side. His shoulder became her pillow, and she fit his side so perfectly he never wanted to move.

He made no demands, not with his hands, nor with his words. Smoothing his palms down her back and up again, he said softly, "Rest, Lexa. You've carried this burden alone all night. For a little while, I'll carry it for you. Rest, Lexi, rest.''

"Lexa," she mumbled. "Not Lexi." Her lashes swept his shoulder as her eyelids fluttered down.

He felt her draw a deep breath, felt every one of her muscles relax against him. She sank into sleep slowly, and Cade's heart beat a heavy rhythm. She'd reminded him, simply and profoundly, that the woman he held in his arms wasn't his wife. She wasn't Lexi, but Lexa. His mind knew the difference. His body didn't care.

He was glad for the cover of darkness, glad Lexa slept and didn't see what her nearness was doing to his body. He could have taken a cold shower, but wouldn't have moved from Lexa's side for the world.

Coming to Roanoke Island had cleansed him of the anger, no matter how undeserved, he'd harbored toward Lexa for leaving him and *forgetting* him. He now understood how difficult it must have been for her. He also understood what she'd given up. Even if she didn't.

The sun came up slowly over the sound, splashing faint light into Cade's room. He could hear Berdie bang a pot in the kitchen below. But Lexa slept on. He'd asked her if she trusted him. She told him she did, and Cade swore he'd live up to that trust if it was the last thing he ever did.

He'd lost all feeling in the arm beneath her a long time ago but hadn't lost the feeling in one certain part of his body, the part throbbing for the woman in his arms. Cade didn't mind even that discomfort. It was a small price to pay for the one thing he could give her. A few hours of undisturbed sleep.

He vowed not to wake her no matter what. That didn't keep his mind from what his body wanted to do. He remembered bumping his hip in the narrow shower. The space was barely large enough for a man his size, but Cade thought it the perfect size to share a hot shower with Lexa.

The close proximity would demand constant contact with Lexa's supple body....

Cade was trapped by his own emotions, by his vow not to wake her and his disturbing fantasies. He breathed deeply and tried to force the images away. Lexa stiffened in his arms, and he turned his head to study her face.

She slept on, but her eyes moved beneath her closed lids. Her lips parted, and she sucked in a quick breath. Her entire body was suddenly rigid with tension. For a moment, Cade worried that his own thoughts had awakened her.

But she didn't open her eyes, didn't move or wake up. He realized she was having a vision. Holding perfectly still, he watched as her vision overtook her. Cade ached for her, but knew he couldn't awaken her. She had to open her eyes on her own, and when she did, he knew she'd tell him more about Callie.

One second the child was inside the car, the next the car was plunging over a cliff. Lexa tried to reach for the little girl, but felt something, like a steel band, hold her back....

As always, her vision was silent, played out mutely by people she could neither hear nor touch. All she could do was see them, and this time what she saw was terrifying. She pushed against the bands that held her down. She fought for a long time to open her eyes, fought to suck a breath into the heaviness in her chest. Her heart pounded beneath her ribs, and her eyes flew open.

"It's all right, Lexa. I'm here."

It was Cade's voice she heard. She pushed against his chest and realized it wasn't his arms that had held her. It was her vision. She bolted upright and clutched both her hands to her chest.

"Lexi, what is it?"

The vision faded. And Cade came into focus. "Don't ever call me that. Never."

"I won't, Lexa. Talk to me."

She heard the desperation in his voice. It didn't bring the vision back.

"What did you see?" he demanded.

She hadn't realized he'd gotten up. He was pacing the narrow room. Stopping a few feet from her, he repeated, "What did you see? Tell me, Lexa. I have to know. What happened to Callie?"

She got to her feet and let her eyes drift down. Taking a deep breath, she remembered what she'd seen. For a fear-blinded moment she'd thought she'd lost her vision. Now she realized she hadn't lost it. At least not completely. If she had, the pressure in her chest would have disappeared with it.

"I saw Callie inside the car. Then I saw the car plunging down a cliff."

His eyes bore into hers. He sucked a breath between his teeth, and before her eyes his dark skin turned pale, as pale as the curtain at his back.

"Was she inside?" His words were barely more than a whisper and spoken as if the words themselves might suffocate him here and now.

Lexa placed her hands to her temples and closed her eyes. "I don't know."

She looked at him again and found his eyes darkened with pain. He clenched his hands into fists at his sides. The fog in her head was clearing, and she searched for something to say, some small piece of hope to give him. "I don't know, Cade. I don't know if Callie was inside. That doesn't mean she was. Hold on to that."

Although he made an effort to pull himself together, his next statement seemed to drain his color further. "I don't know what I'll do if I've lost her. What now?"

Lexa grasped the iron bed frame and leveled her gaze directly at his. "We wait until I have another vision."

"If she's..." He tried to continue, but no sound came. His throat convulsed, and he swallowed. Hard. "If she's..."

"If she wasn't in that car, I'll see her again." She offered a silent plea to heaven to watch over little Callie, to keep Cade's child safe.

A door slammed downstairs, and Ramsey's loud voice echoed up the stairs. A muscle twitched in Cade's cheek, and for a long moment, neither Cade nor Lexa moved. Finally, as if in slow motion, he turned and strode to the door.

"She's alive. I know she's alive. She has to be, Lexa. I can't lose her, too."

With that, he walked on with heavy footsteps, down the hall and down the stairs. Lexa heard both Berdie and Ramsey speak to him, but she didn't hear Cade's reply. The slamming of the back door was his only response.

The wetness on her face surprised Lexa. She stood there grasping the metal bed, sobbing like she'd never sobbed before. These tears weren't for herself, but for Cade, for his pain, his sheer desperation. This case was nothing like the others. She'd known it almost from the beginning. She'd never become so emotionally involved before. She'd never fallen in love with one of the fathers before.

Lexa let her tears fall, let them drain the emotion from her. When every tear had fallen, she walked into the tiny bathroom and splashed her face with cool water.

Cade needed her now more than he ever had. She knew she had incredible inner strength, and she reached down inside, calling on every reserve she possessed. Then she turned and headed for the stairs.

In the kitchen, Berdie and Ramsey both took one look at her face and gasped. "What's happened?"

"Where's Cade?" she asked.

"He slammed through here without a word and drove off a few minutes ago," Berdie answered. "Sit down, child. Sit down. And tell me what's happened."

Taking a seat, Lexa told Ramsey and Berdie what she'd seen. Berdie took a tissue from the deep pocket of her apron and swiped at her eyes, but didn't utter a sound until Lexa had finished. "Great merciful heavens! That poor man. And that poor li'l girl. And what about you, child. I don't like what this is doin' to you."

"Did Cade say where he was going?" Lexa asked.

"No, child, but I wish I hadn't let him leave. Now is no time for him to be alone."

Berdie fixed Lexa a plate of food and clucked over her until she'd eaten as least part of it. Ramsey did his best to keep up a one-sided conversation, and after a long silence, Berdie said, "Tell me, Lexa, what does his li'l girl look like?"

Lexa took the envelope from her pocket and handed the photographs to her friend. Berdie took them into her bony brown hands and went perfectly still. Lexa didn't understand why Berdie didn't tell her what she was thinking. Before she could ask, the outer door opened and Cade strode into the room.

Chapter 7

Cade stopped in the doorway, and Lexa's mind spun, from Berdie's sudden secrecy and from Cade's. His eyes probed hers, asking her a silent question. With a small shake of her head, she answered him. No, she hadn't seen Callie again.

She'd been so attuned to Cade she didn't notice Arnie's arrival. Until he spoke. "Cade and I've been to the sheriff's office. We told 'em all about Lexa's vision, and demanded a little assistance."

"What kind of assistance?" Berdie asked.

"If Lexa saw a car crashing down a mountain, I figure somewhere out there a car's lyin' at the bottom of a ravine. One of the wily deputies scoffed, but the sheriff was real helpful. Said he's heard of people with special powers before and put me through to the state police, who are puttin' it on their computer."

"Oh, Arnie," Lexa said. "That's a wonderful idea. Did the police tell you how long it'll be before they know something?"

Arnie shook his head, and Cade strode toward the doorway leading to the stairs. "Where're you goin'?" Berdie asked.

Lexa watched Cade turn. His gaze took in everyone, and when it settled on her, he hesitated, measuring her for a moment before answering. "I'm going upstairs to pack my things. When that call from the sheriff comes, I'll be ready to leave."

With that, Lexa turned in the opposite direction and strode toward the back door. Again Berdie sputtered, "Merciful heavens, where're you going, missy?"

Lexa's gaze strayed to Cade's, then back to Berdie's. She raised her chin and in a soft but firm voice said, "I'm going to pack, too. When that call comes, I'm going with Cade to help him find his daughter."

Berdie started toward her, but Arnie reached for her hand. "Let her go, Berdette. I think she knows what she's doin'."

All eyes were suddenly on Berdie and the proud man blocking her path. Arnie's expression was serious, and a flush tinged Berdie's dark cheeks. She stared wordlessly into Arnie's eyes, then, like a schoolgirl, glanced down at his hand on hers.

"I'll be gol-darned." Ramsey dragged the word out to at least four syllables, and Lexa laughed in spite of herself.

Berdie cast both her and Ramsey a withering look. "I thought you were gonna pack," she grumbled at Lexa. To Ramsey, she said, "Don't you have nothing better to do than sit there like a bump on a log?"

Ramsey shook his head and declared, "Why, Berdie O'Toole, is that a blush I see on your cheeks? Seems to me I remember someone telling Miz Lexa here it takes a special man to put that particular color on a woman's cheeks."

"You were eavesdropping?"

Ramsey guffawed. "It ain't eavesdropping when yer

voice carries all the way from here to Wanchese and back again.''

Berdie sputtered, and Lexa vividly recalled when Berdie had told her what kind of man it took to make a woman blush that way. That time they'd been talking about Cade, and Berdie had been right. It took a very special man indeed.

She cast a look at Cade, who was staring back at her. She didn't smile, couldn't have if her life had depended on it. She wished she could tell him just how special he was. But a crowded room wasn't the place. Reminding herself why Cade had come to her in the first place—to find his daughter—she realized it might never be the right time. As if by unspoken consent, they both turned in opposite directions and disappeared through different doors.

Cade emptied the drawer of his clothes and stuffed them into his soft case. Trying to keep his mind blank, he strode to the bathroom and swept the shampoo and other scattered items into his hand. He grasped his electric razor and turned to look at the bed, at the slight indentation in the blankets and pillows where Lexa had lain in his arms.

He forced himself to concentrate on packing and found a shirt and one stray sock underneath the bed. He was in the process of writing out a check to Berdie for the use of the room these past several nights when footsteps sounded on the stairs. Cade had signed the check and placed it on the nightstand before Berdette O'Toole appeared in the doorway.

For the first time since he'd met her, she seemed at a loss for words. She hesitated in the doorway, and Cade saw her reach into the big pocket in her flowered apron. Paper crackled, and bringing her hand out, she now clutched the envelope containing Callie's photographs in her hand. Berdie glanced down at the envelope, then stepped into the room, closing the door behind her.

From his position on the edge of the bed, he watched her come closer, take a deep breath and settle herself in a chair a few feet from him. Without speaking, she took the snapshots from the envelope, slowly looking at each. Finally she looked up and said, "There's been somethin' strange about this case right from the beginning. I'm worried about Lexa."

Cade was worried about her, too. To watch what her visions did to her ate away at his insides. He needed to find Callie, but watching what it was doing to Lexa was almost more than he could bear. "You think I should tell her to stay here?"

"It wouldn't do ya no good. When she's searching for a missing child, there's no stopping her. She's been here a li'l over three years, so believe me when I tell ya I've seen her like this before. She's getting closer, I can tell. She'll find yer li'l girl, Cade, and she'll come home and sleep for two solid days. It ain't her health I'm worried about. It's her heart."

"I'll do everything in my power to keep her safe, Berdie."

"You think I don't know that?" Berdie stared into his eyes for a long time before saying, "Lexa's right to go with you. You can't let that woman keep yer li'l girl. But it ain't easy, is it? It ain't easy keeping secrets."

Cade didn't move, not even to breathe. Without making a sound, he stared into Berdie's dark eyes and waited for her to continue.

"I knew there was somethin' different about you from the beginning." She dropped her gaze to the photos in her hand. "But I couldn't figure out what it was. Until I saw these pictures." She shuffled through the pictures of Callie, and Cade watched as she held one up. He took the photograph and gazed at his daughter dressed in her favorite color, purple. She was grinning at the camera, her gray eyes shining. And in her chubby little hand, she held a bouquet of forget-me-nots.

"She has her mother's eyes," said Berdie. "Lexa's eyes. And the forget-me-nots she's holding... Lexa's so tired from her visions she ain't put it all together yet. But somethin's been haunting that girl since the day I met her. And it ain't just the voice she hears in her head. It has something to do with those dried forget-me-nots she keeps in the box in her closet. You know what they mean, don't you?"

Cade stood and strode across the room. With his back to Berdie, he finally said, "She wanted me to promise on Callie's life to walk away if she lived through her surgery, but woke up changed. She'd watched her mother die—slowly, painfully, bit by bit. And she said she couldn't bear to think of our daughter suffering such a fate. That's where those forget-me-nots came from. Her mother's grave."

"You didn't promise her, did ya?"

Without turning, he shook his head. "No. But I never thought she'd leave me. She's strong, Berdie, and she has a capacity to love like I've never seen before. Out of a love so deep and unselfish, she disappeared, and had an attorney draw up divorce papers. She took her maiden name back and signed away her parental rights to our baby. Her note said she'd come back if she could. If she didn't, I was to go on with my life, mine and Callie's. I didn't think there was anything that could have kept her from regaining her strength and coming back to us. I was wrong. There was *one* thing—losing her memories of us."

"How soon after she had the baby did she have her surgery?" Berdie asked.

"The doctors found the tumor the same week she felt Callie move for the first time. The surgeon said it was too risky on the baby to have the surgery while she was pregnant and too risky for Lexa to wait until the baby was born."

"Lexa waited until after the baby came, didn't she?"

Cade nodded. "She said she'd give our child life, then fight for her own. It wasn't surprising it was a difficult pregnancy. Callie was born a month early, and a week later, Lexa was actually thinner than she'd been before. Callie was tiny, but healthy, perfect in every way. Lexa held her constantly, rarely putting her down. I didn't know it then, but I think she was trying to fit all the love she felt for Callie into those few weeks following Callie's birth.

"After Lexa left, I went to see her doctor, who told me he didn't know where she was. Weeks passed and I was frantic. The police knew nothing. No one did. Weeks later I went back to her doctor, who finally told me of a man who might know. I went to see Dr. Jacobiac, and learned that Lexa had survived her surgery, but had no memories of me or Callie. He said her mental and physical health were precarious, and I was afraid I'd make the situation worse by confronting her with the truth. She'd left me, and there was nothing I could do to bring her back. Without her memory of me, it seemed hopeless. I know it could have been worse, a lot worse. Lexa could have died, or she could have suffered severe brain damage. Her surgery saved her life and took her from mine."

A warm hand squeezed his forearm and Cade closed his eyes against the anguish Berdie's touch evoked. "Did you go through with it?" she asked. "Did you divorce her?"

He scowled, ran his hand across his face and shook his head.

"She told me her husband divorced her."

"That's what she'd told Dr. Jacobiac before the surgery, and what he later told her. It's what she believed was true. I didn't know what else to do, so I went home without her."

Berdie shook her head, letting him know without a word that she didn't believe for a minute that he'd done anything less than the honorable thing. "My Tucker, God rest his soul, used to say a man's gotta do what a man's gotta do. Too bad it ain't always easy.''

"I hate what this is doing to her, Berdie. But I can't tell her the truth. If I do, she'll lose her power. She believes that her power is a *gift*, that it was the reason she didn't die on the operating table.''

Berdie didn't say anything for a long time. When she finally lifted her eyes, he read understanding and empathy in their depths. "Yer a good man, Cade Sullivan. Yankee or not.'' She patted his arm before stalking to the bed where his cases were stacked.

"Might as well come downstairs. Arnie'll be happy to keep ya company until you hear from the sheriff.''

"Arnie's a good man, too, Berdie,'' Cade murmured.

At the doorway, she made her sound again, and Cade found himself close to laughter. It helped ease the strain he felt from waiting, from not knowing whether Callie had been inside that car when it plunged down the mountain. Berdie had reminded him there were good people in this world, had somehow managed to renew his faith in humankind.

He took his suitcase and cast a last look around. Then he strode from the room and followed the sounds of Ramsey and Arnie's voices to the kitchen below.

An hour later, that renewed hope within him had been tempered with realism. Lexa had joined them all in the big old cook room, and as Arnie and Ramsey bickered about the price of fish, Cade relived the panic he'd felt when he'd called Lexa "Lexi,'' when he thought she'd lost her vision as a result of that nickname.

She'd told him it had happened before. That's why he'd panicked when she'd answered the phone and heard his father's voice. She'd explained how she'd lost her vision of a missing child when she'd learned about her past. To this day, she kept a photograph of the child she'd never found.

He knew this, but he'd let his guard down. He'd held Lexa in his arms and for a short time had believed in fantasies. He'd believed she could still be his. He'd said, "Lexi," and for a moment they'd both feared she'd lost her vision of Callie.

Cade gazed across the room to where Lexa was peeling apples for Berdie's half-moon pies. When he'd first realized she hadn't lost her vision, he'd felt enormous relief. But watching Lexa now, knowing their lives would never be together, he felt a heaviness grip his heart.

Lexa had felt the pressure in her chest steadily build in intensity all morning. If Callie had been in that car, she wouldn't still be feeling the pressure. Cade's daughter was alive. She could *feel* it.

She'd propped the snapshot against the bowl of apples in front of her. Peeling apples had given her something to do with her hands. Rather than participate in conversation, she'd focused on that photo and felt the pressure in her chest push against her lungs.

The voices around her gradually diminished as if someone had slowly turned down the volume. She saw Callie. Not as she'd been in the photograph, but older, slightly thinner. Her hair was longer, and for a moment Lexa thought her vision was blurry. Until she realized it wasn't her vision, but the very air in which Callie stood. The little girl shivered and wiped misty rain from her face. Winnona tugged on Callie's hand and cast a strange look over her shoulder before stepping onto some sort of wooden walkway.

A commotion at the door drew Lexa from her vision. Blinking to bring her eyes into focus, she watched as the sheriff entered Berdie's kitchen by way of the back door.

Before the sheriff could speak, Lexa said, "She's taken her to the mountains." All eyes suddenly turned to her.

"You've seen Callie?" Cade asked.

Lexa nodded and saw Cade grasp the back of a chair to

steady himself. Ramsey and the sheriff both fired off questions, and Berdie held up a hand to silence everyone. Once again Lexa stared at the snapshot, trying to remember everything she'd seen. "It was beginning to rain, and they were on foot. I saw a few other people, all of them walking across some sort of bridge."

Sheriff Connely stepped forward and cleared his throat. "Your housekeeper's car has been found and identified by the license-plate number you gave me, Mr. Sullivan."

Cade's eyes found hers, and in a steady voice, Lexa declared, "Callie wasn't inside."

"No," the sheriff said. "A witness told the sheriff up in Avery County that the woman drove her car to the edge of a cliff up in the Blue Ridge Mountains and got out before it rolled over the side. Who in her right mind would do something like that?"

Ramsey mumbled, "Sounds to me like she ain't in her right mind. Sounds to me like that woman's crazy."

"Crazy or not," the sheriff said, "why would she want to destroy her own car?"

Lexa remembered asking Cade why Winnona had gone to such lengths to box up all Callie's things, why she'd risked being caught to come all the way to Roanoke Island to get that blanket.

He'd said Winnona had done it so he'd have nothing left of Callie. Lexa thought there was more to it than that, but for the life of her, she couldn't imagine what. Too many nights with too little sleep and too many questions with too few answers were making her mind reel.

"Did the car explode?" she asked.

The sheriff shook his head. "It should have. But it must have been almost out of gas, because it didn't burn." He turned to Cade and asked, "Do you have any idea why your housekeeper would want to destroy her car and everything inside?"

Lexa didn't understand the look Cade shared with Berdie, but stored her questions in some far corner of her brain until later, when she could take them out and examine them more closely. The sheriff was talking, and she focused her attention on his words.

"What exactly did you see in your vision, Ms. Franklin?"

Lexa let her vision replay through her mind like a movie in slow motion. Instead of looking at anyone in particular, she stared at the picture of Cade's child.

In a soft voice she began to speak. "At first it seemed as if my vision was blurred by a gray mist. But I realized it wasn't my vision that was misty, but the air surrounding Callie and Winnona. Winnona held Callie's hand. Callie tried to pull her hand free, but Winnona wouldn't release it. The child wiped moisture from her face and they walked away from me, across a suspended bridge. Before my vision faded, Winnona looked over her shoulder as if she knew I was watching."

Sheriff Connely stared at Lexa and said, "The sheriff there said it was raining up in the mountains. You were right about that. Right about that bridge, too. The woman's car was found at the bottom of a ravine not far from Grandfather Mountain. And the bridge you saw could have been the mile-long suspended walkway near there."

"Lexa, was Callie crying?" Cade's voice sounded hollow, as if his emotions were worn thin, stretched to the breaking point.

"I don't know, Cade. I've never seen her eyes."

Something clicked in her mind, but the weariness enveloping her refused to let her focus on what it was.

Berdie ushered the sheriff out and immediately turned to Lexa. "The only power I have is common sense, but that woman's starting to scare me. The Blue Ridge Mountains are filled with places to hide, ridges and caves and gorges.

I'm fearing that if they get too far into them hills, you'll never find them."

Cade pushed his chair out with so much force it hit the wall behind him. Lexa came to her feet more slowly, steadying her gaze on his. His face hardened and his voice, although quiet, had an ominous quality. "I don't know what Winnona is capable of anymore, and I can't ask you to come with me."

"Then don't ask. Just know I'm going." With that she strode to where her cases sat next to Cade's.

Berdie was immediately at her side. "It's gonna be cold up in the hills. You sure you packed enough warm clothes?"

"Yes, Berdie."

"What about blankets and matches?"

"In my trunk," Cade assured her. "I thought Winnona would take Callie to the mountains to begin with. I packed everything we'll need before I left home."

"Don't worry about us," Lexa murmured.

Berdie looked into her eyes and hugged her, declaring, "You be extra careful, y'hear?"

"I will, Berdie."

To Cade she said, "That goes for you, too."

They stacked their cases in the back seat and climbed into the front. After waving to Berdie and Arnie, who stood close together, and Ramsey, who looked at Arnie as if seeing him for the first time, Lexa and Cade drove away, toward the mountains, toward the Blue Ridge Parkway.

Toward Callie.

Two days earlier, they'd been sightseers sharing a carefree afternoon. They'd driven up and down the Outer Banks, Lexa spinning tales about North Carolinian folklore, Cade committing everything she said to memory. Today neither of them were carefree. They both knew their time together was drawing to an end, and both knew the next day or two would be crucial in finding Callie.

They stopped for lunch in Durham, where Cade filled the gas tank and made a phone call to the sheriff who'd discovered Winnona's car in Avery County. He made another call to the detective he'd hired when Winnona had first taken Callie. The detective didn't have anything new to report, but he did have a general location of Winnona's former address up in the hills.

"What did they say?" Lexa asked when he'd settled himself behind the wheel once again.

"The sheriff said it was Winnona's car, all right. He told me getting that car out of there wasn't going to be easy, but he'd already sent his deputies out to bring back whatever belongings weren't scattered during the fall."

"That's good, Cade. After this ordeal is over and you take Callie home, it'll probably help her to have her special blanket and prized possessions nearby. What about the detective?"

In response, Cade handed her a penciled map he'd drawn from the detective's directions. "This is about all he had for me. Said he'd tried to talk to some of the locals about Winnona but didn't have much luck getting anyone to open up to him."

Lexa nodded, saying, "It's that way in the hills, Cade. I think it comes from living so far from others for so long. They learned to depend only on themselves. And that's who they trust."

She kept a snapshot of Callie in her hand, and Cade's fingers tightened around the steering wheel each time she had another vision. He hated putting her through this, but each time she told him what she'd seen he felt closer to finding Callie.

"If you squeeze that steering wheel any tighter, it's going to disintegrate, Cade. Relax. We have a long way to go."

After a time she said, "I've always thought this whole process would be a lot simpler if I could see into the future. Then we'd know where Winnona was *going* to be, instead of where she *is*."

He glanced at her and found her smiling. She was making light of a serious situation. "What do you mean?"

"If I could see into the future, we could run ahead of them and wait for them to arrive. Like in old Westerns, we'd have the element of surprise on our side and could head them off at the pass."

After a time she said, "I know this isn't easy for you, Cade, waiting for me to have a vision. We clairvoyants should list our qualifications more clearly so you people would know what you're getting *before* you come to us."

"You mean take out an ad in the yellow pages?"

"Something like that. Then you could have gone to a clairvoyant who could see into the future, instead of coming to one who can only see into the present."

Glancing away from the road, he gazed deep into her eyes. "I'm glad I came to you, Lexa. I'm glad for the chance to know you."

Blinking away the tears that suddenly brimmed in her eyes, she tilted her head and smiled a tremulous smile. "So am I, Cade. So am I."

Their teasing had lightened the mood, and their honesty cast a warm glow over them. Two days ago Lexa had spun tales of headless horsemen and land pirates and magic. Now, it was Cade's voice filling the quiet, Cade's voice working magic. For the next hundred miles, he talked about his work, about the different types of apples and peaches he and his father grew. He talked about his father, about Callie and about the life they'd lived.

Lexa continued to have visions. Each time, she described everything she saw to Cade. In one, Callie and Winnona were getting on a bus. In another, they were getting out of a car. She never saw anything specific, like the bus's number or the car's license plate, anything that would lead them directly to Callie, but from the frequency of her visions, she firmly believed they were getting closer. When she heard the child's voice inside her head, she'd be sure.

They stopped for groceries in a small store in the village of Blowing Rock, which was between Boone, the town Winnona had said she was from, and Grandfather Mountain, where she'd watched as her car plunged over the rocky cliff. They stopped for dinner in a small family-owned restaurant about to close up for the night.

The owners, a gray-haired man and his white-haired wife, introduced themselves as Frank and Ida, with no last names, and ushered Cade and Lexa inside like long-lost cousins. Lexa glanced at Cade and found his eyes on her. She smiled and watched the effect it had on him.

Until that moment, she hadn't realized how handsome he really was. Locks of dark hair waved across his forehead. He'd evidently shaved this morning, but now his jaw was darkened with more than a five-o'clock shadow. His features were strong, his nose, his mouth, his chin. But it was his eyes that held her spellbound, those blue eyes that harbored secrets and sent warmth all through her.

"It's so nice to see a pair of lovebirds like yourselves," the old man declared.

"Heavens, yes!" his wife replied. "We don't get many honeymooners, and it does my heart good to see a pair as taken with each other as the two of you."

"We aren't really honeymooners," Lexa said honestly.

Before she could explain why they were there, the woman exclaimed, "Why, that's all the better! A man and woman who've been married awhile and still look at each other the way the two of you are right now..."

Lexa stared wordlessly across the small table, heart pounding, waiting for Cade's reaction. Instead of setting the record straight, he reached for her hand. The almost imperceptible glint of longing in his eyes sent a sense of wistfulness to her heart.

The older couple tactfully excused themselves and went to the kitchen with promises of warm soup and thick sandwiches, leaving Lexa and Cade alone. She'd felt the pull of his attraction since the first moment they met. What she felt now was different. This was more than mere attraction. Her past didn't matter. Neither did the future, and for the first time in her entire scope of memory, she wished she could freeze time.

For this night, live only for the moment. She'd said the words before, but she'd never believed in them more strongly than at this moment.

Plates of thick sandwiches were placed in front of them, and while they ate, the other couple filled the silence with the legend of Blowing Rock. "According to local folklore," Ida said, "two braves fought for the chieftain's beautiful daughter. When one threw the other over the cliff, the maiden begged the god of wind to save her true love. The god heard her plea and lifted her lover back to her, and to this day people come from miles and miles to Blowing Rock, where even the snow falls upside down."

Lexa searched Cade's eyes throughout the tale, wishing there was some way for her life to be entwined with his. She thought of the legend she'd just heard, and knew the god of wind couldn't help her. The pressure in her chest reminded her of her power. The look in Cade's eyes reminded her their time together was nearly over.

When the old man learned they had no place to spend the night, he pressed a key into Cade's hand and gave them detailed instructions to his hunting cabin up in the mountains. "It's nothing fancy," he told them. "Just one room, one bed and a path. But it's private, and the sunrises you can see from the front stoop are pretty enough to take your breath away.''

Arm in arm, the old couple walked them to the front door. From the bottom step, Cade and Lexa turned and called goodbye, then continued on to the car.

Lexa couldn't remember the last time a man had opened a car door for her, and the quaint gesture touched her in ways that had nothing to do with appreciation of gentlemanly conduct. Her heart thumped madly as he smoothed a lock of hair from her cheek, but it was the look in his eyes that drew her closer.

He brought his hand to the back of her neck and grazed her lips with his. His touch was as soft as a caress, and his words as deep as the look in his eyes. ''It's up to you, Lexa. We can go to their cabin, or we can find a motel.''

He didn't say *a motel with separate rooms,* but she knew it was what he'd meant. His eyes spoke of *his* preference, and it was Lexa's turn to touch him, Lexa's turn to whisper a kiss along his mouth. Unlike Cade, she didn't stop with one small kiss. She moved her lips over his and kissed him again, long and lingering, telling him without words where she'd like to go with him.

He lifted his head, and she heard his jagged breath, saw his smile in the gathering twilight. Without another word, she slid into the car and waited for Cade to do the same.

They hardly spoke on the drive up the mountain. Words weren't necessary. Cade kissed her when they reached the cabin, and again when they'd dropped their belongings to the floor inside. Each touch drew them closer, each parting became more difficult.

Cade started a fire in the potbellied stove in the center of the room, and before Lexa had finished spreading the sleeping bags over the narrow bed, strong arms encircled her from behind. She straightened and folded her arms over his.

She breathed in the faint smell of wood smoke and turned to gaze into his eyes.

A lantern flickered from the rustic table across the room, much like the emotions flickering in Cade's eyes. For that moment Lexa thought her wish had come true. For that moment time seemed to stand still.

Her skin turned warm long before the stove removed the chill from the air. Cade's hands moved across her back, squeezing her shoulders and circling her waist. He brought his lips to hers, his kiss surprisingly gentle. She twined her hands behind his neck, and her lids fluttered closed. When he grasped her hips and pulled her fully against him, pleasure radiated through her. She pressed her cheek to his shirt and, turning, placed a kiss to his beard-roughened jaw.

A log popped in the stove, and Lexa opened her eyes. Grasping the hem of her gray sweater, he lifted it over her head. She heard it rustle to the floor, but didn't take her eyes from Cade's. She shivered, but not from the cold. It was as if a flame had been ignited in Cade's eyes, and with his look, that fire spread to her heart.

She sat to unlace her boots, but his hands pushed hers away. He went down to his knees before her, and instead of removing her boots, he slid his hands along her thighs. Squeezing gently, he followed the contour of her legs, kneading the soft skin through the fabric of her gray jeans. Lexa closed her eyes as warmth followed every place he touched and swirled to places he hadn't.

He unlaced her boots and slipped them off. Her socks came next, and then he was on his feet, pulling his own shirt from his jeans. Bending, he removed his shoes, straightening again to unfasten the clasp at his waist. Lexa stood, too, and eased her slacks down her hips, raking her panties with them. She reached behind her back, but Cade's fingers were already there.

He removed her bra and bent to her breasts. His thumb

traced the peak of one, while his tongue explored the other. She heard her own sigh and couldn't stop the moan that rose from deep inside her.

He straightened again, and Lexa felt compelled to meet his look. He placed her hands on the waistband of his jeans, and she couldn't resist his passionate invitation. She pressed her hand over the length of him and watched as his eyelids dropped down. Never before had she felt such power, and it had nothing to do with her sixth sense.

She slid her arms around his waist and pressed her body to his. Her breasts, already sensitized from his kiss, tingled against his sparsely haired chest. She slid his jeans down his hips, and it was his turn to moan. He stepped from his remaining clothes and drew her back with him toward the bed.

She faltered slightly on her right leg, and for a moment she went still, silently wishing she could come to him perfect in every way. But Cade left her no time to feel inadequate. Gathering her close with one arm, he lowered them both to the mattress with the other.

"So beautiful," he murmured. "So beautiful in every way."

The flannel interior of the sleeping bag smoothed along her back, and his words smoothed away any sense of imperfection she might have had. With the palm of his hand, he traced the muscle in her thigh, the one that had faltered, then bent to follow the path with his lips.

The touch of his lips on her thigh was almost unbearable in its tenderness, and Lexa knew she'd never feel self-conscious of her slight imperfection again. As his lips moved onward, feelings welled, and sensation took the place of thoughts.

As light from the lantern flickered off the beams in the ceiling, an overwhelming tremor of excitement quaked through her. She called his name, and he murmured hers.

When she could stand it no more, she brought his face to hers and kissed him, then pressed him to his back. His touch had worked a special kind of magic on her, and she moved over him, touching him with her hands, murmuring praises along his heated flesh in her own magical way.

Their hearts pounded an erratic rhythm. She closed her eyes and called him to her. She wrapped her legs around him like a warm blanket and gasped when he filled her. The degree to which she responded to him stunned her, yet she never wanted it to end. He moved, taking them to the brink of completion, then hurtling them through to the other side.

She called his name, and he answered with hers, and it was a long time before either of them moved.

When his heartbeat had nearly returned to normal, Cade pulled her close to his side and kissed her temple, her cheek and her lips. He knew he'd have to move, knew he'd have to bank the fire. But not yet. It was all he could do not to hold her too tightly, for he didn't want to let her go.

After a long time, she arched against him, stretching every muscle, from her neck all the way down to her toes. Smiling, she pressed a kiss to his neck and settled back into the circle of his arms. "You make me feel beautiful."

Cade rubbed his jaw against the top of her head, wondering at the almost shy tone of her voice. "You *are* beautiful," he answered.

"In your eyes," she whispered. "Because of you, tonight I felt beautiful in mine."

He waited for her to continue, wondering how she could believe she was anything but what he saw. A beautiful, desirable, emotional woman, more beautiful than mere words could express, more desirable than he'd ever imagined possible.

"I've never felt this way, Cade. At least not since I woke up from my surgery. If you could have seen me then, you wouldn't have thought I was beautiful."

Cade wished he could have seen her then, wished she hadn't gone through it all alone. Dr. Jacobiac had told Cade that Lexa had been in a coma for days. By the time Cade knew about her surgery, she was already undergoing physical therapy for her leg, and she already knew about her clairvoyance. Cade had had to face the fact that Lexa had left him, that if she ever came back to him, it would have to be on her own.

"They shaved my head. And my right leg refused to work. I was pale and gaunt, and when I had my first vision, I thought I was going crazy."

"Oh, Lexa," he said in a deep, deep voice.

"I don't want your pity, Cade. I'm telling you so you'll understand. My hair grew back, and after months of physical therapy, my limp improved. But the haunted look in my eyes was harder to mend. It took Berdie's loving care to bring me back, her cooking to fill out my hollows."

"It wouldn't matter if your hair had never grown back, Lexa. It wouldn't matter if you still walked with a limp. I wouldn't care if you'd stayed as thin as a rail. I'd still find you beautiful. More beautiful than any other woman I've ever known."

Her eyelashes fluttered, tickling his shoulder. She pressed another kiss to his neck and whispered the three words he'd waited nearly four years to hear. "I love you."

Cade closed his eyes and clamped his jaw shut to keep from uttering those same words to her. He was afraid to say them, afraid he wouldn't be able to stop there. If he said, "I love you, Lexa," he wasn't certain he could keep from telling her the truth. And he didn't think she was ready for the truth. Lying there, watching light flicker over the rustic beamed ceiling, he wondered if she would ever be.

He got out of bed and crossed to the wood stove. As he threw more wood on the fire, he cursed his need for secrecy, cursed himself for hurting Lexa with his silence. She deserved a future filled with laughter. She deserved to hear the words he longed to say.

Crawling back into bed, he took her into his arms. Maybe he couldn't say the words out loud, but he could show her in at least a hundred different ways. He started with a kiss and followed with a touch, and knew he had at least ninety-eight ways left to show Lexa how he truly felt.

Chapter 8

The propane lantern had gone out hours ago, and dawn was beginning to streak the sky. Lexa had dozed off and on, but the pressure in her chest wouldn't allow her to fall into the oblivion of deep sleep.

The fire in the stove was nearly out, but she didn't want to leave the warmth of the bed to add more wood. Smiling to herself, she knew what she really didn't want to leave was the warmth of Cade's side. Slipping an arm beneath her head, she gazed at him, deciding that being unable to sleep had its benefits. It awarded her the luxury of watching Cade unobserved.

He lay on his back, his head turned to the side, his chin tucked close to his shoulder. His jaw looked nearly black now, and she couldn't believe she'd told him she preferred him clean shaven. To her, he'd never looked better. His hair was mussed, and she knew it had been her fingers, splaying through the thick tendrils, that had made it so.

She regarded him thoughtfully, amazed at the wanton

woman she'd become in his arms. His lovemaking had rocked her with emotion, and she'd murmured her love for him in total honesty. A lesser man might have repeated the words simply because he'd know she wanted to hear them. But Cade had remained silent. She didn't doubt, not for a single minute, that his feelings for her were deep and genuine. It was there in his gaze, in his smile and in his touch. He had his own reasons for his silence, reasons she respected, even though she didn't understand.

Being careful not to jostle him in the narrow bed, she slid from his side. Wrapping a blanket around her, she opened the flue on the stovepipe and lifted the door's handle, then added several logs to the fire. After pulling on her boots, she opened the cabin door as quietly as possible and, glancing all around, followed the path to the rear of the property.

Letting herself back inside minutes later, she smiled at the warmth coming from the stove and imagined that she and Cade lived here together. In her imagination, she had no special power except the one that drew Cade to her. In her fantasies, she and Cade would live here, and love here, and laugh here, just the two of them, alone in the world but not lonely.

No, not just the two of them. Callie would live with them, too. Together, the three of them would become a family, and the emptiness she felt in her chest would be filled with love.

Lexa rummaged through the pockets of her jacket, which was lying on the floor nearby, until she found what she'd been looking for. Taking the snapshots from their envelope, she padded to a chair near the stove and curled her feet underneath her, tucking the blanket securely and snuggling into its warmth.

She looked through each picture, studying the detail in every one. As before, her mind gradually went blank. The pressure in her chest increased, nearly suffocating her, but she didn't let it pull her back.

There, on the screen of her mind, was Cade's daughter. Callie was curled up with her favorite blanket sound asleep in a cabin very similar to the one she and Cade were in right now. The vision lasted no more than a few seconds, but it left Lexa with the feeling that Callie was nearby. They were close. Of this she felt certain.

Cade hadn't moved, and Lexa pulled on jeans and a thick ivory-colored sweater. She laced her boots, remembering when he'd slipped them from her feet the night before. Making as little noise as possible, she opened the door and stepped outside.

Frank had been right about the view of the sunrise from the stoop. It was spectacular, and after gazing at it for several minutes, she filled the pail with water at the hand pump out front, then tiptoed inside again where she filled an old enamel coffeepot and poured the rest of the water into a shallow pan. Placing both containers on the wood stove, she again thought about her fantasy, the one in which she lived here with Cade and Callie.

She sat down at the table, and wondered what her life might have been like had she not needed surgery. What would have happened if she'd met Cade under different circumstances? What ifs swam through her mind. She thought about the kind of happiness she'd found in Cade's arms. Because of him, she understood why people searched the world over to find love. She understood why couples swore undying love. She almost understood happily-ever-afters.

Picking up the snapshots again, she looked through them, thinking that soon another picture would be added to her shelf back home, the one lined with a dozen children's smiling faces. She glanced from the photograph in her hand to Cade, and felt a nagging in the back of her mind.

She'd been trying to imagine her life without her power,

trying to imagine a life with Cade. He'd touched her heart last night. She remembered how she'd felt when she'd said, "I love you." Cade hadn't responded with words. Oh, he'd been wonderful in every other way, but this morning she realized there was a part of himself he kept hidden, a part of himself he didn't want her to see. He'd asked few questions about her past and offered little information about his. At first she'd thought it was because he still loved his wife. Now she realized there was more to it than that.

When the water on the stove had warmed, she washed her face and brushed the tangles from her long hair. She heard the bed creak and the rustle of jeans being pulled on. Without turning, she sectioned her hair and began to weave it into a braid.

Warm fingers stilled her movements, winding through her hair, spreading it across her shoulders. "Good morning." His voice was deep and his fingers infinitely gentle. He kneaded the column of her neck and moved on to her shoulders. His arms came around her from behind, and she rested her head on his bare shoulder and closed her eyes.

One touch and a few words, and he had her as soft and pliant as beeswax. She turned and closed her eyes as his mouth covered hers. His kiss was warm, but far from sweet, the kind of kiss that could almost make a woman forget everything except the touch of his lips and the promise of more.

Her reaction to him was swift, her response instinctive and powerful. She opened her eyes and sighed at the look of desire in his. He gazed down at her, a lazily seductive smile on his face. She traced his cheekbone with her fingertips, silently asking him to tell her what he was hiding. With his black hair and blue eyes and that beard-darkened chin, he looked positively lascivious. But he didn't tell her what she needed to hear.

He kissed her again, the touch of his mouth on hers an

invitation she could hardly resist. His eager response matched hers, but this time she didn't yield to the searing need that had built between them. This time she slowly but firmly pulled out of his arms. "It's morning, Cade. And time to go."

She felt the reluctance in his fingers as he released her and heard the deep breaths he took to bring himself under control. "You're right, Lexa. It is time to go. But first, tell me what I've done wrong."

It was all she could do not to walk right back into his arms. She let her gaze travel over him, from his face, down his bare chest and shoulders, to the fingers of his left hand. Slowly bringing her gaze back to his, she said, "You haven't done anything wrong, Cade. And I meant it when I told you I love you."

He took a step toward her, and she held up her hands to stop his forward motion. "I don't doubt your feelings for me are real, but this morning I realized something I should have known all along."

She didn't understand the look of panic that momentarily crossed his features. It added to her belief that her nagging suspicions were right, that there was a part of himself he wouldn't share with her.

"I've been open with you, Cade, from the beginning. But you haven't been open with me. At first I thought it was because you were still in love with Callie's mother. Now I think it's more than that. Do you realize I don't even know her name?"

Cade gazed into Lexa's eyes and recognized the deep emotion she kept inside. She couldn't remember him, but she loved him. Because of his need for secrecy, he'd hurt her. She believed he'd kept his feelings to himself because he didn't care. How could he tell her the truth? How could he not?

He walked forward, stopping a few feet in front of her.

His heart hammered in his ears as he struggled to find the right words. He breathed in an unsteady breath and began, "You're right, Lexa. There are things I haven't told you. But before I say anything more, tell me this. Would you give up your clairvoyance for me?"

"What do you mean?" she whispered.

"What if I asked you to come back to Hendersonville with me and Callie, to turn your back on your power? Could you do it?"

Cade stared at her for a long time, watching her grope for an answer. Lexa wasn't the only person who'd lain awake last night. He had, too. He'd gone over and over every possible way to be with her. He'd give up his orchards and move to Roanoke Island if it meant they could be a family. But as the minutes had crept by, he'd realized he couldn't do that. He couldn't live with her and not tell her the truth.

And he couldn't tell her the truth. If he did, it would cost her her power. He had to think about what was best for Callie, too. He couldn't let her know her mother's love and keep the truth for her.

When he'd held Lexa in his arms last night, he'd been so certain they'd find a way to be together. Now, looking deep into her eyes, he knew it was up to her. He could fantasize, he could hope, but in the end, it came down to a choice. Him, or her power. As she gazed back at him, her eyes filled with tears, and Cade knew what her answer would be.

"Think about what you're asking, Cade. Because of my visions we're going to find Callie. What about when another child is taken? What about the next parent that comes to me?"

She looked away from him. "No. I couldn't turn them away. Not even for you."

It was what he'd expected her to say and why he loved her with his whole heart. He placed his hands on her shoulders and took a shuddering breath. "I understand, Lexa. And I want you to know how very much I admire you. I never wanted to hurt you."

Without warning, the muscles in her arms flexed and her fingers curled into fists over her ears. He turned her to face him, and realization spread like icy tentacles to Cade's stomach. He'd seen this look on her face before, the day they'd been sightseeing on Roanoke Island, the day Winnona had taken Callie's blanket right out of Lexa's house. He knew she'd heard the child's voice again, and he knew what it meant.

Callie was nearby.

He yearned to hold his daughter so much he ached. But gazing at Lexa, he felt another kind of ache. This ache was for the weight of responsibility she carried. He wanted to curse it, but he couldn't. Instead, he grasped her upper arm, hoping his warmth would chase her torment away.

Hearing the voice had drained her face of color, had deepened her eyes to a dark gray. "We have to leave," she said.

He couldn't tell her how much he wished things could be different. At least not with words. He hoped she saw in his eyes how very special she was to him.

He pulled on his clothes and followed the path to the rear of the property, awarding her a little privacy and himself a little time to get his emotions under control. He'd come to Lexa to find Callie, and he couldn't lose sight of that goal now, not when they were so close.

By the time he went back inside, the sleeping bags were rolled up and Lexa was in the process of setting out the biscuits and honey Berdie had insisted they bring along. Cade walked to the wood stove and poured hot water into two chipped mugs. After stirring in instant coffee, he handed a mug to Lexa.

They sipped their coffee and ate their breakfast in relative silence. When they were through, he pulled a crumpled piece of paper from his pocket and said, "The detective gave me these directions to Winnona's cabin. But I just scouted the perimeter of this property, and I can't find any landmarks indicating exactly where we are."

Lexa took the paper from him and stared at it before saying, "I had another vision while you were sleeping, Cade. I saw Callie in a cabin similar to this one. As near as I could tell last night, we're east of Boone. And according to this sketch, Winnona's cabin is somewhere north of Deep Gap. If the detective and police couldn't find it, I don't know how we will."

Cade spread his big map of North Carolina out on the scuffed wooden table. "There must be at least a hundred cabins like this one in these hills. Without someone with knowledge of the area, it'll be like looking for a needle in a haystack."

"We need a guide."

Looking up from the map, Cade said, "I'll bet that old couple who own this place would know if Winnona used to live in this area."

"Frank and Ida," Lexa whispered.

They dived into action. In record time, the sleeping bags were stowed in the trunk, their suitcases in the back seat. The fire in the stove was extinguished, the mugs rinsed and placed upside down to dry. Neither of them spoke of the change in their relationship, of the distance that now separated them. Neither of them paused to catch their breath.

The ride along the curving road to Frank and Ida's was just as quiet as the ride to the cabin had been the night before. Then, they'd been silent because words weren't necessary. Now, they were silent because neither knew what to say.

Cade parked the car in front of the restaurant and opened his door. Lexa opened her own door, then stopped. She didn't move for several seconds, and Cade didn't like the glazed look that spread over her face. A muscle twitched in his jaw, and worry tightened his throat. She was having another vision, and whatever she saw sent shivers down his spine. He knew the moment it was over, for she closed her eyes, reliving what she'd seen.

She finally looked at him, and he knew there had been something different about this vision. Her voice when it came sounded faraway. "This time I only saw Winnona. Her back was to me. She stepped aside, and I saw a stone marker. On the marker were the words 'Beloved Daughter.'"

Cade grasped Lexa's shoulders. "Not Callie's!" he shouted. "I didn't come this far to only find a grave."

Realization dawned. For both of them. It couldn't have been Callie's grave. Lexa had just seen her hours earlier. But where was she, then? Why was Winnona alone? And whose grave had Lexa seen?

They hurried to the restaurant door and were again greeted like long-lost cousins. "Good morning," Ida called. Her cheery smile turned to worry as she read the anxiety on their faces. Looking over the top of her bifocals, she asked, "What is it? What's happened?"

Lexa hurried to assure her they were both fine, but the old woman looked from Cade to Lexa as if she didn't believe it was true. After Lexa told her why they'd come to the mountains, about her power and Cade's missing daughter, Ida straightened her frail-looking shoulders and hurried away to find her husband.

Lexa and Cade sat at the same table they'd sat at the night before. Even though they were the only people in the room, Lexa whispered, "Maybe you'd better let me do the talking, Cade."

At his raised eyebrows, she rushed on, "Remember, we're in the mountains. I can't tell you how many times

Berdie has said North Carolinians boast easily and often, welcome warily and mind their own business. Remember, tourists are welcomed but rarely wholly trusted.''

Cade scowled and shook his head. ''No wonder the detective I hired couldn't find Callie.''

Somewhere a door opened and slammed shut again, and Lexa felt a draft. A moment later she watched as Frank and Ida entered the room. She couldn't be sure who wore the deepest look of worry. Frank, Ida or Cade.

''What's this about your little girl missing?'' Frank evidently believed in getting right to the point.

Lexa placed a steadying hand on Cade's arm. In a quiet voice she said, ''We're awfully sorry to bother you, but Cade and I came here looking for a woman.''

''This woman related to you?'' Frank asked gravely.

''Not really.''

''Then I don't see how it's any business of yours.''

The muscles in Cade's arms flexed, and Lexa hurried to explain. ''This woman made it our business when she took Cade's little girl.''

The old man refrained from further comment while Lexa reached into her pocket for the photographs and handed them across the small table. Ida exclaimed over the darling child, and Frank asked, ''How long's she been missing?''

Cade answered, ''Almost two weeks. The woman who took her used to be my housekeeper.''

''What's the child's name?'' Ida asked.

''Carolina Joy. We call her Callie.''

Lexa wasn't sure what did it, their honesty or Callie's name, but she sensed a softening in the old couple. Frank narrowed his eyes directly at her and said, ''You're really clairevent, clairessent...''

''Clairvoyant,'' Lexa supplied. ''It means I have more than five senses.''

''You mean you have the third eye?'' Ida asked.

598   *Child of Her Dreams*

Lexa nodded slowly. "You believe in such powers?"

"Egad, who wouldn't?" Frank answered. "Everyone knows there's things we can't explain. We mountain folk call it mountain magic."

Ida added, "Once heard of a woman down Nantahala way who had an inner eye so powerful she could find folks lost in the haunted gorge."

"Then you'll help us?" Cade asked.

Frank and Ida studied him for several nerve-splitting seconds before nodding. After a long pause, Lexa reached across the table and flung her arms around Ida's narrow shoulders, murmuring, "Thank you. Thank you so much."

Ida patted her comfortingly, and Lexa looked at Cade. The blunt worry was gone from his eyes. But the uncertainty had stayed.

Ida looked more closely at the photos and made a clicking sound with her tongue. "Carolina Joy. What a beautiful name for a child. How old is your little girl?"

Cade glanced at the date on his digital watch and went still. His expression became tightly controlled, and he finally said, "She'll be four years old. Tomorrow."

His words brought a nagging sensation to the back of Lexa's mind, but for the life of her, she couldn't understand why. The old man studied the sketched map Cade had made from the detective's directions and shook his head. "Afraid I can't make hide nor tail of this. What did you say your housekeeper's name was?"

"Winnona. Winnona Smith."

"Smith. Winnona Smith. You remember any Winnona Smith up this way, Idie?"

"The last name doesn't ring a bell, but the name Winnona does.... Wait a minute. There was a woman up in the hills north of Deep Gap with a strange name like that."

"Deep Gap? Do you remember what she looked like?" Cade asked.

The old man's eyes narrowed in his direction. "You ain't fronm the South, are you boy?"

Lexa placed her hand over Cade's, saying, "Cade and his daddy own an apple and peach orchard near Hendersonville. Was the woman you're thinking of a large-boned woman with straight dark hair?"

"Yes, but two-thirds of the women up in the hills fit that description," Ida pointed out.

"I've seen this woman in visions, Ida, several times. She came all the way to Roanoke Island to get Callie's blanket, the only thing Cade had left of his daughter. If there's anything you can tell us, anything at all..." She let her voice trail away on a gentle sigh.

Ida said, "You have to remember that some of these mountain folks still live the way their great-great-grand-daddies did. Even though most have television antennas, the old ways die slowly. They're still superstitious. Some still plant their crops and make their soap by the phases of the moon."

"Winnona is superstitious," Lexa murmured. "My friend, Berdie O'Toole, saw her taking Callie's blanket. Winnona took one look at Berdie and screeched, 'Bird in house!'"

Frank and Ida both gasped. It was Frank who finally said, "Bird in the house is the most feared omen there is. I remember now. That woman up near Deep Gap kept to herself, but she did come into the restaurant a couple of times. She was married to a strange sort of man. One day the man came in for some chew on his way off the mountain. Said he was leaving, that his little girl had died, and it was his wife's fault. Evidently she'd seen a bird in their house, but hadn't heeded its warning."

"The child's grave," Lexa breathed. "Was the child buried on the mountain?"

"Folks aren't supposed to. But some do bury their loved ones on their own property."

"Could you show us where she lived?" Cade asked.

Lexa watched Frank assess the younger man and had to bite her lip to keep from pleading for him to help them. But she'd heard Arnie and Ramsey talk about outsiders often enough to know that no amount of pleading would change a man's mind if he decided not to trust a stranger.

"Ida and I have a restaurant to run, and neither of us gets around as good as we used to." Frank looked from Cade to Lexa. "But we also have a little great-granddaughter of our own, and if somebody took her, I'd like to think even a stranger would help us get her back."

A smile spread over Lexa's face as Frank went in search of a piece of paper and pencil. He returned and in a shaky scrawl began to draw the path to Deep Gap and beyond. "Haven't been up there in years," he mumbled. "And the last time was in the fall when the leaves were off the trees. It's gonna be harder to see this time of year."

Ida waited on the odd customer or two who came into the restaurant, and Frank pointed to a line he'd drawn. "This is the same place Daniel Boone crossed the mountains through Deep Gap in 1760. There's a fork in the road right about here. You're gonna want to veer to the right."

Both Cade and Lexa listened to every word, every description, every detail. "Now this trail circles around a bit, but you'll know you're on the right track when you come to a small shack painted pink. Old Morris Burk painted it years ago after taking too many nips from the barrel. This is as far as yer gonna be able to go by car. Tell old Morris I sent you, and he'll let you park your car for free."

Cade cast Lexa a disbelieving look. She shrugged and turned her attention back to Frank, who went on, "Tell Morris I said to help you, and maybe he'll point you in the right direction, too."

By the time the old man had finished, his drawing resembled a maze. Cade took it and, after thanking Frank and Ida profusely, he left the restaurant with Lexa and headed north toward what they hoped was Winnona's cabin.

Although Lexa kept a picture of Callie nearby, she had no more visions and heard no voices calling to her inside her head. Together she and Cade followed Frank's directions, but the closeness they'd shared earlier was gone. Neither spoke of their feelings. It was as if they both knew it was futile. Getting Callie back became their only goal.

They got turned around a few times along the way and had to retrace their path until they found something they recognized from Frank's description of the area. They finally found old Morris Burk's pink house around early evening. After a quick explanation and mention of Frank and Ida, Morris allowed them to park the car, then ambled back to his rickety porch and his old cane-backed chair.

"We're looking for a woman named Winnona who used to live around here," Cade called to the man's back. "Frank said you might be willing to point us in the right direction. This woman's traveling with a little girl. Have you seen them?"

Cade knew the old coot had heard, because he stopped on the top step to listen. But he didn't answer, and Cade cursed the old-timer's ways and his stubborn-as-a-mule lack of trust in strangers.

From the trunk of the car, Cade and Lexa took only what they'd need for their trip—sleeping bags, a change of clothes, matches and food. Lexa waved to the old man on the porch, but Cade didn't bother, which was just as well, because Morris Burk didn't return her wave anyway.

An hour after they began their trek up the craggy slope, they stopped to catch their breaths, and Cade began to worry that they wouldn't reach the cabin before nightfall. They trudged on until they happened upon an old barnlike building that, seventy or eighty years ago, could have been used as a moonshine shack.

Lexa dropped her pack to the ground and asked, "Do you have any idea where we are?"

Cade took the map from his pocket and studied it for a long time before answering. "We crossed this creek about half an hour ago. Frank said it would take us out of our way, and he was right." Looking around, he added, "It's going to be dark soon. We aren't going to reach her today."

Lexa's limp had become more pronounced. She'd slowed Cade down, and they both knew it. Lowering herself to a fallen log, she gently massaged her tired muscles. His hand covered hers, and she slowly raised her eyes to his. The tenderness in his expression almost brought tears to her eyes.

"We're nearly there, Lexa. And I couldn't have gotten this far without you."

She was the one with the clairvoyant powers, yet he'd read her thoughts as clearly as if she'd uttered them out loud. He dropped the sleeping bags near her feet and said, "We'll rest here."

Lexa was thinking that this place looked as good as any to spend the night when Cade said, "I'm going to hike around the perimeter of this area and see if I can spot anything that might lead us in the right direction tomorrow."

She watched him disappear through the heavy foliage, listening to the noises he made. Branches snapped and underbrush crackled long after he was no longer visible. *Daniel Boone, he isn't*, she said to herself.

The sun was lowering and so was the temperature. Lexa buried her hands in her pockets and looked up through the new leaves on the trees overhead. The sky was a beautiful shade of blue, tinged with coral and dusky rose, seeming to change before her very eyes.

Out of nowhere a thought shimmered through her mind.

By this time tomorrow, Cade and Callie would be together again. Even though it was what Lexa wanted more than anything, the realization brought a heaviness to her heart, because it meant they'd leave and she'd probably never see Cade again.

After rummaging through the pack, Lexa lighted the lantern and placed cans of soda and cellophane-wrapped sandwiches on the log next to her. The noise Cade made coming back brought a smile to her lips and helped put her on more even ground where their relationship was concerned.

When he reached the clearing, she called to him in a teasing tone, "You weren't a Boy Scout, were you?"

Her words brought his shoulders around. The wry smile on her face sent an equally wry grin to his. He shook his head and said, "It's that obvious?"

"Afraid so."

They both laughed in spite of themselves, and an inexplicable feeling of rightness settled over Lexa. It felt good to laugh with Cade. It was a release, yes, but it also made her feel as if they were friends.

She began to unwrap her sandwich, and Cade strode to the log where he opened a can and took a sip of warm soda. He spoke little while they ate, seeming preoccupied with his own thoughts. When she lowered her half-eaten sandwich to its wrapper, Cade placed it in her hand again, saying, "Come on, Lexa. You have to eat."

Before taking another nibble, she leveled her gaze at him and declared, "You're beginning to sound like Berdie."

He pretended to pull a dagger from his heart, and she laughed at his surprising humor. They became silent again after that, the color draining from the sky much the way their laughter had drained away the tension they'd felt since morning.

Lexa looked into his eyes, and her laughter trailed away. Even though they were able to laugh with one another,

Cade's eyes still held secrets. She didn't understand why he wouldn't share them with her.

By the time the first star twinkled into sight, she was sure the temperature had dropped at least twenty degrees. She stood and, taking the lantern and one sleeping bag, pushed through the old barn's lopsided door.

Starlight wavered through cracks in the roof, and light from the lantern threw long shadows from floor to ceiling. Wings flapped in the dusty loft. Somewhere, an owl hooted, and a dove roosted, settling down for the night. She spread the sleeping bag on an old pile of dried leaves and turned to find Cade watching from the doorway.

Her heart thumped like the wings of the dove she'd just heard, or like the wings of sea gulls swooping down the Banks back home. Thoughts of home, of Berdie and Arnie and Ramsey, had often sustained her while searching for missing children. Thoughts of them did little to ease the loneliness in her heart now. She loved Berdie and Arnie and Ramsey, but she knew it was Cade she was going to miss.

Averting her face from his gaze, she sank onto the sleeping bag and busied herself with the zipper. "Do you know which direction to take tomorrow morning?"

She heard his boots squeak, heard the rustle of his jeans and the crunch of leaves as he spread his bag near hers. She watched as he removed his boots, and noticed he didn't suggest zipping the bags together as they had the previous night. They wouldn't be murmuring words of passion, of desire, to each other tonight, wouldn't find a night's respite in each other's arms.

"According to Frank's map, Winnona's cabin is only about an hour's hike away. But it's a good thing we stopped here, because the terrain gets rougher. The steep cliffs and rocky ridges rimming the trail would have been treacherous in the dark."

Lexa nodded her head in agreement, then took the lantern and crossed to the door. Cade's voice slowed her progress.

"Where are you going?"

He watched her fluid motion as she turned toward him. The light touched her face with shadow, making her skin appear creamy white, almost translucent. Her eyes held a special glow, and Cade sucked in a jagged breath. In this light, she looked ethereal, and for a moment, he was afraid she'd disappear.

"I'm going outside to, um, use the facilities." With that, she turned and disappeared out the open door.

Cade hadn't realized how stiff he'd held himself until she came inside again. Only then did he relax. She wasn't gone yet. They still had tonight.

She brushed off her jeans and removed her shoes. After climbing into her sleeping bag, she murmured, "What I wouldn't give for indoor plumbing right now."

He felt his tight expression relax into a smile, felt a chuckle form deep inside before it floated up from his throat. Her eyes twinkled with laughter, but she covered her mouth with her hand. Cade raised up on one elbow and took that hand in his.

His chuckle trailed away, and so did her laughter. Gazing at her, he knew he'd never loved her more than at this moment. He squeezed her hand, wanting to convey his feelings, wishing with all his heart they could have found their way back to each other, but knowing they couldn't. He closed his eyes at the stab of loneliness the thought of living without Lexa evoked. When he opened them, it was to find her gazing at him, her eyes serene and brightened with moisture.

He couldn't tell her he loved her, not without explaining why they couldn't be together forever. But there was one thing he could say. "Things will probably get hectic tomorrow."

He heard the faint tremor in his own voice, but no longer

cared if she heard the deep emotion he felt for her. "And in case I forget after we get Callie back, I just want to say thank you, Lexa. Thank you for everything."

She bit her lip and blinked her tears away. Her smile was back, as tremulous as her whisper. "You're welcome, Cade. You're so, so welcome."

She turned to her other side, and Cade slowly lowered the wick of the lantern, casting them in darkness. He closed his eyes and tried to sleep, but couldn't, and he knew it was more than nerves keeping him awake. He was anxious to reach Callie and sad that, after tonight, he and Lexa would never be together again.

Dried leaves crackled, and Lexa's sleeping bag rustled next to his. Her sigh told him he wasn't the only one awake. Straining, he listened for another sound. When none came, he whispered, "Lexa, are you awake?"

For a long time he wondered if he'd been wrong, wondered if she was asleep, after all. When her voice finally came, it flickered through the still air like the starlight flickering through the cracks in the roof. "Yes, Cade, I'm awake. Try to get some sleep."

It wasn't what he wanted her to say. Sleeping wasn't what he wanted to spend his last night with Lexa doing. But she gave him no indication that she wanted the kind of closeness he craved. She wanted him to tell her the truth. He couldn't. He had a feeling she'd turned her back to him to protect herself from heartache, and Cade had to respect her wishes. Even though he wished with all his heart that things could be different.

Chapter 9

Lexa watched the starlight twinkle through a crack in the roof high above. She forced herself to lie still until Cade's even breathing told her he was asleep.

He hadn't touched her, but from the depth of his voice, she sensed he would have welcomed it. One word, one small sign from her, and he'd have joined her. And if she hadn't wanted to make love, she knew he'd have held her through the long night. But she hadn't given him that one small sign. She couldn't. If she wanted to survive with her heart intact, she had to sever the emotional ties binding them together. And she had to get through the night on her own.

She drew a deep draft of air past the heaviness in her chest and sat up, wishing things could be different, wishing their sleeping bags were zipped together, wishing she could reach out and touch him with her hand. But she realized they couldn't go back to the way things were before.

She'd known their lives would never stay together. Cade's father and daughter would draw him back to his

orchards, and her power would take her back to the Outer
Banks and the warmth of Berdie's old kitchen. She had the
wisdom to know this, and the serenity to accept it. But she
didn't have whatever it took to lie there, so close to Cade
but not touching, waiting for the long, long night to end.

Cade didn't know what woke him. Not a sound could be
heard from inside the old barn, not from the loft, not from
the sleeping bag next to his. He fumbled for the lantern and
struck a match, the tiny light shivering through the darkness.
Turning up the lantern's wick, panic rose in his chest as he
took in the empty place Lexa's sleeping bag had been.

His shadow waggled across the wall like a hunchbacked
monster as he pulled on his boots and took his coat in hand.
He swung the lantern in a large arc and stopped just outside
the door.

She wasn't gone. She was there, her back to him, huddled
down in her sleeping bag by the shoulder of a fallen tree.
The arm holding the lantern dropped down, and Cade felt
as if the wind had been knocked out of him. All because he
thought he'd lost her, all because for one blinding moment
he thought he'd never see her again.

"Is it almost morning?"

He should have known she wasn't sleeping, and he cursed
himself for leaving her to face the night alone. Bringing his
watch close to his face, he said, "It's almost five. What's
the matter? My snoring drive you out here?"

"Your snore is quiet compared to Berdie's."

Her laugh was marvelous, and at odds with the dark night.
He'd always loved to hear her laugh. But now it was even
more precious, because she laughed sparingly, and he wondered how many more times he'd hear it before he left.

He strode toward her and, placing the lantern on the log,
shrugged into his coat and sat down. "Have you been out
here all night?"

She sat up and gave a small nod. Cade slid his back against the rough bark until he was sitting on the ground next to Lexa's. Too many nights with too little sleep had left him feeling sluggish. He didn't know how she did it, how she survived on so little sleep or so little food.

Guilt was like a hand closing around his throat, because he knew that this time, she did it for him. "Is it always this difficult, Lexa? Is finding missing children always this hard on you, physically and emotionally?"

"The longer it takes, the more tired I become. But it's always worth it, Cade. In the end, you'll see."

Yes, he supposed it was true. It would all be worth it, all the worry, all the heartache, because in the end they'd find Callie. But he and Lexa would part. And it would be the most difficult thing he'd ever done.

He tipped back his head to gaze at the sky. Stars seemed to wink out before his eyes, and he was reminded of a saying—it's always darkest before the dawn. His life was like that, when stars no longer lighted the sky and the sun had yet to brighten a new day. Lexa was like the light of those stars, seeming to grow farther and farther away before his eyes. Concentrating on finding Callie, he realized his hopes were like the promise of dawn. Of course it would come. It would, but now all he saw was darkness.

"What have you been doing out here all night?" he asked.

"I've been waiting for morning, and I've been thinking," she said.

He turned up his collar and shoved his hands into his pockets, determined to savor what little time they had left. "What have you been thinking about, Lexa?"

He could almost hear her trying to put her thoughts into words. "I've been thinking about a lot of things. About the kids I've found. And the voice that called me back to life during my surgery. And about the picture of my mother back home.''

Cade's heart thumped so loudly he wondered if Lexa heard. She wanted to know about her mother. There were so many things he could tell her if only she didn't care so deeply about the children she'd found, if only telling her wouldn't cost her her inner eye.

Sitting there in the silence of predawn, he knew she still mourned her past, still mourned the fact that she couldn't remember it. He searched for the proper words, words that might soothe, yet keep her power intact.

He drew his legs up, resting his forearms on his knees. The mountain was utterly quiet, and Cade wondered if it was always this way, or if this morning was unique. Staring at the last bright star in the sky, he began, ''Maybe you're looking for your memories in the wrong place.''

She leaned her head back against the tree, and he knew they were looking at the same bright star. ''Maybe you should stop searching your mind and look in your heart, instead, where memories never truly fade.''

She turned her face toward his. There was no disguising the weariness and fatigue in her eyes. But what really amazed him was the infinite tenderness glowing there. He reached for her hand in the semidarkness and found it covering her heart. Placing his hand over hers, he let his voice drop to a husky whisper. Pressing his hand to her heart, he murmured, ''Maybe you'll find what you're looking for here.''

She lowered her eyes and slowly shook her head. ''No, Cade. Since the moment I opened my eyes in the hospital, in my heart I've felt only emptiness, as if I've lost something precious. I can't look into my heart. It only makes me sad.''

He left his hand over her heart, letting the steady rhythm of its beat pulse through them both until the gray light of dawn filtered into the sky. She wasn't happy. She'd as much as told him so. Yet he couldn't change the course of her life. All he could do was hold her hand and wait for morning to come.

Four years ago today they'd sat like this. Four years ago, after Callie's birth. Lexa had been exhausted then, too, but she hadn't slept. They'd huddled together, speaking about the miracle they'd witnessed and the incredible joy Callie's birth had brought them. They'd kept silent about the fear that gripped their hearts, fear of the unknown, of the outcome of the surgery they had yet to face. He'd thought he couldn't love her more. He'd been wrong.

"It'll be light soon." Lexa pulled her hand from his and pushed herself to her knees.

Without a word, Cade drew himself to a standing position. She'd said she felt emptiness in her heart, as if she'd lost something precious. What she'd lost was Callie, and today they'd find her again.

He went back into the barn to roll up his sleeping bag and carry everything outside. They used the fallen tree for a table, drinking juice from boxes and eating the granola they'd purchased in the grocery store in Blowing Rock. By the time it was completely light, they were hiking along the trail Frank had told them to follow, the trail that led farther up the mountain to Winnona's cabin in the hills.

The terrain became rougher, the path steeper, so narrow in places they had to walk in single file. They stepped over fallen trees and rocks and climbed over boulders jutting out from the earth. At one point, the trail was only a couple of feet wide. One side was a wall of rock, and the other fell away into a deep gorge.

"The thought of Callie walking along this path sickens me," Cade murmured. "She's terrified of heights."

"She made it up, Cade. And you'll be there to help her down."

They walked on in complete silence, each step they took bringing them closer to their destination. Lexa was getting winded. Instead of stopping to rest, she breathed in through her nose and out through her mouth, staving off the stitch in her side.

After climbing over a particular difficult stretch of trail, she stopped. "Cade, I smell smoke."

He inhaled and took her hand, helping her over a particularly rough patch. Minutes later they rounded a sudden bend in the trail, and emerged into a clearing. For a moment they both stood motionless, their breathing ragged, their eyes taking in the gray shack with its sagging roof and rotting front steps. A window was broken, and the place looked derelict. Except for the smoke curling from a crumbling stone chimney.

Cade dropped his pack to the ground. "If Winnona sees us coming, she'll run scared. Stay out of sight until I've circled around to the back, okay? When I signal, you go in the front door and I'll go in the back."

He started away from her, but stopped in his tracks and turned back to face her. "Be careful, Lexa."

Her heart nearly expanded to the outside of her ribs. He was on the brink of finding his daughter, yet he'd taken a moment to worry about *her* safety. She sucked in a breath through parted lips, her mouth curving into a smile. "You, too. Now, go. I'm anxious to meet your daughter."

A muscle tensed in his cheek, and Cade turned slowly, as if barely holding a raw emotion in check. Lexa peeked through branches budding with new leaves, using the time to get her own breathing under control and to shore up her heart for what was to come.

Watching the windows for signs of movement was unnerving. She waited for his signal, then slowly crept toward the shack. Lexa wasn't sure what she'd find, wasn't at all certain what Winnona was capable of doing.

Once she was in the open she ran with all her might toward the front door. She took the rickety steps. Crouching below the window, she grasped the knob and listened for the slightest noise inside.

"Now!" Cade yelled.

She turned the knob and flung the door open wide. Jumping to her feet, she strode into the square room. There was a movement from the only other doorway, and Lexa turned, unsure what she would see.

Cade stood in the doorway, and Lexa's eyes gradually became adjusted to the dark interior. The cabin was small and cluttered. And, except for her and Cade, empty of people.

"They're not here," he said, his voice an odd mixture of disbelief and disappointment.

"But the smoke in the chimney..."

A curtain, half-torn from its rod, hung from the doorway, separating the large room where Lexa stood from what appeared to be the only bedroom. She moved past Cade, taking in the child's clothing strewn about the floor. Going down to her knees, she peered under the bed, half expecting to find Winnona and Callie hiding there.

She didn't find them, but she did find Callie's blanket, the one Winnona had taken from her house several days ago. The blanket was dirty and tattered, but Lexa held it close to her heart and pressed her face into its softness.

She could feel Cade's sharp eyes boring into her. Raising her gaze to his, she handed the blanket to him. "They're not here now. But they left in a hurry. Winnona's running scared, Cade. She left the fire in the fireplace unattended. And this time, she left all Callie's things behind."

A muscle twitched in his jaw again, more pronounced because of the stubble on his chin. Eyes that had such a capacity for warmth were cold with disappointment. He

turned on his heel and stalked out the back door. Without
a word, Lexa followed.

She knew he didn't have any idea which direction to re-
sume looking and silently ruled out only the one they'd just
come from. He stopped so abruptly she had to bring herself
up short to keep from running into him.

With narrowed eyes, he scanned the landscape, and Lexa
doubted he realized he still clutched Callie's blanket in his
left hand. They started to go east, but circled around again
when they couldn't find any grass or weeds that looked
trampled.

"Cade, look!" Lexa pointed to a small purple object
barely visible in the bushy ferns several yards away.

Cade ran to investigate. He leaned down and scooped the
object into his hand.

By the time Lexa had caught up, he was gripping a small
purple shoe so tightly his knuckles were white. She looked
from his face to the muddy shoe in his hand and said, "It's
Callie's, isn't it?"

He nodded, and they both cut through the ferns, following
an old trail that hadn't been visible before. A hundred yards
into the thick brush, they came to a stop.

A wan shaft of sunlight filtered through the tall trees,
spilling onto a small patch of cleared ground. In the center
of the clearing was a small stone marker. Chiseled into the
stone were the words "Beloved daughter."

Lexa had spent many a Sunday afternoon wandering
through the old cemetery on Roanoke Island, reading the
names and dates, trying to imagine what the lives of those
buried there had been like. But this was different. This was
a child's grave, untended, and all alone on a desolate moun-
tainside.

"Oh, Cade," Lexa whispered after reading the child's
name and dates aloud. "Be careful when you find Winnona,

Cade. I know what she did was wrong, but she's already suffered, already lost her husband and her child.''

He'd dropped the blanket, and Lexa stooped to get it. Straightening, she looked at the stone marker again. With every heartbeat the mountain grew more silent. The twittering of birds gradually disappeared until Lexa heard nothing. The pressure in her chest pushed against her ribs, and once again a vision played through her head.

She knew her eyes were open, but she didn't see what was before her. Instead, she saw Winnona tripping through brush, clasping Callie's hand, dragging her with her. They emerged onto a narrow trail. On one side of them was a gray wall of rock. On the other only blue sky.

A scream pierced the stillness.

Lexa spun around, the sudden movement making her dizzy. For a moment she thought it came from inside her head. But this scream was different. This wasn't a child's cry, but a woman's high-pitched wail.

Another vision followed so rapidly Lexa felt blackness try to close in on her. She concentrated on the vision, her hands instinctively covering her throat and chest.

Callie's face was dirty, her arms smudged with mud. Her tiny fingers clutched at a jagged rock, her feet, one bare, the other in a muddy purple shoe, dangerously close to the edge of the cliff.

This time Lexa saw Callie's eyes. They were round with fright, nearly the same color of gray as the wall of rock at her back.

This time the child was alone, clinging to the cliff with all her might. Rocks crumbled at her feet, and big tears squeezed from the corners of her eyes. Callie's lips moved, but Lexa couldn't hear her, couldn't make out the words she mouthed. She wanted to tell her to hold on, wanted to assure her they were coming. She tried to reach the child, tried to stretch out her arm and grasp the tiny hand.

The vision faded as quickly as it had come. Lexa blinked against the bright sunlight. Her eyes focused on her own hands. She felt the material clutched in her fists. But the material wasn't Callie's shirt. It was Cade's.

"She's on a cliff, Cade. You have to save her."

"Daaaaaddy!"

Cade turned and followed Callie's scream. He tore through the brush as if being chased by a demon. "I'm coming, Callie. I'm coming. Hold on. I'm coming."

Chapter 10

Lexa followed Cade, barely able to keep him in sight up ahead of her. Branches snapped, hitting her face and body as she ran headlong toward the cliff she'd seen in her vision. She emerged from the trees just in time to see Cade disappear around a bend.

Her breath caught in her lungs, but her feet followed the rough terrain. Rocks lined the path on the right. On the left, there was nothing but blue sky. One false move, and they would fall off the ridge.

The crumbling rocks and jagged uneven ground forced her to slow her pace. Even so, a rock skittered underfoot, rolling to the edge, where it disappeared into nothingness. Lexa listened for it to land below, but heard no sound and knew the drop would be long, fast and deadly.

She moved cautiously, her back against the wall of rock, inching her way toward the voices coming from a short distance away. Rounding the last bend, the path became wider again. She looked just in time to see Cade jump over a narrow gap. Pieces of rock scuttled over the edge and bounced off another cliff several feet below.

Her gaze followed the path those rocks had taken, and she gasped at what she saw. Winnona was sprawled on her side near the edge of the second cliff down below, dead or unconscious, Lexa couldn't be sure.

"Daddy, help me." The tiny voice came from no more than a dozen feet away.

Callie was just as she'd been in Lexa's last vision. She was trembling, clutching a jagged jut of rock with both hands. Her face was dirty, and her feet, one bare and one clad in a purple shoe, seemed to be standing on little more than thin air.

Lexa pressed one hand over her mouth to keep from crying out. She looked into Callie's eyes, and both her hands curled into fists. Pressure pushed against her ribs like a balloon about to burst, and she stumbled backward, clutching her fisted hands to her chest.

"Lexa!" Cade called. "Don't come any closer."

Her head swam, and she shut her eyes against the dizziness coiling tighter and tighter in her head. Callie's voice came again, and through the haze Lexa realized she'd heard that voice before.

You can't faint now. Hold on. Hold on. She fought against the dizziness, fought to open her eyes and forced them to focus.

What little ground there was beneath Callie's feet began to crumble, and her hands began to slip. Cade flung himself toward the wall at his back, his feet searching for a footing. With one hand, he grasped the rock for balance and reached for Callie with the other.

Pieces of earth loosened and fell, landing a few feet from the edge of the lower cliff where Winnona lay. The ground at his feet slowly gave way. As Cade inched lower, his knuckles turned white and his fingers slowly began to slip.

Still fighting back dizziness, Lexa propelled herself forward. Her right leg gave out, and she stumbled, hitting her head on a protruding rock on her way to her knees. Something warm trickled down the back of her head, but she hurried forward on hands and knees, over the rough terrain, to the narrow gap in the rock. Dropping to her belly, she reached her hand toward Cade. With a strength she didn't know she possessed, she grasped his denim jacket and pulled with all her might.

The dizziness closed in on her, but she wouldn't let go. She wouldn't let them die. She couldn't.

Lexa slowly turned her head to the side, squinting against the bright sunshine that slipped through the cracked window shade. She didn't recognize her surroundings, but the slightest movement of her head brought a thundering to her ears.

"Praise the Lord! You're awake!"

She could make out the shape of Berdie's head, and felt the cool touch of her friend's palm on her forehead, smoothing her hair from her face.

The room wasn't familiar, her memories of how she'd gotten there sketchy. "Berdie, where am I?"

Berdie's round face slowly came into focus. "You're in old Morris Burk's rundown shack, that's where."

Realization dawned. Lexa tried to sit up, but her friend gently but firmly held her in place.

"Lie still. Doctor's orders."

"Cade fell!" Lexa pushed against Berdie's strong hand.

"No, he didn't," Berdie insisted.

"But I saw him. Before I passed out I saw him lose his footing. I saw his fingers slip."

"Listen to me. He didn't fall. He's the one who brought you back here. He's safe."

"And Callie?"

"She's fine, Lexa."

It wasn't Berdie's voice. It was Cade's. A smile stole across her lips, and she relaxed into the pillows. Her eyes drifted closed, but she forced them open again and saw Cade standing in the doorway.

Berdie stepped aside, and Lexa saw Callie solemnly inch into the room. The child's face was scratched, and she looked tired and weepy. But she was safe, there with her father, and Lexa offered up a silent prayer of thanks.

"Happy birthday," she murmured from the bed.

The simple greeting chased the fear from Callie's big gray eyes. They took on a gleam of childish wonder and were raised to her father. "Is it my birthday, Daddy?"

Cade swooped down and plucked Callie from the floor. He wrapped his arms around her and hugged her as if he'd never let her go. "Yes, sweetheart. Today's your birthday. Today, you're four years old."

Four years. Lexa felt on the brink of putting together an incredible coincidence, but couldn't quite bring it into focus. She was too tired, and the pounding in her head didn't allow for deep thinking.

"Did you buy me a present?" Callie asked her father.

"Not yet, sweetheart."

Cade looked over the top of Callie's dark head and smiled at Lexa, and her heart began to beat in a rhythm stronger than the pounding in her head.

"I've been a little busy. But this year, you can have anything. Anything you want."

Lexa looked at Cade and Callie. "You're safe. And she's beautiful," she whispered before her eyelids fluttered down again.

"So are you." It could have been Cade's low clear voice, or it could have been the peacefulness deep within her. Whatever it was, it echoed in her ears and shimmered through her mind until she heard nothing, and sleep came.

The next time she opened her eyes, dusk was turning the sky gray. She could hear Callie's small voice, and Berdie's, and an unfamiliar voice she assumed belonged to old Morris Burk. Turning her head, she understood why she didn't hear Cade's.

He was sitting in a cane-backed chair near the bed. His eyes were closed, his head cocked at an uncomfortable-looking angle, his arms folded on his chest. His brows moved and his eyes opened, and she became lost in his look.

"You shaved."

He released half a chuckle and said, "I didn't want anyone to mistake me for old Morris."

Not likely. Looking around the rustic furnishings, she asked, "What am I doing here?"

Cade leaned forward, resting his elbows on his thighs, bringing his face closer to hers. "You hit your head, Lexa. But before you passed out, you reached for me. You steadied me until I found a foothold. You saved my life. Mine and Callie's."

They were safe. He and Callie. They were really and truly safe. "But how did you get me here?"

"Morris helped."

"You're on a first-name basis with a man who painted his house pink?"

He nodded. "He calls me Yankee, and I call him Morris, at least when he's within earshot."

She started to laugh, but stopped when the pounding in her head threatened to crack her skull. "I'm surprised he let you bring me here."

"I didn't exactly give him much choice. Besides, this might look like a mountain shack, but I called Berdie from his telephone. He has a satellite dish out back, and a four-wheel-drive in the shed. The old coot pretends to be a mountain man, but he turned out to be a lot of help in getting you and Callie and Winnona off that ridge."

"Is Winnona..."

"She's alive."

"I'm glad."

"She was only semiconscious when we got her off that ledge. She has a broken arm and a cracked rib or two. She'll undergo psychological testing after her physical ailments heal. Her sister, the one who lives in Raleigh, is coming to be with her."

Callie's voice raised to a whine in the next room, and Cade said, "She wants to go home."

Lexa stared deep into Cade's blue, blue eyes. *So, this is goodbye.*

"Morris called an ambulance for Winnona, and the paramedics checked you and Callie over before they left. Callie's fine except for a few scratches, and they said you have a slight concussion."

"I'll be fine, Cade."

Callie's whine came again, this time stronger and shriller than before. "Listen to her," Lexa whispered. "She's going to be just fine, too. Take her home, and take good care of her."

Her statement made his eyes flicker with pain, but only for a moment. Then his relief took over and he raised himself from the chair. "I will, Lexa. I promise."

The old mattress creaked beneath Cade's weight as he settled himself close to its edge. Smoothing a lock of hair from her face, he leaned over and whispered a kiss along her lips. "I'll never forget you. Neither will Callie."

A tear rolled from a corner of her eye. "And I'll always remember you."

Cade stood up, and strode to the door. He turned at the doorway and gave her one last smile.

The first thought in her mind the next time she opened her eyes was *Cade and Callie are gone.* It was morning, and the pounding in her head had receded to little more than a bothersome tap. She sat up, and Berdie seemed to materialize out of the woodwork.

"They're really gone?"

Berdie made her special sound and slowly nodded her head. "Left last night."

Lexa's gaze followed Berdie's progress from the doorway into the room. From the chair in the corner, she took three items, handing them to Lexa all at once. A piece of paper, folded once, was on top of the other two items. Lexa took the paper, opened it and read the short message.

In Cade's bold scrawl, he'd written, "Lexa, Here's a photograph for your thirteenth frame. The blanket was Callie's idea, something to remember us by."

He'd signed it simply, "Cade."

She placed the note on the bed next to her and took the blanket in one hand and Callie's picture in the other. *Something to remember us by.* As if she'd ever be able to forget.

Morris Burk followed Berdie back into the room a short time later. While Berdie placed enough food in front of her to feed a small army, Lexa smiled at the old mountain man. "Thank you for letting me stay here."

She was pretty sure he was smiling behind his scraggly beard, and his eyes took on a devilish gleam. "T'weren't nothin'. Been a long time since that thar bed's known a pretty li'l thing like you."

Lexa smiled, and Morris let out an "Ow!" He rubbed his arm where Berdie had clobbered him as he shuffled indignantly from the room.

Berdie clucked over Lexa until she'd eaten her fill. Next, Frank and Ida, who claimed they just happened to be in the neighborhood, dropped in, and the doctor from Blowing Rock came to check on her.

When things finally quieted down, Lexa looked at Berdie

and murmured, "Cade and Callie are really safe. They've gone home, Berdie, and I think it's time we did, too."

Back on Roanoke Island, everything was much the same, yet innately different. Arnie and Ramsey continued to play checkers and argue over the price of fish, but more often than not, Berdie's cheeks were tinged with a special glow. And Lexa knew Arnie had put it there.

The tourist season was upon them, and business at the restaurant was picking up. It was nearly the middle of April, and the weather was glorious. But Lexa found little pleasure in the sunshine. She'd been back a week, and for the first time in four years, the pressure in her chest was completely gone. The emptiness had stayed.

She didn't miss the pressure. She missed Cade.

She'd gone to see Dr. Jacobiac, and he'd arranged an appointment with a noted parapsychologist. She hadn't needed his team of specialists to tell her what she already knew. Her power was gone.

"It sometimes happens this way," the old parapsychologist explained. "Clairvoyance sometimes comes on a whim and leaves just as suddenly."

He'd gone on to explain that sometimes an injury to the head brings the power, and another injury takes it away again. Lexa had nodded, but on the drive back to the island, she knew her power had been no whim. It had been her fate, as predestined as her very life. She'd *died* on the operating table. To this day, she vividly recalled how it had felt, how bright the light was that drew her up. Just as vivid was her memory of the tiny voice that had called her back to earth.

The odds were heavily stacked against her, but she'd lived. And it hadn't been luck. It had been fate. Her surgery had saved her life, and in exchange for her memory, she'd been given the gift of clairvoyance. Each child she'd found had been another gift, and each one a stepping stone to the

real reason she'd survived. The real reason had something
to do with Carolina Joy Sullivan and her father.

Lexa hadn't lost her power when she'd hit her head on
the mountain. She'd lost it moments before, when she'd
looked into Callie's gray eyes, when she'd heard her small
voice, the same voice she'd heard inside her head. The same
voice that had called her back to life four years ago.

Four years. Lexa's clairvoyant power had lasted nearly
four years. And Callie Sullivan was four years old.

Day by day, Lexa had put more of the pieces together.
And every day more of her questions were answered.

She unclipped the pins from the clothesline as if in slow
motion, her thoughts far away, as far away as Hendersonville. After carefully folding Berdie's tablecloths, she removed her own towels from the line, placed them in the
basket and carried them into her small house. Walking to
her bedroom, she dumped them on her bed. Instead of folding her towels, she picked up the tattered blanket Callie had
given her, and inhaled the fresh scent. This freshness didn't
come from any bottle, but from the April breeze blowing
across the sound.

Something to remember us by. That's what Cade had said
the blanket and photograph he'd left at old Morris Burk's
cabin had been. Lexa was also beginning to realize she'd
kept the framed photo of her mother and the box of dried
forget-me-nots for the same reason. As reminders of something significant from her past.

Lexa's footsteps took her out to her living room, where
she glanced at the shelf, her gaze taking in each of the
thirteen pictures she'd placed there. Lowering the blanket to
the desk, she silently lifted the thirteenth frame and carried
it into her bedroom. She placed the picture—the one of Callie all dressed in purple, holding a bouquet of forget-me-
nots—on her nightstand.

Those flowers in Callie's hand and those Lexa had stored

in her closet were the final missing pieces. Happiness and hope rivaled for space in her heart, which suddenly didn't feel empty anymore.

Lexa took the clean tablecloths and hurried from her cottage, nearly running over Ramsey at the restaurant's back step. The old fisherman reached out a hand to steady them both. "Whoa, Miz Lexa. What's yer hurry?"

She couldn't suppress the happiness that seemed to bubble from her chest. She grasped Ramsey's shoulders and reached up to kiss his lined cheek. "He loves me, Ramsey. He never stopped."

"Well, of course he does. Who wouldn't?"

She continued up the steps, letting the door slam shut on Ramsey's sputtered question. "Who loves ya, Miz Lexa?"

She hurried into the kitchen, pushing through the swinging door so suddenly Arnie and Berdie had little time to disentangle their arms and step apart.

Lexa stopped, her heart nearly overflowing with feeling. Berdie looked embarrassed, but Arnie leveled his gaze at Lexa's. In a proud deep voice he said, "Berdie and I are gettin' married."

Tipping her head to one side, Lexa's eyes brimmed with tears. She smiled through a haze of happiness and hugged her two friends. "I'm so happy for you."

After eyeing the look the two women shared, Arnie muttered something about catching up with Ramsey and telling him his news. He planted a kiss on Berdie's cheek and quietly walked from the room. Berdie turned her back on Lexa and busily bustled about her cook room.

"How long have you known, Berdie?"

Without looking, Berdie said, "He asked me just now."

"That's wonderful, but it's not what I meant."

Finally Berdie looked at her. "How long have I known what, child?"

"How long have you known that Callie is my daughter?"

Berdie O'Toole was rarely at a loss for words. But Lexa knew she was stalling for time as she took Lexa's hand and led her to the old table where she plopped down in one of the chairs.

Berdie didn't speak, and Lexa said, "I didn't understand why Winnona looked over her shoulder each time I saw her in a vision. It was as if she *knew* I was watching her. It didn't make any sense. Until now. She knew I was watching because she knew about me, didn't she? That's why she took every last item Callie ever touched. It was because Winnona was afraid I'd be able to *see* them if she left anything behind. She knew Callie was my daughter."

Berdie sputtered, "I told you that man was keeping secrets."

"How long have you known, Berdie?"

"Not that long, child. I've known since the day you and Cade left for the mountains. There was just something in that man's eyes, secrets I didn't understand. I knew there was somethin' he wasn't telling us, but I didn't know what it was until I looked at those pictures of his li'l girl. Of *your* li'l girl. Y'see, Lexa, she has your eyes."

Berdie took an old-fashioned handkerchief from her apron pocket and dabbed at her eyes. Lexa reached out a hand to touch her friend's arm and said, "You're quite a woman, Berdette O'Toole."

Berdie made her own special sound before saying, "Yer the second person to tell me that just this afternoon."

Lexa smiled through her own tears. "What should I do, Berdie?"

"What does your heart tell ya to do?"

She remembered Cade's saying nearly the same thing. It had been little over a week ago, the night before they'd found Callie. They'd been waiting for morning to come, waiting for the dawn of another day. Cade had placed his hand over her heart, and Lexa knew she'd never forget what he'd said.

Maybe you're looking for your memories in the wrong place. Maybe you should stop searching your mind and look in your heart, instead, where memories never truly fade.

She'd told him she couldn't look into her heart. It only made her sad. She looked into her heart now. Instead of sadness, she found it brimming with love.

In a voice shaking with emotion, Lexa said, "I can't remember him in my mind, Berdie, but in my heart, I do." After a moment, she continued, "There are still things I don't understand. From the first moment he spoke about his wife, I knew he'd loved her, loved her still. But if Cade loved me, why did he leave me after my surgery?"

"I don't know all the answers, child. But he didn't leave you. You left him."

"Why?"

"Cade told me you'd watched your mama die. Evidently it had been a slow painful illness that took her. He said it was traumatic for both you and your mama, and you wouldn't let your brand-new baby suffer that way. You wanted him to promise, if you lived through that surgery but had been damaged in any way, to let you go. He wouldn't promise, so you left. I think you intended to go back to him. I think that's what those dried flowers you've kept symbolized. But then you couldn't remember him...."

Lexa thought about what Berdie told her. "All along, he felt guilty because he didn't promise to let me go. He's the most honorable man I've ever met."

"If it ain't too late for a set-in-her-ways woman like myself to find happiness," Birdie insisted, "it ain't too late for a young one like you."

Blinded by her tears, Lexa hugged her friend. "You've been like a mother to me."

"I'm gonna miss you, child."

"I'll be back, Berdie. Soon, if I'm right about the look in Arnie's eyes. I don't think that man is going to want to wait long to marry you."

"Merciful heavens! I hope not! I'd say it's about time we both found a little happiness, don't you? How soon do ya plan to leave?"

Lexa went still. "I don't even know exactly where Cade lives."

Berdie bustled away to a drawer and came back flapping a small piece of paper. "This is the check your Yankee left in his room before he left. Ain't it a coincidence I ain't cashed it yet? Look here, missy, it has his address and phone number, too."

Lexa took the check from Berdie's bony hands. Reading the address through her tears wasn't easy. Neither was laughing and crying at the same time.

Chapter 11

It was nearly one o'clock in the afternoon by the time Lexa turned the last corner. No wonder Cade loved it here. Apple trees lined the road on the right, peach trees on the left. According to the teenager behind the counter in the convenience store where she'd stopped for directions fifteen minutes ago, she was almost there.

Almost home.

She swallowed hard against the uncertainties that made her hands tremble on the steering wheel. What if she was wrong? What if what she'd read in Cade's eyes wasn't love, after all?

Apple trees gave way to a large lawn. Tiny purple flowers grew wild near the road and along a sidewalk leading to a lovely white house. She pulled into the driveway, her eyes immediately searching for Cade.

The breeze carried laughter through her open window, and she caught a movement near a tree out back. Her heart expanded at the sight of the tall dark-haired man whose back was to her. She stepped around her car and started toward him and the little girl on the swing.

"Grandpop, look who's here."

The man turned, and Lexa saw it wasn't Cade, after all, but an older man who bore a striking resemblance to his son. Tilting her head, she smiled at him across the lawn. "Hello, Pop."

Walt Sullivan took several long strides toward Lexa, then stopped short. "You recognize me?" he asked.

"I'd know you anywhere," she answered.

"Then you remember me?"

Lexa touched two fingers to her head and said, "Not here." Moving her hand to her heart, she murmured, "But here, I remember."

He made short work of the remaining distance separating them and swooped her right off her feet. "Oh, Lexi, it's so good to see you!"

Finding her feet, she said, "Where's Cade, Pop?"

"He took the truck through the lane to the south orchards. Should be back any time."

She turned her attention to the little girl silently watching from the tree swing. Serious gray eyes so like her own gazed back at her. "Hello, Callie."

The child scrambled to the ground. Suddenly shy, she clung to her grandfather's pant leg. Lexa wanted to grab her up and hug her the way Cade had, but waited for a sign that her daughter was ready. "Do you remember me?"

Carolina Joy Sullivan nodded solemnly, but her words were matter-of-fact. "'Course I do. You're my mommy. The one in the mountain and in all the pictures."

All shyness forgotten, Callie laughed, her impish eyes glowing. As Lexa went down on her knees and reached out her hand, the girl said, "Daddy told me I could have a pony for my birthday. I told him I wanted you to come home."

Lexa wrapped her arms around her child. "What did Daddy say?"

"He said we'd have to wait and see." It was Walt who answered.

With Callie in her arms, Lexa stood, and turned to Cade's father. "And the pony?"

Callie answered, "I named her Bunny. Wanna come see her?"

Lexa tipped her head back and laughed, and the emptiness in her heart began to disappear. "Oh, Callie. Why did you name your pony Bunny?"

"Because Daddy said that's what your pony's name was. You know, the one in the picture."

"What picture?" she asked Pop.

"Cade got back most of everything Winnona took. All Callie's clothes and toys, all the photo albums. And Carolina here's been pouring over everything like one of her curious kittens. Come on, we'll show you."

Lexa cast another look toward the lane leading south, where Pop had said Cade had gone. "He'll come back, Lexi, don't you worry. Knew something was up when he shaved the first day back. He's been waiting for you, all right. We all have."

Cade didn't recognize the car in the driveway. It had North Carolina plates, and the sticker on the trunk said Roanoke Island. His heart beat like a drum on the warpath, then, as he saw the woman standing on the porch, seemed to stop altogether.

Lexa. She'd worn her flowered dress, the one that made her look infinitely Southern, infinitely feminine. He swallowed hard, suddenly afraid to hope too much, suddenly afraid not to.

"Look, Daddy!" Callie called. "It's Mommy!"

Cade wasn't quite sure how he managed to climb out of

the truck and walk the twenty yards or so to the porch. "Callie, honey, she isn't—"

"It's all right, Cade," Lexa said. "She knows the truth. And so do I."

"Carolina," Pop sputtered. "Why don't you and I go inside and sample those half-moon pies we made this morning?"

"Do I hafta?" Callie asked, casting her big gray eyes to her grandpop.

"Just for a little while, darlin'," Pop answered. "Mommy and Daddy need a little time alone." With that, the older Sullivan took his granddaughter's small hand, winked at Lexa, grinned from ear to ear at Cade and disappeared into the house.

Cade heard them go, but his gaze was trained on Lexa. God, she was beautiful. When he'd first seen her standing on this porch with Pop and Callie he thought he'd died and gone to heaven. The breeze caught her hair, lifting it off her shoulders and settling it back again the way he'd have liked to.

"You look wonderful."

"So do you."

"You're a long way from Roanoke Island."

She took a step toward him and gave him a smile that sneaked into his heart and spread through him like warm molasses. She reached for his left hand and, raising it palm side up, said, "Your scrapes have healed. And so have Callie's."

He nodded and waited for her to continue. He didn't know how much to say, didn't know why she'd come.

"My power's gone."

He searched her eyes, but was afraid to trust what he saw. "I'm sorry, Lexa. I know how much it meant to you."

"I'm not sorry, Cade. My power was a gift, a gift I had for nearly four years. But losing it was an even greater gift.

It squeezed from my chest and evaporated into thin air when we were up on the mountain. When I looked into Callie's eyes and when I heard her voice, I knew. The reason I'd been given that power was to save our daughter's life. And the reason it disappeared was so I could live mine.''

Cade's eyes brimmed with moisture, and he squeezed them shut to bring them back into focus. She hadn't released his hand. Without releasing his gaze, either, she moved her fingers across his palm, over his thumb, to his first finger, then the second. She touched him with an inborn gentleness and a steady sense of purpose, her fingers curling around his third finger, covering his wedding band.

"Why do you still wear your wedding ring, Cade?"

She'd never seen his expression more serious, nor heard his voice quake with so much emotion. "I wear my ring because you placed it on my finger and because we made a solemn vow.''

Lexa remained silent, waiting for what he was about to say. "And because I've never stopped loving you.''

Up on the mountain he'd told her she was more beautiful than any other woman he'd ever known. Lexa felt beautiful now. And it had nothing to do with her dress and her hair. It had to do with who she used to be and who she was now. It had to do with the look in Cade's eyes, the look that was making her as warm as the April sun shining above.

"Your eyes have been full of promises, Cade. Promises you've kept for four long years.''

He stepped a little closer, but she still didn't release his left hand. "I didn't do what you asked, Lexa.''

"What didn't you do?" she said, softly kneading his finger above his wedding band.

"I never filed those divorce papers. We're still husband and wife.''

"I love you," she murmured. "That's why I felt so

empty. Because I had so much love in my heart but no one to give it to."

She was suddenly in his arms, holding him, loving him like she'd never loved him before. "I did what you said," she whispered. "I stopped searching my mind for my memories and looked in my heart. And in my heart, I found you, right where you've been all along."

Cade's mouth found hers, and Lexa gave herself up to the feelings spiraling through her. In his kiss she found passion and love, in his arms yesterday's promises. She opened her eyes when the kiss ended, and in his gaze she found tomorrow's.

Callie was suddenly at their knees, tugging them toward the door. "Come inside, Mommy, and see my pictures." She reached for her mother's hand and for her father's, and led them inside.

A flash momentarily blinded them, and Pop mused, "Great shot. I have a feeling I'm going to be using this camera a lot from now on."

In the living room, Lexa sat on the sofa, Callie immediately crawling onto her lap. Cade lowered himself to the floor, where they opened the first photo album. The three of them browsed through Lexa's past, through the photographs he'd saved, those from her childhood, of her mother and her horse named Bunny. She looked at each photo, every one of them a gift. From each picture she received a piece of her past.

Callie was fascinated with the photographs of their wedding. Lexa couldn't help the tears that wound their way down her face as she gazed at the pictures of her holding her newborn daughter. With the pads of his fingers, Cade wiped them away.

"Welcome home," he murmured.

She wrapped her arms more tightly around their child and gazed down into her husband's eyes.

"Why are you crying, Mommy?"

Lexa smiled through her tears, smiled for her beautiful daughter. "Because I've missed you so much. And it feels so good to hold you again after all this time. And because I'm so, so happy." With that, instead of emptiness in Lexa's heart, she felt only love.

"Look up here!" Three heads turned to the other side of the room, and Pop snapped another picture. Callie clapped her hands, and Cade shook his head.

The tears in Lexa's eyes had intensified the circles of light she saw from the flash. She smoothed a lock of baby-fine hair from Callie's forehead with one hand and touched her husband's face with the other.

Cade covered her hand with his own, and Pop snapped another picture. Callie chattered on, and Lexa knew another memory had just been added to her collection. And what a wonderful collection it would be, filled with new memories of laughter and joy, living and loving, memories she'd store in her heart forever.

* * * * *

Dear Reader,

Do you know what I really like about writing romances? I get
to fix things—people, broken hearts, unhappy relationships,
loneliness. All the things that life is made of. If I want to, I
can even fix a rainy day. Of course, the journey to a happy
ending is always a bumpy one, but ultimately, I get there, and
along the way, I get to feel all the joys and the sorrows and
everything in between. But the best part of all is that I get
to take *you*—the reader—with me. I must confess that the
entire process makes me as happy as a preschooler with a
brand-new toy on "Show and Tell" day. Which is why I'm so
pleased that *Patrick Gallagher's Widow* is back.

Jenna Gallagher and Johnson Garth are two people who
really need "fixing." Jenna has lost all her expectations of ever
finding happiness again, and Garth—well, Garth never had
any in the first place. And what an unlikely pair they are. She
is the widow of a respected, third-generation police officer
killed in the line of duty. He is the intense loner and rogue
cop who never quite fit into the highly selective brotherhood
of policemen. But Detective Garth lives and breathes "the
job," and every instinct he has tells him that something is
not quite right about Patrick Gallagher, regardless of the halo
martyrdom has given him. He is certain that the widow is the
key, and the fact that his fellow officers are closing rank to
keep him away from her makes him all the more determined.

Neither Jenna nor Garth is looking for love, but *I* am, and
you are cordially invited to come along with me and
participate in the search. I do hope you'll enjoy it.

My very best always,

Cheryl Reavis

PATRICK GALLAGHER'S WIDOW
by Cheryl Reavis

The strong emotions and engaging plot of
PATRICK GALLAGHER'S WIDOW demonstrate
why the *Silhouette Special Edition* series is so loved.
This line features deeply moving, compelling novels
about true-to-life characters experiencing romantic
relationships as they discover hearth and home.
And in each of the six new *Silhouette Special Edition*
titles every month readers are guaranteed
a *very* happy ending!

To Leslie Kazanjian,
for helping me fly

Chapter 1

*T*he widow Gallagher wanted to dance.

Johnson Garth stood on the other side of the room and watched her, moving whenever someone in the crowd got in his way so he could keep her in view. He suspected that she simply liked the music—Bob Seger and The Silver Bullet Band's rendition of "Old Time Rock and Roll"—and that there was nothing of the "merry widow" about her. If anything, she was trying *not* to respond to the hard, driving beat, and she seemed to be listening intently to the young woman talking to her, oblivious to the partying, off-duty police personnel around her. But he knew that she secretly had one toe tapping, regardless of her apparent attentiveness.

The music was loud, and his head pounded with the bass notes because he'd had too much squad room coffee and too little sleep. The house was already jammed with invited and uninvited guests, and the doorbell kept ringing with late arrivals. All the downstairs rooms were filled with the boisterous laughter and double entendres of wet law enforcement people who had braved the rain to get here. The air hung heavy with cigarette smoke, and past it he could smell wet leather and the aroma of lasagna, pan after pan of it being heated up in the kitchen.

Allegedly, he had come tonight because the party was for some patrolman who'd just made detective and been transferred into the precinct. Garth was one of the few in the Detective Squad without a partner. He liked it that way, but he always seemed to get stuck with the new ones when they first came in—which was surprising to him, considering that he was usually in hot water with the lieutenant for making somewhat liberal interpretations of the *Patrol Guide*. It was true that he did want to see the new man up close. He hated unknowns, and if he had to have a partner, he preferred somebody who was a quick learner, somebody he could depend on to keep his eyes open and his mouth shut. He had no intention of being paired with a dumb kid who thought everything had to be done exactly by the book and who would get on his nerves or get him killed, or both.

But the reason he'd come tonight was Jenna Gallagher. He thought that the new detective must be well connected to get the Gallagher woman out and about. Garth had done the legwork on the investigation of Patrick Gallagher's murder, because he knew the streets and because he had reliable contacts. But he hadn't been able to talk to Mrs. Gallagher, even in an official capacity. The word had come down from the top that Patrolman Gallagher's widow was not to be bothered. All inquiries were to be made through her brother-in-law, Detective Sergeant Hugh Gallagher—which was a joke. Garth didn't trust Hugh to tell him the right time of day, much less something he needed in a murder investigation.

Garth didn't really know Jenna. He hadn't seen her in almost a year, and that had been at Patrick's funeral. He was willing to admit that perhaps she shouldn't have been "bothered" then. He remembered what she'd been like. Pale. Too dazed by the horror of her husband's death to weep, even for the television cameras that dogged her every step.

But he had come to believe that there had been no reason for her to be widowed so young—unless Patrick Gallagher, on this one occasion, had been a fool. The circumstances of Gallagher's death still puzzled him. He had marked Gallagher down as a good cop—not as good a cop as his being killed in the line of duty had made him, but a more than adequate third-generation member of New York's finest, one with a good deal more sense than he'd evidently shown on the day he was killed. Supposedly Gallagher had walked up to a teenage boy who was behaving suspiciously in Central Park. He hadn't bothered to wait for his partner or even to let the man know what he was doing; he hadn't drawn his service revolver—because, his fellow officers surmised, he was Patrick Gallagher, and Patrick Gallagher *cared*. It was true that Gallagher's caring for his fellow man was legendary—particularly now that he was dead—but he had apparently assumed that anyone he encountered would know that, and that colossal stupidity had cost him his life.

Except that Patrick Gallagher wasn't stupid. There was a reason for his behavior that day; there was *always* a reason for people doing what they did. It didn't matter to Garth that the alleged perpetrator had been caught. It didn't matter to him that the case was closed, that Internal Affairs and the police commissioner and Patrick's brother, Hugh, were all satisfied that justice had been done. Garth wasn't satisfied. He didn't necessarily think that Gallagher had knowingly gotten himself into something dirty—it didn't matter now, anyway. It was just that Garth didn't like loose ends, particularly if there was a dead cop on the end of one of them. What he did like was poking his nose into things that made people nervous; more often than not, you came up with answers that way. And in this particular instance, the person who was most nervous was Patrick's brother, Hugh.

Garth didn't like Hugh Gallagher, and the feeling was mutual. Even in the academy they hadn't liked each other. Hugh had moved up fast, making detective long before Garth had, and he had the arrogance that came from belonging to a long line of honored New York policemen. Garth understood Hugh's air of superiority; he was arrogant himself. But his own arrogance had been fostered by the early disadvantages of being poor and fatherless and having a mother who refused to acknowledge the reality of either, not from belonging to an established law enforcement family and, therefore, knowing all the right moves in the unspoken etiquette of the brotherhood in blue. Garth had never really belonged to anything, and he had envied Hugh his inherited expertise in their chosen profession. Hugh had an easy acceptance of the inner workings of "The Job" that often left Garth frustrated and angry. Garth had always been outspoken. He said what he meant and he meant what he said, and somehow that never seemed to work with the police hierarchy. One had to play the game of favors done and paybacks, a game whose existence Garth acknowledged but whose unwritten rules left him more than a little irritated, because he hated having to keep up with who owed whom what.

But there was more than just professional jealousy on his part when it came to Hugh Gallagher. There was a certain wariness between them now—not his, but Hugh's. He worried Hugh. He had ever since Patrick had been killed and he had caught the case. He still worried him, and with a little luck, he'd find out why. That was where the widow Gallagher came in. It was time to bother her.

Garth worked his way through the crowd to get closer to Jenna. She was a pretty woman, he thought. He liked her hair—not quite red and not quite blond, and long and curly and a bit disheveled, as if she'd just gotten out of bed. When he'd seen her at the funeral, she'd been wearing black. The dress she had on tonight was a pale pink. Something soft and clinging, outlining her breasts and the swell of her hips. It was definitely an improvement. She was a pretty woman, he thought again, and he liked pretty women, particularly when they might have information he needed. It made a generally dull and routine part of The Job a little more enjoyable, and he was looking forward to this encounter.

Jenna Gallagher abruptly stopped talking, looking deliberately at the man who stood staring at her from the other side of the room. He'd been looking ever since he arrived, and there was nothing subtle about it. He held her eyes now, refusing to look away simply because she'd caught him doing whatever it was he was doing. In the first few months after Patrick died, she had, by necessity, grown accustomed to being looked at. It was one of the few things that had penetrated her grief. She hadn't been able to go anywhere people knew her without feeling their stares. Some of the looks were kind, sympathetic; most were filled with a kind of morbid curiosity, the same kind of expressions she assumed people wore when they gawked at the scene of an accident.

This man's was neither. His look was filled with determination and frank sexual interest, and in spite of herself, she felt compelled to look back. She assumed he was a cop. He looked like a cop, one of the rogue detectives who did undercover work in Narcotics and who had to dress the part. He wasn't wearing a suit or a tie. He had on jeans. And a white shirt and a zippered jacket. He stood with his hands jammed in the pockets, and he needed a haircut and a shave, and probably a bath.

But he didn't participate in the braggadocio that was so

evident in the room. He was very quiet, the way Patrick had always been quiet, standing apart, tolerating the cockiness that some cops assumed as if it were as much a part of The Job as their service revolvers and their shields. Lord, how the loud and often vulgar machismo of policemen had embarrassed her when she'd first married Patrick. She had been young and abruptly thrust into this strange, always potentially violent world of big-city law enforcement, and she'd spent nearly the first year of her marriage being essentially mortified. She had grown up in a small town on the Susquehanna River, and nothing in her staunch, middle-class upbringing had prepared her for the raucousness of people who had to put their lives on the line every day. Except Patrick. Gentle, understanding, teasing Patrick.

She smiled, remembering, then abruptly suppressed it and looked away. It was good that she could think of Patrick without such pain now, but she didn't want the man on the other side of the room to think the smile was for him.

"Debbie, who is that?" she asked the young woman with her. Debbie was barely five feet tall and had to stand on tiptoe to see.

"Oh, no!" she said immediately. "Why didn't you tell me he was here?"

"Because I don't know who he is."

"Johnson Garth," Debbie said worriedly.

Ah, Jenna thought, recognizing the name. So that was the notorious Detective Garth. She had never met him, but she had certainly heard of him. He had caused a good deal of comment in the Gallagher family a few years ago when he had some kind of public disagreement with Hugh. Garth had subsequently punched him in the nose, and not only had he done it while they were both on duty, but he hadn't been disciplined for it. Or if he *had* been disciplined, the punishment hadn't been harsh enough to satisfy the Gallaghers.

"What is he doing here?" Debbie said, obviously still

worrying. "He never comes to these things—oh, my Lord, you don't think he's after Hugh again, do you?"

"I doubt he was 'after' Hugh the first time." Hugh wasn't the most tactful man in the world.

"Oh, my Lord! He's coming this way! What should I say to him? Jenna, don't go!"

But Jenna had every intention of going—not because she had the "hostess jitters" like Debbie, but because she suddenly didn't want to encounter this man. She found his overt interest disturbing. If she stayed, she had the overwhelming feeling that she would have to deal with him on a man-to-woman basis. There would be no quiet respect for her bereavement on his part, and no hiding behind widow's weeds on hers. She wasn't prepared to deal with that, not because she was still grieving, but perhaps because she wasn't.

Yet she looked into his eyes as he approached, sad eyes, compelling eyes. She felt awkward and uncertain. She shouldn't have smiled the way she had. He must think she'd sent him some kind of invitation.

She was being ridiculous. He was someone who knew Patrick. He'd offer his condolences, and that would be the end of it.

But he had to cross Hugh's path to get to her, and when he did, Hugh grabbed him roughly by the arm. Beside her, Debbie gave a high-pitched squeak of protest, reminding Jenna of a traumatized mouse.

Garth heard the peculiar noise the young woman with Jenna Gallagher made, but he looked around into Hugh Gallagher's eyes.

"Stay away from Jenna," Hugh said, his grip tightening on Garth's arm. Garth looked down at the offending hand, then back into Hugh's eyes. "Jenna who?" he said lightly.

"Listen, you son of a—"

"Excuse me, gentlemen!"

They both looked around. Jenna stepped closer. "I need to borrow Detective Garth a minute, Hugh," she said. "The two of you will have to talk shop later."

She linked her arm through Garth's, and he had the distinct impression that she'd had to dig deep to find the courage to do it. She pulled him away with her through the crowd as if it were a perfectly natural thing she did all the time. It wasn't that he minded going. She was a better-than-average-looking woman, and he wanted to ask her a few questions—he'd go anywhere with her. It was just that he didn't understand. She let go of his arm almost immediately, but he still followed her. The music abruptly changed to something slow and mellow and '50s. The Diamonds, his brain identified automatically, because, like Bob Seger and his Silver Bullets, he, too, liked the old-time rock and roll, and he knew most of the titles and the groups by heart.

"Where are we going?" he asked.

"Nowhere," she said over her shoulder. "I've done my good deed."

"What good deed is that?" he persisted, trying to catch up with her.

She kept going, and she didn't answer him.

"Mrs. Gallagher," he called, because there was no need to pretend that he didn't know who she was. "Would you like to dance?" It was a long shot, but it certainly got her attention.

She turned around, her expression, if he had had to describe it, completely incredulous. "What I would like, Detective Garth, is for you to behave."

It became clear to him then that incredulity must be catching. "Behave? Me?"

"Yes, you."

"What have *I* done?"

He thought Hugh was the one she should talk to about behaving, but he didn't say so. He looked over his shoulder, expecting the man to be coming after them. But Hugh was standing in the same spot—trying to remove himself from the clutches of some woman with big breasts who wanted him to dance. She was all over him, and she kept calling him "Hughie." Garth smiled. If Hugh's wife was here, that little scene had the potential for requiring a very lengthy explanation on Hugh's part.

"Driven your hostess to tears, for one thing."

"My hostess?" He bumped into an overweight patrolman with a huge plate of lasagna.

"Watch it, Garth! Can't you see I'm trying to feed my face here?"

"Yeah, Norm, I can see that. Why don't you let that 'face' of yours take a break? Leave some for the rest of us, will you? What hostess?" he added to Jenna Gallagher. He was beginning to feel a little desperate, because he'd gotten a real opportunity here, and she had clearly finished with him.

She stopped walking—or trying to. They were in a bottleneck of people trying to balance plates of lasagna and hold on to their beers.

"Debbie Carver," she explained patiently. "The wife of the new detective, Alden Carver. The person who is giving this party?"

"Never heard of her," he said in all truthfulness. "So why is she in tears?"

"Because you were going to punch Hugh in the nose. Again."

"No, I wasn't—at least I don't think I was. You didn't give me time to find out. So why should she care if I punch your brother in law?"

"Under the circumstances, the explanation was rather rushed, but I gather that her husband admires you. If you punched Hugh, he'd be on your side. He's got a wife, and he can't afford to ruin his career by trying to help you out when he's only been a detective for three days."

"You think helping me out would ruin his career?"

"Yes," she said evenly, and he smiled.

He rubbed his hand over the stubble on his chin, thinking that he probably should have shaved. "So would you like to dance?"

She looked into his eyes. "You don't even know who he is, do you?"

"Who?"

"Detective Carver!" she said in exasperation.

He gave a small shrug. "No. I don't."

She pressed her lips together, and she took him by the arm again, pulling him along with her toward the kitchen. "He's in there," she said, pointing to a fresh-faced, preppie-looking young man with a makeshift towel-apron around his waist. He was taking yet another pan of lasagna from the oven, and he paused long enough to kiss the young woman Jenna had been talking to earlier.

Garth glanced at Jenna Gallagher. "The kid admires me, huh? What do you know about that?"

He was being facetious, and she knew it—but she wasn't going to put up with it.

"Do you want to be introduced?"

He looked back at the kid with the towel around his waist. He didn't want to annoy Jenna Gallagher; he wanted to talk to her. "What's his name again? Carver?"

"Yes. His wife is—"

"Debbie," he supplied. "Debbie and—" He looked to her for help.

"Alden."

"*Alden?*"

"Skip—to his friends," Jenna added pointedly.

He looked back at Alden "Skip" Carver. He was in the kid's house, and he intended to eat his lasagna and drink his beer, and he wanted to pacify Jenna Gallagher. Those were good enough reasons to walk over there and wish him well.

But someone called Jenna away, and he stared after her, fighting down the urge to follow her. Well, what the hell, he thought. He had his toe in the door, and the few brownie points he might earn by congratulating the Carver kid wouldn't hurt. Apparently Jenna Gallagher was big on that kind of thing—*behaving*.

A couple danced slow and close just inside the kitchen doorway. He pushed his way farther into the room. He should come to parties more often, he decided; otherwise he was never going to get used to seeing two uniformed police officers dancing together, even if one of them *was* a woman.

He sighed and turned his attention to Skip Carver, who was shoveling lasagna into a line of heavy-duty paper plates on the counter.

"Nice going, Carver," he said to make the new detective look up. "Congratulations." He extended his hand, and Alden Carver was so taken aback that he nearly stuck the lasagna-covered spatula into it.

"Garth! I mean Detective Garth!" he said, trying to recover. He laughed and shifted the spatula to his other hand. "Debbie! Debbie, come here! This is Detective Johnson Garth—I told you about him—this is my wife Debbie, sir." He shook Garth's hand vigorously.

It was clear from the look on Debbie Carver's face that her husband had indeed told her about him. It was also clear that she'd been crying and might, Garth thought, start again with very little provocation. "Garth," he said to her, still trying to get his hand away from her husband. "Just call me Garth. Everybody does. Nice party," he added.

"Is it?" she said worriedly, and he couldn't decide whether she didn't believe him or didn't believe the fact that he, of all people, the potential puncher of noses, would actually extend her a compliment.

He smiled. "Yes. It is. It's a good way to get to know the people your husband will be working with." It was a good way, but he wasn't so sure it was a good idea. The police brotherhood in this precinct was very closed, and sometimes it didn't sit well for a young cop to try too hard to fit in.

But wide-eyed little Debbie Carver didn't have to know that. Everybody seemed to be having a good time, and the lasagna certainly smelled good.

"I hear you might be Skip's partner," Debbie said.

"Well, who knows? Nobody knows what the brass is going to do until they do it."

Impulsively she gave him a hug. "Don't be mad because I sent Jenna after you," she whispered. "Please. And don't tell Skip," she added sotto voce.

"No, hey," he said, laughing because she'd taken him by surprise. "Mrs. Carver, I won't."

"What's going on?" Skip asked, looking up from the lasagna to glance from one of them to the other.

"Nothing, kid," Garth answered. "Keep going with the lasagna. You got a lot of hungry people out there." He smiled at Debbie and moved out of the way of another wave of starving guests. To his surprise, Jenna was standing just inside the kitchen doorway. Nice body, he thought as he approached her. Nice eyes. Blue eyes. He liked looking into her blue eyes. And he liked that pink dress.

Now, if she just stayed put.

She didn't run off again. She stood by the doorway, watching him, as if she were waiting for him to get to her.

"That was very kind," she began when he was close enough to hear her. "Talking to Debbie—"

"It wasn't *kind*," he interrupted almost harshly, because, for some reason he couldn't have explained, he didn't want her thinking he was something he was not—not when he was about to put everything he had into getting whatever information he could out of her about Patrick and Hugh. In his life, in his work, he'd been called a lot of things, but rarely *kind*.

They stood there in the crowded kitchen, her eyes probing his, until, unsettled by the assessment he felt she was making, he suddenly smiled.

"So," he said, bending low so she could hear him, "do you want to dance or not?" He realized immediately that under the din of conversation and laughter the music had stopped.

A smile worked at the corners of her mouth. "Actually, Detective Garth, I'd rather eat. If you'll excuse me—" She put her hand lightly on his arm to get by, but he didn't move out of the way.

"I'll get it for you," he said. "Wait right here."

He didn't give her a chance to protest, plunging back through the crowd toward Skip and Debbie. He was counting on the fact that Jenna Gallagher was probably too polite to walk away.

"Skip!" he yelled over the heads of the people in front of him—because he was tall enough to do it, and if he was going to be somebody's hero, he might as well get some benefit from it. "Two!" He held up two fingers in case the kid had trouble hearing him.

"You got it, sir!"

Skip Carver passed him two well-laden plates and two plastic forks wrapped in yellow paper napkins.

"Skip!" Garth called again. "Don't call me sir!"

Carver grinned and saluted with the lasagna spatula.

Garth made his way back toward where Jenna had been standing, carrying the plates of lasagna high over his head. "Coming through," he said to the people in his way, but he didn't see Jenna anywhere.

Damn, he thought.

The music was playing again—The Drifters. "This Magic Moment." There was nothing magic about his being left holding two plates of lasagna.

Someone was poking him in the shoulder. "What!" he snapped.

"That way, Garth," a patrolman said, pointing across the living room. Jenna Gallagher stood in the foyer, motioning for him to come there.

Well, what do you know, he thought. Hugh was definitely not going to like this.

He made his way there without difficulty.

"I found a place to sit," Jenna said, taking one of the plates.

"I'll get the beer."

"No, I've got it," she said, leading the way.

Damn, he thought again.

The place she'd found was halfway up the stairs to the second story of the narrow house. He had to stand back for a moment to let some people come down the steps, one of them Rosie Madden, his partner for a time when she'd first made detective. He'd found her tough and smart and as outspoken as he was himself—which worried him now. God only knew what she'd say if she picked up on the fact that he was about to eat lasagna in the dark with Jenna Gallagher. Rosie had her hair in as many long braids as her head would hold, and as she passed by, she lifted up one of them and waggled it at him the way Oliver Hardy would have waggled his tie. Her eyes cut to the two plates of lasagna he was holding, and then to the widow Gallagher.

"You devil, you" was all she said, and thankfully that was in a whisper, which Jenna seemed not to hear.

Jenna sat down on the stairs. He took a step higher than hers so they wouldn't entirely block the way and so he could look at her without difficulty. He had to be able to see her so he'd know the right time to ask what he wanted to ask.

"Here you go," he said, giving her one of the wrapped forks from out of his shirt pocket. She handed him a beer in exchange.

He stared at her shamelessly, trying to decide how he was going to handle this. Sitting in the dim light on the stairs, she had become very quiet suddenly, as if she'd had to put on a front when she was out there in the middle of everything, but now that she was more or less out of sight, she was letting her guard down.

No more cheerful Mrs. Gallagher, he noted.

He kept watching her. She wasn't eating, but she didn't want to talk, either. Her job, evidently, was keeping the peace, one she'd accepted, albeit reluctantly.

She looked down at the people milling around below them. From time to time she smiled a bit at some overheard remark, because they had a bird's-eye view of all the social interactions going on—the budding relationships, the illicit assignations, the police wives like little Debbie Carver trying to keep things going smoothly for the sake of their husbands.

But he had to get the ball rolling.

"Nice song," he said when The Drifters' music ended.

"Yes," she said. Period.

Great, he thought. She was nothing if not succinct. He was going to have to try thinking of this as sitting in the dark with a pretty woman instead of interrogating a witness. Build your rapport, Garth. Then...

"The Drifters," he offered in an effort at rapport-building. "They don't have good groups like The Drifters anymore."

She looked at him quizzically. He thought that she wasn't dumb by a long shot, and he'd do well to remember that.

"No," she said, looking down at her plate and worrying

a chunk of lasagna with her fork. "You like the oldies, then," she added quietly, carefully, as if her small response might be misconstrued on his part. What could he think from a halfhearted question like that? That she was being disrespectful to Patrick's memory? Disloyal to Hugh?

"Yeah, I like them," he said. "They don't remind me of anything."

She looked at him again—as if she considered that a peculiar reason for liking a certain kind of music but wouldn't say so.

"So what kind of music do you like?" he asked, because she'd given him an opening.

"Jazz."

"Yeah? That random...noodling stuff with no beginning or middle or end, or the quiet kind that makes you want to sit in the dark and chain smoke and feel sorry for yourself?"

"Both," she said. "But I've never thought of it quite like that."

"And you like Bob Seger and The Silver Bullet Band," he said, because he wanted her to think he'd noticed something specific about her—which he had.

"Yes," she said, obviously surprised.

"I thought so."

She smiled. She had a nice smile. Very natural. Warm. Real.

"Why?" she asked.

"I just did." He took a few bites of lasagna, wondering how long Hugh was going to let him get away with this. Hugh had spotted them sitting on the stairs, but so far he was limiting himself to killer looks. If Jenna noticed him at all, it didn't show. "This is good lasagna," he suggested, getting on with the rapport-building.

"Thank you," she said, smiling again.

"You made this?"

"Most of it. Debbie and I worked all day getting it ready."

"You should open a restaurant." It wasn't brilliant, but it was the best he could do—Hugh was coming closer. Jenna saw him, and an expression passed over her face he couldn't identify.

"Are you okay?" he asked.

"Yes, I'm fine."

"Are you worried about Hugh?"

She looked at him. "Are you?" she countered.

"No. I never worry about Hugh."

"Neither do I," she said. He believed her, but that stressed look was still there.

"Is this the first party you've been to since Patrick died?" he asked bluntly.

"I...yes. I've been out to dinner with friends, things like that. But this is the first time I—" She broke off and looked away again, sighing heavily. "I never liked these parties much even before Patrick died, but I..." She trailed off, and he didn't press it.

"You don't have to stay if you don't want to. If you want to go home, I'll take you."

"I wasn't trying to pick you up, Detective."

"I didn't think you were, Mrs. Gallagher." He grinned. "Even if you did drag me all around the ground floor here."

She laughed softly.

Bingo, he thought. Instant rapport.

"So tell me about...Skip Carver," he said. He wanted to ask about Patrick, about his state of mind before he'd been killed, but he suddenly found that he also wanted to be tactful. The truth of it was that he liked sitting here with her on the dark stairs, and it wasn't just because it was creating a buzz in the room. He could smell her fragrance. The scent was soft and womanly—like she was. Citrus, he thought. No, lavender, maybe.

"You're his hero," she said, and he laughed.

"The kid is hard up for heroes. Did Patrick know him?"

"Patrick? No, I don't think so."

"Hugh?"

"I couldn't say."

"Anything else?"

"Anything else?" she repeated, clearly puzzled.

He took a bite of lasagna. "About the Carver kid," he said, gesturing with his fork.

She looked at him thoughtfully. "His mother didn't want him to be a cop."

"Yeah, well, I can relate to that. *My* mother took to her bed for a week—until I told her I might be able to save some rich woman's life if I was one of New York's finest."

"I don't understand."

"See, the Garths don't have much, Mrs. Gallagher. Never have had. Never will. My mother lives in this fantasy from a '40s movie where her poor but handsome son will marry 'up' and change both our lives. She'd like me to marry somebody from the Upper East Side with blue blood and a lot of bucks. Or if I can't do that, somebody without blue blood with a lot of bucks."

"I'm sorry," she said.

He made a gesture of dismissal. "Don't be sorry, Mrs. Gallagher. It's not that bad. I made Hazel sound like some kind of gold digger. She isn't. She's eccentric as hell, but she's a good woman who's worked hard all her life. We all got to have our dreams, you know?"

He looked into her eyes. She did know, but she wasn't going to admit it to him.

"Your mother—Hazel—is she still working?"

"Oh, yeah. She's a waitress in this hole-in-the-wall restaurant in Brooklyn. The Humoresque. How do you like that for a name? Half the people who go in there can't even pronounce it. She's been there forty years. She's the life of the place, you know? Knows all the regulars. Pokes her nose into all their personal business—drags me into it if she things they need a cop. They love it. The place would probably shut down if she retired.''

The conversation lagged. He could feel the interest in the room spreading; people kept wandering by: *Yes, by God, Jenna Gallagher is sitting up there with Garth.*

''You and Skip have a lot in common,'' she said after a time. ''Only he's trying to get *away* from the blue blood and the money.''

''Yeah? The kid's rich, you mean?''

''His family is. He's wanted to be a cop for as long as he can remember. *His* mother sent him for a psychiatric evaluation when he decided to join the force. And then he married Debbie. Her father's a cop, so she's supposed to be all wrong for him. Debbie's afraid she'll do something that will ruin Skip's career, and his mother will say 'I told you so' on both counts. That's why she was so worried about you. She panicked when she saw both you and Hugh were here.''

''And you volunteered to save the day.''

''Not exactly. It's hard to say no to Debbie when she's literally pushing you in the direction she wants you to go.''

''People do a lot of that, do they? Push you into places you don't want to go.''

''Since Patrick died they do,'' she said candidly.

''Why is that?''

''They think I have the Police Commissioner's ear. Or the Mayor's.''

''And do you?''

''Let's just say if there's a neighborhood protest for better police protection in a park or a playground, they'd rather not see Patrick Gallagher's widow carrying a sign in a picket line on the six-o'clock news.''

He smiled. She was the widow of a martyr, a real, media-approved hero. An entire city had mourned with her. He imagined she could make it hot for certain public officials if she wanted to. "So people just come right out and ask you to present their cases to the powers that be."

"Something like that."

"And you do it."

"Most of the time."

"Why?"

She looked at him thoughtfully. "Because I can. Because I don't want Patrick's death to have been for nothing. If it gives me an edge when something needs to be done, I use it."

Like baby-sitting me so I don't get into any trouble with Hugh and ruin Debbie Carver's party, he thought.

"I could use a raise," he hinted.

"Even *I* couldn't manage that," she said dryly.

She was polite, just the way he thought, but she had a bit of the devil in her, too. He found that interesting. And he found that he had a sudden, irresistible urge, not to annoy precisely, but to tease her a little. "Why not?" he asked to put her on the spot.

She only smiled.

"I didn't think my differences with Hugh were *that* notorious."

"Word travels."

"Yeah? What word?"

"The word that you hit him once when you were both on duty. It caused a lot of comment around the Gallagher dinner table."

"I can imagine. Everybody want me hanged?"

"No, I believe they were all leaning toward drawing and quartering. Except for Patrick."

"Yeah? What did Patrick want?"

"Amnesty, I think. He said Hugh probably deserved it, or else the disciplinary action wouldn't have been so hush-

hush. He said one day you were going to clean Hugh's clock for him."

He laughed out loud. That sounded like Patrick. "You know, I always liked Patrick Gallagher."

She looked into his eyes. "So did I," she said quietly.

"Yeah? So why weren't you and Patrick getting along before he got shot?"

Chapter 2

Jenna stood up. Her face felt flushed. She was still looking into Johnson Garth's eyes, and she realized that the remark wasn't the result of blundering social ineptitude on his part. It was callous and deliberate. He knew exactly what he was doing. She didn't say anything to him; she moved quickly down the stairs, leaving her plate of lasagna, and she didn't look back. She was halfway to the kitchen before he caught up with her.

"Mrs. Gallagher—"

He put his hand on her shoulder to make her stop. "Mrs. Gallagher, I…I think you misunderstood."

She looked around at him, and she moved out from under the warmth of his hand on her shoulder. She hadn't misunderstood, and they both knew it. "No, I don't think so. I don't know why you would ask me something like that, and I'm trying not to think you're as rude as people say you are. What I do think is that it would be best if you go annoy someone else. Good night, Detective Garth."

She walked away from him, but he still followed.

"Mrs. Gallagher—"

She turned on him when he would have touched her again. "*Don't* push your luck, Detective!" she said, her eyes locked with his. Her knees were trembling. She felt cornered, trapped; she had to get out.

She didn't bother saying goodbye to Debbie. She didn't even look for her. She slipped away through the kitchen to the Carvers' glassed-in back porch where she'd left her coat and purse in a corner among Debbie's potted plants. Her car was parked in the small yard behind the house by a chain-link fence that separated the Carvers' yard from the property next door. It was raining still, and she ran the last few steps to the car. She didn't have her keys out, and she had to fumble in her purse for them. The rain was cold, and she couldn't keep from shivering. She could hear her heart pounding in her ears.

When she was about to get into the car, Johnson Garth called her from the back porch steps. She could not believe this man! She hurried to get inside the car.

"Mrs. Gallagher!" he called again as she reached to close the car door. "I had a reason—"

She slammed the door hard. Whatever he had to say, she didn't want to hear it. Incredibly she was close to tears—when she had thought she was all right now. She had thought she had her guilt in perspective, that the persistent physical response to it was now under control and she could get on with her life.

"*So why weren't you and Patrick getting along before he got shot?*"

That one question had brought it all back again—all the pain, all the regrets. She didn't care about Johnson Garth's reason for asking. Reasons didn't matter. Reasons never changed the final outcome of things. She had had her reasons for making Patrick so unhappy those last few months.

She had had her reasons for sitting with Johnson Garth on the stairs—ostensibly because Debbie had forced her into it. If there was anything she hated more than the loneliness of her widowhood, it was the assumption people made that not only could she somehow take care of their problems, but that she would *want* to do it. She had always been happy on the fringes of life, yet since Patrick had died, she kept letting herself be pushed right into the fray. Tonight, she'd suddenly found herself in the position of having to intervene in a long-standing feud between two hotheaded detectives who would be better off if they settled their differences once and for all. It was nothing to her that they were at odds with each other, except that she liked Debbie, and she didn't want her to be so upset.

"You do a lot of that, do you? Let people push you into places you don't want to go?"

"Yes, Detective Garth, I do."

And because she did, she was going to have to deal with the Gallaghers, too. Hugh hadn't liked her interference. And Mamie—Patrick and Hugh's mother—would like it even less when Hugh told her about her daughter-in-law's improper behavior. Jenna had spent a long time sitting on a dark stairs with Johnson Garth. The reasons wouldn't matter.

You don't have to justify it, she thought. She had been married to Patrick—not to the police department and not to the Gallagher family.

In truth, she wouldn't even have considered having to justify her behavior—if she hadn't been enjoying herself. For the first time in a very long while, she had actually *enjoyed* herself, with no thought of Hugh and Mamie Gallagher and how things might look. After the initial awkwardness, she'd found Johnson Garth easy to talk to, and he'd made her laugh. He hadn't been loud; he hadn't been drunk. He had needed a shave, but he hadn't needed a bath.

And until he'd asked his too-personal question, he hadn't been anything but quietly friendly in a way that reminded her all too much of Patrick.

And she wasn't quite sure why. He didn't look like Patrick. He wasn't handsome in the way Patrick had been. Johnson Garth had a kind of youthful, boyish look about him, but his eyes were very old; old and tired and sad, she supposed, from seeing whatever he'd seen, doing whatever he'd done. All too many of the men on the force had eyes like that. It had made her want to comfort him, when she knew personally how difficult it was to do that—comfort a cop. They didn't want it, no matter how much they needed it—not from the women in their lives. They didn't want to talk about the problems of The Job. Baring their souls they saved for their fellow police at the precinct watering holes, so that they worked an eight-hour tour and then spent another two—or more—winding down, and the women who cared about them sat alone and waited. She had always hated it, the collective assumption that civilians in general and women in particular either couldn't understand or had to be protected from the realities of police work. Patrick had been a good and caring man, but he was a cop, and he'd shut her out when he'd needed her. And, in spite of all that, she had been on the verge just now of letting herself become attracted to another one. She had let herself become all too aware of Johnson Garth, of his nearness, the warmth of his body, and his masculine scent, of his strong-looking hands and the small scar over his left eyebrow.

You've been alone too long, Mrs. Gallagher, she thought wryly. That had to be the problem when someone like Garth appealed to her.

She took a long, deep breath and tried to force his image from her mind. She didn't want to think about him staring at her from across the room, or sitting in the dark with her on the stairs, or standing on the porch steps in the rain.

She knew what was expected of her. She was expected to preserve Patrick's memory; she was expected to do exactly what she'd told Johnson Garth to do—behave.

The shaky feeling, the pounding heart, was passing. She switched on the car radio and turned the dial until she found one of the public radio stations. At least for the duration of the drive home there would be nothing in her thoughts but windshield wipers and oncoming headlights in the rainy night. And back-to-back sorrowful jazz.

What were you going to say, idiot? Garth thought. *I didn't mean it? I thought you might know something you aren't telling about your husband's death?*

He had meant it—and she knew it. He stood on the steps and watched her drive away. He just hadn't meant to upset her that much. She looked so pale, the way she'd looked at Gallagher's funeral.

He gave a one-word assessment of the way the evening had gone and walked to his car, his mind replaying his conversation with Jenna Gallagher over and over on the way home. He turned down the street of old two-story buildings where he lived, driving slowly, as if he were still in uniform and on patrol. Time and the weather meant nothing in this neighborhood. People still milled around in the streets, regardless of the late hour, regardless of the rain. But he had no difficulty finding a parking place. There was an asphalt parking lot next to the brick building that housed the small family restaurant where Hazel worked, and he pulled into it, the beams from his headlights bouncing over the wet pavement. He could get to his apartment through The Humoresque when it was open, but when it was closed or when it suited him, he entered using the metal fire escape that zigzagged up the side of the building to a second-story door.

He parked close to the building in case he had to leave in a hurry or in case somebody tried to strip his car.

"Good evening office-r-r-r-r," a group of boys standing in the doorways on the other side of the parking lot sang in falsetto voices as he climbed the metal steps.

He gave them his approximation of what they should go do with themselves in concise street terms, but he did so without malice. Since he'd begun living over the restaurant, they'd developed a kind of symbiosis. They knew what he did for a living; he knew what they did for sport, but they'd all come from the same place, and they took great satisfaction in hurling pseudoinsults at each other. He made no effort to try to establish any kind of rapport with them—if tonight was any kind of example, he was no good at it, anyway. All he wanted was for them to understand that when they needed rousting, he'd roust them. Or if they needed help, he'd do that, too, if he could. There was no need for any kind of personal relationships. He was from the streets himself. He knew what a delinquent kid thought of a cop with a social conscience. That kind of law enforcement officer was right up there with Santa Claus and the Easter Bunny—only worse, because nine times out of ten, he wanted something in return.

He worked his key into the lock, listening intently as he opened the door slightly. Then he pushed the door back until it was flat against the inner wall and he knew no one was hiding behind it. His eyes scanned the huge loft for anything amiss, but he saw nothing. There was no place for anyone to hide, really, except the bathroom, and that door opened outward, and he always left it ajar and the light on so he could see into it when he came home. He could also see into the galley, and the iron support posts that ran in two rows the length of the place were too narrow for anyone to hide behind. The sofa and the one matching chair were turned so that he could see all but the far ends. He supposed that someone could be hiding under the bed, but he hadn't yet grown that cautious.

He closed the door behind him and double-locked it. He understood those boys down below, but he didn't trust any of them. He'd once been just like them, and since he'd become a cop, he had seen too often what some punk kind with the wrong mind-set and an illegal weapon could do.

His mind went again to Jenna Gallagher. Supposedly she knew, too—*if* the boy charged with Patrick's murder was guilty. Maybe he was; maybe he wasn't. The kid had been one of Patrick's pet projects. Patrick's partner, people on the street, said the two got along well together. Why would the kid just up and shoot him?

Now Garth also knew that there had been some kind of problem between Patrick and Jenna. He'd gone on a hunch, and the stricken look she'd given him when he asked about it, and her reaction afterward, confirmed it. But how bad was it? *She* thought it was bad, apparently, but how had it affected her husband? Garth had seen men so emotionally traumatized by their personal problems, by the breakup of a marriage, for example, that they carelessly put themselves in harm's way—sometimes, he felt, not so much carelessly as deliberately. But if something *had* been wrong with the Gallagher marriage, it still didn't explain this nervousness of Hugh's. Unless there was some kind of triangle going on.

He shook his head. Patrick and Jenna and Hugh? He didn't believe that that was the case, but he wasn't quite sure why he didn't—except that he didn't *want* it to be. He had liked Jenna Gallagher, and he couldn't see her letting herself get involved with a self-serving bastard like Hugh. She wasn't Hugh's type. He liked the rowdy, big-breasted ones like the woman who'd tried to get him to dance with her tonight. Jenna Gallagher was quiet and a little shy—except when he'd upset her with his tactless question and when she'd had to come put herself between him and Hugh.

She had guts, and he liked that. She'd let people push her around for a good cause, but she had her limit.

He sighed heavily. He was tired. He took a long, hot shower and put on a pair of sweatpants and a T-shirt. He wasn't sleepy, for all his tiredness. He kept thinking about Jenna. He walked around barefoot on the hardwood floor, roaming into the galley for a beer and to the "conversation area," as his mother called it, to turn off lights.

Conversation area. He didn't need a conversation area. Who the hell did he ever talk to? Certainly not to the few women he'd brought here. He didn't like bringing women into his home, and when he had, it hadn't been so they could talk. He'd brought them here because he needed a quick fix for the emptiness he felt almost all the time. They were always women he liked but not ones who would make any demands on him. They were women who understood that he was committed to no one and nothing but The Job.

He reached to pick up a framed photograph sitting on the telephone table. It was one of the few he had in the apartment, a picture from the old neighborhood he kept to remind him of why he was a cop. He stared at the young, smiling faces—his, Roy Lee Anderson's, Mary Zaccato's—the three of them standing arm in arm with Buono's Fish Market in the background. Smiling. All of them smiling. He couldn't remember why. He knew only that none of them was smiling now. Mary was gone, and Roy Lee was aimlessly wandering the streets somewhere, his life essentially wasted. Garth had cared about these two people; he had loved Mary—almost as much as he'd hated her brother Tony. Good old Tony, who had made Garth's life a living hell from grammar school on, beating him up for his lunch money when they were kids, keeping him away from Mary when he was a man. He sighed heavily. He was a cop because of Tony Zaccato, because he didn't think the Tony Zaccatos of the world should always win. It was wrong to be victimized because one was too young or too old or too poor or didn't understand.

Blessed are the meek, he thought. Maybe so. But the strong like Tony Zaccato ate them alive if somebody didn't try to stop them.

He set the picture down and picked up the phone book. Jenna Gallagher's number was still listed in Patrick's name. He dialed it quickly, before he changed his mind, but there was no answer. He had the sudden mental picture of Jenna staring at the ringing telephone and knowing it was probably him.

He walked to the big double-arched windows that reached nearly floor to ceiling at the end of the loft. The windows looked out on the street below, and the apartment suddenly smelled too strongly of fried food—onions—from the restaurant kitchen below. The onion smell had been the reason he'd been able to get the loft in the first place. The owner of the restaurant downstairs had lived here for years—until he made enough money to be able to afford to let the smell of fried onions offend him. He'd moved to a renovated brownstone in Park Slope—and Hazel had gone to work on him. How would he like to rent his place and get a certain amount of on-the-premises police protection all at the same time, cheap? Garth smiled to himself. Luckily for him, onions or not, the man had liked the proposition. Now Garth had more room than he knew what to do with, but the downside of that was that he kept meeting his loneliness head-on.

He pushed open the upper half of one of the windows to let in some air. It was raining still, and the air that came in was damp and cold. It would be winter soon. He hated winter. Winter was the time of dead things, dead trees and grass, dead memories.

Again he thought of Mary.

Maybe that was why he was so down tonight. Maybe he

was about to do it again—let himself become personally involved with someone he needed for a case. He had loved Mary, but there had still been his need to finally, *finally*, get Tony. But for the accident of their environments, he mused, Hugh Gallagher and Tony Zaccato were a lot alike. Maybe he'd transferred his obsession for one to the other. Maybe—

He swore out loud. He wasn't going to worry about this. He'd do whatever he had to do; he always did. He popped the top on a can of beer he didn't really want and walked to the radio, flipping around the dial until he found some music. Jazz. Nobody seemed to play golden oldies at one o'clock in the morning, and he didn't want to hear the usual contemporary rock stuff.

He walked back to the window, sliding a folding, corduroy-covered lounge he liked close to the windows. As he sat down and propped up his feet, a woman on the radio began to sing. He could hear the rain, the voices carrying up from the street below. The loft filled with the soft strumming of a jazz guitar and her husky, poignant voice. She made promises. You're my man, she sang. And she made him believe it. He closed his eyes, and in his mind, with no thought as to how it came to be, he made exquisite love to Jenna Gallagher.

Chapter 3

He awoke with a start, trying to identify the sudden noise from the outside. Gunshot? The noise came again. No. Fire-crackers. Somebody was celebrating the Fourth of July nine months early.

He was cold and damp, and he had a crick in his neck. He got up from the chair and closed the window, then carried the half-drunk can of beer back into the galley.

"Here's to you, Mrs. Gallagher," he said, and he poured the beer down the sink.

He glanced at one of the several clocks on the nearest wall. He felt like hell, and he had the day watch, and there wasn't enough time to go back to sleep. He had to start taking better care of himself. Eat better. Exercise. Sleep more. The mere thought of all that healthy living made him groan.

He looked out the arched windows. The rain was gone, and the sun was just coming up. The street was already alive with its legitimate and not so legitimate doings. An old man was sweeping the water off the steps of the A.M.E. Zion Church just down the block, the broom worn down on one side and curling on the other, his breath coming out in white puffs in the chill morning air. The "fences," with everything from hot watches to temporary oblivion, were out and ready to haggle, drawing small, interested groups of men into some of the doorways. It didn't matter whether they had any money or not. It didn't cost anything to look.

He wondered how Jenna Gallagher was feeling this morning. Better than he did, he hoped. In the cold light of day, he knew that he wouldn't have done anything any differently. He had asked her exactly what he meant to ask her. Only it was the cop who had asked it, letting the question zing her in an almost automatic response to her increasing vulnerability. It was the man who couldn't forget the way she'd looked. He hadn't wanted to hurt her, but he'd done it, and he had no idea why it should matter to him. He was going to have to do something about her today, and he wasn't quite sure what.

He started to make coffee, then changed his mind. For the first time in a very long while, he dressed and went downstairs to the restaurant for breakfast.

"My God, if it's not my only son, the detective," Hazel announced to the clientele when he walked in. She was wearing her usual hair net and a green cotton smock with a plastic "Hazel" name tag pinned to it. Not that everybody didn't know her name already. The place probably hadn't had a new customer in years.

"Don't do that, Ma," he said, dutifully giving her a kiss on the cheek. "What if I'm undercover?"

"Undercover or not, there ain't nobody in here that don't know you're a cop already. Am I right?" Hazel asked the crowd. "All of you know he's a flatfoot, right?"

They all mumbled and nodded.

"See?" she said. "So what'll it be? You come to eat or what?"

"To eat. Give me some oatmeal."

"*Oatmeal!*" his mother and the counterman, Luigi Lufrano, said in unison.

He sat down on one of the stools at the counter. "Didn't I say that? I want oatmeal. It's good for you—lowers your cholesterol and stuff like that."

"What's the matter?" Hazel asked suspiciously. "You sick?"

"No, Ma. I'm not sick. I *like* oatmeal."

"You haven't eaten oatmeal in twenty-five years," she said, unconvinced.

"Look, have you got oatmeal or not?"

"Yeah, we got it. We keep it for the old guys with the ulcers."

"Well, am I going to get any, or do I have to go down the street?"

His mother threw up her hands. "Coming up. Luigi, what do you think of this? Oatmeal, yet!"

"I think we give him some nice peaches with it, he'll like it even better," Luigi said, giving Garth a big wink.

Garth grinned in return. He couldn't remember when he didn't know Luigi Lufrano. Luigi was the closest thing to a father he'd ever had. And the old man was right. The peaches were just the right touch. He ate two bowls. Oatmeal. Peaches. Real cream. So much for lowering cholesterol.

Hazel was watching every spoonful.

"So how come you're eating breakfast?" she persisted.

"I was hungry?" he suggested.

"When you're hungry, you eat junk. You always did. You're sure you're not sick? You can tell me—I'm your mother."

"Ma, I'm not sick, okay? Quit worrying, will you? I've got to go."

"Okay," Hazel said. She suddenly smiled. "Hey, you. You got a new girlfriend? Some woman's making you do this—making you take care of yourself, right?"

"No, Ma! Jeez! Eat a little oatmeal and look what I have to put up with."

"So why not? You need somebody to take care of you—somebody with a little money..."

"That's it!" he said, kissing her on the cheek again. "Goodbye! The oatmeal was great, Luigi!" he called to the old man as he went out.

He smiled to himself on the way to the station house. Hazel should have been the detective in the family. She had the instinct for it, and she probably had more contacts in the street that he did. As he drove past the building that housed the patrol precinct to which he had the dubious privilege of being assigned, he thought he saw Jenna Gallagher on the front steps, but by the time he'd parked the car in the basement parking garage, she'd gone—to lodge a formal complaint, no doubt. The lieutenant would just love this. One of his detectives harassing Patrick Gallagher's widow at a party.

"Garth!" the desk sergeant called to him as he passed by—an ominous sign.

"Yeah, Sidney, what?"

"Himself is looking for you, lad. Were it me, I'd be getting my tail into the Detective Division with the utmost haste."

"What does he want?"

"He didn't say, and what he *did* say wouldn't bear repeating."

"Great," Garth said, more to himself than to Sidney. He headed for the lieutenant's office, encountering Hugh along the way. Hugh had his morning coffee in his hand, but it

was obvious that it had done nothing for his disposition.
Garth looked past him for Jenna, but he didn't see her.

"Good morning, Hugh," he said to annoy him. His good
wishes went ignored, and if looks could kill, Garth would
have been on his way to the city morgue.

"Garth! Get in here!" the lieutenant yelled out his door.

Garth went, but no faster than he would have under normal circumstances. As far as he knew, circumstances *were*
normal, and he'd learned in grammar school not to act guilty
until he was caught. "Good morning, sir," he said as he
came in. "Nice morning, after the rain."

"If I want the weather report, Garth, I'll watch Channel
Nine. And don't call me sir. We both know you don't mean
it, and it just pisses me off. Shut the door!"

Garth shut it. Oddly enough, when Garth called the lieutenant "sir," he did mean it. The lieutenant was an old
street cop, and he knew his business. He was one of the few
men around for whom Garth had enough respect to show it.
That wasn't to say that they didn't have their differences.

He waited to see if the lieutenant wanted him to close the
blinds. There were certain detectives in the squad room
proper who could teach lipreading for a living, and the lieutenant knew it. The seriousness of this meeting would be
indicated by whether or not he wanted the blinds left open
or closed.

Open—this time.

The lieutenant leaned back at his desk and belched loudly.

"You ever have trouble with your gut, Garth?" the lieutenant asked, his face screwed up as if belching had only
compounded his misery.

"Ah, no, I don't."

"No, you wouldn't, would you? You *give* ulcers, you
don't get them. You do whatever the hell you please, and
to hell with it. Well, some of us can't do that, Garth, you
know what I mean?"

"Not exactly."

"This new kid—Carver. I got people all over me about him. His old man's got clout with the big boys downtown—they play squash together or some kind of ball us poor working stiffs never heard of. *I've* been playing 'Yes, sir, yes, sir, three bagsful' ever since I got here this morning. Now, I'm giving the kid to you, and I don't want him shot up his first day out, you got me?'' He eyed Garth closely. "You got something to say here? Keeping in mind, of course, that with my gut the way it is, I'm in no mood for rebuttals.''

"I was just wondering—"

But Garth lost his train of thought, because Jenna was standing out in the squad room with Hugh. She was wearing a black coat—something left over from her mourning, maybe—but the severity of the coat was relieved by a black-and-gold striped scarf. She looked in his direction, her eyes catching his, and she didn't look away.

"Am I boring you, Garth?'' the lieutenant barked.

"No, sir. I was just wondering why Carver's not at Midtown,'' he said forcing his eyes away from the window. "He wouldn't get his hands dirty there.''

"Because he asked to be put where he was 'needed,' even if it's someplace like here. The kid's got a bad case of the noblesse oblige—only Mummy and Daddy don't like it too much, see?''

"So what am I supposed to do with him if it looks like we're going to get into something?''

"Listen!'' the lieutenant said, jabbing his finger in the air. "You do your job! The kid's been through the academy. He's supposed to know how to handle himself. And he was a good patrolman from what I hear. Just don't go running around kicking ass with him along—at least not until my stomach settles down. I don't need any new aggravation, you hear?''

Garth glanced out the window. Jenna was still talking to

Hugh, and Skip Carver had joined them. "Anything else, Lieutenant?" he asked. He moved a little closer to the window, and Jenna turned and walked away.

"You catching a plane, Garth? When I'm done, you'll be the first to know." The lieutenant got up from his desk and opened the door. "Carver!" he yelled with his usual aplomb. The kid was standing with his back turned, but he didn't jump. When he turned around, Garth could see the edge of anxiety in his face, but he was trying hard not to show it.

Not bad, he thought. The kid had a handle on it.

"You called me, sir?" Carver asked with just the barest edge of amusement—as if there could be any doubt in a three-block radius that the lieutenant had.

"Meet your new partner," the lieutenant said. "Detective Johnson Garth."

"We've met," Garth said, extending his hand.

"Garth here'll show you the ropes. I expect good work from the two of yous. If there happens to be some personality conflict between yous, feel free to settle it yourselves, because I don't want to hear about it, understood? Now get out of here. I got work to do."

"Does he always yell like that?" Skip asked when they were out in the squad room.

"Nah. He's a little under the weather today. His volume's way off," Garth said, scanning the area to see if Jenna was still on the premises. He walked toward the hallway, and Skip trailed along after him.

"She's gone," Skip said.

Garth stopped looking. "Who's gone?" he said, annoyed that Carver had second-guessed him.

"I thought you were looking for Jenna."

"Now, why would you think that?"

"I thought something happened between the two of you last night—or Debbie did."

"Well, you and Debbie thought wrong."

"She was here to—"

"Did I ask you why she was here?"

"Sorry," Skip said. "I thought maybe you were interested."

"I'm not interested."

"My mistake then."

They stared at each other. Garth turned and walked back to his desk.

"So why aren't you interested?" Skip asked, tagging behind him. "She's a nice person. She's intelligent. She's pretty. Of course, she's not feeling up to par this morning, and that takes away some of her usual vivaciousness."

Garth picked up a folder on his desk and shuffled some papers in it. Skip Carver waited. He didn't presume. He wasn't impatient. He just stood there.

Garth suddenly snapped the folder shut. "So what's wrong with her?"

"Who?" Skip said obtusely.

"Jenna Gallagher!"

"Oh. She was at the hospital most of the night."

"Why?" Garth asked abruptly, and from the look Carver gave him, he realized he wasn't exactly being nonchalant.

"She was with a rape victim."

"Why?"

Skip Carver took a deep breath. "Because," he said, patiently, "she does volunteer work with the Family Crisis Council. She got a call from them last night after she got home from the party."

"I thought she just championed losing causes before the community relations board."

"Yes, she does that, and she substitute teaches at Saint Xavier's with Debbie."

"Anything to stay busy," Garth said to get a rise out of Skip. Not that he wasn't familiar with the work cure. The busier you were, the less time you had to think. He could feel Skip looking at him. "What?"

"I admire her," Skip said a little testily.

"Yeah?" he said, feigning disinterest by shuffling papers in the folder again.

"It's not easy for her to go into a hospital."

"Why not?"

"Because she—it's a problem she's had since Patrick was killed. He was still alive when she got to the emergency room that afternoon—she could hear him calling her, but they wouldn't let her in to see him. And then it was too late. Sometimes she has acute anxiety attacks when she has to go into a hospital now—especially Bellevue. She told Debbie the smells, the hospital noises, anything she associates with that day, bring it on."

"What kind of anxiety attacks?"

"Palpitations, the shakes—you know."

"Then why the hell does she do it?" Garth barked.

"I imagine because she needs to prove something to herself."

"Are you going to go around like that?" Garth asked abruptly, because the expensive suit Carver was wearing suddenly registered and because he didn't want to know any more personal information about Jenna Gallagher. It made her too real, made him too much at fault for her abrupt departure last night. He looked Skip up and down, realizing that he was going to have to spend his working days with somebody who looked like a Ken doll—or an undertaker.

"Are *you*?" Skip countered, returning the inspection. Garth was wearing his usual—jeans, shirt with no tie, a jacket that zipped up the front.

"Yeah. I am."

"Me, too," Skip said mildly.

"I don't know how the hell you think you can work with me dressed like that."

"Oh, no problem. They told us in the academy that men from the affluent part of Manhattan sometimes go into the rough neighborhoods—purchasing pleasure, as it were. I expect I'll look like a customer."

"*Whose* customer?"

"Yours."

"Mine. And what am I supposed to be selling—just in case somebody should ask?"

"Oh, about anything, I guess."

"You guess? Carver, this is not some kind of police academy role play here. This is the real thing."

"Oh, I know that, sir. So what should I do first?"

"First? First, you stop calling me *sir*."

"Right. What else can I do?"

"You can invite me to your house for dinner. And you can make sure Jenna Gallagher is there."

Chapter 4

"I...I think I've found out why Garth hit Hugh that time," Debbie said.

Jenna looked at her sharply but didn't comment. She had had nearly a week of Debbie's campaigning to get her to come to dinner. Debbie had made no secret of the fact that the invitation was at Johnson Garth's request, and thus far she had covered everything from Garth's brilliant, if somewhat checkered, career, to his flaming youth, to his apparent availability, as evidenced by his total lack of a social life. Jenna had been expecting yet another pitch, but this approach was a little different. And the worst part was that she was interested. She had been interested from the first, or perhaps *intrigued* was a better word. She and Garth had certainly not parted on the best of terms, and yet he'd elicited Debbie and Skip's help to mend his fences. If that was what he was doing. She really didn't know what he was doing, and she constantly puzzled over possible reasons for his wanting to see her.

"It wasn't easy," Debbie continued. "I had to name-drop— Everybody line up for hand washing!" she called to the five-year-olds who milled around them.

"Whose name?"

"Yours, silly. I told my dad Garth wanted to have dinner with you, but you were worried about whatever that thing was between him and Hugh— Hand washing!" Debbie called again as the children more or less got into line. "Hernando! Leave that lumber alone! Jenna, if we don't get all that stuff for the new cubbyholes out of here, Hernando's going to either set fire to it or sell it."

But Jenna wasn't concerned about the disposition of the precut lumber. "Debbie, I wish you wouldn't go around letting people think I'm somehow involved with Johnson Garth."

"The man wants to have dinner with you, Jenna. If you know some of the particulars about him, you can make up your mind better."

"I've made up my mind."

"Hernando! Leave the gerbil alone! What did you do with the soap! Oh, Lord, Jenna—you can't make a gerbil eat soap, can you? You take him this time. I'm liable to pinch his little head off."

Knowing that it was Hernando Cooley, the "old man" of Saint Xavier's kindergarten class, whose head was in danger and not the gerbil's, Jenna went to frisk him. Hernando was almost six, and he was one of Sister Mary John's finds, a little boy who was learning-deprived in every area except how to survive on the streets. Jenna doubted that he'd ever been a child, and the fact that he tried so hard to hide how much he wanted to be one made him all the more endearing. He was completely fascinated by the simplest of things crayons, coloring books, wild animal pictures—when he wasn't causing complete chaos. In the past few days she had begun to think of him as an early version of Johnson

Garth, and it was becoming apparent to her that something needed to be done about both of them.

"Hernando, why did you put it in your pocket?" Jenna said, trying to scrape the wet, slimy clumps of soap out.

"'Cause you find it everyplace else," Hernando said matter-of-factly. He gave her a charming grin. "You're smart, Miss Jenna. I didn't think you'd ever find it in there."

"Yes, well, lucky me," Jenna said, looking for something to do with it now that she'd retrieved it.

"I don't like washing my hands," Hernando said, watching her try to press the soap back into shape. "That's all you do—make peoples wash their hands."

"Washing your hands will help keep you from catching a cold."

"I ain't washing mine no more," he informed her.

"Fine," Jenna said. "It's up to you. No clean hands, no cookies."

He thought this over. "You mean everybody else gets a cookie and not me?" he asked, apparently to make sure he understood all the particulars of her pronouncement. "Just because my hands ain't washed?"

"You got it," Jenna said.

"You're crazy," he informed her further.

She smiled. "Give me a hug anyway."

He hesitated only a moment, then flung himself into her arms. There was progress in that direction, at least. Hernando was learning to accept affection from her and Debbie both, even if clean hands were sometimes the price.

"How come you ain't mad at me?" he asked.

"Crazy, I guess. Go wash your hands."

"You ain't got no soap no more," he said.

"You wish," Jenna advised him, pressing a small blob of what used to be the bar of Ivory into his palm. "Use that."

"Do you want to know what I found out or not?" Debbie

said when Jenna had Hernando pointed in the right direction and the hand-washing line was moving again.

"Tell me," Jenna said in spite of herself. She couldn't have dinner with Johnson Garth, but Debbie was right about one thing: she might as well know as much as she could.

"Well, it's just a rumor Sidney, the desk sergeant at the precinct, told my dad. I don't think anybody knows for sure except Garth and Hugh—and probably the lieutenant. I don't know if it got to Internal Affairs or not." Debbie paused long enough to check on the progress of the hand washers. "Anyway, there was this kid from Tennessee— Juanita something. She'd hitchhiked all the way to New York looking for her boyfriend. He was supposed to send her the bus fare, but he never did, so she came anyway. Can you imagine that? Some kid from Tennessee trying to find a guy who probably didn't want to be found—in New York City—with no friends and no money? She ended up on the streets, of course, and it didn't take her long to get into harm's way. Sidney said he remembered her because she had the saddest eyes he'd ever seen. He said she reminded him of a little sparrow someone had deliberately stepped on. Anyway, Hugh and Garth caught the case. When they were questioning her, trying to find out about the men who had—" She broke off.

"Go on," Jenna said.

"I'm sorry, Jenna. I know Hugh's your brother-in-law."

"Go on, Debbie."

"Hugh asked her if she'd enjoyed it. And Garth hit him. It would have been worse if Sidney and some of the others hadn't broken it up. I...don't think it's just a rumor. I think it's the truth."

Jenna stood watching the children waiting to wash their hands. She thought it was the truth, too. She was a part of a volunteer support team for women who were victims of violent crimes. She knew the harassment they sometimes still had to endure from investigating officers, regardless of the efforts toward more humane treatment for the victim. And she knew Hugh Gallagher. She had no trouble imagining it, Hugh with his arrogance, and his perfectly barbered little blond mustache, and his piercingly cold blue eyes. How he must have scared a little girl from Tennessee.

"What?" Jenna asked, because Debbie had said something.

"I said I think he's a very complicated man. I tried to find out this business about his name, but Skip doesn't know. Even Sidney doesn't know about that."

"Who are we talking about?"

"Garth, Jenna. His first name is Johnson. Everybody knows that, but nobody calls him by it. They don't call him Johnson, or John, or Johnny. Nothing except Garth. That's what he said to me in the kitchen: 'Just call me Garth.' I think— Hernando! Leave that lumber alone!"

The kindergartners, Hernando notwithstanding, were getting too restless for their just-before-going-home cookie and milk for Debbie to go on. It was standard practice to give the children something to eat before they left for the day, because it was a long time before dinner for many of them— if they got dinner. Jenna wasn't at all certain Hernando was fed anything after he left here. She didn't think he would have washed his hands for the cookie otherwise.

"I think—" Debbie began again as soon as the last of the peanut butter cookies were given out.

"That I ought to come to your house for dinner," Jenna finished for her.

"Well, I do. You ought to at least *talk* to him. You aren't going to find out what he's up to any other way. Lord knows, Skip can't find out, and he's tried. He thinks Garth likes you."

Jenna laughed.

"Well, he does. Why don't you come to dinner tonight, Jenna? Let me tell Skip to bring Garth home and—"

"No."

"For the love of Pete, why not? For curiosity's sake, if nothing else."

"Because," Jenna said firmly, "I have something else in mind."

Garth had been waiting all day to hear whether Jenna had changed her mind about coming to dinner. He hadn't asked because he didn't want to seem too eager. He didn't need word getting back to Hugh that he was hotly pursuing his sister-in-law.

Skip waited until they were in the middle of a traffic jam to tell him.

"Debbie said Jenna couldn't make it."

"Couldn't?" Garth asked offhandedly.

"Wouldn't," Skip answered. That was one thing about Skip. Garth could trust him to tell the truth. There was no denying the pang of disappointment he felt, just as there was no denying that he was beginning to dwell less and less on his original reason for wanting to talk to Jenna Gallagher in the first place and more and more on the woman herself. He found himself thinking about her at odd times of the day, remembering the way she had looked and the way she'd smelled. There was a lot to be said for a woman who took the trouble to smell nice—not loud, but nice. Soft and womanly. Of course, that could be false advertising on her part. This particular woman was turning out to be anything but soft. When she said no dice, she apparently meant it.

"Did she say why?"

"No. Do you want to come to dinner anyway?" Skip said.

"Why?"

"Why? Because you're my partner and Debbie told me to ask you to come anyway."

"Why?" he said again.

"I just told you why. Debbie thought you might like a hot meal. Look, if you don't want to come, just say so. I can tell Debbie I asked you, and you said no. No problem!"

"Skip—"

"It doesn't matter that she's been knocking herself out trying to be your go-between with Jenna. It doesn't matter that she's been practicing on *me* so she can cook something she thinks is good enough to feed *you*. It's nothing to you. It's important to her, Garth, but trust me, the Carvers will survive your absence."

"Skip!"

"What!"

"Did I say I didn't want to come?"

"You don't have to. I'm not *that* dense."

"Since when?" Garth asked mildly. The kid had made a few mistakes in the last few days—not bad ones, but bad enough that Garth wanted to keep him from thinking he was Super Detective.

"I'm ignorant about some things, Garth. Ignorant, not stupid."

"If you say so. You're the one with the big Harvard education."

"Princeton. It's Princeton. And I do say so. I'll just tell Debbie you don't want to come."

"Hey—I want to come, okay?"

"Don't do us any favors, Garth."

"What is it with you, today? I'm not doing you any favors!" And he wasn't. He liked Debbie and Skip, even if he did overdo it with the Bill Blass suits. "You can tell Debbie I'll be there!"

Skip kept cutting looks at him as they inched along.

"What?" Garth said in exasperation. "What!"

"Okay, I'll tell you 'what.' I want to know what it is with you and Jenna. Debbie's all worried about her. It's the first thing I hear when I get home—'What is it with Jenna and Garth?' It's the last thing I hear before I go to bed. And when I'm at work, you're working me over about her, too. I want to know why."

"It's nothing— watch where you're going!"

"Watch where I'm *going*? I'm not going anywhere, Garth. There's a bus in front of us and cabs everywhere else. You're changing the subject."

"I'm not."

"Yes, you are! I'm your partner. If you're up to something that's going to get both our butts kicked, I want to know what it is. What do you want to talk to her about?"

"It's personal."

"Personal? Have you got the hots for her or something like that?"

"Yeah, something like that— watch the bus!"

Skip slammed on brakes just short of a rear-end collision.

"Look, Garth, Jenna is a friend of ours. I'm not going to help you get her in the sack."

"Skip, I just want to get to know the lady. That's all."

"Maybe so, but there is no way in hell she's coming to dinner if she knows you're going to be there."

"Thanks a lot, Skip. Why don't you build up my social confidence here."

They sat in silence, waiting for the traffic to move, ignoring the free-lance pedestrian windshield washers who ran around the car spraying and wiping and making a pitch for a "donation."

Garth suddenly rolled down the window on his side, because he recognized one of them. The wind was blowing, and the shadows were deep. It was cold on the street today. Very cold.

"Roy Lee!" he yelled, and the man he recognized came trotting over. "Get in," he said, unlocking the back door.

Roy Lee hesitated, bending low so he could see into the car and hugging himself to stay warm. His rheumy eyes darted around as if he expected something worse than passing conversation.

"Get in," Garth said again, and Roy Lee suddenly smiled.

"Garth! What's happening?" he asked as he crawled into the back seat. His voice was hoarse. He tried to clear his throat, but it didn't help. That it had been a long time between baths for Roy Lee became rapidly apparent in the small confines of the car.

"I've been looking for you, Roy Lee," Garth said mildly, and he left the window down.

With his usual reluctance to play stool pigeon, Roy Lee feigned surprise. "Yeah? I been around, Garth. You know I ain't going noplace."

"What have you got for me?"

"Nothing, Garth."

The old familiar holding-out pattern. Garth turned around in the seat. "Don't you start with me, Roy Lee. I'm not in the mood. Am I, Skip?"

"No," Skip said with great sincerity, and Garth smiled.

"This is my new partner, Roy Lee. His name is Skip. Skip's caught all kinds of hell today because I couldn't find you. I can do that, see, because I'm the top dog. I can take out all my annoyance on him. Can't I, Skip?"

"Damn right," Skip said on cue.

Roy Lee tried to clear his throat again. "No, hey, Garth, I been working for you. I said I would. You know I don't lie."

"You owe me, Roy Lee. Cut the crap and tell me what you've got."

"I got—I got a message for you, Garth. From Tony—

Tony Zaccato,'' Roy Lee offered. Clearly Roy Lee was going to try to fob him off with some useless piece of information about Tony Zaccato, but Garth played the game anyway.

"Tony's out of the country, Roy Lee."

"No! No, he's back, Garth! He said if I saw you I was to tell you that."

"Roy Lee, what is this?"

"I don't know, Garth. It's just what he said."

"Here," Garth said, digging into his shirt pocket for the bills he'd gotten back when he paid for a hot dog at lunch. "Go buy yourself some thermal underwear, man." He slapped the money into Roy Lee's hand without counting it. "Now beat it. Get off the street before you catch pneumonia."

Roy Lee looked down at the money in his hand, and for a brief moment Garth thought he was going to cry.

"Beat it," Garth said again, and Roy Lee opened the door.

"Garth," he said before he got out. "That cop that got whacked—Gallagher. It's still the same. Nobody's talking."

"Yeah, yeah, you told me. See you around, Roy Lee."

"You know what that means, Garth," he said anxiously.

"Yeah, I know, Roy Lee. It means somebody doesn't like me asking about it."

"It means that cop was doing just like you—poking his nose where people didn't want it. You better take it easy, Garth."

"I always do that, Roy Lee. Tell Tony I'm glad he's back. Tell him the three of us will get together sometime—for old times' sake."

"No—Garth—you watch your back. I mean it. It ain't just Tony you got to worry about. Hugh—"

"What do you know about Hugh Gallagher, Roy Lee?"

"He knows you're still asking about his brother. He don't like it."

"Good. You make sure he keeps on knowing it."

"Garth…"

"Beat it, Roy Lee. I got things to do."

Traffic was finally moving, and they left Roy Lee standing on the windy street. Skip was very quiet. Garth could almost feel him weighing information.

"You know what Roy Lee's going to do with that money," Skip said after a long time.

"Yeah," Garth said absently, his own mind once again working on how to see Jenna, apologize after a fashion and get her to talk about Patrick.

"He's not going to buy underwear," Skip persisted.

"Skip, I know what he's going to do with it!"

"Then why did you give it to him? He didn't tell you anything. We already know about Zaccato."

"Because we go back a long way, okay? Roy Lee and Zaccato and I, we all go back a long way."

"So what do they have to do with Patrick Gallagher?"

"Nothing, as far as I know."

"But you think they might."

"Why do you say that?"

"Because all three names *and* Hugh's came up in the same conversation, and because you're acting as if it's not important. That's the way you work, Garth. The more important it is, the more you behave as if it's not."

Garth gave an indulgent smile. "If you say so, Detective."

"You think Patrick was a dirty cop?"

"If he was or wasn't, it doesn't matter now."

"I'm beginning to see what you want with Jenna."

"No, you don't."

"Yes, Garth, I do. Hugh doesn't want you asking questions about Patrick. The only reason I can think of is that one or both of them was dirty, right? Right?" Skip insisted. "You've got a score to settle with Hugh, and you think poking into Patrick's death for something is the way to do it."

Garth didn't answer.

"Look! I told you before if you're doing something that's going to get both our butts kicked, I want to know about it!"

"Skip, will you take it easy? This has got nothing to do with you, okay? Nothing. Just…don't say anything to Jenna about it. Or Debbie."

"Yeah, right."

"I mean it."

"I know you do. That's what worries me."

They rode the rest of the way back to the station house in silence.

"I understand why you'd want to take Hugh down if he's into something," Skip said when they were in the parking garage. "What I don't see is why you have to use Jenna to do it."

"I'm not using Jenna. I told you before, Skip. I like her."

"Yes. *That* worries me, too."

The shifts were changing, and inside the building was the usual madhouse.

"Garth!" Sidney called over the heads of several patrolmen hanging around his desk. He had a bunch of pink slips in his hand. "You're popular today, lad. Several calls from the D.A.'s office. And two from a Mrs. Gallagher."

"Thanks, Sid," Garth said, reaching for the slips and shuffling through them until he found the two that interested him. But they only had the CALLED box checked, and there was no return telephone number on them. "What Mrs. Gallagher is this, Sidney?"

"Now, how would I be knowing that, lad? She said what she said, and what she said is on them pink slips."

"This doesn't tell me anything."

"Ah, well," Sidney said philosophically. "Perhaps she'll be calling you again."

Garth looked down at the slips. The only Mrs. Gallagher he knew was Jenna, but she wouldn't call him. Would she? Twice?

Frowning, he walked to his desk.

"Garth!" Sidney called after him. "Line one! I believe it's the lady again!"

Garth looked at the telephone on his desk. Only line three was blinking, but knowing that Sidney refused to be intimidated by a multiline telephone system, he answered it. Everything to Sidney was generally "line one," and when one answered the telephone in this station house, one took one's chances.

"Detective Garth," he said into the receiver, feeling Skip's undivided interest. No one responded, but he could hear background noise on the line. It sounded like a bunch of children. "Detective Garth," he said again.

"Oh," a woman's voice said. "I'm sorry. I thought I'd be on hold longer. Sidney must be getting better. This is Jenna Gallagher."

He glanced at Skip, who suddenly got busy shuffling papers, but who was still listening.

"Yes," Garth said noncommittally, because he couldn't think of anything else.

"Is this a bad time?" she asked. "I can call back later."

"No, now is fine."

"I was wondering if you would consider doing some volunteer work. I know tomorrow is your regular day off—Debbie told me. Do you think you might have several hours free?"

She was short and to the point. He waited before he answered, glancing again at Skip.

"Detective Garth?" Jenna said.

"Sorry," Garth said, making up his mind quickly. "To-morrow? I could manage a few hours tomorrow."

"Could you come to Saint Xavier's, to the school—Skip can tell you how to get there—around ten o'clock?"

"Yes, I could do that."

"Good. You'll need to wear old clothes. And could you bring a hammer?"

"A hammer? Yeah, I've got one." Somewhere.

"Good," she said. "Ten o'clock then."

"Jenna, wait—" he said just as she hung up. He sat for a moment pondering this unlikely situation, wondering if she'd noticed that he'd been so agreeable he hadn't asked for any details. *Come to the school. Bring a hammer. Anything you say, Mrs. Gallagher.*

Skip was fidgeting.

Garth looked up at him. He was not about to discuss the phone call, and he meant it.

Skip's eyes shifted sharply to the right—where Hugh was standing.

Chapter 5

Garth stayed too long after dinner at the Carvers, over-sleeping the next morning in spite of his numerous clocks. He was nearly an hour and a half late when he arrived at Saint Xavier's. There was a locked car with the engine running in the parking lot. He thought it belonged to Debbie Carver, but he wasn't certain. He assumed there was a good reason for burning up a tank of gasoline like that, but none came to mind. It was cold today, but not that cold.

He crossed the lot to the old brick building behind the church itself and tried the first door he came to. It, too, was locked. When he turned to leave, the door suddenly opened, bumping him hard on the shoulder.

"Oh! Garth! I'm sorry!" Debbie Carver said. "You can come in this way." She stood back to let him inside, but the little girl with her didn't. The child was carrying a huge plastic bag with what looked like a winter coat in it; the bag was nearly as big as she was. "Let Detective Garth inside, Becca," Debbie said, maneuvering the child out of the way.

"You know your car's running?" Garth said. Debbie seemed a little high-strung to him, and he thought he'd better mention it.

But then, as he stepped inside the building, he was distracted from the gasoline issue. He suddenly understood Jenna Gallagher's difficulty in going into Bellevue Hospital—that the smell and feel of a place could bring back a flood of memories. Saint Xavier's had several annexes, but this wing appeared to be the oldest. It smelled of books and mimeograph fluid and creaking, varnished wood. It smelled of his own school days, and for a brief, painful moment, he was the Garth in the picture on the telephone table, young and smiling and in love with Mary Zaccato. It took a conscious effort on his part to thrust the sudden attack of nostalgia aside.

"Oh, yes," Debbie was saying. "I've got to take Becca home. The Phantom Coat Flusher's struck again, and I had to get the car warm."

"The what?"

"The car."

Garth frowned. "No. I mean the other thing. The phantom?"

"The Phantom Coat Flusher," Debbie said. "Jenna will explain it. You're late, by the way. We'd given up on you— are you all right this morning?"

"Yes, I'm all right. Why?" He was late not just because he'd overslept, but because he'd had to go buy a hammer. He didn't want to tell Debbie that. He'd bought wine to impress a woman before, flowers even. Never a hammer.

"Well," she said, taking the little girl by the hand, "with my cooking, you never know. See you!"

Garth laughed and held open the door for her. "How many times do I have to tell you, Mrs. Carver? The dinner was fine. You want me to carry the coat?" he called after her because Becca wasn't doing too well, and Debbie didn't seem to notice.

"No, thanks. Becca's coat is new, and she's very territorial. Jenna's inside. Just go straight down the hall to the end."

The Phantom Coat Flusher? Garth thought as he firmly shut the outside door. He started down the long hallway, once again fighting down the feeling of déjà vu. And he halfway expected to meet Hugh somewhere along the way. Hugh must have known he was talking to Jenna yesterday, and sooner or later Garth expected him to do something about it—a little "friendly advice" on Hugh's part, prompted by his concern over the vulnerability of his brother's widow, no doubt. Or maybe he'd just cut the crap and get right down to it. It would, Garth supposed, depend on how nervous he was getting.

The cafeteria was somewhere close and in high gear. He could smell something cinnamon baking. He saw no one, and he kept walking. There were classrooms along the way, but they all had their doors shut.

"And just who are you?" someone said sharply as he walked by the one door that was open.

He backed up. A diminutive nun sat behind a desk in the room he'd just passed. Saint Xavier's certainly had a penchant for undertall staff people, he thought. Jenna only came to his shoulder, and she was the tallest he'd met so far. If this little person's feet touched the floor at all behind the desk, it was just barely.

"Detective Garth, Sister. NYPD," he said.

"Jenna's policeman?" she inquired, trying to get him in the right place in her bifocals. Apparently she couldn't, because she pulled them off and put them aside.

"Yes," Garth said. He supposed he was that.

"You don't look like a detective."

"I do the best I can, Sister," he said without apology.

The sister smiled. She had a beautiful smile, and very dark, merry brown eyes.

"Oh, but, you see, that's exactly what we want, Detective Garth. We want someone who doesn't look like what most of these children are used to seeing. You look very... suburban and leisurely. Very Saturday morning. And you have your hammer, of course?"

"Of course," he said, showing her where he had it stashed in an inside pocket of his jacket. She was clearly delighted.

"Excellent, Detective Garth! This is going to be so wonderful!"

"I...certainly hope so," he said vaguely.

"Now. There are several things I insist upon while you're here. You will be under the most exacting scrutiny. You must not swear under any circumstances. You must not smoke on the premises. And at lunchtime, you *will* drink your milk, won't you?"

He opened his mouth to say, but she didn't let him.

"Well, run along, Detective Garth. The children are waiting for you."

"The children?"

"Yes, Detective Garth. That way!"

She shooed him; he went, thinking that the time to bail out of this thing was now. He didn't like milk, and he backslid and had a cigarette now and again, and he had certainly been known to swear. If a conversation with Jenna Gallagher hadn't been the prize, he doubted that this—whatever this experience was—would be worth the aggravation.

Ah, well, he decided as he continued down the hall. If he ran into The Phantom, at least he had a hammer.

He could hear voices coming from the last door on the left, but the long hallway gave them a hollow, echoed sound. He couldn't tell if it was Jenna he heard or not.

She came out of the door just before he got there, and he

was infinitely aware of his own response. He was glad to
see her—and not just because she was the possible means
to an end. Yes, he wanted to rattle Hugh's cage as much as
humanly possible. But no, that wasn't the reason he felt the
way he did now. It was difficult to describe. There was
sexual attraction certainly; she was a good-looking woman.
Her hair was tied back in a black ribbon, and she was
dressed in dark green today—a soft-looking sweater he immediately wanted to put his hands on, and a long wool skirt.

But he also wanted to sit down and talk with her. He
wanted to explain about the other night—as much of an
explanation as he could give, at any rate. He wanted to know
about the anxiety attacks and what she was doing about
them. He wanted to know how she was today. He
wanted...everything.

It may have been that she was a little glad to see him,
too—until she remembered herself.

"Detective Garth," she said, her eyes reserved but looking directly into his.

He smiled. "Don't look like that, Mrs. Gallagher. I'm
supposed to be here."

She didn't return the smile. He was late, and she had
nearly given up on seeing him. She wasn't looking forward
to explaining why she'd asked him to come, the official
reason or the real one. Her eyes scanned over him. He
looked...himself. He dressed the same for a kindergarten
visit as he did for a party, but he had shaved, and that was
something, she supposed. She was worried that he was going to immediately insist on talking about her declining his
invitations for dinner, or that he'd want to launch into some
explanation as to why he'd made such a prying remark
about her relationship with Patrick.

But he didn't. He merely stared back at her. And that was
more flustering for her than his questions or apologies would
have been.

She took a deep breath. She was in control of this situation. It was she who had initiated it, and for no other reason, she wanted to assure herself, than to relieve Debbie and Skip of the obligation Skip felt toward his new partner. They both took Johnson Garth too seriously; they were too career conscious not to. But they were in no way accountable for her refusals to join him at the Carvers for dinner—*he* was. And before the day was over, she intended that he understand that. She also intended that, from now on, she would be able to get through an entire day without being bombarded by thirdhand dinner invitations.

She looked into his eyes, hazel eyes with thick dark lashes. She *wanted* to assure herself. But she couldn't. There was still the other thing. Insensitive or not, enemy of the Gallagher family or not, Garth had stayed on her mind. All morning she'd been thinking about him and about some lines of dialogue, something she remembered from a movie she'd seen when she was a girl growing up by the Susquehanna River. Joanne Woodward and Thelma Ritter perhaps. She didn't think she had ever really understood the emotion involved until now:

"*What's his name?*"

"*I don't know.*"

"*What does he want?*"

"*I don't know.*"

"*Is he coming back?*"

"*I don't* know! *I just know if I don't see him again I'll die.*"

She had wanted to see Johnson Garth again, and there was no use pretending otherwise. There was something about him, some sadness that she could feel when she looked at him. And she thought that he knew she felt it, and that he let her empathy draw him to her in spite of himself.

"Yes, well," she said. "I think I need to explain a few things to you."

"That would be good. Belated, but good."

"Belated?"

"I just had a very puzzling conversation with a little nun about so high." He held out his hand to show her how high he thought the nun would have been if she'd stood up.

"Puzzling?"

"Yeah. Something about children and a hammer?"

"Oh, yes, it's very simple. Sister Mary John—"

"The short one," he interrupted, because he sensed her nervousness and because, once again, he had an irrepressible urge to tease her. She was already angry with him. It couldn't hurt.

"Yes. She's—"

"She's even shorter than Debbie."

"Right. She—"

"She didn't tell me who she was."

"Sister Mary John," Jenna repeated, and she paused in case he had yet another two cents he wanted to put in. His eyes were full of mischief, and she tried her best to ignore it.

"Go on," he prompted.

"Sister Mary John," Jenna said carefully, "saw a television special about Scotland Yard. It dealt with the Golden Thread."

"What Golden Thread?"

"The policy Scotland Yard has for dealing with the public is called the Golden Thread. The Golden Thread is Courtesy, Compassion, and something else—I've forgotten what. Anyway, Sister Mary John said they lost it in the '60s because they stopped having their police officers walk a beat. But then they realized how important it was for a policeman to know his people and for them to know him."

"Go on," he said again.

"Especially the children. This one bobby knew all the children in a school on his beat by name. So, Sister decided

yesterday that she wanted a police officer to come spend
the day with the kindergarten—because you need to start
young. And she didn't want him to *look* like a policeman.
And she didn't want a policewoman because more of the
children don't have fathers than don't have mothers, and
she thought they'd benefit more from a male role model.''

"Is that what I have to be? A father figure?"

"In a manner of speaking, yes. I don't think it will be
too difficult. The only one who may be a problem is Hernando Cooley."

"Tough guy, huh?"

"Well, he's five going on thirty. Yesterday he tried to
start a game of strip poker."

Garth smiled again, and this time she smiled with him.
Not much, but a little.

"And what did Sister Mary John have to say about that?"

"Some things, Detective Garth, are better kept from Sister. You know what I mean?"

His smile broadened. "Yeah, I know what you mean. I'm
just surprised that you do."

"Are you going to stay?" She tried to sound neutral, but
she was very well aware of how much she wanted him to.

"That depends."

"On what?"

"On what I have to do with the hammer. Or is it for
protection?" *That's more like it,* he thought. She smiled
genuinely this time, no holding back, no trying not to give
him an opening because she thought he was going to presume.

"The hammer is so you can put the cubbyholes together.
We've run out of space for the children to keep their things.
One of the parishioners donated the lumber. It's already pre-
cut and grooved, so it's just a matter of putting it together—
I knew you'd hate it," she finished abruptly.

"I don't hate it, Mrs. Gallagher. If I hated it, you'd know before we got this far."

He was looking into her eyes. She glanced away, and he waited for her to look back again.

"It beats the hell out of sleeping till noon," he said when she did. "What with The Phantom Coat Flusher and everything."

"How did you know about that?"

"I met Debbie on my way in. So why isn't Skip in on this? It's his regular day off, too."

"Skip went to Southampton. He was summoned to the palatial estate. Debbie thinks it's the family's formal announcement that he's been cut out of the will."

"I don't think he'll care, do you?"

"Not a bit. Are you ready to meet the children?"

"Not until I find out about The Phantom."

She gave a small shrug. "Somebody—one of the children—keeps trying to flush coats down the toilet."

"You have an idea who it is?" he asked, thinking that this was one problem he'd never run across before.

"Of sorts. But we can't catch him at it. The Phantom is very diabolical."

"You don't need a carpenter, ma'am. You need a detective."

"Does that mean you're staying?"

He was still looking into her eyes—as much as she'd let him—and enjoying every minute of it, because she was still trying not to smile. "Oh, yeah," he said. "Just watch where you hang my coat, okay?"

She smiled after all, a warm smile that made him glad he'd come.

"Boys and girls," Jenna said to the small upturned faces. "This is—" She was all set to say Johnson Garth, but he cleared his throat sharply to interrupt her. She glanced at him, and he mouthed the word "Garth."

"This is Garth," she continued, and he nodded. "Garth is a police detective."

"He don't look like no police detective," Hernando said immediately. "Where's his gun?"

"Detective Garth is going to build the new cubbyholes for us today. He doesn't need a gun. He has a hammer." She looked at Garth, who dutifully produced the hammer from inside his coat and held it up as if he were a letter-turner on a television game show.

"How old is he?" Hernando said suspiciously, looking Garth up and down. Jenna had no idea what that had to do with anything, but apparently, to Hernando, it signified.

"I don't know," Jenna said. "Why don't you ask him?"

"How old are you, man?" Hernando said without compunction.

Garth scratched the side of his face with one finger. "Um...thirty-five."

"You're *old*, man."

"Yeah, well, I used to be just *plain* five," Garth said ominously. "Like you."

"Now," Jenna said, trying to regain some control here. "I want all of you to get your name necklaces out and put them on so Detective Garth will know who you are."

"I don't want him to know who *I* am," Hernando said, folding his arms.

"I already know," Garth advised him.

"Do not."

"Do, too."

"Oh, yeah? Who?"

"Hernando Cooley. Himself."

Jenna tried not to smile at Hernando's incredulous look. She waited while the children shuffled through the stacks of papers on the tables in front of them, looking for the laminated circles of construction paper that had been threaded onto long pieces of yarn. She glanced at Garth, who grinned and raised and lowered his eyebrows once.

"What is it, Mallory?" she said to the little girl who was pulling desperately on her skirt.

"I can't find my name necklace, Miss Jenna," Mallory said. "It's all lost!" Everything was a major crisis to Mallory, and she was very near tears.

"Don't worry. I'll help you find it."

"But—but what if we *can't*!" Mallory wailed.

"Then I'll make you another one. It'll be all right. Let's go look."

"You're not going far, are you?" Garth asked when she took Mallory by the hand.

"Don't worry," Jenna said to him, too. "You've got the hammer."

"Yes, but I'm seriously outnumbered."

She smiled and went to help Mallory find her necklace, feeling Garth's eyes on her as she bent over the low table. She was certain that nothing was showing, no cleavage, no lace on her underwear. Her skirt was too long to do anything but hide the backs of her legs, and yet she felt as if he could see *something*, something he rather liked, and the feeling made her want to pull at her sweater and fuss with her hair. She glanced back at him. He looked entirely innocent—rather like Hernando with the missing soap in his pocket.

"I'll take your jacket," she said when she came back.

He gave it to her, but with some reluctance.

"Do *not* let The Phantom get that," he said as he handed it over.

"I'll do my best," she promised.

She took it and hung it with her coat in the small closet at the back of the room. When she returned, Garth had taken matters into his own hands. He was reading the name necklaces and having the children "give him five," all except Mallory, who was afraid to do it.

"Come here, Hernando, my man," Garth said. "Show Mallory how."

Hernando slapped Garth's open hand with his—hard.

"Way to go, Hernando!" Garth said. "Now tell Mallory what that means."

"It means you're cool, man," Hernando said. "It means you're cool and *I'm* cool."

"Right," Garth said. "Come on, Mallory. Let's see you be cool."

She stood hesitantly with one finger in her mouth and tentatively slapped his hand. "Good, Mallory! One more time!"

This time she struck harder.

"All right, Mallory!" Garth praised. "Now a 'high five' like the Jets do—all right!"

Mallory was beaming, and Garth moved on to the next child, who had definitely been inspired by Mallory's success. Jenna could only hope that Garth's hand held out through the rest of them.

But, not only did it hold out, he had enough left to insist that she "high five," too.

"Okay, Miss Jenna," he said, holding his hand up and giving her a mischievous grin.

Jenna slapped his palm.

"You call that a high five? Come here, Mallory. You show her."

Mallory was on the scene in an instant, slapping Garth's hand like a pro.

"See, Miss Jenna?" Garth said. "Like Mallory does it—all right!"

Jenna's palm stung from "high fiving." She looked into his eyes too long, and they both glanced away. He *was* kind, she thought, regardless of his apparent aversion to the term.

There was a kindness, a gentleness, evident in him in spite of what he might intend.

And there was a part of him that was not so kind, too. She'd already had experience with that.

She looked at her watch.

"What's the matter?" he asked. "Have I worn out my welcome already?"

"No, I was just wondering what was keeping Debbie. We'd planned to keep the children out of your way for a while so you could hammer in peace."

He looked at her, but he didn't comment on the obvious: She hadn't planned to have to deal with him alone.

"It won't bother me if they watch," he said.

"Are you sure?"

"I'm sure. I might need a couple of helpers. How about you, Hernando? You want to be my Main Man?" As he said it, he caught a glimpse of Mallory's crestfallen face. "And you, too, Mallory."

"Both of us can't be no Main Mans," Hernando said, a small frown between his eyes that Jenna recognized immediately. Illogically she felt as if it were a kind of caste mark—not of his birth, but of his environment—a symbol of frustrated anger she'd come to associate with violent and potentially violent young men. It was the same expression the boy who had shot Patrick wore.

"Yeah, you can," Garth said. "Miss Jenna, too. You want to be a Main Man, too, Miss Jenna?"

"Yes," she said after a moment, realizing that Garth was looking at her with some concern. But he didn't say anything. He started on the cubbyholes instead, and he was a whiz at organizing. He assigned her to be the Main Man With The Official Lumber Loaders, who put cubbyhole pieces into the red wagon that was part of the kindergarten play equipment. Then there were The Official Wagon Escorters, who pulled or walked alongside the wagon until it reached its destination—Garth. He supervised The Official Lumber Unloaders and fitted the pieces together with the help of Mallory, who held the bag of nails, and Hernando, who stood by with the hammer.

Amazingly enough, with Jenna on one end of the operation and Garth on the other, it worked, though Jenna was filled with misgivings about giving Hernando anything so lethal as a hammer.

But Garth seemed to know how to handle him, and in a short time it became apparent that Hernando liked his job as one of the three "Main Mans" and intended to stick to Garth no matter what.

Now and then, Jenna could hear bits of their conversation.

"You have to be smart, Hernando. Everybody gets ticked off. Everybody. But when you get mad, you got to put it someplace where it does some good. Like out this hammer and into this nail, see? You want the nail in the wood, right? And that's a good thing. It's going to hold these shelves together. When you're ticked off, you put it where it doesn't hurt you and it doesn't hurt anybody else—then you're a smart guy. Now hit that sucker! Harder!"

When they stopped for lunch, the cubbyholes were almost finished. Garth was escorted royally to the cafeteria by his adoring new friends, and he seemed to enjoy the attention. Because they all wanted to sit at his table, seating arrangements precipitated a small riot, one Jenna averted by pushing two tables together.

"Be strong," she told him when he looked down at his plate—chicken and noodles, carrot sticks, cinnamon pumpkin cookies with raisins, and milk.

"This is not bad," he said a little too earnestly after a bite or two.

"I'm glad you think that. Sister Mary John is very big on setting an example."

"Is that why I have to drink my milk?"

"That's why."

"Well, here goes," he said, picking up his milk carton and clicking it against hers—which led to having to toast everybody else's as well. "I keep forgetting you have to do everything here in twenties," he said to Jenna. "To your very good health," he said to the children. "Now you say that back to me—To your very good health!"

They said it with enthusiasm, and he tipped back the carton and drank. "Okay, who's got to burp?" he asked when he'd downed the last of the milk.

"Detective Garth!" Jenna said.

"Miss Jenna, you stay out of this. We're going to burp really loud—and then we'll be good, won't we?" he asked the group. But most of them were already warming up and, therefore, too busy to answer.

Jenna sat surrounded by giggles and rude table noises. "Sister Mary John is coming," she nonchalantly advised them when the school's principal appeared in the doorway.

Garth desperately tried to shush everybody, but he had started this impromptu concert, and he was about to find that five-year-olds were nothing if not difficult to deprogram.

"Aren't you going to help me?" he whispered frantically to Jenna as the noise escalated.

"No way," she whispered back. "I've never seen any of you people before in my life."

"Ah! Detective Garth!" Sister Mary John said, coming over immediately. Every child at the table had the giggles. Garth had Hernando's head in a combination hug and hammerlock in an effort to keep him from really letting one rip. He smiled broadly, but he didn't let Hernando go.

Sister Mary John looked from Garth to the top of Hernando's head and back again. "Having a nice lunch?" she wondered.

"Oh, yes, Sister," Garth assured her. "Very nice."

"And you, Hernando?"

"Yeah!" came the muffled reply, punctuated by a giggle.

"What about you, Jenna?" Sister Mary John inquired.

"Oh, I don't know when I've had a lunch like this," Jenna assured her.

"Good. Very good," Sister Mary John said. She wandered away, and Garth released Hernando. He came up grinning.

"I wasn't going to do nothing!" he said.

"The he-heck you weren't," Garth said.

Mallory put her hands on her hips. "Garth! I thought you were going to say a *bad* word!"

"Who me? Mallory thought I was going to say a bad word," he said to Jenna.

"She's not the only one," Jenna assured him, and he grinned. He was a rascal all right; she had no doubts about that. And the children loved him.

"You've got to loosen up, Miss Jenna," he had the nerve to suggest.

"No, thank you. I don't have the stamina for it. And I'm supposed to be in charge here. Could we go now, or do you have some other totally gross thing in mind?"

"How would you feel about a food fight?" he asked, clearly still trying to annoy her.

"Are you the target?" she countered, and they both laughed.

But he could tell the very instant Jenna Gallagher remembered that she intended to handle him, not enjoy him, and her smile slid away.

"So what's next?" he asked to cover the moment.

She stood up and began getting the children into line. "It's time for them to go outside."

He got up from his chair. "Can I come along?"

He was standing too close to her—much too close. "I think we've taken up enough of your time."

"It's my time, Miss Jenna. I haven't finished the cubbyholes yet, and I'm supposed to get to know the children, right? I'll come along."

He went with her to take the children out to the playground—because there was no way to stop him, and because, she reasoned, Debbie still hadn't gotten back, and she needed the help. Fortunately The Phantom hadn't struck again, and dressing for the outing went smoothly. No one had misplaced anything, not even Mallory, though it took a while to retie all the shoes that had come untied. Even the children with Velcro fasteners wanted help—if Garth was the one helping. He sat patiently on the floor, surrounded by small lifted feet.

The group opted for the sliding board, with Garth supervising the climb up the ladder and Jenna catching at the bottom. The sun was bright, but the wind was brisk, and she huddled in her coat, watching him furtively. He was certainly good with the children, and he seemed to know all their names now without having to refer to the necklaces. Sister Mary John should be pleased. As for herself, she was acquiring a grudging respect for him, one that conflicted strongly with her need to be left alone. He didn't behave like Patrick and yet he...

She didn't know what he did—except disrupt everything. Her hard-won serenity. Her emotions. Her life.

He caught her looking at him, and she glanced away. She couldn't escape the fact that she was glad that she'd asked him and glad that he'd come, even if she hadn't addressed any of the reasons behind it. But when they got back inside, she tried once again to release him of his obligation to the class if he needed to go. Talking to him about his unwanted dinner invitations would be awkward at best.

"They'll be taking naps now, so you can't hammer any—" she began.

"I'll wait until they're awake," he interrupted. He looked

into her eyes, giving her the opportunity to tell him the real reason she was so determined for him to leave.

But she didn't press for his departure, and he walked away to supervise hanging up coats on the pegs along the back wall of the classroom and to get down the sleeping mats, letting Mallory and Hernando show him exactly what he was supposed to do. Then he helped tuck all the children in, covering them with the beach towels they'd brought from home. Jenna might have worried about the logo on Hernando's towel if kindergartners could read. CERTIFIED BEACH DOCTOR, it said. FREE CHEST EXAMINATIONS GIVEN HERE. She saw Garth smile when he read it and pat Hernando on the head.

"Go to sleep, man," he told him. "You've worked hard today. You deserve a good nap."

Jenna turned off the overhead lights and closed the blinds, then sat down on one of the two adult-size chairs to watch over the room. Everyone grew quiet, and after a moment Garth dragged up the other chair and sat down close to her.

"My God," he whispered. "They're actually going to sleep. I didn't think they ever wound down."

"Amazing, isn't it?" She looked at him. "Tell me, how is the investigation coming?"

"Investigation?" he asked, a bit taken aback.

"The Phantom Coat Flusher," she said.

He looked out over the sleeping children. "You've only got one slick enough, angry enough, to do it."

"Hernando," she said without hesitation, and he nodded.

"Why would he do that, do you think?" He had been very close to Hernando all day, and she found that she wanted his opinion.

"Well, one good thing about a Catholic school is the uniforms. Everybody dresses alike. Theoretically, nobody gets the business about what they wear. Except they aren't alike when it comes to their coats. That's the one place you can tell a difference in them. Hernando's wearing a third hand-me-down ghetto kid special, and he knows it. It's adequate, it keeps out the cold, but it's got 'Poor Kid' stamped all over it.''

"I don't think any of the children have said anything."

"They don't have to. *He* knows it."

"I'll talk to Sister Mary John."

"If you don't mind, I'd like to take care of it. If Sister Mary John or the school arranges a new coat for him, it'll make him feel worse, see?"

"Not exactly."

"The coat he's wearing now is a kind of symbol to him—of what he is and what he hasn't got. He already knows he's different, and if you single him out with a new coat, he'll know it all the more. Understand?"

She didn't precisely. "Won't your getting him a new coat make him feel bad, too?"

"Nah," he said blithely. "I'll think of something." He yawned and stretched his arms over his head. She was so aware of his body suddenly, of his strength and his masculinity, that she shifted in her chair. She had been alone for nearly a year, but no one had made her feel her aloneness as much as he did with that simple gesture.

"I could use a nap myself," he said.

"I could use the official kindergarten teacher for this class," Jenna said to take her mind off his physical presence. "I wonder where Debbie is?"

"Are you worried?"

"Yes and no. She was only going a few blocks to take Becca and her coat home. But she's—"

"What?" he prompted.

"A little addleheaded. She's been known to get sidetracked."

"You want me to go look for her?"

"No, not yet. She's been needing to talk to Becca's mother about some things. She's probably doing that."

The conversation lagged, until Jenna suddenly looked at him.

"I want to ask you something," she said.

"Go ahead." He expected that she'd get to the real reason she'd invited him here, but she didn't.

"I was wondering about your name…"

"My name?"

"Your first name—why you don't want anyone to use it."

He smiled slightly. "Because I'm a lot like Hernando."

"I don't understand."

"It's—" He shrugged. "I told you about how my mother wanted me to marry rich."

"Yes."

"Well, I wasn't just kidding around. It's the truth. Some people think winning the lottery or the magazine sweepstakes would be the answer to all their problems. Hazel thinks it's one of the two of us marrying money—not in a calculating way, but, like I said, the way it happened in the old movies. Luigi—he's the counterman at the Humoresque—he says she's always been that way. And she thinks if you can't be rich, you ought to *act* rich. She read someplace that in wealthy families a lot of times a son is given his mother's maiden name as his first name. That's why I'm 'Johnson.' I don't like it because it's a symbol to me—like Hernando's coat is to him." His eyes searched hers. "Do you understand?"

"I understand," she said. She understood completely. She just hadn't expected such candor. She didn't think he'd told many people that, and she felt as if he'd just given her a small but precious gift.

The minutes passed. They sat quietly. She could feel him

looking at her. The door at the end of the hallway banged loudly.

"Mrs. Gallagher," he said, his voice low. "About the other night, at the Carvers' party—I was out of line."

She didn't say anything. She was sitting with her arms folded, and he couldn't see her face.

"Mrs. Gallagher, don't you ever say stupid things? You don't know why you say them, you just…do?"

"Yes," she said evenly. "I sometimes say stupid things." She looked around at him. "But I don't think you do, Detective Garth."

He could feel himself flush. He wasn't being entirely honest with her, and she knew it. "Mrs. Gallagher—"

"Your remark was cruel at best—I'm sure you know that. I'm sure you've had no problem understanding why I didn't want to spend an evening over dinner with you."

She abruptly got up and went to cover the children who were out from under their beach towels. Then there was a commotion in the hall—Debbie arriving out of breath and harried. As she came into the room, she tried to smile but didn't quite make it. She kept looking over her shoulder.

"What's wrong?" Jenna whispered to keep from waking the children.

"I…thought I saw someone," Debbie said, looking over her shoulder again.

"Who?"

"Oh…" Debbie said airily. She glanced at Garth. She had a slight frown, and she gave an offhand shrug. "Looked sort of like Hugh." She started to take her coat off but then apparently changed her mind. "Garth," she said, her agitation apparently growing. "Garth, could you take Jenna home this afternoon?"

Chapter 6

"Debbie—" Jenna protested. Debbie was distracted at best, and Jenna was totally unprepared for this last-ditch attempt at matchmaking.

"Jenna, I'm sorry," Debbie said, moving away. "Something's come up. I have to take care of it today, and I don't know how long it'll take me. You don't mind, do you, Garth?"

"What?" he said, because he'd only heard his name in the middle of Debbie's run of conversation.

"Taking Jenna home," Debbie said.

"Sure," he said, glancing at Jenna. He'd do it, but from the look on her face, he was going to have one hell of a time getting her into the car.

"I'll take the bus," Jenna said—not unsurprisingly.

"Don't be silly," Debbie insisted. "It'll take you forever on the bus. Garth said he'd take you."

"Debbie, I don't want to impose any more on Detective Garth."

"It's no imposition, Mrs. Gallagher," he said lightly. She was feeling cornered again; he could see it in her face. But here was yet another opportunity—if he didn't screw it up.

Debbie looked at her watch. "What are you going to do, stand on the street in the cold and wait for the next bus?"

"I've done it before."

"When you had to," Debbie agreed. "This time you don't have to, does she, Garth?"

"No," he said. Some of the children were waking up and beginning to mill around. "Mrs. Gallagher, I would hate for you to do that on my account. It's the least I can do."

"See?" Debbie said, though clearly she didn't understand the obscure apology he was making.

"You don't have to *do* anything," Jenna said.

"I know that, Mrs. Gallagher. But I want to."

"Why?" She looked into his eyes, waiting to hear the answer.

"Because you were a cop's wife. Because you're my partner's friend. I don't want to leave you standing on the street in the cold waiting for a bus," he said evenly, and he didn't look away.

"It's out of your way."

"Yes," he agreed, because he felt as if this were some kind of trial suddenly. Would he tell the truth, the whole truth and nothing but? Or would she catch him in a lie— even a socially appropriate one—so she could dismiss him and his unwanted offer? "But today that isn't a problem."

"Detective Garth, I—"

But she was suddenly swamped by children. Mallory and at least two others were pulling on her skirt, and she turned her attention to that. He glanced at Debbie. She was frowning, and she kept watching the door.

"What's the matter?" he asked, walking over to her. She jumped.

"Oh, Garth! You scared me!"

"In broad daylight in the middle of a kindergarten class?" he asked, not quite teasing.

"I was thinking about something." She gave him a strained smile. "I forgot to tell Jenna I had this...errand this morning. Otherwise she could have driven herself instead of riding with me. I hate forgetting things the way I do—I don't know why I do it. Just me, I guess. Thanks for taking Jenna home."

Garth wasn't as certain as Debbie seemed to be that they'd gotten that settled, but he didn't say so. "Okay to get back to hammering now?" he asked. He'd been solicited to put cubbyholes together, too, and at least he knew he could finish that.

But he didn't get very far. Children, as they got their things gathered up and their coats on, kept coming to him, unabashedly hugging him before they lined up to go home.

Mallory was first.

"You are a very fine person, Garth," she said, hugging him hard.

"So are you, Miss Mallory," he responded.

"You are a fine person, Garth," the next two said.

Jenna was standing close by, watching.

"What is this?" he asked her when the children had trotted off to get cookies and juice, realizing now that he was participating in some kind of ritual.

"We always have hugs and positive reinforcement before they take their naps. I forgot today, so they're doing it now. Too many of them only hear that they're all right just the way they are from us—or from 'Mr. Rogers' on television. It's very important to them. They want to share it with you."

He gave up any further ideas of hammering, staying on his knees and waiting for the rest of the children to come and be hugged. Hernando was last.

"*I'm* a fine person," he said in typically Hernando fashion.

"The best, man," Garth agreed.

"I don't like cops."

"Yeah, I know," Garth said, giving him his hug. "What can I say?"

Hernando leaned back to stare at him for a moment. "Are you coming back here?"

"If I get invited."

"You ain't coming back, man. You're telling a *lie*."

"No. I'm telling you I haven't been invited yet."

Hernando studied him closely. "Okay," he decided. "Maybe I'll talk to Miss Jenna and Miss Debbie for you."

"You do that," Garth said.

Always "cool," Hernando slapped Garth's hand.

"Detective Garth," Jenna said, and he looked up at her. "I...can't leave until all the children are gone."

She was looking at him gravely. He thought that she was agreeing to let him take her home. He also thought that he could still blow it.

"Fine," he said. "I still have to finish the cubbyholes."

He went back to work. The less said on the matter, the better. The room grew quiet as Jenna and the last of the children went outside for whatever the going-home procedure might be. All in all, it had been a satisfactory day, he thought. Hammer or not, he certainly hadn't envisioned doing even minor carpentry, but his old high school shop training had apparently survived the years of police work, and the cubbyholes had been put together with minimal amount of aggravation. He'd had a conversation—of sorts—with Jenna. He'd liked the children. He would have liked to have had more time to work on whatever it was Jenna might know about Hugh, but maybe that would work out, too, if she'd decided to let him take her home.

The door at the end of the hallway slammed again, and

he could hear someone coming—hurrying—down the long corridor.

"Forgot my purse," Debbie said, bursting into the room. It was lying on the desk, and she snatched it up in a hurried dash around the room. "Thanks for taking Jenna home," she called again as she went out the door, leaving him no time to reply. "You didn't have a date or anything, did you?" she asked, abruptly sticking her head back into the doorway.

"No. No date. I told Hazel I'd come to the Humoresque for dinner."

"Why don't you take Jenna?" Debbie said. "She'd love it."

He grinned. "Yeah, sure." He was trying to gain Jenna Gallagher's confidence, and a hole-in-the-wall café straight out of the pages of a Damon Runyon short story wasn't likely the place to do it.

"No, she would. She likes people. There are people there, aren't there?"

"I'm afraid so," Garth confessed.

"Look. Jenna isn't a snob. She'd like it. Really. I have to go," she concluded abruptly, disappearing from the doorway. He could hear her break into a run as she neared the outside door.

A bell rang somewhere, and the school emptied out in earnest, all the upper grades being let loose and all the appropriate commotion. He hammered the last few nails into the shelves and checked them for stability, remembering his own exhilaration at being let out of school for the day. As a boy, he'd considered school something just short of prison. But for Hazel's determination, he probably would have dropped out and ended up in a real one. He owed Hazel a lot for that, for making him stay in school.

He looked up, thinking Debbie had come back again.

"What did you forget this time?" he asked, but it was

Jenna. They were both wearing black coats and the gold-and-black-school-colors scarf. "I thought you were Debbie," he said before she could reply.

"No, she's off on her errand. Are you finished?"

"Except for moving this section wherever you want it to go."

"Oh, next to the others, I think."

Jenna helped him slide the unit of cubbyholes across the floor and align it the others. *It was very kind of you to do this,* she almost said, but she didn't. She'd heard, loud and clear, that he didn't want to be thought of as "kind."

"Very nice," she said instead. "This should help cut down on some of the confusion."

He smiled. He'd spent the day here, and he was nothing if not battle scarred. "You think so, do you?"

"I hope so," she answered, smiling in return. "Every little bit helps."

"How often do you work here?" he asked idly, but he was more than aware of the fact that they were alone now, more than aware of how pretty she was and how nice she smelled.

"As often as they need me. The other regular teacher is pregnant, and she's having all the upsets that go with it. I'm hoping for something permanent. This gets my foot in the door anyway."

They stood there awkwardly. Garth couldn't keep from staring into her eyes. He wanted to know what she thought of him, and he supposed that he might see it there. The silence lengthened, and it occurred to him that he'd better tread lightly if he wanted the opportunity of taking her home.

"So," he said abruptly, "are you ready to go?"

She looked relieved.

"Yes. Sister Mary John would like to speak to you on the way out."

"I'm not in trouble, am I? I drank my milk, and I didn't swear—out loud."

"You should be in good standing then." She moved to the windows to open all the blinds. "When I was a little girl," she said over her shoulder, "we closed all the blinds at the end of the day to help keep the heat in. Now they have to be left open so anyone passing by can see if there are any suspicious lights or vandals or burglars."

"That's what the world's come to," he said, opening the last few blinds for her. She went to the small closet at the back of the room to get his coat.

"Are you sure you don't mind going all the way to Park Slope?"

"I don't mind, Mrs. Gallagher."

She handed him his coat, and their fingers brushed. Hers were warm, soft. He put the coat on on the way out, opening the door for her for no other reason than it would allow him to get closer to her, albeit briefly.

Jenna walked alongside him to Sister Mary John's office, a bit disconcerted because the place was deserted now. A school with all the children gone was a bit eerie, she thought, though that wasn't entirely the reason for her disquiet. The primary reason was Johnson Garth—kind, accommodating Johnson Garth.

She glanced at him. She was a policeman's widow. She was his partner's friend. Why shouldn't he offer to take her home? There was nothing wrong with his offer. What was wrong was her response to it. She wanted to be with him. And she wanted to run for her life. And she was perfectly aware that both responses were overreactions on her part.

Perhaps the duality of her feelings was because she was lonely. And because she was still having some kind of watered-down version of her anxiety attacks. She didn't have the weakness or the palpitations, but part of her certainly wanted to run away. From him—or from herself—was the question.

"About the dinner invitations," she said when they were nearly at Sister Mary John's open door.

"Yes," he said without surprise.

"Detective Garth?" Sister Mary John called through the doorway.

"They're still good—the invitations," Garth said with a wink just before he stepped inside the principal's office.

Jenna waited outside, exasperated because she was going to have to go into this after all. She should have known that subtleties wouldn't work with Garth. Not that it was entirely his fault. She *had* agreed to let him take her home.

She stood in the hallway, rubbing a small ache between her eyebrows that threatened to become a major pain.

"I thought you understood," she said when he came out again.

"I understand. I just wanted you to know the invitations stood anyway."

"Garth—"

"Friend of yours," he interrupted, nodding toward the end of the hallway.

But it wasn't a friend at all. It was Hugh.

"Hugh," Garth said when he reached them.

"What is he doing here?" Hugh said to Jenna, ignoring Garth, his eyes cold, his manner tense.

"I usually speak for myself, Hugh," Garth said. "What is it exactly you'd like to know?"

"I'm talking to Jenna," Hugh said, taking her by the arm.

Jenna pointedly removed it from his grasp. "And if I thought it was any business of yours whatsoever, Hugh, I'd tell you," she said.

Hugh hesitated, looking from Jenna to Garth and then back again. He suddenly smiled. "Jenna—Jenna, hey, I'm sorry. Patrick was my little brother. I was so used to looking after him—and with him gone, I guess it spills over to you sometimes.''

"What are you doing here, Hugh?" Jenna asked. If he'd come because he'd somehow found out Garth was here, she wanted to know about it—and she didn't need him to remind her about Patrick.

"I was supposed to pick up Mom. She's here for some meeting about the Fall Bazaar or something. You haven't seen her, have you?" He continued to ignore Garth, but he was trying to handle her with that unsubtle charm of his that he could turn on and off at will. His assumption that he could cajole her into a better frame of mind grated on her nerves even more so than usual.

"No, I haven't," Jenna said, refusing to be assuaged. "If she's here, she'll be talking to Father Kevin."

"So how about helping me find her?" Hugh said, the smile still firmly in place.

This time Jenna smiled in return. "I think you know where Father Kevin's office is, Hugh. Patrick told me you were sent there enough when you were a student here."

Garth, who'd seen fit to stay out of the conversation thus far, spoke up. "I believe that's Mrs. Gallagher coming now."

Jenna looked around. Mamie Gallagher was coming down the corridor. She smiled broadly for a moment, but then, as she recognized Garth, the smile slid away.

"I was looking for you, dear," Mamie said to Jenna with the same studied indifference to Garth her son had displayed. "And how nice you look. Hunter green is your color, isn't it? So becoming. It's nice to see you taking an interest in that kind of thing again."

Mamie said the words, but her meaning was clearly the opposite. Mamie Gallagher still wore black, unlike her disrespectful daughter-in-law, who stood here in dark green—with another man.

Jenna smiled, a smile she had to dig deep for and strain hard to keep. "Mamie, you know Detective Garth."

"Mrs. Gallagher," Garth said, leaning forward to shake her hand before she had time to decide whether she wanted to or not. In the process, he shot Jenna an are-you-sure-you-know-what-you're-doing look.

Jenna did know what she was doing. She was working very hard at not being intimidated. Garth was here at her invitation, whether the Gallaghers approved or not, and she wasn't going to behave as if she'd been caught doing something wrong.

Because Mamie Gallagher had been schooled to be gracious, she smiled politely—for a second and a half. "Detective," she said, dismissing Garth without so much as a second glance. "You're coming to dinner tonight, Jenna." It wasn't quite a question. "We haven't seen you lately."

Jenna had no excuse for not coming, none except that she didn't want to have to explain her association with Garth. Garth was unexplainable—to herself, much less to Patrick's mother. "I—"

"You didn't forget about Hazel, did you, Jenna?" Garth interrupted.

She looked at him blankly.

"She's waiting at the Humoresque," Garth said. "You didn't forget, did you?"

She looked into his eyes. Hazel?

"Oh, Hazel!" she said abruptly. "I did forget," she said. She had forgotten that Hazel was his mother, certainly, and that she worked at the Humoresque; she wasn't playing entirely fast and loose with the truth.

"I think we'd better get going," he prompted, putting his hand on her shoulder. "Nice to see you again, Mrs. Gallagher," he said to Mamie. "Hugh."

* * *

"Nice going," Garth said as they crossed the parking lot to his car.

"Oh, sure—I can't believe I let you lie for me!" He now had her by the elbow, as if he thought she might not come along otherwise.

"I didn't lie," he said. "I only asked if you'd forgotten Hazel—which you had."

"It's the same thing—no, it's worse. It's...manipulation. I didn't have other plans."

"You didn't want to have dinner with the Gallaghers, did you?"

"No, but—"

"And you're all the old lady has left of her son, aren't you? You loved Patrick, and you don't want to hurt her feelings, right? So you can't very well tell her to take a hike, no matter how much you want to—"

She abruptly stopped walking and looked up at him. It was incredible to her that he understood the situation so perfectly.

"—can you?" he finished.

She sighed. "No."

"All right, then. Sometimes you gotta do what you gotta do, for your own sanity. This is the car."

He unlocked the door and opened it for her.

For my own sanity, she thought as she got in.

She looked back toward the school. Hugh and Mamie were coming out—to see if she was actually leaving with Johnson Garth, she supposed. She sighed again. "I live at—"

"I know where you live," he interrupted.

She didn't ask him how. She sat staring straight ahead, thinking about Mamie, thinking about what she should have said, but she gave a small wave as the car went past Mamie and Hugh on the way out of the parking lot. She was *not* going to behave as if she were doing something wrong!

"You're coming to dinner tonight, Jenna."

Thank you, no, she should have said. A big smile and a simple no, without explanation or excuse. It couldn't be any worse than letting Garth invent excuses for her. Why couldn't she just say that? Thank you, no!

Because she'd loved Patrick and because she was all his mother had left of him. And because sometimes you have to do what you have to do, for your own sanity.

"You still beating yourself up?" Garth asked when they'd gone a few blocks.

She glanced at him. "Yes," she said truthfully. She realized suddenly that they weren't going to Park Slope.

"Where are we going?" she asked abruptly and not without some alarm.

He looked over at her. "Take it easy, Mrs. Gallagher. I got you into a guilty conscience. I'm going to get you out of it."

She pursed her lips to ask how, then didn't ask after all. There was no point in it. For whatever unlikely reason, she believed him. She couldn't feel any worse; perhaps she'd feel better. Wherever he intended taking her, as it stood now, she'd go.

Chapter 7

Jenna would remember their entrance into the Humoresque as a series of double takes—from the older woman in a green smock and a hair net waiting tables, from the old man in a T-shirt and a white apron working behind the counter, and from a nervous, ragged street person just inside the door, who stared at her, then immediately left.

The Humoresque was long and old and narrow. It had a big front window boasting its name, the lettering faded and barely still visible, and when Garth opened the door, it smelled of fried onions and fresh coffee and tired, down-and-out people. The floor was made of tiny hexagonal black-and-white tiles that made a whispery sound against the soles of her shoes when she walked, and everyone in the place looked up when she and Garth came in.

To her right was the grill behind a long counter with a row of wobbly wooden stools, and against the opposite wall, high-backed wooden booths with an assortment of patrons' initials carved into them. There were several small tables with bentwood chairs farther in back. Jenna looked up at the high ceiling. Probably the original embossed tin, she thought, and in spite of needing some repairs and paint, quite beautiful.

"Whatever you do, don't mention Walter O'Malley," Garth said as they made their way through the patrons to find somewhere to sit. The place was crowded with elderly couples, taxi drivers and little old men who slurped soup at the counter.

"All right," she said agreeably. "Who's Walter O'Malley?" She was feeling better already. Telling the truth in reverse like this was something she'd never done, but she had to agree that the guilt was fading. Somewhat.

"Who's Walter O'Malley?" Garth asked, his voice so incredulous that she shrugged and gave him an apologetic grin.

"On October 8, 1957," he explained hurriedly, "Walter O'Malley announced that he was moving the Brooklyn Dodgers to California—that's who Walter O'Malley is."

"I take it he hasn't been forgiven."

"Not in this world or the next. Ebbets Field—"

But he didn't get to tell her about Ebbets Field. The waitress in the green smock and the hair net swooped down on them.

"Well, what do you know?" she said loudly, giving Garth a hug. "My son the flatfoot," she continued in an exaggerated whisper. "And who is this?" she asked in a normal tone of voice, smiling at Jenna.

"This is Jenna Gallagher, Ma. I'm making an honest woman out of her."

Jenna gave him a hard look, but he only grinned.

"Good," Hazel Garth said, patting him on the cheek as if such announcements were commonplace from her irrepressible son.

"Jenna, this is the notorious Hazel of whom you've heard me speak."

Jenna extended her hand. "Mrs. Garth, it's nice to meet you. Actually, we just—"

"—came by for dinner," Garth finished for her.

"No, we didn't," she countered as nicely as she could.

"Yes, we did," he replied just as nicely.

Hazel was looking from one of them to the other. She shook Jenna's hand.

"Call me Hazel, Jenna. Everybody does. So how come you're out with a nice girl like this dressed like *that*?" she demanded of Garth. "You look like Roy Lee. How many times I got to tell you you got to dress for success, huh?"

"That makes about seventeen million, five hundred thousand and six, Ma," Garth said.

"Oh, you. You make the jokes. He ain't never serious, Jenna. So you want dinner? It's too early for dinner. Luigi's not ready for the dinner crowd. Who eats dinner this time of day?"

"Working people, Ma. People who've only had chicken and noodles and carrot sticks."

"You go find something else to do for a little while. Jenna! You seen the loft, Jenna?"

"Ah, no."

"You take Jenna up to see the loft." Hazel patted her on the arm. "It's a great place. There are people who'd give their eyeteeth for a place like that. You go show her," she said, giving Garth a little push. "Then you come back."

"Want to see a loft?" Garth asked, smiling into Jenna's eyes.

"Garth…"

"I'm telling you, it's a lot easier to just go. Trust me on this." He cut his eyes toward his mother.

Jenna smiled in spite of herself. "All right. Why don't I go see the loft?"

"Smart woman," Garth said, taking her by the arm. "Luigi!" he yelled down the counter. And apparently it was that kind of place, because hardly a head turned—even Luigi's—for a raised voice. Clearly only entrances caused the clientele to take note. "Luigi!" he called again, motioning for the old man behind the counter.

This time the old man looked around, and he seemed delighted at Garth's summons, hurrying down the length of the counter and wiping his hands on his apron as he came.

"Luigi, posso presentare la mia amica, Signora Jenna Gallagher," Garth said to him.

"Signora, Giovanni?" Luigi said, eyebrows raised. *"Dove é il suo marito?"*—And where is her husband?—he continued in Italian, clearly bracing himself to have his sense of propriety offended.

"Lui é morto"—dead—Garth hastened to explain, glancing at Jenna to see if the conversation was disturbing her. No, he thought. She didn't understand Italian.

"Assassinato," he continued, because he knew Luigi had the gentlest of hearts, and it was suddenly important to him that the old man think kindly of Jenna. *"Lui era un poliziotto."* A policeman, murdered.

"Ah!" Luigi said in sympathy. *"Felice di conoscerla,"* he said to Jenna, clasping her hand warmly in his two big ones.

"Jenna, this is my friend Luigi Lufrano."

"Mr. Lufrano," Jenna said, smiling.

"Luigi, please, *Signora*. So. It's good to have so pretty a lady be your friend, Giovanni," he said to Garth. "You stay with us a while, Jenna. I fix you the best dinner you ever have."

"That would be nice," Jenna replied, because she liked him instantly. She glanced at Garth. If there was any complicity here, she couldn't tell it from Garth's face.

"You like...hamburger steak?" Luigi asked earnestly.

"Yes," she said.

"Good! I give you the best. Lots of onions and garlic." He squeezed her hand. "You go with Garth now while I get ready."

"This way," Garth said, leading her out through the back of the restaurant into a narrow hallway. "Through there." He pointed toward a door at the far end, one of dark wood with a textured, frosted panel of glass in the upper half. It reminded her of an office door out of a 1940s private-eye movie. In fact, the whole place reminded her of a 1940s movie set. No wonder Hazel Garth believed in Frank Capra miracles, working here every day.

"Luigi calls you John," she remarked, and he looked at her in surprise.

"You speak Italian?"

"No. I know Giovanni is John, but that about covers it."

"Interesting language," he said.

"You speak it very well," she said, wondering why he looked so relieved.

"Not really. I can hold my own with simple pleasantries. That's about it. And some simple *un*pleasantries," he added with a mischievous grin.

"That must come in handy," she observed. "Being able to swear in more than one language."

"Oh, it does, Mrs. Gallagher. Did you mean what you said to Luigi about staying here for dinner?" He fumbled in his jeans pocket for his keys.

She looked into his eyes. "I...think it would be nice," she said again.

"Good," he said, unlocking the door. It opened with a loud squeak. "I've got one question, though."

"What?" she said, waiting to see if he wanted her to lead or follow.

Follow.

"What's Luigi got that I haven't got?" he asked over his shoulder on his way up the stairs.

"Manners," she said dryly, and he laughed.

"Well, you've got me there. Hold on to the rail. And watch the steps. Some of the metal strips on the edges are coming up."

Her toe caught even as he said it, and he grabbed her arm to steady her.

"Easy," he said. His touch was warm and pleasant, but he let her go immediately. "I'd get these stairs fixed, but in this neighborhood you need all the booby traps you can get. So when's the last time you toured a loft apartment?"

"Never," she said, stepping well into the wooden steps as she climbed.

"Never? That's hard to believe. Housing is the only way New Yorkers know how to impress each other. You go to L.A., they want to show you their cars. You come to New York, all you hear about is apartments. I thought you would have seen everything by now—brownstones, penthouses, the works."

"No. Lofts I've missed."

"Well, you're going to love this. I figure this loft is right up there with, say, an '84 Porsche."

"I'm sure," Jenna said.

At the top of the stairs they came to another door with frosted glass.

"After you," Garth said, unlocking it. "The light switch is on the wall on your left."

She found it without difficulty and switched it on. The loft was huge and well lighted—the one switch seemed to turn on everything. As big as the area was, there were no dark corners. But there was a draft. One of the windows was slightly open, and the room was cold. She was glad to keep her coat on.

"So, how do you like it?" he asked, walking ahead of

her, snatching up discarded clothes as he went and rolling them into a ball—which he tossed unceremoniously into a corner for lack of a better place.

"This isn't an apartment. This is a skating rink with furniture," she said, impressed by the vastness of the place. Some of the apartments she and Patrick had lived in when they were first married would have fit into this place twice.

"Not much furniture," he said, and he was right. There was a small grouping not far from the arched windows across the front of the loft—a sofa and a chair and a table with a telephone and a floor lamp. There was a double bed, made up but without a bedspread, at the far end of the room—a long way away. There was no kitchen table in the galley area, or anyplace else for that matter. She supposed he ate on a stool at the counter.

"But plenty of clocks," she said, noticing that there were four of them on the wall, identical except for the time. "Do you need this many clocks?"

"Yeah. I hate being bothered by bureaucratic nonsense like daylight saving time. You know how much aggravation that is? Setting and resetting clocks?"

"Yes," she said agreeably.

"Well, the first clock is Eastern Standard Time. The third one is Eastern Daylight Savings Time. This way I only have to reset my alarm clock."

"What are the other two?"

"Well, the second and the fourth one is what time I'll get to the station house, God willing, if I leave by whatever time is on the first one or the third one. See?"

She was grinning. She had no idea if he was serious.

"*No,*" she said pointedly.

"See, it saves a lot of wear and tear on the Whip if I'm not late. The lieutenant *hates* ten o'clock scholars."

"I'm not surprised. Does the lieutenant know you go to all this trouble on his behalf?"

"Nah. I don't think he'd believe it, do you?"

"No," she said. "I don't believe it myself."

He gave her an incredulous look that made her laugh.

"This way for the view," he said, pointing to the arched windows.

As she walked in that direction, she noticed the photograph by the telephone. "This is you," she said, bending down to inspect it more closely. How handsome he was, she thought. And how happy. Somehow she'd never thought of him as being as young and carefree as this. She studied the other two people in the picture—the beautiful dark-haired girl Garth had his arm around and the skinny boy whose ears looked too big for his head.

"Who are the people with you?"

"Just...friends."

"You don't have any brothers or sisters?"

"No."

"The girl—she's so pretty. How old were you in this picture?"

"I was eighteen," he said, and something in his voice made her look up at him.

Something in his face made her stop asking questions. She straightened and walked to the windows to look down at the street below.

"You can see everything from here," she said, because she felt awkward suddenly and needed something to say.

"Sometimes more than I want to." He paused. "But sometimes it's nice. In the summer especially. Most of the businesses on the street are family owned, and everybody'll drag folding lawn chairs outside and sit on the sidewalk in front of their stores when business is slow. Parents, grandparents, the kids. It's...nice."

She looked back over the apartment. "Well, I'm impressed. I'm surprised Skip hasn't tried to talk you out of it."

"Skip hasn't seen it. I don't bring many people here."

He was standing close to her, and she looked into his eyes again. And once again, she believed him. She didn't think it was some kind of line he used on women. Perhaps that was why Hazel had insisted he show her the place. Jenna was someone new in Garth's life, and perhaps his bringing or not bringing her up here was, to Hazel, some kind of indicator, some kind of clue.

Signifying what? Jenna wondered, looking away from his eyes and back out the window to the street below. She had no idea what she was doing here—at least from his standpoint. Or was this still part of some police code of honor? She was a policeman's widow. She was his partner's friend. He'd been rude to her, and now he owed it to her to be a little more civil than was his custom?

She gave a soft sigh. She didn't think Garth *had* a code—at least not one that he wouldn't chuck at a moment's notice if he needed to.

What, then? What did he want? Maybe it was some kind of locker-room bet. Some plan to get even with Hugh. Or some plan to prove his sexual irresistibility to his skeptical peers. She'd been to enough department social gatherings to know the mind-set. *Five will get you ten old Garth can make it with the widow.*

She had to be careful. She had to stop feeling the things she was feeling. She liked him. And, while she couldn't help herself in that regard, it had to stop there, before someone got hurt. Her.

"What?" she said, because she realized that he had said something, her eyes searching his for some glimmer of intent.

"I said, he wouldn't like the onions."

She frowned, not knowing what he meant.

"You said you were surprised Skip hadn't tried to talk me out of this place. I said he wouldn't like the onions—

the smell from the restaurant. It drifts up here. I have to leave a window open.''

''Oh,'' she said absently.

He watched her closely. He'd lost her somewhere. Again. She'd remembered that she didn't want to like him, and the wall had gone up. He had to give her credit for determination. When she'd decided not to like someone, she stuck with it.

But, God, he wished she wouldn't look at him like that! Those beautiful, sad, *knowing* eyes of hers. It was as if she knew he wasn't being straight with her, but she was going to let it play out anyway. Because she couldn't help it. Because neither of them could help it. The truth of the matter was that he had to keep reminding himself what this was all about. He wanted to know if Hugh had even remotely had anything to do with Patrick's death. It was important, damn it, and she was making him forget that. Standing here now, he wanted to touch her. He wanted to put his arms around her. He wanted to get as deep inside her as he could get. He wanted to take away the sadness in her eyes and promise her she'd be all right with him.

Like Mary?

The thought rose unbidden, and there was nothing he could do about it.

''Are you ready to go?'' he asked more sharply than he had intended.

They went back downstairs—to a booth Hazel had ceremoniously held for them with a small, worn RESERVED sign she'd placed in the middle of the table. Jenna took her coat off and put it with her purse in the corner.

''So, what'll it be?'' Hazel asked as they slid in, order pad out. ''And if it ain't hamburger steak, it'll break Luigi's heart.''

Jenna smiled. ''Hamburger steak will be fine—and this goes on separate checks.''

"You can have it well done or well done," Hazel advised her. Hazel's eyebrows had gone up at the request for separate checks, but apparently she wasn't going to comment.

"I'd like it...well done," Jenna decided.

"Way to go. Two hamburger steaks, separate checks, with the trimmings. You do want the trimmings?"

"With all our hearts," Garth said.

"Hush, you. You get what you get."

"Ever wonder why business is the way it is, Ma?"

"Listen, we got all the business we can handle. You want sweet talk, you let Jenna sweet talk you."

"I wish," he said, looking into Jenna's eyes. She smiled tolerantly, the way she would have smiled at some outrageousness of Hernando's.

Hazel left, taking their order—which surely would be no surprise—to Luigi. Luigi read it carefully, exchanged a few words with Hazel, then yelled "Giovanni!" in their direction.

"Excuse me," Garth said. "That's me."

"I know," she said dryly, and he grinned.

She watched him go. Apparently it was all right for Luigi to call him John, as long as it wasn't in English. The two men had a small conference, with Garth shaking his head no, then nodding.

He was grinning again when he came back. "Luigi wondered if you wanted french fries or hash browns."

"And what did I want?"

"Well, you'll try both," Garth said. "Because you don't know for sure."

"Ah," Jenna said. "Good thinking on my part. You two go back a long way, don't you?"

"He's the closest thing to a father I ever had. He even busted my butt good for me one time when I needed it. Man, he let me have it. And you know what? *He* cried. Big

guy like that, crying because he had to put a good-for-
nothing punk like me in his place.''

"Giovanni!" Luigi yelled again.

"Luigi, what!" Garth yelled back, but Luigi had lapsed
into a whirlwind of Italian. "Excuse me again," Garth said
to Jenna.

Jenna sat smiling to herself, watching the drama at the
grill. It was obvious that these two, regardless of the history
of "butt busting," harbored a great affection for each other.

She suddenly looked up, realizing that someone was
standing at the edge of the booth. It was the street person
who'd been waiting just inside the door when she and Garth
came in. He was nervous still, pulling at the grimy collar
of his shirt. His eyes met hers briefly, then shifted away.

"Tony wants to talk to you," he said.

"Tony?" Jenna asked, looking in the direction he indicated. A man in a business suit was getting up from a table
way in back. At a distance, he looked like any successful
businessman in a well-tailored suit, and he was definitely
out of place in the Humoresque. But as he came closer, the
flashiness became more evident. The walk, the attitude, was
all wrong for the world of legitimate business. He was wearing a pink silk shirt and too many rings—big diamond rings,
two on each hand. He had his hair in the "wet look,"
combed straight back from his high forehead and into a
queue. She could smell his cologne, expensive cologne—
Drakker Noir, she thought—well ahead of him.

Jenna looked at him quizzically. She was certain they'd
never met before. He smiled, but she didn't return it.

"I just wanted to say you are one beautiful lady," he
said, his voice low and urgent, his dark eyes boring into
hers. "Sometimes people don't take the time to appreciate
beautiful things. Tony Zaccato takes the time. Life's too
short—"

"Have we met?" Jenna said, growing uncomfortable under his scrutiny.

"Not exactly. You've got a nice body, beautiful lady." The smile became sly and knowing. "I noticed that when you took off your coat." His eyes slid down to her breasts and back again. "You be good to the cop there," he said, his head jerking sharply toward where Garth stood talking to Luigi. "You make him *real* happy, because he's not going to get—"

But Garth was coming, and he didn't finish. Jenna could feel the tension in him as he watched Garth approach. No, not quite tension. Expectation, perhaps, as if he'd deliberately wanted to provoke a reaction. When Garth was near, Tony Zaccato deliberately stepped closer to her. She thought for a moment he was going to put his hand on her shoulder.

"So," Garth said quietly, his gaze shifting from Jenna to the man. "Tony. It's been a long time."

"You know how it is, Garth," Tony Zaccato said. "It takes time to get over a great sorrow—for some of us, that is." He turned his attention to Jenna. "She's very beautiful. Even Mary would say so. Are you going to introduce me to her, Garth?"

"No," Garth said.

"No?" Tony said, both eyebrows raised. He gave a small smile. "You shouldn't be ashamed of such a beautiful woman, Garth."

"You're not going to start anything with me, Tony. You're back, and you've made sure I know it. That's the end of it."

"No, Garth. Not the end. But I don't want to start anything with you. I want to finish it, don't I?"

"Listen, you—"

Tony held up both hands. "Ah! Not here, Garth. Not in front of the beautiful lady. Another place. Another time."

He sidestepped Garth and walked toward the door, the

street person hurrying to catch up with him before he got outside.

"Garth?" Jenna said, but he wasn't listening to her.

"Luigi!" he yelled. "You know he's here and you don't bother to tell me?"

"Hey!" Luigi said, throwing up both hands. "What, am I cooking with eyes in the back of my head now? Who sees Tony Zaccato? The man is a snake! He comes, he goes, like a snake!"

"Hazel!" Garth said.

"Yeah, I knew he came in and I didn't say anything!" Hazel yelled before he could start in on her. "And you want to know why? Because you'd act like you're acting now, that's why! Crazy! You can't do anything about Tony Zaccato! The less you see of him, the better for everybody. Now, sit down with Jenna—or do you want to chase him down the street so he can file charges of police harassment? Again!"

Garth swore under his breath; everyone in the place was looking on with great interest. He sat down, but he was still fuming. It was all he could do so sit still.

"Do you want to go?" Jenna asked, and he looked up at her as if he'd completely forgotten she was there.

He gave a short exhalation of breath. "No," he said. He shrugged. "The sonofa—Zaccato gets to me."

"Really?" Jenna asked quietly, and he half smiled.

He made a concentrated effort to get himself in hand. He'd expected to encounter Tony Zaccato sooner or later; he just hadn't expected it to be here, with Jenna. He had no idea what Tony had said to her. She didn't seem upset, but then he knew that Jenna Gallagher could keep a rein on her emotions if she had to. He took a deep breath. He was rattled, and not because Tony had turned up unexpectedly. It was because he'd been afraid for Jenna. When he'd looked up and seen Tony hanging over her, it had been all he could do not to behave like the street kid he was whose territory had been invaded. "Yeah," he said. "Really."

Hazel came by the booth carrying a pot of coffee and somebody's dinner. "Now look what you done," she whispered to Garth. "You got Luigi all stirred up. You know he can't cook when he's upset."

"Ma, tell him I'm sorry."

"*You* tell him you're sorry! You're the one who made him think he let Tony Zaccato sneak up on you."

Hazel went on with her plate, and Garth leaned against the back of the booth for a moment and closed his eyes. When he opened them, Jenna was regarding him thoughtfully.

"What did Tony Zaccato say to you?" he asked, his voice quiet but filled with purpose.

"Nothing I understood. Some kind of macho pick-up line, I think."

"Did he know who you are?" he interrupted.

"Who I am? No. I asked him if we'd met—"

"He didn't mention Patrick or Hugh?" he asked, interrupting again.

"Why on earth would he do that?"

"Tony likes to name-drop. He might—if he knew who you were."

"He didn't. He only told me to—" She stopped. She hadn't wanted to tell him that part, but she fully realized that she was dealing with Garth, the cop, and not Garth, the man, and that the barrage of questions was his way of working, of getting information. He didn't give a suspect time to manufacture alternatives to the truth. And that was exactly the way she felt. Like a suspect.

"He wanted you to what?" he persisted.

She hesitated, then decided to tell him. "To...be good to you."

Garth frowned. "Be good to me? He said that? Tell me exactly what he said."

"Garth, I don't remember exactly. I think he misunderstood. He thought I was your girlfriend. But that was the gist of it—he told me to be good to you."

They stared at each other; she couldn't begin to read his expression. Hazel came by again, this time carrying only the coffee decanter. She cleared her throat with great significance as she passed, and Garth looked around at Luigi. He sighed heavily.

"Excuse me," he said—for the third time since they'd come in the front door. He stood up, but he caught her by the hand and pulled her along with him. "I need the moral support."

That wasn't precisely the truth. What he needed was to touch her, and he couldn't think of any other way to do it. "I don't make apologies often. You can give me pointers."

That Garth would make the effort to soothe Luigi's ruffled feathers or that he would want her along while he did it was incredible to Jenna. But she went, letting him take her by the hand, his fingers warm, strong on hers. All day she'd had to keep changing her mind about him. The people at the Humoresque were his family, and he'd brought her here when there was no reason for it, or none that she could discern, regardless of his claim that he was making her an honest woman. Garth was a complicated man, and now he made a sincere apology, ignoring Luigi's gestures of dismissal until he had the old man in a better mood. The conversation ran in half-Italian, half-English until Luigi glanced around at Jenna.

"It's not a good thing to let Tony Zaccato see what you treasure," Luigi said, and Jenna wasn't certain if it were an explanation for her or a warning for Garth.

Luigi suddenly smiled. "Your pretty friend is hungry,

Garth. You stand here a minute. I give you your dinner, and you can save your poor mama's feet."

They both waited, carrying their own plates back to the reserved booth as soon as Luigi pronounced the hamburger steaks done. The steak was excellent, Jenna thought, just the way she liked it, smothered in fried onions. Garth was very quiet.

"Tell me about Tony Zaccato," she said after a time.

Garth looked up at her. "You want more coffee?"

"No, I want to know about Tony Zaccato. Why did you think he might have mentioned Patrick or Hugh?"

She could feel him trying to decide—could he get out of answering her question or not?

"He's a two-bit hood," he said, apparently deciding the latter. "Drugs mostly, but he's not above a little prostitution and auto theft. I told you he likes to name-drop. If he knew who you were, I thought—" he shrugged "—he might have mentioned it." He looked into her eyes. "You never heard Patrick or Hugh mention him, did you?"

"No," she said. "Not that I remember. Can't you get anything on him?"

"Nothing that sticks."

They ate for a time in silence.

"Who is Mary?" Jenna asked.

Garth looked up at her as if he were startled by the question.

"Mary?"

"Tony Zaccato said, 'Even Mary would think so.' Who is Mary?"

He was growing restive again. He suddenly smiled, but his eyes shifted away. "So, how do you like Luigi's cooking?"

She didn't answer him. She was waiting for her own answers.

"Obviously you're worried about whatever this is with Tony Zaccato," she said.

"I'm not worried."

"You're a liar, Detective Garth," Jenna said mildly. "And as a participant or the bait or whatever I was just now, I think I'd be a little more at ease if I knew some of the details."

"I told you. Tony Zaccato is a two-bit hood."

"And what about Mary? Is she a hood, too?"

Garth looked into her eyes, and he realized he was going to tell her, that he wanted to tell her.

"Mary...is the girl in the picture, the one you saw upstairs. I was crazy about her when I was eighteen. After high school, I went into the Navy, and we lost track of each other. And then one day, about three years ago, she came walking into the Humoresque. I hadn't seen her in fifteen years. Fifteen years, and it was still there. All of it. I wanted to marry her. She was Tony Zaccato's sister."

"Was?" Jenna asked quietly.

"She's dead. Tony thinks it's my fault."

"Is it?"

He looked into her eyes. "Yeah."

They rode to Park Slope in silence. The streets were foggy. He had told her that he loved Mary Zaccato and Mary was dead because of it. He didn't know quite what he expected her reaction would be, but this wasn't it. He'd thought she'd be shocked, not uninterested. But she must be uninterested, because she hadn't said a word. He flipped on the radio to fill in the silence. Jazz. The radio station was playing jazz. He left it.

"You can let me out here," she said when they turned down her street. But it was dark, and a light rain was falling. He drove on and parked in a tight space.

"I'll come in with you," he said.

"You don't have to."

"I want to see where you live."

He opened the car door and got out, leaving her perplexed and uneasy. Again. He kept doing that to her—completely disarming her with the truth, when all the while she sensed that he would more likely be lying. And, though she couldn't explain it, she *believed* him. She believed the reason he'd given for wanting to be called Garth. She believed him about Mary Zaccato. She believed that he didn't take many people into his home and that he wanted to see where she lived.

She opened the car door to get out, and he was there to help her, offering her his hand. She took it, because she wanted to, and she pushed aside all her questions and misgivings to do it.

"I liked Luigi's cooking," she said as they walked along in the rain.

She could feel him smile. "Best short-order cook in Brooklyn," he said. "Which one?" he asked about the white or beige or brown row houses.

"The brown one there," she said, and he walked with her up the stoop.

Ten steps. Crazily he counted them. Ten. Somewhere in his flaming youth he'd learned that brownstones had a ten-step stoop.

The foyer was dark and smelled of the tenants' varied dinners—hot bread, coffee, seared meat with peppers and onions. Her apartment was the first one on the left. He waited while she unlocked the door and let him in. He was standing close enough to smell her perfume, or perhaps it wasn't perfume but simply her. He savored it, wanted more. He'd been with her all day, and he wanted more.

He followed her inside.

"Nice place," he said of the softly lit room.

She was about to take off her coat, and he reached to help

her, then didn't help at all. He turned her around and, grasping her coat by the lapels, brought her to him.

Her mouth was both cold and warm. Cold lips from their brief walk from the car. Warm mouth because she parted her lips immediately.

She wants this, he thought incredulously.

He gave a soft moan as she returned the kiss and let him taste her, the way he'd wanted to for a long time now. A long time.

God, Jenna, he thought, perhaps said.

She leaned into him, and a warm, urgent pleasure suffused his body. His hands slid inside her coat, touching her soft breasts through the dark green sweater.

She had forgotten, she remembered—all at the same time. A man's touch. A man's smell. She'd been alone too long. She wanted to weep. She wanted—

"Garth, no," she said, trying to break away. "I don't—"

But he wasn't listening. His mouth came down on hers again. It was wonderful. She was afraid.

"Garth! I don't want this!"

He leaned back to look at her, his eyes searching hers. They were both breathless. She pressed her lips together to keep them from trembling.

"I don't want this," she said again, her voice barely a whisper.

He reached to touch her cheek—the way he might have if she had been Hernando or Mallory—and he gave a soft laugh.

"You're a liar, Mrs. Gallagher."

Chapter 8

So. They were *both* liars, he thought as he walked back down the ten steps. It was raining harder now, but he didn't hurry. Walking in a cold rain was as good as a cold shower, he supposed. He hadn't wanted to leave her; it had taken everything he had in him to do as she asked—because he'd wanted her, because he knew she didn't mean it. He'd had the advantage. He could have persuaded her—into bed *and* out of any information she might have.

But he hadn't done it. She was afraid of him. He knew that, and he'd let the moment pass. But when had he gotten so altruistic? She was a very pleasant means to an end, and he kept letting himself forget that.

He suddenly smiled to himself, remembering the look on Jenna's face when they were about to leave the Humoresque—when Hazel had suspiciously asked her just how much she liked oatmeal, followed by a heavy-handed query into the status of her bank account.

Jenna. She'd let him take her into an absolute nuthouse,

and she'd seemed to enjoy it, Hazel's unsubtle questions and Tony Zaccato aside.

He'd enjoyed it. He'd enjoyed the whole day.

Mrs. Gallagher, Mrs. Gallagher, what the hell are we getting into?

The headlights of an oncoming van lit the street. Garth could see the silhouettes of two men sitting in a car parked at the curb ahead of him. The car was expensive.

Two men. Now what would two men be doing sitting in a car here? Waiting for the rain to stop so they wouldn't get their Armani suits wet? Anyone but a former street kid might think so.

He hunted in his jacket pocket for the pack of stale cigarettes he carried. He didn't really smoke anymore, but cigarettes sometimes came in handy. When another car came down the street, he paused just short of the parked vehicle and lit one. And he read the license plate number.

The men in the car were watching, not waiting. He could feel their eyes on him as he passed, but he didn't hurry. He walked on, and he listened for the sound of a window rolling down or a door opening.

When he reached his car, he was careful not to look in their direction. He opened the car door and got inside, but he didn't leave. He got on the radio instead, and he waited for the report on the license plate number.

It didn't take long.

"*Be advised that the vehicle in question is NYPD property.*"

"NYPD?" he asked to make sure he'd heard right.

"*Ten-four.*"

A tail car. Not Tony Zaccato. NYPD.

He opened the door and got out, walking down the middle of the street toward the other car. When he was a few feet away, he held up both hands where the men in the car could see them. He could tell there was a hot discussion going on in the car, but after a moment the window on the driver's side slid down.

He immediately recognized the man behind the wheel.

"Rex," he said quietly. "And Putnam." He couldn't actually see the other man, but he had a good idea who it was. It was rare to see one without the other, even when they were off duty. They were both cronies of Hugh's.

"Garth," they both said.

"What are you two supposed to be doing?" Garth asked, because he knew they wouldn't tell him, and because anything they did say, he could check.

"Nothing," Putnam said testily. "Not a damn thing."

"Yeah? Well, as long as you're not doing anything, you can tell Hugh I left at—" he looked at his watch "—19:08. And tell him if he wants to know anything else, he can just ask me." He indicated the car. "This is a hell of a waste of taxpayers' money, guys."

He turned and walked away.

"I told you he'd get a make on us!" he heard Rex say as the window went up.

"Yeah, yeah, you told me," Putnam said. "You told me."

Jenna sat in the dimly lit living room, staring at nothing. She reached up and ran her fingers lightly over her lips. She could still feel the urgent pressure of his mouth on hers, still taste him. Garth and the peppermint candy Hazel had given her when they left the Humoresque.

I want him.

The thought presented itself, its import as significant as if it had been chiseled in stone. She didn't love him. Maybe she didn't even like him. But she wanted him.

What about Patrick? I loved Patrick.

Patrick was dead. She was alone. All the time. Patrick was dead.

She closed her eyes and took a wavering breath.

I don't want any more pain.

What else would she get from Johnson Garth? She could guess what his ideal woman would be like—overly willing, more than available, someone who would let him come and go without explanation and who would make absolutely no demands. But that aside, Garth was a cop. She didn't want to get involved with another cop! She didn't want to live on the fringes of a man's life; she didn't want to be afraid every time he left that she'd never see him again.

And she didn't want a purely sexual relationship between two strangers. She was certain of all these things, and yet...

She gave a heavy sigh. And yet she could still feel his kiss. Her body was alive with sexual desire, not just for a man, but for him. She was playing with fire, and she knew it.

The telephone rang, making her jump. She expected it to be Mamie, but it was someone from the Family Crisis Council.

"I hope you've had dinner, Jenna," the familiar voice said. "We need you to go to the hospital."

"Yes, all right," she answered, and she wrote down the particulars. For once she was glad to go. For once, going into a hospital would be better than staying here alone. She resolved that she would do whatever it took to get Johnson Garth off her mind. Maybe she'd even go out with the public defender she'd met in court who had asked. She would stay busy. That had always helped to take her mind off Patrick; it would help to take her mind off Garth. And she would stay away from Johnson Garth.

But she needn't have worried. She heard nothing from Garth. There were no more dinner invitations forthcoming, no telephone calls. She kept her resolve to stay busy, going to work in the Saint Xavier kindergarten the last three days of the week. But Garth was never far from her mind. One of the first things she saw when she arrived at Saint Xavier's was Hernando—sporting his new, pint-size, genuine leather bomber jacket. He proudly showed her all the zippered pockets and the World War II military patches. His father brought it to him, he said. Just like a surprise.

Jenna had no doubt about that, though the one most surprised was probably the heretofore notoriously uninvolved senior Mr. Cooley. She wondered how Garth had managed to persuade him to provide his son with a coat. With a well-placed foot to the man's behind? Garth would have done whatever it took, she decided. He had said he would get Hernando a new coat in a way that wouldn't make him feel worse about his poverty, and clearly he had.

Debbie didn't mention Garth at all. There were no questions about his having taken her home. Nothing. In fact, Debbie suddenly had little to say about anything.

"Do you feel all right?" Jenna finally asked her, and Debbie looked at her in surprise.

"I feel fine. Why?"

"Oh, you just seem...quiet. You're not pregnant, too, are you?"

"Good gracious, no!" Debbie chuckled. "Me, pregnant? What an idea!"

"Then what's wrong?" Jenna felt she had to ask.

"Nothing! I'm fine," she said blithely. And she became very busy somewhere else.

She's afraid I'm going to ask about Garth, Jenna decided. She knows something, and she doesn't want to tell me. Maybe that Garth had believed her when she'd told him she didn't want anything to do with him. He must have. Otherwise, given his earlier persistence, she would have heard something from him.

If anything, she told herself, she was relieved that he'd

finally respected her wishes. Relieved—and disappointed that he'd apparently given up on her so easily.

But today was the day she'd know for certain. She had to be at the police station in the late afternoon. Family Crisis Council volunteers were meeting with a police representative, and Garth would likely be somewhere on the premises.

She left Saint Xavier's early, impulsively taking the writing exercises the children had done the first of the week with her. They had each drawn and colored a picture of Garth in the blank space at the top of the page, and on the blue lines below, they had laboriously copied the sentence: *Thank you, Detective Garth, for being our friend.* She found the exercises stuffed in the desk drawer, and she wondered why Debbie hadn't already given them to him. Or at least given them to Skip so he could pass them on. Pictures and a copied sentence were something the children did for all their guests, and she was certain that Garth would want his. She could leave them at the precinct for him; she didn't have to see him.

But she looked for him. From the moment she entered the front door until she went into the meeting. And then when she came out again. He wasn't there. She had the manila envelope with the pictures in it under her arm, and impulsively she went into the squad room.

"Where is Detective Garth's desk?" she asked a patrolman who was walking through.

He pointed it out, but she probably could have guessed. It was piled high with papers and folders, and if there was any rhyme or reason to the stacks, she couldn't tell it. She hunted down a pen from her purse and wrote his name on the manila envelope, hoping to put it in a place where he would see it—sooner or later.

"Is that for me?"

She jumped at the question.

"Garth—yes," she said, completely flustered because she

hadn't seen him come in and because she had no business hanging around his desk, pictures or not, and because her knees went weak when she looked into his eyes.

"Yes," she said again, and she tried to walk away.

"Well, wait a minute," he said, catching her by the arm as he picked up the envelope. "What is it?"

"Some drawings. From the children at Saint Xavier's. They're...thank-you notes for spending the day with them."

He smiled and opened the envelope. "So what did they draw?"

"You."

He looked up at her and grinned. "Me? I can't wait to see this." He dumped the pages out and began to shuffle through them, chuckling from time to time, obviously pleased. "This is my favorite," he said, glancing up at her. "I look like Ma Kettle standing on a red boa constrictor."

She looked at the picture he showed her and smiled. He did look like Ma Kettle standing on a red boa constrictor.

"They're very...free-spirited," she said. "We try to let them do the pictures however they want."

He picked up another one. "Hernando did this one. That little sh—rascal knew I had a gun," he said incredulously.

"You had a gun?" Jenna said, not without some incredulity of her own.

"Under my pants leg—right where he drew it," he said, showing her the picture.

"You weren't supposed to come into the kindergarten with a gun, Garth."

"Old habits die hard," he said absently. He looked up from the pictures he had spread all over his already-messy desk. "Thanks for bringing these. Tell the kids I really like them."

She nodded and turned to go.

"Jenna?" he said, and she looked back at him. But looking into her eyes, he didn't know quite what he wanted to say. Well, he did know; he just couldn't say it here. "Nothing," he said.

"Jenna!" the lieutenant called from his office. "What is this? You come by and you don't take the time to say hello? Come in here. Come tell me how you're doing."

Jenna immediately walked toward the lieutenant's office, her relief at getting away from Garth written plainly on her face, but mixing with her dread of having to make a courtesy call on the lieutenant and listen to him reminisce about Patrick.

She's still in love with her husband, Garth thought.

He gathered up the pictures and put them back into the envelope, watching Jenna all the time she talked to The Whip, watching her when she left the lieutenant's office without a backward glance.

"My God," Skip said at his elbow. "There must be fifty case folders here. Did we get put on the scut detail or what?"

"Scut detail," Garth verified, sitting down at the desk and shoving some folders aside.

"Was it something we said? No, strike that. Was it something *you* said?"

"Probably. I'm not known for my tact."

"Do I get to know who's pissed off?"

"Alden!" Garth chided him. "Your language! What would Mummy and Daddy say?"

"Now, don't you do it again, Garth."

"Do what?" Garth said innocently.

"Stonewall me, that's what! You don't want to answer the question, so you give me a dig about my background. I know how you work, Garth, and since I'm the one who's got to help with all this, I want to know what's going on!"

"Take it easy, kid. You're going to give yourself ulcers."

"You're doing it again, Garth!"

"Okay! Okay! Hugh Gallagher's doing this. He doesn't

want me seeing Jenna, and he's trying to help me understand that my happiness is going to be directly proportional to his. Unfortunately you get caught in the fallout.''

"Hugh can't do all this," Skip said, gesturing to the piles of folders.

"He can call in a favor from someone who can."

"You think so?"

"I think so."

"This is crazy. You aren't seeing Jenna. She's going out with some lawyer, a P.D.''

"Since when?" Garth wanted to know. "Who is it?"

"Since...tonight, I guess. She's going to the Peking Opera—or maybe it's tomorrow night..."

"Who is it?" Garth said again.

"I don't know. Debbie said Jenna was going out with some P.D. she met when she was in court with one of her Family Crisis Council cases—and that's all she said. Except that he has money."

"P.D.'s don't have money."

"This one does."

"What the hell does she want to go out with a lawyer for?" He realized that he could have used a bit of Hernando's "cool" at the moment, because his own had somehow escaped him. He didn't like the idea of Jenna going out with a shifty lawyer any more than he'd liked Tony Zaccato hanging all over her—money or no money.

"How should I know? Women can overlook a lot. Maybe if *you'd* asked her out, she wouldn't be hanging out with such trash. The Peking Opera, maybe even dinner at Lutèce—poor woman. What a downhill slide."

"Very funny, Skip. Very funny."

"Garth!" the lieutenant yelled out his door.

"You, too," Garth said to Skip as he wearily got up from his chair.

"My name's not Garth," Skip assured him.

"It's going to be crap if you don't get up off your can.
That's his now-hear-this voice, and whatever's caused it,
I'm not taking the heat alone."

"Gee, thanks," Skip said, reluctantly following.

"What are partners for?"

For more scut work.

"Don't take the time to sit down," the lieutenant said.
"One of our favorite gentlemen has inadvertently given us
what we need to make an arrest."

"Who?" Garth said.

"Tony Zaccato."

Garth could feel the sudden rush of adrenaline. Zaccato.
Another shot at Zaccato. "What have we got?" he asked,
hoping against hope that this time it was something Tony's
high-priced legal staff couldn't circumvent.

"Midtown got a really good collar from one of their buy-
and-bust operations," the lieutenant said. "Tony's been trying to cut into this guy's territory of late, and the guy thinks
Tony fingered him. It really pissed him off, so he's been
singing like a songbird—names, dates, places. Seems he
kept a lot of documentation for just such an eventuality."

"He'll testify? He's not scared of Tony?"

"Sure, he's scared of Tony. But like I said, he's pissed
off. By the time he gets over it, he'll be in too deep."

"Do we know where Tony is?"

The lieutenant handed Garth a slip of paper. "This is the
address Hugh got from one of his snitches. Maybe it's legit.
Maybe not. I want you and Carver to go over and see."

"So how come Hugh's not going after him?" Garth
asked, feeling Skip cringe beside him. It was not a proper
question. Even Skip knew it.

"You got some problem with how I'm making the as-
signments, Garth?"

"No, sir. I understand." He looked into the lieutenant's

eyes. He knew why he'd drawn the job, and it wasn't because no one else in the department knew Tony Zaccato as
well as he did—though he had no doubt that that might have
been Hugh's subtle suggestion at the time the lieutenant was
making up his mind. And apparently the honeymoon for
Skip was over as well. Garth looked again at the address.
He wanted to get Tony Zaccato, but, God, he didn't want
to try to do it using anything that came from Hugh Gallagher.

"Just how bad is this little task?" Skip asked on the way
back through the squad room to the lockers.

Garth needed a few extra things, and he could feel the
tension in the squad room when they passed through.

"Bad."

"You think it's the same thing as having all those case
folders on your desk?"

"Something like that." Worse, he thought but didn't say
it. A lot worse.

"Are you worried?"

"Yeah."

"*Yeah?*"

Garth gave a sharp sigh. "What do you want me to do,
Skipper? Tell you it'll be a piece of cake?"

"That would be nice."

"It *won't* be a piece of cake. Nobody messes with Tony
Zaccato, not even the official representatives of Truth, Justice and the American Way. And I'm not exactly at the top
of Hugh Gallagher's Favorite Person list, now, am I?
There's only one good thing about this, Skipper, and that's
the chance, even a small one, of getting at Tony Zaccato."

"Are you going to carry all those guns?"

"Are you going to stand there and ask me all these damn
questions? Yeah, I'm going to carry all these guns!"

"They're not regulation, Garth."

"You want me to be unofficially armed or both of us officially dead?"

Skip pressed his lips together and swallowed hard. "Do I need to carry something extra?"

"Nah. You're not used to it. You'd probably forget where it was and blow off something important. The only thing you have to do is what I tell you."

"You really think it's going to be bad," Skip said again on their way out of the station house.

"Skip, I really, *really* do."

He took a deep breath. "Okay, then. Just so I know."

It was bad. Very bad. Bad timing. Bad backup. Bad luck. Two patrolmen and a civilian wounded, and they didn't get Tony Zaccato. Garth had wanted Zaccato's arrest so bad he could taste it. Even if Zaccato had walked an hour later, he'd still wanted it. But once again the Tony Zaccatos of the world had triumphed. All he'd gotten was a spot on the six o'clock news.

"Can you explain what went wrong here, Detective? Detective? Detective!"

Yes, hell, he could. The other team played better ball. We just couldn't get it together out there, coach.

But he couldn't explain it to himself. He had more puzzle pieces than ever, and none of them fit. Tony never gave them a chance to say why they wanted to see him. And even though Garth had been ready for any eventuality, he had still been surprised by Tony's reaction, a reaction that came *before* he supposedly knew the you-know-what had hit the fan. Why hadn't Tony assumed that this little visit was like a thousand others, that they had just wanted him to come in and answer the same old routine questions they always asked, simply because it was part of the cat-and-mouse game. Big offenders like Tony expected it. A little cage-rattling. A little war of nerves. Tony had always cooperated. He was full of big-mouth threats, but he always came in willingly for those little sessions. In fact, Garth had always believed he enjoyed them.

But not this time. Why? *Why?* Because he'd known they were coming? No. Tony hadn't expected them; he wouldn't have been there if he had. Garth suspected that Tony had reacted the way he had because he knew that *if* they came for him, this time it would be the real thing, and that whoever had dropped the dime, whoever had pointed the finger, could make it stick. So who was Tony afraid of? Not some punk dealer in Midtown.

Who then?

Hugh Gallagher, Garth thought.

Maybe Hugh had wanted to get rid of two major aggravations at one time. In Garth's mind, it fit. *If* Hugh had some deal with Zaccato and wanted out of it, who would he want to bring Zaccato in? Somebody who would play it by the book? Or somebody who had a long-running feud with Zaccato, someone who was likely to provoke a major exchange of gunfire on sight. And they'd certainly had that. He had two bullet holes in his jacket sleeve.

It was well after midnight when Garth finished writing up the report. He was tired, hungry and depressed, and Skip was into Act III of "The Junior Detective, On His First Big Shoot-Out, Blunders."

"That little kid was in the way," Skip said for the hundredth time. Some cops internalized and said nothing. Skip Carver wasn't one of those. He was pumped up and talking.

"I know that," Garth finally said, knowing it was better for the kid to let off steam.

"I didn't freeze, Garth. I just couldn't take him out with the kid in the way."

"Skip, you're the one with every damned Annie Oakley shooting award the department gives. If you said you couldn't, you couldn't. Will you lighten up?"

"The whole damned thing was a mess!"

"I know that, too. Get out of here, will you? Debbie'll be worried. I'll see you tomorrow."

He sat at his desk for a while after Skip had gone, until he realized he had no alternative but to go home. But he didn't go home. He drove through Park Slope instead, telling himself that he was crazy—Jenna wouldn't still be up at this time of night.

But her lights were on.

He'd never find a parking space.

But there was one halfway down the block. Or at least three-quarters of one. With much juggling and not-so-gentle nudging of a Ford Escort and a Honda Civic, he parked. And sat in the car for a long time. Then he got out, walking up the dark street to the brown row house.

Her lights would surely go out before he got there.

They stayed on. And halfway up the ten steps of the stoop, he ran out of excuses. He also ran out of nerve. Maybe the lawyer was there. He just wanted to be with her for a little while; he didn't want to cause her any trouble.

He turned abruptly and went back down the steps.

Jenna saw him from the front window. She saw him come up on the stoop, and she saw him turn away again. She hurried out into the foyer, running the last few steps until she reached the front door. But she couldn't go any farther. She didn't have her keys, and she had to keep the door from closing.

"Garth!" she whispered, leaning out as far as she could. She could just barely see him, and he kept walking. "Garth!" she called out loud, and this time he heard her.

He came walking back, and she stood waiting, holding the door. The night was starry and cold. She didn't ask him what he wanted. Debbie had already called and told her about the day's events.

"Come inside," she said, shivering against the cold.

Tonight was lawyer night, all right, he thought. She was still dressed up. She looked so pretty. *Ah, God, Jenna, you look so pretty!*

"It's late," he answered. He was standing on the bottom step.

"Well, you're the man with the four clocks. You should know."

She could feel him smile in the darkness, and he climbed two steps.

Is the lawyer gone? he almost said, but he bit down on it. She wouldn't have asked him to come in otherwise. And surely he had some remnants of street kid "cool" left. But he was tired of tiptoeing around with this; she might as well know how he felt.

"I made a mistake," he said. "I was feeling sorry for myself, and I came here because I wanted you to feel sorry for me, too. I wanted you to feel sorry enough to let me into your bed. But I've changed my mind. I don't want the first time to be like that. I...think maybe we've got more going for us than mutual pity."

With that, he turned to go, not giving her time to say anything. Not that she could think of anything to say. He'd caught her completely off guard. Again.

"Garth?" she called when he'd reached the bottom step.

He looked up at her, and he was so handsome to her. She couldn't even *see* him and he was still handsome, rough, standing-with-his-hands-in-his-jacket-pockets Garth.

"I'm sorry about Zaccato," she said quietly, because she understood enough about the man to know how he must feel.

He shrugged, not asking her how she knew. "Story of my life, Mrs. Gallagher, you know?"

* * *

Jenna was awakened by the telephone shortly before seven. It was Debbie. In distress.

"Jenna, I need to talk to you," she began, her voice little more than a whisper.

"Now?" Jenna asked. She was awake, but just barely. "Why are you whispering?"

"I don't want to wake Skip. Jenna, I need some advice." There was a pause, and Jenna imagined Debbie checking to see if Skip were still sleeping or not. "I'm no good at being a cop's wife, Jenna. I thought I had the hang of it because I was a cop's kid, but I don't. Skip had a hell of a day yesterday—he thinks he's no good and Garth is going to dump him. I need you to tell me how to help him."

"Debbie, I don't know how to help him."

"Then just listen to me talk, okay? I don't have anybody who understands but you. Can you meet me at my dad's apartment this afternoon? I have to pick him up at the doctor's after work and take him home. He'll be tired, and he'll want to rest. We can talk there, and I won't have to worry about Skip coming in. Okay?"

Jenna didn't say anything. She had things she needed to think about, things that were disturbing enough to have kept her awake most of the night.

Garth.

She and Garth lied to each other about their true feelings. She and Garth considered each other pitiful. Was there more to their relationship than that? Yes, she thought. There was lust, at least, apparently in both directions.

"Okay?" Debbie said again, and Jenna gave a quiet sigh.

"Okay. I'll be there around six."

"Jenna, thanks. Thanks—I know you're busy today."

She *was* busy today. She had to go to court with a young rape victim who had sought Family Crisis Council support. The testimony for the defense was the worst kind—long and tedious and intimating that the victim was at fault. There was little Jenna could do for the young woman, nothing she could say that would lessen the ordeal of relentless media attention and having to relive the rape. All she could do was be there and hope that her presence somehow helped.

Jenna was emotionally exhausted by the time court adjourned for the day, and the last thing she wanted to do was play sounding board for Debbie and have to deal with even more distress.

But she went. Because she remembered what it was like to be a young cop's wife. Because she remembered the feeling of helplessness that came from being excluded when the man one loved couldn't share his failures and his pain. She remembered, too, how quiet Patrick had been before he'd been killed, and how little she'd been able to ascertain about what he was feeling. She had always thought it was because she'd had another miscarriage, her second, the month before, because he'd wanted lots of children and he certainly wasn't getting them with her.

Patrick's death had more than compounded the guilt she'd already felt. Had he been distracted, thinking about the disappointment, the unhappiness she'd caused not just in losing the babies, but in refusing to discuss future pregnancies? She hadn't wanted another pregnancy, not until she could distance herself from the ones that had already gone wrong. Twice she had lost a child, and she simply hadn't been prepared to face the prospect of losing yet another.

Had she said that to him? Yes. Yes, she had, but she still hadn't been able to break through the wall of silence he'd built around himself. It was only when he was dying that the wall had cracked, and then she couldn't get to him. He'd wanted her then, and she couldn't reach him.

Hugh. Hugh had kept her out of the room where Patrick was being treated, holding her back, keeping her away from him when he'd called and called her name.

"Oh!" she said, surprising herself that she'd spoken out loud. She hadn't thought of Patrick like that in a long while, and it was only because of Garth that she was doing it now. Garth with his pointed questions: *So why weren't you and Patrick getting along?* Garth with his surprising candor: *I want to see where you live. I wanted you to feel sorry enough to let me into your bed.*

Garth.

She didn't know anything when it came to him, except that she physically desired him. She wanted to lie with him in the dark and make love with him and fall asleep in his arms. She couldn't look at him without wanting it. She couldn't *think* about him without wanting it. It made things much worse knowing that he wanted it, too. And it was so hard *not* to think about him, now that she'd been to the Humoresque and to the loft. It was easy to imagine him in those places, being his irrepressible self, listening to The Drifters, bantering with Hazel and Luigi.

But she forced her mind back to the problem at hand, finding a parking space so she could go talk to Debbie. That wasn't so easy. She finally squeezed into a cramped space nearly two blocks away.

She walked briskly to the apartment house where Debbie's father lived. It was cold, but she needed the fresh air to clear her head. She liked Debbie's father, a stereotypical cop from the old school like Sidney, who monitored the precinct's telephones. Joe Eagan had been wounded in the line of duty and was paralyzed from the waist down. Still, he was self-sufficient and determined to be useful, going regularly to the police academy in a wheelchair to lecture from his vast storehouse of knowledge about being a New York cop. Debbie had met Skip when she accompanied her father on one of his lectures. New York's police brotherhood looked after its own, and he lived comfortably enough. The apartment house was in an older but nice neighborhood. Jenna had no qualms about the two-block walk.

In the building foyer, she located Joe Eagan's name and pressed the intercom button. Debbie answered almost immediately, releasing the lock so she could get inside. Jenna didn't see the man who came into the foyer behind her. He reached over her head to keep the inner door open, pushing his way in with her. She turned immediately, and immediately she recognized his intent. He lunged at her; he had on layers of old clothes, and he stank. She knew she should scream, make noise, but nothing came. She was terrified, and yet her mind registered such peculiar information—the faded blue-and-gray flannel shirt, the dirty navy-blue knit cap, the tattered raincoat with all the buttons missing. He kept shoving her backward toward the stairwell door. She looked around frantically for another person, but there was no one.

Surely it was money he wanted, credit cards.

"Here, take it," she said, thrusting her purse at him, but he slapped it out of her hands. The contents spilled out and skidded across the floor. He said nothing, grabbing her by the lapels of her coat, slapping her hard when she finally tried to scream. He slammed her against the door, knocking the breath out of her, and then dragged her through it into the stairwell.

"Please..." she managed with what little air she had left in her lungs.

He hit her again, hard enough to make her knees buckle. She had to grab on to him to keep from falling backward down the stairs. She held on tightly, so that he couldn't get in another blow, and she tried again to scream,

How unusual, she thought as she fought him. He was wearing thermal underwear. This close, she could read the inspection sticker just below the band on the neck. INSPECTED BY No. 2.

Chapter 9

Roy Lee was out washing windshields again. Garth saw him from a block away.

"Don't make this next light," he said to Skip. "I want to talk to Roy Lee."

"You think he knows anything about Zaccato?"

"Yeah, he knows. They all do. But the question is, will he tell me?"

Skip drove slowly so as not to make the light, much to the ire of the cabbie behind them. When they got closer to the place Roy Lee had staked out for himself, Garth began to roll down the window. Roy Lee glanced in their direction.

"Roy Lee!" Garth yelled at him. But Roy Lee was already backing away. As Garth opened the car door, Roy Lee broke into a run, dodging through moving traffic toward the far side of the street.

"Roy Lee! Hey!"

But he didn't stop, and Garth couldn't get to him for the flow of traffic around them. He stood watching as Roy Lee disappeared into an alley.

"Now what the hell does that mean?" Garth said as he got back into the car. He had an understanding with Roy Lee. Sometimes he got information and sometimes he didn't, but because of the old days, there were no hard feelings.

"It means the answer to the question is no," Skip said dryly.

Sidney was looking for Garth when they got back to the station house.

"Line one, lad," Sidney said as he walked in. "Be a good lad and answer it now and save me the trouble of writing one of those piddling pink slips."

"Yeah, Sid," Garth said in passing. He went to his piled-up desk and uncovered the telephone, pushing the Line One button on the off chance that Sidney might, just this once, know what incoming call he was talking about.

"Detective Garth," he said.

"Yo! Garth!" a familiar voice said, and he smiled. "This is your old partner, Rosie Madden."

"The Rose!" Garth said. "What can I do for you?"

"This ain't no social call, honey. You see Hugh around anywhere close?"

Garth looked around him.

"No. Why?"

"I heard on the QT you've been trying to get into Hugh's sister-in-law's pants, you devil you, and Big Hugh ain't too happy about it. I got enough troubles, life being what it is. I don't want *my* desk covered up in case folders, too, and I want you to make sure he don't catch on to what I'm telling you."

Garth was shuffling papers as she talked, but Rosie certainly knew how to get his attention. "Jenna?" he said, responding to the only part of her spiel that interested him.

"Shh!" Rosie snapped at him. "Didn't you hear what I

just told you? I don't want Hugh to know I'm calling—and how many of Hugh's sister-in-laws' pants have you been trying to get into? Yeah, Jenna!"

"What is it?" he asked, feeling the cold fist of anxiety in the pit of his stomach.

"Jenna's over here at Bellevue, Garth. Somebody roughed her up and—"

"I'll be right there," he interrupted.

"Wait a minute, will you! She doesn't know I'm calling you. She doesn't want anybody called, especially the Gallaghers. But like I said, I heard about you and her, and I thought you'd want to—"

"How bad is—"

"Will you quit interrupting and listen? She's not hurt too bad, but this is getting to her. It's about all she can do to hold it together. If she means anything to you, you sneak out and get your butt over here. She's still in Emergency. I got a partner with an itchy dialing finger, and he would have called Hugh already if he wasn't too dumb to think of it. I got to get off this phone before he figures out what I'm up to."

"What happened to her?"

"I'll tell you the details when you get here. I got to go!"

"Rosie, wait! She wasn't—"

"She wasn't raped, Garth," Rosie said, and he realized how tightly he'd been holding the telephone.

"I've done something maybe you won't like," Rosie Madden said.

Jenna looked at her sharply. She was sitting on the side of the stretcher in the cubicle they'd put her in, sitting because she couldn't bear lying down. She had the sheet over her lap, the top edge clutched tightly in both fists. Her hands were icy cold. She felt weak, dizzy; her heart was pounding, but she still couldn't lie down. The only thing she wanted was out of this place. Intellectually she knew that she needed to be X-rayed, examined, but it was all she could do to sit quietly and let them do it. It took everything she had to keep her anxiety hidden. If she let them see it, let anyone see it, she might have to stay. Every time she closed her eyes, she could see Patrick here. Every time she closed her eyes, she could see her assailant's face. So she sat rigid on the side of the stretcher and tried not to shake.

"What?" she asked Rosie Madden warily. There was a tremor in her voice she couldn't do anything about.

"I...called Garth."

"Why would you call Garth?" Jenna said, her voice rising, the control she was working so hard to maintain threatening to snap.

"Because," Rosie interrupted, equally loudly. "Because," she repeated in a softer tone, "I saw you and Garth sitting together on the stairs at Skip Carver's party. Because the word is you and Garth have a thing going. Because you need somebody here with you. Because Garth used to be my partner, and I care enough about him to make sure he knows what he ought to know."

Jenna swallowed hard and looked into Rosie's eyes. "Is he...coming?"

"Is he coming?" Rosie asked incredulously. "Now what kind of question is that? Is he coming? Of course he's coming. The man's crazy about you, honey. It was all I could do to keep him on the phone long enough to tell him what I wanted to tell him."

Jenna abruptly bowed her head, feeling the tears that had been so close to sliding down her face.

"Hey," Rosie said. "Now don't you go bawling. You don't bawl because a man cares about you and he's coming. You bawl because he don't and he ain't, see?"

Jenna understood the logic perfectly, but it didn't help. She tried to smile—Rosie Madden was trying to be kind to

her—but she couldn't. She didn't want Garth here, and she
wanted him here more than anything else in the world. Was
she never going to feel anything but completely contradic-
tory where he was concerned?

It didn't take him long to get there. She heard him before
she saw him. The long time seemed to be until he actually
reached her cubicle. She knew when he was finally standing
right outside. She knew when he pulled back the curtain,
and slowly she turned her face to let him see.

At first he thought she wasn't hurt; seeing her in profile,
she looked fine. But then she looked at him and gave him
a funny, lopsided smile that faded almost before it had begun.

Oh, God, baby.

He didn't say anything. He reached for her instead, holding her tight, careful of her bruised and swollen cheek and
eye. He could feel her trembling, and she clung to him with
all the desperation he'd seen in her face.

"Get your clothes on," he said, leaning back to look into
her eyes. "I'm taking you out of here."

She stared back at him, not knowing whether to believe
him. She was going?

"Hurry up," he said, "before the doc changes his mind."

"The X rays—" she began, her voice husky with unshed
tears.

"They're okay. I told him you'd be better off at home.
You're not going to tell me you want to stay in this joint,
are you?"

She shook her head, overcome by the sense of relief.
"No," she managed. "No—Garth—thank you."

"Hey, Mrs. Gallagher. What are friends for?" He gave
her a mischievous smile that belied the concern she saw in
his eyes. "Now get your clothes on." He stepped outside,

fully aware that that particular phrase was one he'd certainly never expected to ever say to her and mean.

But he did mean it—this time. He needed to get her out of here before Hugh turned up. Rosie had been right in her assessment of Jenna's emotional state. And in his estimation, a confrontation with Hugh or Mamie Gallagher would just about push her over the edge.

Jenna took off the hospital gown and gathered up the clothes she'd been wearing when she came in. She tried to hurry, but in her haste, she fumbled with buttons and zippers.

"You decent?" Garth asked once.

"No," she said, putting her hands to her face in exasperation. But that hurt, and she took a long, deep breath.

"Now?" he called a moment later.

"Yes, all right," she answered. She was more or less together.

Garth slid back the curtain. "Where's your coat?"

She gave him a bewildered look. "I don't know."

"You know where her coat is?" Garth asked a nurse who stood nearby.

"She wasn't wearing a coat when she came in."

"Were you wearing your coat, Jenna?" Garth asked her.

She shook her head. "I don't know—yes. I don't care about the coat. I just want to get out of here."

"No coat when I got here," Rosie put in.

"Here," Garth said, stripping off his jacket. "You can wear mine."

"I don't want to take yours," Jenna said, but she let him put her into it anyway.

"It's not what you want in this world," he said philosophically, "it's what you need."

"Get," Jenna corrected as he turned her around to lift her hair out from under the collar. "It's what you get." She felt like one of the kindergartners. She felt like a woman who was being gently cared for by the man she very much needed right now.

"Whatever," Garth said. "It's cold as a witch's—"

"Whatever," the nurse and Rosie supplied, and he grinned.

"Could we go find the doctor? I'd rather not wait here," Jenna said to Garth.

"Let's go," he said, taking her by the arm. "When we find the doc, try to look a little perkier, okay? He wants to give you the lowdown on the X rays and stuff like that."

"All right," she said, taking a deep breath and working on "perky."

"Can you make it?"

"I can make it," she assured him.

Her knees were wobbly, but she managed to listen to the doctor's report on her condition and his instructions about rest and the names of the over-the-counter medicines she could take for the pain. But all the while she could feel the panic rising, the illogical fear that somehow something would keep her here and she wouldn't get out after all. She was finding it hard to concentrate. She felt that the lights were too bright, the noises too loud. But she stood firm. She'd been through enough anxiety attacks to know that that was what she was experiencing now, and that they were only that—a rush of adrenaline and her body's response to it. She'd had counseling for them; she understood them; she just didn't want to have to explain them. So she tried to look "perky" instead.

"I'm sorry you were hurt, Mrs. Gallagher," the doctor finally said. "But you were very lucky. I know it's been a bad...year for you."

It didn't surprise her that he recognized her name; she'd made a lot of public appearances in the past few months. But she made no comment. He, however, apparently felt the need to explain. "I was working the day the officer—your husband—was brought in...."

The sentence hung in the air, and Jenna swallowed hard, giving Garth a plaintive look. "Let's go," he said, cutting the physician short.

"She can wait here while you get the car."

"It's close," Garth said, and he hustled her out.

"You okay?" he asked as soon as they were outside.

"Yes," she said, not really knowing.

"I lied about how close the car is."

"I know," she answered. He put his arm around her as they walked.

"It's down there. I thought the hike to the car was the lesser of two evils."

She nodded. "Why?" she suddenly asked, because she knew her reasons but she didn't know his.

"Skip...told me you have a hard time in hospitals."

"Not always," she answered, wondering what else Skip had told him.

"Panic attacks, right?"

"Yes," she said.

"And you keep going back into hospitals anyway."

"I'm...supposed to. The first thing anybody does after an attack is to try to avoid the place where they had the anxiety—because they think it will happen again."

"Can't it?"

"Sometimes. But if you keep doing that, pretty soon you aren't going anywhere."

"So what do they do for panic attacks—give you pills for them or what?"

"Sometimes. Why are we talking about this?"

"To take your mind off your other troubles."

"This is taking my mind off my troubles?"

"Okay—because I want to know. Do you take something?"

"No, I wait."

"For what?"

"For the attack to be over. I know I'm not dying, so I just…wait."

"And then you go on about your business."

"Something like that. Did you say something to the doctor to get him to let me go?" it suddenly occurred to her to ask.

"I told him the truth. Mrs. Gallagher, don't look so incredulous. The truth comes in very handy now and again. I think we'd better hurry—unless you want to talk to Hugh."

She had thought they *were* hurrying, but she picked up the pace as he hustled her toward the parking lot. The wind was sharp and cold, scattering bits of trash and leaves across the pavement.

"No, I don't want to talk to Hugh. And it doesn't matter if you told the truth or not. I was leaving anyway."

"Well, let's don't let the doctor find that out. Let's let him think he was persuaded."

They walked on, and she stumbled once.

"Maybe I should have let the car warm up for you," he said, hurrying her on.

"For me? I'm the one with the coat."

He suddenly grinned. "You know what I like about you, Mrs. Gallagher? You had a hell of a day, and you've *still* got enough spark to be a smart-ass."

She didn't say anything to that.

"You'll feel better when you get home," he said.

She stopped walking. Home. She didn't want to go home. Somebody was surely going to tell Mamie her daughter-in-law had been beaten up in an apartment house stairwell. She closed her eyes. She didn't want to have to deal with Mamie. Mamie was high-strung, emotional, still mourning Patrick. She'd weep; she'd use the incident to try to talk Jenna into coming to live in the Gallagher house, where Mamie thought she belonged. With her. So they could wear black and talk about Patrick.

"What?" Garth was saying.

"I don't want to go home, Garth. I don't want to go home!" She couldn't keep her voice from rising, and she was doing it again—running away because she didn't want to have to deal with the Gallaghers. Sneaking out before Hugh got here. Panicking, because she'd have to see Mamie if she went home. She was ashamed of it, and she couldn't help it. "I don't want to go home," she said again, trying to sound more reasonable this time.

"Okay. No problem."

"I just...don't want to have to talk to anybody," she said, feeling that she had to make some kind of explanation or Garth would think she was crazy.

"Okay," he said again.

"If you could—"

"Take it easy, Mrs. Gallagher. I'll take care of it. The car's over there."

She believed him. He'd take care of it.

He opened the car door, and she got inside. She huddled on the cold seat, and, relieved of the responsibility of deciding what to do next, she suddenly gave herself up to physical and emotional exhaustion. She hurt. Her body. Her soul. No one had ever deliberately hurt her before. Nobody.

She tried not to shiver as Garth got in on the other side. She could feel him looking at her, but he didn't say anything. She was thankful for that. She didn't want to talk; she didn't want to explain. She drew inward, because she didn't want to think about anything anymore. She just wanted to sit here, thinking nothing, feeling nothing.

No. There was feeling. She hurt. Her face hurt. Her eye. She reached up to tentatively touch the place that throbbed so, but Garth caught her hand.

"Leave it alone," he said. "If you think it hurts now,

just go poking around.'' He pulled her closer to him, and he slid his fingers between hers. She didn't try to move away.

"How...bad is it?'' she made herself ask.

"You look like hell.''

Of course, she thought. I look just the way it feels. She closed her eyes.

"Jenna?'' Garth said, and she opened them.

Not Mrs. Gallagher. *Jenna.*

But he wasn't holding her hand anymore. He was outside the car, holding the door open. She looked up at him. "Come on,'' he said kindly.

She slid across the seat to get out, wincing when he took her arm.

"Sorry,'' he said.

She didn't answer.

She looked around. A deserted parking lot. She looked up. The moon was full. Frosty and full in the night sky. It was so cold out here.

"I'm not going to take you in through the Humoresque,'' he said. "It's still open, and Hazel and Luigi will go nuts if they see you. Come on.''

She went.

"Come on,'' he said again when they reached a fire escape. "Can you make it?''

"I can make it,'' she answered.

It was a long way up.

"Okay,'' he said when they reached the first landing. "You need to rest?''

"No,'' she said. "Do you?''

He chuckled softly. "Smart-ass,'' she thought he said.

But she did need to rest. She needed to rest so badly. Just to sit down. Here—anywhere—for a few minutes—forever.

"Come on, baby," Garth said, his face close to hers. "You can do it."

"I know." She could do it—because he wanted her to.

She climbed, and she stood on the last landing while he wrestled with the door locks. She looked up at the moon again. Beautiful—unlike herself. She lifted her battered face to the moonlight.

Garth had the door unlocked, and when he said it was all right, she followed him inside. He went around closing windows; it was nearly as cold in the loft as it was outside. Why was it he left the windows open? Oh, yes. Onions. Luigi's fried onions.

She stood where he left her, shivering.

"Come sit down," he said, and she went to sit in the chair next to the table with the telephone. She looked at the picture again, the picture of Garth and Mary Zaccato.

"It'll take a while to get warm in here."

"She was very beautiful," Jenna said.

There was a pause before he answered. "Yes. She was."

"And you loved her very much."

"Mrs. Gallagher…"

"Don't call me Mrs. Gallagher."

"All right," he said, his tone of voice indicating that he'd humor her.

"And you loved her very much," she repeated.

This time he answered. "Yes. I loved her very much."

Jenna nodded. It was important to her, knowing precisely how he'd felt about Mary. She felt better, knowing. She had loved Patrick. And he had loved Mary Zaccato. She looked down at his jacket. It had holes in it, holes she didn't remember from the day he'd spent at Ft. Xavier's.

"Jenna?" Garth said, and she looked up at him. "Will you take some advice from an old hand at having the living daylights kicked out of him?"

She tried to smile. "Why not? I don't have any...prior experience."

"I know you're tired, but I'm going to run the tub. I want you to take a hot bath. And then you can take some aspirin and go to bed. You won't be nearly so sore in the morning if you do that, okay?"

She looked into his eyes. He was going to take care of it. Of her. Of everything.

"Okay?" he asked again, and she nodded.

"Good. Maybe it'll be a little warmer out here when you get done."

She did as he suggested, but it took her a while to get past her reflection in the bathroom mirror. Garth had been right about both things. She looked like hell, and if she thought her eye hurt left alone, she should just try poking around. She didn't seem to have many other bruises—a few on her arms, scraped knuckles on one hand.

Garth had a huge clawfoot tub—necessary for a man used to having the living daylights kicked out of him, she supposed. She slipped gingerly into the hot water, and she lay with her eyes closed, savoring the warmth until the water grew cool.

But it wasn't warmer when she came out. The loft was too cavernous to have recovered from an all-day airing out. Garth had given her one of his flannel shirts to put on, and a pair of sweatpants, and wool socks, but she was still shivering.

"Nice outfit," he said when she came out, but she couldn't smile. She was too dammed up with feeling. She wanted to smile, but she wanted to cry more, and as a result, she could do neither.

He took the clothes she'd been wearing out of her hands and put them aside. He gave her two aspirin, and he gave her his bed, making her sit on the side of it while she drank what she thought was going to be coffee.

It was hot chocolate. She had thought she had no appetite for anything, but it was wonderful.

"Courtesy of the Humoresque," Garth said. "Luigi wanted to send you a dish of ice cream, but I told him you were too cold. When he was a young man—when he first came to the United States—he had to have his tonsils out. They gave him ice cream in the hospital. Impressed the hell out of him, even if he couldn't eat it. He thinks ice cream fixes everything."

She did manage to smile at the anecdote about Luigi, and she drained the whole cup of chocolate, sitting there on the side of the bed. Then she crawled between the crisp, cold sheets. It was so good to lie down. Garth had been right about the hot bath. She lay quietly, trying to get warm while he covered her in blankets and a quilted brown comforter. He had music playing softly.

"The Drifters," she murmured, her eyes growing heavy as the bath and the aspirin and the hot chocolate did their work.

"Yeah," he said.

"I like The Drifters."

"Good. They kind of go with the territory."

"Garth?"

"Yeah?"

"Thank you."

"It's okay, Mrs. Gallagher—Jenna."

She felt so tired, but sleep didn't come.

"Garth?" she said after a time.

"Yeah?" His voice was still close by, but she didn't open her eyes to see exactly where he was.

"Hernando's coat. How did you get his father to buy it for him?"

"You don't want to know," he said.

She gave a half smile. "That's what I thought. He's so...proud of it. Garth?"

The telephone suddenly rang, and he went to answer it.

"Yeah, Debbie," he said, and she turned her head to look at him. He gave her a questioning look, and she shook her head no. She didn't want to talk to anyone—except him.

"No, she's all right," Garth continued. "No. I'm sure, Debbie. I wouldn't tell you she's all right if she wasn't. Yes, she's out of the tub now, but she's just about asleep. Yeah, I talked to Skip. No, Debbie, it's not your fault. No, Jenna doesn't think that. I'm sure—I'm positive. Okay. Good night." He hung up the phone.

"Second time she's called," he said. "She thinks it's all her fault. She let you in, and then she got busy on the telephone and she didn't realize how long it was taking you to get upstairs. And then she couldn't find out what had happened to you. She's pretty frantic."

"I'll call her tomorrow," Jenna said. She suddenly put her hands to her face. She was going to cry again. Suddenly she was going to cry.

"Don't," Garth said quietly. "Not now. I want you to talk to me instead. I want you to tell me everything that happened. Everything you remember, no matter how minor or how silly it seems to you. And I want you to do it now."

"Garth, I can't. I've already told Rosie."

He came and sat on the side of the bed. "Yes, you can, and I want you to tell *me*. You tell me, and then you can sleep. But there's one other thing first. I need to ask you a question."

She tried to wipe her eyes with her fingertips, and she looked at him. "What?"

"Your name."

"My *name*?"

"I promised the doc every two hours I'd make sure you knew what planet you were on."

She sighed. If he'd promised, he'd promised. "Jenna Gallagher."

"And today is..."

"Friday," she supplied.

"The date?"

She told him that, too.

"Very good. Joe Eagan called while you were in the tub."

"Is that the truth, or are you still testing?"

"Both. You get to tell me who Joe Eagan is."

She looked into his eyes. He was so serious about this. "Joe Eagan is Debbie Carver's father. He's a retired cop—retired because of wounds received in the line of duty. He's in a wheelchair. He lectures regularly at the police academy about things like keeping a little notebook—an 'auxiliary brain,' he calls it, because a street cop never knows when an unimportant detail might become an important one—how am I doing?"

"Well, *I'm* impressed," he said. "How did you know about the auxiliary brain?"

"Patrick told me. He kept one. A lot of you do, don't you?"

He looked away; there was a long pause.

"Yeah, I guess we do," he said finally. "The test is over. Now, tell me what happened to you."

Garth paced around the loft. The moon was shining in the arched windows, leaving patches of moonlight on the floor. And damn, this place was still cold! He glanced from time to time at the clocks and at Jenna sleeping quietly in his bed. He'd have to wake her soon for another name and day of the week run-through to make sure she was all right. But at the moment, he had other things on his mind.

Patrick Gallagher kept a notebook. Had anybody looked in it? *He* certainly hadn't. That unofficial spiral pocket notebook Joe Eagan advocated hadn't been part of the murder investigation, and he hadn't thought to ask for it.

He still remembered Joe Eagan's lecture from when he had been at the academy. "If you got a great memory, don't keep a little book," he'd told them. "I had a partner like that. Remembered everything he ever heard—names, addresses, everything. Of course he got hit by a bus over on Second Avenue one night, and everything he could remember didn't do anybody a damn bit of good."

Where was the notebook now? Garth wondered. If it was significant, Hugh would have done something with it—*if* he had known it existed. But maybe he hadn't thought of it, either. Some rookies took Joe Eagan's advice to heart; some didn't. Which brought him to the problem at hand. If the book still existed, Jenna must have it. How was he going to get it?

Ah, Jenna.

He closed his eyes. He'd been scared for her. He was *still* scared for her. The mugging hadn't been a robbery. Attempted rape? He didn't think so. What, then? All he had were questions.

He went to the telephone, quietly dialed the station house and asked for Skip.

"Skip!" he said when his partner answered. "What's the word?"

"Quiet," Skip said. "Hugh's not around. Some of us have to pull a twelve and some of us don't. I imagine he's heard about Jenna, though. Everybody here has. The brotherhood is pretty riled about this happening to her. She made the evening news, complete with clips of Patrick's funeral. How is she?"

"Asleep."

But she wasn't asleep. Even as he said it, she made a soft whimpering sound.

"Skip, I want Roy Lee picked up," he said hurriedly. "Take care of getting that out, will you?"

"You got it. And you take good care of Jenna."

He hung up the phone and walked toward the bed to see if Jenna was all right. She was quieter now, her breathing deep and even again. He stood staring down at her. She was so beautiful to him—even with a black eye. Her hair was loose and spread out over the pillow. She had a black eye, no makeup; she was wearing a man's flannel shirt, and she was still beautiful to him. He tried not to think about how much this had scared him. If something had happened to her...

Like Mary.

He realized that he was scared for her and for himself. He was scared of what he was feeling, scared of this need he had to be with her, to bring her into his life and keep her there. He didn't want any encumbrances; he *knew* that, and yet...

He was about to move away from the bed when she suddenly sat up.

"Jenna?" he said, but she didn't hear him. "Jenna," he said again.

"Don't!" she cried out. He reached out to touch her, because she was on her knees. "Don't!"

"Jenna!" he said sharply, taking her by the shoulders. She began to fight him, flailing out with both arms.

"Don't! Don't!" she cried.

He caught her to him, holding her tightly. "It's all right. You're all right," he whispered urgently. "Jenna!"

She suddenly went limp in his arms. "Oh, Garth! Oh, Garth! He wouldn't take the money—I tried to give him my purse. He wouldn't take it!"

"It's okay," he soothed. "It's just a dream, baby. It's okay."

"Don't go anywhere, Garth. Please!" She clung to him desperately.

"No, I won't. Here. Cover up. It's cold." He tried to pull the covers up around her, but she wouldn't let go of him so

he could. She was trembling. Careful of her bruised face,
he stroked her hair, rocking her gently, as if she were a
child.

But she wasn't a child, and in a very little time, they both
knew it. She suddenly stiffened in his arms, pushing herself
back so she could see his face. She regarded him gravely,
and he was lost again in her eyes, those sad, knowing eyes
of hers that saw everything and still forgave.

The Drifters sang.

Her hands rested lightly on his shoulders. And slowly, so
slowly, she lifted her mouth to his. He tried to stay passive
under the tentative sweetness of her lips.

She tasted him.

Again.

And then again. He let her, his breathing growing heavier,
his hands moving over her back in spite of everything he
could do.

Don't do this, he told himself. He understood, and he
wanted to tell her that he did. He wasn't the one she needed.
She'd been hurt, and she needed her husband to comfort
her. She needed Patrick; she didn't need him. He didn't
want to take advantage of a moment of weakness. Hers. Or
his. In the cold light of day, she'd be sorry, and he didn't
want to see that in her eyes.

But he was all she had, and her kisses were warm and
soft. Her body was warm and soft. He shivered with desire
and buried his face in her sweet-smelling neck.

Ah, God, he wanted her.

"Jenna," he whispered, some part of him still needing to
protest.

But she slid her hands into his hair, and she parted her
lips under his, so that he wouldn't be passive anymore. His
arms tightened around her.

"I don't want to hurt you, baby."

"You won't," she promised him. "You won't." She

knew that he didn't necessarily mean now. She knew that he was giving her the chance to stay Mrs. Gallagher.

But she didn't want the chance. She wanted him. He'd been watching over her while she slept, and he was so cold. She wanted to warm him. She wanted to be close to him. She wanted to belong to him, and she purposefully moved his hand to her breast. She could feel the trembling in his body and in her own, and she wanted to shut out everything but him. The physical pain she felt was nothing compared to the pain in her heart. She wanted his comfort and, yes, his kindness. She would ask for nothing else.

"Jenna," he said, holding her away from him.

She gently placed her fingertips against his lips. "Don't say anything. You don't have to say anything. I don't want any promises in the dark."

He took her hand and slid his fingers between hers the way he had in the car. "Yeah?"

"Yeah," she answered.

He pulled her closer and placed both her arms around his neck. "Well, I do," he said quietly, staring into her eyes. "I want you to promise me everything. I want you to sweet-talk me and make me feel good. What do you think of that?"

She thought she would die from the pleasure of it.

Making love with him was not the way she had thought it would be. He talked to her, touched her, looked at her, made her laugh, made her cry. He filled her with urgency, an urgency that the effort to discard clothes and emotional baggage didn't diminish. Her body sang the familiar refrain that had come into play almost from the beginning:

I want him.

She felt no jealousy that he was prepared for the possibility of lovemaking, that he kept what he needed near the bed for just such an eventuality as this, regardless of the

fact that supposedly he rarely brought anyone here and regardless of the fact that he most certainly hadn't intended
them for her.

She didn't care.

She didn't care about the women he'd had here or the
potential liaisons he'd bought condoms for. She didn't care
that he didn't meet the Gallagher standards of what an ac-
ceptable police officer should be. She didn't care that he'd
come from a world she couldn't begin to understand. It was
only Garth himself that mattered. She'd sweet-talk him.
She'd make him feel good.

He sat up and piled pillows behind his back to lean
against, bringing her leg over his so that she sat astride his
thighs. They were face-to-face; she could look into his eyes.

Hide me, Garth. Just for a little while.

"Are you all right?" he asked her.

"Yes," she whispered, her voice so tremulous she hardly
recognized it.

"Where can I touch you? I don't want to hurt you." His
fingers moved lightly over her shoulders to her breasts.

"I'll tell you if you hurt me—oh, Garth—"

"What? What? Did I hurt you?"

"No," she murmured, her mouth finding his. She kissed
him deeply, reveling in the moan of desire she elicited from
him.

She pressed her body against his. Her breasts flattened
against his chest. She wrapped her arms around him and
held him tightly. "You're so cold."

He laughed softly against her ear. "No, baby. I'm *not*."

Even so, he took his time. He wanted to make it last. He
had no illusions about her need of him. He knew that this
would likely be his only time with her, and that when the
morning came, they would both remember who they were.

What if I love you? he thought. But he didn't say it. He
tried to make her feel it instead. It was such an ache within

him, that he might be in love with her and that she might be thinking of Patrick.

When he entered her, she could still look into his eyes.

Don't be sad, Garth, she thought. Why was he so sad? Because she wasn't Mary?

And then she said it, cupping his face in her hands, kissing his eyes, his mouth. "Don't be sad, Garth. Please."

"I'm not," he whispered, thrusting into her, trying not to hurt her and yet trying to take all the pleasure she could give. It was so good with her. So good. "You—make me happy. You—"

She clung to him, letting the rise of his passion fuel her own. Incredible, she kept thinking. Incredible, her need of this man. She loved being with him like this. She loved the smell of him and the taste and the feel of him. And she found that she was jealous of his other women after all. And Mary.

"Garth," she murmured. "No, don't stop—oh, Garth—"

But it was he who did the "sweet-talking." He told her how good she felt around him. He told her how long—how *long*—he'd wanted to do this, how he'd thought about making love with her ever since the night they'd met. He told her she was beautiful, so beautiful—shiner or no. He told her—showed her—how much he wanted her.

And even when their passion had peaked, even when she thought she would die from the pleasure he had given her and she began the slow spiral downward into reality, she believed him.

Chapter 10

They lay together, bundled under blankets and the brown quilted comforter. Her body was warm against his, and her hand rested lightly on his chest. He didn't think she was asleep.

He covered her hand with his. Who was he kidding anyway? He was crazy in love with this woman.

What do you think of that, Jenna? I love you.

But he didn't tell her.

"The lawyer you went out with," he said instead. "The Peking Opera one," he added in case she had any doubts about which one he meant.

"What about him?" she asked sleepily.

"Whoever he is, I hate his guts. I just wanted you to know that."

There was a long pause.

"I wasn't too crazy about him myself," she said finally, and they both burst out laughing. He hugged her to him. She made him so happy. Just being with her made him happy.

Until he remembered—Mary, and Hugh Gallagher, and how he'd come to have Jenna in his bed in the first place.

I love you, Jenna, and by the way, could I have Patrick's notebook? You see, I want to break his mother's heart and ruin his family.

But he didn't want to think about that. Not now. Not now. He abruptly rolled her over on top of him, and his mouth found hers. She gave a soft cry of surprise, but he didn't stop.

"That dress you wore to the opera," he whispered against her ear. "One day I want you to wear it for *me*." His hands moved over her, as if he could memorize the feel, the softness of her body before she was gone. "Jenna."

"Yes," she said, returning his kiss. For now, for this night at least, he was her lover. And she wanted him.

She must have slept, because she seemed to have awakened, but what had awakened her she couldn't say. Some disturbing dream not quite remembered—the man in the stairwell again?

She gave an involuntary shiver and moved closer to Garth.

"You okay?" he asked, pressing a small kiss on her forehead. He brought the covers more snugly around her.

"Yes," she said. "I...can't stop thinking about the man—oh!" she said softly as the memory returned, strong and disturbing and not at all muted by the pleasure she'd shared with Garth.

"You're safe here. Try to sleep."

But she couldn't go back to sleep. Not because she was afraid of the night, but because she dreaded the morning. She wouldn't be able to hide then. She would have to deal with everything—with the memories, with the fear, with Patrick's family, with the possibility that Garth would resent her intrusion. She would leave early, she decided. Before he even wanted her to. She couldn't bear the thought of being here when he wanted to be rid of her. He was a private man, and she'd imposed upon him without mercy.

Still, she thought, lying here with his breath coming soft and warm against her neck and his hand cupping her breast, her imposition wasn't without compensation. The problem was that she wanted to be more to him than a double-edged sword.

She finally slept, only to be wakened for another of Garth's orientation quizzes. She knew who she was—she knew only too well who she was, and what planet she was on, and whatever else it took to prove that her mental faculties were intact. It wasn't her mind she was concerned about. It was her heart. In spite of herself, she'd given it to him—and he didn't even know it. She understood the kind of man he was, that he would be driven to isolate himself from personal involvement. And she had never wanted just a sexual relationship between strangers.

Neither had she wanted to become involved with another policeman. It was too lonely, too filled with worry. And commitment, if Garth were capable of it, would be on the run, falling somewhere well behind his mistress, The Job. Yet what was the alternative? Quietly returning to her widowhood, the way Mamie wanted? Going back home to live along the Susquehanna River?

She gave a sad smile. Hazel had wanted Garth to marry "up." Jenna's mother had wanted the same—only where she came from, marrying up would be to a nice white-collar worker from IBM instead of someone from the shoe factory—neither of whom would be anything at all like Garth. No one was like Garth. No one. She suddenly tightened her arms around him.

"What?" he asked.

"Nothing. Nothing…"

She left his bed at dawn, dressing quietly in the bathroom

because the best she could do for him would be not to bother him anymore. She still looked like hell, or perhaps worse. Her eye was still swollen, and her cheeks tingled from the chafing of his beard. The pleasant memory of his lovemaking immediately surfaced, making her give a soft, ragged sigh.

When he finally woke, she was standing in front of the arched windows, waiting, her arms folded over her breasts.

"What are you doing?" he asked, trying to rub the sleep from his eyes.

She turned to look at him. "I'm going to go home now, Garth," she said quietly.

"Now? What time is it?"

"It's early, but—"

"What's wrong?" he asked, cutting in the way he always did when he wanted answers.

"Nothing."

"Don't do that! Tell me what's wrong."

"Nothing is wrong. I...need to get home."

He stared at her across the room. When he was right, he was right. He'd known her regrets would get the best of her this morning. Regardless of the night they'd spent, in the cold light of day, she was done with him. And he, *he* had said too much, revealed too much about what he was feeling. He knew enough to keep things to himself, and he hadn't done it. And that lapse made him angry.

"You mean you need to get away from me, don't you? It's all right, Mrs. Gallagher. You can tell me. I can take it." He got up from the bed, looking for his shorts.

"That's not what I meant."

"You mind if I shower first? Or can't you wait that long?"

"You don't have to take me. I've called a cab."

"I see," he said. "So what's the hurry?" he asked as he

crossed the room. "Are you afraid somebody will see you leaving?"

She had only meant to relieve him of the responsibility he'd had to take for her, a responsibility he'd really had little choice about, but instead she'd insulted him somehow. Because they'd rushed their intimacy, she thought. Because they really didn't know each other. "You know better than that," she said.

"Do I? You know Hugh has you watched when you're with me, don't you? You know that?"

"No, I don't know that!" she said sharply. "Hugh wouldn't—"

"Yes, Mrs. Gallagher, he would. So tell me. How was I? Was I worth that aggravation? Was I worth the guilt you're feeling now for your little lapse in propriety? Am I as good in bed as Patrick was or not?"

She walked toward him with every intention of hitting him, and it surprised her that he didn't realize it. Even when she swung at him, he hadn't anticipated her intent.

He caught her hand, pulling her around and pinning her arms, his eyes filled with incredulity that he'd misjudged her.

"What is the matter with you!" he cried.

"Why don't you tell me if I'm as good as Mary Zaccato, Garth! Did you tell her the same things you told me? And while you're at it, you can tell me what's the matter with *you*! Why are we having this conversation!"

"Because I don't want you to go, that's why!" he yelled at her. He held her away so he could see her face. "Because I don't want you to go," he said, bringing her to him, wrapping his arms around her and holding her tightly.

"Garth—" she said, leaning into him. She put her arms around his waist and laid her uninjured cheek against his bare chest. "Garth—"

"What, damn it!"

She gave him a hard hug. "I'm trying not to bother you anymore, you big dummy."

"When I'm bothered, lady, I'll tell you."

She leaned back to look at him. "Maybe I don't want you to tell me. Maybe I'd rather—" She stopped because someone was knocking on the outer door at the fire escape.

"I'll get it," she said, because he wasn't dressed.

"No," he said, picking up his jeans and getting into them. He didn't bother to button and zip, and he quickly crossed to the chair where he'd hung his gun holster. He took the gun out.

"Garth?" Jenna said, but he held up his hand to keep her quiet. He walked barefoot to the door as the knocking continued. He stood well to the side against the brick wall.

"Who is it?" he yelled to whoever was outside.

"Open the door, Garth! I want to talk to Jenna!"

They both recognized the voice immediately. Hugh.

Garth cursed softly and unlocked the door. "About what?" he asked Hugh as he opened it.

"Now, that's not any business of yours, is it, Garth?" Hugh said, pushing his way into the loft without an invitation. Jenna watched as his sweeping glance took in everything—her, the rumpled bed, Garth's half-dressed state. Hugh, on the other hand, was wearing an expensive suit and a tailored winter coat, but neither his unexpected arrival nor his wardrobe rattled Garth in the least. He slammed the door shut behind him and casually walked to put his gun back into the holster.

"Making your rounds kind of early, aren't you, Hugh?"

"I want to make sure Jenna's all right."

"You want to catch somebody with his pants down."

"Well, I didn't miss by much, did I?"

"I'm fine," Jenna interjected before this got out of hand.

"That's just great, Jenna," Hugh said. "But none of the family would know that, would they? It didn't occur to you that we'd be worried? A phone call would have been nice. You know mother hasn't been well since Patrick died, and—''

"She wasn't thinking about making telephone calls," Garth cut in.

"You stay out of this!" Hugh said, turning on him. "This is a family matter."

"Is Mamie all right?" Jenna asked, but no one heard her.

"She wasn't thinking about making telephone calls," Garth said again. "I could have done it for her, but I thought it might make things worse for your mother to get a telephone call from me. And I was sure it wouldn't take you long to find out where she was. I really expected you sooner, Hugh."

"Look, do you mind? I'd like to talk to Jenna alone!"

"That's up to her," Garth said.

"It's all right, Garth," Jenna said. She might as well get it over with. "Hugh, say whatever it is you want to say— and, Garth, this is your home. You don't have to leave."

"No problem," he said, looking into her eyes. "We don't want to get Hugh any more bent out of shape than he already is. I'll be in here. Yell if you need me." He walked into the bathroom and closed the door. In a moment, Jenna could hear the shower running.

"I can't believe this," Hugh said, running his hand over his cropped hair. "I cannot *believe* this! Jenna, what are you doing here with him? Don't you know what people are going to say!"

"I know what your friends will say, but, for me, that isn't a consideration. Garth helped me when I needed help."

"Yes, I can see how he *helped* you. I understand your problem, Jenna—a woman as attractive as you is bound to get lonely. But don't you have any respect at all for my brother? Patrick was a good man. He was worth ten of Garth."

"Don't talk to me about Patrick, Hugh! Patrick is dead. I loved him, but he's dead."

"Jenna, use some sense, will you? I read the report on your so-called mugging. The man who attacked you didn't want your money. It was deliberate—he probably would have raped you if he'd had the time. I think—a lot of us think—it was because of him," he said, jerking his thumb toward the bathroom door. The water abruptly shut off. "He's got a foot on both sides of the law, Jenna, and his old friends make bad enemies. If he steps on their toes, if they even think he's stepped on their toes, they're not above setting up some kind of retribution. I want you to stay away from him. I don't want to see you hurt."

"Hugh, I appreciate your concern, but I have to make my own judgments. I know you and Garth don't get along, and I'm sorry about that. But it doesn't have anything to do with me—"

"It's got everything to do with you! Do you think he'd come sniffing around if it didn't? You're not even his type, Jenna. Don't you see?"

Her temper rose at Hugh's choice of words, but she didn't get the chance to say anything. The bathroom door opened, and Garth came out wearing one towel around his waist and drying his hair with another.

"Sorry," he said to Hugh. "I was getting pruney."

"I've said all I came to say," Hugh said, heading for the door.

"I think you're right, Hugh," Garth said when he reached it. "I think Jenna's mugging was a message—but I don't think the message was necessarily for me."

"What is that supposed to mean?"

"It means, Hugh, that fifty case folders on my desk or a hundred and fifty case folders on my desk—or playing clay pigeon for Tony Zaccato—I'll find out."

* * *

"What was that supposed to mean?" Jenna asked as soon as Hugh had gone.

"What?" Garth said, his tone of voice neutral enough to make her angry.

"Don't give me that, Garth! I want to know what that 'fifty case folders' and the 'clay pigeon' thing means."

"I don't want to tell you."

"I'd suggest you do," she said evenly.

He looked at her from under the towel and grinned. "You have got a lot of sonofabitch in you, Mrs. Gallagher. You know that?"

"Yes. It comes from having to deal with condescending police officers. And——"

"Sure you weren't raised on the wrong side of the tracks, too?"

"Don't change the subject! I want to know what that means."

He sighed and dropped his towel—the one that mattered—and walked blithely toward the sleeping area, hunting through various drawers for his underwear. The sight of his bare backside caused an immediate internal flutter in her. He knew she liked his body—she'd certainly done everything she could last night to convince him of that—but she was determined not to let him get away with this flagrant ploy to distract her from the topic of conversation.

"Garth..."

"Jenna, it means that Hugh has seen to it that I keep busy." He put his shorts on.

"Why?" she asked pointedly.

He didn't answer.

"Let me guess. Another message?"

"Something like that."

"Because of me?"

He didn't answer that, either.

"All right—that brings us to the mugging, which all of

a sudden isn't one at all. Were you going to tell me about that?''

"Nope," he said easily. He put on a T-shirt.

"Why not!" she cried, trying not to think how seductive it was to stand and watch a man put his clothes *on.*

"Because I know what I think it *isn't.* I don't know what I think it *is.* So there's no point in it."

"Who's the message for then, if it's not for you? Hugh?"

"Maybe. Maybe not."

She rolled her eyes upward in exasperation. "Maybe the message is for me, Garth. Maybe *I'm* the one who stepped on somebody's toes with these committees I'm on. Or maybe it's because of somebody I've gone to court with."

"Maybe," he said noncommittally.

"Maybe it's not a message at all. Maybe I was just in the wrong place at the wrong time."

"Maybe," he said again.

"But Hugh—and some of the others—think it's your fault. And you think it's Hugh's fault. And Debbie thinks it's *her* fault, right? And don't say 'Maybe'!"

"Don't forget Joe Eagan," he put in.

"Joe Eagan?"

"Yeah. He thinks it might be *his* fault. He's made a lot of enemies in his time, and you were on your way to his place."

"Good Lord," she said in aggravation. "And just who would know that?"

"Debbie said some man called Saint Xavier's looking for you when you were in court. Something about a change in a meeting. He wouldn't leave a message. *Had* to talk to you. Debbie told him she was meeting you at Joe's apartment yesterday afternoon so he could call you there."

Jenna stared at him.

"What else haven't you bothered to tell me?''

"You weren't feeling up to hearing this last night," he said instead of answering.

"Today I'm feeling better! What else?"

"I've got a couple of things I want to check out."

"Like what?"

"Oh," he said airily, "like the sticker on your assailant's underwear."

"That's very funny, Garth." A car horn blew several times in the parking lot below. She went to the window to see if her cab had arrived. "Very funny. I'm not stupid. And I'm not weak, regardless of the way I behaved last night. If you explained things very carefully, I could probably follow it."

"I told you I didn't want you to go," he said as she picked up her purse.

"Nevertheless, I'm going. Thank you for your... hospitality."

"Take my coat," he said when she reached the door.

"I don't need it."

"Take the damn coat!" he yelled, grabbing it and shoving it at her. "Have you got money?"

She stood staring at him, then finally accepted his jacket. "Yes. I have money."

"We won't be seeing each other," he said, trying to look into her eyes. She wouldn't let him.

"No," she agreed.

"Until we know more about your assault," he qualified. "In case I am the reason."

She opened the door to go down the fire escape. He was trying to be kind to her. He was a kind man, regardless of what he said.

"Jenna?"

She looked back over her shoulder at him.

"I want you to be careful. Don't go anyplace alone. Don't take any chances."

"I won't."

"Jenna," he said again. He wanted to say something about last night, something so she'd know how special it had been to him. But he didn't. He knew the price of revealing too much. "The notebook you said Patrick kept," he said instead. "Do you still have it?"

"I think so. Why?"

"I'd like to look at it. I'll...pick it up when I pick up my jacket."

He stood in the arched window staring at nothing for a long time after she'd gone. The sun was just coming up. He had a lot to do and no inclination to do it. He could see what she had done. She'd tried to take away every trace of her having been here. Nothing was out of place. She'd put the sweatpants and flannel shirt he'd loaned her into the dirty laundry. The bathroom was straight. She'd even washed the cup that had held the hot chocolate.

And yet she was still everywhere he looked. He hadn't wanted her to go, damn it all, and he hadn't known how to keep her. The only thing he'd known to do was to *say* that he wanted her here, and that certainly hadn't worked.

He went to the station house—early, because he didn't want Hazel and Luigi to give him the third degree about Jenna and because he had to think. He wanted to get Skip so they could go looking for Roy Lee. If anybody on the street knew what getting to Jenna was all about, Roy Lee would.

He was surprised to find Skip already at work on the pile of folders. The kid looked like hell, as if he hadn't slept at all.

"What's the matter with you?" Garth asked, and none too kindly. The last thing he needed was a partner who was ailing.

"Oh, nothing much," Skip said, waving a folder in the air. "Debbie's having an affair."

Garth laughed, when he thought that he felt nothing at all like laughing. "Sure," he said. On the way here, he'd formulated a plan, and he needed Skip to carry it off. "Skipper, I want you to—"

"I tell you my marriage is over, and all you can say is *sure*?" Skip demanded, causing a few heads in the squad room to turn.

Garth leaned back to look at him. The kid was serious.

"Look, Skip, you can't stay in bed *all* the time. Sometimes you have to get up. And when you do, words fly. It's nothing to—"

"How the hell do you know? You don't know a damn thing about it!"

"Well, you got me there," Garth said, trying to humor him. "You want to tell me what's going on, or do you want to keep acting like a complete idiot?"

"Oh, so I'm acting like an idiot. Sure, blame me."

Garth's temper snapped. He was worried about Jenna. He did *not* have time for this. "Knock it off and tell me what's going on!"

"Read my lips, Garth! Debbie is having an affair!"

"Damn it, Skip—" Garth began, but he needed to exercise more control here, before he hit the kid on the head with something. "Skip," he said, trying hard, "what makes you think that?"

"What makes me think that? She's been acting crazy! That's what makes me think that!"

Crazy for Debbie or crazy for everybody else? he almost asked. "Like what?" he said, revising his first impulse.

"She keeps disappearing—going places with some kind of vague explanation of where it is and when she'll be back. She's all nervous. She's scared of the telephone."

"Did you *ask* her what's wrong with her?"

"Ask her? No, I didn't *ask* her."

That did it for Garth; he cuffed Skip sharply on the ear. "What is the matter with you! Don't I have enough to worry about? You get me all involved in this thing with you and Debbie, and you don't know any more about the situation than I do!"

"Don't you hit me, Garth," Skip said, bristling and pointing his finger into Garth's face. "I don't like it!"

"Don't hit you? You don't *like* it? I'm going to throw you out the damn window, kid!" Garth jerked him up by his lapels.

"Teacher's watching," a patrolman said in passing.

"What the hell is going on out here!" the lieutenant yelled, bursting out of his office. Garth let go of Skip's lapels. The Whip would stay out of most squabbles unless it came to breaking up the furniture, and he and the lieutenant both knew he was only a hair away from that.

"What the hell is the matter with you two? Didn't I tell you I don't want to be bothered with personality clashes! We got television people coming in here today—all I need is for them to see two of my detectives kicking the holy crap out of each other!"

"It's nothing, sir," Skip said, straightening his jacket. "A hands-on learning experience. That's all."

The lieutenant made a noise of disgust and went back into his office.

"Here!" Garth said, shoving the telephone receiver into Skip's hand. "I want you to call your old man."

Skip gave him an incredulous look. "I don't call my father, Garth, and you know that."

"Today you do. Today you call him and you tell him what happened to your friend James Gallagher. And you tell him you and your partner want the case. You remind him of who Jenna is and the tragedy she's suffered, and you tell him it's really important to you. Then you tell him to mention that to his squash-playing friends at One Police Plaza or Gracie Mansion or wherever the hell they are so they can pass the word down ASAP.''

"I'm not going to do it, Garth."

"Yes, Skip, you are."

"I don't ask my father for favors!"

"The favor isn't for you. It's for me. I want Jenna's case, and I won't get it any other way. I'm your partner, and sometimes you have to put yourself out for your partner. You're going to do this for me, do you understand?"

"What do I get out of it?" Skip asked.

"I don't kick your butt all around the squad room?" Garth suggested.

"No—you talk to Debbie for me."

"Talk to Debbie? I don't want to talk to Debbie! I'm not a marriage counselor."

"She likes you. She respects your opinion. You talk to her. That's the deal."

Chapter 11

The day, for Jenna, was an incredible study in extremes. She was exhausted emotionally and physically, but she had no time to recoup her strength. She had to deal with a visit from Mamie and with the news that Mamie had seen fit to call Jenna's mother and tell her that she'd been beaten senseless in an apartment house stairwell. She had to talk again with Rosie Madden—this time about the matter of her missing coat. She didn't *know* what had happened to it— perhaps she'd been beaten as senseless as Mamie had led her mother to believe. She got a special-delivery letter from a lawyer in the city who represented the college friend of Patrick's from whom they'd sublet the apartment four years ago when he'd taken a job abroad. He was back. He was very sorry about Patrick, but he wanted his apartment. She had a message on her answering machine from a rather ha-rassed-sounding Sister Mary John.

She had all these phone calls to make—to her mother, and to the lawyer, and to Sister—if the phone stopped ring-

ing long enough so she could. Television people were
hounding her for an interview about the mugging, the overly
sympathetic tones of voice suggesting that they all believed
"mugging" was a euphemism for "rape." And while she
was at it, perhaps she'd talk about her life since Patrick had
died and her ideas for making New York a safer city. In her
desperation, she referred them all to Detective Rosie Madden of the NYPD.

She didn't have an apartment anymore. She didn't have
a winter coat. All she had was her battered self and a misplaced devotion to Johnson Garth. She couldn't stop thinking about him. She didn't want to deal with any of this; she
wanted to hide some more. With him. She wanted to go to
the Humoresque, where black eyes wouldn't be so out of
place, and eat one of Luigi's hamburger steaks. She wanted
to sit in Garth's lap and have him tell her everything would
be all right.

But she was a responsible, mature person. She called her
mother, trying her best to reassure her that she was fine—
not an easy task, because she could see her reflection in the
mirror in the foyer as she talked. It was hard to sound con-
vincing when one was looking directly at one's black eye.

"Jenna, honey, don't you want to come home now?" her
mother pleaded. "Mamie was so upset."

"No, Mama."

"But, Jenna, it's not safe—you shouldn't be living by
yourself!"

"I'll come for a visit as soon as I can. We'll talk then."

"When?" her mother asked, trying to pin her down.

"Soon, Mama," she repeated, because she couldn't say
"as soon as the black eye's gone."

She called Sister Mary John next. Incredibly it was an
offer to work at Saint Xavier's full-time. She wanted—
needed—the job, but Sister Mary John wanted her to start

tomorrow. She tried to explain about her black eye. Sister wasn't impressed. She'd start tomorrow.

The lawyer Jenna ignored. Her current coping limit seemed to be two major demands per day.

She set about looking for the notebook Patrick had carried instead, finding it in a desk drawer where she'd put it just after he'd died. She hadn't looked at it then or since. But she sat down to look at it now. How strange it was seeing his handwriting again. Patrick. She smiled to herself. He had terrible penmanship, but she could read his entries. None of it made much sense, however. There were names, addresses, notes to himself: *Don't forget Jenna's birthday!*

Her eyes fell on Joey Malaga's name, the boy who had shot him. Patrick must have written it down the first time they'd met so he'd know it the next time he saw him—so the boy would know that his name, that he himself, had mattered, to at least one cop. She silently shook her head and continued to turn the pages. There was nothing significant to her until several pages later. At the top of the page was a vaguely familiar address. In the middle, Patrick had drawn a triangle. At two of the corners he had a question mark. At the other corner, he'd written a name. *Mary Zaccato.*

"Are you going to sulk for the rest of the day?" Garth asked when they stopped long enough to buy something to eat—a luxury Garth allowed only because they were going to eat on the move. He wanted to find wherever Roy Lee was holed up before it got dark.

"I'm not sulking," Skip said. "I'm worried about my wife. When are you going to talk to her?"

"Skip, I can't do it today. I want to find Roy Lee. I'll...do it tomorrow. I'll come by and—"

"You can't come by, Garth!"

"Well, how the hell am I going to talk to her?" he

snapped. His head ached from lack of food, and as far as he knew, Skip's old man hadn't come through with the favor. So he'd taken it upon himself to start the hunt for the whys behind Jenna's being hurt anyway.

"You can't talk to her with me there, Garth. You'll have to meet her someplace."

"Oh, sure. I just ask Debbie to meet me and she's going to do it, particularly when I tell her I want to talk about the affair you think she's having."

Skip gave him a stricken look.

"Yeah, well, see? It's not going to be easy, kid."

"You could say you wanted to talk about Jenna," Skip said as they got back into the car.

"No, I couldn't."

"Yes, you could. You're crazy about her. Everybody knows it."

Everybody knows it, he thought. *Except Jenna.* For once he didn't waste his time trying to deny it. Okay. So he was crazy about her.

"I'll…stop by the school tomorrow. I'll talk to Debbie there. Pull into that alley."

"Now where are we going?"

"We're looking for Roy Lee, remember? You look for a rat where he lives. Hold that," he said, handing Skip his Polish sausage. "And don't eat the damn thing while I'm gone."

Garth walked the length of the alley, stepping over sleeping men, staring into old faces, into young faces with old eyes. He didn't see Roy Lee. He moved on toward a pile of cardboard boxes, knowing Roy Lee used to sleep in one of the bigger ones.

"Roy Lee!" he yelled because he didn't want to stick his head into some wino's sanctorum if he could help it. "Roy Lee!"

"Roy Lee ain't here, man," a voice said crabbily.

"Where is he?"

"How the hell do I know? He ain't here. That's all you need to know, sucker."

"Which box is his?" Garth asked the voice coming from a refrigerator box to his right. The voice didn't answer, and Garth kicked the side of the box hard.

"Hey, man, are you crazy?"

"Which one is his!" Garth yelled.

"That one!"

"Which one!"

"Kenmore!"

Garth knelt down to shine his mag light into the box with the Kenmore logo, making certain first that no one was behind him. The pavement was wet with God only knew what, and the box stank of unwashed human, as if it had just been vacated. There was nothing inside but a rolled-up coat. He pulled it out. It was a woman's coat—black. He held it up so he could see, running his hands into the pockets. He found a piece of paper. A memo from Saint Xavier's.

"Let's go!" he said to Skip.

"What is that?" Skip asked, dodging as Garth threw the coat into the back.

"Jenna's coat."

"Don't tell me we've got a crazy who falls in love with women's coats?"

"No, we've got a crazy who sleeps on the street and needs all the insulation he can get." He didn't tell Skip what he was thinking. That for once Roy Lee *had* spent the money he'd given him on something besides booze, and that he'd taken Jenna's coat because he'd been living on the street too long to let a chance like that pass him by. An INSPECTED BY No. 2 label and the missing coat in a Kenmore refrigerator box in an alley full of winos wouldn't stand up in court, but it was enough for him. Roy Lee had worked Jenna over, but the question was *why?* Roy Lee had no animosity toward anyone. Unless it was bought and paid for. "Where's my sausage?" he asked abruptly.

"Oh—I, ah, gave it away."

"You gave it *away?*" Garth said incredulously.

"Well, this old guy was staring in through the window. He was hungry...."

"What the devil do you think *I* am?"

"I told you the guy was hungry!"

"Yeah? Why didn't you give him *yours?* Jeez! A man could starve to death with you for a partner!"

They kept looking, checking the bars, all the places Roy Lee hung out, Garth taking one side of the street and Skip taking the other. He wasn't there. He wasn't anywhere, and no one would admit to having seen him. Just before sundown, it began to rain.

"Now what?" Skip said tiredly.

"We call it quits."

"Why is it I don't believe you?"

"No, I mean it. We've looked everywhere I know to look. Go home to Debbie."

"Good idea—if she's there. What are you going to do?"

"I may look some more."

"If you're still looking, so am I."

"Or I may go see Jenna."

Skip grinned in the dark interior of the car. "Yes, sir. Old Garth has bitten the dust on this one, hasn't he?"

It was late when the telephone rang. Jenna had been crying for a long time, and she wanted desperately to let it keep ringing. But it would cause more problems than she already had if once again she couldn't be accounted for. The last thing she needed was to have Hugh or Mamie come over because she hadn't answered the phone.

She wiped her eyes and picked up the receiver. "Hello?"

For a moment all she could hear was traffic and some kind of steady background noise—the rain, she supposed. She didn't hang up. She knew it wasn't a crank call or a wrong number. She knew Garth was there, and she waited.

"I want to see you," he finally said, and her knees went weak.

She marveled at her loss of resolve. She didn't spar with him; she didn't pretend to be coy. There was no token "It's late" or "You said we wouldn't." He was the source of her unhappiness, and he was the only one who could comfort her. She didn't have to be persuaded. She had only one thing to say, and she said it.

"Hurry."

He closed his eyes at the need he heard in her voice. "Baby," he whispered into the receiver. He could feel it— a loneliness and a longing that matched his own. He didn't say goodbye; he didn't say anything. He stepped out into the rain. And he hurried.

She washed her face in cold water and waited for him, answering the door ahead of his knock, not knowing what she would do until she saw him face-to-face.

He looked so tired—and so good. He was a beautiful man to her. She stared into his eyes; she tried to find her anger and couldn't. She didn't care that he was rain soaked; she stepped into his arms, her body warm and soft against his.

How pretty you are, he thought. Her hair was hanging free to her shoulders. She was barefoot, and she was wearing what looked like a man's white cotton nightshirt. He buried his face in her neck and hair. She smelled so good! Sweet, sweet woman smell.

"You make me crazy," he whispered against her ear. "You make me crazy."

"Good," she answered simply. Her arms slid around his neck, and her mouth found his.

So good, he thought. Her kisses, the feel of her body pressing against his, drove him immediately to the brink. It was as if they'd never made love before. He reached down to find the edge of her nightshirt, sliding his hand up under it.

Soft, soft skin. Warm, dewy places that were already ready for him. He was so hungry for her. Nobody did it for him the way she did.

Nobody.

He leaned back and lifted her up off the floor; she locked her legs around his hips. He carried her through the apartment, looking for the bedroom door.

He found it easily because she'd left the light on. Her bed was full of pillows, pillows and pink-and-purple flowered sheets. He had the vague concern that this was the bed she'd shared with Patrick, but then he realized that it was narrow. This was *her* bed, a replacement, not the one she'd had with Patrick, and if she brought a man into this one—if she brought *him* into it—it was because she wanted him there.

He set her down among the pillows and the flowers, trying to get out of his jacket, his clothes, and still touch her. He didn't want to break contact, not for a second. She helped him. On her knees at the edge of the bed, she undid buttons, unsnapped snaps. He kept one hand on her, stroking her unbruised cheek, her soft breasts through the opening in her nightshirt.

He held her close for a moment before he sat down with her, hugging her to him. Once again Jenna could sense that he didn't want to hurt her—physically, at least. She was still on her knees on the edge of the bed, and he kissed her forehead, stroked her hair. She didn't want him to feel her desperation, but she couldn't keep from clinging to him.

She should have told him immediately about Mary's name being in the notebook, but she didn't. Even knowing that its being there had ended everything between them, she didn't. She would tell him about the notebook—but not now. Not now. She wanted this one last time. She would tell him goodbye in a way she hadn't been able to say goodbye to Patrick.

He was aroused, and so was she. She could feel him, hot and hard against her belly.

He could feel her trembling, and he leaned back to look into her eyes. "What is it?"

She shook her head, giving him a small smile to fool him, and she kissed him tenderly, deeply, to fool him more.

"Love me, Garth," she murmured, the words flowing from her mouth into his. She moved backward to make room for him, holding up the covers in invitation. He slid into bed beside her, and she held her arms out to him.

He lifted her up and took her astride his thighs, so that he could see her face, touch her breasts. She surprised him. God, she surprised him. When they'd first met, he'd thought her buttoned-up and shy. She *was* shy, and that made this all the sweeter. He caught the edge of her nightshirt and pulled it off over her head, giving it a sling and not caring where it went. He put his arms around her and pressed his face against her breasts. She smelled so good, felt so good. He could get lost here. He wanted to get lost here.

She gave a soft moan when he took a tightly budded nipple into his mouth. When he gently suckled her, her head arched back.

Her hands slid into his hair.

"Garth," she whispered. "Garth—"

And, God, he loved that, too, hearing her say his name.

She brought his mouth to hers, and for a moment, he did his best to stay passive. He liked for her to kiss him; he liked the taste of her warm mouth. He liked the feel of her warm hands stroking his chest, her warm, *bold* hands that now moved downward. He closed his eyes. She kissed his eyelids. And all the while her hands—her clever hands—stroked and encircled and caressed.

"Yes," he hissed in her ear. "Like that—oh, baby—Jenna!"

He was awash in pleasure. His hips thrust upward. "Wait—" he whispered urgently as her ministrations continued.

But she didn't want to wait, and she told him so. He wrapped his arms around her and thrust himself into her. He tried to hold back as the exquisite pleasure she'd begun intensified. It was torture not to move. She was so hot and tight; he trembled with the effort to make the pleasure last while everything in him screamed for release.

In a moment, he made the first tentative thrust. It was so good! He needed this—no, he needed *her*. "Jenna."

She gave herself up to pure sensation, to his loving intrusion into her body. She wanted him inside her. He filled that great emptiness she'd had since Patrick died. He filled it, but he was not a substitute for Patrick. He was himself. The emptiness she would have after he'd gone, no one else would be able to fill. She wanted to cry again, but suddenly there was nothing but the sweet oblivion of his body joining with hers. He made her feel so good! The pleasure swirled around her, took her away from everything but him, until at last it peaked and shattered, and she tumbled earthward, her face covered in her own tears.

"Don't cry," he said after a long time of listening to her try to hide it.

"Can't help it," she answered, trying to sound reasonable and in control. But her voice was husky and strange-sounding even to herself.

"What's the matter?" he insisted, trying to make her look at him.

She sighed. "Just…one of those things, I guess."

She lay quietly in his arms, and her silence made him afraid. She wasn't telling him the truth.

"You know I...care about you," he offered.

"Don't!" she said sharply. She turned on her side to look at him, wiping quickly at her eyes with her fingertips as if by doing so she could minimize the emotion she was feeling. "I told you before. I don't want any promises in the dark."

"What do you want?"

"This is enough," she said, but she avoided his eyes.

"Great sex, you mean? Making the earth move?"

She forced herself to look at him. "We don't know each other well enough for anything else." It was both the truth and a lie. Chronologically, she hadn't known him long, but he had been giving her small pieces of himself ever since they'd met. She knew him well enough to admire the person she thought he was and to care about him; she knew him well enough to care a great deal.

"What if I want more?" he asked.

"Do you?" she countered.

He didn't answer.

"I think we'd better end this conversation while we still feel kindly toward each other," she said. She moved to get up, but he wouldn't let her.

"I'll tell you what I don't want. This is a small bed. I don't want three of us in it."

"Or four?" she asked.

"Mary is dead."

"I have something for you," she said, moving to get up again. This time he let her. She picked her nightshirt up from the floor where he'd slung it and put it on.

"What is it?" he asked, but she was already going into the living room.

He heard her opening a drawer someplace, and in a moment she came back again. She handed him a small book with a black plastic cover.

His lips were pursed to ask what it was when he realized that she'd given him Patrick's notebook. He looked up at her, but she was already going back into the other room. He stared after her for a moment, then down at the book.

Jenna stood in the dark by the bow window, looking out at the rainy street. Every now and then a car went by. She could see the raindrops in the headlights. She took a deep breath to gather up her courage, and she walked back to the bedroom.

Garth was sitting on the edge of the bed—fully dressed.

"I have to go," he said when he glanced up and saw her. He stood. "You read this?" he asked, sticking the notebook into his shirt pocket.

"Yes. I read it. But I don't know what it means."

He didn't offer to enlighten her.

"Mary—and Patrick. That's what this has all been about, hasn't it?" she said, moving out of his way as he bent to pick up the change and keys that had fallen out of his pockets in his haste to make love to her.

"I don't know what you mean."

"I mean, Garth, there was some connection between the two of them. And you've been using me to try to find out what it is."

He came and stood closer, and he reached out to touch her, but he didn't at the last moment, letting his hand fall to his side. "Not exactly," he said, and she gave a short laugh.

"Not exactly? For a cop, you are the worst liar in the world, Garth."

"Jenna—"

"Take the notebook. Take it, and your jacket, and your half-truths and go. Or is there something else I can do for you? I've already told you I never heard Patrick or Hugh mention Tony Zaccato. I'll tell you now that I never heard either of them mention Mary, either."

"Jenna, it's not what you think—"

"It doesn't matter what I think. I certainly can't pass any judgments. I'm the person who figured out this afternoon that there was some kind of rhyme and reason to your sudden interest in the widow Gallagher and your unsubtle questions. I figured it out, and I went to bed with you just now anyway. You see, I always thought you were doing a number on me, but I wanted you, so I let you do it. That doesn't say much for my integrity or my good sense, does it? But tell me. At Skip's party, if I'd said no, Patrick and I weren't getting along before he was killed, what would your next question have been? Would you have asked me right then and there if he was having an affair with Mary Zaccato? The truth is, *I don't know.*"

"I didn't think he was involved with Mary!"

"The thing I can't understand is, what does it matter? They're both dead. What does it matter?"

"I can't explain it to you. You have to trust me."

She smiled; a tear ran down her cheek anyway. "Now, that's the strange thing, Garth. I do trust you. Or I did. Even thinking you had to be up to something, I believed everything you told me. I guess you're a good liar after all." She gave a tremulous sigh. "Ah, well. Live and learn."

"Jenna, don't—"

"Don't? You needn't worry about this, Garth. I'm all right. If I can get over Patrick's dying, I can certainly get over you."

"Jenna, I can't explain this to you," he said again. "It's too complicated. I don't know all the answers myself."

"Then we'll just have to let it go, won't we?"

"We have to talk about this—"

"No! Please, please! Just go, and we'll call it even."

He stood staring at her; it was all he could do not to try to take her in his arms. But he saw in her eyes that he had been relegated to another place, to that place where she put pesky television cameramen, and demanding Gallagher in-laws, and anybody else who wanted to take a piece of her for their own gain.

"Okay," he said finally. There was nothing he could say to her. Nothing.

Chapter 12

He hadn't slept. He'd looked for Roy Lee all night. And all morning he had vacillated between being hurt and being angry. He didn't know what to do, and indecisiveness was an entirely new emotion to him. Should he call her? Try to see her, talk to her?

Damn it all, Jenna!

She was a strong person; he knew that. Last night he'd looked into her eyes and listened to what she said, and he'd had no doubt whatsoever that she meant every word of it.

"Just go, and we'll call it even."

Well, he couldn't just go. She had tried to make it sound so simple. He'd used her, she'd used him, and that was supposed to be the end of it. It wasn't the end of anything. The idea that he couldn't see her, that she'd been so loving and then so cold, was a relentless ache in him he couldn't do anything about. He kept remembering the way she'd made love to him. Why had she done *that* if everything was over?

He couldn't think about anything else, but how the hell was he going to explain anything to her? He didn't know himself. All he had was bits and pieces and one of those gut feelings a cop got and could never explain to anybody— except another cop. All he'd known was that Hugh Gallagher hadn't wanted him investigating Patrick's death. But, my God, how had Patrick known Mary? It was incredible to him that this mess might somehow have cost him *both* women he'd loved.

But what to do about it? He'd never been a man who could just wait. He had to *do* something, talk to her. God, he wanted to talk to her.

And I can't, damn it! I can't!

He worked at his desk when he should have been out looking for Roy Lee again, fiddling with the endless paperwork that always needed doing. But he didn't register any of it. His mind filled with idea after idea for making Jenna understand—none of them worth a damn. His temper grew shorter and shorter, and even the news that Skip's father had come through and he and Skip would take over Jenna's case from Rosie Madden did nothing to improve it. Once again he marveled at the inner workings of the police department. After all his years of being a cop, it was still incredible to him that somebody's squash partner could influence a detective's assignment. Not that he didn't welcome it this time. He intended to take care of Jenna, whether she wanted him to or not, and if he couldn't be with her, the least he could do was find out for certain who had hurt her and why.

"Just how involved are you with Jenna Gallagher?" the lieutenant asked before he made the assignment change.

He looked the lieutenant in the eyes and told him the current truth. "I'm not."

"That's not what Hugh says."

"Hugh is full of—"

"Be that as it may," the lieutenant interrupted. "I'm not

having you harass Patrick Gallagher's widow—for what reason, I don't even want to think about. What I want is for you to tell me what the hell's going on. Now, you may think I don't see your heavy hand in all this, and if you do, you're not as good a cop as I thought. Before I do or don't do what I'm being leaned on to do, I want you to fill me in on why you're using your partner's contacts to get this case.''

He didn't say anything.

''Hugh suggests that of late his sister-in-law has been the victim of your unwelcome attentions. He suggests that you won't take no for an answer. He further suggests that your having this case will compound and aggravate the misery you have already caused her by your uncouth behavior.''

''Have you had any complaints from Mrs. Gallagher?''

''No. And that's why we're having this little tête-à-tête instead of me busting your butt. The only thing I've had is a letter from a Sister Mary John at Saint Xavier's telling me how kind and helpful a Detective Garth was to the children there. Jenna Gallagher also signed it. As you are the only Garth we've got, I put it in your file—it's kind of lonely in there, considering some of the past complaints that have come in, but I like to be fair. Now,'' he continued, his voice unnaturally controlled and quiet, ''this is where you tell me why you're rattling cages to get this case. And, I might add, this is your last chance to do it.''

Garth gave a short exhalation of breath. He'd learned a long time ago that sometimes you had to give to get—and this was one of those times.

''I don't think Jenna—Mrs. Gallagher—was mugged. I think it was more.''

The lieutenant's eyes narrowed. ''Like what?''

''Maybe the company she was keeping me. The day I was at the school I took her to the Humoresque for dinner. Tony Zaccato saw us there. He even made a point of talking to her.''

"You're going to all this trouble because of that old grudge you've got with Zaccato?" the lieutenant said, shaking his head.

"Yes."

"The Job is no place for personal grudges!"

"No," he agreed, but they both knew that that was neither here nor there.

"You got any hard evidence?"

"No. A gut feeling. That's all. I think I know who did it. He's from my old neighborhood, and he owes me. If I can put enough heat on him, I think he'll drop a dime on Zaccato."

The lieutenant looked at him over the top of his glasses. "Okay. You got until something else more important comes up—and *I* decide what that is. Now get out of here. Garth!" he said sharply when Garth reached for the door. "I hope you and Carver get the sonofabitch, but, personally, I think he's vacationing in sunny Colombia."

"He's here," Garth said. "He wouldn't give the nod to get to Jenna and not be around to see what I'm going to do about it."

"Is this as good as it gets?" Skip asked. "Or can I look forward to some small improvement in your current disposition? Anything, anything at all, Garth, no matter how minute, no matter how seemingly insignificant, would be ever so appreciated."

Garth glanced at him but didn't feel the remark was worth a comment—tossing him out the window, but not a comment.

"You're supposed to talk to Debbie today," Skip persisted. "Remember? The mood you're in, I'll end up divorced."

The fact of the matter was that he hadn't remembered.

He had other things on his mind. No, he had *one* other thing: Jenna.

"So what's wrong with you?" Skip asked.

"Nothing," Garth said.

"Oh, yeah, everybody in the whole station house can see that it's nothing. Didn't you see Jenna last night?"

"I saw her—and I don't want to talk about it."

Unfortunately the only way he could manage that was to leave—in which case, he might as well go talk to Debbie. And he didn't tell Skip he was going; the kid was strung out enough already.

He arrived at Saint Xavier's shortly after the end of the school day. As before, Sister Mary John flagged him down when he passed her door. He liked Sister Mary John—even before he knew she'd written a complimentary letter—and, for some reason, she seemed not in the least surprised to see him. The reason for that became apparent when he came out of Sister Mary John's office and walked into Jenna. The stricken look she gave him made his heart sink. He had kept trying to tell himself that maybe things with Jenna weren't as bad as he thought, but they were. He had only to look into her eyes to know that.

"I didn't know you would be here," he said immediately, because she looked so upset. She was tired, and her face was still bruised, and he had never wanted to put his arms around anybody so bad in his life. But he knew from experience that she wasn't above taking a swing at him if she thought she needed to. It was one thing he'd admired about her—her feistiness. One of many, many things, all of which came to mind when he looked at her.

"What are you doing here, Garth?" She had a stack of papers in her arms, newly mimeographed papers, he could smell the familiar, pungent smell of the mimeograph fluid. She held them tightly in front of her, as if they were some kind of barrier that would keep him at bay.

He decided to tell the truth. "I'm here to save Skip and Debbie's marriage. Well, it's the truth!" he said when she frowned.

"That's what worries me," she assured him. "I didn't know there was anything wrong with Skip and Debbie's marriage."

"He thinks there is. He's been driving me crazy. He thinks she's having an affair."

"Is he crazy or are you?" she said incredulously.

"Yes," he said, and he thought for a moment she was going to smile.

But she was an old hand at not letting him amuse her, and she squelched it immediately. She started walking down the hall, and he went along with her.

"I want us to talk," he said, his voice echoing in the deserted hall.

"There is nothing to talk about."

"Jenna!" he said in exasperation, but she stopped walking and turned to him.

"I understand how you must have felt. You loved Mary. You wanted to know the truth. I would have felt the same way. I do feel the same way. It's just that I would have done it differently." With that she walked off, and he would have followed if Hernando hadn't appeared.

"Garth! You came back, man!"

"Yeah, Hernando. I came back," he said, watching Jenna until she went into the classroom. He looked down at Hernando. Hernando was frowning now, his head cocked to one side.

"You going to give me five?" Garth asked, holding out his hand, but he got no response.

"Did you hurt Miss Jenna?" Hernando asked, watching Garth closely, apparently for some sign that he might lie.

"No. I didn't hurt Miss Jenna," Garth said, because he knew that Hernando meant her black eye.

"You looking for the sucker that did?"

"I'm looking."

"You ain't going to find him."

"I don't know, sometimes I get lucky. Hey, that is some coat. Turn around here and let me see."

"The *real* kind of leather," Hernando said proudly.

"The real kind? Yeah, it looks like the real kind. And a Screaming Eagles patch. You are one tough dude."

"I know it," Hernando assured him. "Did you get your pictures we drawed? Did you get *my* picture?"

"Yeah, I got them. I've got them on the wall in my apartment."

"*All* of them?"

"All," Garth said.

"Mallory can't draw, man," Hernando pointed out.

"I put her picture up anyway."

"You crazy, man—you don't supposed to put up *ugly* pictures in your apartment."

"It's the thought that counts, Hernando," Garth said, wondering if someone had told him that about his own pictures. "Beauty is in the eyes of the beholder. Give me five."

"You crazy, man," Hernando said again, but he slapped Garth's hand and ran down the hallway toward the outside doors.

Garth walked on toward the classroom Jenna had gone into, catching bits of conversation as he neared the open door.

"—I'll make the visit," Jenna said.

Debbie responded, but he couldn't hear the words.

"No, Garth's here. He wants to talk to you," Jenna said.

"Has something happened to Skip?" Debbie said, alarm clearly evident in her voice.

"No," Jenna said quickly. "I'll make the visit. You stay and—"

Their voices dropped again, and he couldn't understand

any more. When he reached the doorway, Jenna came out of it, wearing a coat—a new or borrowed coat, he supposed. She looked into his eyes, but she didn't say anything. He stepped aside to let her pass.

"Jenna!" Debbie said, running out into the hallway and all but bumping into him.

"Easy!" Garth said, catching her briefly by the elbows to keep her steady. "Debbie, I need to talk to—" He stopped because she wasn't listening to him. She was staring distractedly after Jenna. "Debbie," he said again.

She looked at him.

"I need to talk to you."

"I can't talk now, Garth. I have to—" She was wringing her hands, and she didn't tell him what was so pressing.

"Debbie, Skip sent me to talk to you."

"Skip?" she asked, her eyes darting from him to the far end of the hallway. And she kept trying to edge away from him. Her hands were shaking, and he thought she was about to cry.

"Honey, what is the matter with you?" he asked, deciding that Skip had cause for concern after all. "Are you all right?"

"No," she said, her face crumpling. "I'm not all right, Garth."

"Debbie—"

"You have to go get Jenna. Don't let her go there—I should have *said* something, but I'm afraid they'll hurt Skip. Garth, stop Jenna—she might see them!"

"Who? Honey, I don't know what you're talking about—"

"They'd know her. Everybody knows her. Garth, do something!" Debbie was pushing her way back into the classroom. She ran to the desk and picked up a small index card. "Here! Take this!" she cried, shoving it into his hands.

Becca Sullivan he read on the card, and then the address. The address was the same as the one in Patrick's notebook.

Chapter 13

He could see Jenna ahead of him, walking briskly down the sidewalk, piquing the interest of the unoccupied males who loitered on the steps and in the doorways along the way. He had no idea what he'd say when he caught up with her but, nevertheless, he would do what Debbie asked and deter her visit to Becca Sullivan. He was reasonably content to find out *why* he was doing it later. Even if he didn't know what the hell Debbie was so upset about, he didn't consider the action entirely inappropriate. He had specifically told Jenna not to go anywhere alone, yet she'd parked her car three blocks away—in this neighborhood—and elected to walk rather than circle for a closer parking space. He himself didn't waste the time looking; he simply double-parked, leaving the vehicle with its dubious talisman on the dashboard for protection—a NYPD Official Business plate.

The day was cloudy and cold, and a panhandler waylaid him at the end of the first block. By the time he disengaged his arm from the man's persistent grasp, Jenna was well into the third block. He ran to catch up, but she went into the building before he got to her. As he entered the ground floor, it occurred to him that Jenna wasn't likely to let him dissuade her from doing whatever it was she was doing—in which case, he'd just have to go along. She wasn't apt to like that, either, but he considered his company the lesser of the two offenses.

He took the stairs two at a time, catching up with her on the second landing. She turned sharply around at his boisterous approach, clearly frightened for a moment, and he damned the impulsiveness that had let him forget her recent experience with Roy Lee.

"Garth, what are you doing here?" she said. She looked relieved, regardless of the exasperation he heard in her voice.

"I'm going with you."

She gave a small sigh. "I thought you were busy saving marriages."

"Well, Mrs. Gallagher, as far as I can tell, it's become a matter of shifting priorities. I told you not to go anywhere by yourself. You didn't listen to me. So here I am. What are we doing here—aside from the fact that this is the same address that was in Patrick's notebook?"

She stared at him, her lips pressed into a tight line. He tried not to look at them, tried not to think how much he wanted to hold her and kiss her until her mouth became soft and responsive.

"You did make the connection?" he said, looking into her eyes.

"Patrick's notebook has nothing to do with this—and, yes, I made the connection. I'm here to see Becca Sullivan's mother. Becca hasn't been coming to school, and Sister Mary John wants to know why."

"Couldn't she telephone?"

"She tried. The number has been disconnected—why am I explaining this to you?"

He ignored the question.

"You know, of course, that there was a reason for Patrick to have written this address down. And Debbie's all to pieces over this little jaunt of yours."

"Debbie's *always* all to pieces of late."

"Right—hence my other quest. But you take precedence."

She looked into his eyes, then looked away. "I didn't come here because of some whim I had about Patrick, Garth. Sister is anxious to know about Becca. Debbie was supposed to come, but then you arrived to save her marriage or whatever it is you think you're doing—"

"Right," he said again. "So here you are, in spite of what I told you. How many times do you have to be roughed up to get the message?"

"Do you mean literally or figuratively?"

"Touché, Mrs. Gallagher. Pardon me while I bleed."

They stared into each other's eyes.

"Nobody followed me, Garth."

"I did."

"Please!" she said, holding up both hands. "Can we stop this? I have to see about Becca."

"Lead the way," he answered.

"You don't have to go with me!"

"I know that. But I'm going. Now we can stand here and argue, or we can get on with it." He held out his hand for her to go first.

She went, climbing the stairs quickly.

"Your face is looking better," he called after her, but she didn't respond.

"New coat?" he asked on the third landing.

She gave him a hard look.

"It's very nice. Not as nice as the other one, but nice."

"Thank you," she said, but she certainly didn't mean it.

"You're welcome," he said, knowing it would annoy her even more. But he'd rather have her angry than the way she was last night. "So which one of the Terrible Twenty was Becca? I can't place her."

"She wasn't there. She had to go home early—her coat was flushed."

He suddenly remembered meeting Debbie and Becca at the outside door. Becca had been carrying her coat in a plastic bag, and Debbie had stayed gone all day. She'd been here in this building, and she'd been very worried about Jenna's coming back.

"Garth," Jenna said when they reached the fifth floor. "I don't want you to—"

"Jenna, don't start up with me. We've covered this. Let's find the apartment. You look on that side."

She hesitated, but he walked off without her, reading apartment numbers. She followed, and she sensed that the people on the other sides of the doors they passed were watching through their peepholes to see where she and Garth would stop.

"There is no reason for you to be here!" she suddenly burst out.

"Yeah, well, that's a matter of opinion—it's down that way."

He took her arm, walking her in the direction he'd pointed, but after a few steps Jenna balked, digging in her heels so that he would stop.

"Garth," she said, turning to face him. She held on to both his arms, her eyes searching his for understanding. "You're going to have to leave me alone. Do you understand? I can't..." She abruptly looked down, and he could feel her struggling for emotional control. She looked up at him. "I can't make it if you don't."

"I'd do anything for you," he said. "Anything. But not

this, not now." He reached up to lightly touch her cheek, and she turned away. He tried to keep her close, but she pulled free of him. She couldn't explain it to him; he didn't understand at all. She cared about him; she couldn't be near him and have him touch her in that gentle way he always seemed to use with her.

"Hey!" someone—a man—yelled. He was standing at the end of the hallway, and from behind the nearest door a child suddenly began to cry.

"What do you think you're doing?" the man demanded.

Jenna thought he meant the argument she and Garth were having, but he didn't mean that at all. Their argument was the least of this man's concerns. "Get out of the hall! Now!" he yelled. "How many times do we have to tell you people!"

The child behind the door cried louder. She expected Garth to do something—and he did. He was going to leave and take her with him.

"Come on," he said, taking her firmly by the arm. "Now."

"I have to see Becca's mother," Jenna insisted. The Sullivan apartment was just in front of her, and she stepped up to the door, intending to knock. The child's crying was coming from in there, and the door opened abruptly before she could knock on it.

"Mrs. Gallagher, come in here!" Becca's mother whispered urgently. "Get out of the hall!"

She went in—with Garth right behind her. Becca sat on the couch sobbing, clinging to her mother frantically when the woman took her into her arms.

"What's going on?" Garth said, but Becca's crying only escalated.

"You were a big help," Jenna whispered to him.

"You get the civilians out of the way first, and then you

find out what's going on. *Then* you help. Mrs. Sullivan, what's happening?''

Becca's mother looked up at him. "Who are you?"

"Detective Garth, NYPD."

"Oh, God! Why did you bring him here?" she cried, looking at Jenna and rocking Becca back and forth.

"Mrs. Sullivan," Jenna said, "I didn't bring him. I just ran into him on the stairs. Detective Garth was concerned about my being out alone. I was mugged a few days ago." She stopped, glancing at Garth. The woman was too distraught to listen.

"Mrs. Sullivan," Jenna said, beginning again. She waited until the woman looked up. "Sister Mary John has been worried because Becca hasn't been in school for a while. I just came to see if she was all right. We weren't able to telephone you."

"How could she go to school with *that* going on!" she said, flinging one hand toward the door. "What are you going to do?" she asked Garth. "I haven't said anything. None of us has said anything!"

"Mrs. Sullivan," he said quietly. "I'm going to ask you again. What's going on?"

"If you don't know, *I'm* not going to be the one to tell you."

Garth stared at her, then moved to the door.

"What are you doing!" she cried.

"Be quiet!" he said sharply. He cracked open the door enough to see down the narrow hall. The "hall monitor" was still there, and some nondescript people were coming up the stairs. These people, however, seemed not to be trespassing. He watched them—three men and a woman—disappear into the next apartment, stay a few minutes and then leave one at a time. And they left happy.

He looked back at Mrs. Sullivan. Jenna was holding Becca now. "What are they selling?" he asked. "I'll find out,'' he said when she remained silent. "Sooner or later. The guy in the hall—he's seen me come in here. He's going to think you told me anyway.''

Her eyes shifted to Becca before she answered. "You remember Alice's Restaurant?'' she said obscurely, reaching out to touch Becca's hair. She gave a wavering sigh. "Crack mostly.''

He nodded, understanding that her concern now was for her child. "Are you willing to relocate for a while—maybe let us use your apartment?''

She looked hesitant, worried, and he didn't blame her. She was in a dangerous situation, and they both knew it.

"Jenna, can you get them shelter with the Family Crisis people?'' he asked.

"Either there or through Saint Xavier's,'' she said, letting Becca go back to her mother. She stood up and came to stand beside him. "What are you going to do?''

He gave a heavy sigh. "Clear out the civilians. Mrs. Sullivan, how long will this go on? How long are you supposed to stay out of the hall?''

"It goes on as long as it takes them to get rid of whatever they've got,'' she said. "Sometimes into the middle of the night.''

"We aren't going to wait that long. Is there another way out?''

"Just the fire escape.''

"Get your clothes together. Go on,'' he said when she didn't move. "Pack whatever you and your little girl will need for a few nights. We all have to do our part, Mrs. Sullivan,'' he added. "Inconvenience isn't such a big price, is it?''

"We're talking about more than inconvenience here, and you know it!'' she answered.

"Yes. I know it. But I don't know of any other way to deal with it. They're not going to just disappear. How long has it been going on already? A year? Two? I'll do my best to help you, but I need your cooperation.''

"That's what you think now," she said doubtfully. "You'll help us?"

"I give you my word."

"Excuse me if that doesn't exactly thrill me, cop."

"Look! What choice do you have?"

She stared at him. "Yeah, right," she said. She got up from the couch, taking Becca with her into the next room.

"Garth—" Jenna began.

"Yeah, yeah, I know. You *hate* going up and down fire escapes.''

For a moment, he thought she was going to smile. "I'm not crazy about it," she admitted, her brief flash of amusement taken away by the seriousness of the situation. "What are you going to do?"

"Whatever it takes," he said.

When she was about to object to his vagueness, he held up his hand.

"These people shouldn't have to be living like this. Nobody should have to live like this."

He went back to watch through the crack in the door. Whoever was involved in this operation was certainly confident about it. The man in the hall hadn't been the least bit concerned about who he and Jenna might be, certainly not that they might have been working narcotics. It only mattered that he didn't recognize them as customers.

"Do you think Patrick knew about whatever is going on here?"

"I don't know, Jenna," he said, but he did know. He believed that Patrick had written down the address of this apartment building for a reason, just as he believed that Debbie had been caught here in the same way he and Jenna had. It must be that that had her so rattled.

But if Patrick had known what was going on here, why

hadn't he done something about it? Or Debbie, either, for
that matter? Mrs. Sullivan and the rest of the tenants had
apparently been living like prisoners in their own homes,
staying out of the way of the drug transactions because the
man in the hall ordered it.

But Garth's concern was that Mary's name had been written down on the same page as the address. And if Patrick
knew about Mary, then it logically followed that he must
have known about her brother Tony and that Tony must be
in this somewhere.

"Mrs. Sullivan," he said when she came back into the
room. "Why haven't you called the police?"

She gave a short laugh and shook her head. "Why
haven't I called the police? These people—these animals
who have to sell their drugs here—they *are* the police."

Becca, at least, enjoyed the jaunt down a rickety fire escape in a high wind. Some part of Jenna's mind presented
the fact that she'd never even been on a fire escape before
she met Garth, and she was now embarking on her third
trip. This fire escape, however, didn't go all the way to the
ground, and it took some determined maneuvering on
Garth's part to get the last segment of ladder down. He
managed, swearing under his breath in a way Jenna found
all too endearing. He carried Becca down, and Jenna stood
on the sidewalk, guarding Becca's hastily packed Barbie
overnight case and holding her hand while he went back up
to help her mother and get the other suitcase.

The street was more or less deserted. A few men in a
nearby doorway watched with jaded interest. Everything
around her was cold and bleak, but not as bleak as she felt.
She tried not to think about Patrick and Mary Zaccato, or
why he might have come here.

"Using the fire escape is something you do only in an

emergency, Becca," she said as the teacher in her reasserted itself. "Fire escapes aren't to play on or anything like that."

"Where is it, Miss Jenna?" Becca asked, sniffing heavily, her nose red and running from the cold.

"The emergency? Not down here where we are."

Becca looked up at her. She had the hiccups from crying so long. "Is my mommy scared?"

"Not so much now," Jenna promised her, hoping it was the truth. But what did she know about it? Where she had come from, people didn't have to live in a self-imposed prison in their homes in order to survive.

"I was scared. And I cried and cried," Becca said, her voice quavering.

"I know. But Detective Garth is going to help, and we're going to find another place for you and your mother to stay for a while."

"Not here?"

"No, not here."

"Okay," Becca said.

Jenna watched as Garth came the rest of the way down the fire escape ladder. *The Job,* she thought. He'd become even more intense and purposeful than he usually was; he reminded her of the night they'd met at Skip's party. He was completely in his element, and she and the Sullivans were impediments to his ultimate goal. He wanted to do what he got paid to do, and he wanted the civilians out of the way so he could do it.

She fell in step with Mrs. Sullivan and walked down the street ahead of him, still holding Becca's hand. In a moment, he was at her side, but he didn't say anything. She glanced at him. His face was grim.

She understood his quandary. Becca's mother had said the men involved were police. It was likely the truth. But was it a legitimate undercover operation? Or were they dirty? The problem would come for Garth if the latter were

the case. She knew that the best compliment a cop could
get from his peers—from his superiors, too, for that matter—was that he was a "stand-up kind of guy," a guy who
would do anything—look the other way, perjure himself in
court, anything—to preserve the honor of the brotherhood.
What kind of choice was that for a man like Garth who put
personal, individual honor first?

She understood the situation perfectly; she had been a
policeman's wife. But because she'd been a policeman's
wife, she knew that it would likely never occur to Garth that
she, someone outside The Job, could be capable of such
empathy. And that was yet another thing that made their
being together so impossible. She didn't want to live on the
outside of a man's life again; she wanted to be part of it.
She wanted to matter enough to share the good times *and*
the bad.

She glanced at him again, and this time he caught her at
it.

Ah, Garth, she thought. It wasn't the choice that troubled
him. She thought he'd already made it. It was the consequences of his choice that would bring him pain.

He helped get Mrs. Sullivan and Becca and their suitcases
into her car, but when she was about to open the door and
get in herself, he stopped her.

"What?" she asked, because he *still* wasn't saying anything. He was looking into her eyes, and he reached up to
take a strand of hair the wind had blown across her face
and tucked it behind her ear.

"I love you," he said simply and without prelude. "You
understand? I didn't want to, but there you are. I can't help
it. I love you a lot, and regardless of what you think of me,
I want you to know that."

She wanted to say something, but she couldn't. Her heart
soared, only to have the reality of their situation bring it
down again. First Garth had seen her as a means to an end,

and now he claimed to love her. And he'd actually said so—and not in the throes of passion, but on a windy New York street in broad daylight when he didn't have to say anything at all. Her mind couldn't get anywhere past that or past the fact that once again, fool that she was, she believed him.

His eyes, his beautiful eyes, searched hers, and then he suddenly smiled.

"Bowled you over with that one, didn't I, Mrs. Gallagher?" He opened the car door for her, but he didn't wait for her to get in. He turned and walked away, leaving her with her bewilderment.

Chapter 14

Jenna waited. To hear something from Garth. To see something on the evening news or in the papers. There was nothing. Becca and her mother were safely tucked away in a shelter for women and children, and they, too, waited.

She tried to find out something from Debbie when they were together at Saint Xavier's, but that was entirely futile. Debbie didn't want to talk about going to Becca's apartment building, and, if anything, she was more addled than ever. She claimed no knowledge about whatever Skip was working on at the moment, and she knew even less about Garth. Her only concern seemed to be her supposed betrayal of Jenna's friendship—which she couldn't explain without dissolving into tears. Jenna tried pressing her, but it only upset them both. There was no sense in mentioning Garth's assertion that the Carver marriage was in difficulty. Debbie was so distracted it was likely she didn't even *know* she was having marital problems. Finally, Jenna just let it alone. The bottom line, anyway, was that she wanted to see Garth.

How like a cop, she kept thinking, to announce his love and then disappear. She spent every free minute of her time trying to decide what he had really meant. It couldn't have been a simple declaration of affection. Nothing was simple where he was concerned. But what ulterior motive he might have, she couldn't decide. And she didn't know which worried her more, that he might have an ulterior motive, or that he might not.

She missed him. She *missed* him. It was all too apparent to her that she needed him in her life, just as it was apparent to her how crazy she was for wanting him there. Everything was turned upside down; she had to pacify her mother and her mother-in-law, she had to find a new place to live, and she understood nothing about Patrick and Mary Zaccato. And all she could think about was Garth.

And she began to have nightmares about the man in the stairwell. She woke up repeatedly, thinking she heard noises, dreaming he was there in the apartment. Suddenly it all seemed to catch up with her. She didn't want to go out alone. She didn't want to go out at all. Once, she even dialed Garth's number, hanging up after the first ring.

Three days later, Rosie Madden telephoned her at Saint Xavier's, asking her to come to the station house to look at some pictures. She went, without seeing Garth anywhere in the place, and after nearly an hour of looking at what had begun to seem the same basic faces, she recognized two men. The man who had been with Tony Zaccato at the Humoresque, and the man who had assaulted her—Roy Lee Anderson.

"Well, this is a surprise," Rosie said, looking at the second mug shot Johnna indicated. "You're sure?"

"Yes, I'm sure. Why is it a surprise?"

Rosie looked up at her. "This dude is from Garth's old neighborhood. They kind of looked out for each other when they were kids. I always thought they still did. Well. Thanks for coming in. I'll let you know if we need you again."

Thus dismissed, Jenna had no alternative but to leave— or to swallow her pride and ask the question she'd been trying not to ask ever since she'd arrived.

"Rosie, have you seen Garth?" she said, letting the question out before she had the time to agonize about it anymore.

"This afternoon, you mean? Nah, I haven't seen him this—" She broke off and looked at Jenna closely. "Oh, you mean have I *seen* him? Yeah, yeah, I've seen him here and there. He and Skip have been running around here doing their Frick and Frack, Two Stooges impersonations. No, that's not what you mean, either, is it? The question is, why haven't *you* seen him, right? Well, Jenna, I don't know. All I know is there is something going down around here. Garth's been in there with the lieutenant with the blinds shut—nobody knows nothing, and nobody can find out nothing. But unless I miss my guess, our Garth is knee-deep in the middle of some heavy you-know-what. Now you know how a cop is when he's working—especially if he loves it like Garth does. He don't know he's on the planet. It's just him and The Job. You know what I mean?"

Jenna gave a small smile. "I know what you mean." She turned to go.

"Hey," Rosie called after her. "I'm going to hand you some advice, okay?"

"What is it?"

"When he does show up, be glad he did, okay? Don't give him a lot of grief about why he wasn't there sooner. Believe me, we all hate that. You were married to a cop. You know how it is."

"Yes," she said quietly. "I know how it is. I was just…worried about him."

Rosie grinned. "Jenna, if you don't worry about a man, he's not worth having, I always say."

Again, Jenna turned to go.

"Hey," Rosie said. "I think he could use a friend about now. You wouldn't happen to know where he could get one, would you?"

"Maybe," Jenna answered.

"Good. I'll tell him. You know, that sucker is one lucky dude—having two fine women like us caring about what happens to him."

Jenna didn't know about that, but she left in a better mood than when she came, and she couldn't say precisely why, except that it was a relief to talk to someone who understood. Rosie Madden knew she cared about Garth; she didn't have to pretend otherwise for fear of offending or for fear of being thought a fool.

She headed for home, intending to have a hot bath and a quiet meal. She still had nights when she didn't sleep well, and she was so tired suddenly.

But her mind kept presenting her with worrisome information, things she'd rather not consider—like that the man she had identified as the one who had beaten her was a friend of Garth's. Coincidence or not? She didn't know, but she was almost certain that Garth did. Perhaps Hugh had been right. Perhaps her association with Garth had been the reason the man had hurt her.

She had her bath and her dinner, but, as tired as she was, she didn't want to go to sleep early and then lie awake half the night. She put on a sweat suit, and, just to keep occupied, she began to pack up the books and the bric-a-brac she had in the apartment, putting as much as she could into what few boxes she had. Another chore to add to the list. Finding boxes. Finding an apartment. Finding Garth.

She tried not to think about him as she methodically put away the pieces of her life with Patrick—books he'd given her, a photograph of the two of them the day he'd graduated from the police academy, a David Winter cottage he'd bought her for her birthday, an old celluloid Kewpie doll with pink and blue feathers he'd won at Coney Island when he was a little boy.

She worked on, not stopping for anything as long as she had space in the boxes, until someone knocked at the door. It was too late for visitors, and she reluctantly went to see who it might be, checking through the peephole and not failing to note how hope flared that it might be Garth.

But it was a woman, one she didn't recognize, standing on the other side of the door. There was a man with her, and perhaps one other person.

"Who is it?" Jenna called.

"Mrs. Gallagher," the woman called back. "I'm Jay Jay Coleman. I'd like very much to get your—"

The woman turned her head toward the man with her, and Jenna couldn't understand the rest of the sentence. She opened the door, leaving the chain on. The minute the door was cracked, a bright light hit her full in the face.

"Mrs. Gallagher!" Jay Jay Coleman said. "What do you think of the investigation and the arrests?"

"What?" Jenna said, shading her eyes. Someone stuck a microphone through the crack in the door.

"The investigation! Did you know about the alleged drug dealings?"

"I don't know what you're talking about," Jenna said, trying to close the door. The man in the hall was holding it.

"Our information is that you're personally involved with one of the detectives on the case. Did you know about the lengthy investigation? Don't you think it's ironic that the cop who was instrumental in solving your husband's murder case is also responsible for—"

Jenna managed to get the door shut.

"Please, Mrs. Gallagher!" Jay Jay Coleman yelled through the door. "We'd like to have your comment!"

The telephone was ringing, and Jenna dashed to answer it, looking back over her shoulder at the door. They were still out there, still calling out questions for her to answer.

My God, what's happening?

She picked up the telephone. "Hello?" she said, her voice wary.

"Jenna, it's Garth."

"Garth, what—"

"I'm coming over. I'll tell you when I get there."

"No! Don't come. There's a television crew outside the door."

"I'll be there in a few minutes."

"Garth!"

But he hung up. She looked at the front window. Someone was hanging over the banister on the steps outside, trying to see into the apartment. She crossed quickly and pulled down the shades, knocking one of the plants on the windowsill onto the floor. She left it lying there with half the dirt spilled out.

She kept pacing around the apartment, trying to make some sense of Jay Jay Coleman's questions. The only reason the woman could be here is that it had something to do with Patrick.

She abruptly sat down, only to get up again and pace. She could tell the moment Garth arrived. There was another barrage of questions outside the door, all of which he apparently ignored.

"Can you give us your name, sir!" Jay Jay was calling as Jenna opened the door. She let him in quickly, standing well back out of Camcorder range.

"I wanted to get here ahead of them," Garth said, slamming the door closed behind him. "At least they don't know who I am."

"What have they found out about Patrick?" Jenna said. "Garth, you tell me what it is!"

"It's not Patrick, Jenna. It's Hugh."

"Hugh?"

"Hugh was arrested a little while ago—let's get away from the door. I wouldn't put it past one of them to have an ear at the keyhole."

She followed him into the living room.

"Garth, tell me!"

"I'm going to turn on the music," he said, walking to the stereo on the nearly empty bookshelves. "I want to make sure they can't hear." He punched the radio on, adjusting the volume so that the room filled with quiet jazz.

He turned to look at her. "What's all this?" he asked about the boxes and the packed books.

"I have to move. What about Hugh?"

"Jenna, why are you moving?"

He was stepping on the ends of her questions again, the way he did when he wanted to know something, and her temper flared. She had such a contradiction of feelings where he was concerned. She was glad to see him, and upset about his arrival, and annoyed with his questions all at the same time. But she still wanted to be with him. She remembered her mother giving her a piece of sage advice once about how to gauge your affection: If a man makes you mad enough to kill him, but you never think of leaving—it's love.

"I have to move," she said evenly. "The apartment belongs to an old school friend of Patrick's. We were renting it while he was out of the country. He's back now, and he wants it. Now will you tell me what is going on!"

"I'll tell you what I know," he said.

"Well, that would be a refreshing change."

"Now, don't start up with me," he warned her. "I've had a hell of a day. I came here to tell you about Hugh in person because I didn't want you to hear about it on the six o'clock news or read it in the newspapers. It was really *very* nice of me."

She stared at him, then threw up her hands, half in capitulation, half in token apology. He looked so tired, she suddenly realized.

"So tell me," she said, not yet willing to be pacified.

"Becca's mother was right. The drug operation in the apartment house was being run by cops. It wasn't part of a sting. It was being done on the sly for a big cut of the profits."

"And Hugh's in it?"

"Hugh—and others."

"How?"

"I don't know for sure, but IAD—Internal Affairs—does. From what I've heard, it may have started as a joke."

"A joke?" she said incredulously.

"Jenna, you know how cops are. They raided the place, and somehow this guy came looking to make a buy. He was either too dumb or too strung out to realize he was shopping in the middle of a bust. As a lark, they sold him an ounce or two. They asked for a ridiculous price, and they got it. And all of a sudden there was all that stuff just lying there waiting to be sold. They stayed open. They even cut a deal with the original supplier to keep it running—only his percentage was suddenly a lot less. But a quarter of a pie is better than no pie at all."

"How do they know Hugh's in it?"

"They picked up the guy we saw in the hall first. He was from another precinct. They gave him a choice of taking the heat alone or wearing a wire to get what they needed to nail the rest of them. He went for the wire."

"Does Mamie know about any of this?"

"Hugh was at her house when they picked him up."

"Did they have to do that?" she said sharply. Poor Mamie. Her police officer sons were her reason for being, and Hugh was all she had left.

"Jenna, when the word comes down to pick him up, that's what you do."

"You arrested him?"

"No, not me. I had very little to do with that part of it—because of the fight Hugh and I had that time. IAD didn't want a defense lawyer to be able to suggest that I might have planted evidence to get back at Hugh or anything like that."

"So you just had your little talks with the lieutenant with the blinds closed."

He frowned. "What is it with you?" he said. "What are you mad at me for? I'm not the one running drugs and terrorizing five-year-olds!"

She looked into his eyes. What was it with her? He'd just given her very bad news about her late husband's brother, but all she could think about was that he'd said he loved her, and she was desperately afraid that she loved him back. *That's* what it was with her.

She stepped away from him, because she was perilously close to throwing herself on him. Once again she wanted his comfort, his closeness. Nothing seemed as bad if he were near. How could she tell what she really felt about him, if she could never get past that? And how incredibly unfair it was to have one's only source of comfort also be one's source of pain.

"Tell me the rest," she said.

"They're going to indict him. I don't think he'll get off."

"I'd better call Mamie," she said, crossing to the telephone. She quickly dialed the number. A woman whose voice she didn't recognize answered the phone almost immediately, and there seemed to be a lot of commotion in the background.

"I'd like to speak to Mrs. Gallagher," Jenna said, not certain she had the right number.

"Who is this?"

"Jenna Gallagher."

Jenna could hear a hand being put over the receiver and then muffled conversation. A voice in the background began to rise.

"Hello?" Jenna said.

"I'm sorry," the woman said in a rush. "Mamie asked me to tell you that she can't talk to you at the moment—"

"That's not what I said!" Mamie cried in the background. "You tell her what I said!"

"Mamie..." the woman on the telephone said. And then she spoke to Jenna. "I'm sorry. Mrs. Gallagher is very upset. It would be better if you didn't call again."

She hung up, and Jenna stood holding the telephone receiver. She looked at Garth. "She wouldn't talk to me."

He didn't say anything.

"What's going on, Garth?" she asked, hanging up the phone.

"She...thinks you have something to do with Hugh's being arrested."

"Why would she think that!"

He shrugged. "Hugh has her ear. I don't."

"You're not answering me!"

"Hugh and I are enemies. You and I have been seeing each other," he offered.

"And?" she said, because she sensed there was more to it than that. Much more.

He looked into her eyes. He was going to have to tell her, so he might as well do it. "I think—" He broke off. He didn't *think* anything. He knew it; the lieutenant had told him. Mamie Gallagher had called the lieutenant personally to ask him, with all the influence she had, to get rid of Detective Garth, to make him admit what he'd done to her son—to both her sons. But Garth wouldn't tell Jenna that part of it. "Hugh told her that you and I were together... before Patrick was killed. He told her that that was the reason for his fight with me. He said he'd kept it to himself all this time out of respect for his brother."

"Garth, he wouldn't do that!" She didn't want to believe it, couldn't believe it. Still, she asked the question. "Why would he say that?"

"He knows I have Patrick's notebook. There's only one way I could have gotten it."

"There's nothing in the notebook, Garth. Nothing but the address of that apartment house."

And Mary Zaccato's name. The unspoken phrase lay heavy between them.

"Hugh doesn't know that," Garth said.

He wanted to look away from her, but he couldn't. He could see the worry and the pain in her eyes, both of which he'd helped put there. He wanted to tell her that Hugh had always been a man to cover his bases, and that he was certain Hugh was doing it now. If Mamie Gallagher thought the worst of Jenna, she wasn't likely to listen to anything Jenna might have to say about what was in that notebook. Maybe Hugh thought he could bluff his way through all the rest of it—with his mother at least. He could tell her he was undercover, that things went wrong and now his superiors were letting him take the blame for it. It wouldn't work on a street-wise woman like Hazel, who knew human nature inside and out, but it might work on someone like Mamie Gallagher, who needed desperately to keep intact whatever prestige her husband and sons had given her. The only thing that could throw a wrench into a plan like that was whatever Patrick knew and had written in his notebook.

But Garth didn't say anything. Hugh was Patrick's brother, and Jenna had loved Patrick.

"What else?" she asked.

"That's it."

"What about Patrick?"

"He wasn't in it."

"How do you know?"

"I don't *know*. I just don't think he was."

She closed her eyes for a moment and took a deep, steadying breath. Her mind was whirling. Hugh. And Mamie. My God, how was she ever going to convince Mamie that she hadn't known Garth until a few weeks ago?

"We have to talk," Garth said.

She walked away toward the spilled dirt and the overturned plant. She began to scoop up the dirt with her hands, dumping it back into the pot.

"Jenna," Garth said, following her. He stood to one side as she worked at cleaning up the mess, and she worked at it as if it were a matter of life and death.

"We have to talk," he insisted.

She didn't look up at him.

"You don't think so?" he asked. "Will you stop doing that! Sometimes keeping yourself busy isn't the way to go."

She looked up at him. "I don't know what you mean."

"I mean sometimes you can't hide from your troubles, Jenna. You have to deal with the problem head-on, because it isn't going to go away. Sometimes keeping yourself busy—the way you did after Patrick died, the way you're doing now—doesn't work. Look. Do you think I'm going to tell you I love you and not want to hear what you have to say about it?"

"I don't have anything to say. I've told you how I felt about you."

"You told me you ignored your personal principles because you wanted to go to bed with me. Period. I want to know how you feel about us."

She got up from the floor, wiping her hands on her sweatpants. She picked up the pot and put it back on the windowsill. "There's a lot more we need to talk about before we get to that, Garth."

"Like what?"

"Like the truth about why you came looking for me at Skip's party."

He didn't try to deny his duplicity in what had seemed a chance meeting. "It doesn't matter now," he said instead.

"It does to me. At Skip's party, you suggested that Patrick and I weren't getting along before he was killed." She looked into his eyes. "Sometimes I think you did that because you wanted to find out if Patrick and Mary were involved with each other. Sometimes I think you did it because you suspect me of having something to do with his murder."

"If you think that," he said, "then we're a hell of a lot farther apart than I thought."

"That's the problem, Garth, don't you see? We *are* far apart. We were...lovers too soon. We were intimate before we really knew each other. I think now that maybe I can't trust my own judgment where you're concerned."

"I never lied to you."

"Didn't you?"

"No, goddamn it!"

"Is omission a lie?"

"I don't know what you mean."

"I mean that the woman out there with the television crew suggested it was ironic that you were the cop who was instrumental in solving Patrick's murder. I didn't know that, Garth. No one ever told me it was you—or if they did, I was too upset about Patrick to remember it. And you certainly never mentioned it."

"Jenna, I did the legwork on Patrick's murder investigation. Somebody dropped a dime on Joey Malaga. I went out and found him—"

She could keep from wincing at the sound of Joey Malaga's name. She could see him in her mind's eye, angry, unrepentant, a boy murderer.

"—but it wasn't because I knew it might upset you that I didn't say anything about that. I didn't tell you because the whole thing with Malaga was too easy. It was so easy it worried me. I never thought it was you who might have had something to do with Patrick's death. I thought it was—"

"Who, Garth?" she asked when he didn't continue. "Tell me."

"Hugh. I thought it was Hugh."

She turned from him. "My God, Garth, they were brothers!"

"I told you before, I can't explain it to you. I don't have anything concrete. It was a thousand little things that don't add up to much separately. Hugh was scared of something. He didn't want me asking questions on the street. During the investigation, he wouldn't let me talk to you about Patrick. At Skip's party, he still didn't want me anywhere near you. I said what I did that night because I wanted to know if Patrick was worried or distracted enough not to be paying attention to what he was doing. I was looking for a reason not to think what I was thinking. I was looking for an alternative."

She stood staring at him. He didn't go on because he didn't think she was listening anymore. He could feel it, her distancing herself from her feelings and him. He wanted to touch her, hold her, *make* her understand that, no matter how it had started, he loved her now.

"We weren't getting along," she said after a moment, her voice very quiet.

"What?" he asked, because he didn't understand. She was standing so rigidly in the middle of the room, her arms folded over her breasts as if her only source of comfort was herself.

"Patrick and I. We weren't getting along. He was very... unhappy. We couldn't have children—it was my fault. I kept having miscarriages. I didn't want to try anymore. It hurt too much, losing the babies. But he—"

"Don't," he said, reaching out to touch her shoulder. She didn't move away, but he didn't take it as an invitation. "Don't go beating yourself up again, Jenna. You can keep doing that, but the guilt's still there when you're done. I know."

He came closer. She could feel how close he was; his breath ruffled her hair.

He could smell her scent, the soft, tantalizing essence that was her and no other. He felt the faint stirring of desire, and she suddenly leaned against him. He put his arms around her. She gave a resigned sigh and rested her head against his shoulder. She felt so good to him, but he didn't press his advantage, if indeed he had one. They were on the very edge of not making it, and he didn't want to do the wrong thing.

She said something he couldn't hear.

"What?"

She lifted her head and looked at him. "I said, tell me how you know."

"Mary," he answered simply and with a candor that surprised him. He'd been all through his relationship with Mary Zaccato for IAD the last few days—because her name was in the notebook and because IAD field representatives liked to impress upon the rest of the department just how much so-called personal information they knew. The ordeal had left him touchy, defensive, the old wounds raw. He hadn't intended to speak of Mary to anyone again. Ever.

But he looked into Jenna's eyes, and he had to make her understand. "I loved her. I cared about her. But she was my chance to rattle Tony Zaccato's cage. I should have gotten her away from him, gotten her out of this town, but I waited too long. She was caught in a raid of one of Tony's operations. He was her brother. He was the only family she had, but she'd had enough of it. She wanted out." He paused. "She didn't make it. She was killed."

"Did you know about the raid beforehand?"

"No. I was off duty, waiting for her to meet me at the Humoresque."

"Did Hugh know about it?"

He'd forgotten how quick she was. He wondered if Patrick had known what he had in this woman, if he'd ever bounced ideas and problems off her, ever made use of her intuition and her logic.

"It's all tied together, isn't it? Hugh and Mary and Patrick."

"I don't know."

She walked a few steps away, then turned to look at him. "I think you do know, Garth."

"Jenna..."

"I'm not stupid, Garth!"

"Baby, I know that—"

The telephone rang, and she went to answer it.

"For you," she said, holding out the receiver to him.

He hesitated, then reached for it. No one knew he was here but Skip; it would have to be important for him to call.

"Garth," he said tersely. But it wasn't Skip. It was Sidney.

"Your Roy Lee Anderson's been run aground, lad," he said. "He's at St. Vincent's, and if you want to talk to him in this world, you'd best be getting over there."

Jenna watched Garth closely. He suddenly frowned as he listened to whatever the desk sergeant was telling him. She could see him changing; how easily he made the switch from Garth, the man, to Garth, the cop.

"I have to go," he said to her as he hung up the phone.

"Yes," she answered without surprise.

"I have to go to St. Vincent's Hospital to see Roy Lee Anderson."

She was surprised he told her, but she didn't ask him for details or whether he knew that Roy Lee Anderson was the man who had attacked her. She turned away, expecting to hear the front door closing behind him.

"Jenna," he said, his voice close, startling her because, in her mind, he'd already gone. "Jenna..."

She looked back at him. The jazz still played quietly in the background, the kind that made a woman want to sit in the dark and feel sorry for herself.

He reached for her hand, his fingers closing over hers, and he brought her to him. His arms slid around her, and, for a moment, he held her tight.

She gave him a brief hug in return, savoring the feel of his body against hers. *I love you, Garth.*

"Be careful, will you?" she said, because she knew he wanted to go and because she could do that much for him—help him take his leave. And because she hadn't said it enough to Patrick.

"I'm always that," he answered.

"The hell you are," she said, and she could feel him smile. She closed her eyes tightly so that she wouldn't cry.

"I love you, baby." The words were soft and warm against her ear. "You hear me?"

"I hear you, Garth."

He leaned back to look at her, his eyes searching hers. She thought he was going to say something else, but he didn't. He was in too much of a hurry to be gone.

Chapter 15

It suddenly occurred to Garth that he hated hospitals as much as Jenna did. He'd certainly never been in one except when something bad had happened. He could see Skip at the end of the corridor, motioning for him to hurry up. He walked quickly, nearly colliding with one of the housekeeping staff who was pushing her cleaning cart out of a side room.

"Sorry," he said to the woman, and he kept going.

"Where is he?" he asked Skip, falling into step with him as they moved rapidly down the corridor.

"Down this way. Intensive Care. He's in isolation."

"Is he going to make it?"

"The doctor said if he'd been worth killing, he wouldn't have made it this far. But since he's not, it's fifty-fifty either way—sorry," Skip added as if he suddenly remembered that Roy Lee Anderson and Garth used to be friends.

"For what?" Garth said. "I know what Roy Lee is. Are they going to let me see him?"

"Yeah. He's been asking for you. And there isn't exactly a line ahead of you."

No, Garth thought. No line. As far as he knew, he was the closest thing to a family Roy Lee had.

"Did he say who did it?"

"No. He didn't say much of anything except to get you here—that way," Skip said, pointing around a corner. "You'll have to put on a gown and a mask before you go in."

"Why?"

"Third-degree burns," Skip answered, and Garth didn't ask how Roy Lee got them.

He could see through the glass partition ahead of him, but he couldn't tell if the patient in the first bed was Roy Lee or not. He rapped lightly on the glass so that the closest nurse would look up.

She seemed to be expecting him. He didn't have to wait to get in. He didn't get any hassle about upsetting schedules or trying to visit in the wrong quarter-hour. All he had to do was get the gown and mask on and come inside.

"Mr. Anderson is right there," the nurse said, pointing out a bed in a small glassed-in cubicle.

He looked at her doubtfully. At first glance, he had thought the patient in the bed was an old man.

"That's him," the nurse assured him, and he walked forward, letting himself into the small, closed-off room.

The door shut behind him, cutting off the whirring and beeps of the medical machinery outside. Of course there was machinery in here as well, but none of it seemed to be doing anything, except the green screen that flickered with the path of a heartbeat. And the closer he came to the bed, the more inclined he was to think the nurse had made a mistake about who was in here. This couldn't be Roy Lee; this man had no hair.

But he could see the name tag on the side of a bag of IV

fluids that hung on a pole at the corner of the bed. ANDERSON, ROY L. The name was the only thing that was familiar, certainly not the man in the bed. Whoever Roy Lee had offended had more than meant to pay him back.

He moved closer, trying to decide if Roy Lee was conscious or not and trying not to bump into any of the medical paraphernalia that stood ready for whatever the rest of the night might bring.

"Roy Lee," he said after a moment, and Roy Lee's eyes flickered open. His eyelashes were gone.

He turned his head slightly. "You took your time, man," he said, his voice hoarse and grating. "Where the hell have you—been?"

"I've been busy."

"With her? Jenna—Gallagher?" Garth didn't answer him, and he smiled. "You're pissed, aren't you, man? Because I did the job on her."

"Yeah, Roy Lee. I'm pissed."

"How did you know it was me?"

"You didn't take the sticker off your new thermal underwear," Garth said. "And I found her coat."

"Big shot cop."

"That's me, Roy Lee. Why don't you tell me why you did it?"

"She could have got worse than me, man," Roy Lee said, his raspy voice now hardly more than a whisper.

"What is that supposed to mean?"

"It means I did you a favor."

"You hurt her, you bastard."

"No! No, I didn't hurt her—not the way Tony wanted her hurt, man. I hurt her just enough for you to get the message."

"What message?"

"How the hell do I know?"

"What message!" Garth said again.

"Tony Zaccato always wins, man. *That's* the message. You got to be careful now. He's mad, Garth. He's *real* mad—you can look at me and tell that." Roy Lee tried to laugh, but it deteriorated into a string of coughs.

"I know all about Tony, Roy Lee."

"Not just Tony, man. Hugh. Hugh Gallagher. You got to watch Hugh, too."

"Hugh's in jail."

This time Roy Lee did manage to laugh; at least the sound he made Garth took for a laugh.

"Now I—see what it is. Now I see."

"See what, Roy Lee?"

"I—thought I got this for cutting out the dude that was supposed to work her over. I thought Tony found out it was me that beat his man to it. She's pretty, Garth. Real pretty—I seen her on TV one time. I tried not to hurt her face much."

"Roy Lee, I don't know what you're talking about."

"I'm talking about *this*, man. This! They did me good. I thought it was because Tony found out I got to Jenna before he could. But it wasn't—"

"It wasn't Tony?"

"Yeah, it was Tony, man! Can't you *listen*? It was Tony—but it was for the *wrong thing*. He kept saying how I told you, how I *told* you. I didn't know what he meant." He tried to smile. "He was a little too cranky for explanations, you know? But he must think I dropped a dime on his little business with Hugh. He didn't even know I took care of Jenna for you."

"For me?"

"So she don't get hurt the way Tony wanted. It was better that it was me that did the job first, see? I hurt her just a little bit. Not bad. I owed you, Garth. I wouldn't hurt her bad, see?"

Garth looked away for a moment. The worst part was that

he *did* see. He understood perfectly the convoluted logic that would let Roy Lee hurt Jenna himself, only a little bit, because he owed Garth for a pair of thermal underwear, rather than coming to him so that he could try to keep it from happening in the first place. Tony Zaccato had ordered Jenna hurt; to Roy Lee's mind, it wasn't negotiable. And what kind of track record did Garth have against Tony Zaccato? None. Nothing.

"Why was Tony sending me a message, Roy Lee?"

"You know why—"

"Tell me again."

But Roy Lee drifted off, telling him nothing.

"Garth," he said abruptly after a moment.

"What?"

"You got to teach her, Garth."

"Teach who, Roy Lee?"

"Your woman—Jenna. She don't know—nothing, man. She don't know how to take care of herself, how to fight. If she's yours, you got to teach her, Garth—take her and *show* her what to do, so when Tony..."

Roy Lee drifted off again.

"Is it night or day?" he said abruptly.

"Night, Roy Lee."

"Jeez, I hate the night. You remember how I always hated the dark? Ever since I was a little kid."

"Yeah. I remember."

"Mary and me, we were scared of the dark, but not you. You weren't scared of nothing. Don't go yet, Garth, okay? Stay here till the sun comes up. Please, Garth—"

"Take it easy, Roy Lee—"

"Please, Garth! I don't want to be by myself if it's dark—" He was trying to sit up, and Garth would have restrained him if he could have found a place to put his hand. But Roy Lee had no place where he could touch him.

All over, he was either bandage or raw skin. The pattern on the green screen darted around crazily.

"Lie down, Roy Lee," Garth said. "They'll throw me out of here if you don't."

Roy Lee suddenly relaxed. "You know what, Garth?"

"What, Roy Lee?"

"I think I'll get to see Mary."

The sun was coming up, and Skip was sleeping in the waiting room. Garth was half-surprised to see him still here, and watching him snoring softly with his head thrown back, oblivious to everything, Garth suddenly felt worn-out, used up, old. He'd felt that way before he'd ever become a cop, and The Job certainly hadn't made it any better. At this particular moment he couldn't have said why he was so hell-bent to have Jenna. She was loving, giving. What would she want with a burned-out cop like him? He had nothing to offer her, and she probably had the good sense to realize it.

He kicked Skip on the bottom of his shoe to wake him up, handing him one of the cups of coffee he'd brought with him.

"Thanks," Skip said, sitting up and taking a sip. "Where did you get this? This isn't the machine stuff. This is good."

"From the nurses' lounge."

"Do they know it or do I have to hide the cup every time I see one of them?"

"Yeah, they know it," Garth said, sitting down heavily. "Two cups of real coffee, free of charge. If there's anybody nurses feel sorry for, it's two dumb cops—and vice versa."

"I'll remember that. So how's Roy Lee?"

"He died," Garth said without emotion.

"I'm—sorry, Garth."

"Don't be. He's been dead for years. This was just the official leave-taking. He's a damn sight better off—" He felt a sudden lump rise in his throat, and he abruptly got up and walked to the window. The sun was just topping the buildings across the street. He took a deep breath. He wanted to see Jenna. He wanted to go to her and put his head in her lap until he felt better. She'd be kind to him, even if she'd never once said she loved him.

I need you, Jenna.

He closed his eyes against the great emptiness he felt.

Don't give up on us, baby. Not yet.

He realized that Skip was talking to him. "What?"

"I said Debbie told me what happened."

He looked around. "What happened where?"

"At the apartment house the day she took the kid with the wet coat home."

Skip had his attention. He walked back and sat down. "And?"

"She recognized a couple of the men hanging around in the hall as cops. She didn't say anything to them because she didn't want to inadvertently blow somebody's cover. They didn't seem to recognize her, so she just kept quiet. But then she realized what they were doing there—the drug deals going on. The walls in the Sullivan apartment were thin, she said. She could hear voices in the next apartment. Loud voices. A fight about somebody not getting his fair cut. She thought she recognized one of the voices—Hugh's. She kept hoping it was some kind of legitimate operation, but then Hugh came to the school just after she'd gotten back from that place. She thought he'd followed her—to see if she knew anything, I guess. And then Jenna was beaten up. She thought it was meant for her—she and Jenna both wore black coats, and they both had one of those gold-and-black school scarves, and it was done in her father's apartment building. She was afraid to say anything—she knows enough about the way things work to know that Hugh could probably have gotten out of it if it were just her word alone. She was afraid Hugh and his friends might do something to

me if she came forward or if she told me about it. That's
why she's been acting so crazy. She's been scared to death,
and she was ashamed because she didn't do anything and
Jenna got hurt.''

"It wasn't her fault about Jenna," Garth said. He told
him about Roy Lee's "favor." "Hugh must have been giving Tony trouble about his share. That's why Zaccato
wanted to kill two birds with one stone—to make sure Hugh
understood his family wasn't safe, to make sure I knew he
hadn't forgotten me, all of it—by getting to Jenna.''

"What are you going to do?" Skip asked, apparently because he'd been Garth's partner long enough now to know
that the question was appropriate.

"I'm going to go home and shower. And then I'm going
looking for Zaccato. I'm going on the street. Anybody I can
scare, I'm going to scare. Anybody I can't scare, I'll bribe.
But I'm going to find him. I want him bad, Skip."

"Yes, well, count me in on that."

"I'd rather work alone."

"Well, that's tough. You've got a partner, and there's not
a damn thing you can do about it."

But they split up to cover more territory, and they stayed
out until midafternoon, when Skip summoned Garth with a
loud whistle across a windy waterfront parking lot.

"Come on!" Skip yelled at him. "They want us in!"

"Did they say why?" Garth asked as he jumped into the
car Skip didn't bother to completely stop. He was half expecting Skip to tell him that Hugh had slipped the noose
after all.

"No."

"Did you *ask*?"

"Yes, I asked.

"Well, what did they say?"

"They said to come in! And don't you start about what

a lousy partner I am just because they wouldn't tell me anything! You're damn lucky to have somebody who'll put up with you, and you know it!''

"Is that a fact?''

"Yes! It is!''

"Drive the car, Skip. And don't hit the bus—''

"Don't tell me how to drive!''

"Somebody's got to.''

"I told you not to start with me! Didn't I tell you that?''

"You told me, Skip. You told me.''

"Garth!'' a patrolman yelled as soon as he hit the front doors at the station house. "Sid's got some kid tying up the 911 line. He won't tell anybody what's wrong—he just keeps asking for you.''

"What kid?'' Garth asked.

"I don't know—the kid won't say. He's crying a lot and—''

Garth could see Sidney hunched over the telephone. He caught sight of Garth and motioned for him to hurry.

"Here you go, son,'' Sidney said kindly into the receiver as Garth approached. "Detective Garth's here to speak to you.''

"Where's the call coming from?'' he asked Sidney as he took the phone. "This is Garth,'' he said into the receiver.

"Saint Xavier's,'' Sidney said.

"Hello?'' Garth said, because no one answered. He made hand motions for the people gathered around him to cut the noise. "This is Garth,'' he said again, holding his other ear so he could hear better.

He heard a long sniff. "How do I know that, sucker? You could be anybody.''

"Hernando?'' Garth said.

"How come you know my name?''

"Hernando, I told you the other day. I know who you are. What's the matter?"

"Are you Garth?"

"Yeah, kid, it's me. What—"

"You got to come over here, Garth! You got to bring your gun!"

"Hernando, what's the matter?"

"*He's* here, man! He's going to hurt Miss Jenna! Bring your gun, Garth!"

"Who, Hernando! Who's there?"

Hernando was crying, and Garth was wasting time.

"Hernando, I'm coming. Now you get out of there! You hear me? Hernando!"

Hernando said something and dropped the phone.

"Hernando!" Garth called, but he knew he wouldn't get an answer. He understood the last thing Hernando said:

"Tony's coming!"

"Skip," Garth said, hanging up the phone. "Call home and see where Debbie is."

It only took him a second. Garth could see the relief flood Skip's face when his wife answered. Skip covered the receiver with his hand. "Jenna stayed late, Garth."

Jenna heard the crying distinctly. And so did Tony Zaccato.

"Who is that!" he hissed in her ear, the arm he had around her neck tightening.

"I don't know."

"Who else is here!"

"Nobody else is supposed to be here."

"Hey!" Zaccato yelled. "Who's there!"

He dragged her along with him, and Jenna couldn't keep from crying out in pain.

"Don't you hurt Miss Jenna!" a small voice called from the far end of the hall. She recognized it immediately.

"Hernando, get out of here!" she cried, and Tony Zaccato made sure she suffered for it.

"Don't you hurt Miss Jenna!" Hernando yelled again. "You're going to be sorry, man, when 911 gets here. You'll be sorry!"

Tony Zaccato chuckled to himself. "Little dummy thinks 911 is a person. Yeah, I'm scared to death, kid!" he yelled at Hernando.

"Garth's going to bring his gun!" Hernando warned him, and Jenna closed her eyes.

"What did he say?" Zaccato demanded. She shook her head, pretending she didn't understand him.

"Hey, kid! You know my friend Garth?"

"He ain't your friend! He's *my* friend, sucker. And he's coming to shoot you!"

Tony Zaccato laughed. "Well, well. Looks like we'd better be going, Mrs. Gallagher, before your hero gets here. Hey, thanks for the tip, kid!"

But Hernando's tip came too late. Zaccato forced her down the long hall, and by the time they reached the end door, there was no traffic going by Saint Xavier's. The street should have had cars bumper-to-bumper at this time of day, and Tony Zaccato knew it. He stood cautiously in the doorway, then pressed forward just enough to still hold the door open, keeping her in front of him, the gun pressed under her chin and forcing her head back. She couldn't see where she was going, and she stumbled on the raised weather stripping on the threshold. She didn't have her coat, and the cold wind—and the fear—made her shiver.

She couldn't see anyone—no police, no patrol cars anywhere. Everything was so quiet. Too quiet.

"Where are the bastards?" Tony muttered to himself. "I know they're out there—where are they!"

A nondescript car pulled in at the end of the block. And then another. And another.

Tony Zaccato swore under his breath and dragged her back inside.

"What did you see?" Garth asked. He jerked off his jacket and put on the bullet-proof vest, standing outside the car in the biting wind. His hands were shaking, but he wasn't worried about it. His hands always shook at the beginning of an operation, but once he was into it, he was calm. He was always calm.

"The guy's in there. He's got the woman. He brought her to the door with him, but he didn't come all the way out." The patrolman's voice had a quaver in it. He wasn't used to this.

"How did she look?" Garth asked.

"Scared—he's got a .45 automatic under her chin."

"Did you make him?"

"Nah, I don't know him."

"Six feet tall?" Garth said. "A hundred and eighty pounds? Black hair, combed straight back? Probably wearing a big cashmere coat—gray?"

"Yeah, that's him."

"Did he say anything?"

"Nah, I don't think he knows for sure if we're out here."

"He knows," Garth said. He put his jacket back on and stuffed extra clips into his pockets.

Another car pulled up, and the lieutenant got out.

"This is your call, Garth," he said immediately. "How do you want to handle it?"

"I want to go in. Alone."

"He's not going to let you just walk in there, Garth."

"Yes, he will. Tony's been waiting a long time to get his revenge. And he'll want me there to see it."

The lieutenant stared at him, clearly understanding what Garth *didn't* say. "You go in ahead of the others—but not alone. That's all I'm going to give you."

Garth nodded, and he listened while the lieutenant said what he wanted done. Skip and Rosie Madden would go in with him, but not close. Garth took a slip of paper and rapidly sketched the layout of the building, indicating the two doors that were in most of the classrooms.

"I'm not looking to make an arrest," he said under his breath to Skip, and Rosie heard him. "If that bothers either of you, you better jump off now." He picked up the bullhorn. "Tony!" he said over it. "It's Garth! I'm coming in."

Jenna made a small sound of protest, and Tony Zaccato laughed.

"Looks like he thinks you're worth the trouble, Mrs. Gallagher. That's good. That's real good. Ah! Pretty lady! You going to cry about it? That's good, too. You let Garth see you cry—"

He jerked her around and made her sit on a kitchen bar stool someone had just donated to the kindergarten. She and Debbie had laughed earlier that day about what to do with it, dunce corners no longer being in vogue. It put her at just the right height to shield Zaccato, just at the right height so he could keep the gun under her chin. She struggled to stop crying. She didn't want to distract Garth in any way.

She heard running footsteps, but it wasn't Garth she heard. The footsteps were too quick and light.

"Hernando!" Garth whispered fiercely, reaching out to grab him up as he went flying past. "I told you to get out of here! I could have shot you, man!"

"You got your gun, Garth!" Hernando said, clearly more pleased than intimidated.

Garth wanted to shake the child until his teeth rattled, but he gave him a brief, hard hug instead. "Where are they?"

"Down in my class. You got to get Miss Jenna."

"I will. But you take your butt out of here."

Garth could tell by the look on Hernando's face that there was no way in hell the boy was going to do that. He didn't waste time arguing. He scooped Hernando up and hurried back toward the end doors, keeping an eye on the classroom where Tony was supposed to be, as he went.

"Hey!" Hernando bellowed. "Hey!"

The patrolmen on backup were on the ball, and the door swung open before Garth got to it.

"Handcuff him to something," Garth said, slinging Hernando into a pair of waiting arms. He couldn't help but smile at the elegant convolution of street names Hernando called him. "And wash his mouth out with soap while you're at it."

Garth stood for a moment and stared down the long hallway, listening intently. He could hear a murmur of voices, much as he had on other occasions.

He took a deep breath and walked forward, trying not to think about Jenna and how scared she must be. A noise in another direction made him stop. Rosie and Skip were supposed to be coming in, but he didn't know exactly where they were now. Hernando had said Tony was in the classroom—but then, Hernando was only five years old.

He listened. Everything was quiet.

He tried not to make any sound as he approached the classroom door.

"Please!"

The word stopped him; it was Jenna. He hugged the wall, willing himself not to be stampeded. He didn't want to do anything stupid; he had to forget that she wasn't a nameless civilian.

"He's not going to care!" Jenna said next. "You can't threaten him with what you might do to me!"

"Oh, I can threaten him, pretty lady. You're going to see how I can threaten him—Garth!" Tony suddenly yelled.

"You're not saying anything, Garth! You think I don't hear you out there?"

"I didn't come to talk, Tony. I came to kill you."

Zaccato laughed. "Now, how are you going to do that, Garth?" he asked, his voice patronizing, as if he were speaking to a naïve child. "I got something you want here. I got something you want real bad."

Garth's heart contracted at the small noise Jenna made. From where he stood, he could just see her. He couldn't see Zaccato, at least no more than his hand and arm and the gun under her chin. He couldn't see his other hand at all. He moved back a little.

"Yeah, but she understands, Tony," he called.

"Understands what?" Tony snapped, his jovial manner sliding away.

"She understands that first things come first. She understands that I owe you. For Roy Lee. For Mary."

"You don't talk about Mary! Mary is dead because of you!"

Garth wiped at his eyes. He was sweating. The vest was heavy and cumbersome. But he didn't take it off.

"An eye for an eye, Garth! You ever hear of that? Mary is dead because of you, Garth! You knew there was a drug bust going down, but you didn't tell Mary!"

"Who told you that? Hugh Gallagher? I wasn't working narcotics, Tony. *He* was. You think he didn't know the bust was going down? You're the one who sent Mary to make the drop for you. *You* sent her in there!"

"She always made the drop for me! They don't trust me if she doesn't go!"

"Oh, well, then, Tony, why didn't you *say* so? That makes everything all right. Business is business, right?"

"You shut up! I'm going to show you *business*, Garth! You move where I can see you—where *you* can see *me*. I want you to watch when I do this pretty lady of yours. We'll keep it in the family. I took care of her cop husband, I'll take care of her, too.''

"What's this, Tony? You down to taking credit for some kid's nickel hit?"

"Nickel hit! What do you know!"

"I know Joey Malaga whacked Patrick Gallagher."

"Not Joey, Garth. Me. *I* pull Joey Malaga's strings. Patrick Gallagher wouldn't stay where he belonged. He started sniffing here, sniffing there. Hugh said he could handle him, but I don't get where I am waiting for somebody to be 'handled.' Anybody bothers me, I want him taken out so he don't bother me no more. You think it was a nickel hit? No! Joey owes me, so he does his cop friend—for nothing! Ah, Garth!'' Tony said. "See what you did? You made the pretty lady cry again.''

"Jenna!'' Garth called, his heart twisting at what she must be feeling now. He caught a glimpse of Skip crossing the hall at the other door of the classroom and slipping inside. "Jenna!'' he called again to keep Tony's attention focused in the other direction.

"Garth!'' Jenna cried, her voice strong. "I want you to do what you have to do, Garth! For me! For Mary! Don't you let him walk out of here!''

She suddenly stopped as Tony grabbed her by the hair and yanked her head back.

"I told you, Garth!'' Tony yelled. "An eye for an eye!''

"Yeah, right, Tony! Hugh took Mary. But you didn't even know he did it, you dumb bastard! You took Patrick on a whim—not for *her*, not for Mary. Mary's in her grave, still waiting for you to catch on.''

"You shut up!''

"Mary's dead because of *you*, Tony, not me.''

"I said shut up!''

"You're right about what this is, Tony. It's an eye for an eye!''

With that, Garth abruptly stepped into the doorway, showing himself, counting on Tony's anger to be at a fever pitch.

"For Mary, Tony!" he yelled at him, and Skip was quick and deadly, Annie Oakley all the way—but not quick enough to keep the shot Tony got off from hitting Garth midchest.

Chapter 16

He opened his eyes. He could see the blue sky, and he was very cold. He turned his head slightly, trying to focus on the face that suddenly peered down at him. *Jenna*, he decided. She was wearing that dark green sweater he liked so much. Or was it the way she filled the sweater that he liked?

"What's the matter?" he asked, because she was obviously very upset.

"What's the *matter*? I thought you were too much of a damned hardhead to wear a vest, that's what's the matter!" Her voice was on the verge of cracking.

"No, I've got it on," he said, because she was about to cry and he didn't want her to. "I told you I'd be careful. Didn't I tell you I'd be careful?"

She nodded, but she was going to cry anyway. She suddenly bowed her head.

"Hey," he said softly, reaching up to touch her cheek. "You're not going to bawl, are you?"

"Yes!" she informed him, wiping furiously at her eyes.

He tried to sit up. The effort made him cry out in pain.

"Lie still, for God's sake!" Jenna said, putting her hands on his shoulders. He struggled briefly, then lay back against the parking lot pavement. It wasn't at all comfortable.

He looked up at the sky again. "How did I get out here?"

"You walked, you big dummy!"

He managed a grin. "Tell me something, Jenna. When you call me a big dummy, do you do that because you like me, or what?"

"Garth…" she said in exasperation.

"I was only wondering," he said. "God, my chest hurts."

He suddenly remembered. "Tony—"

"Skip shot him, Garth."

"Is he dead?"

"I don't know. Rosie jerked me out of there. I didn't have time to find out—and you were going for your walk."

He reached up to touch the center of his vest. "Damn thing works, doesn't it?"

"It works," she said, putting her hand on his. "But you've probably got some broken ribs."

He tried to sit up again.

"Garth, don't!" Jenna pleaded. "Don't. If you love me, please just lie still. I can't—take anymore." Her voice had gotten all teary again.

"Hey, Garth, how are you doing?" a patrolman said, squatting down beside him.

"Down but not out, Russo," he said.

"The bomber pilot's giving us a fit. Can I kick him loose?"

"Yeah," Garth said. "Let him come over here."

He could hear Hernando's running approach and the skidding halt his shoes made on the asphalt.

"Garth!" Hernando said. "Garth! You ain't killed, are you?"

"No, Hernando."

"Hey, man! You had me arrested! Them suckers put me in a car, and I couldn't get out. You can't have me arrested! I'm only five years old!"

"I'll remember that," Garth promised him. He closed his eyes against the pain in his chest.

"Garth," Jenna said. "Garth!"

He forced his eyes open. "Yeah, baby, what?"

But she didn't tell him what. She just looked stricken. But by then the paramedics had arrived.

"I can walk," he said to the one who began listening to his chest with a stethoscope.

"Maybe you *can*, but you *ain't*, got it? You're going to be wearing the print of that vest on your chest for a month. Brace yourself, macho man, you're going for a ride," he said as his associate rolled the stretcher up close.

Garth suffered the indignity of being lifted onto the stretcher, fighting down the wave of dizziness and pain that suggested that perhaps he couldn't walk after all.

"Jenna?" he called, or thought he called—his chest hurt so bad!

But he couldn't see her. Anywhere.

"Where—?"

"Officer, if you don't keep your butt still, you and me are going to tangle, you understand me?" the paramedic said. "You got broken ribs and a bruised heart, and I ain't having you bouncing around. So far you ain't got no holes in you, and I mean to keep it that way."

"What is it I've got?" he asked weakly as the pain threatened to overwhelm him again.

"Broken ribs. Bruised heart."

No, he thought. It was the other way around.

Jenna...

* * *

He opened his eyes. No blue sky this time. Blue ceiling. And he wasn't cold anymore. His chest, however, still talked to him with every breath.

He turned his head. Someone was asleep in the chair by the bed. He watched for a moment—Skip again, he decided. Every time he'd opened his eyes, it seemed that Skip had been here. The kid was a good partner, took all his duties seriously, even the bedside vigil.

"Hey," he said, or tried to. His throat was dry, and he wanted desperately to cough. But he knew what kind of havoc that would wreak, and he fought it down until his eyes watered. After a moment, he tried again. "Hey, Skip!"

"What!" Skip said, jerking awake. "What—"

"Can't you sleep at home, Carver?"

Skip grinned. "Yes, I can sleep at home. But I decided I'd hang out here for a while."

"How long is 'a while'?"

"Oh…" he said airily. "About two days."

"Two—" He had to stop, because he was going to cough again.

"Maybe three. You had some trouble with your heart. Fluid and swelling from the trauma of being hit in the chest so hard. And you were exhausted, I guess. You've been asleep a long time."

"Where's…Jenna?"

Skip didn't answer him.

"I know you heard me," Garth said. "Where is she?"

"She's—I'm not sure—well, I know where she *is*, I just don't know why…she's not here," he finished lamely. "Well, I do know why—or I think I do.…"

"Will you make up your mind and tell me?" The outburst caused him to cough in earnest; there was no holding back this one. Excruciating pain shot through his chest, making his breath catch and his eyes water.

"Go ahead," Garth said when he could.

"Garth…"

"Go. Ahead."

Skip sighed heavily. "I think hearing what Tony said about having Patrick killed has really thrown her, Garth. I think it's been like having him die all over again. And then *you*—"

"Okay," he said abruptly. He didn't want to hear after all. "She's all right?"

"She's all right, Garth. Tony didn't get the chance to really hurt her."

"Well, that's good. That's good."

Skip suffered for a moment in the awkward silence that followed.

"Well…can I get you anything?"

"No. Nothing."

"Hazel and Luigi will be here later."

"That's good," he said again, because the words seemed to fit and he didn't feel like thinking up any others.

"Well, I guess I'll go on then."

"Yeah," Garth said. He waited until Skip had reached the door. "Skip. How good was the shot you made?"

They stared at each other across the room.

"You got what you wanted, Garth," Skip said quietly. "No arrest."

Garth nodded, the relief he felt knowing Tony Zaccato was dead nearly as acute as the sorrow he felt knowing he'd lost Jenna.

"Thanks, Skip," he said, turning his face away. He heard Skip leave and quietly close the door.

Now what? he thought. But there was only one thing he could do. Think. Whether he wanted to or not. About Roy Lee. About Mary. About Tony. About Patrick Gallagher. About Patrick Gallagher's widow.

He closed his eyes. Maybe he slept again. He didn't know. Maybe he dreamed. The face he saw in his half-waking state was Jenna's—smiling, angry, stormy with passion.

I need you, baby!

But he couldn't tell her that. He'd told her he loved her. Twice. And that was as far as he would go.

Someone was in the room. He braced himself to have to deal with a worried Hazel and Luigi. They'd both be wringing their hands, and how was he going to cope with that when he already felt like bawling?

He turned his head; Jenna stood at the foot of the bed. His heart, bruised and battered as it was, lurched.

He forced himself to look away; he'd been working hard to get used to the idea that she wouldn't be coming, and now here she stood.

"What are you doing here?" he asked, his misery making him less than kind.

"Where else would I be?" she asked.

"You don't have to come here and be nice to me."

"Well, that's good, because I can see already what a chore *that* would be."

He looked back at her, and he made a grand effort at small talk.

"Find an apartment yet?"

"No," she said. "I...haven't been up to looking for an apartment."

It was suddenly clear to him. She was only here because she wasn't going to duck the issue. She was an honorable person. She'd tell him to his face that she didn't want any more to do with him. He wondered if the lawyer was still waiting in the wings somewhere, and that thought left him more depressed than ever. He lapsed into silence, dreading what he was sure she would tell him.

"Are you upset because I wasn't here sooner?" she asked.

"No. Why should I be upset?"

"*I* would be. I…wanted to come, Garth, but I—I guess things just sort of caught up with me." She tried to smile. "I'm…better now, though."

"Glad to hear it," he said, sounding cold and petulant even to himself.

She looked at him thoughtfully. "Rosie told me something once, Garth. I was worried because I hadn't heard from you. She told me when I *did* see you, not to give you any grief about why you weren't there sooner. She said I should just be glad you were there *now*. I thought it was good advice."

He considered this, wondering if he dared to hope what it might mean. He decided to behave like an adult.

"What? You couldn't pick up the telephone? Send me a card?" he said in spite of his decision.

"You were asleep for a long time, Garth. They didn't want you disturbed. And the card's in the mail. All the children at Saint Xavier's signed it. They all write big, so we had to get a really *big* card—"

"Okay. Okay. I understand how bad you must have felt going through everything you did with Tony, and with Roy Lee. I understand how hard it must have been hearing about Patrick. I know it's hard for you to go into a hospital, but—"

"But what?" she asked when he didn't continue.

"But my feelings are hurt! It ticks me off, Jenna!"

"Oh," she said. "Do you want me to go?"

"No, I don't want you to go!" he said, alarmed.

"Well, what do you want?" she said in exasperation.

"I want to…pout, okay? And you can't pout unless somebody's there to see it."

He glanced at her. She was trying not to smile.

"That sounds reasonable." She came and sat on the side of the bed. "You pout. I'll wait."

She made herself comfortable, careful not to jar him. And she looked into his eyes. *Her* eyes were full of mischief, and she was humming, of all things. In a moment, he recognized the song.

He couldn't keep from smiling. "'Some Kind of Wonderful,'" he said.

She smiled in return, and she began to softly sing the words.

"I'm not as good as The Drifters," she said after a moment.

"Well, it's the thought that counts," he answered, smiling still. The smile slid away. He could feel his eyes welling up. "Isn't it?"

"Yes," she answered.

He reached up to touch her cheek, finally, and she turned her face to press a kiss into his palm.

"You shouldn't be here. You hate hospitals."

"I know," she agreed. "But I *love* you."

Epilogue

She wouldn't move in with him. It was the perfect solution, *he'd* thought. She was homeless; he was needy. In his whole life, he'd never been so needy. And, God knows, he had the room. He had talked to her—explained, discussed, argued and, yes, even pouted. Roy Lee had said that Garth should teach her to fight, but Roy Lee should have seen her, determined to do what she had to do and not let anyone push her around, not even Garth.

"I love you!" Garth had been reduced to shouting.

"I love you," she'd countered with maddening calm.

But she wouldn't move in with him.

And it wasn't that he hadn't understood. He understood perfectly. Why she hadn't come to him at first when he was in the hospital, and why she had needed more time afterward. She had her panic attacks in hand, but she had still had a lot of loose ends to tie up. She loved Garth, whether she'd wanted to or not. But she had to get used to that, and she had to put Patrick to rest once and for all. And she had to try to make some kind of peace with Mrs. Gallagher. With *both* Mrs. Gallaghers. Patrick's mother—and Patrick's widow. She even had to stand with her in-laws during Hugh's trial, all the while knowing that Hugh's association with Tony Zaccato had likely cost Patrick his life.

That had been hard for Garth. Even if it was harder still for Jenna.

"If I'm not there, people will think it's because I know he's guilty," Jenna had said.

"You do, and he is!"

"I know that, Garth! But he should be tried by the court, not by the media. You know how it will go—'Martyred brother's widow refuses to attend trial.' I have to do this— for Patrick's mother, if nothing else."

And he began to understand a little what it cost a woman, what it cost Jenna, to wed a policeman. To wed herself to The Job.

Garth had understood, but it hadn't helped. He wasn't a patient man, and he'd been afraid. He was still afraid. Happiness—life—was so precarious. He'd learned that the hard way. And Jenna had, too. She *knew* firsthand, just as he did, how easily everything could slip away. But she was still willing to risk it all. It ticked him off—even if he *did* understand.

"Everything has to be right for us," she kept telling him. "As right as I can make it. I'm not going to hide anymore. I'm going to deal with my problems head-on."

He agreed. He didn't like it—he hated having his own words come back to haunt him—but he agreed. And he'd worked hard to help her get everything settled. By keeping his mouth shut about the Gallaghers—even when Hugh was convicted. By *not* keeping his mouth shut about The Job.

By sharing the good times—and the bad. By doing everything in his power to allay Jenna's fears, especially her
worry that perhaps she wouldn't be able to have his baby.
It hadn't been easy to convince her once and for all that she
wasn't a means to an end to him, or a reparation for Mary,
or an adjunct to The Job, or anything remotely peripheral
to his life, that she simply *was* his life. *She* was his life,
with children or without.

And so, here he stood, all these months later, a nervous
wreck.

"Garth?" Skip said behind him—again. "Oh, Garth," he
said, when Garth didn't turn around.

"What!" he snapped.

"Are you...all right?"

"Yeah, fine," he said, and he didn't miss the looks Skip
and Luigi exchanged. "I'm fine!"

"You don't look fine. Does he, Luigi? Maybe if you
could just blink your eyes now and then so we could tell
you're not in a coma—"

"Look! I'm nervous, all right? I'm getting married, and
I'm nervous! Weren't you nervous when you married Debbie?"

"Who, me? All I had to worry about was whether or not
my mother was going to crash the ceremony with a bunch
of men in white coats and a court order. Why would I have
been nervous?"

"Yeah, well, at least you were sure the bride wouldn't
back out," he said.

"Garth, Jenna isn't going to back out. How many times
do I have to tell you? She's here—Luigi's seen her. Tell
him you've seen her, Luigi."

"I see her, Giovanni," Luigi told him earnestly. "I see

her. I even give her a little kiss on the cheek. I say it's from you.''

Garth suddenly laughed. "You want to go around kissing brides, old man, you get one of your own and leave mine alone." He boxed Luigi once on the arm. "God! How much longer before this thing starts?"

"Minute, thirty-seven seconds," Skip said without looking at his watch. He cracked the door so he could see out into the congregation. "The church is full," he noted.

"Thanks a lot, Skip! That's all I needed to know—the church is full!"

"Take it easy, Garth! People have to come see this miraculous event, don't they? Hazel finally getting old Garth married? How else are they going to believe it?"

"Very funny," Garth said.

"A miracle is a miracle," Luigi said philosophically.

And you don't know how close to the truth that is, Garth thought. It was a miracle all right—not that he'd asked Jenna to marry him, but that, with all their problems, she had finally agreed.

"No Mrs. Gallagher," Skip said, still peeping out the door.

"What?" Garth said in alarm.

"Not Jenna, Garth! The old lady. She didn't come. Jenna said she wouldn't, but I think she was hoping— you *are* in bad shape."

Luigi came and put his arm around Garth's shoulders. "Giovanni, you listen to this," he said, squeezing hard. "You *love* Jenna. You want her to be your wife. So all you got to do now is say so—to God and to the people. What is so hard about that?"

"God and the people," Garth echoed vaguely. "What's so hard?" he exhaled sharply.

The organ music started in earnest.

"Now!" Luigi said. "You go and do it, right?"

"Right," Garth said, hoping this was like all the other times he'd had the jitters—shaky at first, but then, once he got into it, everything settled down and he was all right. "You got the ring?"

"I got it! I got it! Don't ask me that no more!" Luigi said. "And if I don't got it, Skip's got a spare one for me to use. So go on! We go get you married!"

In spite of Luigi's shoving, Garth took a deep breath before he stepped out into the church proper. Then he walked purposefully to stand where he'd practiced standing just the night before.

It was even worse than he had imagined. He wasn't used to being stared at, and there wasn't a damn thing for all these people—many of them police personnel—to look at but him. Garth, held captive before them and actually wearing a suit.

And Hazel was bawling her head off. She gave him a little wave, which in no way interfered with her crying. Jenna's mother stood at a pew on the opposite side. She wasn't crying, and she didn't wave. She did, however, look at him kindly. They were both holding up well, Garth thought, for two mothers who had had their dreams for their children dashed the way they had. Jenna wasn't a blueblood with money, and Garth didn't work for IBM. He smiled briefly at them both.

Ah, God, he thought, resigned and trying to endure. His tie was choking him to death. It was all he could do not to tug at it—he might even die up here. Of suffocation. But he kept his eyes on the back of the church, looking—waiting—for Jenna. No matter what Skip and Luigi said, he wouldn't be surprised if she didn't appear. He wasn't much of a catch, and he knew it. He was mortally afraid that, as the time for the ceremony drew near, she'd suddenly know it, too.

The music changed; the bridespersons were coming—Rosie Madden and her braids, and Debbie and all of Saint Xavier's kindergarten. He couldn't keep from grinning. The children had on their school uniforms, but in honor of the occasion, all the girls wore flowers in their hair, and all the boys had boutonnieres. He could see Hernando marching along, taking big steps and grinning from ear to ear. Just as he was supposed to file into the front row, he broke away and dashed to where Garth stood, giving him "five" before Debbie shooed him back to where he was supposed to be. The congregation loved it.

Jenna was standing at the back of the church.

Oh, baby, he thought. *You are so beautiful.*

So beautiful. She was dressed in pale pink lace, and she had flowers in her hair, the same kind of flowers she carried in her arms. Her eyes held his all the way down the aisle. When she was close enough, he gave her a wink so she'd know that no matter how rattled and choked he looked, he wasn't going to break and run for it.

Jenna smiled and took his arm, and as it always was with him, his nervousness vanished the moment the action began. His voice was strong and clear, his hands steady and warm as he made his promises to her.

"Love...Honor...So long as you both shall live?"

No problem. Piece of cake. I love you, Jenna.

Suddenly it was all over.

"...man and wife."

The words rang in his mind, in his heart. He kissed her,

hugged her, kissed her again.

"So," he whispered in her ear before they turned to face the congregation. "*Now* will you move in with me?"

* * * * *

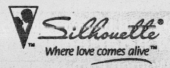

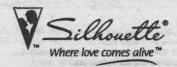

SILHOUETTE'S 20TH ANNIVERSARY CONTEST
OFFICIAL RULES
NO PURCHASE NECESSARY TO ENTER

1. To enter, follow directions published in the offer to which you are responding. Contest begins 1/1/00 and ends on 8/24/00 (the "Promotion Period"). Method of entry may vary. Mailed entries must be postmarked by 8/24/00, and received by 8/31/00.

2. During the Promotion Period, the Contest may be presented via the Internet. Entry via the Internet may be restricted to residents of certain geographic areas that are disclosed on the Web site. To enter via the Internet, if you are a resident of a geographic area in which Internet entry is permissible, follow the directions displayed on-line, including typing your essay of 100 words or fewer telling us "Where In The World Your Love Will Come Alive." On-line entries must be received by 11:59 p.m. Eastern Standard time on 8/24/00. Limit one e-mail entry per person, household and e-mail address per day, per presentation. If you are a resident of a geographic area in which entry via the Internet is permissible, you may, in lieu of submitting an entry on-line, enter by mail, by hand-printing your name, address, telephone number and contest number/name on an 8"x 11" plain piece of paper and telling us in 100 words or fewer "Where In The World Your Love Will Come Alive," and mailing via first-class mail to: Silhouette 20th Anniversary Contest, (in the U.S.) P.O. Box 9069, Buffalo, NY 14269-9069; (In Canada) P.O. Box 637, Fort Erie, Ontario, Canada L2A 5X3. Limit one 8"x 11" mailed entry per person, household and e-mail address per day. On-line and/or 8"x 11" mailed entries received from persons residing in geographic areas in which Internet entry is not permissible will be disqualified. No liability is assumed for lost, late, incomplete, inaccurate, nondelivered or misdirected mail, or misdirected e-mail, for technical, hardware or software failures of any kind, lost or unavailable network connection, or failed, incomplete, garbled or delayed computer transmission or any human error which may occur in the receipt or processing of the entries in the contest.

3. Essays will be judged by a panel of members of the Silhouette editorial and marketing staff based on the following criteria:

   > Sincerity (believability, credibility)—50%
   >
   > Originality (freshness, creativity)—30%
   >
   > Aptness (appropriateness to contest ideas)—20%

   Purchase or acceptance of a product offer does not improve your chances of winning. In the event of a tie, duplicate prizes will be awarded.

4. All entries become the property of Harlequin Enterprises Ltd., and will not be returned. Winner will be determined no later than 10/31/00 and will be notified by mail. Grand Prize winner will be required to sign and return Affidavit of Eligibility within 15 days of receipt of notification. Noncompliance within the time period may result in disqualification and an alternative winner may be selected. All municipal, provincial, federal, state and local laws and regulations apply. Contest open only to residents of the U.S. and Canada who are 18 years of age or older, and is void wherever prohibited by law. Internet entry is restricted solely to residents of those geographical areas in which Internet entry is permissible. Employees of Torstar Corp., their affiliates, agents and members of their immediate families are not eligible. Taxes on the prizes are the sole responsibility of winners. Entry and acceptance of any prize offered constitutes permission to use winner's name, photograph or other likeness for the purposes of advertising, trade and promotion on behalf of Torstar Corp. without further compensation to the winner, unless prohibited by law. Torstar Corp and D.L. Blair, Inc., their parents, affiliates and subsidiaries, are not responsible for errors in printing or electronic presentation of contest or entries. In the event of printing or other errors which may result in unintended prize values or duplication of prizes, all affected contest materials or entries shall be null and void. If for any reason the Internet portion of the contest is not capable of running as planned, including infection by computer virus, bugs, tampering, unauthorized intervention, fraud, technical failures, or any other causes beyond the control of Torstar Corp. which corrupt or affect the administration, secrecy, fairness, integrity or proper conduct of the contest, Torstar Corp. reserves the right, at its sole discretion, to disqualify any individual who tampers with the entry process and to cancel, terminate, modify or suspend the contest or the Internet portion thereof. In the event of a dispute regarding an on-line entry, the entry will be deemed submitted by the authorized holder of the e-mail account submitted at the time of entry. Authorized account holder is defined as the natural person who is assigned to an e-mail address by an Internet access provider, on-line service provider or other organization that is responsible for arranging e-mail address for the domain associated with the submitted e-mail address.

5. Prizes: Grand Prize—a $10,000 vacation to anywhere in the world. Travelers (at least one must be 18 years of age or older) or parent or guardian if one traveler is a minor, must sign and return a Release of Liability prior to departure. Travel must be completed by December 31, 2001, and is subject to space and accommodations availability. Two hundred (200) Second Prizes—a two-book limited edition autographed collector set from one of the Silhouette Anniversary authors: Nora Roberts, Diana Palmer, Linda Howard or Annette Broadrick (value $10.00 each set). All prizes are valued in U.S. dollars.

6. For a list of winners (available after 10/31/00), send a self-addressed, stamped envelope to: Harlequin Silhouette 20th Anniversary Winners, P.O. Box 4200, Blair, NE 68009-4200.

Contest sponsored by Torstar Corp., P.O. Box 9042, Buffalo, NY 14269-9042.

ENTER FOR
A CHANCE TO WIN*
Silhouette's 20th Anniversary Contest

Tell Us Where in the World
You Would Like *Your* Love To Come Alive...
And We'll Send the Lucky Winner There!

Silhouette wants to take you wherever
your happy ending can come true.

Here's how to enter: Tell us, in 100 words or less,
where you want to go to make your love come alive!

In addition to the grand prize, there will be 200
runner-up prizes, collector's-edition book sets
autographed by one of the Silhouette anniversary
authors: **Nora Roberts, Diana Palmer,
Linda Howard** or **Annette Broadrick**.

DON'T MISS YOUR CHANCE TO WIN!
ENTER NOW! No Purchase Necessary

Where love comes alive™

Visit Silhouette at www.eHarlequin.com to enter, starting this summer.

Name:

Address:

City: State/Province:

Zip/Postal Code:

Mail to Harlequin Books: **In the U.S.**: P.O. Box 9069, Buffalo, NY
14269-9069; **In Canada**: P.O. Box 637, Fort Erie, Ontario, L4A 5X3

*No purchase necessary—for contest details send a self-addressed stamped envelope to:
Silhouette's 20th Anniversary Contest, P.O. Box 9069, Buffalo, NY, 14269-9069 (include
contest name on self-addressed envelope). Residents of Washington and Vermont may
omit postage. Open to Cdn. (excluding Quebec) and U.S. residents who are 18 or over.
Void where prohibited. Contest ends August 31, 2000.   PS20CON_R2

Multi-*New York Times* bestselling author

Nora Roberts

knew from the first how to capture readers' hearts.
Celebrate the 20th Anniversary of Silhouette Books
with this special 2-in-1 edition containing her fabulous
first book and the sensational sequel.

Coming in June

Irish Hearts

Adelia Cunnane's fiery temper sets proud, powerful horse
breeder Travis Grant's heart aflame and he resolves to
make this wild *Irish Thoroughbred* his own.

Erin McKinnon accepts wealthy Burke Logan's loveless
proposal, but can this ravishing *Irish Rose* win her
hard-hearted husband's love?

Also available in June from
Silhouette Special Edition (SSE #1328)

Irish Rebel

In this brand-new sequel to *Irish Thoroughbred*, Travis and
Adelia's innocent but strong-willed daughter Keeley discovers
love in the arms of a charming Irish rogue with a talent for
horses...and romance.

Where love comes alive™

Visit Silhouette at www.eHarlequin.com   PSNORA

USA Today Bestselling Author

SHARON SALA

has won readers' hearts with thrilling tales
of romantic suspense. Now Silhouette Books
is proud to present five passionate stories from
this beloved author.

Available in August 2000:
ALWAYS A LADY
A beauty queen whose dreams have been dashed in a
tragic twist of fate seeks shelter for her wounded spirit
in the arms of a rough-edged cowboy....

Available in September 2000:
GENTLE PERSUASION
A brooding detective risks everything to protect the
woman he once let walk away from him....

Available in October 2000:
SARA'S ANGEL
A woman on the run searches desperately for a reclusive
Native American secret agent—the only man who can save
her from the danger that stalks her!

Available in November 2000:
HONOR'S PROMISE
A struggling waitress discovers she is really a rich heiress—
and must enter a powerful new world of wealth and
privilege on the arm of a handsome stranger....

Available in December 2000:
KING'S RANSOM
A lone woman returns home to the ranch where she was
raised, and discovers danger—as well as the man she once
loved with all her heart....